As in her earlier novels, *The Four Winds of Heaven*, *Encore* and *The Eleventh Year*, Monique Raphel High has drawn from the diaries of her family as well as from personal recollections of friends. Ms High lived in France for many years, and now lives in Beverly Hills.

By the same author

The Four Winds of Heaven
Encore
The Eleventh Year

MONIQUE RAPHEL HIGH

The Keeper
of the Walls

Published by Grafton Books 1986
First published in Great Britain by
Granada Publishing 1985
This edition published 1993 by
Diamond Books
77-85 Fulham Palace Road
Hammersmith, London, W6 8JB

Printed and bound in Great Britain by
BPCC Hazells Ltd
Member of BPCC Ltd

FOR GAN-GAN, MY BELOVED GRANDMOTHER
You never needed to be 'liberated':
you were always free.

A grandam's name is little less in love,
Than is the doting title of a mother.

SHAKESPEARE, *King Richard III*, IV, iv

'I am the rose of Sharon, and the lily of the valleys.
As the lily among thorns, so is my love among the daughters.'

The Song of Solomon, 2: 1, 2.

'The watchmen that went about the city found me, they smote me, they wounded me; the keepers of the walls took away my veil from me.
I charge you, O daughters of Jerusalem, if ye find my beloved, that ye tell him, that I am sick of love.'

Ibid., 5: 7, 8.

Foreword

This is a story about Time. How time changes the delicate relationships between men and women; how it transforms children to adults sometimes almost overnight; how a woman's heart can change, as life puts its stamp on her.

And it is the story of a particular time, when countries went through changes more quickly than people. It was a time when passions soared high, and men were cannibals. It is a time none of us should ever forget existed.

I've always wanted to write this book, in memory of Sonia de Gunzburg, my grandmother. Her courage knew no bounds, in the face of disaster. She thought it her duty to help those in trouble, even if she might have been risking her life. Much of this story, therefore, is hers: I am merely the seamstress who sewed it all together.

But Sonia is not Lily. Lily must stand on her own.

This book tells stories of many people. I was privileged to hear some of these stories firsthand. Most of all, I was touched by the openness of Mihai Berkovits, of Los Angeles, who shared the most painful part of his life with me, that I might write about it. And my father, David Raphel, revealed an aspect of his past that I had never heard him discuss. Most of us shelve our past because it hurts too much, or because it has little bearing on our present. But in this case, I believe that the past can help us to see clearly into the future: what happened then, in the thirties and forties, must never be allowed to happen again.

My editor, Charles Spicer, put almost as much love and

enthusiasm into this project as I did. And his professionalism came through at every turn of the road. Thank you, Charlie.

March 1984

Prologue

Nothing ever happened in Chaumontel. The hours slipped through one's fingers like so many potato peelings, Lily thought, wiping her hands on her apron. In the sink, the new potatoes shone a nice clear yellow, perfect for soup.

One thought about one's daily chores, and chatted about the weather. It was as if one had been caught in a time warp, and isolated from the turmoil outside that was rending Europe apart. No, she thought, I will not think about it, I will not think of those who aren't here, of those who might have died without my knowing. It's better just to pretend that things will never change, that tomorrow a new batch of potatoes will have to be washed and cleaned, and that Paris, and all that was mine, was only one of my delusions.

'Lily,' her companion said, her voice low and taut: 'Something's wrong. Look what's coming.'

Something's wrong. Lily felt the sudden sharp stab of fear. She didn't want to look, because she didn't have to. She realized, in that split second, that she'd been waiting all this time for those words, and for what they meant: *something's wrong.*

What's wrong in this quiet little village is *me*, and my daughter, she thought. We're the odd ones, the ones people pretend blend in, but don't. And yet, you can't ever run away. Like a time bomb waiting to explode, you carry your destiny inside you.

She breathed in, very slowly, and raised her eyes to the windowpane. And she saw him. Trim, in his martial *feldgrau* uniform, he stood beside the two young French policemen from the county seat of Luzarches, who always smiled and nodded to her on the road, like friendly acquaintances. He was like a martinet, and the swastikas embroidered on his sleeves kept her eyes riveted to him, fascinating her in their horror.

For the Gestapo never came to Chaumontel. As far as the Nazis were concerned, the hamlet didn't exist.

'You just have time to hide in the basement,' the older woman whispered.

'No. They've seen me.'

'Then run out the back. Go down the street, into any house. They'll hide you.'

'And endanger the whole village? Maybe it's just routine. Maybe they're not even looking for *me*.' Lily tried to smile, couldn't glue it on, and abandoned the effort.

The older woman seized her hands, and squeezed them. 'There's our powerful friend in Paris, the actress,' she whispered. 'She'll help you, won't she?'

Lily shrugged, lamely, too numb to think. She kept seeing images of the Nazis seizing a man in the middle of the Champs-Élysées, right before her eyes, months ago. She'd understood then that, within the week, this man would have begun his descent into Hell … God knows where. They took people like him … people like her and her daughter … far away, and no one ever heard from them again after that.

Incredible images were parading through her mind, of her mother, of her wedding, of her children, of the man she loved. She'd lived a rich, full life, even if recently it had become a nightmare. She'd be forty next year. But her young daughter wasn't yet twenty, and had only just begun her time as a woman. She, too, deserved a normal life, with marriage and children and maybe a profession. Her daughter loved children, and wanted to teach in a nursery school. That's where she was now: in Paris, at her college, finishing her class.

'Oh, my God,' Lily cried, turning to fully face Madame Portier. 'If we don't warn her, she'll come back, and they'll take her, too.'

'I'll go and wait for her at the station.'

'And he'll have someone watching you. If they know about me, they know about her.'

She knew the Nazis. It had, after all, only been eighteen months or so since she'd stood in her silken evening gown at the German Embassy, her long, delicate fingers lightly kissed by Otto Abetz, the ambassador. All around her the French collaborators had been toasting the success of the Third Reich, which, like a poisonous oil spill, had been spreading its conquering edges past the borders of enemy nations that stood in its way.

The Nazis left no stone unturned. They left no family unscathed.

Madame Portier was moving to the door in answer to the sudden intrusive knocking. And then the Gestapo officer had wedged himself in, his lips curved in a smile, his eyes hard and flintlike and unreadable.

'Madame Portier? We don't aim to disturb you. I understand that all your papers are in perfect order.'

The older woman's chin jutted forward, arrogantly. 'This is a proud French home,' she declared. 'What do you want?'

Again the mellifluous voice of the German, his accent flawless, inserted itself into the cool, calm atmosphere of the small house.

'We just want a word with your boarder. The lovely Parisian lady you've been hiding.'

Lily, in the kitchen, felt a moment of disembodied panic, and couldn't move. She stopped hearing what Madame Portier was replying. She kept thinking about her daughter. There had to be some way to stop her from coming home. There had to be a way to let her live. They'd already come

11

this far, and Germany, everyone said, was on the verge of losing the war now. Only a few more months . . .

The figure of the Gestapo officer had materialized before her, right in front of her. He was still smiling. Suddenly his fingers slid around her arm, and she felt them tighten, like a vice, cutting off her circulation. 'So you're afraid,' he remarked softly. 'The incomparable, the illustrious Liliane Bruisson is actually afraid. We've never met, but I've seen your photograph, fair lady, in all the tabloids of France. And my ambassador was right: you *are* a beauty, even in these rags.'

She tried to control her breathing, and stammered: 'Thank you.'

'But it's time the princess stopped pretending she's Cinderella,' he continued, his face so close to hers that she could smell his faint odour of cologne. 'It's time she stopped hiding in her pumpkin.'

So they knew who she was. All exits were cut off to her now. There was nothing left to do, at least not for herself. It was too late to panic; she was, to all intents and purposes, already dead.

Two thoughts tormented her, however: how to get word to her daughter on time.

And who had betrayed her? It had to have been someone she knew . . . someone close to her or her family. But *who?*

I'm not going to die, you bastard, she thought, her eyes all at once blazing in her pallid face. But she said, softly: 'Just let me get my things.'

And it wasn't until she'd turned around, to go back to her room, that the floor tilted up to meet her, and her knees buckled.

Book I
The Twenties

Chapter One

'Lily, for God's sake, no one can wait for you forever!'

Claude's voice sounded harsh, cutting into the quiet tranquillity of the blue-green room with its four-poster bed and its delicate pastel watercolours on the walls of raw silk. The girl quivered, almost imperceptibly, and picked up a white beaded bag and the ermine stole that had been lying on the bed. She slipped the stole around her shoulders and touched her long dark hair, almost as if seeking reassurance from its thick, glossy presence, and opened the door.

Below her curved a stone staircase, covered with dark red carpeting, and at the bottom stood her brother, resplendent in his tuxedo and frilled shirt. Lily lifted her skirt of pale yellow muslin, and went quickly down the stairs. Claude stood looking at her, his head cocked to one side, critical. She felt the blood rush to her cheeks – a moment of acute embarrassment. She was always self-conscious, especially about her height, which, at five feet nine inches, was unusually tall. He said: 'Why don't you cut your hair? You're six years behind the times.'

She felt the words reverberating inside her body, like a series of small, consecutive stabs. Her eyelashes stung. She said softly, taking his arm: 'I can't think of being without my hair. Don't you remember? Grandpa always said that hair was a woman's ornament.'

'Grandpa died ten years ago, Lily, and he was an old fuddy-duddy. You're eighteen years old – it's time you thought for yourself.'

15

As tall as she was, he was three inches taller. She looked up at him, and replied quietly: 'But that's what I'm doing.'

They were standing in the vestibule, with its mahogany coat-rack and umbrella stand, and the grandfather clock ticking in its gleaming wooden frame. Claude said: 'I'll get the car. There's no use your getting your feet wet in the puddles.'

As she stood alone, waiting, she glanced at her own reflection in the ornate, gilt-framed mirror. How many guests had done the same, while waiting to be received into the inner sanctum of her father's study or her mother's sitting room? And how had they reacted to their own image? She thought: Why do people think I'm good-looking? Beauty was Madame de Noailles, with her amethyst eyes, or Gabrielle Dorziat, the actress, with her tender face and soft, feline curves. I am too dark to be beautiful.

Outside, a car horn was honking. She pulled the wrap more tightly round her, and ran out of the door. In the night-time, the Renault 40-*chevaux* loomed large and grey, like a metal carriage. Claude was opening her door from the inside, and she climbed in. Without a word, he started the motor.

Lily sat motionless, afraid. It had only been six months since she had come home from the finishing school in Brittany and left the comfortable cocoon of the nuns. Women were safer than men, and the sisters safer than anyone but her mother. They didn't ask her to be sophisticated or *dernier cri*, just to be docile, obedient, studious. More than anybody else, she feared her brother. She'd left him six years before, she a child of twelve, he already a man at eighteen. They'd lived in different worlds, and seen each other only once in a while, at dinner or a Sunday outing. He'd already been leading a life of his own and she'd been the baby of the family.

Suddenly she'd come to the end of her studies, and the

peaceful life she'd grown to love had ended. Passed so swiftly. She hadn't wanted to return to Paris.

She was glad to be with her mother. But how much of the house was really Mama's? Father was such an imposing man, so loud, so peremptory. She felt she had nothing in common with him, and remembered how, as a child, she'd imagined that her mother had fallen in love with a foreign prince, and had her. She'd finally admitted this in confession, and had been severely reprimanded. Now she smiled about it.

Claude's voice sliced into the softness of her thoughts. 'The Comtesse de Béhague has a splendid mansion, and receives the most elegant people in Paris. Many are of foreign extraction. Try to think of interesting things to say, Lily. Not just hello, how do you do. You've no idea how much this invitation cost me.'

'I don't understand. You *paid* to be invited there?'

He was lighting a cigarette. 'Don't be silly. I didn't pay in money. I paid in favours. I passed somebody a handsome client.'

'But . . .'

She was frankly bewildered, and uncomfortable. Before, they'd lived in a small house in Bougival, on the outskirts of Paris, and her father had handled small to average construction jobs. They'd had one maidservant. But after the war, things had begun to change. Two or three years after the Armistice of 1918, the French government had announced that it would pay for the rebuilding of the northern and eastern sectors of the country, from which the inhabitants had fled one step ahead of the German invaders. Nothing had been left of their properties, and now those in power had proposed to pay four times the estimated value of each lost building, as long as what was rebuilt coincided exactly with what had been razed. Where there had been a house, a house had to be built; where a factory, a factory. And because the franc had been greatly devalued, the government had set the rate at four times the original worth of the property. Those who had fled their homes could return, and industry could begin again in the blighted parts of France. For contractors like Paul Bruisson, Lily's father, a gold mine had been uncovered. And now the family lived in the Villa Persane, in Boulogne-sur-Seine, just ten minutes on foot from Paris, with a butler, two maids, and a cook. Only the chauffeur worked part-time, for the women.

Lily didn't like the Villa Persane. It rose proudly near the beautiful Boulevard d'Auteuil, bordered by old, majestic trees. It was entirely covered with enamel mosaic in small squares of blue, white, and green, with some black ones thrown in for a more modern look. 'See how geometric this design is,' her father had expostulated to a guest. 'It's the design of the future!' But Lily thought it devoid of good taste, and the turret failed to resemble a Moorish minaret, and seemed, in its pretentiousness, no more than ridiculous.

Lily, in that house, where the furniture was heavy and dark, felt like a small cloud imprisoned in a dungeon. Only her mother's boudoir and her own room were light and soft and delicate, because everywhere else her father's will had imposed itself.

She didn't like what Claude had told her. Ever since she had returned from Brittany, she'd noted things he'd said that didn't feel right. He worked with their father. He solicited new clients. He drove a medium-priced car 'in order not to seem richer than the clients'. He was a young man-about-town, but there was no joy to him except when he could speak of money, of benefits, of contracts. Although he'd inherited their mother's dark good looks, he was, Lily thought, a younger replica of their father.

But it wasn't only that. Father was straightforward, and he was honest. He dealt with facts, with figures. Claude went beyond that. He manipulated. She wondered if there was anyone at all for whom he felt respect, or genuine caring. Maybe for their mother, because no one could remain immune to her gentleness or fineness of spirit. Certainly he didn't love her, his sister. Then . . . what was it he wanted with her? Why couldn't he leave her alone, to paint or to read, instead of insisting that she go to endless fittings that made her ankles swell, and to gatherings with people she'd never met, whose extreme stylishness made her feel like a small child peeking into a world where she didn't belong?

'The Comtesse de Béhague won't even notice me, Claude,' she said. 'It won't matter what I say. She doesn't know me and doesn't care about me.'

'But I want people to notice you! What do you want to *do* with your life, Lily? You have no profession. In society we don't yet have a name. It's up to you to make this name, because you're lucky, you're a beautiful girl, and men will notice.'

'So what are you hoping for? That some elderly marquis will build a castle for me? In return for what?'

'I just want you to have an opportunity to marry well.'

'And if not, to become a rich man's whore.'

He turned to her, amazed, and started to laugh. 'I didn't know they taught you these words at the convent!'

But she wasn't amused. When he chucked her under the chin, in an effort at friendliness, she remained impassively staring ahead of her, at the lighted streets of the Paris winter. He withdrew his hand, and once more they were strangers sharing the same name, the same space, but nothing else.

Mikhail Ivanovitch Brasilov plucked a *coupe* of champagne from a passing tray, and leaned against a panel of the wall. From his vantage point, for he was excessively tall, he could peer through two reception rooms clear into the vestibule, where the Comtesse de Béhague's *maître d'hôtel* stood at attention. He was restless, bored. He'd worked all

19

day since six that morning, going over all the company books with the chief accountant, and he'd come here to feel around him the atmosphere of his early youth, in Kiev and Moscow. He'd thought that since the countess entertained a great many exiled Russians, like himself, his usual nostalgia for the golden moments of a dead era would be assuaged through the company of his compatriots. But so far it hadn't been so. He'd been disappointed. Yussoupov had talked endlessly of his antique business, and the delicious prattlings of Tessa de Pulszky, Nijinsky's sister-in-law, had been like thick moths buzzing around his head. He felt tired, irritable. He shouldn't have come – but if not this, then what? He'd had enough of that little model from the Latin Quarter, and nothing new had appeared on the horizon.

He half closed his green eyes, amused, detached. The *maître d'hôtel* was letting in two late arrivers, a man and a woman. The man was ordinary. He might have been any one of a dozen young Frenchmen always on the lookout for an opportunity to mix with the right crowd. They bored him. Every day two or three came to his office and opened the conversation in the same fashion: 'My dear Prince, we met two days ago at – ' and there would follow the name of a famous hostess, directly in front of a petition for a job. Inevitably he turned them down. On principle. He never mixed work and fun.

But the young woman was different. Mikhail Brasilov's eyes widened. She clashed with everything that spelled 1924. She was too tall, and her breasts and hips were too ample. She wasn't large – merely statuesque, slender but full. He liked that. The woman of today had no breasts worth mentioning, and was flat as a board – Madame Chanel at the forefront of them all. She wore a long gown of lemon-yellow muslin, and her arms were a dark creamy colour. Girls of today liked to be white, bleached out. And this one didn't wear makeup. Her dark, almond-shaped eyes were fringed with curling black lashes, and her complexion was the same bronzed colour as her arms. She looked exotic, not French at all – perhaps Arabian, or Greek. Mikhail Brasilov picked up his *coupe* and sipped from it, eyeing the girl.

She had long brown hair, almost black, that undulated down her back and over her shoulders. Her posture was erect, proud. But she looked very young. Certainly, he thought, a virgin. And that, added to all the rest topped off his fascination. He strode forward, nearly upsetting a passing tray of caviar on toast points, and followed the angle of his vision towards the girl.

She was alone, on the threshold of the first reception room, and nobody had noticed her. Where, Mikhail wondered, was her escort? And, more important, who was he? Her husband? She looked like the sort of person who'd be happily married, who'd never venture anywhere without her escort. But now she looked confused, ill at ease.

Reaching her, he said, bowing slightly: 'Are you looking for someone? May I help you?'

She blushed. What girl had blushed in the last year? She looked up, tried to smile. She was shy, but not overwhelmed. 'I was waiting for my brother,' she answered. 'He went to say hello to somebody he knew . . .'

Then he must be the last of the boors, Mikhail thought. It was incredible to leave her standing there, not to introduce her! Surely that brother of hers was a *nouveau riche* social climber of the worst sort. But he said: 'Allow me to present myself. Prince Mikhail Ivanovitch Brasilov. You are . . . ?'

'Liliane Bruisson.' She was holding out her hand, long and well kept, and he bent over it and touched it with his lips.

'Would you like me to introduce you around? Are you curious about all these people?'

21

Her smile widened. She said nothing, but he caught the irony in her brown eyes. 'You couldn't care less,' he said.

'It's not that. I just – I'm not sure why I'm here. What I can possibly have in common with most of these people.' Then she turned red again, looked aside. 'I'm sorry. You're here, and what I just said was terribly rude . . .'

'It was merely terribly honest, mademoiselle. I hope to God that I, like you, don't have too much to share with the rest of this crowd.'

He laid her fingers over his arm, and had started to walk. She wondered if this was all right, to go with this stranger into another room, without waiting for Claude. But there was something so powerful, so hypnotic, about this man, that she matched his step instinctively. She'd worry about her brother later. Prince Brasilov rose at least six feet four inches, with shoulders that matched, wide and strong. But his waist tapered down, and his hips were no larger than Claude's. He had long legs with thighs that showed muscle under the broadcloth of the evening suit. She liked his largeness – it made her feel small, while at the same time allowing her to walk in her usual bold stride, which Claude had told her was decidedly unfeminine. She didn't feel self-conscious.

But – he was a prince. Princes belonged in fairy stories. A Russian prince. She said: 'You do belong here. Why do you reject your peers?'

'Because they're not. I came from Russia with my father, a little man with a pointed beard and the best mind this side of Asia. We lost my mother to the Bolsheviks. We came here penniless – not like Felix Yussoupov, or even Felia Litvinne, the diva. But we brought with us four sacks of sugar beets from our plantations in Kiev. And because we were hungry, because we couldn't be satisfied with anything less, we built from these four sacks our own empire. I got up at four thirty this morning, mademoiselle. I was at the office at six. If I danced all night, or spent it

22

with a *chanteuse de café-concert*, that is nobody's business but my own, and my work was not affected by it . . . No, I am not at home with those who waste their life in cognac and coffee conversation.'

He'd spoken in a rush of words, and as she looked into his face, she was struck by the passion of this man. There was something savage about him. He had a large face with strong cheekbones, a large nose, and big white teeth. She caught herself abruptly, surprised at the turn of her thoughts. His green eyes, under the soft arch of their brows, were appealing to her, suddenly vulnerable. He was everything she didn't know, everything foreign, everything male. Not at all like her father, with his plump stomach hanging ridiculously over his belt – or like her civilized, cut-and-dried brother, Claude. Lily was afraid and fascinated, at the same time.

He had stopped a valet with a tray with small sandwiches, and was saying to her: 'What is your preference? Foie gras? Smoked salmon? Caviar?'

She wasn't sure. At home Mama gave pastries for tea, and sometimes small pieces of round bread covered with a cheese pâté. At school, tea had been even simpler: a brioche with hot chocolate. This wasn't tea, it was evening, it was . . . cocktails? She wanted to make sure this man wouldn't desert her when he learned how simple she was, how backward. 'I'll take anything,' she said. 'Thank you.'

He took the tiniest sliver of smoked salmon on pumpernickel, and held it before her. 'Open your mouth, Cinderella.'

She laughed. He listened, delighted. Then he popped the tiny morsel into her mouth, and watched her astonishment. He laughed too. It was a moment she thought she would always remember. The Russian prince feeding her and laughing with her in the midst of a crowd of elegant people, in a strange house, waiting for her brother.

And then the magic bubble burst, Claude was at her

elbow. 'We've met before, my dear Prince. At the Baronne d'Oettingen's costume ball, six months ago . . .'

'Yes, yes,' Mikhail Brasilov muttered, barely acknowledging the hand that was thrusting itself at him.

'We spoke then about the government contracts to repair the war damage in the north – and how our firm could be useful to you.'

'Perhaps we did,' the Russian said, already beginning to look over Lily's head into the next reception hall. 'I really couldn't say . . .'

Lily felt waves of mortification washing over her. A young woman was coming near them, her hips flat, her hair cut short, chin length. Her lips were outlined in carmine red, and her cheeks were dotted with rouge over white powder. Rows and rows of long strands of pearls were knotted over her small, perky breasts.

'Misha, darling, where have you *been?* We need your counsel. Tessa says the best Negro jazz club is Le Boeuf sur le Toit, but I myself prefer – '

Mikhail Ivanovitch Brasilov smiled, laid a finger over the painted girl's lips, and took Lily's hand. 'Mademoiselle,' he stated, raising it to his lips. 'It's been a pleasure. Perhaps we'll meet again . . .'

No, we won't, Lily thought. You've met my brother, and now you know exactly who I am, where I come from. And she was furious with Claude for bringing her here, for letting her meet a man who would laugh with others behind their backs, who would say: Guess who came to la Béhague's reception? They didn't belong with the cognac-and-coffee set, with the fast set and the cream of French society. No matter how well she dressed, she'd never be comfortable with these people, who weren't her kind, weren't her people.

'Bravo, my dear sister,' Claude was whispering. 'That's the richest bachelor in Paris. He's of the oldest Kiev aristocracy.'

* * *

The Villa Persane was, to Lily, a monument to bad taste and the desire to flaunt new money. And the worst part about it was that its location was superb. The Boulevard d'Auteuil began in Paris, a block or so away from the Porte d'Auteuil, and in Boulogne-sur-Seine there were houses only on one side, all with gardens. Only the Villa Persane had its gate on the boulevard. In front stretched the nursery of the Bois de Boulogne. Why Paul Bruisson had insisted on creating a Persian monstrosity amid such typically French surroundings was beyond his daughter's understanding.

The vestibule was flanked by the kitchen and the garage, and on the first floor were the reception halls; on the second, the family bedrooms; on the third floor were the laundry and the servants' quarters. Paul had fitted the windows with heavy velvet drapery, but the reception rooms were furnished in the style of the First Empire. Every piece was encrusted with mother-of-pearl inlays, with curlicues and complicated drawers, and had borders of carved bronze representing swans and cupids. Lily thought them hideous. She never went into the living room if she could help it; and for meals, she sat erect in the dining room, trying to avoid looking at the enormous oil painting of her grandfather in frilled shirt and curled hair – her grandfather Bruisson, who'd been a carpenter in Lille and had never worn a frilled shirt at any time in his life.

She liked her mother's boudoir. At forty-three, Claire Bruisson was still a handsome woman. She was tall, like Lily; but with the years her figure had grown more ample. She had dark eyes in a beautiful cameo face, and wore her dark hair in a topknot at the crown of her head. She dressed simply but tastefully in greens and reds, which went with her somewhat sultry colouring. Light hues didn't enhance her looks. But in the boudoir she had selected walls of beige raw silk, a Louis XV *bergère*, a small secretary

25

with delicate, unobtrusive inlays of lighter woods, also Louis XV, and a pale green and pink and beige silk, hand-painted, for her bedspread and canopy.

Lily felt at home with her mother. They didn't have to talk to feel each other's moods. Lily sometimes took a book into the boudoir, and read there while her mother embroidered. Claire was a quiet person, reserved, contemplative, and rarely talked about her childhood, about the parents who were now dead. But Lily remembered her grandfather. He'd been from Brussels, where he'd owned and managed a small business. Lily didn't know, and perhaps had never known, what that business involved. But she'd been told that Claire had been an only child. Lily couldn't remember her grandmother.

Knocking on the door to the boudoir, Lily hugged her shawl closely around her. Claire told her to come in, and she did. At once the feeling of constriction around her throat eased off.

'Claude tells me you were quite the belle of the ball,' her mother said, smiling. She was sitting on the *bergère*, repairing a lace napkin.

'It wasn't a ball, and I was by no means a belle,' Lily replied crossly. She drew up the hassock near her mother's armchair, and plopped down. 'Claude humiliated me. He has a horrible way of insinuating things . . . of . . .'

'Claude has ways about him that are disconcerting. I've never quite understood him. But darling, don't *mind* him so! If you're a lady, nobody else can bring you down. And besides – I'm sure he means well, taking you out and showing you to society. That's what your father wants.'

'And you?'

Claire's shoulders rose and fell, and she sighed. 'I want to see you happy. You were cloistered for too many years. You've forgotten what Paris is like. But it's your home; you have to fit into it. I know you didn't enjoy the ball your father gave for your *début* in the autumn. But sometimes, Lily, you must make an effort to do what's expected of you.'

'I didn't like the ball because I didn't know a single soul there. And Papa wouldn't let me invite Marisa.'

Claire kept her eyes on her work. 'Marisa Robinson is always welcome here. I know you two have loved each other since before you left for Brittany. But your father has his ideas about this – about Jewish people.'

'That's ridiculous! Marisa's family is the real thing, not like Papa's absurd pretensions! They live in a palace, almost, and they've had money and servants and fineries for generations. What does it matter if they're Jewish, or Protestant – or Buddhist, for goodness' sake?'

'It's just how your father feels.'

'But it's unjust. Papa's never been religious. It's all just another one of his pretensions.'

'Lily, he's your father.'

Their eyes locked. Lily asked, almost in a whisper: 'And you never disagree with him?'

Claire laid a long smooth hand over her daughter's. 'In my head and in my heart, I'm free to think what I like. But marriage is a compromise. Your father has been good to us all. He works very hard to give us a life of ease and comfort.'

Lily knew that her mother was closing the subject. Claire never really spoke her intimate thoughts. Lily stood up, conscious of all the unresolved, unanswered questions. Her mother was looking at her. 'You didn't tell me about the Russian,' Claire said softly.

Lily wheeled about, her cheeks red. 'I didn't tell you because it didn't amount to anything. I met a man – a Russian prince. There are thousands of them roaming the streets of Paris. He couldn't wait to get away from me. And I don't blame him. Claude standing there, as if waiting for a handout – and then the pretty girl who came

27

along, who *belonged*, not like me! Maybe Claude's right: I *am* six years behind the times. Her hair was bobbed, and she wore makeup – outrageous makeup. I'd die if I had to look like that. But *he* liked it. He didn't even really say goodbye – '

'But you'd like to see him again.'

Lily said, her hands clenched so tightly that the knuckles shone white: 'I hope I never see him again. My brother's never going to sell me for thirty pieces of silver!'

Claire's eyes, so large and dark, stayed on Lily's face until, the passion wrung out of her, the young woman sat down again. I'm never going to have another outburst, she was thinking. I'm never going to lose control because of someone else's behaviour.

And then, as she watched Claire resuming her needle-work: I'm never going to be like my mother, trapped into a marriage that isn't right.

Marisa Robinson was small and very frail, and wore her short ashblond hair waved in tight curls around her pixie face. Lily always felt awkward and big when she was with her. They'd met ten years before, when they'd been eight, at a ballet school where their mothers were sending them. Marisa had been the best student, executing all manner of steps, but she'd also been the class clown, losing points for bad behaviour. Lily adored her. Only with Marisa could she feel free of the oppression that hung around her, from the sadness brought on by living in a house dominated by a strident, self-important man like her father, and by her brother, whom she didn't trust.

Sometimes Claire came with her to the beautiful apartment in the Avenue Henri-Martin, where the Robinsons lived. Claire liked Marisa, her mother, her young brother. Claire laughed, easily, the worry lines around her mouth and eyes disappearing for a few hours during these visits. David Robinson, Marisa's father, was the most important confectioner of sugared biscuits in France. His family had started this business generations ago. Marisa remembered being told that Czar Nicholas II and Queen Victoria had ranked among her grandfather's preferred customers.

The Robinsons lived, with their six servants, in an enormous high-ceilinged apartment close to the Bois de Boulogne. Marisa's mother, Eliane, had furnished each room with exquisite taste. Marisa's room was hung with pink-and-white striped wallpaper, and her furniture was all white, with pink-and-white striped curtains and bedspread. The living room was delicate Louis XVI, but Eliane Robinson had mixed Impressionist paintings with this period decor, and scenes from Manet and Dufy in no way took away from the curved armchairs and enamel-inlaid tables that adorned the room.

Lily, always conscious of underlying thoughts and motives, couldn't help but feel awkward coming again to a tea at the Robinsons'. Claire made certain to invite Eliane and Marisa at least once a month to the Villa Persane, but Lily realized that tea was always served early on these occasions, so that by the time Paul and Claude Bruisson returned from their offices, the guests had left. She was as glad about that as her mother, because she was afraid that her father might speak coarsely, or too loudly, to Madame Robinson, so fine and distinguished. Nevertheless she felt ashamed. In Marisa's house, one inevitably became involved in a long discussion, and suddenly David Robinson would appear, cheerful and gallant, to add yet another note of brightness to the occasion. Unlike her father, Monsieur Robinson was a charming, easy man, one who could get along with women and not be bored or boring in their company.

Sometimes Lily had wondered if Marisa had been the reason her parents had insisted on sending her so far away to boarding school. The girls had planned to go together to a tutor chosen by Marisa's mother. Then, suddenly, Lily's father had declared that she was to go to a convent school in Brittany. The only sort of school where Marisa wouldn't have been able to follow her.

That summer of 1923, when Lily had come home for good, her parents had organized her *début*. She was eighteen; it was time to enter society. Since the war, it mattered only if one was rich enough to do so; *débutantes* abounded, from all sorts of backgrounds. Granddaughters of factory workers married sons of famous noblemen – the war had changed everybody's values. What held meaning was, above all, to have money in the bank, which many aristocrats no longer had. And Paul had refused to invite Marisa Robinson.

'You're part of the élite, now, Lily,' he'd said to her. 'You don't need people like that anymore.'

'But the Robinsons have been part of society longer than we have! Madame Robinson is a Rueff!'

'The Robinsons are not our kind of people.'

She couldn't help but recall this conversation as she and Claire stepped out of the lift into the hallway that led to the Robinsons' door. Another invitation that might or might not be returned.

A young maid in uniform opened the door. Behind her came Eliane Robinson, holding out her hands to Claire. She kissed Lily, and an expensive perfume filled the air around them. 'Welcome, darlings. We have quite a gathering here today. David's sister sent us a fascinating young American journalist. He tells of such things . . .' She let the sentence hang, to tantalize her guests, and Lily saw Claire's half-smile of amusement. The Bruissons had never met David Robinson's sister, who had committed the intrepid act of marrying an American architect in the Deep South. But of course they'd heard of her.

They entered the salon. Marisa almost upset her cup of tea in an effort to reach her friend and kiss her. Lily, always so quiet and controlled, loved and envied Marisa's exuberance. It was so foreign to her own nature, yet winsome and warm. Everybody liked Marisa Robinson. Five hundred people had'flocked to her *début*, and, Eliane had confided to Claire, the telephone never stopped ringing. Marisa was a woman of the world who went three times a week to hear jazz at small, exclusive, intellectual clubs, or to listen to the *tziganes* at the Russian cabarets. Yet nobody had one word to say against her reputation. Nobody ever saw her alone with a young man, in a compromising situation.

She had been sitting on the brocade love seat next to a stranger with fine features whom Lily assumed to be the American journalist. Lily was intrigued. Marisa, in her cowl-necked, short-sleeved blouse tucked into her tight, knee-length Kiki skirt, seemed as sleek as a kitten. Lily felt too tall, and blessed the fur trim that lengthened her own Maggy Rouff afternoon dress of soft green silk.

'Lily, this is Mark MacDonald, of Charlotte, North Carolina,' Marisa declared. 'Liliane Bruisson, my oldest and dearest friend. We tripped over our own feet and fell over each other's in ballet school.'

The young man laughed. He rose, and Lily noted that he was exactly her height. He was built in a tight, compact manner, like a small panther. He had an oval face with a straight nose and hazel eyes, and his hair was a soft brown mass of curls. He went well with Marisa: two small, well-shaped young people. He looked to be about twenty-four years old – Claude's age.

There were six or seven other people present, and Lily had met some but not others. She made her rounds politely. Mark was the only man present, except for an elderly gentleman leaning his chin on a silver-tipped cane, who had accompanied his silver-haired wife. Lily turned back to the love seat and saw that Marisa had disappeared. She sat down next to Mark, suddenly awkward.

'Do you know, Mademoiselle Liliane, that Marisa speaks nearly perfect English?' he said to her.

'Marisa has many talents. But I wouldn't have the temerity to judge her English. I didn't learn it. In Brittany, where I was in school, the nuns taught us Latin and Greek.'

'My heavens!' he cried, playfully moving away from her on the sofa. 'Marisa's introduced me to an intellectual!'

'Oh, I'm really not. We had no choice about taking Latin and Greek. With the nuns, one seldom has any choice.'

'You're so serious. I was only teasing you. Tell me, mademoiselle, are you always so serious? With Marisa, a person can't ever fit in a serious word.'

'I suppose,' Lily said, 'that's one of the reasons our friendship has survived ten years. She brings me out of my brooding moods, and I tone her down a bit. But I don't like to do that. Marisa's perfect – don't you think?'

'I never try to find a perfect person. They're unwholesome. But I like Marisa. I like the whole family. Eliane is great. She reminds me of my mother.'

'But Madame Robinson is so typically French! Is your mother of French origin, perhaps?'

Mark laughed. 'No. We're what is called a Family of the American Revolution. Our ancestors were Pilgrims who came over on the ship *Mayflower*. You must understand, Mademoiselle Liliane, that this doesn't mean a thing. I couldn't tell you whether my great-great-grandfathers were Puritan scholars or criminals let out to free the congested jails of England. But in the United States, people are very snobbish about having ancestors that came over on the *Mayflower*.'

Lily was silent, listening. Yes, she thought, he would make a fine husband for Marisa. He has humour, charm. She felt curiously at ease with him. How different from what she had felt in the strange company of the imposing, somewhat frightening Mikhail Brasilov . . .

'You see,' Mark was saying, 'the Deep South isn't at all like New York or San Francisco. It's still the stronghold of Old World gentility. My parents live in a white mansion with doric pillars that has been in our family for many generations. My mother receives magnificently with nothing but the best. That's life in Charlotte.' Mark MacDonald smiled, raising his brows: 'Boring.' She laughed. He took out a cigarette case of tortoiseshell and gold, and a gold lighter. 'Do you mind if I smoke?'

She motioned no, and he looked at her, squarely in the eye. For the first time she fell silent, embarrassed. Why was he staring? He said: 'You're remarkably beautiful. I've never seen a woman like you. You're a real *ingénue*, born yesterday, and yet you're full of the wisdom of the ages. Ceres, the goddess of the earth.'

She felt her cheeks burning. 'I don't know anything. I don't even know much about Paris. I don't go out much.'

'That's what I like about you. Tell me, what do you do for amusement?'

'I embroider, I read, I listen to music.'

'Things one does alone.'

'Or sometimes with my mother.'

'And what dreams do you have?'

She looked back at him, surprised. 'Dreams? I'm afraid of dreams. Life always seems to disappoint the dreamer.'

'But if you weren't afraid? What would you dream?'

'I'd be married, with a household of my own, and I'd have friends – intelligent people, like Marisa. I'd have a gentle husband who never shouted, never gave orders – just suggested his wishes to me. Or maybe – maybe I wouldn't be married. Maybe I'd be a poetess, or a concert pianist.'

'You play the piano?'

'Yes. I've been playing since I was five. You asked me

33

what I like to do best. My favourite pastime is my piano. It's a beautiful Pleyel and it plays with a deep, mellow resonance that lifts up one's heart ... Do you think I'm odd?'

He shook his head, and the hazel eyes remained on her face, pensive. 'Never odd. But somewhat lonely.'

'My brother wants me to get out more. But I'm not sure I like it. Six years in a convent haven't helped – I'm awkward in society. I'll never be,' she stated wistfully, 'like Marisa.'

'But you are every bit as charming as Marisa. I doubt that the world will forget you.'

She opened her mouth, amazed, and didn't close it. He remained looking at her with a steadfastness that studied her features and tried to read her mind. They were silent thus, for a few minutes. And then Marisa returned, holding out a chain of perfect rubies in a gold clasp. 'Look, Lily,' she said. 'Papa brought this back from Amsterdam last week. Aren't they wonderful?'

Above her curly head, Lily caught a gently ironic expression on Mark MacDonald's face. And then she realized that she'd been speaking to him with such honesty and candour because she'd thought he belonged to *Marisa*. She felt suddenly disconcerted, and a little angry. He'd won his way into her thoughts on a pretence.

But that's not fair, she thought. He never pretended. It was I who assumed.

She didn't know why, but the softness of the afternoon seemed warped, like a fine Stradivarius left out in the sun and rain.

The girl closed the door of the tall, thin confession box, and knelt in front of the grating. Her long hair was held back by a silk ribbon and covered by a woollen scarf. Beyond the grating she could discern the vague, ominous shadow of the confessor.

'Oh, Father, I have sinned.'

'How long has it been since your last confession?'

'One week.'

'How have you sinned, my child?'

Her voice, strong and clear in its purity, wavered. 'I have had indecent thoughts.'

'That is not good, my child. You must renounce such thoughts.'

'Father, I am afraid.'

'Those who honour the Lord's commandments have nothing to fear. Why are you afraid?'

'I'm afraid of myself.'

'My child, who is the man who has not entertained self-doubt? As long as you use the word of our Lord Jesus Christ as your protective shield, no harm shall come to you.'

'And . . . about the man?'

'You shall recite five Hail Marys, and forgo the morning meal for one week in penitence. And you shall not see him.'

She bowed her head, and felt the tension letting go, the pain slowly ebbing, the guilt being washed away by centuries of Latin litanies. 'In the name of the Father, the Son, and the Holy Ghost, I absolve you of your sins.'

The disembodied voice was like the soothing, impersonal hand of the Mother Superior when she had passed out pictures of the saints to reward a particularly deserving pupil. *Mea culpa, mea culpa, mea maxima culpa.*

'There isn't any reason why you shouldn't try for a career as a concert pianist,' Mark said. They were walking in the gardens of the Tuileries, their collars turned up to ward off the freezing cold of the bleak January day. In the distance, Marisa was romping in the snow, a small ball of fur among the statues.

'You heard me play Brahms. I'm not so good.'

35

'You're beyond-this-world good. Why don't you have more confidence in yourself, Lily?'

She stopped, hugging herself in her wool coat with the full skirt and large sleeves that let in the wind in great, bone-chilling gusts. She stood facing him, her long hair blown away from her face, her cheeks stung red. 'I'm not sure what I have that should give me confidence. I play for my own pleasure. In concert halls the artist is dramatically good – not just agreeable. And then, I was taught that self-importance is a great sin. Jesus was humble.'

He started to laugh. 'You believe such things?'

She shrugged, embarrassed. 'In the United States, people don't have faith?'

'Some do, some don't. I'm a confirmed sceptic.'

'But a person can't ignore the Bible. It's such a beautiful testimonial to God's love for His people.'

Mark MacDonald reached for her gloved hand, and brought it to his lips. He remained holding it, looking into the velvet brown eyes of the young woman in front of him. 'You make me want to be young again,' he said softly, mild humour in his hazel eyes.

'But you *are* young. Why do you say that?'

'Because I'm a journalist. My job has been to print facts, and most of the time, facts are ugly, raw, crude. I used to work on a newspaper. It disgusted me what countries can do to one another. Then they put me to head the society column. I had to go to all the fine houses in Charlotte to interview its leading citizens, the women with their diamond rings and their fur coats, the men with their three-piece suits and shining spats. What exists among members of the same family is far, far worse than anything you can imagine.'

'Not so far,' Lily whispered.

'But you are unchanged. You are like a lost illusion.'

'No,' she said, her tone stronger. 'It's just that I'm waiting. I'm not sure what exactly I'm waiting for, but there's a life outside that must have some meaning. My mother says that life is composed of compromises. Maybe I can't become a great pianist. But I know that *they* think I'm worth something. Even if Claude criticizes me without stop, even if he doesn't like me – he knows I'm worth something. So I have to wait.'

'I'm not quite sure I understand.'

'They think I can make their life good for them. I just want to make sure that they don't hurt my mother. I'm not like them, and neither is she.'

'Who else is "they" besides your brother?'

'My father. He never knew I was alive until my *début*. And now he sends me for fittings twice a week, and makes sure my shoes aren't scuffed.'

'Poor little Lily,' Mark said affectionately, squeezing her hand. 'We shall have to give you a better existence.'

'No,' she said. 'I have to learn what exactly I want, and then I'll make my own decisions.'

All at once Marisa Robinson bobbed up between them, her fur hood dotted with snow. 'What a great day!' she cried. 'And what have you two serious people been talking about?'

'World revolutions,' he said, letting Lily's hand go. 'Come on, let's go to the Marquise de Sévigné for a triple order of hot chocolate.'

Chapter Two

The sumptuous offices of the Brasilov Enterprises stood on the second and third floors of a large granite mansion on the Rue de Berri, just off the Champs-Élysées, on the other side of which rose the elegant Hotel George V. Mikhail Ivanovitch Brasilov occupied the second largest office, which had once been the sitting room of a French duchess. Its walls, white and clean, met the high ceiling with a scalloped piping, and when Mikhail had to think out a complex problem, his eye inevitably fastened itself on the geometric design, so pure and so repetitive, which drew him like a magnet.

But the room had long since become strictly masculine. It was decorated in gleaming Louis XIII ebony and rich mahogany, and the desk was adjusted to the large proportions of the prince. On the walls hung only two paintings, both oils, both framed in simple, understated gilt wood. One was a painting of the Princess Maria Brasilova, Mikhail's mother, done by Jean Édouard Vuillard according to a tiny photograph that had been smuggled from Russia; the other was a pastoral scene executed by Manet, all frivolous colours of the rainbow. Apart from these two testimonials to Mikhail's love of beauty, the room was functional, and spare.

He sat now, this January morning of 1924, with a series of legal documents in front of him, not looking at them, but thinking. The government of Raymond Poincaré, the Bloc National, was about to be changed; this he could predict. Poincaré had been the answer in '22; then, he had heralded a new prosperity, and his conservatism had matched the

38

nation's. He had been a middle-class premier in a country dominated by the newly rich bourgeoisie. But now, especially after last year's ill-thought-out expedition into the Ruhr valley, the franc was devalued. France seemed to be turning to a more plebeian leadership. This would mean changes, in the economy as well.

Work never bothered Mikhail Ivanovitch. As a child, in Kiev, he had so rapidly absorbed his tutor's teachings that at the age of twelve he had already surpassed them. His father had moved the family to Moscow and sent Mikhail to a *Gymnasium*. At fifteen he had graduated, passing his baccalaureate examinations with a series of unsurpassable 5's. He had entered the university with a special dispensation from the czar, because he hadn't reached the normal age; there he had entered two faculties at the same time: that of law, which all businessmen had to master, and that of history, which was his passion. Within three years he had obtained both degrees, where other young men took four years to complete a single course of study. And then his father had put the eighteen-year-old boy at the head of most of his enterprises.

The Brasilov Enterprises had stretched over a vast continent, and had comprised diverse businesses. Prince Ivan, Mikhail's father, had a nose for where the money lay. He bought all businesses that he thought could prosper; if they were failing, he saved them; if they were already successful, he tripled their gains. He owned a great number of sugar refineries in Kiev; windmills; mines of semiprecious stones in the Urals; land in Siberia; a boat company on the Volga; and a tramway business in Odessa.

Prince Ivan paid his son a million roubles in gold per annum. This represented an enormous sum of money, especially for one so young. Mikhail – Misha to his intimates – began then to spend all his nights out, to entertain himself with the mad passion of the 'golden youth', and to spend a small fortune. His father wasn't exactly happy with this, but left him alone. First of all, it was his own money, not even money received through gift or inheritance, but money earned through his own work. Misha had the right to do what he pleased with his money. Furthermore, he furnished the business with an enormous load of work. Sometimes he didn't arrive home until seven in the morning, just in time to bathe, change, and read the newspaper in an armchair to freshen his mind. But never did his nights of sleeplessness prevent him from arriving at the office at nine on the dot, the first one there, his mind lucid, ready to make complicated calculations and solve difficult problems.

Then came the Bolshevik Revolution. Being so phenomenally rich, the Brasilovs moved to Kiev, then went to Odessa, and finally ended up in the Crimea, once the summer paradise of many aristocratic families. From there, father and son were able to leave for Constantinople.

But, like many emigrants, they weren't able to take their fortune with them. Prince Ivan took only what he judged to be most important: four sacks of sugar beets. Arriving in France in 1921, he bought sugar plantations in the departments of the Nord and the Oise, and sold seeds to be planted. The sugar that resulted was far superior to the French sugar, and in 1923 Prince Ivan was awarded the French Legion of Honour for having bettered the French sugar beet by breeding it with the Russian. Then he and his son began to expand their business. They founded a Metallurgy Works that built large garages, storage areas, and factory hangars. Then they bought a sardine canning factory in Brittany, a duck-liver factory near Bordeaux, a factory of silk stockings in Troyes, and a paper factory. Now they were solidly established, and, once more, money flowed through their pockets.

Like many entrepreneurs, the Brasilovs had benefited from the government policy of repaying for the war damages in the north and east of France. The business of buying and selling war-damaged properties had become a most complex affair. At each moment rules were modified, others withdrawn. Articles of law mounted up in the large register of the Ministry of Finance. Those who were interested consulted this ledger, and having reached the article they were looking for, stopped there. In the middle of building they suddenly found themselves in trouble with the government, for they hadn't known about modifications added after the article they'd supposed would be the last change.

Misha Brasilov was a thorough researcher. He read the ledger from A to Z, and studied it. If he needed Article 59, he continued beyond it. Often, at Article 123, he saw that the latter contradicted number 59 and erased it without even referring to it. With his prodigious memory, Misha kept all the articles on the tips of his fingers and never experienced difficulties. He and his father rebuilt two sugar refineries in the Nord and the Pas-de-Calais, and one in the Oise. He bought land to replant sugar beets. And this was how Prince Ivan came to receive the Legion of Honour. It gave the two men much cause for laughter, but nevertheless the head of the Brasilov Enterprises never failed to pin the distinguished red ribbon on his lapel when he was in full dress.

Now, Mikhail Brasilov was examining a paper containing the facts surrounding a newly purchased building damaged by war. They would have to reconstruct a sugar refinery in Ribécourt, in the Department of Oise. Because of some intricate specifications, they would have to use German material. In view of the huge war debt that Germany owed France according to the Treaty of Versailles, the French government had agreed to help put back in motion some of Germany's industry. But, Misha knew, there were few French contractors willing to go to Germany to bring back the raw materials. He pressed a button on a panel on his desk, and soon the door to the office opened and a middle-aged man in nondescript black clothes appeared.

'Your Excellency rang?'

'Yes, Rochefort. I'm stumped on the factory in Ribécourt. None of our usual suppliers will do. Any ideas?'

The secretary scratched his chin thoughtfully. Finally he said: 'We don't deal with them usually, but perhaps this time . . . I was thinking of Bruisson et Fils.'

Misha looked up, alert. 'Bruisson? I've heard the name recently. Tell me about the firm.'

The secretary cast his eyes to the side, embarrassed. 'They aren't so well thought of. Before the war, they were hardly known. The son – Claude, I believe his name is – he was very young then – served as a pilot during the war, and speaks fluent German. They've made a pile of money from war damages. I quite believe they'd be the ones for us to send to Germany. They have . . . few . . . scruples.'

Misha laughed. 'Well, business is business. We don't have to invite them to dinner. Claude, you say? Young, fairly attractive? A social climber of the worst pretension?'

Rochefort half smiled. 'Quite so, your Excellency. Though naturally Madame Rochefort and I do not associate with them personally.'

'I'm sure you don't. Not to worry. No one will force you to be seen in his company – Claude's. Nevertheless, get me the number. I shall ask him to come to the office. He'll be here within the hour.'

Rochefort executed a small bow, and departed. Misha shook his head, and chuckled. Then he laced his fingers together and laid his chin over the lacing, remembering. A beautiful, surprisingly beautiful young innocent – the sister. It had been a long time since he'd encountered that type. He'd thought he'd forgotten her, but now the memory returned.

Rochefort knocked on the door, and came in. He was

holding a piece of paper. 'The telephone number, your Excellency.'

'Thank you infinitely. It was a brilliant suggestion.'

Rochefort regarded him sceptically. 'Brilliant, sir?'

Misha sighed. 'A good idea. Send a memorandum to my father . . .'

Paul Bruisson was of average size, but his *embonpoint* filled out every crease of his elegant tailored navy blue suit. His double chin pressed out over his stiff collar, and his stomach strained the buttons of his white silk shirt. So, Misha thought, our contractor is the image of the prosperous French bourgeois. He didn't stand up, but motioned with a flip of his hand for the two men to sit in the large Louis XIII armchairs facing his oversize mahogany desk with its piles of neatly stacked documents.

Paul Bruisson was all smiles. He had a double chin and a fleshy mouth. Claude, however, was serious, almost sombre. Dressed in a dark grey suit with waistcoat, he appeared tall and brooding. His dark eyes were like his sister's, Misha thought, but without the kindness, the compassion. This man was hard.

Misha was fighting a strong desire to give in to the revulsion he was feeling. As a child, of the oldest Kiev nobility, he had been arrogant, and his mother had reprimanded him gently, but not too severely. 'Let the boy know his place,' Prince Ivan had cautioned her. Later he had trained himself to overcome his antipathy for the lower classes. One had to work with them. One had also to work with the greedy old Jews from the Pale of Settlement, who would gladly have sold their mothers for a hundred roubles. Misha liked the cleanness and directness of his father, who smiled only when something pleased him, and who seldom made pretences of anything. He was honest to the last kopek, the last sou. But when he was angry, a towering, burning fury erupted from him. He wasn't a man of compromises. Prince Ivan was his son's best friend, and his exemplar.

On the other side of the human scale was Paul Bruisson. Misha was not a Frenchman, but he hated the Germans because of the stupid war that had killed millions of Russian men and made his own nation weak enough for the Bolsheviks to take over. He had seen the devastated lands in the north and east of France. How could a French patriot ever agree to go to Germany, then, even for the cause of business, after what that country had done to his people? Misha looked at the Bruissons cautiously, not to give away his feelings. He tried never to give them away. They were the only treasures worth holding on to.

The door swung open, and the erect figure of Prince Ivan appeared. Then Misha rose. His father was small, thin, angular, with a trim grey Vandyke beard, and, unlike Paul Bruisson's, his suit, made on Savile Row in London of the purest dove-grey flannel, fitted exactly to the measure. His grey pearl cufflinks gleamed, matching the pin on his thin silk tie. 'Gentlemen,' he said.

Immediately the Bruissons rose, proffering their hands. Prince Ivan ignored them, and chose a small chair near his son's desk. 'My son tells me that you could handle the building of our factory in Ribécourt,' he said.

Paul Bruisson, his face red and beginning to show beads of unwelcome perspiration, nodded. 'Our firm has built quite a few factories, of all types,' he said. His voice was sweetly unctuous.

Prince Ivan nodded. 'I have seen the records. And whom would you send to Germany for the materials?'

Claude cleared his throat. 'I would be the one, your Excellency. I speak fluent German.'

Misha was chewing on the left side of his lower lip, listening. 'And you can select the best materials?' he asked.

Claude turned to him, and Misha was surprised to see

44

the smug look on his face – almost a look of silent triumph. 'Oh, most certainly, my dear Prince.'

Misha heard the words as if they were chalk grating on a blackboard. 'My dear Prince.' It wasn't the first time Claude had called him that, instead of 'your Excellency'. He'd used the words in front of the girl, at la Béhague's party. He focused his green eyes fully on the young man, and smiled. He knew how to make his lips smile alone, and the effect was chilling. 'We always check,' he said evenly. 'Nobody's word is good enough. If the factory is built wrong, we can lose a harvest. If we lost a harvest, we can lose a season. It's a game of dominoes. Don't ever forget that when dealing with us, Bruisson.'

Claude had coloured. But it was his father who replied. 'Oh, we wouldn't have it any other way. Business is business.'

'Then tell your lawyer to call mine, and we'll draw up the contract,' Misha declared.

To signal that the interview was at an end, Prince Ivan rose. Misha rose. The Bruissons scrambled to their feet, hands extended. This time they both held out their hands to the son, not the father. For a second Misha stared at them, levelly. Then, inclining his head with an ironic half smile, he put out his own hand and allowed the two contractors to shake it. But from Claude, he withdrew his own almost at once.

At the door, the young man suddenly turned, and Misha noted that his eyes were once more glittering with something not unlike bravado. 'Your Excellency,' he said softly, 'I forgot. My sister, Liliane, sends you her best regards.'

Misha smiled. 'How charming of her. Please convey to her my humble greetings.'

The two men exited, and Prince Ivan sat down again. He looked at his son. They both started to laugh. 'The father is a pork and the son a weasel,' Prince Ivan stated.

'Would that we didn't have to deal with such scum.'

'Nevertheless, this is France. We can't ignore these people. They're still one step above the Blums and the Herriots who will soon be leading this country, pushing it closer and closer to what we fled from in Russia. . . . Tell me, you know this young man's sister?'

Misha nodded, offhandedly. 'I've met her.'

'Is she like the father, or like the son?'

'Like neither.' There was a silence, and Prince Ivan's eyes stayed on his son. Misha was not elaborating. Prince Ivan's scrutiny became more intense.

'Clean up your life, my boy,' he whispered softly. 'It's time, don't you think?'

But Misha didn't answer.

Lily's room was separated from Claude's only by her bathroom, to which, unbeknown to her, he possessed a key. Now, as his footstep passed her closed door on the way to his own, he stopped, hearing her voice. She was chanting something, in a low, soft tone. Claude held his ear to the door panel, but the voice was muffled. He walked into his own room, slipped off his jacket, and went to a hardwood box on the secretary. He opened it and withdrew a key. Then, smiling, he inserted the key in the lock of the door that connected his room with Lily's bathroom.

He slid in, soundlessly. She'd left her own connecting door ajar, as she often did. Good. Crouching, he approached the basin. From there he could see perfectly what his sister was doing. She was kneeling by her bed, her hand on her rosary. And she was speaking.

'Holy Mary, Mother of God, pray for us poor sinners, now, and at the hour of our death . . .'

He let out a sigh, exasperated. Just a Hail Mary. But just as he was about to tiptoe out through his own door, he heard her again. 'Blessed Virgin,' she said, her voice beginning to break. 'Help me not to think of him, because it isn't meant to be. Help me not to have images of him, but to forget.'

Claude stood tense, alert. *Him?* That young American, Mark what's his name?

He'd call Marguery tonight and arrange for a meeting.

The nightmare pursued him. Hours before, his father and Rochefort had gone home, and the subaltern employees, receptionists, and female secretaries had locked up their work before leaving. Beyond the velvet curtains, Paris gleamed black, with dots of yellow from the streetlamps. He tried to think of the apartment on the Avenue de la Muette, off the Place du Palais de Chaillot in the distinguished Sixteenth Arrondissement, where his father was probably sipping cognac and warming his feet by the fireplace. The Russian *maître d'hôtel*, Arkhippe, whom Prince Ivan had hired in Paris, where he had found him waiting at tables at Maxim's, himself a refugee from St Petersburg, would be standing discreetly at attention, and in the kitchen, the cordon bleu chief cook, Annette, and her two assistants would be preparing a delectable five-course dinner.

But Misha couldn't concentrate on this soft image of habitual luxury. He knew he wouldn't be able to sleep again that night. He pressed his fingertips against the sockets of his eyes, pushing out the dull, aching throb. He saw red dots on the inside of his eyelids, from the pressing of his fingers. Red dots that became swirling crimson flames rising in the air, and suddenly, a young, anonymous woman screaming as the flames engulfed her. Misha's fist banged on the desk, and he knew that his face was wet. In his nostrils he could breathe the smell of burning flesh, a smell he would never forget. If this was Hell, then it existed, and he'd seen it, like Nebuchadnezzar.

Like all the times before, he thought desperately: My country is no more – my past is dead. Who *am* I?

He stood up, his legs shaking. In his breast pocket he found the neatly pressed linen handkerchief with his monogram. He wiped his face. Always a vain man, he carried with him, like a woman, a small hand-mirror. He glanced at his reflection and realized how he had aged in these three years. Below his eyes, the skin was puffy. He was thirty-three.

Abruptly, he buttoned his jacket and turned to leave the office.

When he'd been young, and visited Paris during his university days, the place to go had been Montmartre, dominated by the white cathedral of the Sacré-Coeur. Now, in the twenties, the place to go had shifted to the Left Bank, in Montparnasse. Misha was aware that he knew almost all the *bistros* and cabarets of the area; he was on first-name terms – one way, of course – with all the owners of the *dancings* and all the eating-places and bars and jazz clubs on the Left Bank. It didn't help.

He'd been a member of the 'golden youth' of Moscow, all the young aristocracy who chose to spend their nights carousing till dawn. He'd enjoyed being young, being rich, being single. He had to answer to no one but himself. Now he thought, in his customary brutal way, that his conscience was clean. He'd had hundreds of women in his day, and if they'd suffered, it hadn't been through any fault of his. He'd never lied. Brasilov princes never lied. They told the truth and got away with it.

Once in a while he worried. About the possibility of a child somewhere, unknowing and unclaimed. *That* would have been wrong. But he didn't think one existed. The women had been honest. He'd helped all the ones who'd been in trouble. He'd known a midwife, in Moscow, and she'd taken care of each one he'd sent, and brought him the bill. He'd always been kind, never derisive. But usually that was the last the girl had ever seen of him. He was afraid. Afraid of being trapped by a pregnant woman, the wrong woman.

Until now he'd never been faithful: he'd had every one, the princesses, the milliners, the married women and the virgins. He'd had them all.

As he parked the royal blue De Dion-Bouton between two Citroëns on the wide Boulevard Edgar-Quinet, Misha pushed the vague guilt of the Casanova out of his mind. Next to a secondhand dealer's was the Cossack *boîte de nuit* Les Djiguites. He pushed open the door and smelled shish kebab and cheap perfume. The muscles in his neck, along his spinal cord, began to relax.

It was dark, but he could make out familiar faces at the bar and around the tables. Cossack music made his eyelids sting, as it always did the first moment. He'd spent some years doing military service in the distinguished Division Sauvage in the Caucasus. Memories. Drinking songs. Before the end of his Russia, the mutilation of his people.

His eyes were becoming accustomed to the darkness. He needed some vodka. He sat down at the bar, listening to the hum of human voices. Good. This way he couldn't think. The barman said: 'Your Excellency, Prince Michel! A lady was just looking for you!'

'Looking for me *here?*'

'Well, we all know you come here two or three times a week. I put her over there, in the corner . . .'

Misha stood up, depressed. He'd hoped not to run into anyone he knew well. He possessed too many nodding acquaintances to ever have the luxury of being alone. But maybe that was why he'd come here. Aloneness meant the recurring nightmare. He'd never told his father that. Maybe then Prince Ivan would have understood . . . Maybe he already understood.

He walked over to the corner table, and saw her. She was very thin, and wore her hair in a pageboy around her oval face. She'd dyed it burgundy, which shocked. Her

K.O.T.W. - 3   49

face was dusted with white powder, and kohl rimmed the slanted amber eyes. She was pretty, in an elfin way. Her dress was a simple red sheath hiding the smallness of her bust but emphasizing the trim hips. She wasn't alone. With her was a young man with a headful of curls, and another elegant young woman with a washed-out, exhausted face. Too much opium, he guessed, and the next instant he was enveloped in a warm, slightly moist embrace that smelled of Shalimar.

'*Chéri*,' she said, and he was amused, because he hadn't seen her for some time. 'This is Mark MacDonald, of the Charlotte *Clarion*, and Nini, the newest model *chez* Lanvin. Meet my beautiful Russian prince. His name is Charming.'

Her name was Henriette, Rirette to her intimates, and he supposed that if she'd been looking for him, he was one of them. He remembered they'd met some months ago. She'd been a model *chez* Poiret, and at night she sometimes danced naked for private parties. She had a nice, firm, strong, athletic body. They'd made love almost right away, and he'd wanted her with an urgency that had made his performance passionate. She'd wanted more. He'd taken her to Deauville and spent three days and nights locked up in the Hotel Normandie with her. Then he'd cooled off. She was too vital, and seemed too old. She wasn't quite thirty, but looked as if she had been through it all, and had turned hard. He didn't need that: it was too demanding.

But still, when he'd wanted a woman to take his mind off everything, he'd often come back to her. Now she'd been looking for him. He sat down. The washed-out model from Lanvin bored him without even opening her mouth, but he wondered about the reporter. The reporter, too, was evidently wondering about *him*. 'I don't suppose we'd be polite to call you just "Charming",' he was saying, smiling.

Misha thought he looked intelligent, but with an American that was hard to tell. 'Mikhail Ivanovitch Brasilov,' he said, holding out his hand. In passing he thought that he had shown more familiarity to this stranger than to the two men who had been in his office that day. There was something genteel about the young man, something agreeable about his classical features in the small face.

'Mark was telling us all about the United States. He hopes to become a great novelist one day,' Rirette said.

'Actually, your Excellency, I was telling Rirette and Nini the dull story of my apprenticeship on the *Clarion*. But probably you've never even heard of my hometown of Charlotte, North Carolina. It's beautiful – but it's not that large. The city editor was a college friend of my father's, and so he took me on as a junior reporter. Later he discovered that I am in some ways like my mother – I love gossip. So he put me in charge of the society section.'

'And how did you make the transition from town gazetteer to international novelist?'

'Hardly that. But I wanted to get out of the South. I tried New York for a while, but it was too harsh for me. I met some good people. I found some others I already knew. I'd been at Princeton University with Scott Fitzgerald. He advised me to get out of the whole bloody country for a while, and write a book. Somehow, my mentor helped me. He thought it would shake up Charlotte to have a Paris correspondent to relay news of what other American artists were doing here. I'm afraid I've been so excited by what I've encountered so far, that I haven't even begun the Great American Novel.'

'You're very honest. Would you like to do an interview of my father and me, to show how two destitute Russians have adjusted to life in Paris, and how we started our business from four sacks of sugar beets? We aren't exactly American artists. But perhaps your readers would find us . . . exotic.'

Over the heads of the two young women, Misha's green eyes pierced the darkness, keen and expectant. Mark

MacDonald, younger and less experienced, met those eyes with his own. If you can figure out my motive, more power to you, the prince's eyes were saying. Mark smiled. 'Your Excellency wants to expand his business enterprises to the United States,' he said softly.

'And why not? Your country is young, my country is gone. Mine was the past, France is the present, and the United States is the future. The Brasilovs cannot be stopped by a simple frontier, nor by an ocean.'

'Then, by all means, I would be honoured to come to your offices for an interview.'

Mark took out his wallet, where a tiny gold pen lay attached to a small pad of tear-off paper. He tried to remove the pad, but it was stuck to a photograph wedged between it and the rest of the wallet. Mark removed the photograph, laying it on the table. Then he unhooked the pad and raised his eyebrows, waiting. Misha said: 'Thirty-six, Rue de Berri. Second floor. Tomorrow?'

Nini had picked up the photograph, and was holding it up to the light of the red candle on the table. 'Oooh, she's beautiful,' she sang. At once Rirette crowded near her, to take the photograph from her hand. She showed it to Misha. 'She *is*. Who is she, Mark, darling?'

Misha felt the muscles of his face tightening again, and the vodka ran through his body in small staccato pulsations. Haughtily, he plucked the snapshot from Rirette's fingers, and handed it dryly back to Mark. The young journalist took it with a suddenly embarrassed smile. 'You wouldn't know her,' he said. 'She's a friend of a friend.'

'That's what they all say,' Rirette said coyly.

'But it's the truth,' Mark answered.

In the candour of his hazel eyes, Misha saw that he'd told the truth. He could feel the relief flooding his body. All his life he'd believed that women were whores, because with him, they'd behaved this way. But somehow . . . this girl . . .

What did it matter about the girl? he then thought. She was too young, and her background wasn't quite right. New money, and the wrong relatives. He looked carefully at Rirette, and knew that she was far more interesting than the other, far more experienced, far more sexual. 'Come on,' he whispered in her ear. 'Let's get out of here.'

He was making a mistake, he felt it in his bones. But he couldn't help it at that moment. He wanted the girl, and he wanted her with a poignancy that made him vulnerable. But at the same time, right now, he wanted Rirette. One was a sentimental longing and the other was a basic, primeval need.

I'll make it all work out, he thought desperately.

'I think he's in love with you!' Marisa cried. Then: 'If he is, would you marry him?'

Lily, by nature, disliked to be the centre of attention. It embarrassed her. Now she clasped her hands together and stared at a spot on the carpet in Marisa's room. 'I've never considered it. Of course he doesn't love me.'

'He took the photo of you and me at the Bois, and cut me out of the picture so that he could put you in his wallet.'

Lily looked up, her eyes widening. 'He did that? But how do you know?'

'I needed change, and we've become such friends that he simply told me to find it in his wallet. He'd left his jacket upstairs, and was in his shirt sleeves. We'd been playing chess and the fire was strong, so we were both hot. I ran upstairs to find the jacket, and took out the wallet. Out tumbled the picture, one-two-three.'

Lily passed her tongue over her upper lip. 'You know how to act,' she said softly. 'But I really don't. Those six years in Brittany, I simply wished ahead that I was out of the house. I imagined myself married. But – I couldn't visualize being courted by a young man.'

'He's very decent. You should consider him, Lily.'

'He's an American. Someday he'll go back there. And besides, I like Mark, but I don't love him. So I guess that's that.'

'You've never even kissed him! You can't judge whether or not you're in love with a man until that first kiss.'

'I'm not going to kiss a stranger,' Lily countered.

Marisa burst out laughing, and took her friend's hand in her own. 'Oh, Lily, Lily, you are so Victorian! You remind me of a maiden aunt I have, who turns beet red whenever somebody kisses her hand!'

On the second floor of 13 Rue d'Anjou, Bruisson et Fils had a small suite of offices. Claude's office, down the hall from his father's, was furnished in a way he didn't approve of, but which he tolerated. Paul Bruisson, who had spent a fortune on his house, felt that at the office, one should exercise restraint. This went along with the advice he had given Claude in the selection of his car. The client should never feel that those who provided a service were richer than they, nor even as rich. If they did, they would begin to suspect that the wealth had come from plumping up their customers' bills. So the offices at Bruisson et Fils were uniformly decorated with furniture from the Galeries Lafayette: nice, clean pieces, but not of luxurious design, nor of the top quality.

Claude always wondered, when he was alone, if his father's customers even gave the offices a second glance. But he kept these comments to himself. Now he heard the knock on the door, said: 'Come in!' and waited. It was already dark outside and the offices had, to all intents and purposes, closed down. But he'd stayed behind to receive his last appointment.

The man who came in was small, pointed, and sharp, with a beak nose and a receding hairline. He was uncomfortably middle-aged, and equally uncomfortable in his black suit. Claude didn't rise, but he smiled. 'Marguery, you're never late.'

'In my business, that would be disastrous, monsieur.'

'Sit down,' Claude said, and when he had, raising his brows with expectancy, the young man cleared his throat. 'I'm going to ask you to investigate two people. Both are foreigners, so it's rather delicate, and of course more complicated. You'll be well remunerated, so don't worry about your expenses.'

The other smiled, inclining his head. 'I never worry about such things when I do a job for you, Monsieur Claude.'

'Then listen. The first is a young man, like myself – an American. I believe he's on an assignment from his home-town paper. I want to know all there is to know: character, family, and, naturally, financial disposition. The other will be more difficult. He's a Russian aristocrat who's made quite a fortune here, branching out into a number of unrelated businesses. I know almost nothing about him, except that he's reputed to be a man-about-town, and all the elegant hostesses love him at their parties.'

'And who may these two men be?' Marguery asked softly. His intelligent brown eyes were fastened to Claude's face.

'Mark MacDonald. I believe he rents a small apartment on the Left Bank, but I'm not sure where. He's visited my mother once or twice, but I wouldn't want to ask her for details. The other' – Claude pressed the palms of his hands together – 'is Prince Mikhail Ivanovitch Brasilov. You can find him easily enough during the day, in his office on the Rue de Berri.'

'But of course I shan't look for him there,' Marguery stated, smiling. Claude laughed. This was as close to a joke as Marguery had ever reached.

'When do you need this information?'

Claude sucked in his lips, pushed them out again. 'As soon as possible,' he answered.

Claude knocked on the door to Claire's boudoir, and when he heard her reply, he opened the door and let himself in. He'd hoped to find her alone, but Lily was there, sewing. For a split second his eyes rested on the delicacy of her long, tapered fingers, with their well-shaped pink nails. Then he smiled, took his mother's hand, kissed her on the cheek. 'Good evening, Mama.'

'This is indeed a surprise, my dear,' Claire said. She patted the seat of the small chair next to her, and her son obediently sat down. 'Are you on your way out, or will you be having dinner with us?'

'I'm tired. I have no plans for going anywhere. I thought I might speak with you for a few moments . . .'

Lily, blushing, stood up, but Claude said: 'Don't go away, my dear. I didn't mean to interrupt your tête-à-tête with Mama.'

Lily sat down again, disquieted. He wanted something. She waited, her breath a little short. Did Mama know him as well as she did? She was never outwardly revolted by his ways. She'd say, smiling: 'I am his mother, just as I am yours.' Without comment or criticism. The wisdom of Solomon.

Claire was looking now at her son. 'We rarely see you. _I_ rarely have the pleasure of your company. I sometimes wonder what shall be my fate, when Lily marries.'

Lily heard this with some shock. Her mother was lonely. She felt an impulse to say: But of course you will live with me! and then remembered that her mother, though so often alone, was a married woman. She said nothing.

'I worry about all these things,' Claude said. 'You, me, Lily. Lily doesn't go out enough, but she doesn't appreciate her evenings with me. Perhaps a woman today prefers not

56

to go out escorted by her brother. There are so many more interesting escorts to have!'

'It's all very sudden for her, that's all,' Claire replied quietly. 'She's shy – and she hasn't been out in society for many years.'

'Still, she's not a nun. She must find a way to swallow her shyness, to blend in.'

In the few moments of silence that ensued, Lily squirmed on her seat. She wondered how her relatives could speak this way about her, as if she were a small animal or an inanimate object whose character and predilections could inoffensively be discussed in front of her.

Then Claude said: 'Mama, I wonder if I might beg a favour of you. Papa and I have entered into a limited partnership on a project of great importance, with a distinguished and powerful man. I'd like you to invite him to the house, for a special dinner.'

'So soon in the relationship?' Claire inquired.

'It's most important. He needs to meet you, to see what a lovely table you set – to understand that we aren't just *nouveau riche* upstarts from nowhere.'

Lily thought: Mama isn't. And again she wondered why her parents, such different people, had ever come together. Claire asked: 'And who is this most distinguished personage? A deputy?'

'Prince Mikhail Brasilov.'

Lily blinked. Claude wasn't looking at her, but at their mother. She could feel her anger mounting, and her disgust. Claire said: 'But – I'm not sure. It might be quite wrong.'

'Why wrong? To invite someone to dinner?'

'Wrong,' she said, with emphasis 'because of Lily.' And her large dark eyes didn't leave his face. They spoke for her, and made him shift on the little chair.

'But Lily hardly knows him. They said hello, and that was that. For Papa and me, this would be important.'

57

'But for me, it would be wrong. And *that*, my dear boy, is *that*.'

'Very well,' Claude said tightly. He rose, but his lips were pinched. Perfunctorily he bent down to kiss his mother, and then he was gone. The two women remained alone, sewing, silent. But neither was concentrating on what she was doing.

At the end of dinner, some hours later, Paul Bruisson raised his head from his *pommes de terre à la Dauphinoise* and said to his wife: 'Next Thursday, we shall have Prince Brasilov to supper. Plan something really fine. These Russians are used to seven-course dinners in the privacy of their own homes – so do your best. Lily can help you.'

Claire's face, very pale, met her husband's eyes, and she said nothing. But she turned to Claude and looked at him with silent reproach. He smiled back, guiltlessly, and turned his hands palms up in the air. 'You see,' he murmured. 'Papa had the same idea.'

'But Prince Mikhail will refuse to come,' Lily spoke up suddenly. The compressed revolt inside her showed in red patches on her cheeks. 'He's a man of dignity – he'll refuse.'

'He'll accept,' her brother countered, smiling at her. 'You'll see.'

Misha held the monogrammed vellum in his strong fingers, and was perplexed. Clearly this was the writing of a woman of breeding, of a lady. Under normal circumstances he'd want to meet her, his curiosity aroused. But not if it meant having to socialize with the Bruissons, father and son. He'd categorically refuse, so that they'd feel the extent of his rejection: so that they'd know it had been improper even to suggest it.

He put the note down on his desk, and brought forward a thick folder. The sardine canning factory. He leafed through the first few pages, then suddenly set them down and picked up the note from Claire Bruisson. Such fine, elegant handwriting! The girl's mother.

He'd thought of her on and off for the last few weeks, even though he knew he should have forgotten her. And now, this note. They were trapping him, he knew it. They were holding out the girl as their bait. How could he refuse the dinner invitation if he ever planned to see her again?

There had to be some other way, a way of his own, not controlled by them. Misha sat at the large desk and thought. Then, impulsively, he reached for his pen and notepaper. He began to write:

Chère Madame,

I beg you to accept my sincere apologies for having to decline your kind dinner invitation. A previous engagement prevents me from complying.

I would, however, be most unhappy if this meant that I must miss meeting you. Would you be so generous as to let me know when you would be free to receive me during the afternoon? I should be honoured to make your acquaintance and call on you and your charming daughter, to whose memory I commit myself.

With my compliments, I remain

Your humble servant,
Mikhail Ivanovitch Brasilov.

Misha folded the letter and inserted it into a matching envelope embossed with the family crest. Then he rang for his secretary. 'Rochefort,' he said. 'See to it that this note is hand-delivered today, and have the messenger wait for a reply.'

Mikhail Brasilov was hardly surprised by the Villa Persane. The *maître d'hôtel* was well trained, but as soon as the prince was inside the house, he began to feel shivers of revulsion. All his life he had liked simplicity; the villa was anything but simple. The salon into which he was ushered was an orgy of ornate Empire furnishings. *Chiffoniers* of mahogany and bronze lorded it over gilt wood ceremonial armchairs that resembled thrones, with bronze swans holding up the arms. On one of these *bergères* with sphinxes under the armrests sat one of the most beautiful middle-aged women he had ever seen. And this took him aback on the instant when he first crossed the threshold.

Claire smiled at him with a kind of motherly understanding. He realized that he'd stood without moving for too many seconds, taken in by the cameo loveliness of the woman's face. She was alone, out of place in this sitting room, but in no way ill at ease. *He* had been ill at ease, confused like a child. Now he stepped forward and brought to his lips the hand that she offered him.

'I am Claire Bruisson,' she said, and he thought her accent was not quite French. 'Welcome, your Excellency. My daughter and I were charmed by the thoughtfulness of your letter.'

'I am pleased that you could receive me at such short notice, madame.' He sat down near her.

'I have heard much about you. You and your father have accomplished a virtual miracle of readaptation. The fate of the Russian exiles has touched our hearts. To have to leave such a beautiful country . . .'

'France, too, is beautiful. But you, madame, unless I am mistaken, are not French.'

She inclined her head, smiling. 'How good an ear you have, Prince Mikhail. I was born in Belgium. I am, naturally, a French citizen, but my formative years were spent elsewhere. And you? Are you planning to become French now?'

He sighed. 'Unless it becomes a necessity, I doubt it. I shall always be a Russian. I would see it as a form of treason to abandon my citizenship. My family is from Kiev, which is where Russia first began. But I don't wish to bore you.'

It was strange, but he was closer in years to this woman

60

than to her daughter. Only ten years separated him from Claire, but fifteen from Lily. Perhaps that was too much. He was afraid his thoughts would betray him, though, after all, sooner or later he would have to come forward and speak to the girl. He wondered where she was, and, without thinking, turned around.

She said, softly: 'Lily is supervising the cook, and our tea. She will be here presently.'

He felt the blood rushing to his cheekbones. 'You have a most special daughter, madame. Direct, unpretentious – when she is without doubt the most beautiful woman I have seen in France – with the exception of her mother, of course. Mademoiselle Liliane takes after you.'

'Thank you, Prince Mikhail. But my daughter is not sophisticated. She wouldn't know how to be pretentious. She comes from a completely different world – one which must be understood and handled with tact and gentleness.'

Was she advising him not to hurt her daughter? He said, somewhat harshly: 'Her brother doesn't always take this precaution.'

'Claude is another kind. He's like our French youth, more concerned with material things than with things spiritual. He's not a bad boy, but he isn't like Lily, and he gets impatient with her sometimes.'

'He doesn't understand what a rare privilege it is for him to have such a sister.'

Claire regarded him fully. 'Quite the contrary,' she murmured. 'He knows it only too well.'

Misha caught the expression in her eyes, and froze. He glanced surreptitiously around him, and the sense of claustrophobia that had enveloped him from the start became more acute, more pressing. He had a feeling that somehow, some way, Claire was asking him to take Lily out of this house, to protect her. At this moment he instinctively glanced around again. Lily was coming in, and behind her came the *maître d'hôtel* carrying the tea tray.

She was wearing a 'one-hour dress', so named for the simplicity of its execution. It had wide, kimono sleeves and a simple skirt that reached the middle of her calf. It was a green dress, and at her ears she wore tiny emeralds. He watched the progression of her legs and had to rise hastily before appearing rude. She'd worn a full-length evening gown the first time, and her shapely calves had been hidden in yellow muslin. She wore her brown hair low over her forehead and ears but tucked into a Psyche knot at the back of her head. Her tallness pleased him again, as it had the first time.

Lily smiled, but he could see the strain on her face. 'Your Excellency,' she said.

'Mademoiselle Liliane.'

Lily sat down on the other side of her mother, and the servant disposed the tea tray laden with pastries and the teapot, with a hot-water pot and a jug of cream, the sugar bowl and the dish with the lemon slices. Claire busied herself pouring, and Lily's eyes, so frank and unassuming, met Misha's over her mother's bent head. He thought: She's exactly what I've always needed: the cool poise of a tall lily, to calm my own combustible Russian nature. I've only met her once before, and already I know her: she's honest, she's modest, and she's intelligent.

And Lily thought: He found a way to come that didn't place him, or me, in checkmate. But I know nothing else about him.

'I saw your photograph a few nights ago,' he said easily, to test her.

She looked surprised. 'Mine? I don't understand.'

'A young man came to interview my father and me. A bright, agreeable young American.' He didn't want to mention the evening with the two models, and was suddenly afraid that Mark might have mentioned it – and him.

'Mark MacDonald?' she asked. 'We see him quite often.'

But she suddenly looked away, and he knew then that she realized Mark's infatuation. Did she return it? She knew Mark far better than she did *him*. Mark was attractive. Why shouldn't she have liked him? He, Misha, hadn't even made the effort to see her again – until today.

She handed him his cup of tea, and he noticed that her fingers trembled. He wanted to speak with her, alone. This entire episode was beginning to seem off-key, in 1924. Women slept with men on the first encounter, and here he was, playing a comedy with a demure young virgin and her proper mother. But this was exactly how he had wanted it.

On an impulse, he turned to Claire and asked: 'Madame, would you and Mademoiselle do me the honour of accompanying me to the theatre?'

Claire's smile touched him. Her eyes, which so rarely reflected her feelings, now shone with limpid pleasure. 'We'd be delighted.'

'It's been so long,' Lily added, and he noticed the bright colour in her cheeks. 'Hasn't it, Mama?'

He imagined the two women locked up in the Villa Persane, growing old and dry among the bronze and gilt furniture. 'Mademoiselle, is there a particular play you've set your heart on?'

She didn't hesitate. '*Romance.*'

'Then *Romance* it is.'

He sat back, enjoying the Ceylon tea and the small, cream-filled pastries placed at his disposal . . . imagining himself in a soft decor with ashes of roses and dove-grey upholstery, Monet and Dufy on the walls, and small wooden Louis XVI tables where she would lay out the tea set, to serve him. He imagined her this way, so young and naïve, but without the line between her brows. To possess this girl in her entirety, to have her be his . . .

* * *

Marguery seemed to have shrunk in his black suit, and his dark little eyes looked everywhere but at Claude. There was a soft beading of sweat over his brow.

'Well?' Claude sat forward, his elbows on his desk, his head supported on the palms of his hands.

'With Mark MacDonald, everything seems to be all right. He's twenty-four, the elder of two sons. His father is a doctor in Charlotte, North Carolina. There's considerable money from both sides of the family. Mark was educated at the Hill School in Pennsylvania, and at Princeton University – both excellent institutions. He worked as junior reporter on the *Clarion*, and apparently impressed the city editor. He then was moved on to the local society column. Now he's the Paris correspondent – quite a feat for someone working for a small city paper like the *Clarion*.'

'And?'

'Prince Mikhail Brasilov is a different story. His father is the legendary Ivan Vassilievitch Brasilov, founder of an empire of businesses in Kiev and Moscow. Everything he touched turned to gold. Mikhail was an only child. He grew into a prodigy, finishing the university with two degrees at the age of eighteen. He was always a carouser, however.' Marguery's nostrils twitched.

'Most of this is known territory. Please continue.'

'The Brasilovs came to France in '21. They were able to rebuild their financial position by fortifying the French sugar beet. They live on the Avenue de la Muette – quite sumptuously.'

'For God's sake!' Claude cried. 'Will you get to the point, Marguery?'

The little man hesitated. 'I've never asked before – but why do you need this information?'

Claude said, through tight lips: 'It's a personal matter, Marguery. A family matter.'

'I asked only because, to touch such a high-placed, well-connected man as Prince Mikhail . . .'

'No one will ever know. You won't be linked to this.'

'There's only one black point I was able to discover. But it took me some time and not a little effort to uncover the facts. Prince Mikhail made a most unexpected marriage.'

Claude leaned forward, amazed.

'He got married two years ago, shortly after he came here.' He stopped, seeing the incredulous expression on Claude's face. Then, licking his thin red lips, he plunged ahead: 'She's known as Jeanne Dalbret, one of the dancers in Mistinguett's revue, *Paris qui Danse*.'

'He's *still* married?'

'There's no divorce decree on file, Monsieur Claude.'

Chapter Three

At the dinner table that night, Claire said brightly: 'If we aren't very hungry, it's because Lily and I had *such* a charming guest for a well-furnished tea: Prince Mikhail Brasilov.'

Paul smiled at her above his double chin, but Claude sat up, suddenly tense. 'Well done, my girl,' the father said.

'In fact, he invited us to attend a performance of the play *Romance*. The Russians really know how to charm people. But I was surprised to find out how *warm* he is.'

'They know how to charm, because they take us all for benighted idiots!' Claude said.

His father turned to look at him, taken aback. His mother said: 'There's nothing supercilious about Prince Mikhail. You led me to believe – '

'I think it's splendid my girls are going to go to the theatre!' Paul crooned. Lily thought it ironic, and half smiled. She could well remember how she'd begged and pleaded six months ago, and what her father had replied: 'All this ridiculous acting is a waste of time and of hard-earned money. I'll be damned if I let you go, Claire!'

But suddenly Claude was standing up, trembling. 'Lily,' he ordered. 'There's a matter of some delicacy I must discuss at once with Mother and Father. Go to your room.'

Claire opened her mouth, but Paul glared at her across the table. He spoke up: 'Lily, you heard your brother. Some things aren't for a young girl's ears.'

Lily rose, without looking at anyone, and started to walk away. She strode, without hesitation. It didn't mean anything to her that Claude had dismissed her so curtly.

She didn't wish to waste her time listening to Claude's dissertations, anyway. At moments like these, she felt more than ever her alienation from her father and brother. She went into the sitting room, and sat, thinking. He wasn't exactly beautiful, but his large features fitted in his wide-boned face, and his legs were so long, so powerful. He'd sat in *that* chair, talking of this and that, and she'd imagined herself alone with him, in a garden. Imagined his taking her hand, his pulling her towards him. Abruptly she stood up and went to the grand piano in the right-hand corner, and sat on the small stool. Her hands began to hit the keys, and there was a violence unleashed suddenly in the form of music, rich, cascading arias from Bizet. She didn't even notice when the pins slipped from her Psyche knot and the dark, glossy hair came tumbling down over her shoulders, magnificent and wild. She was angry, excited, oddly exhilarated, alone and apart.

In the dining room, Claire spoke out: 'Claude, you have an extremely disagreeable manner when you speak to your sister.'

'What's all this about?' Paul demanded. He detested being interrupted during a meal.

'It's about Prince Mikhail. We have to stop considering him for Lily. He took advantage of our goodwill, of Mama's hospitality, to treat her like a common tramp!'

'I didn't see it,' Claire objected.

'Because you only saw the surface of the man. He's a married man!'

Claire blinked, stunned. Claude said, his voice a reedy whisper: 'He's married to a dance-hall girl he keeps hidden somewhere.'

'Then . . . I shall have to find a polite way to decline the theatre engagement,' Claire murmured.

Suddenly, Paul stood up, his double chin shaking like gelatin. 'No,' he declared, narrowing his eyes. 'You'll go. I want to see exactly how far this man will try to take us.

You saw how he received us in his office, Claude — all arrogance, all superiority, as if we were scum to be pushed away with his foot. And why? Does my money smell any different from his? He's a tradesman, just like the rest of us, even with his fine aristocratic airs. This isn't Russia, and he shouldn't feel so confident. I'll catch him, and then, Claude, we'll crush him.'

Claire shivered, and closed her eyes.

Misha was not overly interested in the play. Certainly it was charming, but he'd seen his share of charming plays all over the European continent. He was dying for a cigarette, but the two women didn't smoke, and so he concentrated on watching them while they watched the stage.

Claire wore a fur coat of grey astrakhan trimmed with mink, and, in the box that Misha had rented, she had slipped the coat off, revealing a gown of soft beige silk, with wide sleeves and a high collar. He'd been looking forward to spending the evening with her, for she was a witty conversationalist: and so he'd been disappointed by her unusual reserve. But the girl was a dream. Her long hair had been swept into a topknot, but rebellious tendrils escaped charmingly over her ears and neck. She wore a tubular gown of white chiffon and a stole of white mink, with pearls on her ears and around her neck. She wasn't wearing makeup.

He watched her rapt attention, the small tongue that protruded between her parted lips — her wonder. It was painfully obvious that she wasn't used to going out. He felt protective, compassionate. All his life he'd given in to the need to protect the weak and the suffering. Just as easily he'd come to be known as ruthless because when he saw corruption, he sought to crush it without thought to his victims. In a game played outside the rules, Misha always won, for when someone played a dirty trick, he didn't realize that Misha could be dirtier.

In the interval, Claire excused herself to go to the ladies' room, and for the first time Misha found himself alone with Lily. She was embarrassed. She didn't dare to look at him. And so he said, gently, 'Do I frighten you?'

She looked at him then, and smiled, colouring. 'You're of a different world, Prince Mikhail. You're older, and you're foreign. I'm afraid my conversation is dull for you.'

'On the contrary. I see in you one of the most beautiful women in Paris. And you possess a rare talent: imagination. You're intelligent. It's fashionable to be shallow and you are not. You are worth spending time with – much time, mademoiselle.'

She looked down at her hands, pensive. It seemed incredible: the most beautiful woman in Paris. Only seven months ago she'd left the convent, where humility was considered the first quality to live by: to give up one's dreams to serve other people. The teachings of Christ. Self-abnegation. Was she destined to put aside her fancies in a supreme effort at helping others to fulfil theirs? Part of Lily rebelled against this. Another part accepted it as her fate, the way she'd always accepted the dicta of the Church, and its punishments for her sinful mind.

Claire was reappearing, and Misha stood up politely. The play was starting again.

But this time, Lily hardly watched. Misha, observing her, wondered how much woman she was already. Lily sat with her head bowed, absorbed. Then, at one point, he caught her looking at his legs, at his hands as they lay clasped over his knees. She was staring at them as if in a trance, fascinated. He was suddenly touched: she *was* a woman, aware perhaps of her first man, and taken with the strangeness of the man-woman 'thing', for which she had no name yet.

The next day, he sent her a dozen red roses, with his compliments.

His father had told him to clean up his life. Misha remembered an episode from his youth, in Moscow. He'd been an ace at billiards. But in this great city the billiard halls were set up in the most downtrodden, ne'er-do-well neighbourhoods, and Prince Ivan, who so rarely interfered in the life of his son, had said to him: 'I can't allow you to return there again.'

The game, however, was stronger for Misha than his father's reprimand. Like metal to a magnet, he'd felt himself drawn irresistibly to the pool halls. One evening he was so absorbed in his game, winning against clever opponents, that it was morning before he lifted his eyes from the felt table. And then his gaze had encountered a most unusual sight. Among the thieves and low-lives stood his father, in his top hat and tails, fresh from a formal dinner and ball, standing erect and incongruous, looking at his son. Misha had felt himself change colour, and had dropped his cue and followed Prince Ivan out of the door.

They'd never exchanged a single word about the episode. But Prince Ivan had made his point.

It wasn't the game, however, that had caused the most trouble in Misha's life. It had been women. As careful and meticulous as he was in his work, he couldn't handle his women. His private life was messy and disordered, overflowing with women of various ages and all sorts. It had always been this way.

In Moscow he'd been involved with a married woman, Varvara Trubetskaya, older than he by five exciting years. She'd been a society woman, the wife of a general. But she'd loved Misha so! She'd thrown her reputation to the winds in the hope that he would ask her to leave her husband and marry him. But that hadn't been in his plans.

And then the Bolsheviks had moved nearer, and the

70

Brasilovs had pushed on to Kiev, to the safety of their refineries. As he had never actually broken with Varvara, she'd found a way to convince her husband to go to Kiev too. And they'd met each other.

Misha remembered the scandal. Even in those troubled times, when everyone had had only his safety on his mind, when the rich were rich no longer and were afraid for their lives, the remnant of the upper crust had discussed Misha's shameful behaviour with the general's wife.

The Bolsheviks had been coming closer and closer. The Brasilovs had fled. In the Crimea, by chance this time, he'd run into Varvara and her husband, on their way to Constantinople, too. He hadn't resisted the insistence of his married mistress, and they'd started all over again, practically under her husband's nose. And yet . . . for all their sexual exhilaration, he didn't think he'd ever *loved* Varvara. He'd never loved *any* woman.

He entered the quiet apartment, where Arkhippe had left two hall lights on to greet him. He loosened his tie, unbuttoned his crisp evening shirt. He was very tired. It had been one of those pleasant evenings at Cécile Sorel's. The actress had gathered to her Quai Voltaire Palace the cream of Parisian society. He'd enjoyed her guests, but at the end, as usual, they had bored him and pressed on his nerves. Now he poured himself an armagnac and went to the silver mail tray.

It hit his eye and, a minute later, his stomach. The pale blue paper, lightly scented with Chanel No 5. He'd introduced her to it. By an odd coincidence it was the perfume that Lily used, too. He'd have to change that. Misha tore the envelope open with suddenly clumsy fingers, and held the letter to the light.

She'd written, in her strange, angular scrawl:

You won't be able to forget me. You keep trying. But I'm still your wife, and I won't sign the papers, no matter what you do. I don't need your money. Remember that I work, too, to support myself. You can't buy me.

She'd signed it, simply, 'V'.

His father had said: 'Clean up your life, my boy.' But how would he be able to do it with this new hitch? He'd all but pushed the consciousness of her existence out of his mind. The hasty wedding in Biarritz, during the 'Russian season'. A wedding that had been a lark, a joke, because the gods had burned away his motherland, because, in the midst of despair, you had to be a clown, you had to spit at Fate. He'd regretted it as soon as he'd done it, and told her so. 'We'll have to live in separate residences. You can stay my wife, because I never intend to marry again. But we won't make it public.'

Strangely enough, she'd accepted, nodding with her proud head, tossing the mink stole over her shoulder in a sign of bravado – for she was a reckless adventurer like him, one who gambled on life, and lost well. He'd admired her for it, and because of this he'd treated her well. He'd let her live her life, but he'd gone to her in moments of tension, to drink from her the courage to continue, to persevere against all odds. She'd never asked for help, and had gone on to learn a whole new career, one of which he disapproved, but who was he to make a criticism? They were no longer in Moscow, where appearances mattered. They were in Paris during the Roaring Twenties, when women did far worse than to become dancers in a revue. She'd banked on the loveliness of her legs and on her hours of practice with her private ballet master from the Bolshoi – her hobby as a wealthy Muscovite matron.

But what had seemed irresistible in Moscow, and even in the Crimea, one step ahead of the Bolsheviks, had all at once lost its lustre in Paris. He'd seen the chinks in the armour: her small wrinkles, her tired jokes. She'd lived too much, lost too much, ever to be fresh again for him. The five years yawned between them. He was, pure and simple, out of his spell. The young women of Paris were more alluring, new, different. The Russia that she brought to his mind was not the Russia he wished to remember.

He'd asked for a divorce, to make it clean between them. She'd accepted. They'd signed the preliminary papers together, a year ago. He had seen her maybe three times since then, amicable, distant moments. She was hurt by his desire to break completely – he'd felt this, and experienced a short instant of guilt. But she'd always known he hadn't loved her. If she'd accepted things on his terms, he couldn't really blame himself.

Varvara. Her husband had died so quickly after they'd reached Paris! Had she even mourned him? She was a hard, violent woman, a street urchin reared like a princess. He needed a real princess. Lily Bruisson was like a fairy princess, like his mother, the restrained, tactful Princess Maria.

It was impossible to think Varvara was refusing now, at the last moment, to sign the papers. Why? Could love survive the humiliations he'd put her through – the rejections? He'd offered to maintain her for three years at five thousand francs a month. She'd be able to resign from her job. Why, now, was she suddenly being proud?

If Lily learned of her existence, he'd lose her. Misha knew that he couldn't let it happen.

There had to be a way out. Wasn't there one?

He remembered now. She'd decided to shed her Russian image, to become French. She'd called herself 'Jeanne Dalbret'. A simple name. Hadn't she also signed the marriage certificate that way, to add to the fun? Had they recorded her as Varvara, or Jeanne? His attorney had the licence, and it hadn't mattered before, because the officials had known her true identity. They'd never be able to involve her in a fraud. He'd married her, pure and simple.

So he'd have to make her change her mind.

Mark had never felt so relaxed in his entire life. He was in Paris, fulfilling the dream of a lifetime – a dream that for many years had lain nameless in the back of his mind: to travel, to acquire a cosmopolitan polish. And, of course, to write what *he* wanted. He paid the rent on his small mansard apartment on the Boulevard Saint-Germain with money from the articles he sent to the Charlotte *Clarion*: bright bits of gossip on the Americans he'd met: Gertrude and Leo Stein, Natalie Barney, the Fitzgeralds and the Murphys. But this took up very little of his time. The rest was his own, to do with as he pleased. In a sense, then, the newspaper provided him with a sinecure – a stipend to develop his own writing.

Since he'd met Lily, he'd started serious work on his novel. He didn't talk about it to anyone except her. He wasn't quite sure why he'd chosen to open his heart to this young middle-class girl who'd so obviously only just left the strictures of a provincial convent school. Marisa, better educated, more sophisticated, and as Parisian as the Arc de Triomphe, possessed a mind better disposed to help him. She read English, too. But Mark saw her as a little sister not to be taken seriously. Lily was different. She was already a woman, even if Marisa was more liberated. And she could quietly listen to his ideas without interrupting him with her own.

She asked questions. Why did Mark feel that every American who came to Paris had to be running away from his own past? Why were the young American protagonists so self-destructive? Why couldn't Mark put more of himself into the main character? He tried, as best he could, to reply to her satisfaction. 'I had all I wanted in Charlotte,' he explained. 'But I prefer being less spoiled in this big city than to have everything handed to me on a silver platter in my hometown.'

'Your life's been much like mine,' she commented, sitting down next to him. They were in the overcrowded Empire sitting room in the Villa Persane, where he often came to visit.

'In which way?'

'Parochial. Money, but not travel, not independence.'

'There's a small difference, Lily. As a young woman, you've been sheltered. I was a man. My family made no effort to keep me in a cocoon. Perhaps it was I who kept myself there for so long.'

He showed her the ten new pages he had finished, and translated them as best he could for her. She sat back, occasionally passing her tongue over her full red lips. 'I've never read anything like that before,' she said.

'Does that mean you like it?'

'I do. I feel so bad for Theresa. She's going to fall in love with Trevor, and then – I fear for her.'

'But falling in love can be wonderful.'

She said, not looking at him: 'It's frightening. What if the love isn't returned? We live in such a strange society!'

'Maybe so. But you have to take risks, Lily, to feel alive.'

'I know that's what your Theresa believes. She'll try *any*thing to prove to herself she isn't just a doll.'

They fell silent. He cleared his throat. 'Lily,' he asked. 'Would you play something for me?'

'Something sad, or something happy?'

'Whatever you feel like playing.'

She stood up, went to the shining black Pleyel. She sat down and hesitated, her fingers poised above the keys. Then she plunged in, and he closed his eyes to listen to the joyful notes of Chopin. After a few moments, he opened them again and looked at her. She was playing like a virtuoso, moving her torso slightly to the rhythm. When she finished, he clapped. She closed the lid over the keyboard and rose, and he was conscious of her twin breasts as she breathed, of the colour in her cheeks as she smiled with what resembled triumph.

'Have you found the right teacher yet?' he asked her.

'Yes, I have. Her name is Sudarskaya – a garrulous Russian woman who was a concert pianist in the days of the czar. Mama's agreed to hire her, three times a week. But we haven't dared to broach the subject with Father.'

'Is your father, then, such an ogre?'

'If he thought that I could find a husband more easily if I perfected my playing, he'd pay double the price of Sudarskaya. Otherwise he'd consider it a waste of his money. I don't think he's ever gone to a concert.' She laughed. 'Of course, he's gone to the Moulin Rouge. I saw some tickets once lying on his dressing-table. He turned bright red and told me they were Claude's.'

She turned serious then, and he could decipher pain on her features. All at once, taking his courage in his hands, he said: 'Lily. Do you think you could be happy living with me for the rest of your life?'

She wheeled about; her eyes widened. 'You mean – '

'Yes. I want to marry you, Lily. As soon as you'll have me. I'll never hurt you. I'll treasure you always.'

She sat down on the first available chair, a heavy *bergère* of gilt wood and velvet. 'Mark,' she said. 'I – ' But she couldn't finish. She'd known he cared, but she'd thought he was taking his time, giving her time. She'd thought that the proposal would come a year from now – or would recede into the folds of friendship.

'You don't have to answer immediately.'

'I really must think about it, my dear.'

'I realize that. I shouldn't have been so abrupt.'

Suddenly there was a wall of awkwardness between them, where before there had been ease and comfort and pleasure. She looked at him, noting the regularity of his features, the adorable curls that made him look like Cupid. But Cupid had been a baby. No woman could have fallen

76

in love with Cupid. She wasn't in love with Mark. She loved him, but she wasn't in love. She never awakened in a sweat from a dream of him, of them.

Maybe she was like Mark's heroine, Theresa, who wished for cataclysms and fireworks, and wouldn't settle for anything less. Maybe, Lily thought, she was a fool.

Mark had never asked a girl to marry him before. He was nearly twenty-five, and now he was ready. But he'd frightened her — he knew that. What a fool he'd been! He was consumed with embarrassment, and wanted to leave her alone as soon as possible. There was nothing he could do to retract his words. And, furthermore, he'd meant them. So he took her hand and pressed it, and before she could react, he walked out of the door, closing it behind him.

He stood in the vestibule, his bearings lost. He put on his camel's-hair coat and his muffler, to ward off the cold. Who could he talk to?

Marisa. He'd talk to *her*. But no, he couldn't. Marisa would feel caught in the middle. He had no one else who was a close friend. Rirette and Nini? They were just amusing people to spend an evening with. They didn't believe in marriage.

At that moment he heard the hall door opening, and Claire Bruisson walked into the vestibule, wrapped in furs. She seemed surprised to see him, and held out her hands. 'Mark! I didn't realize you were here. You're leaving?'

'And you, madame?'

'I'm on my way to the dentist's office. Dreary, don't you think? Why don't you let the chauffeur drive us both?'

On an impulse, he accepted. He always came in a taxi, and had no car of his own. He felt beaten, miserable. In the large Citroën, he was silent. Claire asked: 'What's wrong? You can tell me, Mark. I'm a mother — I might understand.'

77

He looked at her, at her beautiful cameo profile. She jarred with the atmosphere of the Villa Persane as much as Lily. He began to feel resentful, thinking of Lily. In Charlotte there were any of half a dozen girls of better family than Liliane Bruisson who would gladly marry him. And the girl he'd dated when he'd been at Princeton – Judy, the girl from Wellesley . . . Claire was staring at him with a strange insistency, and so he said: 'I asked Lily to marry me. It was an idiotic thing to do – I hadn't planned any of it . . .'

'Young men seldom do,' Claire remarked softly. And then she laid a soft gloved hand on his arm. Her eyes shone large and sad. 'Of course, she didn't answer?'

'No.'

'You shouldn't take it so hard, Mark,' she said. 'It's only normal for her to want to think it through. She's a devout Catholic: divorce doesn't exist for someone like Lily. Marriage, for her, means a one-time event.'

'But had she loved me, she'd have answered at once.'

Claire made no comment, but her hand remained on his arm until the moment when she disembarked at the Place de la Concorde, telling the chauffeur to drive Mr MacDonald wherever he wished to be taken. As she watched the Citroën pull away from the kerb, she wondered for whom her heart ached more: for Lily, who was still blindly hoping, or for Mark, who'd gambled and seen the truth.

In the evening, when she came home, she knocked lightly on the door to Lily's room. She turned the knob, and entered. Her daughter was sitting quietly in the gathering darkness, leafing through a book without seeing the pages.

'Mark told me,' she said.

'I put him off.'

'I know. And he's smart enough to understand why. Lily – '

'What, Mama?'

'Prince Mikhail is a married man. Claude told us, but

we were afraid to upset you. It was wrong of us. We should have told you.'

Lily simply repeated: 'Married? To whom?'

'Claude didn't say.'

She stood up then, angry, and cried: 'But you still allowed him to take us to the theatre! And to send me roses – Why? *Why?* What does he want with me, then, Mama?'

Claire sighed. 'If I knew, I'd tell you. I don't know any part of the story.'

'And so you want me to accept Mark's proposal.'

'*I* don't want you to do anything. It's you who must decide, based on how you feel about Mark, not on your anger against Prince Mikhail. It serves no purpose to marry a man unless you're sure of your love for him.'

She looked at her daughter, long and hard. But Lily remained perfectly erect, although her eyes seemed suddenly bloodshot. She was courageous, and she was proud. She'd never cry in front of anyone. Claire felt helpless, and shook her head. Then she quietly left the room.

Lily walked over to the vase of red roses, and picked one out. In the semi-darkness she examined its firm perfection. She'd had a stupid, childish dream, just because he was tall, imposing, larger than life – a Prince Charming come to lift her away, all the way from Moscow on his white horse. She'd fallen in love with a man she'd hardly spoken to – because he was the first man who'd ever picked her out of the crowd. Foolish, silly Lily. She plucked a rose petal from the bud, then another, then a third, ripping them off like the wings off a fly. *Married.*

If I don't marry Mark, maybe nobody else will ever come, she thought. Mark is the gentlest person I know, except for Mother. He could make me happy, and I'd be good to him, in gratitude.

Mark understood her, he approved of her, he wanted her to continue with her piano studies. He'd take her away

79

from her father, from Claude. He'd be a kind father to their children. What, really, did it matter that she'd wanted another man to hold her in his arms?

The next morning, when the basket of out-of-season fruits was delivered from Fauchon, she said in her even, poised voice to the messenger boy: 'Send it back to the person who ordered it. But wait – I have a message.' And she went to her room, returning moments later with a small envelope.

When the boy had left, she went upstairs into her father's study. She went to the telephone on the desk, dialled a number. When it was picked up at the other end, she said, softly: 'Mark? I've thought it through. If you're sure you love me, let's get married as soon as possible.'

Misha was sitting in his office when the messenger was ushered in from Fauchon. 'What's this?' he asked. 'I ordered it delivered to Boulogne.'

'The young lady refused it, and said to bring it directly back to you, with this note.' He laid the small envelope on the massive mahogany desk.

'Thank you,' Misha said, but in his heart he felt a deep shock, a premonition of pain to come. After the messenger had departed, he opened the envelope. 'Dear Prince Mikhail,' she'd written in her round schoolgirl hand: 'This wonderful basket would be more fittingly displayed on your wife's table.'

He stared at the note, stunned. Such incisive, harsh words from this sweet child, this fresh young girl. What pain must have prompted her to display such uncharacteristic sarcasm! How had she found out? He was tempted to leave his office and rush over to Boulogne, to try to explain. But – to explain *what?* That, although he wanted to ask her to marry him, he was already bound to somebody else, someone he'd married on an impulse, someone he didn't love? She'd have to find this yet another strike against his character, and, of course, she'd be right.

It was the middle of the business day, and his desk was littered with folders and typed papers. But he knew he wouldn't be able to concentrate. He buzzed Rochefort. By the time the secretary had entered the office, Misha was already standing, his jacket buttoned. 'I have an appointment,' he said shortly. 'I'm not sure when I'll be back.'

It wouldn't do to play the buffoon to an eighteen-year-old girl, but he had to settle the issue with Varvara. At this hour she'd still be at home. He manoeuvred the royal blue De Dion-Bouton through the afternoon traffic, up the Champs-Élysées, down the Avenue Wagram to Place Péreire. In that part of town all breathed of quietude, and the granite building where she rented a medium-size apartment stood behind some tall plane trees that, leafless in the winter mist, stood as skeletons beckoning to the passersby. He parked the car and went through the street door into a covered yard, past the janitor's lodge and up a dark, winding staircase to the second-floor landing. He rang the doorbell and waited.

Varvara Trubetskaya opened the door herself. She was a spectacular woman: of medium height, she possessed the lush figure of a courtesan, sheathed in a peignoir of yellow silk embroidered in Chinese fashion with black and red dragons. Her triangular face was of translucent pallor and great blue saucer eyes opened wide over pronounced cheekbones. She didn't look a year over twenty-seven or twenty-eight, although she was ten years older. Her pale red hair haloed her face, and was of chin length, but thick and tousled.

She stepped back, pinching her lips together, and he entered. The apartment was interesting, eclectic. Ming vases were set on Louis XVI tables, in front of soft, Art Nouveau sofas, two of them forming an L shape in the large living room. She motioned for him to sit, and did so herself, tucking her bare feet beneath her on one of the sofas. 'I take it you received my note,' she finally said.

'I did, and I'm baffled. You went along with all the motions to this point.'

'But I'm a woman. I can change my mind.' She smiled then, and rang a small silver bell on the table before her. Presently a tall black man appeared, bowing from the waist. He was clothed in bright red and green satin, and wore a turban around his head. She said: 'Dragi, bring us some interesting libation – like Scotch and water for me, and vodka on the rocks for his Excellency.'

When he'd left the room, Misha raised his eyebrows. 'Where did *he* come from, Vava?'

'From a club in Montmartre. He played the clarinet. But when the club closed down, he lost his job. So I took him in. He makes an interesting *maître d'hôtel*, don't you think, darling?'

'Why "Dragi"? And why this strange African attire? If he's a jazzman, then he must be American.'

'But these days, that's already *passé*.'

He smiled. She'd been outrageous in Moscow already. He remembered when she'd arrived at a costume ball dressed as a lion tamer . . . with a live lion manacled to her wrist. She was afraid of nothing. But what had attracted him in those days wasn't sufficient to hold him now. He needed to find stability, gentleness, calm. He said, as kindly as he could: 'I want this divorce, Varvara. The case is coming up within two weeks, and if you play me foul, I'll play it your way, but by *my* rules.'

She raised her head, showing off the tiny, pointed chin, without an age fold underneath. 'Is that a threat, Misha?'

He inclined his head. 'Maybe.'

At that moment Dragi reappeared, balancing a lacquered tray on which were two crystal highball glasses. Bowing in front of his mistress, he brought it first to her, and then repeated the performance in front of Mikhail. Then, with little steps, he disappeared through the swinging doors behind Varvara.

Misha took a swallow of vodka, and said: 'Five thousand a month is a small fortune. It will be written in the divorce decree.'

'I'm not a whore,' she answered softly. 'You've always done with me exactly what you wanted. You're totally without shame.'

'You knew why from the beginning. This marriage was never a real one.'

'I'm told you send dozens of roses to a young French girl who could be your own daughter.'

'Who told you that?'

'It's true, isn't it? That there's someone?'

He nodded. 'It's true. Won't you help me, Vava?'

She slammed the crystal glass on the coffee table. 'You're really too much, Misha! I didn't care about the marriage licence until you began to pressure me about dissolving it. I'd thought – somehow – that we might have our chance, after all these years. In Moscow, in the Crimea, it was different. Why not me, Misha? Why her?'

He said, quite coldly: 'I need a lady, Vava, and you're an Amazon, a firefly, a Fury – but not a lady. I need someone to come home to – someone whose only interest in life will be to take care of my needs, to comfort me, to listen to my problems.'

'What you want is a nursemaid – a nanny. You're afraid of getting too close to a real woman. Perhaps she'd be smart enough to find the chink in your armour.'

He breathed in and out, fully, and repeated: 'Five thousand a month. This is my final offer. You really should consider it, because in any event, I won't be your man. I'm in love with this girl, and if you once get in our way, I'll crush you, Varvara.'

She stared back into his green eyes, and saw the steely

purpose in his tiny pupils. She said: 'Seven. Seven thousand, payable on the first of every month. For five years.'

'Five. For three years. It won't do you any good to argue with me. My lawyers will know how to make you look ridiculous in court.'

She opened her mouth, but he'd already risen. She could feel her heart pounding, but saw no response on his face. He didn't have a heart. She should have known that, long ago. He was saying: 'Thank you, Varvara,' and turning his back on her to reach the hallway. There was nothing she could think of saying, no irony strong enough for the occasion. She couldn't think, couldn't react, and when he'd opened the door and let himself out, she felt only the pain of her own lost illusions, hammering at her. These five thousand francs were the only things he'd ever offered her, she knew. He'd never promised to love her, and so she couldn't blame him for any lies, only for the cold way he chose to live his life, separate from any touching being – a selfish man, protecting his entity from the groping hands of those less strong than he.

She took a long sip of Scotch, and thought, with a half smile, that the poor girl on whom he'd set his sights would have no way of knowing that it was useless, most of the time, to fight against him.

Mark gave Lily a gold ring inset with a two-carat diamond, from Van Cleef and Arpels, as an engagement present. This seemed to please Paul Bruisson. He felt that the young man had proved his wealth, and so, as was customary, he spoke to him about the dowry he had put aside for his daughter when his business had begun to improve, after the war. But Mark shook his head. 'I'm not marrying Lily for money,' he stated. 'I can earn enough for her to live well, and besides, I have a trust fund set up in Charlotte to supplement my income.' Paul could hardly believe this good luck, and rubbed his meaty hands together, chuckling.

The American had turned out to be much worthier than anyone had anticipated. Maybe he wasn't a Russian prince, but Paul thought that on the whole, those Russian aristocrats who now flooded Paris had done very little to contribute to the French economy.

Americans, on the other hand, were a strange breed. The women seemed to possess no sense of decency. Those who married well, like Winnie Singer de Polignac and Marie-Laure Bischoffsheim de Noailles, hid their eccentricities and sexual depravities behind the elegance of their Old World French husbands. The others – like the wife of that author Fitzgerald – were openly, shamelessly scandalous: drinking to excess and sleeping with men on the spur of the moment. But the men were strong, no-nonsense fellows, and if they drank too much, one could excuse them more because of their sex. Still, Paul Bruisson didn't like artists, and most of the Americans in Paris purported to be artistic in one form or another. Mark, however, was a journalist. To Paul that seemed more solid.

Thank God that Mark had promised Paul not to take Lily back to the United States. He was happy in Paris. At least, he'd said, not within the next few years. He, Paul, would have to sweeten the pot to make sure Mark and Lily *never* went back. And he'd agreed to a Catholic wedding, and to rear the children, when they came, as Catholics. Paul would see to it that his grandchildren grew up as decent, clean-cut French children. On the whole, Paul was pleased at the intended marriage. The wedding was set for 6 June.

One afternoon in the early part of February, Lily was in the dining room, showing the maid how to set the table for a late supper she was planning for the next evening. Paul approved. His little girl was learning how to be a hostess. She had Claire's good taste. He thought: I've built my family the perfect house, and I've furnished it as it deserves.

Now it's up to them, the women, to work within it, to fill it with the right sorts of guests. He knew he didn't know how to arrange a centrepiece, or how to place the crystal. For these things he'd always trusted Claire – and now Lily.

He was reading in the living room, feeling good, as always, when he raised his bespectacled eye to appraise the furniture. How he loved the brass and gilt swans and sphinxes that adorned his chairs! He'd sent Claude to the office and, just this once, had decided to take the day off because he could feel a tickle in his throat. It was that damned Parisian winter again, chilling his bones. He heard a noise – the doorbell sounding. The *maître d'hôtel* was letting somebody in. He thought he heard a man's deep voice, and was suddenly interested.

Paul rose, setting aside his newspaper, and peered out into the hallway from the living room. And then he was really surprised. Prince Mikhail Brasilov was walking briskly behind the *maître d'hôtel* into the dining room. He followed, shuffling his slippered feet.

Lily had stopped laying out the silver, and stood looking at the Russian with an air her father couldn't describe: remote, withdrawn – the way she sometimes looked at Claude. Prince Mikhail went to her and took her hand, brought it to his lips. Still, Lily said nothing. The *maître d'hôtel* hovered by the entrance, waiting for a signal, and the small maid had scampered away. Paul waited, interested.

'Please, mademoiselle, tell your servant to leave us alone,' Brasilov finally said, annoyance seeping into his voice.

'It's all right, you may go,' Lily said. Her own voice was completely toneless. 'But my father is here, and I'd like him to be present if you have anything to tell me, your Excellency. I'm engaged to be married – and I don't want to speak alone to any man except my fiancé.'

Paul entered now, straightening out his tie and filling his chest with air to make it stand out. 'My dear Prince,' he stated, not knowing what to add because he had no idea of the purpose of this visit to his home. He couldn't help but feel proud of Lily – of her upright morality at a time when other young women had forgotten what decency meant. He extended his hand, and Brasilov hesitated less than before until he shook it.

The Prince didn't look so proud this time. He had turned a ruddy colour at Lily's words, but he didn't resist. 'Mademoiselle,' he said. 'Your engagement – I just heard about it.'

'Mr MacDonald is the best of men.'

'Indeed he is. I've had the pleasure of meeting him. But – still – '

Lily said, her voice thin and clear: 'Prince Mikhail, it was kind of you to take us to the theatre, and to send me flowers. But you are a married man, and now I, too, shall marry. I'm afraid all contact between us must stop because of these two facts.'

'I think,' Brasilov said, clearing his throat, 'that I must explain my behaviour to you. You must think me a boor – a liar and a cheat. But you were misinformed. I am no longer married. I was in the last stages of a divorce when we met last month.'

Paul Bruisson knew then that he had the advantage, and so he said, with a little smile: 'My daughter isn't a dance-hall girl, your Excellency. You cannot treat her as you did your wife.'

Brasilov turned around, and his eyes were cold. He said: 'You, too, were misinformed, monsieur. My wife is a dancer, yes, but she is first and foremost a lady. I am a free man now – but this gives no one the right to criticize the woman I divorced.'

'Papa,' Lily said. 'I would like to hear from Prince Mikhail why he came here today.'

'I wanted to beg you to reconsider. To propose marriage to you myself. I want you for my wife, mademoiselle.'

Lily looked at him, her wide eyes unforgiving. 'Why?'

'I don't know! Maybe I'm bored with the life I've been leading. Maybe I'm looking for some kind of peace, and you could give it to me. I can't be more clear-cut than that!'

'But Mr MacDonald *loves* me, Prince Mikhail.'

'If you lived with me, you would see in a thousand small ways the extent of my feelings for you. I am not, like Mr MacDonald, a man of big words.'

'But "love",' Lily countered softly, 'is a very small word. One that matters.'

'It's the thought that matters, Mademoiselle Liliane. I am a man of action, not of words.'

They remained staring at each other, and Paul Bruisson wondered what to do. He coughed. Lily had never spoken this way to anyone – had never sounded so sure of herself. And he? He wasn't sure what would be best: to leave well enough alone, or to encourage her to let the American go in favour of the Russian. Prince Mikhail had a much greater fortune than Mark.

'But I have pledged my faith to a good man, a man who came to me with clean hands. I can't reject him now.'

'You could, if you wanted to. You aren't married yet. I came here to beg you not to marry him, but to marry me.'

Suddenly, Lily sat down on one of the dining room chairs, and passed a weary hand over her brow. She shook her head, overcome. She didn't look so strong now, so resolved. Her eyes went to her father, and he read in them the plea: decide for me.

He'd always made all the decisions in the family. But this one time, somehow, he couldn't. The mute appeal in Lily's eyes softened his heart. He thought he understood, and felt nervous, lest he hadn't. He didn't know his daughter very well, and wished Claire had been there, to help him read her.

He said to Lily: 'And you, my girl? What do *you* want? I

can only guide you, but I can't force you in this important matter.'

'And how would you guide me, Father?'

'They are both good men, good providers. But with Prince Mikhail, you would be a princess, and life would be easier. I'd never have to worry about you anymore.'

He thought that he detected a small smile on Brasilov's face, but just for a moment. The Prince was waiting, poised at attention. Lily looked at him, her eyes full of an intense, wordless feeling. Then she dropped them to the floor.

Mikhail Ivanovitch Brasilov stepped forward, took her hand, and held it until she looked up into his wide-boned face, and then he declared, gravely: 'You'll have me, then. I am glad, Liliane.'

She was still staring at the floor, but her eyes had filled with tears, and so Paul said: 'We'll go now into the study, your Excellency. I think my daughter wants to be alone.'

At the Avenue de la Muette, Misha sat at his desk, thinking. Dawn was slowly rising, setting its pink and lilac mantle over Paris, bathing his still hands in its roseate light. He sat, still in his evening clothes, and thought.

Another night come and gone, in the arms of Rirette. Another night. He imagined Lily, kneeling by her bed, making her morning prayer. Lily's fine brown hair covering her shoulders and her back. Lily was a creature of the morning, and Rirette, a night witch. They inhabited two different worlds.

Why hadn't he learned to stay away from them, the night witches? Rirette was like Varvara, like the conflagration that had consumed his country. A night with her drained him of all his juices and his energies, but, like a moth, he was drawn to the light instinctively. Lily was quiet, sensitive, gentle, compassionate, kind. He couldn't hurt her. He'd won her away from that American reporter, who'd loved her sincerely, and therefore he owed her all the more his protection and care.

I'm getting married next month, he thought, making a fist with one of his hands. And as a wedding present to you, Liliane Bruisson, I shall give up Rirette the same way that I let Varvara go, for good.

He wanted to be faithful, welcomed the experience as a novelty in his life, a purging, a cleansing. Maybe by being faithful to his new wife, he would finally put an end to his guilt about his lifetime of infidelities.

Lily sat on her bed, in her silk nightgown, thinking. It felt like being on a wide river, alone in small canoe, propelled by a tremendous current that pulled her along she knew not where. This was what was happening to her, with Mikhail. He was the current, a natural life-force that controlled her destiny, that gave her no choice.

She didn't want to fight back, but she shivered slightly, because she didn't know where the current would lead her. A waterfall would topple the canoe. And she would have no warning of its presence ahead, beyond the wide river.

She couldn't sleep, frozen by that image.

Chapter Four

Prince Ivan sighed, wondering. It hadn't been his style to involve himself in his son's life, yet he thought that it was time for grandchildren, for an end to a past era that was irrecoverable, like his wife Maria. An era that lay buried in a distant land that it was better not to regret too passionately.

On the night of the engagement dinner, he watched the Bruissons carefully, from under hooded lids. The long table gleamed with engraved crystal and with Sèvres china, and the centrepiece of exotic flowers exuded its musky odour that mingled with the roast pork and the chestnut purée. He wondered why it was that the brother, Claude, seemed so ordinary. He wore perfectly tailored clothes with the ease of a gentleman; his hair was parted on the side, and his features were regular, pleasant. Then, what was it? His dark eyes were hard, expressionless, his smile automatic. He seemed to pass over his mother, his sister, in an unspoken condescension that tightened the muscles in Prince Ivan's stomach. This was the sort of man who in Russia would have been let in through the back door – a tradesman. But an opportunistic tradesman, crafty and shrewd, where the blustering father seemed only self-important and uncultured.

Claire Bruisson, he had to agree, was different. So dark and charming, like the face on an Italian cameo. Her skin, so creamy, unwrinkled. He had spoken to her of Diaghilev's ballet and found her delightfully up-to-date. She was composed but not timid.

Lily was timid. He tried to see her from the point of view

of a young man, and smiled. She was like an exotic fruit, ripe and open. Her body was supple and young, but full, the way he remembered his wife's. If she'd been older, much older . . . He could understand Misha. With this girl he might erase the past.

When Misha showed him the ring he had ordered at Cartier, a large tear-shaped diamond banked by two emeralds, Prince Ivan ordered matching earrings as his own present to his son's betrothed. He approved of Lily.

Lily stood awkwardly twisting the ring on her left hand, and Mark's eyes, unable to bear looking into her face, were instead drawn to that enormous diamond, so different from the smaller, daintier ring she'd worn in the weeks of their own engagement. He'd come because she'd sent him a note to meet her, wishing that he'd had the good sense to be rude and stay away. The pain was worse than he'd played it out in his mind – much worse, more searing and brutal in this confrontation.

They had her father's hideous parlour to themselves, each as uncomfortable and embarrassed as the other. But finally, thrusting her fingers through the mass of her dark hair, she spoke. 'I wanted to tell you that I'll never forgive myself,' she began. 'I should never have promised to marry you, then to go back on my word. You're such a good man, Mark – and I was never worthy of your love.'

He sighed, and shrugged, rather inelegantly. Ah, well, to hell with it. 'Look, Lily,' he cut in. 'It was probably as much my fault as yours. You weren't really in love with me, and so I had no right to push it – because I saw clearly what you felt and didn't feel.'

Her large, almond-shaped eyes rested on him then. 'Oh, Mark . . .'

'I think perhaps that I can understand. My love for you, Lily, is like a fountain gushing out of me that I can't control. You cared, but your caring was like a civilized

92

faucet whose knob could be turned on or off. And you love Brasilov. What can I do? What could I *ever* do? You have to go with your feelings, Lily. I can't challenge him to a duel, or threaten to kill myself, or – or anything. Because whatever I chose to say or do – the fact would remain that you loved *him*.'

'But what I did . . . It was so irresponsible . . . And I *do* care, Mark. I'll always care. I want us . . . to be friends, if that's possible.'

He smiled then, and she saw, in that tired, used smile, just how callously selfish her statement had been. 'My dear,' he said, 'I just told you that I still love you. I'm going to try to ease myself out of this love, because it's a hopeless case, and I've never had much admiration for literature's unrequited lovers. Most of them, if you'll pardon me, were fools.' His expression softened. 'But whatever happens, I'll never want to lose the tenderness that flowed between us. You're not my girl anymore, but you'll always be Lily . . . and it's going to be hard not to wake up each morning and think of you when I open my eyes. Of course we'll be friends – but not right away. You do understand that, don't you? That I'll need to stay away for a while?'

Tears hovered on the edges of her lashes. She nodded, wordlessly. And then held out her hands, and saw him hesitate only a second before seizing them warmly in his own.

She closed her eyes, felt his lips touch the extremities of her fingers, and then he was gone, the door closing gently behind his retreating back.

She found herself hoping, fervently, that she'd done the right thing.

Misha seemed composed, almost distant as he spoke. 'We'll be married simply, at the city hall of the Sixteenth Arrondissement. I don't want a formal wedding. I don't like pomp and ceremony. Weddings should be intimate affairs. Don't you think so, darling?'

Lily nodded. 'I want whatever you want, Misha.'

'Thank you, my love.'

The truth was that she felt a bit intimidated. She'd finished school less than a year ago, and had never formulated dreams to fit her new circumstances. She'd known nothing about the Russians who had come, sixty thousand of them, to Paris after the Bolshevik Revolution. She wasn't even sure if she was prepared to get married – to anyone. What would Prince Mikhail – Misha – expect of her?

'What's wrong?' Prince Ivan was asking her, gently.

'It's just that . . . well . . .' Suddenly she was near tears, and confused.

'Don't be afraid of what's ahead,' Ivan Vassilievitch said. 'You'll always be able to lean on Misha, and on me, for our experience. You'll never be alone.'

But in spite of the old man's understanding words, she was more afraid than ever of what her life would be, and was suddenly sorry she'd given in and agreed to be married to this tall, massive, self-possessed man who thought, and rightly so, that he controlled the lives and destinies of thousands of people: those who worked for him, with him, even against him; those who were his friends; and those who, to their own consternation, had come to realize that he was not their friend.

Some time later, when Prince Ivan had left, after kissing her, she was sad to see him leave. His presence had been reassuring, benevolent. Alone with his son, she looked away. She really was at a loss for words.

'I found us a very nice apartment on the Molitor,' he was saying, turning her palm over in his own, and touching the diamond on her finger. 'It's exactly what we need. It's near the Bois de Boulogne, for the nurse to take our children for their daily walks. We'll have eight rooms: a master bedroom, a boudoir for you, two children's rooms and the nurse's room, a living room, dining room, and a study for me. Perhaps I should have thought of a music room for you – but you won't have two children at once, I hope, and so we can turn one of the rooms into a piano room. Upstairs, there are four servants' rooms. Papa is letting us take Arkhippe, our *maître d'hôtel*, and Annette, our cook. Arkhippe is getting married, and his wife Madeleine will be your maid. Annette's husband will be my chauffeur. And we'll have two young girls to help with the cleaning and the cooking. Six servants in all, until the nurse when our first child is born.'

She looked up, with wonder. He was really still a stranger. Locked within the outer shell, the large, well-muscled body and the strong-featured face with the unexpectedly vulnerable eyes, there lay a human being whose force magnetized her, but whose motivations were foreign to her understanding. She'd felt so comfortable with Mark. When he'd kissed her – she'd felt . . . protected? With Misha, she always felt on the edge of fear, a sensation that could be exhilarating or terrifying, depending on the circumstance.

He'd made all the decisions, like her father. But, unlike Paul Bruisson, he hadn't shouted to make himself heard. She hadn't had to tremble. Nevertheless, Lily felt a twinge of discomfort. She asked: 'And the furniture?'

'The apartment has high ceilings, and the rooms are spacious. We are large people. I chose furnishings to fit our size. Besides, I'm Russian, and in my country all is built massive.'

Lily visualized sofas of cavernous proportions – something as hideous, in its own way, as the decor at the Villa Persane. Seeming to read her mind, he traced ellipses on the back of her hand, and said: 'The dining room is all Chippendale. It's an elegant room. The study, however, was chosen for its comfort. The sofa and two armchairs are blue and yellow, and the desk is a beautiful rich mahogany, to match the bookcase and chairs. For our bedroom, I tried to read your mind, and so your vanity table is of light wood with charming mother-of-pearl inlays, but the mirror is large and modern. The living room is Louis XVI, light green with gilded wood. And all the rooms have Aubusson carpets to match the particular colour scheme. Of course, you'll have to find everyday dishes and kitchen utensils, but I suppose that you won't have trouble, because the Rue de Paradis is lined with china stores, and the Printemps has a good kitchenware department.'

He'd made all the decisions, and what he'd left to her, he was telling her how to accomplish. She said, her head swirling a little: 'Thank you.'

He still hadn't told her he loved her. Sitting there, so close to him, breathing the musky odour of his maleness, she thought perhaps that she was in a trance. His leg was lightly brushing against her, and the contact was like electricity. She wasn't thinking of apartments, furniture, or dishes, but of his lips on hers, of other, more elemental mergings. In the convent, she'd been taught about sins of the flesh. But what of one's future husband? In just a few weeks he would be married to her. Just a few weeks. He didn't believe, he'd told her mother, in long engagements. He considered himself too old for that.

It's because he wants a family right away, she thought. He'd made all his plans as if I were already pregnant. The thought made her strangely embarrassed, as if he'd kissed her in the most intimate way, instead of having outlined an apartment for her. If I fail him, she thought, he will not hesitate to divorce me. Like Napoleon with Josephine.

'I won't be able to get away for too long,' Misha was saying, and she realized that he had begun to speak about their honeymoon, a bit apologetically. 'The Loire valley is beautiful, Lily, at this time of year.'

She nodded. It wasn't really important where they went, so long as they could be alone together. She needed time to get used to him, to feel that he was hers. Yes, the châteaux of the Loire would be a fitting decor. Kings had loved inside the thick grey walls, and had begotten heirs, legitimate and illegitimate. Maybe there, she would stop feeling intimidated by this man who had made her act dishonourably, breaking her engagement to another man – hurting Mark so, he who had covered her in a velvet mantle of love, given her security and trust. She'd let that nameless something, that dark instinct against which she had fought so many mornings on her knees, break all other commitments and all other plans.

She touched his cheek, and saw that the soft gesture had startled him. His skin was smooth, ruddy, healthy. He was smiling, but his eyes were tender, deep. She wanted him to kiss her. Slowly she moved, putting her hands on his shoulders, looking into his face, and finally he swept her to him, crushing her in a tremendous embrace. She trembled against his heartbeat for a moment, and then he found her lips and parted them with his own. She could feel everything: his tongue, his heart, his life's breath.

Lily felt the kiss descending to her throat, and was afraid. If he continued, she knew that she wasn't going to stop him. But after a while it was he who gently disengaged himself, and she was relieved, first, and then a little disappointed.

'Princess Liliane Brasilova,' he said. 'You're a wind of madness.'

The wedding had been set for 4 March 1924. In the short intervening weeks, Lily had much to prepare. Claire ordered several outfits for her honeymoon, at Lanvin. For the wedding, Lily picked out an apricot lace dress with a small toque hat of egret feathers. For in the matter of a formal wedding, Misha had stayed firm.

But Paul prevailed in one area. He wouldn't hear of his only daughter getting married without any festivities. He insisted on a luncheon party following the wedding. This was something Lily herself could have lived without.

On the morning of her wedding day, Lily got dressed quickly, donning the apricot dress and the small hat. She'd insisted on Marisa as a witness, and her brother was imposed on her by Paul. Oddly enough, she hadn't felt a great enthusiasm on Misha's part for her best friend. She'd asked him why. 'I can't really explain it,' he told her. 'It's just that in Russia, most Jews we met were uneducated and greedy – totally without finesse.'

'But Marisa's just the opposite! They're the finest people I know!'

'Perhaps you're right. But it's difficult to overcome one's basic feelings, Lily. It may not be generous, and it may even be unfair: but in Russia, Father and I never had Jewish friends, and for good reason.'

She was sure that in time he would see she was right about the Robinsons, and so she didn't argue any further. Claude and she drove to pick up Marisa, and from there it was only a few minutes to the city hall of the Sixteenth Arrondissement. She stepped out of Claude's car into the building, and was met by Misha, Prince Ivan, and Rochefort. He'd asked his secretary to stand up for him – not even one of his friends. She felt the slight shock but said nothing. Even if this wasn't how she'd dreamed of getting married, this was still her wedding.

Afterwards he kissed her, and she knew that they were bound together for life, and that they now belonged to each other. It wasn't important how they'd got married. She was his wife now.

In the Villa Persane, Claire had prepared a splendid luncheon. Misha was at first taken aback. He hadn't anticipated so many people in attendance. Lily helped her mother pass the sandwiches, and she thought: It's the last time I'll be doing this in this house. She passed the food and heard the compliments and felt the soft rush of blood to her cheeks, every time someone called her 'Princess Brasilova'. It was really true: he'd married her, he hadn't changed his mind before the wedding. Maybe he loved her. She knew for certain that she loved him, that she wanted to feel his arms around her, his lips upon her.

She wanted to leave, couldn't wait for the moment when she would go upstairs to change, to leave with her new husband for the Loire valley. Neither one of them belonged here, and both were awkward. But it's the last time, she told herself. The last time anyone will force me to be with people I don't care for, people who don't care about me, but only about the name I bear. 'Liliane Brasilova; Princess Mikhail Brasilov.' She loved its sound but was a little afraid of its importance.

In the royal blue De Dion-Bouton, she sat silently, watching his hands on the steering wheel – surprisingly delicate hands, though large and strong. It was a strange sensation, to be sitting next to a man she still knew so little, but who was now her husband before God and all men. She glanced at her ungloved hands, folded together on her lap. The large diamond gleamed coldly at her. She felt the small gold medallion of the Virgin around her neck. 'Misha,' she said timidly. 'I'd like to stop somewhere, in a small chapel. It would be nice, to consecrate our wedding.'

He turned to her, and she saw the kind concern in his eyes. 'If that's what you want.'

'Don't you?'

'God is always with us, Lily. Wherever we are.'

He was stronger, more powerful, wiser than she. She'd wanted a husband like that, to protect her. She didn't want to feel alone, battling with the world. A surge of affection filled her then. He was stopping the car in the countryside, in front of a small, dilapidated church.

Unlike Claude, he always came around to her side to open the door for her. Next to him, she didn't feel awkward about her size. She was still small beside him. They walked hand in hand up to the church, and he held the wooden door to let her pass inside. The church was small and deserted, grass growing between the bricks of the pathway. The altar was well tended, however, with a shining statue of Christ on the cross at the rear wall. Lily plucked a candle from a sconce, and went up to the altar with it. Misha remained behind, watching her as she knelt, as she prayed.

In a few moments she stood up, pressing out the creases in her skirt. She looked up, and encountered his eyes. Suddenly she felt embarrassed. He went halfway up the aisle to hold out his hand to her, and silently, she put hers into it. They walked hand in hand into the hazy March sunshine, timid with each other, a little uncomfortable.

They were standing in a field, near the road, among the poppies. They were alone. Far off, sounds of mooing cows reached their ears. He cupped her chin in his hand, looked deep into her eyes. 'It's the timing,' he said gently. 'You're my wife, but you don't *feel* like my wife yet.'

She nodded, amazed at his perception. Maybe it wouldn't be this hard after all. He bent over, tasted her lips, and with a suddenness that took her breath away, swept her up into his arms. He strode towards a lone tree in the meadow, away from the dirt of the road, and laid her down on the soft grass. Then, to her complete incredulity, he began to take off his jacket, his tie, and then his shirt. 'What . . . ?' she murmured.

'I *want* you to feel like my wife,' he answered simply. 'Now.'

She would never forget their first coming together in the meadow, when she'd first felt him as a man inside her, while she trembled for fear that somebody would see them, and he laughed, gently, about her bourgeois fears. Afterwards, there was a new bond between them. Although

100

she still felt that he was an iceberg, seven-eighths unknown, there was something touching and vulnerable about the sex act with him that revealed more of the man's sensitivities than all the words he'd ever spoken to her. He called her 'Lily,' and spoke in deep tones the language of his past, which had at first surprised her, because all Russian noblemen spoke French from the cradle. She supposed that at the most elemental of times, a man spoke the most instinctive tongue that came to him. But he never praised her, or filled her ears with terms of endearment. He was spare in the expression of his feelings: she'd learned that early on.

Together, they wandered through the vast stone castles of the Loire valley, imagining scenes from the Middle Ages taking place in their gardens. They ate lunch at small taverns and drank *vin du pays*. He ate and drank enormous quantities, always with relish. And always he pointed out to her the things he thought would broaden her mind. For hers was a parochial mentality, carved by the nuns away from the world.

She tried to ask him about his life. Whenever she touched on the subject of Varvara, he closed himself off. It was visible, this closing off. His eyes became remote, he raised his head in proud rejection. But he described to her with amusement the things he'd done as a youth, and some facets of his father's business. Lily felt that she'd entered a world greater than life. He was a giant among men. She whispered to him: 'I love you, I love you,' to make him happy and to chase away the past. But he simply held her head against his chest, and never answered her. It was all right: she could survive without the words, she could learn anything to please him, to make him smile.

In the early spring, she felt herself grow into a woman beside this man whom six months ago she hadn't even known. He never let her far away from him. He liked to touch her, to link his fingers with hers, to surround her shoulders with his arm. Lovemaking was a strange experience. He was so smooth in his nudity, his chest muscled but hairless, with the two round brown aureoles of his nipples flat and strong against the boyishness of the hairless chest. He was like a statue, every muscle finely delineated and visible. She always knew when he was aroused, she always felt it was something so incredible, a man excited. He was careful not to hurt her, not even to embarrass her. He kept himself above her, moving in and out smoothly, letting her feel him inside her. Nobody had ever told her what to expect from sex, but she liked it.

She said to him, once, over a candlelit dinner in a small inn: 'I'm glad you've lived a full life before me. Women often worry about their husbands' fidelity. But you've had your fill of women – haven't you?'

He smiled. There was always something a little sad about his smile. 'I'll never dishonour you,' he said.

'And I'm – enough?'

Again a little smile. 'I'm here, Lily. With *you*.'

He wanted her to understand by half words, by facial expression. If she'd hoped to learn much more about him during their honeymoon, she learned it from the tone of his voice, from his body language. But somehow she felt that he loved her, that she would be protected forever.

It was with regret that she entered the De Dion-Bouton to return to Paris. She realized that never again would they be so totally alone, so completely at peace together.

The next few weeks took care of themselves. Lily went to the Rue de Paradis with her mother, and bought everyday dishes; to the Galeries Lafayette, where they purchased all that a kitchen would need. Claire came every morning by chauffeured car, only it was Lily who sent the car for her: a metallic Rolls-Royce that was a present to the young woman from her father-in-law. They spent the day shopping, taking tea at La Marquise de Sévigné, and at six o'clock Lily sent her mother home again. It gave her just enough time to bathe, brush her hair, and be dressed and ready for dinner with her husband. Often Prince Ivan came along, and they would dine as a threesome.

She slipped without too much trouble into the role she realized he wanted. All her life she had been afraid of confrontations. The idea that an entire household depended on her management had at first frightened her. But after a few weeks she knew that her authority had been established: that her gentle ways had made inroads with everyone.

She met, one by one, all the great hostesses of Paris: the Baronne d'Oettingen, the Vicomtesse Marie-Laure de Noailles, the Marquise Casati, the Princesses Murat and de Polignac. They were kind to her because she was so young, and by nature she was a quiet one, listening and learning. The nuns had taught her well, giving her a solid foundation in the classics. And twice a week she and Misha went to the opera, the ballet, or the theatre. She came to know Gabrielle Dorziat, Cécile Sorel — the foremost actresses of the day, hostesses in their own right. And the languorous Anna de Noailles, poetess and patroness, and Misia Sert, who had helped the careers of many famous poets and painters.

Inevitably, he asked her to plan a dinner at home. It was something small, intimate. She asked him to include Marisa Robinson, to bring her confidence. 'Marisa knows all these people,' she explained. 'She's my best friend. She's been out in society much more than I.'

'Invite Marisa. But don't see her too often alone, Lily. She's unmarried, and a bit too free for my taste.'

She couldn't help herself, and said: 'You don't like her for the same reason Papa didn't: because she's Jewish.'

He raised his eyebrows and looked at her. 'Not at all. I told you before, Lily: it was a prejudice founded on the behaviour of some people in Russia. I haven't let it influence me here.'

'But still – you hold it against her.'

He shook his head slowly. 'I hope not. Maybe I do, in my subconscious. Don't judge me, my dear. I'm trying very much to like your friend. My objections are of a different nature. I don't approve of young women of good family going all over Paris with gentlemen friends – unchaperoned.'

'But Marisa is very decent. This is 1924, darling. Mothers don't accompany their daughters anymore the way they did ten or twenty years ago.'

'If I remember correctly,' he interjected, 'I never called on you to be alone with me until after we became engaged. I knew how to respect you.'

She was silent then, pleased. He'd treated her differently from his other women. As much as she tried to keep her mind clear of his past, people spoke. Be it in veiled allusions, in small *apartés* concealed behind a laugh – people spoke. They said: 'You've become a good boy, Misha.' Or: 'We don't see you anymore at all your old hangouts.' She heard his own laugh, hearty and full, responding. And then she felt left out. He'd led a rich, ribald life before his marriage. A life that in her wildest fancies she couldn't even begin to fathom. But she was pleased. He'd given all this up, because of her. She was happy.

Even the first dinner had gone well, and Misha had bent to kiss Marisa's hand, while she'd flirted with him in her innocent, elfin way – only once, for a split second, had Lily caught him looking at her friend with a strange, pointed stare.

But Lily noticed that whenever Marisa and Misha were thrown together after that, her small blonde friend always appeared just a touch selfconscious. Oh, well, thought Lily: I must let them come together in their own way, each in his and her own good time.

104

And she lay back and relaxed, enjoying her life.

Marisa Robinson slipped the black Chanel chemise dress over her tiny body, and fluffed up her golden curls. The only thing that was missing was rouge. She dabbed some over her cheekbones, smoothed it over her lips. Then, without looking back, she stepped out of her room and half ran to the living room, where Mark was waiting for her, with Eliane.

Her mother rose, at the same time as the young reporter. 'Well, dears, have a good time,' she said lightly. 'Don't keep her out too late, Mark. She spent all afternoon at Lily's, and they always wear each other down with girl talk.'

Marisa laughed. She kissed Eliane on the cheek, and allowed Mark to slip a sable stole over her frail shoulders. They walked out together into the April coolness. Mark had bought a Citroën, and now he opened the door and let her into it. 'I want to go to the Jockey Club,' she declared.

'Then that's what it'll be, mademoiselle.'

As they drove, Mark seemed preoccupied. Suddenly he asked: 'Tell me about Lily. Is she happy?'

Marisa shrugged. 'I think so. Misha's very kind to her. And she's very much in love with him, of course.' She looked sideways at Mark, bit her lower lip. 'I'm sorry. I shouldn't have said that.'

'Don't be silly. I want her to be happy. I thought perhaps I'd run into her now and then, but so far, I haven't.'

'They don't go out to clubs. Only to the theatre, and society parties. He keeps her sheltered.'

'Just like her father. I wouldn't have done that, but maybe he understands her better than I. He must: she chose him, didn't she?'

Marisa let that stand, understanding the bitterness. As she had never loved anyone with great passion yet, she wondered how he must be feeling about the rejection. He'd come so close to marrying Lily, only to be thrown over for another man – older, more imposing, richer. She shivered inwardly, glad to be free of the tempests of love.

The Jockey Club stood on the Rue Campagne-Première in Montparnasse, and Marisa loved it. She'd introduced Mark to it and turned him into a regular patron. They entered, and Marisa left her stole with the cloakroom lady from Normandy. In his black tails, the owner, Hilaire Hiller, an American painter, was greeting the new arrivals. 'You'll see,' Marisa had whispered. 'There's always gossip to be written about here. Hemingway comes here – all the American expatriates. They brawl and they make passes and they think up their next short story.'

The Russian pianist was accompanying a jazz combo, and Mark and Marisa sat at a small table and ordered *amourettes*, the anise-flavoured aperitif that was customary before the unique dish of Welsh rarebit. Slowly, their eyes became accustomed to the darkness, and Marisa laid a small hand on Mark's. 'There, in the corner,' she whispered. 'Zelda Fitzgerald and a man who isn't her husband.'

He smiled. He was always amused by Marisa. He looked where she had motioned with her chin, and saw a blond woman with bobbed hair drinking from a highball glass with a thin, dark man. His eyes shifted to the bar. There was something familiar about the sensual redhead who was sitting there, chatting to the bartender. She was of average height, but her silk dress clung to overripe breasts and the beginnings of appetizing calves. Coloured beads were knotted midway between her cleavage and her waist. 'Who's that?' he whispered to Marisa.

'I'm not sure. But she does look like someone we've seen before, doesn't she? Is she perhaps an actress?'

It was the legs that kept his gaze riveted to her. He'd seen *them* before. But it didn't matter. He turned away and raised his hand to signal for the waiter.

They picked at their food, talking of this and that. It distressed him that Marisa didn't seem to care about making a future for herself. She just wanted to have a good time. 'Lily always talked about wanting to be a concert pianist. What's become of that?'

Marisa shrugged. 'With *him*, what do you expect? Sudarskaya comes three times a week. She's a small Jewish woman with the worst taste in clothes, but she plays like a dream. Of course, he can't stand her. Lily takes pity on her – she has so little money – and has sent her some students. Whenever Misha's retained in town for a business dinner, she keeps her to eat with her. Lily only invites her when she's alone. Like tonight. He had something or other to do – a meeting with a commissioner – '

'But he doesn't want her to reach the stage.'

Marisa laughed. 'Are you joking – Princess Brasilova?'

He held out his hand to Marisa, and she rose to join him on the dance floor. A tango had begun.

Over the head of his small partner, Mark looked about. The stunning redhead at the bar was turning around, smiling. She had wide, sensuous lips painted a carmine red. A man was striding up to her – a tall, massive, well-dressed man in a dark silk suit. He, too, looked familiar. The man took the woman's outstretched fingers, brought them to his lips, but she laughed, and closed both arms around him in a single fluid embrace. It was then that the man turned and Mark caught his full profile. He froze on the dance floor, and Marisa stepped on his foot and stopped, bewildered. 'What on earth's got hold of *you?*'

'Look,' he breathed into her ear. 'That's Misha Brasilov.'

Marisa turned around, and saw them. She shook her head. 'But – the meeting with the commissioner . . .'

'Let's sit down before they see us,' Mark said tightly, taking her arm in a strangely vicelike grip and leading her back to their table.

The rarebit had got cold. There were lines around

107

Mark's mouth. She was suddenly a little afraid of him. She'd always thought of him as the gentlest man on earth, but now she could feel something else – a sort of fierceness.

'Look,' he was saying. 'It's none of our business, is it?'

She looked at him, appraisingly. 'But *you* think it *is* . . . just as I do. You're still on Lily's side. You still love her.'

'That's neither here nor there. But I don't like what I've just seen. If I'd been lucky enough to have just married Lily – '

At that moment, a waiter holding a drinks tray moved deftly behind Marisa's chair. On an impulse, she turned, and touched his arm. He stopped in his tracks, bewildered. 'Madame?'

'I was just wondering if you could tell us who the redheaded lady at the bar might be. We both felt we might have met her before, somewhere – only we can't quite place her.'

The waiter smiled. 'Oh, you'd have seen her on the stage. She's called Jeanne Dalbret, and she's become one of Mistinguett's best support dancers. Many people feel she'll be ready soon to form a revue of her own.'

'Thank you,' Marisa answered. Then, when he had left, she pressed her lips grimly together.

'Jeanne Dalbret is Misha's ex-wife,' she stated. 'Her real name's Trubetskaya – Varvara Trubetskaya. I guess . . . he still likes her.'

'Let's go home,' Mark said, reaching for Marisa's hand across the table. 'It's best neither of them sees us.'

'Don't you *see?*' Marisa cried. 'He lied to you!'

'He must have had his reasons,' Lily said in a low voice. 'I respect Misha. He wouldn't ever do anything improper.'

'But he was with *her!* Don't you even care?'

'He has to pay her money every month. Maybe he was giving it to her last night. It's his business, Mari. Let it be.'

'He lies to you and goes out with another woman, and you don't *give* a damn?'

Lily closed her eyes. She could feel the room spinning and spinning, her stomach lurching. She'd felt this way all yesterday, all the day before. It came in waves, the nausea, the dizziness. Now she simply whispered: 'Mari, please go home. I'm so tired. I just have to sleep.'

It was the first time she'd ever sent her friend away, and she felt a twinge of remorse. But really, everything was too much. She couldn't be bothered with Marisa's feelings when she felt so dismally bad. She felt Marisa's kiss on her cheek, held out her hand. 'I'll see you on Thursday,' she said in a strange, muffled voice. Then she heard her friend's footsteps, and knew she was alone. She curled into a small ball on the sofa, and fell asleep at once.

When she awakened, her whole body was drenched in perspiration. Madeleine was standing over her, sponging off her forehead. 'I've called the doctor,' she stated.

'No, Madeleine, you mustn't.'

'But it's the middle of the day. Monsieur le Prince won't be home for several hours. You should really be examined, madame.'

'It's probably just strain, or a small virus.'

Madeleine peered at her, sternly. 'I think I know what it is. But the doctor needs to confirm it. How long has madame been married?'

'Almost two months,' Lily answered.

She allowed Madeleine to lead her to the boudoir, to change her clothes for a loose, soft housedress of green silk. Then the doctor came, and told her to lie down on the bed. He examined her and she felt the stirrings of shame, as always. Madeleine hadn't left the room. As the doctor poked and prodded, she thought again of her conversation with Marisa. Why had Misha lied to her? And if he just needed to pay Varvara, why hadn't he just had Rochefort send the cheque? She remembered bits and pieces that

109

she'd put together. He'd known Varvara a long time. Maybe he was, as Marisa suspected, still interested in Varvara as a woman. Oh, God, she thought. It would be too horrible – too painful and humiliating . . .

'When was your last menstrual period?' the doctor was asking.

'A little while before I was married. But I've never been very regular.'

'I think this time there's a reason for it. Princess, you're six weeks pregnant. You can expect a little prince or princess at the end of the year – about Christmastime.'

Lily sat up, her heart pounding. It couldn't be true, so quickly! She felt the thrust of joy, the incredible exhilaration. 'Thank you, Doctor,' she said breathlessly. And then, to Madeleine: 'Please call the chauffeur with the car for me. I'm going to the Rue de Berri right now!'

'But madame – '

'Do it, Madeleine. I've got to tell my husband right away!'

During the drive, she thought chaotically about Varvara, and about the baby. She was happy, she was afraid. The chauffeur helped her out of the car and into the office building, and she took the lift up, realizing for the first time that she was still in the green silk housedress. She was embarrassed, then waved away the shame. Her news had been too great for waiting, for changing, for the amenities of decorum. Misha would have to understand . . .

'*Bonjour*, Rochefort. I have to see my husband.'

She was amused by the secretary's look of dismay, but he was quickly on his feet, knocking on the boss's door. He opened it for her, but she pushed past him, into the light room, to Misha's desk. He was looking up from a file of papers, his face displaying total astonishment, even shock. 'Darling,' she cried, crossing to him. 'I simply had to tell you *now!* Dr Châtel came to the apartment, and he told me we could expect our baby at the end of the year!'

110

She felt his arms around her, holding her up against the light-headed feeling, against the sudden dizziness. He was sitting her down, fanning her with some bills. 'Are you sure?' he was asking.

'Positive. That's why I came.'

Their eyes locked, and she could interpret his joy, his delight, his infinite pride and gratitude. In this supreme moment of intimacy, she knew that she would never ask him about the Jockey Club, that it was a closed issue. And then he rang for Rochefort, and said to him: 'Call my father. And get us some champagne – the best! The line of Brasilov has been brought forward: we'll have an heir by Christmastime!'

Chapter Five

The year 1925 was a memorable year: the Exposition of Decorative Arts revolutionized the world of fashion, design, and architecture. And Marisa became engaged to a young Viennese doctor.

At the end of December 1924, Nicky had been born: smooth, strong, long-limbed – like both his parents. He was a serious child now, looking straight into people's faces with Claire's dark, pensive eyes. They'd hired a Swiss nurse, Yolande Bertrand, only a few years older than herself but already with sound references, to take care of him. And at once they'd fallen into the Swiss pattern of calling her 'Zelle', an affectionate shortening of the more formal 'Mademoiselle'. Zelle was efficient, discreet, polite – and knew what to do with a baby. Lily realized that for all their talk of matrimony and its duties, the nuns had taught her nothing about what was needed in the handling of a small infant. She'd felt shy at first – awkward – in front of this stalwart little being who had come from her, but who was still very much a stranger. She didn't understand his needs. Zelle relieved her of the immediacy of the problem, but the nagging guilt remained that somehow, she was failing as a mother. And only three months later, before he'd even developed his first secret language – when he was barely learning to push his pudgy hands down and lift his head to look around – she'd found out she was pregnant again.

She and Sudarskaya had made a lovely music room out of an unused bedroom. For the last few months of her pregnancy with Nicolas, she hadn't used it much. But after his birth, she'd found herself in it more and more, learning new pieces and practising the old. She'd put up a magnificent oil of one of Degas' dancers on the wall, and had textured the walls with pearl grey silk, for a soothing effect. Plants with creeping tendrils finished off the decor: it was *her* room.

Misha was exuberant about Nicky, and the joy he felt in expectation of this second heir was, to Lily, touching. Lately he'd been absorbed in all sorts of complex business issues that had taken him to various parts of France, that had resulted in late-night meetings between him and sombre, elegant men who greeted her when they came in, bending with understated graciousness to kiss her hand – men whose names had strange resonances, and who, she felt, wielded much more authority over the fates of Frenchmen than those poor harassed premiers, Herriot and his successor, Paul Painlevé. In drawing rooms, people laughed about the Radical cabinets, about the finance ministers who had come and gone like elusive comets in the sky, flickering but a moment before fall and extinction. But people didn't laugh about Ernest Mercier and François de Wendel. She wished she understood everything that was happening around her: her husband's affairs, the true facts about France's present situation. Maybe, she thought, she was just too stupid to sort it all out.

She didn't regret her choice, her marriage to Misha. She'd wanted fireworks and shooting stars, and sometimes she had them. When there was time. She understood, completely. He had built an empire and made her his empress, but it was his duty to make sure the colonies didn't rebel. But she realized how right she'd been during their honeymoon, when she'd supposed this would be the last time they would be alone, truly alone. Now, when she sat with him in the study, he was most often absorbed in his papers – or in his thoughts. And other times, she'd find him in the nursery bending over Nicky, crooning to him in Russian. She felt lonely.

But sometimes the mood would lift, and she would walk through the house, imagining what she could do, *she*, Lily, to turn this apartment into something special, something that she'd always dreamed of during those barren years in Brittany. She had taste, and she knew it.

When the Exposition set up its pavilions on both sides of the Seine, Misha said to her: 'Go, see, feast your eyes on what delights you. I want you to have everything, Lily.'

'No, Misha, you must tell me what *you* want.'

'I've put in what I thought was essential. Money is no object.' But she knew that this was a man who had selected everything down to the last detail, and that she was expected – because this was how his mind worked – to amplify his taste, to fill in the blanks. She couldn't complain. How many women her age had been told: 'Money is no object'? And so she went.

The weather was beautiful. She willed the slight nauseous feeling of her pregnancy to go away. The metallic Rolls-Royce slid down to the Alma, where the pavilions began. They wound all the way to the Concorde, and her driver asked her where she wanted to be let out. 'At the Palace of Elegance,' she said.

They drove past incredible architectural displays: a church, an entire cemetery, landscapes of gardens like veritable cities, with strangely shaped fountains. The Palace of Elegance was like a museum of all that dealt with the clothing industry. It lay, asymmetrical, behind an enormous hedge draped with white and silver silk. She secured her egret hat and walked in, breathtaken.

She had never minded being alone – it was, sometimes, comforting. Now she was glad she wouldn't have to think of clever things to whisper to Marisa, for example. Under delicately carved chandeliers reflecting all the colours of the rainbow, lay the displays from all the great *couturiers:*

Lanvin, Chanel, Worth, the Callot sisters, Jean Patou. The furniture was simple, clean, linear, and the dresses went with it: little bits of nothing shimmering in the refracted lights. She could feel herself blooming out below the breasts, and her breasts held firmly up by the custom-made brassière. A pang of envy went through her. She'd never be the Woman of the Twenties, who went to sleep in skin-thin pyjamas like a boy: this boy-woman, this *garçonne*. Marisa had told her of the new book by that name by Victor Margueritte, illustrated by Kees van Dongen. A naughty book. Marisa read everything, and apparently under the eyes of her mother. Lily thought: But if she passes it to me, I'll not know where to put it so Misha won't see it.

She stopped in front of a display of gossamer materials, by the designer Paul Poiret. An attractive woman was rearranging some silks. Fascinated, Lily watched her. She was lithe, very thin, with eyes that might almost have been Oriental – long and narrow, gleaming a kind of amber. Her hair was short and of different shades of maroon. Not beautiful – but somehow striking. Lily felt strange, standing there, pregnant and awkward. She wanted to ask something, but felt suddenly shy in front of the efficient, sleek employee. It was she who saw Lily, and inclined her head: 'Madame?'

'I was wondering . . . these materials are from the fashion house, or from the interior decorating shop?'

The woman said: 'From the Atelier Martine. But, of course, if the design pleases madame, I'm sure Monsieur Poiret could create something beautiful at the Avenue d'Antin.'

Lily bristled. She's trying to see whether I'm a provincial who doesn't know the ins and outs. She wondered whether she'd ever seen this girl before, and decided she hadn't. She'd bought few outfits from Poiret because of her pregnancies, but she did know the famous *maison de couture* in the Avenue d'Antin. The Atelier Martine was his decorating house in the Rue du Faubourg Saint-Honoré, where those who dared all commissioned entire rooms redone as Buddhist temples or Chinese pavilions. She stared, wondering how such delicate cloth could find its place on the back of a chair or on a headboard. And the other woman continued to stare at *her*, her head cocked to the side.

'Who,' Lily asked softly, 'is brave enough to put his house in the hands of the Atelier Martine?'

'The great *Spi*.'

The singer Spinelly, Lily thought, feeling an unexpected pang of envy. A woman who'd made it on her own. 'There are many others. Gabrielle Dorziat, Jeanne Dalbret.'

Lily's eyes widened: Jeanne Dalbret. For a few seconds the pavilion seemed like a mausoleum, and Lily alone in the silence. Jeanne Dalbret: Varvara Trubetskaya. She never spoke about her and refused even to think of her, and avoided reading the variety section of the paper because, a year ago, it had chronicled her ascent from revue dancer to solo artist in some of the best showhouses in Paris. 'Jeanne Dalbret is at the Gaîté-Lyrique right now,' the young woman said to her.

I should have stayed at home, Lily thought unhappily. And then she said, raising her chin: 'I should like to have them do something for *me*.'

'I'll be glad to relay the message of a new client to monsieur,' the maroon-haired girl said dryly. 'Who may I say is interested?'

She knew it had been an impulsive mistake, that the Atelier Martine was much too avant-garde for her and Misha. But she'd wanted to jump in, to join the crowd of women who dazzled the world, who did more than have babies and play the piano for their husbands and mothers. Around her, smooth Lalique crystals beckoned near lacquered screens by Dunand: an entire world of luxury such

116

as she had never witnessed before in her life. Misha had said: 'Money is no object.'

She had been about to respond to the unmotivated arrogance of Poiret's representative by saying that she was the Princess Mikhail Brasilov. But now, suddenly she felt ashamed, and shook her head. The Cartier display suddenly seemed sickening, the finely crafted silver and gold work of Christofle excessive. Many in France were still devastated by the effects of the war.

She left the Palace of Elegance lost in thought, chewing on her lip. Behind her she could hear a woman's voice asking: 'Who was that, Henriette?' and the employee's reply: 'Nobody.'

Claude looked around him. His sister had redecorated, or at least completed the decorating of, the apartment at 34 *bis*, Rue Molitor. As always, when he was there, he had to admire the easy grace of his surroundings. A bare five minutes' walk from the Bois de Boulogne, it was convenient for the nurse and the baby. The Brasilovs lived on the second floor, and Lily had made the eight rooms warm and pleasant. In the immense living room, she had left the green and gilt Louis XVI chairs and the small sofa, but had intermixed them with some exquisite, larger Louis XIV furniture in crimson silk and gilt wood: a large divan, four armchairs, and six chairs. Just lately, he noticed, two *bergères* of Louis XVI style, in mauve silk and the same gilt wood, had been added. They had tall backs that curved outward at the top. Lily had told him they were called 'Voltaires'. She was very proud of them and of her salon. Like her, it displayed classical refinement that was in opposition to the trends of the extravagant twenties.

It was a room that, for all its careful style, looked alive. Old books lined a full wall. On another was displayed an oil painting by Hubert Robert: a castle in ruins on a cliff, overlooking a small river. It breathed of calm – Lily's own serenity. And on another wall, the portrait of a cardinal by Philippe de Champaigne. Claude approached it, felt almost in spite of himself the rich texture of the painted robes. He knew enough about art to remember that Champaigne had executed only a few canvases; most of them were catalogued. Misha had undoubtedly paid a small fortune for this unique work.

Lily came in, smiling. Two years ago he had told her to cut her hair and modernize herself. Now he was glad she hadn't listened. Paris was full of petite, flat women with bobbed hair. His sister was different – a rare bird. She had swept her hair up, and still strode, in spite of her pregnancy. So. The Russian was going to use her as a spawning mill for dozens of little heirs – one after the other. He felt a pang of regret. It was a shame, really, to ruin a beautiful body in this fashion. Because, truly, his sister was one of the most beautiful women in Paris.

She said, kissing his cheek: 'You're not at the office?'

He sat down opposite her, and watched her hands. The elongated fingers gleamed with rings. He was using her as a spawning mill, but paying for it. He couldn't remember the young girl who had come home from the nuns – full of hope, brimming with the most incredible naïveté. He'd thought, in his detached fashion, that they would never have a thing in common. He'd always been alone, with all the problems. Women, like his mother and sister, were fine in a drawing room. But what kept them in their drawing rooms were the practical, unrelenting males like himself who somehow kept the money rolling in the coffers.

He asked: 'Where did you find the Champaigne, Lily? Surely it wasn't easy.'

She shrugged, simply. 'It's rather a funny story. Somebody owed Misha money. A lot of it – thirty thousand francs. Misha kept waiting and waiting for the man to

118

come to him with the money. He was a great collector. So finally, when Misha pressed him, he asked us to come to his house and choose five paintings.'

'Tell me – do a lot of Misha's associates owe him this kind of money?'

Lily raised her brows. 'I don't know. Misha's business is very convoluted, and he doesn't usually tell me the details.'

'But have you ever thought that if this kind of thing takes place frequently, Misha might stand to be in a real cash-flow problem?'

Lily was silent. He could see her pupils contracting to tiny black points. She said, finally: 'But Misha didn't really press this man too much. He really didn't seem to *need* that money. But the principle was another thing: the man owed him and had to be made to pay up honourably.'

Claude was tempted to rebuke her angrily, the way he'd used to when she'd been a girl. Now he controlled himself. She'd been a silly young girl he could rebuke. Now she was the wife of a powerful man. He'd come for a reason, anyway. It wasn't his custom to pay her social visits with no purpose in mind. When he was with Lily, he never knew what to say or do: they'd been brought up virtually as strangers, because of the difference in their ages and because by the time she'd grown, financial difficulties had all but been eclipsed. He'd been the one who'd had to struggle – never she. Again he glanced at the ringed fingers, and felt anger.

'It's very grand to be generous with one's debtors,' he stated. 'But today, things are more difficult than they were some years back. I don't suppose you've ever given any thought to the current economic crisis?'

She sat quietly, her eyes intent on his. She said, slowly: 'But people are spending a great deal of money. The *grands couturiers* are doing more business than ever. And the jewellers, and the restaurateurs, and the antiquarians . . .'

'Oh, my darling, the very rich are richer than ever. The

119

Rothschild fortune will never go dry. That's why, at the Bank of France, there's strong disagreement between the bankers and the industrialists – people like your husband, who invest their money in capital and not dividends. Who rely on products being manufactured and then being sold in order to make their profits. What you're witnessing are the fireworks before the deluge. People are spending madly, while there's still money to spend. Taxes are still low enough not to have disturbed the big earners, and inflation's reduced the national debt we incurred when we had to borrow to finance the war. But that's *right now*. And that's just the very rich.'

She leaned forward. 'And Papa's firm?'

'First of all,' Claude said, 'I run the firm now. Papa hasn't been well. His heart is bothering him. Mama's tried to put him on a diet, hoping it will help . . . and they're planning to go to take the waters during the summer . . .'

They said nothing for at least a minute. Then she asked, in a curious voice: 'But still, your visit doesn't make sense. I can't believe you'd leave the office just to give me a lesson in economics.'

'No, that isn't why I came. I wanted to ask you to sign a paper for me. We're a small firm, but we're trying to grow, and all this talk of taxing businesses could weaken us a great deal. That's why I want to set up Bruisson et Fils as a multiple-vote company. Then we are not going to seem so big, and we won't be taxed so high. I need you to sign as shareholder.'

'Is that fair? I'm a member of the family.'

'It really doesn't matter. The truth is' – and he laughed dryly – 'nobody checks too closely. It's the setup that counts, that's all.'

As he began to fumble in his briefcase, she cleared her throat. 'Claude. I can't sign anything without Misha's approval. Leave the papers and I'll show them to him when he comes home tonight.'

Claude's eyes hardened. 'You're a Bruisson, aren't you? This is a family matter. As you yourself just finished pointing out.'

For a moment her fingers interlaced, tightly, so that her knuckles gleamed with tension. Then she asked, softly: 'Aren't you a bit too late, Claude? Don't forget, it was primarily you who sold me to the Brasilovs. But now that you need me, you find it convenient to forget that I was once considered matter for trade — like the poor franc. Only, unlike the franc, my value's gone up. And now I'm first and foremost a Brasilov. I don't act behind my husband's back.'

Claude stood up, pale and straight. 'I always knew we were complete strangers,' he said. 'But I did believe you were a helpful person. Yes, maybe I wanted you to marry a rich man — but you chose him, Lily. You loved him. Nobody pushed you into this.'

'You're right. I married him because I loved him. And I love him now. I told you: leave the papers, and I'll discuss everything with him when he comes home. If you expected me to turn into a free-thinking Amazon, like Elisabeth de Clermont-Tonnerre or Gertrude Stein, then you are mistaken. I was reared to be traded in for a business advantage — not to be independent and clear-thinking, with sufficient education to be able to make my own decisions. I won't be your pawn, Claude. If Misha approves, I'll sign.'

Claude closed the briefcase, and said, tightly: 'Goodbye, Lily.' He didn't wait for her to escort him to the door, and when Arkhippe, the courtly *maître d'hôtel*, held out his coat for him, he shrugged him off impatiently and slung it over his arm.

In the street, the Renault 40 sat waiting for him. It was a solid car, but nothing compared to the metallic Rolls that was his sister's exclusive property. At the moment when he stepped inside, he felt hatred. He'd wanted Lily to marry Brasilov, but he'd imagined an alliance, two brothers-in-law equal partners in a fast-moving venture into industrial progress. He'd never thought to be left behind, by everybody.

What was his life, except for business deals made from behind the mass-produced desk the Galeries Lafayette had manufactured identically for hundreds – thousands – of offices like his? He'd never taken the time for fun, for sports, for shows, for women. He didn't know what it was like to be loved. He felt jealous and bitter. But his time would come.

In the study, Misha didn't quite seem so overwhelming, such a force of nature, for the room was very spacious and had been furnished for his measure. An immense library covered one whole wall, and his desk was six feet long. The sofa where Lily was sitting was large enough to seat six people. The room had been decorated with pieces of stark, polished simplicity, English furniture from the late eighteenth century, and on the wall behind the desk were some Russian hunting scenes that he had bought from an impoverished countryman.

'If this is what goes on when I'm not here,' he was saying, pacing up and down in front of her, 'then I shall have to tell Arkhippe not to let him in next time.'

Lily said nothing. She watched him. Then she said, gently: 'It's all right, really. I'm not at all upset.'

'You're my wife. You are not to get involved in any outside affairs with anyone – not even your own brother! You are not here to make deals with anyone, to sign papers as a favour to anyone. You're going to have a child, and you're supposed to take care of yourself, to do only the things that give you pleasure and that don't require a strain.'

'But . . . is Claude right? That the economy's in trouble?'

He hoisted himself onto the edge of his desk, and crossed his legs. Her eyes were anxiously lifted to his. He

122

compressed his lips and said: 'Yes and no. There *is* a problem. It's a wealth caused by inflation. And if inflation makes the state richer, it also pushes everything else up: prices of goods and services, primarily. Devaluation weakens the franc, while at the same time, inflation creates a false sensation of wealth that sooner or later catches up with everyone except those rich enough never to feel anything.'

Lily asked, hesitantly: 'Misha . . . are we part of those who never feel anything?'

He looked at her, wondering. She was so serious – so young and earnest and caring. He was furious that Claude had dared upset her quiet, serene life with his petty, materialistic reality. He felt a profound pang of vulnerability when he looked at her, at the trust in her eyes.

Yet it was also, in a touching way, amusing. Like a child's naïve and hopeful question: 'Papa, are we millionaires?' He'd once asked his father if they had enough rubles to buy the Winter Palace in St Petersburg. He remembered Prince Ivan's answer: 'No, my boy, but we do have enough to build one just as nice.' Now he wanted to laugh: the arrogance of the Brasilovs, the ease with which they'd lived, generation after generation, always secure in the knowledge that they were the *ne plus ultra*, that no one sprang from a better lineage, that Russia was their land and that, from this land, they would always be able to extract millions of rubles to build palaces of marble and gold . . . An irony that was so bitter that the past now seemed ludicrous, God's harsh joke on those who had been too sure of themselves.

'No, Lily,' he answered softly. 'We aren't that kind of rich. Ours is the wealth of newcomers, of foreigners trying to make a new beginning. Our wealth is a vulnerable wealth, for we must invest our benefits right back into our capital, to make it prosper, and there is little in reserve in

123

case the capital itself disappoints us. We're not Rothschilds, nor Monsieur de Wendel.'

'But you told me that money was not an object.'

'I was speaking to you about the sorts of things that women want: jewels, furs, lovely furnishings. You know we have money. But you also know that we don't live in a five-storey palace, like some of the people we know whose families have been accumulating millions for centuries. I had that in Russia – but here, it is yet to come. And it will come, I can assure you of it. When Nicolas grows up, he will be able to build his palace.'

How sure he was! Lily thought, admiring him. He possessed the force and drive of a bull, and the intelligence, she was sure, of a genius. Yes, he would do what he had set out to accomplish.

'In any case,' Misha continued, 'the Radical party instigated taxation of businesses.'

'That's why Claude was here. You are not upset by this?'

'I'm not upset because, as your brother saw, there are legal ways to get around this. A Radical tax levy means that it provides loopholes. I've done what hundreds of other large firms are starting to do: formed subsidiaries, with multiple shares so that we can't be accused of monopolizing business.'

'You didn't ask me to sign for some shares.'

'There's a simple answer for that: you're my wife. I automatically have power-of-attorney over you. There are many shares in your name in three different companies, and shares in Nicky's name. And your mother gave me her signature.'

'I didn't know.'

'It wasn't important between you and me. So you see, all that Claude did was to stir up unnecessary anxieties in you.'

'But if you went to Mama, wasn't that the same thing?'

Misha shook his head, almost sadly. 'I'm afraid not. Your mother may soon be alone in the world, and I did this to make sure that she would always have a steady income. Claude never intended to pass any dividends on to you – he just wanted to control his affairs without having to pay an extra tax.'

Lily turned away, and he could see the pain of her conflicting emotions. Her old family, her new – old loyalties betrayed, new ones still untested. She'd never had the chance to find out who *she* was, Liliane Bruisson Brasilova, and he wanted to tell her to go ahead, that it was all right to set out in search of her own self, that everybody had to do it. But the words stopped in his throat. Another feeling had taken possession of him, twisting his insides: fear. Fear that if she found out who she was, she would no longer be satisfied to remain what he had made her.

'Don't worry about Claude,' he said almost brusquely. 'I'm planning to absorb his firm into our own, and give him a vice-presidency.'

He was as shocked as she was by his words, because until that very moment, he'd never considered such a thing. He felt the most profound antipathy towards his brother-in-law, and to top it all, he distrusted his business ethics. The Brasilovs had always prided themselves, father and son, on the cleanliness of their books and on the lack of corruption of their firm. Yes, one could take advantage of a loophole – if it was legal. And one could compete to the bitter end of a financial rivalry, if one's methods were fair and aboveboard. Claude Bruisson's ways were like those of the Radical party: he was an opportunist, whose alliances could swing wherever he could hope to gain a point. Misha didn't respect him and found him potentially dangerous. Then why had he promised Lily to make him a partner?

It would have been a convenient self-deception to say he'd thought of Claire, or even of Lily. But Misha was too honest to lie to himself. He'd done it to bind her more to him, to make sure that not one string lay untied between her and him. Not merely to make her feel a debt of gratitude, but able to see to it that Claude never withdrew his total approval of the marriage. And, Misha realized, he intended to exercise control over Claude in business as well.

It was his right, now, to fight to keep what was his, what was dear. Lily was rising, coming towards him, and putting her arms around his neck. He buried his face in her hair.

Chapter Six

Marisa had met Wolfgang Steiner in a library. True, one had to admit that it wasn't your run-of-the-mill sort of library, for Adrienne Monnier, the owner, enjoyed a certain renown among the literary avant-garde. She had sponsored the Rumanian Dadaïst poet Tristan Tzara, and other young French poets such as Valéry Larbaud. She held informal readings in her shop in the Rue de l'Odéon, across the street from that other literary haven, Shakespeare and Company, the lending library for American and English expatriates run by Adrienne's friend Sylvia Beach.

Marisa had gone to Shakespeare and Company first, looking for *The Beautiful and Damned*, Scott Fitzgerald's latest book, which had been highly recommended by Mark. Actually, to be honest, she'd gone there in the hope of glimpsing the author in person. But the shop had been sadly vacant of intriguing activity, and Miss Beach had been out of *The Beautiful and Damned*. So Marisa had wandered across the street to see what might be happening there. She'd found a lovely old volume of the memoirs of Ninon de Lenclos, bound in decaying leather, the corners of the pages swollen out of shape – with the wonderful ancient way of spelling *s*'s like *f*'s. But somebody else had been holding the book. She'd tried to squeeze herself between the bookshelf and this person, clothed in a camel's-hair coat and muffled in a hat and scarf, and had stolen a peek or two.

He'd looked at her then, and she'd seen spectacles and a trim brown beard and moustache, and intelligent brown eyes behind the spectacles. 'You are interested in this, mademoiselle?' he'd said in a strange, somewhat clipped accent.

'No, really, I was just . . . passing by,' she'd answered, blushing and trying to shrug in an offhand fashion.

'It's all right. It's quite a charming old book. Allow me to purchase it for you, mademoiselle.'

He'd been so serious, and so courtly. A Frenchman would have been ironic. She hadn't been able to gauge his age, with all that clothing. On an impulse, touched by his sincere appreciation of her interest in Ninon, she had accepted the gift, and then, a coffee at the Café des Deux-Magots. He had removed his hat and muffler, and she'd seen a pleasant face with a slightly receding head of hair. He had told her he was Dr Wolfgang Steiner, specialist in neuropsychiatry in Vienna. He was on his winter vacation, which he customarily took in Paris. His French was good and his English even better. He came from an old Viennese family of Jews who were somewhat lax in the upkeep of the old traditions, but who nevertheless were proud of their ancestry and treasured the teachings of the Torah. He was thirty-two years old and steadfastly single, and his passions were the symphony and the opera, and, yes, a good game of tennis on a warm day.

Marisa, who had never loved any man before, and who had wondered curiously what it was that had led so many of her friends into sometimes totally unexpected alliances, surprised everyone when she brought the young man home to meet her parents, and when she continued to see him every day and every evening of his vacation. At the end of February, two days before going back to his practice in Vienna, he proposed to her. And, to the astonishment of the dandified young Frenchmen who had tried in turn to bed her down or marry her, she accepted without a moment's hesitation. Her parents were delighted. Wolf was everything they'd always hoped for in a husband for their irrepressible, lively daughter: the perfect match as well as the perfect counterpart.

Now it was Wolf who was escorting Marisa and Lily to their fittings for the wedding. It was November, and very cold. Marisa had wanted a winter wedding, so that she could start her life in Vienna ice-skating and driving around in the snow. She'd wanted a wedding where the guests would warm themselves in front of her mother's fire at the luncheon – where the women could wear furs, and the gentlemen, elegant spats and dark overcoats trimmed in astrakhan. Lily was eight months pregnant, uncomfortable and enormous, and had hoped for something after Christmas, so she could have been slender and normal. She felt ashamed in front of Wolf, ashamed of her awkwardness and lack of elegance. But Wolf was so sweet – not like the men she knew, who revelled in their maleness and made a woman feel silly and childlike, or else taunted her with ill-concealed provocation – Wolf was so sweet, so serious and kind and *accepting*. He made one feel *good*. There was a sensation of being appreciated for inner qualities, of being accepted as a mental equal, that she could only remember having encountered in Mark MacDonald. 'Feel not that you have lost your friend,' he said to her in his slightly stilted French, 'but that you have gained a loving brother to watch over you.' She'd felt suffused with emotion, touched to the core. Wolfgang Steiner was almost a stranger, certainly a newcomer in her life – but already he had made inroads into her heart that Claude, her blood brother, never had and never would.

Marisa's wedding was one of the big events of the season, and, at the Maison Poiret, Avenue d'Antin, the *première* was in a flurry, sending the girls for this and that to finish off Mademoiselle Robinson's veil, petticoat, and train. The gown was shimmering white silk with small seed pearls sewn into the skirt and bodice. Lily and Wolf stood to the side, he with his customary gentle, amused smile, she with an admiration tinged with sudden sadness. Marisa's wedding was exactly what she herself had wished and hoped for: the gown a perfection of froth, the guests warm and loving. But where would Liliane Bruisson have found such guests – people who had been coming for years to see Eliane and David and their children, intelligent, intellectual people, funny people, fashionable people? Her parents hadn't known anyone like the people who had sent in their acceptances to Marisa's wedding.

Marisa went into the fitting room, and Wolf helped Lily to sit down. She was wrapped in sable, he in his usual muffler and topcoat. The *première* said, 'If Madame la Princesse can be patient for just a few minutes . . . we had to do an alteration on your dress, given the . . . situation . . .'

'It's perfectly all right.'

When they were alone, Lily turned to Wolf and said: 'Before I had Nicky, I came here quite often. Now I feel strange. In almost two years I've had two pregnancies – and I haven't been wearing anything very wonderful.'

'But I like you very much the way you are today, my dear Lily.' She was wearing a mint-green maternity dress of the finest cashmere, and had opened the flaps of her coat because of the heat in the *maison de couture*.

'I feel bad for Misha. I'm not very nice to look at, these days.'

'Misha is a man who wants children. He can only appreciate your condition.'

She thought: But I wonder if he does. And thought again of the day she'd learned of her first pregnancy. She'd made it a point from that day on never to ask where he had been, never to question his comings and goings. But for the past two months he hadn't asked her to come to him. He'd been the best of husbands – kind, generous, affectionate – but he hadn't touched her as a woman. She, who had been reared such a strict Catholic, who had always been discreet and private by nature, suddenly felt a tremendous urge to empty her mind to Wolf – a man, yes, but also a doctor, a doctor of people's feelings and secret longings.

An assistant had brought hot tea. Wolf had turned slightly, and half risen in his chair in polite deference to a woman who had just walked in. Lily thought there was something in this woman that would make any man take notice. She was older than Lily, but still young, and was of average height. Thick, softly curling hair of the palest red – almost strawberry blond – aureoled her head beneath a tiny strip of black velvet topped by a single mauve feather. She wore her dark mink coat open, revealing a simple sweater set, English style, over a fitted skirt. Pearls came down to her waist, knotted over her breast. And the legs were long, strong, sensual in their silk stockings. She nodded to Lily and Wolf, and sat down on the small sofa to the right of their armchairs. She opened an alligator bag and extracted a gold cigarette case, and took from it a long, thin cigarette. For a split second in time, while Lily and Wolf watched her, mesmerized, she waited, cigarette poised – and then Wolf was lighting it for her while she smiled.

I've been saved, Lily thought, somewhat regretfully, by this strange woman. Otherwise, God knows what stupidities I might have confided to Wolf. But she knew that she would never again have the courage to begin such an intimate conversation with anyone.

'Madame la Princesse, we'll just be another minute . . . a thousand apologies . . .' The *première*, confused, was back again. 'Would you feel ready, in five minutes, for a quick *essayage?*'

'Certainly.'

'I'll send Henriette to model the gown, so you can get an idea of what it's like from all sides again. But, of course, we had to pad her a little . . .'

131

Lily didn't remember which of the models was called Henriette. She smiled – and the redhead, near them, started to laugh. She laughed with mirth, with unsuppressed lack of restraint. The *première* turned to her, embarrassed. 'I'm so sorry, madame. I've been so preoccupied with the gown for the Princess, who's been so patient and kind. I – '

' – didn't notice I was there. Believe me, it happens all the time.'

For some reason, they both started to laugh, and Lily and Wolf looked at them, bewildered. The *première* turned to them, smiling: 'Isn't that something for madame to say! Of all the people . . .'

So the woman was a personality. But no one she'd met. No. If Lily had been introduced to her, she would never have forgotten her. This wasn't somebody that she or Misha knew. So she wasn't a member of the Sert group, nor of that aristocratic enclave that socialized with the Murats.

The model was coming, decked out like a pregnant woman in the most sumptuous dress of purple velvet, with fluid lines that softened the stomach. Lily stared, fascinated. Then her gaze travelled upward, and she started. The model was the same impertinent girl who had been short with her at the Palace of Elegance some months before. But that shouldn't have been such a surprise. After all, she was an employee of the Maison Poiret.

The woman with red hair, smoking her cigarette, raised her thin, arched brows and commented: 'My, my. Quite a different look for you, my dear Rirette.' The model smiled, once, coolly ironic.

'We'll fit you when you're ready, Princess,' the *première* stated.

Lily felt overcome with self-consciousness. It was as if the *première*, the model, and the strange, alluring woman near her were all in on some secret that excluded her. The model, perfectly adept, was turning on her toes, her back slim and arched almost unnaturally. Everyone was looking at her. Lily thought: they are all more worldly than I. And she thought, almost jealously, of Marisa's impending wedding: Wolf was the sort of man who would want his wife to understand all, to absorb, to question, to accept or reject in conclusion. Misha was less liberal by a long shot.

And then there was a small commotion, and Marisa appeared, a cloud of white tulle and silk, holding up her skirt and bursting with uncontrolled exuberance: 'Look! I'm a vision of nubile grace, don't you think?'

'Aphrodite in miniature,' Wolf said, with a smile.

Marisa clapped a hand over her mouth: 'Oh, my God! You aren't supposed to see me in this until the wedding. I forgot!'

Wolf said, gently: 'Don't worry about it. You know me, I'm a scientist. I don't believe in superstitions.'

Marisa giggled, then turned to Lily and the *première*. All at once, her eyes fell upon the elegant redhead sitting on the side, looking at her with an indulgent smile. She stayed rooted in place, her face paling. Automatically she nodded back, then made a quick motion for Wolf to join her in the opposite corner.

'What's wrong?' he demanded, when they could speak away from curious ears. 'Are you all right?'

'I'm fine. But that woman over there is Misha's ex-wife. You've got to get Lily away from her, as fast as you can.'

'I'll do my best.'

'Then I'll go and change, at once, so we can all leave.'

She left him pondering the issue. Marisa had already darted back towards the fitting room. Wolf, striding back towards Lily, overheard the *première* whispering sotto voce: 'They say it's going to be the wedding of the season among the Israelites,' and the model's ironic retort: 'She'll be Queen for a Day in the golden ghetto.' A quick anger threaded through him, which he shoved aside, concentrating instead on Lily, looking at him in some bewilderment.

133

Gently, Wolf circled her shoulders and drew her aside. 'Marisa recognized the redhead,' he murmured. 'It's your husband's first wife. Do you want – '

But Lily had stopped listening. Her lips stood slightly parted on an intake of breath, and he felt rather than saw her dark eyes suddenly drawn to the seated woman, like magnets to steel. Lily's entire body had gone rigid, then had started to tremble in small waves of shock. Amused, the woman who had once been married to Misha, who had shared his life, his bed, turned aside with a small, good-natured nod. Then she rose and gathered up her wrap, and began a conversation with the *première*, while gracefully manoeuvring her out of the room. Their voices, raised in pleasant small-talk in the hallway beyond, trailed behind them. '. . . more of a physical drain to have my own revue. And the Gaîté-Lyrique isn't always properly heated backstage . . .' Lily shivered once, then looked into Wolf's quiet, concerned face, and tried to smile.

The model, Henriette, still stood in the room, staring at her. Lily brought a hand to her throat, suffused with embarrassment. Wolf half turned, and saw the strange, pointed look on the other woman's face. It unnerved him. 'Thank you, mademoiselle,' he said to her. 'The Princess has approved her outfit. But she prefers to try it on another day.'

Afterwards, when they were at last alone, Lily stammered: 'She knew, didn't she, about Jeanne Dalbret? That she and I – '

'Perhaps that wasn't it at all,' Wolf reassured her. 'Maybe she was only envious of your beauty.' And then, to take her mind off the entire episode, he sighed. 'She made a nasty comment about Marisa, too. Not really "nasty", actually – but ungenerous. People who envy Jewish social-ites tend to set them apart by their religion. It's as if they're saying: "She thinks she's *somebody*, but she's only a Jew. We'll pretend to play her game, but the truth is, *we*

know that *we*, as good Christians, are better than she is."
I've tried to tell myself it doesn't matter – that I don't
really care. But sometimes, you know, it still can sting.'

'I'm so sorry,' she whispered. 'Sorry, and ashamed. For
all the *bad* Christians who feel that way, and who have
hurt you.'

He shrugged, half smiling. 'You needn't apologize, Lily.
It's something people like Marisa and me have had to
learn to live with. And if we find ourselves reacting in spite
of our common sense, then, truly, we're as much at fault as
the poor fools who seek to bring us down. We should know
better. Most of us, after all, have had to deal with this
since early youth. I remember what my mother told me
when I was five, and we went to the seaside for a summer:
"Wolf, when you meet another child, you must first tell
him that you are a Jew. Like that, if he refuses to play with
you, it will hurt less than if he finds out later, and you two
have already become friends." I did what she had said,
and I was lucky: most of the families we ran into were
broadminded and accepting. But a few were not.'

'But Marisa never told me anything like this. And we've
been like sisters, since we were both eight. Why wouldn't
she have confided this sort of thing to me?'

'Because you are not Jewish, and would not have been
able to understand.'

Lily stared at him, shocked. 'But – why not? I'm a
person! You don't have to be Jewish or not Jewish to
understand a human problem!'

'Yes?' he asked, gently. 'I don't think so. That's why the
Jewish communities in most cities are so tightly knit.
Because they share the same problems since birth. You're
a wonderful girl, and Marisa and I both love you. But you
know that even in your own family, there's quite a lot of
anti-Semitism. You can disrespect your father, and be
angry with your husband, because they feel this way – but
the problem ends there. It doesn't touch you personally,

and it won't affect Nicky, or the child that's going to be born now. Lily, darling, it's quite simple: anti-Semitism just *is not your problem*. And it was wrong of me to impose it on you, even now, in conversation.'

'No,' Lily said. 'You weren't wrong, Wolf. We're friends.' But for the first time in twelve years, she felt that a wall had been erected between her and Marisa. It wasn't fair. She'd never been prejudiced, against anyone. She'd argued with her father, with Claude, with her husband, for Marisa. She'd even gone so far as to impose this friendship on Misha, she who was always a little afraid to face up to him and run the risk of displeasing him. And now she was being told that she didn't understand, that she was outside the problem.

Hurt, she thought: Maybe sometimes the Jews build their own ghettos, and exclude the rest of the world. That, too, had to be another kind of prejudice. Now Marisa would be more and more within this ghetto, because she was marrying Wolf, another Jew. She remembered what Misha had once explained to her, about the Rothschilds and the Gunzburgs, two of the wealthiest, titled Jewish families in Europe: that they had the practice of intermarriage, of cousin marrying cousin, in order not to have to go either outside the faith, or outside the rank and financial circle of the family. A kind of golden ghetto, formed of their own free will ...

There was so much, Lily thought, that she really didn't understand. For, after all, there was only one God, and everyone agreed to that. What possible difference could it make how a person chose to express his faith?

It was a Tuesday, at two o'clock, that Marisa Robinson was to become the wife of Dr Wolfgang Steiner, of Vienna. Because it was to be a grand wedding, the two janitors of the large synagogue in the Rue de la Victoire had required extra help with ushering, and the Jewish Consistory next door had to send two of their office boys, who were now dressed in black, with coloured sashes and cocked hats, and were escorting the elegant guests down the aisle to their assigned places. The carpet extended outside onto the pavement, so that the ladies would not have to feel the November cold against the thin soles of their delicate shoes. They passed underneath the great red awning, with the initials *R* and *S*, into a lobby filled with flowers, and then into the main hall of the synagogue, also profusely decorated with flowers. Lily knew that Eliane Robinson had sent especially to Nice for blooms that were now out of season.

All the lights were on. Lily could see the choir in the back. She felt the solemnity of the occasion catching at the back of her throat, which was clasped by a choker of pearls and amethysts to match her purple dress. Misha, on one side of her, stood tall and elegant, holding her by the elbow so that she would not miss a step. How careful men are of the women who are carrying their babies, she thought. On her other side, Claire, in a light mink coat over a beige outfit, seemed expectant, absorbed in the surroundings. They sat down, on the bride's side, behind old Madame Rueff, Eliane's mother, and several aunts and uncles.

The music began. A pianist, a violinist, and a cellist were playing for the entrance of the wedding party. Lily wondered what Misha was thinking, and stole a look at his profile. He was sitting, erect and impassive, waiting. Little children, boys and girls from the Robinson, Rueff, and Steiner families, came first down the aisle, in neat pairs, the girls with long, curled tresses and flowers, whose petals they scattered ahead of them over the red carpet. A cantor began to sing. Lily saw her mother's face, her lips parted with rapt attention, as the strange sounds of the Hebrew words fell upon the room, soft, swaying, hypnotizing.

The chant ended abruptly, and Mendelssohn's nuptial march filled the temple. Eliane walked first, on her son's

137

arm, followed by a middle-aged couple, a little plump and overdressed for Paris, he in tails, she in lamé: the Steiners, Lily supposed. From the sacristy beyond, Wolf, in a morning suit, more elegant than she had ever seen him, came up with his best man to wait for his bride. She could see the nervousness on his earnest, bespectacled face – that good face that she had learned to love. And then the music swelled, and everybody stood, turning slightly to catch Marisa with her tall, courtly father, her train flowing endlessly behind her, held up by the smallest of the little cousins. It was impossible to see the expression behind her thick tulle veil.

The entire wedding party was now lined up under the huppah. The cantor began to intone a prayer. Lily looked beyond into the crowd of guests. Most of the men were wearing small satin skullcaps, and Misha's vital crest of black hair seemed like an angry protest. She felt suddenly ashamed that she hadn't thought to ask Marisa if she would have preferred for Misha to wear one too. There were so many distinguished faces! Some, like the Baron Robert de Rothschild, she had met before. Strange: She hadn't realized that the young composer Darius Milhaud was a Jew, but his lips were moving in tune to the prayer. Marie-Laure de Noailles was there – but she was half-Jewish on her father's side. There were other important guests who were not Jewish at all, of course – she could see Hélène and Philippe Berthelot, and Paul Valéry. Her heart beat faster when she caught sight of this *paterfamilias* of French literature.

Because the words were in Hebrew, Lily lost track of what was going on. Then the Grand Rabbi of France, Israel Lévi, began to speak. He was a magnificent orator, the words falling from him with ease, with grandeur, with resonance. He spoke of Eliane's family, the Rueffs; of David's, the Robinsons; and then he went on to describe the great Steiner family of Vienna, and what humanitarian contributions had fallen from their hands. He spoke of the Jewish tradition, and how the two young people, Wolfgang and Marisa, had been brought together to carry on this tradition, to uphold the Mosaic faith, and to continue the unbroken chain. Lily forgot where she was: what he was saying mesmerized her, took her beyond this ceremony into the ancient land of Palestine, back to the Twelve Tribes of Israel. She felt, in her heart, that Wolf had told her, that afternoon *chez* Poiret, only half the story: he had left out the glorious history of the Jewish people, and their pride.

Maybe, she thought, remembering her feeling of hurt and anger, the Jews had come together in a feeling of pride, and had stuck together to make certain that no enemy, however great, would ever destroy this noble sentiment. Maybe it hadn't been prejudice, on their part – but just fear of the alien, who had to be turned away. And I am part of this alien body, Lily thought, shaken. If I can't understand the tradition, then maybe I'm not worthy of sharing the problem. Wolf had said: *It is not your problem.*

She looked at Claire then, and saw that tears were brimming from her large brown eyes, and that she had made no effort to wipe them away. Lily was stupefied. She had almost never seen her mother weep, even in the worst of circumstances. But now she wept unashamed, and at the words of a rabbi whom she didn't know, who was speaking of traditions that were not hers and a family that didn't include her. Lily didn't understand, and was flooded with an odd anxiety. Beside her, Misha stared at the dais, formal and attentive, manly and distant. The words hadn't touched him at all. He was on foreign ground, like a polite visitor, marking time.

Music followed. Marisa, unobtrusively, was removing her right hand from the suede glove that covered it. The rabbi was whispering words to Wolf, who repeated them in Hebrew: the marriage vow. He was placing the ring on

Marisa's finger. Lily found that her eyes had moistened, too. The rabbi was giving them the benediction, was reading the act of marriage in Hebrew, and then Marisa and Wolf drank from the silver chalice. An attendant brought a small cushion with the traditional glass, which Wolf set on the floor, in his methodical fashion, then ground strongly under his foot.

Just as Wolf was gently lifting his bride's veil from her small face, Lily saw for the first time a refined middle-aged man whose picture she had seen in the newspapers many times before. My God! she thought, her lips parting: it's Léon Blum, leader of the Socialist party ... the man who Misha had said was 'a real menace' because of his intelligence. He was totally different from what she'd imagined: extremely well dressed, he might have been yet another French society man attending the wedding of a dear friend.

So the Robinsons were friends with the 'real menace'. As she looked again at the nuptial dais, and caught Wolf's kiss on Marisa's lips, she couldn't help but see again the face of Léon Blum superimposed upon her mind. The music to accompany the exit march of the newlyweds towards the sacristy had begun. Claire was soundlessly wiping the tears from her cheeks with a linen handkerchief, but her face reflected absorbed serenity, and no sign of shame. Lily wondered if Misha had seen Blum.

An usher came to the row where they were sitting, and Lily felt her husband's hand on her elbow again. They followed in the train of guests towards the sacristy, where a receiving line had been set up. The sacristy, too, was filled with flowers. Lily stood in line between her husband and her mother, hearing the laughter, the jokes, and thinking again about the ceremony and her mother's tears, about Léon Blum, about Misha. He didn't like socialists, he didn't like Jews, and he had reasons for both those feelings. But – did that necessarily exonerate him? Léon Blum, in his expensive suit, hardly looked like the sort of man who – like Lenin, who had died last year, or like the new man, Joseph Stalin – started revolutions. He was just a man who thought that poor people deserved a chance.

Misha, in his office, had always treated his employees with respect and fairness. Where, then, was the difference between them?

Ahead of her, Misha was kissing Eliane's hand, congratulating Wolf and Marisa. And then it was her turn. She hugged the bride and groom, she hugged David and Eliane, and answered the perfunctory question about when the baby was due. Suddenly it was over, and she was hungry. She said to Misha: 'On to the luncheon, then.'

He shook his head. 'I'm afraid not. I have much business waiting for me at the office. But I've arranged for François to be waiting for you and Claire outside the temple, with the Rolls. Make my excuses to the Robinsons, and to Wolf, will you?'

She opened her mouth, but the words didn't come. He kissed the top of her head, caressed her cheek. 'Don't come home too late,' he whispered in her ear, affectionately. And then he was gone, his broad back disappearing among the guests, last of all his head, which always towered over other people's. She stood alone, uncertain, resentful – abandoned.

'Don't be so upset,' Claire said when they were riding across town in the silver Rolls. 'Business is business. Your father didn't even come – it's a workday.'

'Papa didn't come because he's never socialized with the Robinsons. But Misha – I can't explain it. He left us there, alone – on purpose. Papa didn't come at all: you could use any excuse you wanted. But what can I say that Marisa and Wolf could possibly understand? That my husband didn't think they were important enough to miss a small meeting for their wedding reception? They *saw* him there: they *know* he wasn't ill. He did it to slight them.'

Claire was looking at her, puzzled. 'And what makes you so belligerent?'

She shrugged, sighing. 'It's just something that Wolf told me, not long ago. About people's reactions to Jews. Misha is purely and simply an anti-Semite. No different in any way from Papa.'

'No, no, there *is* a difference. Be fair to him, Lily.'

'It's not I who's unfair – it's him!' she cried. And then she closed her mouth and didn't speak until they arrived at the Avenue Henri-Martin.

On the drive back from Boulogne, where François, the chauffeur, had first dropped off Claire, Lily sat back, exhausted, and closed her eyes. For her, it had been a long, strenuous afternoon. The magnificent luncheon in the Robinson apartment, the good food, the shining cut crystal, Marisa's radiant face, Wolf's jokes – she saw all in chopped succession, like a series of quickly flashing snapshots.

She'd wanted so much to meet Léon Blum. But of course, he'd been surrounded by a group of gesticulating gentlemen, and she'd stayed on the outside, hearing bits and pieces. Aristide Briand was sure to win the Nobel prize for peace in the coming year, because of the Locarno agreements. Yes, she recalled hearing about that: the treaty among the French, the Belgians, the Germans, the British, and the Italians. Germany had promised to respect the Rhine frontier, set up in the Versailles agreements after the war. Everyone was happy about that. There wasn't going to be another war, even though Hindenburg, that war criminal, had recently been elected President of Germany. And anyway, just in case . . . there had been, last year, the mutual defence pact signed with Czechoslovakia. The gentlemen had all been in a good mood. In the end, she'd gone away, seeing that there was little chance for a word with the 'real menace'.

And yet, at one point, Marisa had gone to him and put her arms around his neck, and said, gaily: 'Well, Uncle Léon, are you really going to go into the kitchen and make our servants go on strike?' And he'd laughed, and swept her into the air, and answered half jokingly: 'Is it necessary?'

At the door, on his way out, Wolf had detained him, and she'd gone over, once again. Wolf had made the introductions: 'Monsieur Léon Blum, the Princess Brasilova.' He'd been quite charming. Inclining his head, bending over her hand, he'd said: 'When a man meets such a lovely woman, does it really matter that he and her husband are on opposite sides?'

But she'd asked curiously: 'Is it true, really? That you and my husband are, as you say, "on opposite sides"?'

'As gentlemen, I'm sure we're not, Princess. But in the area of politics, certainly. Your husband is the last of the capitalists, and will fight to the end to maintain a capitalistic state. As for me, I've long since reached the conclusion that capitalism doesn't work. Too many people are hurt by it.'

'Then – why not participate in the formation of a cabinet?' Wolf had asked.

'Because we don't yet have a majority in the Assembly. And because power corrupts even the best of men. I'm trying to protect my people, Wolfgang.'

'But Misha isn't trying to hurt anyone,' Lily had interjected.

'Of course not, Princess. I'm sure the Prince is a very good man.'

'And a kind, generous one.'

'But what a man will do at home, and to what extremes his political feelings can drive him, are two entirely different things.'

She thought about that now, about the gentle, fatherly tone of the man who had told her this. And she wondered, suddenly, what Misha did or didn't do in the parts of his

143

life from which she was excluded. And she was oddly troubled. What, really, were Misha's beliefs? After almost two years of marriage, she still wasn't exactly sure.

She felt the bumps on the road, opened her eyes, yawned behind a gloved hand. That other troubling moment: Claire's tears. And superimposed upon that, the vision she had caught of the Grand Rabbi of Paris, Julien Weill, better-looking than his brother-in-law, the Grand Rabbi of France. He'd been going to get a refill of poached salmon, when he'd suddenly noticed her mother, standing by the table, waiting for Marisa's brother to return with a glass of champagne for her. He'd seen her, because her person had crossed his field of vision: and he'd lifted his brows in surprise, the surprise of someone chancing upon an acquaintance one isn't expecting to encounter – an acquaintance who is liked. Lily had watched her mother, had seen the smile, the extended hand. She thought she'd heard him say: 'Claire! And how are you?'

A brief encounter, to say the least. Afterwards, in the car, she'd hesitated to bring any of this up, and she'd decided that the tears were too private a matter, but the rabbi, not. So she'd said: 'I didn't realize you knew Grand Rabbi Weill.'

Claire had nodded, pensive. 'Yes. I've known Julien Weill for quite some time.'

'But – *how?*'

'Well, my dear, when one is forty-five years old, as I am today, one can count any number of interesting acquaintances.'

No, Lily thought: she is trying deliberately to evade me.

In front of her, François, his cap neatly on his head, was manoeuvring the car in front of the house on the Rue Molitor. Lily wondered if, when he and Annette went to bed, they ever discussed the speeches of Léon Blum, and if they, too, were 'on opposite sides' from the Brasilovs. For

144

whatever Misha thought or did, she was his wife, and she owed him her allegiance.

Why is it, she asked herself, that no one sees fit to tell me their own truths?

Chapter Seven

In December 1925, Kyra was born, almost exactly a year after the birth of her brother, Nicolas. Like him, she was born at home, under the supervision of Lily's doctor from the American Hospital in Neuilly, and a nurse who remained for two weeks. After that, Zelle was able to take care of both children. Kyra was different from Nicky: where he possessed his mother's equanimity and serene disposition – a French calm – she was highly-strung and nervous from the start, a true little Russian princess. She had her father's interesting colouring: his green eyes and black hair, his healthy, ruddy complexion. And like him, she was given to moodiness, even as a very small infant. It was impossible to predict if she would accept the bottle or reject it; and sometimes she cried insistently for no apparent reason.

After Kyra, Lily didn't regain her strength. Somehow, when she wanted to climb out of bed, her head would begin to spin and she had to lie down again. She spent hours of the day lying down, the door of her boudoir closed against the noise of the babies and the servants. A long corridor separated the nursery from the rest of the apartment, and she felt little inclination to walk the distance more than once or twice a day to see what was going on there. Nicky had accepted the intruder: in fact, he took his toys into Kyra's room every time Zelle permitted it. The servants had welcomed the new arrival. And Misha, when he came home from work, always spent the first hour playing with his son and holding his small daughter. Lily felt guilty; but also, the enormous exhaustion that swept over her daily was a good enough excuse not to spend much time around her children. It wasn't that she didn't love them; and it wasn't that they bored her. She simply couldn't face the corridor, and the noise, and their young vivacity.

Counting the hours during the day, Lily felt a wrenching loneliness for Marisa. The Steiners wrote to her often: bright, interesting letters about what they were doing in Vienna. Marisa loved it there, and had already made a circle of friends. She went to the theatre and the opera and the ballet with her husband, and during the day she took walks in the Prater with her mother-in-law and visited art galleries. The Steiner family was phenomenally wealthy. Wolf was the only child left, for his only sister had died ten years before, in a riding accident. His father owned a large mansion at number 2 Schwindgasse, where Marisa and Wolf had their own sumptuously furnished apartment, and Wolf his office. For weekend retreats they owned a beautiful villa in Baden, near Vienna, and for longer vacations, a magnificent old castle in Tobitschau, in the province of Moravia. The Steiner fortune came from seemingly inexhaustible coal mines in the heart of Austria, and people called them, respectful of their wealth, the 'Barons von Steiner'. The famous diva Lotte Lehmann was a frequent visitor, and three times a week Wolf, who was an aficionado of the cello, was joined by a violinist and a pianist from the Philharmonic Orchestra, and played for his pleasure and Marisa's. The household servants were wonderful: at the last minute, they could put together a dinner party for twenty, or a picnic lunch for Marisa and a dozen friends. By the time Lily and Misha had celebrated their second wedding anniversary, in March, Marisa was still sending photographs that showed her slim and girlish, unmarked by pregnancy and unstoppable in the flow of her activities. If anything, she was busier and happier than during her

147

single years in Paris, when she had been courted by every eligible bachelor who'd known her.

No, it wasn't exactly jealousy that Lily felt. But she was sad, when Misha left for work and she was alone. Except that she wasn't ever really alone: there were seven servants and two small children whose presence was felt even when her door remained closed. She was trapped. Marisa, in Vienna, was free. She came and went as she pleased, and her husband was delighted by all her friends and her stories about them. Wolf was a kind of confidant for his wife: they could talk for hours, analysing people and events, or they laughed over any number of silly things that they had heard or seen. She, Lily, wouldn't have dared tell any such stories to Misha. He was, first of all, too judgmental; and, second, he would not have been amused by the foibles of people who didn't truly touch the sphere of his own life.

Lily stayed in her room, and steadfastly refused to enter the living room, where her piano, the Pleyel, elegant and noble, gleamed like a forgotten jewel at the bottom of a bank safe. And March rolled into April, and then into May. Raïssa Sudarskaya's telephone calls, never returned, became less frequent, and her notes, never answered, scarcer. And Misha, when he came home from work, went straight into the nursery to take note of the changes in his baby daughter, and to play some simple games with his little boy. He no longer asked how many times his wife had been there before him, and he didn't question Lily when he returned to her boudoir. Their conversation was quiet, polite, and impersonal. Neither knew how to bring it back to the present, to themselves, and to their family. He sat awkwardly at the dinner table, and tried to speak of events in the arts. And she sat across from him, always elegant in her understated fashion, pretending to care about what was going on outside their home. They sat, avoiding each other's eyes, and after dinner he sometimes asked her if she wanted to go somewhere, and when he did, she always demurred, because she was tired and felt weak. Then he would get dressed and go out, kissing the top of her head, and she never asked him where he was going, and he never told her.

But in the morning when Arkhippe's wife, Madeleine, came into the boudoir to wake her with the breakfast tray, Lily was always on one side of the bed, curled up like a small child; and when Arkhippe knocked on Misha's door, he always found his master sprawled out alone in the seven-foot bed, the pillow rumpled under his head, while on the other side, the other pillow sat starched and clean like a toy soldier at attention. The two servants never discussed this, but when they turned off their light in the privacy of their own room, they instinctively moved closer together, into the middle of their own double bed, to ward off the scent of bad luck.

Misha parked his car, locked it, and stepped outside, smelling the spring air of the city after nightfall. He loved the enveloping medieval quiet that always fell upon the Ile Saint-Louis, pulling him out of himself and into the scents and sounds around him. Sometimes he thought that he could almost feel the presence of Restif de La Bretonne, pungent chronicler of the last days of the French monarchy. Like Restif, he was always drawn to the unusual, to the strange, to people who, by occupation and status, ought never to have touched his existence. In Moscow, he had been irresistibly drawn to the pool halls of the underworld – and here? His acquaintanceships were certainly not limited to the élite of Paris whose palaces he frequented with his wife. He thought for a moment of Lily, imagining her reading quietly in her bed while he was out walking the streets of Paris.

He never liked to pursue thoughts that caused him guilty feelings; Lily was where she belonged, where he had placed her. She represented the most unsullied part of himself –

the best, and the safest. Unlike him, she needed protection: she couldn't stand alone. He felt tremors that touched the deepest places of his heart, and stilled them.

He walked along the Quai de Bourbon, alongside the dark, silent waters of the Seine. Around him, the sculptured architecture of the seventeenth century spread itself out in elegant *hôtels particuliers* that had witnessed the presence of Chopin and Baudelaire. In the distance, he could see the lighted ribbed arches of the cathedral of Notre-Dame. He crossed the street, and looked up. He was standing in front of an arched passage that led into a delightful enclosed garden. Le Vau had built the mansion to which it belonged, and, he thought with sudden anger, when Varvara had bought the place last year, relinquishing the more modest apartment on the Place Péreire, she'd paid a small fortune for the privilege of living here.

He crossed the garden, and rang the doorbell. Cécile Sorel, *grande dame* of the Parisian stage, had a palace on the Quai de Voltaire, not far away. Undoubtedly Varvara had wanted to reproduce Sorel's way of life, the way all parvenus sought to imitate the grandiose life-styles of those with old money. She'd done incredibly well for herself – especially when one remembered that she was forty years old, and fairly new to the stage. But she had ambition, and colour. She'd been just exotic enough to conquer Paris. And now she was *somebody*, with her own place in the entertainment world of Paris. He'd done her a decided favour by divorcing her – even though she still, perversely, insisted on getting paid her five thousand a month no matter what: money that she no longer needed in any fashion.

Dragi, his thin black head wrapped in a turquoise turban, opened the door. 'Ah, Monsieur le Prince . . . Madame is in her room.'

Misha smiled. Tonight he knew that she'd had no performance. 'Please tell her I'm here,' he said, and watched the black *maître d'hôtel* undulate away, like a Magi prince, from the entrance hall into the inner recesses of the mansion. Knowing his way around, Misha passed the enormous jade Buddha from whose lips emanated a blasphemous jet of water that fell into a shell-shaped marble basin filled with oriental fish. He climbed down three steps into the living room, hardly glancing at the domed ceiling composed of myriad small mirrors. He went past the Coromandel screens to a set of lacquered armchairs, and sat down. Perhaps he liked the unbelievable exoticism of her taste because it represented everything that he, in his own home, would find unacceptable. She was a person who left her indelible signature on everything she touched: a phenomenon that set his nerves on edge while at the same time fascinating him.

Dragi had silently made his appearance, and executed three Indian bows. 'Madame would like Monsieur le Prince to come to her bedroom,' he said. It was difficult to recall, from the mellifluous accents of his voice, that he was actually an American from Ohio.

Misha stood up, and followed. They passed silk paintings of dragons spitting flames, and brass ornaments whose function he could not have guessed at. A pervasive scent of cinnamon and ginger seemed to cling to the very walls. At the opened door to his mistress's bedroom, Dragi turned, bowed almost in half, and eclipsed himself. Misha wondered how much money she was paying him to play this absurd charade, even in front of him, a familiar visitor privy to the truth.

Varvara was sitting cross-legged on her bed, which was elevated on a pedestal of black marble. It was sculpted in brass, and its cover matched the Chinese red of the raw silk walls. The ceiling was of cut crystal, and small tables and chairs of Chinese design, all of lacquered wood, were strewn around. A magnificent Persian rug, black, jade green, and red, had been set underneath all of this.

'Hello, Misha,' she said. She was wearing loose pyjamas of gold silk, and no makeup. Even so, she seemed smooth and young, and strangely vulnerable with her large baby blue eyes. She was smoking a cigarette, blowing out the smoke in little circles in front of her. 'I was just playing patience.' She waved at the cards in neat rows over her bedspread. 'Do you want a drink?'

He shook his head, and went to sit on one of the chairs. He watched her as she carelessly gathered up the cards and tossed them down on her bedside table. Five nights a week, *le tout-Paris* came to see her in her own revue, a great painted Russian bird, on display; but he'd known her for almost twelve years. He remembered meeting her, at a dinner, and being captivated by the way she held her head, by the way she moved, the way she'd laughed when somebody had paid her a compliment – and noticing, all the time, her nervousness, her boredom, her restless unhappiness. He'd been oddly moved by that, more than by anything else: a still young society woman, exciting to look at, admired and probably even desired, who felt alone. Now, watching her moving around in the comfort of her room, he thought again of that sadness, and of the defiant way that she had sought to disprove its very existence.

'I'm always surprised,' he said softly, 'when I come here and find you alone, doing the everyday things that other women do.'

She cocked her head at him, amused. 'I think that's why you still like me. You think that I'm some sort of sphinx-woman, larger than life. But I'm very simple, and down-to-earth, compared to you. *You're* larger than life, Misha. To me ... to me, you're like the vastness of Mother Russia, hungry and demanding, spoiled and grand. That's why I fell in love with you, eons and eons ago, when both of us were young, and living was an art, and a passion, instead of commonplace and brutal.'

'But you haven't become commonplace, have you, Vava?

152

Perhaps just a little brutal, though.' He smiled at her, and added: 'I'll have that drink. I'm tired. God, how weary I feel! France does this, somehow. In Russia, when we set out to purchase land, or to add a new company to our growing enterprise, I could feel the taste of the hunt, and electricity all through my body. But the French are a nation of civilized sheep. How could any hunter worth his mettle go after a foolish, bleating sheep? Too much civilization stunts a people, Vava.'

She laughed, a low chuckle, and rang for Dragi. When the *maître d'hôtel* appeared, after a discreet knock, she ordered two tall vodkas on the rocks. Her elegant, quick fingers had gathered up the cards in front of her, and had begun to riffle through them, with mechanical adeptness. 'But Catherine the Great still needed Voltaire, didn't she?'

'Ah, yes: the man-eating empress and the quintessential man of the mind. Not at all like our own encounter, was it?'

Dragi was tiptoeing back in, holding up a small brass tray that he set down on an end table. He brought Varvara her drink, then bowed in front of Misha. 'Your Excellency.'

Unobtrusively, the black man exited, leaving them in a cool, refreshing silence, listening to the ice tinkling in their glasses. He raised his first. 'To you, O great Sphinx. May you find answers to all of life's mysteries.'

She took a long swallow. 'Do you still find life mysterious?'

He sighed, suddenly seeing Lily in his mind's eye, and his children. Things had unaccountably changed between him and his young wife. *She'd* changed. He knew *he* hadn't. He opened his mouth, then closed it again, knowing full well that it would destroy the mood to bring up his marital problems to Varvara. And yet ... If things had been better at home, would he still have gone looking for another woman?

153

'Not exactly "mysterious",' he answered, suddenly serious. 'But puzzling. I don't understand women, for example. They're so inexplicably complicated – like exotic dishes that are wonderful to eat, but that only the cook knows how to prepare.'

She burst into peals of laughter, and rocked back and forth on her haunches. 'You *would* think of us as delectable morsels, wouldn't you? Well, darling, I'll have you know that in today's world, especially here in France, women have pushed their way out of the boudoir and into almost every facet of contemporary achievement. Some of us, dear heart, like the great Natalie Barney, have even elected to live without you men *inside* the boudoir. You are no longer the focal point of our existence. And that, I believe, should explain why our sex bewilders you. You're still lost somewhere in the past, when women were either ladies or whores, wives or courtesans. And now some of the most well-known courtesans have turned into model wives, and some of the best-bred ladies have turned blatantly promiscuous.'

He shook his head, feeling childish and put down. Perhaps she was right. He, however, was the most normal of men, and what he longed for was a well-ordered world where everything fell into place, logically and predictably. It was true that his hungers were enormous, that in his quest to assuage his boredom, he sought for unexpected distractions. But even these had to be placed well within the context of the manageable ... of what he knew he could control.

She was examining him, frankly and directly. 'You may not have understood why you rejected our marriage,' she murmured. 'But I did. I was never malleable, Misha, and I was too wilful and impulsive. You were attracted to me for short periods, but somehow, you were afraid I'd wear you down, that our passion would burn you out, and that I

154

wouldn't look to you to dot all my *i*'s. I loved you, but you were not my God.'

'And what about now? Do you still love me?'

Her expression softened, and she caressed her chin with a lazy finger, thoughtfully. 'I don't know. I've learned to live my life in bits and pieces. There are many things that I still love *about* you. But . . . no, I don't suppose I still love *you*, the total man, the way I once did when my horizons seemed boundless, and I thought I could change you into a full-time hedonist, like me.'

'If I'd been that, Vava, we would surely have burned each *other* out. Our union, like the phoenix, would have ended in ashes.'

'Not necessarily. Pleasure doesn't have to mean decadence. Look at me: I've built a life around my own pleasure, haven't I? And yet I'm still surviving, and no one's been destroyed by anything I've done. Even Anton, when we were married – our marriage survived the fact that I was in love with *you*, and not with him. I knew what he needed from me, and I gave it to him.' She fell silent, her face grave in the soft light of the room.

'Sometimes,' she stated, 'those who try to shape the world instead of just letting things happen naturally, create the greatest series of disasters. Because nature has a way of rebelling against artificial interference – and people do, too. I knew better than to fight for you – because I knew I couldn't, shouldn't, change you.'

Was she obliquely referring to Lily? But no, that was impossible; Varvara didn't even know his wife. It had been his own mind playing tricks on him, trying to trap him into feeling guilty. She was laughing now, a low, amused laugh, female and ribald. 'No woman could change Mikhail Brasilov,' she declared. 'But watch out, lover, that all your women don't get you in over your head. Not everyone's as entertained as I am by your antics.'

155

'What are you talking about?' he demanded, momentarily jolted.

'That girl Rirette. She's a tough cookie, my darling. I can see why you like her, but can *you* really see *her*?'

He grinned, relaxing, and pretended embarrassment. 'Vava – no woman compares with the Sphinx; you know that, don't you?'

She shrugged, ironic. 'There's always the phoenix, isn't there?'

'I don't believe I've met her,' he retorted, downing the last of his drink.

Varvara yawned, catlike, and stretched. Then: 'Come to bed,' she said, pulling the gold pyjama top over her head in a single fluid gesture.

That summer, while France continued to be the stage for fallen ministry after fallen ministry, and the franc's value plunged from a pre-war value of nearly twenty cents to a scant four, Paul Bruisson suffered a massive heart attack from which his doctors felt that he would not be strong enough to recover. Lily packed her own bag and telephoned Rochefort to announce that she was moving out to Boulogne to be with her mother.

She hadn't been inside the Villa Persane for many months. Claire always made it a point to come to her at the Rue Molitor apartment. Lily felt the familiar chill upon entering. The *maître d'hôtel*, Alphonse, seemed older, his parchment face a tinge more yellow. All was the same, except that her own clothes were more finely made, and that, on her hands and ears and around her neck, jewels shone where before her marriage only the translucent cream of her skin had been exposed. Her long hair was swept up into a Psyche knot, and she thought, glancing briefly at her own reflection, that she too had come a long way in these two years. 'Madame is with monsieur,' Alphonse murmured, and she left him in charge of her suitcase while she climbed the staircase hurriedly, a little out of breath.

When Lily opened the door to the master bedroom, what she felt the most was an overwhelming sense of pity. Her father lay propped up on many pillows, his plump face suddenly lined, its usual red colour replaced by a washed-out white. He was an old man. Near him, on a hard-backed chair, Claire was reading to him, her face grave, spectacles on her nose. She, too, seemed all at once to have taken on a mantle of years. They're not young anymore, Lily thought, with the consternation of all children faced with the vulnerabilities of their parents. She'd always thought of her father as perennially middle-aged, but a healthy, ruddy middle age; and of her mother as still young, fresh, seemingly untouched by time. Now she saw old faces, faces that had lived through years when she had not even been of this world — years that had made them strangers in spite of their familiarity.

She felt her heart going out to her father. He was smiling at her, and she wondered why, all during her adolescence, she had thought of him as such a forbidding ogre. He was a florid, loud man given to bullying; but underneath, there was the man who had refused to seal her fate, the day that Misha had come to propose to her: and had allowed her, a young girl, to make her own decision. He'd been a little like Misha: a man who, for reasons of pride or of shyness, she was never sure which, couldn't give free vent to his feelings. 'Lily,' he said, and she came to him and knelt by the bed, laying her head in the crook between his neck and his face.

Claire said nothing. Lily thought that her mother seemed to have grown harder — or maybe it was just that they hadn't seen each other much over the last few months. She'd been resting, from Kyra's birth, and her mother had been here, taking care of her father, hoping against hope to

157

find a way to hold back destiny. My God, Lily thought: I've failed everyone, haven't I, by my selfishness?

A few hours later, she tiptoed out of her father's room, and her mother closed the door gently behind them, to let Paul sleep. Without speaking, they made their way to Claire's boudoir, where the maid had placed a tea tray. Claire took off her shoes, and lay down on the *chaise longue*, closing her eyes wearily. Lily tried not to look at her, and busied herself pouring tea.

Suddenly, Claire spoke, almost coldly: 'He's not going to pull through.'

Lily set down the cup and saucer, shocked. 'Why not, Mama? He's not yet sixty. And he was always a healthy man.'

'I know he's dying. He's even lost the will to live.'

Lily said, her voice vibrant in the late afternoon shadows: 'Then we must pray. Pray to the Virgin, Mama: she's never failed us.'

Claire's brown eyes fastened themselves on Lily's. 'I've prayed all I could,' she replied, picking up her cup and averting her face.

Then Claire's tone became gentler. She said, touching her daughter's cheek: 'Parents are meant to die before us. But our children always need us. The children from the marriage we go into. It was God who said to Adam: "Therefore shall a man leave his father and his mother, and shall cleave unto his wife." And He also said: "Be fruitful and multiply, and replenish the earth."'

Lily whispered: 'I had no idea you could quote from the Old Testament, verbatim.'

Claire shook her head. 'There are so many things you still don't know.'

'Why did you marry Papa?'

Claire said: 'For many reasons. You always felt that you could judge your father. No one has this right, unless they've lived with a person in the most absolute intimacy.'

158

'Did you love him?'

Claire laid a finger upon her lips. 'Shhh. Someday Kyra may ask you the same question.'

'But my answer is set! Of course I love Misha!'

Claire smiled, and sighed. 'You love what you think is his perfection, because you're still so young. And if now you feel an estrangement from him, isn't it partly because you realize that no one can be perfect?'

Lily was silent. So her mother had understood that all was not as it should be between her and Misha. But she felt so helpless that she couldn't think further. Too many things were happening at once, too many emotions, to sort them out now.

Claire was standing, and slipping on her shoes. Instinctively, Lily rose too, and followed her out of the boudoir. Twilight had settled outside, its roseate hues filtering through the windows. Claire opened the door to the master bedroom, and stopped suddenly. Behind her, Lily tried to peer into the room, and what she saw amazed her. Misha was sitting by the sick man's bed, and the two men were listening to the radio, quietly, their faces intent.

Then Claire walked in, her hands outstretched, and Lily saw her husband rise and take the hands, drawing Claire into a tight embrace. She blinked rapidly to prevent tears, holding herself together with an effort of will so that he wouldn't see her cry. He came to her, and for a moment neither said a word. Then his arms came around her, and he held her close, and she shut her eyes and listened to his heartbeat, to the sound that was proof of his existence, of his permanence.

Holding hands, they sat down on the other side of Paul's bed, opposite Claire. Still, the radio announcer was trumpeting out the news, his voice strong and clear, as if no one were dying. 'When the Briand-Caillaux Cabinet fell on 17 July, the franc had reached an appalling low of four cents. During the last four days, while Edouard Herriot has vainly attempted to form another ministry, it has continued to plummet, reaching the frightening value of two cents or two hundred and fifty francs to the pound sterling. President Gaston Doumergue has been forced to call back "France's lawyer", Raymond Poincaré, who, in spite of the left-of-centre majority in the Assembly, may be the only man who can save France and the franc after two years of mismanagement at the hands of the Radicals.'

Gently, Claire rose and switched off the voice, and there was quiet in the room. Lily was watching her father, whose face seemed more ghostlike now in the gathering darkness. Misha's profile, his crest of black hair, the sharp outline of his nose, the set of his chin, contrasted with almost painful distinction. One was so alive, the other so near death. She felt the warmth of Misha's fingers interlaced with hers. He'd always had the most profound dislike for her father, she knew this; and yet, when he'd learned the news, he hadn't hesitated.

'You should have left the news on,' Paul was murmuring to Claire. 'Mikhail and I were trying to guess the announcer. Did you hear? Poincaré's coming back, to save us the way he did after the war!'

'Don't excite yourself, Paul,' Claire said.

'Are things really that bad?' Lily asked.

'Things will get better,' her husband said.

'As long as he doesn't tax us,' Paul commented.

'He'll have to tax,' Misha said, with a tone of kindness that she hadn't ever heard him use with her father. 'But we'll concentrate the firm, make some of our profits flow through your and Claude's business. Then the taxes won't have to hit us so hard.'

'You'll work things out?'

Paul's voice, suddenly pathetic, made everyone start. Misha said, quietly: 'Yes. I'll work everything out.'

Then Lily felt as though her father had already died, and understood why her mother had told her he wasn't

160

going to pull through. Misha was drawing her to him, holding her shoulder, and she wondered what would have happened if this crisis hadn't come up. Her father was dying, and his death had brought back her husband. She thought then that if he wanted another child, she would want it too, to cement their love and to atone for her own errors as a daughter. She'd have this child for Misha, but also for Paul.

Why was it, she asked herself, that families so often wronged each other until the moment when somebody died? When people thought about what they could lose, they realized its worth.

Chastened, she listened to her father's laboured breathing, knowing that he wasn't going to last out the week, and loving him for the first time.

Chapter Eight

After Paul Bruisson's death, Lily tried to persuade Claire to move into the apartment with them. She had decided to ask Zelle to share Kyra's room, to make space for her mother. But, to her surprise, Claire declined.

'You can't stay *here*,' Lily said. 'You've always hated the Villa Persane. And alone, with just Claude, you aren't going to need such a large house, with so many servants.'

Claire shook her head. 'Claude can't be alone,' she answered softly.

'He's twenty-seven. It might be better for him to be on his own in a *garçonnière*, too.'

Claire sat down in an immense *bergère*, its feet and armrests of mounted bronze, and looked at her daughter. 'Claude is a very lonely young man, Lily. Even if he goes out, it's for business only. And now, the entire business of Bruisson et Fils is going to be resting on his shoulders.'

'Not really. You know that Misha's taken over most of the administrative functions by absorbing Bruisson into Brasilov Enterprises. Besides, Mama, Claude was never close to you. We need you.'

'I'll be here when you do. But it's Claude who needs me more. He doesn't know it – but I do, and because of this, I have to stay.'

There were so many things that baffled Lily! At the funeral, Claude had stood apart, his face impassive. She'd always assumed that father and son had been close: certainly, their ideas had been much alike. But now she was beginning to see that Claude had never been close to anyone. Claude was much more remote than her father had ever been, for Paul had not been a complicated man. He'd been a bully, but he hadn't been an island of ice, closed off to the rest of the world. She felt that in his fashion, he'd loved his wife and children, but that Claude had never allowed himself to love anyone.

Did he even feel gratitude for Misha's goodness in giving him a vice-presidency in the firm? And did he understand that their mother was sacrificing the chance to be with the daughter and son-in-law who wanted her, and with her grandchildren, just to make sure that he was never too alone?

After Paul's death, Claire auctioned off some of the heavier pieces of furniture, and changed the drapery to lighter, softer shades and materials. But she didn't make a complete refurbishment, as Lily would have thought. Maybe she was worried about finances. She kept Alphonse and the chauffeur and the cook, and one maid, dismissing the rest. And Lily knew that she was keeping the old *maître d'hôtel* only because, at his age, he would have found it difficult to obtain new employment.

Lily saw, with profound emotion, how Misha arranged for Claire to be with them at least two or three times a week. He reserved theatre seats, took the two women out for dinner. Once, he suggested a fitting for his mother-in-law at Worth, and had all the bills sent to his office. Claire was discreet in showing her appreciation. She was deeply touched, and whenever he came home from work and she happened to be there, she always tried to spend a little time with him, alone, talking of this and that – to show him how fond she was of him, and how important she considered him to be. For she understood that he was a man who needed to be needed; and also, that he was someone whom lavish displays of gratitude would have made uncomfortable.

Lily spent half her week with her mother. They took the children for walks in the Bois, and went together to gallery openings and matinées at the Comédie-Française. She realized that her mother was an eminently self-sufficient woman. Claire was a private individual, and didn't discuss her life. And she rarely spent a night with the Brasilovs. Discreetly, she usually asked François to drive her home after supper, and sometimes before. She had her own programme.

Sometimes she rushed through the end of an afternoon, glancing at her watch to make sure she wasn't late for an appointment. Once, laughingly, Misha had asked her what mischievous plans she had that didn't include them. She'd smiled – that cameo smile that was a touch like the Mona Lisa's, distant yet humorous. 'My dear children,' she'd replied 'I do have appointments of my own.'

'But you never really had many friends, when Father was alive,' Lily said.

'I just didn't have as much time to see them. Don't forget, my love, that you were in Brittany for six years, and that, shortly afterwards, you married Misha.'

Lily had renewed her connection with her old piano teacher. Misha didn't much like Sudarskaya. He thought her coarse. And, truly, Lily couldn't blame him. Raïssa Sudarskaya was middle-aged, short, and plump, with a round face that looked like a polished pink marble. She had been born in Moscow and had attended the Conservatory there. She was a widow, and lived in almost desperate straits in a mansarded room in the Rue des Sablons in Neuilly. Whenever she came to Rue Molitor, Lily made sure that Annette prepared a delicious high tea, knowing that Sudarskaya, near starvation, would be only too happy to assuage her hunger. Lily tried to put herself in Misha's shoes. Refined, a gentleman, he would never be able to tolerate Sudarskaya's lack of manners and delicacy near himself or his children. So Lily tried, as tactfully as she could, to send Sudarskaya home before he returned from his day's work.

Lily herself didn't find the woman personally appealing. She enjoyed the beauty of her playing: her velocity, her neatness of rendition, her feeling and comprehension when she played some of her favourite pieces. But when Sudarskaya looked around a room, her small, pig's eyes darting this way and that, it was annoying to behold. When she peered at a canvas or touched the silk nub of a chair seat, Lily felt an absurd sense of violation. Lily tried to excuse her behaviour as the result of poverty, but Sudarskaya was the most indiscreet woman she'd ever met. She pried, even when all she was really doing was looking at a postcard on the table, or at a child's toy left behind on the piano bench. Lily had the sensation that if left alone in a room, Sudarskaya's first impulse would have been to unlock the secretary and examine all the bills, and read all the letters.

Great indeed, therefore, was her surprise when she came home one afternoon to hear that her mother was there, conferring with Annette in the kitchen about leftover food. She went there, and saw Claire putting some cake and sandwiches into a large bag, while Annette folded some salami slices into some wax paper. 'I didn't know you were coming today,' Lily said, kissing Claire on the cheek.

'I was at the Musée Galliéra, and so I asked the driver to take me here.'

'Are you staying for dinner?' Lily asked. 'We're not having anything fancy. Annette made a delicious meal last night for Ivan Vassilievitch, and there's a lot left over.'

Claire smiled. 'I know. Nicky told me that already, as soon as I arrived. So I thought you wouldn't mind if I took just a few things over to Sudarskaya later on.'

'You're not eating here tonight, then?'

'I'm afraid not. Raïssa Markovna asked me to come to see her. She wants me to help her sell tickets for her concert next month.'

Lily was astounded. Claire abandoned the packing to Annette, and followed her daughter into the blue and yellow study. Lily said, feeling ridiculous: 'Mama, I'd no idea you knew Sudarskaya that well.'

'But you knew I was the one who selected her for you.'

'Of course. But ... piano teachers come well recommended. I myself have found some new students for her among the sons and daughters of our acquaintances. But she'd never think to ask me to ... sell tickets for her.'

'And you think I'm too good for such a thing?'

Lily shrugged, embarrassed. 'No. I didn't mean it quite like that. It's just ... such an act of familiarity ... and I never thought Sudarskaya knew you more than to say hello to. How did you meet her?'

Claire sighed. 'Julien Weill sent her to me, some years ago.'

'The Grand Rabbi of Paris? The one who was at Marisa's wedding?'

'That one. Sudarskaya had just arrived from Russia. She was a poor refugee, and came to him at the Consistory, for help and referrals. He sent her to me.'

'But – *why?* Why not send her to the Baronne de Rothschild – or Eliane Robinson? Why to you?'

'First of all, because he knew that you were interested in a good piano teacher. And then, of course, because we're friends. Friends help each other, Lily.'

Lily's mouth opened, but no sound came out. She could feel her heart pounding. She said: 'Mama. *Friends?* But you live in Boulogne, and aren't even Jewish! What possible connection could there be between you and one of the foremost rabbis in France? I thought your only Jewish friends were the Robinsons. Did you meet Weill through them?'

'It was the opposite. I met Eliane through Julien Weill. It wasn't by accident, Lily, that I took you to that particular dance studio when you were eight. I took you there because Eliane had recommended its teachers.'

'But – Marisa and I thought that *we'd* started the

friendship! Why – why did you let us believe that, all those years?'

'Because that was the way it had to be. For everybody's sake.'

Lily stood up, began to walk slowly towards her mother. Her expression was puzzled. 'Why?' she finally asked.

Claire turned away, and Lily went to face her. She saw such grief in her mother's face that she was momentarily ashamed of her relentless hounding. But for once, she couldn't contain herself. 'Tell me!' she exclaimed. 'Isn't it time I knew why you couldn't tell me the truth?'

Claire whispered: 'Sometimes it's better not to know.'

'I don't agree!'

'But if your husband were involved with another woman, would you want to know everything about *that?*'

'It's not the same thing. No, I wouldn't want to know. Of course not.' Lily had a fleeting image of Jeanne Dalbret with her egret feather, and pushed the image out of her mind. 'But this is different. You're my mother.'

'And mothers should be open books to their children?'

'Maybe they should. It would save them from many disillusionments later on.'

'Oh, my God, what a child you still are,' Claire murmured. She passed a weary, trembling hand over her forehead. 'I wish I hadn't told you anything about this small concert of Sudarskaya's. Then all this could have been avoided. I wish I hadn't come to see you, to kiss the children. It was just an impulse – and it was ill-timed.'

'It's never ill-timed for you to be with us.'

The two women faced each other. Lily knew that her hair had come undone, that her skin was moist with perspiration. Claire's face was strangely white, the small lines around her eyes more visible this way. 'It doesn't matter about Sudarskaya,' Lily said. 'Ever since Mari's wedding, I've felt something strange between us. Something . . . not like before. I attributed it first to my illness after Kyra's birth, and then to Papa's death. But it wasn't that at all. It was ... you and Rabbi Weill, standing together at Mari's reception – smiling at each other like two old friends. Someone you weren't even supposed to know. Someone ... of a different world entirely.'

'Someone ... Jewish.'

Lily thought for a moment, then nodded, suddenly self-conscious. 'Yes. I suppose that's it.'

'And this made you feel – how, Lily? Uncomfortable?'

'No. Just – baffled.'

'Your father would have said: "out of your skin". Your mother wasn't supposed to know a rabbi. And why *not?*'

'Because. It makes sense to me, why not. Wolf shocked me when he told me, one afternoon *chez* Poiret, that non-Jews couldn't be made to understand all that a Jew might feel in a hostile, anti-Semitic situation. But afterwards, I understood him.'

'I understand him, too,' Claire said.

'Then why can't you understand *me?* Rabbi Weill is part of Wolf and Mari's world, part of what holds it together against the intruders. How could a man so close to the fundamentals of Jewish society have any connection to you: a matron with grown children, living in the suburbs of Paris in absolutely typical bourgeois style, à la Poincaré?'

'Sit down, Lily,' Claire stated, in that odd, almost cold tone that she had used the day Lily had come to her father's bedside. Lily went to the sofa, sat, crossed her legs. She felt drained, and yet nervous, expectant. 'I'm going to tell you a story, but you have to listen without interrupting. Can you do that?'

Lily nodded. Claire cleared her throat, stared at her hands, then concentrated on a pattern in the Persian carpet. 'Every human life is a network of complexities that weaves together into a tapestry of many threads. You never knew my mother. She was a beautiful woman. She was a native of Braila, in eastern Rumania. Her parents were well-to-do merchants – they dealt, I believe, in some sort of dry goods that they exported on a line of freight ships which they owned, on the Danube River. When she was sixteen, a young man from Belgium came to town, to see some relatives. He fell in love with my mother, and married her, and took her home to Brussels with him. This was in 1878. The young man was my father.

'My parents were very happy together. The community where my mother had grown up, in Braila, had had the tradition of speaking French and German more than Rumanian: so, in Brussels, my mother didn't feel lost. My father was running a series of very successful workshops where women of all ages handcrafted lace. In those days, every well-to-do matron owned hundreds of lace items, from table linen to personal lingerie. A woman could hardly have survived without her trousseau of lace. My father employed about two hundred women, and they had the best reputation in the city for turning out the most elegant lace at the fastest speed. He sold to private customers and to the big stores, such as the Maison de Blanc here in Paris.

'Then, two years later, I was born. But my mother hadn't had a healthy pregnancy, and never fully recovered from my birth. It wasn't anything like your problem after Kyra. My mother was a small woman, and I was a large child. My mother suffered horribly, and afterwards, was never again the same. I adored her; but the brief years we were together, I can't remember seeing her once on her feet. She suffered intermittently from internal bleeding, and eventually, when I was twelve, she died from a haemorrhage that couldn't be stopped. Medicine wasn't so sophisticated in 1892.'

Claire closed her eyes, and continued. 'After that, everything seemed to go wrong. They'd been so happy – *we'd* been so happy ... Papa couldn't keep his mind on the shops, and his competitors took advantage of our tragedy to close in on the business. By then, of course, women weren't relying so exclusively on handmade lace, so this, too, contributed to his collapse. By the time I was eighteen, there was almost no money left.

'And so Papa decided that in Brussels, I would have no future. He collected a small sum, and sent me to Paris to study art at the Académie Julien. I, like you, possessed a few talents. He made a tremendous sacrifice, both financial and personal: for I had become his right hand, and his dearest companion. But he wanted me to make something of my life. What could I have become, in Brussels: poor, without dowry?

'Through some connections, I was able to find a room in a small boardinghouse on the Left Bank. My life was very frugal. I studied, I painted, and I made my own meals over a Bunsen burner when I couldn't afford to pay the landlady for my board. Of course, I considered myself the Marie Laurencin of the turn of the century. I wasn't nearly so good – but I wasn't bad.

'But I was very lonely. There were so few people I knew in Paris, and my student friends were all so much wealthier than I! I couldn't afford to go anywhere. I felt lost in my room, or walking alone on the edge of the Seine. I needed to feel that there was one place where I belonged. And I found that place. It was the Jewish Consistory.'

Lily was staring at her, her eyes wide, her lips parted. Claire nodded. 'Because, Lily, my parents were both Jews. In Braila, my mother had grown up in a kosher house; and in Brussels, she and my father had dutifully observed all the traditional holidays. I wasn't just brought up a Jew: I was brought up a religious Jew, with respect for all the Jewish laws and taboos. You are right: Marisa's world, Wolf's world, is a very special place, where customs are venerated and culture is prized, and where the outsider has no place. Because the outsider, Lily, is never absent. He lurks just outside the borders of the golden ghetto, which, however gilded, is still a ghetto. And, as a lonely young art student, I found comfort in the synagogue, and comfort in the friendship of a young rabbi whose wisdom helped me through many a tear-streaked moment.

'Thus began my friendship with Julien Weill. But I was eighteen, living alone in Paris. All the kind words of Rabbi Weill weren't enough to fill my life. Inevitably, I met a young man. He was rich, he was attractive, he was Jewish. I met him at the synagogue, where his parents were great patrons. I fell in love with him. He was tall, dark, slender – and spoiled, by generations of incredible wealth. He said that he wanted to marry me, and I accepted. I never really found out the truth. I suspect his love was only words, but Julien Weill told me that it was his parents who sent him away when they learned of our plans and of my expectations. It doesn't really matter, though, does it? I was already pregnant when I learned that he'd sailed for New York.'

She looked pointedly at her daughter, her face impassive. Lily was sitting, hands clasped beneath her chin, her neck muscles taut – waiting. Not breathing, it seemed. Claire wet her upper lip with the tip of her tongue. 'I couldn't go home, to face Papa like this. And Julien Weill really couldn't help me. In all my desperation and sense of betrayal, I blamed the rich French Jews who had allowed this injustice to happen: these selfish philanthropists who had sent their son away because the girl had been too poor. But I did listen to Julien when he advised me not to have the pregnancy . . . taken care of. Somebody like me, reared in the utmost respect for human life, couldn't have ended the new life that was being created inside me. And so, without resources, I waited until my baby was born. Claude was born when I was not yet twenty, and I did the only thing I could: I gave him up to the Assistance Publique.'

Claire's eyes had filled with tears, and she let them fall,

twin streaks upon the fine cream of her cheeks. She sat, wringing and wringing her hands, the tears falling unheeded down her cheeks – exactly the way she'd sat in the synagogue during the ceremony of Marisa and Wolf's wedding.

Then she appeared to turn in on herself, and the weeping stopped. She said, in a trembling voice: 'All that they gave me in exchange for my child was a number, written on a piece of cardboard! That was all I had of my son. All day and all night, I used to think about him, to wonder what he had become. I sat in my small room, holding that cardboard number, thinking about my own mother, who might not have died if I hadn't been born – and wondering if I would ever have the chance to see my son again.

'But life is so unpredictable. I was sitting by the Seine one day, eating a piece of cheese and watching the barges sliding by – dreaming, maybe, of my Rumanian grandfather's ships on the Danube – when a young man came up and started to speak to me. It had never been my custom to acknowledge strangers. But I was so alone – more alone now than ever – that I simply listened, and nodded my head, and let him talk. He wasn't good-looking; not bad-looking, but without distinction. He obviously hadn't had my education. He was pure French, a working-class boy – but full of life, full of ambition. I listened to him and imagined a different life: without the old traditions, those traditions that I felt had betrayed me. Without the old elegance. But with a roof over my head, with a big stove on which to cook a meal, instead of a miserable Bunsen burner. I listened to him, but after, when we had coffee, I told him that I could never see him again, because I was an art student who had a brilliant career ahead of me, and no time for stupid courtships. But he persisted, following me home, calling for me after his job ended. He was called Paul – the name of Jesus Christ's most devoted apostle. Paul Bruisson. He was a simple construction

172

worker, and he brought me daisies with enormous yellow centres and big happy white petals. As if I'd been a virgin who'd deserved this, and not an unwed mother who had given up her son.'

Her tone had turned hard again – bitter. 'I married him. One day, when he came, with a half-dozen eggs and a bottle of wine, he told me of his plans. He was saving money and learning all he could about construction. He was going to become a building contractor, and build me my own big house on the outskirts of Paris. And I? I'd spent the last two years dreaming of a high-ceilinged old apartment on the Ile Saint-Louis, with tall, louvered windows of bevelled glass. But I realized that the rich couple who had sent their son away were only exemplary of their entire class, of their entire world: I no longer could belong there, because my father had lost his money. Who, if not Paul Bruisson, would have married me and given me a child I could keep, my head held high? I accepted Paul's offer, and we were married. And he never asked me my religion. He was a Catholic, of the nonpractising sort, and so we were married like you and Misha, in the city hall near where I lived.

'I didn't love him. In fact, not a day went by that I didn't feel I was better than he. I'd hoped to become pregnant at once, to take my mind off Claude. But – I didn't. Paul worked hard. How he loved me! He used to come home at lunchtime and sit across the simple wooden table in our kitchen, in the small house we rented in Vaucresson, and tell me of how he was progressing, and how he would make my life beautiful and meaningful in the only way he knew how: with money. We were poor. I never wrote to my father about the poverty we lived in. To him, it was bad enough that I'd married a gentile. I was trying to keep all my lives separate, so none would impinge upon the other: my Jewish upbringing, my Jewish father; my working-class French husband, who knew nothing of my past; and my child, of whom I had retained only a cardboard number. For I'd learned to listen to Paul, and knew that he, like many outsiders, was so afraid of Jews that he had learned to hate them. What, then, would he have said about my child?

'One day, he came home early, and found me weeping, holding the number in my lap, my old suitcase on the bed. I was frightened, and ashamed, and tried to stuff it back inside and close the lid. But he stopped me, and asked me what this number was. I burst into tears. It wasn't that I loved him – but I didn't want to lose him, because who else did I have?

'And so I told him that I'd borne a son, and given him up. And then, he did the most extraordinary, unexpected thing: he took me in his arms and held me. He told me that he'd always surmised that I was better than he, and that it didn't matter about the child. He said: "If this is your son, then I want him as my own. I'm going to help you find him, and he will grow up as my eldest child."

'But, Lily, there was one thing I'd omitted from my story. I was afraid to tell Paul I was Jewish. I'd heard him speak against the Jews, and was certain he'd find my background even more objectionable than the fact that I'd been an unwed mother. You see ... he came from an uneducated, prejudiced family, the kind that believed that the world's catastrophes, beginning with the Crucifixion, could be blamed on the Jews.

'At the time of my marriage, my dear friend Julien Weill advised me to be honest with Paul, and even to bring him to the temple. He offered to speak to him about our religion. But I was adamant. Perhaps I was merely young, and stubborn. But perhaps, too, I knew the man I planned to marry. And so, when I admitted my "feminine mistake", I realized that he might forgive me this foible. Many of the girls he'd grown up with had committed similar "errors".

174

In his society, this was a venial sin. Whereas being a Jew was like being a pariah.

'After Paul's generous offer to look for Claude, I went to Julien Weill, and begged him for his help. I showed him the number. He gathered the oldest employees of the Consistory together: Monsieur Walbert Salomon, the accountant, Georges Salomon, his brother the cashier, Monsieur Muslack, in charge of weddings, and Oscar Berg, janitor of the temple, who knew useful bits and pieces about how everything worked in Paris. They all decided that even though Paul Bruisson wasn't a Jew, he had acted beyond the call of duty: he, a poor man, wanting to take in his wife's illegitimate child! They thought that he deserved their help. And so, anonymously – so that Paul would never know of my connection with the temple – the Jewish Consistory assisted us in our search for Claude.

'It took two years, Lily, for us to locate him and have him back. And Paul recognized him as his and gave him his name. I wasn't a better person than he, never; he was always better than I, even if he sometimes shouted and if he had opinions I didn't agree with. I suffered during my marriage because he wasn't the kind of man I'd hoped for as a husband. But he remained faithful, and he always treated Claude as his own son. And God repaid him more than I ever could have: for Claude came to *be like* Paul . . . much more so than you, his blood child, ever were.

'And so, Lily, I was always two people: the wife of Paul Bruisson, the mother of his children; and a woman who could not practise her religion freely: a religion she had deeply loved, but which she'd also blamed for the loss of the man she had once hoped to marry. I was always torn between my love of Judaism, and my hatred for the family that had shattered my dreams. And it was Rabbi Weill who helped me to understand that the religion was not to blame, only the particular individuals. It was he who showed me how similar had become my hatred to the

175

hatred of all the gentiles, like Paul, who were afraid of the "foreignness" of Jews, the "difference" of Jews, the power and arrogance of some Jews. It wasn't their Jewishness I hated: it was, simply, *them*. And it was Rabbi Weill, also, who helped me to accept my family: the good man who, for all his faults, had become my son's father; and you, my daughter, who had turned into such a devout Catholic. I learned to accept Paul's anti-Semitism, and your own devotion, because there is only one God, and as long as you believed, it was all right.'

They were sitting in the opaque darkness, both of them unaware that dusk had fallen. Finally Claire asked: 'Was it really worth it, Lily, to dig up these memories? What good can it possibly do you, to know these sad secrets that don't really belong to you?'

Lily shook her head. She couldn't speak. In front of her sat a woman she had never known. The quiet little Belgian bourgeoise had been anything but that; and her father? Not an ogre, although surely a limited man. Where was the point beyond which human beings transgressed from purity to sin? Where was the neat, clean definition in her catechism lessons? 'Father, I have sinned . . .' But who, here, had sinned?

She sat staring across the darkness at the dim outline of her mother, the beautiful mother who, all her life, had been her symbol of goodness and fineness and nobility, the ethereal model for her own femininity. She'd loved Claire more than anyone – more even than Misha, from whom she'd sometimes felt estranged. She didn't understand why her whole body was trembling, nor why she felt twin, conflicting impulses. She rose, unsteadily, and stood over her mother, looking down.

And then, when the words came out, Lily spoke them with a bitter intensity she had never known before. 'You lied. You lied to everybody, all your life. You lied to your own father, you lied to Papa – and you lied to me!'

Claire was holding her hands over her breasts, and whispered: 'I lied to protect us all.'

'You lied to protect yourself – all your selves! And to protect Claude, because he was, finally, the only one of us you ever loved! He was the son of the man you'd wanted; I was the daughter of the man you settled for! Oh, damn it, *damn it* – I don't know what to say, I don't know what to think! I hate you right now – for not telling me this before, when I could have helped you – when I might have felt you were trusting me with your life. I don't think you love me, Mother. I think you never loved me. I was the child you had to pay him back with for accepting Claude.'

Claire stood up, unwrinkling her skirt. Her hands were shaking. She said: 'I'd better go home,' but the words came out muffled. Lily remained standing, and Claire sidestepped her hurriedly, her footsteps making small staccato noises in the hallway. Lily heard the footsteps, felt them like small stabs inside her heart, and the words: Don't let her go! rang inside her head. But she tamped them down, shutting out the noise of the front door being opened, and Arkhippe's voice.

When Misha came in, he found her sitting on the floor, her hair over her shoulders, her eyes dry but rimmed with red. Kneeling beside her, he touched her cheek, but she bristled away from his fingers. 'What's wrong?' he asked.

'Lies. By the time the first lie's been told, it's too late to stop the rest. And then, there's no turning back. The truth has ceased to exist.'

'What are you talking about?' he demanded.

She smiled then, uncertainly, and shook her head. 'Nothing. It's nothing, really.'

'Arkhippe and Nicky told me that Claire was here.'

'Yes. But she left a while ago. She had to go and help somebody arrange a concert.'

He looked at her quizzically, and she shrugged. 'Maybe I misunderstood her,' she murmured. 'I thought that's

177

what she said, but then I fell asleep here, and had a bad dream.'

Giving her his hand, he pulled her up, and said, with joyous relief: 'Oh ... so it was only a nightmare ... Thank God, because you had me worried.' And then he pressed her close.

There was an odd moment of awkwardness when Lily stepped into the hall of the Villa Persane, to pick her mother up for Sudarskaya's recital. They hadn't seen each other since the afternoon when Claire had told her story to her daughter. Neither had been able to take the first step. The memory of Lily's words had wounded Claire; as for Lily, she couldn't forgive her mother for having hidden the truth from her for so long, and about so many things. She felt as if her entire life had been based on a lie: or worse yet, on a series of lies.

She hadn't been able to sort everything out for herself. But somehow, she hadn't gone to confession once in the intervening month. Something stopped her going there. Her foundation of faith had been shaken by all that her mother had told her. Her mother didn't believe in the same things she did. And so now, what had seemed so natural for all these years appeared, all at once, questionable. She'd been a Catholic not simply for her faith, but also because she'd thought it had been the familiar faith of her whole family – of her whole world. Yet, all the time, Claire had been going to the Rue de la Victoire to hear prayers in Hebrew that Lily had never imagined existed – because she'd simply never thought about the question at all.

She kept Claire's story a secret, knowing, without having to be told, that somehow, threads of her life, Claire's life, and even the lives of her children would come apart if anyone else learned the truth. She felt that with Misha she was being deceitful for the first time in their marriage, and

178

had the sensation of being unclean. But how could she tell him when she had no idea of how he would react? And Claire had called her story 'these sad secrets that don't belong to you'. It wasn't her right to reveal them, therefore, to her husband.

She wished she might have been able to write freely to Marisa and Wolf. But obviously they hadn't been told the truth either. She wondered how much Eliane knew – how much Rabbi Weill had told her; how much Claire had confessed. Knowing her mother's extreme discretion, she thought: probably very little. And so she had no one to confide in. She was beginning to realize the cell of loneliness in which Claire had had to live, all these years. She understood it; but this didn't make it easier to bridge the gap and make peace with her mother. Somehow, Lily couldn't help thinking that the truth had come *at the wrong time*. And so, instead of bringing them closer, it had destroyed a fabric of trust between them – and initiated a thin wall of distrust now between Lily and Misha, because of her inability to tell him everything that had happened.

She waited in the hall, fingering the shawl around her shoulders. Suddenly, Claude appeared, dressed for the evening. Lily scrutinized him for a moment, the regular features, the slender nose, the dark hair and eyes. She'd always thought he resembled Claire. Now, for the first time, she saw traces of another influence, a more pronounced . . . exoticism. She'd never spent much time wondering about her brother; now she was filled with a new curiosity: Who was he? Who was his father? And she thought, shocked: He's completely Jewish, and I'm only half. I know all about him, and he knows nothing.

'Hello, Lily,' he said, kissing her on the cheek. 'Waiting for Mama?'

'Yes. We're going to Sudarskaya's recital. And you?'

'Just a dinner party at a client's. Really, Lily, if I were

179

you, I wouldn't encourage Mama to associate with that woman.'

'Why?'

He shrugged, a little exasperated. 'Come on. She's not really our sort.'

'Oh?'

'She's common,' he said.

'She's a fine pianist,' Lily answered. 'We're going to hear her play, not criticize her habits.'

'Suit yourself,' he tossed off. 'But if I were you, I wouldn't waste my time.'

He picked his coat from the rack, and put it on. 'Well,' he murmured. 'Good night, little sister.' And he was opening the door and stepping outside, leaving her alone.

A few minutes later, when Claire arrived, there was no time to break the ice between them. They were late, and hurried to the car and to François. And in the car they were conscious of his presence, and spoke, somewhat perfunctorily, about the children.

Sudarskaya's recital was at the home of Raymond Duncan, brother of the celebrated Isadora. He and his wife lived on the ground floor of an old two-storey house in the Fifth Arrondissement. They had covered the interior yard and set up a stage, and had bought about one hundred chairs. They were standing at the entrance to greet the guests. Lily remembered that Sudarskaya had told her that they were Quakers, dedicated to helping others. So as not to have to pay the thirteen per cent tax, Sudarskaya had accepted their offer to give the recital in their home and to sell the tickets as if they were for a private performance.

They were dressed in long white robes belted with a cord, and their feet were shod only in sandals. Raymond was tall, thin, grey-haired, and his face was interesting, his voice deep. His wife was shorter and plumper, her pretty face animated by enormous black eyes. They had no children. Lily and Claire shook their hands and went to

180

sit down. The covered yard was already full, and soon Sudarskaya came in and sat at the piano. There was a silence, and then she plunged into one of Chopin's nocturnes.

Lily clasped her hands on her knees, and leaned forward. Her piano teacher didn't often play for her, and it was amazing to hear such beautiful sounds coming from her short, pudgy fingers – those same fingers that could stuff a tart in its entirety into her small, round mouth. The tone was clear, the notes moving, and one forgot one was in Paris, sitting in someone's courtyard. One thought only of the sounds, of the emotions that rose to the surface through Sudarskaya's hands. It was, Lily realized, like a miracle. This small, vulgar, prying woman was creating magic.

Lily stared at her, and wondered. She'd always accepted Raïssa Markovna Sudarskaya as someone who was in her house for only one purpose, to teach her to improve her playing. As someone who was better got rid of when her husband came home, and in whose presence it was best not to be seen by friends. Now she felt acute shame. Sudarskaya was a magnificent artist. But she was also a *person*. A lonely, hungry person whom her mother had befriended out of kindness. Her mother had been right; not her, not Misha.

Feeling the trembling notes in the air, she felt, all at once, a surge of empathy toward this virtual stranger at the piano. A connection had sprung up from one's ears to the other's heart. Lily felt proud of Sudarskaya. It was almost as if her piano teacher had been her own child, performing for a hundred people in awe of her magic. She thought, with consternation: But why should I feel this way?

Afterwards it was late, and François dropped Claire off first, then drove home in the dark, starlit night. Misha was waiting for her in the study. 'How was it?' he asked.

'It was moving, and beautiful.' She sat down, letting the

181

shawl slide from her shoulders. 'Her talent is spectacular. I hadn't expected this.'

He smiled. 'There's something about the Jews,' he remarked, 'that connects them to the arts. I saw and heard it before, in Russia. Maybe it was their confinement, in the Pale of Settlement, that left them only this outlet. Men and women who were ugly and ill-bred, like your Sudarskaya, could make a violin or piano suddenly alive.'

'Yes,' she agreed. 'That was it, exactly.'

'The Jews,' he said, 'are born merchants and artists. They're like those strange people who are retarded, except for one or two areas where they are geniuses. You know? They can multiply millions by millions, in their heads, in the fraction of a minute; but they can't read or write, and their talk is stupid, like children's talk. Idiot-geniuses: isn't that what they're called?'

She blinked, in slow motion. He had begun to speak of something else, but she wasn't listening. She watched his face, pleasant, alert – loving. And she thought: My God. He thinks the Jews are different, oddities – like clowns in a circus. And then her mind went back to the little woman playing Chopin in the covered courtyard. She understood, all at once, the connection between them.

Somewhere in her blood lay the same mysterious element as in Sudarskaya's. It didn't matter if the Dniester River had separated their ancestors. She came from the same corner of the world as the pianist, and their families had felt the same constraints, the same joys. For among Jews, it didn't matter if one was Rumanian and the other Russian. The Jews, as Wolf had told her, had their own strength, their own heritage.

For the first time since Claire had revealed her story, Lily felt what it meant to be a Jew. It didn't matter, really, how she worshipped God. Judaism wasn't merely a religion; it was a culture – even a race. That was why Claire had accepted her daughter's Catholicism; she'd known, all along, that what had made her a Jew was much stronger than a simple manifestation of her love of God.

I am a Jew, like Sudàrskaya, like my mother, she thought. It's in my bones, in my blood. I have to recognize this, and go on from here. I also love Christ, and the Virgin, and the Apostles. But it's all right. I must accept all sides of who I am.

Chapter Nine

'It's going to rain,' Claire said. 'We could have a cup of coffee there, across the street, and avoid the showers.'

Lily looked up at the sky; it was grey, forbidding, angry. They had been walking along the Champs-Élysées, hardly speaking, simply enjoying a breath of fresh air on a clear spring day. 'April showers, May flowers,' Lily said. Together, they held up their skirts and ran across the great avenue, watching for cars. Under a red and white awning, a large café appeared, inviting. They slipped underneath, and went to the table furthest to the back. Claire and Lily sat down, and just as they did, drops began to hit the pavement. 'We made it just in time,' Claire said.

They ordered coffee, and some pastries. It was pleasant, the air still warm, but the café was nearly empty. When the waiter had left, leaving them with coffee and brioches, she turned suddenly, and asked: 'Mama, do you think you'll ever remarry?'

Claire laughed. 'What kind of question is that? I don't know. When a person was married to the same man for all her grown life, she can't really imagine what it would be like to be with someone else in that same intimacy.'

'But you're still young. You could meet a widower, and have the sort of life you never had with Papa: evenings at the theatre, trips to Italy.'

Claire smiled. 'I hardly think trips to Italy would be in order,' she commented. 'Mussolini's rearming – have you heard?'

'Misha says he's only a silly little man strutting about to

make himself look important. You shouldn't worry about him.'

They sat quietly, sipping coffee and eating their brioches. It was amazing how time had taken care of mending their relations. This April 1928, they were almost back to the way they'd been, before that afternoon some ten months back. It had been the children who'd made everything normal. At first, both women had hidden behind Nicky's eager questions about the world, and Kyra's progress as she learned to walk and talk and to assert herself over the household. Kyra was a strange little being, so impulsive and unpredictable, less intellectually developed than her brother had been at the same age, but much more interested in how things worked, how people reacted, and where she fitted into this whole structure. An anarchist, Misha called her, laughingly.

Then Claire said, shyly: 'You know, Lily, I'm not a romantic anymore. The life I had with your father – it wasn't so bad. He was a good man, fundamentally, and a loyal man. I wouldn't want to run from that life into another. It isn't like that for me.'

'How do you mean?'

'I mean that at my age, after all my life has been, marrying again would have to be for different reasons. I'm not looking for the stars.'

'Still, it makes me sad when I think of you, all alone.'

Claire said, thoughtfully: 'I don't like to think of myself alone, either. I mourned for Paul, with all my heart. These last few months, I've been less concerned about Claude, you know. I think he's started to see a young woman.'

'Really?'

'He's not communicative, of course. But he's out a lot, and he's telephoned the florist, and somebody's been telephoning him, too, at the villa. A woman's voice. Very *French*. Probably not someone terribly refined – but it

185

doesn't matter. I doubt he'll marry her; but it's good to know he's less alone.'

'Yes,' Lily remarked. 'It *is* good news.'

'And so,' Claire continued, setting down her cup, 'I too have started to . . . well . . . see someone.'

Lily turned to face her. 'Mama! *Who?*'

Claire said, blushing: 'An older gentleman. Older than I. He's never been married. A retired businessman from Basel, Switzerland. His name is Jacques Walter. He's been . . . a very pleasant companion, when we've gone out. We like the same books, the same artists. He wants to marry me.'

'And if I hadn't pried – would you have told me?'

Claire laughed. 'One can't very well hide a thing like that. I might not have told you *today* – but yes, I was planning to tell you soon. I want you to meet him.'

Lily felt an odd breathlessness take hold of her. 'And so you've decided to accept his proposal?'

Claire shrugged. 'I'm not sure yet. You see – it's what I said, at the beginning. After so many years with Paul, it wouldn't be so easy to be with another man. But he's a fine human being.'

In front of them, sheets of water were hitting the pavement. Lily said: 'He's good, you have things in common, and he's well off. I'm really happy for you, Mama. You took me by surprise – but it's a good surprise.' She pressed Claire's hand. 'But – you amaze me. I'd absolutely no idea.'

'I met him quite some months ago, through Eliane and David. You see, he spent most of his life in Switzerland, and the idea of retiring there didn't hold much excitement at this point in his life. He sold his business, and came to Paris for a short visit – a kind of vacation. He'd known the Robinsons – you know how *everybody* seems, at some time or another, to have crossed paths with them! – and so

186

naturally, he looked them up, and they gave a party for him. That's when we met each other.'

'And he fell in love, and decided to stay?'

Claire laughed. 'He fell in love with Paris, and stayed. We began to go out together, to learn something about each other. It was ... enjoyable. Of course, at first it wasn't anything special.'

'Do you love him?'

'My darling,' Claire stated, 'I'm afraid of big words like that. But I *can* tell you that I feel good with him.'

The rain was starting to die down, the sheets being gradually replaced by patterns of distinguishable drops. Lily cleared her throat. 'Mama – you mentioned the Robinsons. What do they say about Mark? How is he?'

Claire pushed away her plate, dabbed at the corners of her mouth. 'He's finished his novel. In fact, it's already come out in the United States. He's very pleased about it.'

'You've seen him?'

Claire looked at her. 'Lily. All these years, you've never once mentioned him. He's never tried to see you, has he?'

She felt herself colouring. 'No. Why should he?'

'Well, then. It's better that way, for both of you. He does ask about you. But he has infinite respect for you, and wouldn't want to cross you in any fashion.'

'But it wouldn't cross me. I always liked him. That was the problem, really: I liked him too much to love him.'

Claire sighed. 'I'm sorry to hear you say that,' she remarked. 'The best part of a marriage is the friendship. Or, it ought to be.'

They sat for some moments, and then, to their surprise, a timid sun began to peek through the rain clouds. 'Look,' Lily said, 'good luck. God's smiling at us.'

'You always used to say that,' her mother told her, fondly. 'Ever since you were Nicky's age, practically. Taking every small quirk of nature to be a sign of God's moods.'

'Well, shouldn't it be? Manifestations from heaven, no?'

Lily laid some money on the table, and stood up. She walked to the edge of the café, and stood looking out into the wet avenue. Claire came up beside her. Across the street, some young men in blue raincoats and berets were marching, in orderly, almost martial fashion. 'Who are *they*?' Lily asked.

'Surely not a manifestation from heaven. I believe they're part of the Jeunesses Patriotes.'

'They're very right-wing, aren't they?'

'They're dangerous people,' Claire said, her tone suddenly angry. 'They like to go around breaking up the meetings of those they don't agree with.'

'Like Blum?'

Claire said: 'You mean, you haven't heard about them?'

Lily peered across the street, her body still, feeling pinpricks erupting all over – signs of tension. She said, softly: 'They can't be so bad. They're just young people, maybe a little crazy at times – '

'They're Fascists,' Claire stated. 'And frankly, I can't agree with Misha about that "silly little man strutting about" in Italy. I don't agree with Blum. I wasn't brought up to be that liberal, and I lived with your father for too long not to have become infected with some of his opinions. But still – to beat people up just because their ideas don't agree with yours – that's unacceptable, I'm afraid.'

They were silent. Then Lily said: 'The elections are just a month away. Nothing much can change just because of these blue berets. This isn't Germany, where one man's reactionary views can suddenly make his small party an enormous one.'

'Let's go home,' Claire declared.

That evening, when they were alone, Lily said to Misha, excitedly: 'I wanted so much to tell you the news: I think

Mama's going to remarry. His name is Jacques Walter. He was a businessman in Basel. Have you heard of him?'

Misha rubbed his chin. 'Walter? No, I don't believe so. I've done very little business with Switzerland. But if your mother's chosen him – then I'm all for him. Let's give them a dinner.'

She kissed him. Then she said: 'We saw some strange people on the Champs-Élysées: members of the Jeunesses Patriotes.'

He looked up, alert: 'Really?'

'Tell me, Misha – are they very bad? Can they really hurt people?'

He took in some air, let it out. 'Their ways aren't always very nice,' he answered, slowly. 'But then, their aims are understandable. They don't want this country to go the way of Russia.'

'That can't happen here.'

'We thought it would never happen *there*. Your Monsieur Blum – it's best he stay out of office, with his Red ideas.'

Lily rose, went to the large gilt mirror, pushed back a strand of hair behind her ear. She could see her own face, cool and immaculate, the creamy skin unwrinkled and glowing, the dark eyes almost liquid. The dark, dark hair. The face of an Italian madonna, the Mother Superior had so often remarked. Behind her reflection, Lily could see Misha sitting on the sofa, smoking a cigar. She said: '*My* Monsieur Blum?'

'Well, you have rather an admiration for him, don't you? He charmed you at Marisa's wedding, if I recall.'

'Well, then,' she said, turning around, 'then he belonged to *all* the women there. I'm sorry you didn't have a chance to speak with him.'

'I know all about him, my dear,' Misha declared, blowing out circles of smoke.

Lily opened her mouth, closed it again. She really wasn't

189

feeling well tonight. 'I think I'll go to bed early,' she murmured. 'You don't mind?'

He shook his head. 'It's all right. I have some work to finish, anyway. I'll be up in a while.'

She bent down to kiss him, felt the strong pull of his soft lips on hers – a hypnotic, magnetic effect that never failed to make her forget where she was and what she was doing. With an effort, she drew herself straight. 'Good night,' she said, and walked out of the room.

In her boudoir, she combed her hair and let her clothes fall to the floor. She looked at herself again, this time in her own full-length mirror. She wondered. Could it be that she was pregnant again? It was hard to tell just by looking. If so, it must have happened within the month. She sat down on the bed, thinking.

She'd decided, two years before, that if Misha were to want a third child, she would have it. But Misha hadn't spoken, since Kyra, of more children.

Maybe, she thought, I'll have this one for *me*. Nicky had been for the continuation of the Brasilov dynasty, and Kyra, for Misha's pleasure. She loved them both equally, with all her being. But maybe *she* deserved a baby in peace, in health, now that she'd had two years between Kyra and this. Now that she'd given up on ever becoming a concert pianist. Now that she was twenty-three and no longer a child herself.

Her mother was finally doing what she wanted. It was only right, after so many years of having lived a compromise. She slipped the lace negligee over her head.

I really didn't tell Mama how happy I am, she reflected, climbing between the cool sheets of her bed. It's late, but she'll be up reading. I have to make her forgive me. It's time to stop resenting her for something she felt she had to do. In her position, would I have told Kyra, or Nicky?

She reached for the telephone extension, and picked it

up. But when she put it to her ear, she heard Misha's voice speaking: 'You didn't receive the cheque?'

Lily started to put the phone down, and then held it back to her ear, picturing a redhead with an egret feather. But a man was answering: 'No, it must still be in the mail. May I ask how large was your contribution, your Excellency?'

Damn, she thought, angry with herself: he's long since stopped paying her. The agreement only stipulated three years. What a fool I am. Misha's voice was saying, with a touch of irritation: 'Look, Taittinger, I've done all I could. Fifty thousand francs. And don't forget, I'm not even a French national, so I really have no business getting involved in these elections.'

She held the telephone rigidly. 'That's something else,' the man Taittinger declared. 'You *should* really become French. Because to be Russian, in our times – '

'There's absolutely nothing anyone can say about my leanings. I came here to escape from Communism – not to hold on to it. And this fact is known even to President Doumergue.'

'I was only saying this as friendly advice, your Excellency. I myself have always respected your good name. We strive to uphold it. If there are foreigners among us, my dear Prince, we should perhaps look more closely at some of our *own* nationals. To be foreign doesn't simply mean to be born abroad, like you. Some of those who want to destroy France were born right here on our shores.'

'The socialists?'

'Worse: the *Jewish* socialists. Remember Marx, your Excellency.'

Lily could hear her heart beating. As quietly as she could, she set down the telephone. Her fingers were trembling. Where had she heard that name before: Taittinger? . . . 'the *Jewish* socialists.' Something was strangely, disturbingly familiar.

As her hand turned the knob of her lamp, and the room grew dark, she saw them again: marching like automatons in their blue berets and blue raincoats, their boots echoing on the puddled pavement. The Jeunesses Patriotes. Pierre *Taittinger's* Jeunesses Patriotes. Her mother exclaiming: 'You mean, you haven't heard about them?'

Yes, Lily thought, hugging her body so tightly that her ribs hurt: I've heard about them. And my husband just sent them fifty thousand francs.

Claude wondered, as he walked up the steep Rue Lepic, holding the small bouquet of rosebuds, whatever had possessed him, to find himself in such a place. It had all happened a few months before this balmy May evening, at the *vernissage* of an art collection. He hadn't wanted to attend, but Misha had told him that it was most important, for business reasons, not to turn down this invitation. A rich client was unveiling his carefully put together collection of fauve paintings. Claude had protested that he knew nothing about art; but Misha had insisted. For some reason he himself hadn't wanted to go, and had thrust the obligation upon his brother-in-law.

Claude had gone, and found himself staring at Matisse oils of overweight nudes that he had felt were not worth the canvas they'd been painted on. A young woman had approached him, and with somewhat shocking familiarity, had leaned over to whisper to him, her feline hand on his arm: 'It's a lot of nonsense, isn't it? To waste a fortune on these boring middle-aged nudes. Most of these fellows are just a bunch of perverts, anyway.'

He'd laughed – almost in spite of himself. And had turned to look fully into the proffered face. She'd been a strangely vulnerable street urchin, with absurd burgundy hair cut very short, and slanted amber eyes. Very thin, and with an elegant little nothing of a black dress. He'd asked: 'And how do you know that?'

She'd lifted her shoulders, dropped them again. 'Simple. They send their rich wives *chez* Poiret, where I work, and while I twirl before them, when the *première* goes away, the well-heeled ladies whisper an invitation to a private party, and slip a thousand francs into the bodice of the dress I'm modelling.'

'And? You go?'

She'd made a face. 'Sometimes. You have to look reality squarely in the eye. What I make as a model hardly pays the rent. And I'm not going to stay a nobody all my life – that's for sure!'

At that point, he'd felt something: a sudden stab of recognition. She was ambitious, and self-made. And she wasn't going to stop at conventions to arrive where she'd set her goals. Although he'd never been attracted to women who were in any way outrageous, he'd liked her. But it had been her initiative to get him out of that town house and into a small bar, where they'd sat over gin fizzes, talking about their lives. He'd been touched by her candidness, and responded with a strange protective feeling he had never felt before – not even towards his sister when she'd been younger.

It wasn't that he loved her, Claude thought, ringing the doorbell of a small apartment on the top floor of an old house. He didn't like Montmartre, with its small, steep, winding streets, and its atmosphere of poverty and cheap art.

She swung the door open, and he found himself smiling, his heart beating just a little more rapidly. She really did look like a child, with her slender, vulnerable face, and her thin, athletic body. She was older than he – maybe five or six years, but somehow, he never felt the age difference when they were together.

'I've cooked for you,' she said, presenting her elfin face to be kissed. Moving with quick grace, she put the rosebuds in a small vase. She was wearing an old plaid bathrobe, and looked exactly the opposite of when he'd met her, or when, subsequently, he'd taken her out on the town. Then she'd been in the height of fashion, in her Poiret clothes – the only point of luxury in her life, for she received them for free. Now she looked like a somewhat rumpled child in her father's Sunday-morning bathrobe. He found this charming.

'What have you been cooking?' he asked. The small living room was filled with green plants and charcoal drawings of herself in various poses and modes of dress, but the sofa where he sat down was soft and curvaceous, the latest design. She'd received it from Poiret after the Exposition of Decorative Arts, as a bonus for her work.

'*Pot au feu*,' she answered, laughing. 'You can't ask a country girl from Meaux to cook you something more tasty. You can't get it *chez* Maxim.'

'It's funny,' he remarked, lacing his arm around her and walking into the kitchen. 'Long ago, before we had money, my mother used to cook things like that. And my father's mother. I love good French food – unpretentious. My sister would never serve *pot au feu* for any of *her* guests.'

'I've seen her once or twice,' Henriette said, somewhat tightly. She lifted the cover off a large pot, and stirred the contents with a big wooden spoon.

'My sister is what one calls a *lady*: her tastes are artistic, her culture is sound, her political and economic background is nil. And she's very devout – the kind of woman who'll want to procreate because that's what the Church believes in.'

'You don't sound as though you like her.'

'I don't. The fact is,' he said, surprised at his own vehemence, 'I really detest that husband of hers. He can convince *her* of his inherent goodness – but in reality, he's a selfish bastard. He took our company under the awning of his large firm, and gave me a general vice-presidency. Lily thought that was so generous on dear Misha's part – he made sure she'd think that. But he didn't fool *me*: he wanted to control us, to skim the profits legally. How else do you think he's made it so big? He's been absorbing smaller companies from the start – threatening to ruin them in the competition if they didn't sell to him. And then he's milked them dry.'

'You have no proof of this, do you?' She was bringing soup plates and ladling the stew into them, little by little.

'No. You see, darling, he's very smart. He won't do anything illegal. What he does is just one millimetre within legality. So he's never been caught.'

He found himself with a soup plate in hand, and followed her into the tiny dining room, where the table was set. They both put their plates down and sat down. She put her elbows on the table and held her head up with her hands. 'Claude,' she said. 'You know, I was involved with him for a while.'

He stared at her. 'With Mikhail Brasilov?'

'Yes. When he was still married to Jeanne Dalbret. She was a nice woman – let him do what he pleased. Then he divorced her to marry your sister.'

'Did you like him?' Claude asked.

She began to attack the stew before her. 'Mmm. I liked him a great deal. He was . . . an adventurer. He adores women. A lot of women. I never imagined a man like that could ever be happy with a person like your sister.'

'They do seem a rather ill-matched pair,' he agreed, starting to eat. 'But maybe not . . . Lily inherited a sort of queenlike demeanour from my mother.'

She said: 'Don't talk about them! There are so many fascinating things and people for us to discuss! Let's let them be, okay?'

'Were you in love with him, then?'

She shrugged. 'I just wanted to tell you about us, that's all. So you'd hear it from *me*. People in this town have such big mouths . . . And then, of course, you might decide to

195

have *me* investigated!' She sat smiling at him, still holding her glass up. Tilting her head to one side, she asked, seriously: 'Tell me the truth, Claude. You're such a . . . well, *distrustful* person . . . and you've told me a bit about the way you work. Have you already had me investigated?'

His fork poised midway between his plate and his mouth, he shook his head. 'No. Not you. Somehow, I had the feeling that . . . how can I put it? . . . you'd tell me your own story.'

She set the glass down. 'Well,' she declared. 'I did, didn't I? I haven't been a saint, like the immaculate Lily – but then, I'm not married, and I'm almost thirty-four. A girl has to survive, in a tough, ugly world where good guys almost never win. And for sure, not good girls.'

'You're not such a bad girl,' he said, reaching across the table and covering her hand with his. And then, clearing his throat during a moment of embarrassment, he added: 'And you're *my* girl.'

'And you're the only serious man I've ever known,' she answered.

In the stillness that ensued, Claude thought, almost with awe, that this conversation was the closest he'd ever come to a declaration of love with anyone, including his family. This small room, with its slightly discoloured wallpaper, with the warm, familiar smell of *pot au feu*, and the girl, with her long amber eyes and that tattered bathrobe, felt more like home than any place he'd ever been. Maybe, then, he was in love with her after all.

Jacques Walter's suite at the Ritz was all subdued opulence, like the man himself. At fifty-eight, he was tall, erect, well dressed, his silk shirts always impeccably pressed, his silk ties a marvel of hues to match each one of his suits. He had a long, well-sculpted face, topped by a head of white hair that shone like a silk bonnet. His eyes were a sharp blue, his long, aquiline nose aristocratic. Now he stood before Claire and put his hands squarely on her shoulders. 'I don't see why we have to get married out of town,' he declared.

'It's the only way of avoiding a public wedding.'

He passed his tongue over his upper lip. 'You mean, it's the only way of having a quiet Jewish wedding without your family.'

She looked away, fumbled uncomfortably with her rings. 'Jacob,' she murmured, 'I've tried to explain it to you. You and Lily are the only two people besides Julien Weill who know the whole story. Even Eliane doesn't know all.' She whispered, not looking at him: 'I've told the children you're . . . a Protestant, like many Swiss people.'

He burst into short, hard laughter. 'To go with my lean and hungry face. But darling – isn't it time all this stopped? I can understand how things were for you, when Paul was alive. But now –'

'I have to protect Claude. And Lily, too. Misha would never be able to accept a Jewish – or half-Jewish – wife. Even a Jewish stepfather could be held against Lily.'

He sighed. 'I can't argue with you. I know something of Prince Brasilov. He and his father were not exactly Semitophiles in their country.'

'Misha's a good man, Jacob.'

'I'm certain of it. But nevertheless, you're afraid to tell him the truth.'

She said, wringing her hands: 'Please don't force me to! I'm just asking you to lead a quiet life, the way you've always done, even in Basel. To be discreet – for my sake.'

'All right,' he stated, stopping in his tracks. 'I'll meet your Misha, and I'll do what you ask. *For the time being,*' he added.

'Then,' she whispered, kissing his cheek, 'we'll go to the Riviera, and be married there. I'd like that, anyway. It's infinitely more romantic than Paris.'

* * *

197

It was a wonderful, warm day, and Lily felt good as she walked out of the Galeries Lafayette, holding the small parcel. There were always things there for the children. She'd bought a nightgown for Kyra, and a little sailor suit for summer, for Nicky.

She'd told François to come back in two hours, and now there was still an hour to go. She was glad, hugging her time alone like a precious commodity. She'd always enjoyed walking alone along the boulevards, like a common, every-day French bourgeoise. It was like an escape from being, twenty-four hours a day, the Princess Brasilova, who was only allowed to do certain things. It was a small rebellion, but, Lily thought, one that made her feel good.

She strolled along, stopping to look in shopwindows. She wasn't showing yet, but she was constantly aware of the new pregnancy. She hadn't told Misha yet, and wondered why. Perhaps it was because, for a few weeks, she'd wanted to be the only one to know.

'Lily,' a voice called, and she turned, surprised at the voice she hadn't heard in so many years. Beside her on the pavement stood Mark MacDonald, in a light raincoat. She felt a sudden wave of warmth, and her heart beat quickly.

He took her hands. 'You haven't really changed,' he said. 'Where are you going?'

'Nowhere in particular. I just had a free hour. I'm glad to see you, Mark.'

'Would you like to stop for a cup of coffee? I have some time, too. I'd like to catch up with you.'

For an instant only, she hesitated. Why was it that she never really dared take an initiative, sensing always a presence behind her, looking over her shoulder? She nodded, feeling squeamish. She was indulging herself in a perfectly legitimate pastime, catching up with an old friend – but still, the old guilt persisted. He had taken her arm and was walking with her across the street, to a small outdoor café that beckoned invitingly. She realized that

Mark's reassuring presence was like the answer to a prayer. She hadn't felt so happy to be with someone since Marisa and Wolf had got married, moved away, and deprived her of the joys of their companionship.

They sat down, and all at once Lily was afraid to look up and encounter his eyes. She could feel a wave of heat and a concurrent tightness in her stomach. This is ridiculous, she thought, and resolutely forced herself to look at him.

His hands had folded over some cutlery, and he was twirling a fork through his fingers, seemingly concentrating on the movement of the silver tines. So he, too, was somewhat embarrassed. She saw, for a few brief seconds, a replay of the last time they had met, when she'd sent for him at the Villa Persane, and he had promised to stay her friend, adding that he'd have to keep away for a while because of his pain.

'Your book's doing well,' she remarked, to break the silence.

He smiled. It was a smile tinged with a certain ironic sadness, which touched her. Lines had developed between the sides of his nose and the corners of his lips, and she had to admit that she liked this sign of maturity. 'I'm pleased with the sales,' he said. 'I've quit the *Clarion*, and haven't even had to touch my trust fund. No, professionally speaking, I can't complain.'

'And . . . otherwise?'

Why was it she was hoping that his face wouldn't light up, that he wouldn't suddenly reveal the name of a new love? She was being unfair. She'd rejected him, and had never really been in love with him. He deserved to be happy with another woman. Why, then, was she selfishly willing him to still care? He'd told her that men who pined for long-lost loves were, in his opinion, fools.

His hazel eyes opened warmly to her, gold flecks like sunlight over green waters. 'Otherwise? I've kept up old friendships, and met some new people. You'd be surprised how the world flocks around a man when he's been lucky enough to have had one minor success.'

'It wasn't minor, and people always knew that you were special. Don't put yourself down, Mark.'

He laughed. 'I used to tell *you* the same thing.' Slowly, the amusement seeped from his face, and he asked, softly: 'And . . . did marriage bring you what you wished for? Fireworks, like my character Theresa?'

A sudden cloud seemed to fall over her spirits, which she tried to ignore. 'Well . . . fireworks tend to burn out, don't they? A nice warm hearth seems more enduring – don't you think? For real people?'

'Perhaps.' He was silent then, a bit withdrawn, his eyes far away. Abruptly, he looked at her again. 'I hear you have two children. That's nice.'

Still trying to sort out her feelings, and to shrug off the cloud, she burst out, 'And I'm expecting a third!' and then immediately wanted to bite her tongue at the foolishness of having revealed this.

'Oh?'

'But – nobody knows yet. Misha . . . I haven't told him the good news. It has to be a special moment, a – '

'Yes, of course, I see.'

'I'm so sorry we lost touch, Mark,' she then stated, her voice unexpectedly warm. 'You were speaking of having kept up friendships . . . yet with me . . .'

'It wasn't quite the same, Lily, was it? You were never just another Marisa for me, nor a Claire. I've seen *her* a few times, by the way – your mother. And I've met Jacques. What a fine man he appears to be! I think they'll have a happy life together.'

Glad to be once again on neutral grounds, and to be able to give free vent to her feelings, she relaxed. 'I agree. He's exactly what Mama needs – what she's always needed.

But I *do* wish they hadn't planned to elope to Saint-Paul-de-Vence. I'd hoped to be . . . well, her matron of honour. And now *I* feel like a mother whose eloping daughter has cheated her out of a wedding!' She laughed, nervously. 'Perhaps it's because I didn't have a formal wedding either. I'd counted on Mama to have one in my stead!'

Mark sat chewing thoughtfully on his lower lip. 'I might be entirely wrong,' he said, 'but somehow I'd gotten a vague impression that Jacques Walter's a Jew. And if so, you'd have to understand why they wouldn't want a religious service. People of different faiths very often prefer to be quietly married by a justice of the peace.'

Demitasses of coffee had been placed in front of them, and Lily's hand, halfway to her mouth, put down her cup. 'But – that's not true. Jacques isn't a Catholic, but I think Mama said he was some kind of Protestant – Lutheran or something. And . . . and . . .' Her voice trailed off, and she found herself trembling.

Puzzled, Mark asked: 'Would you *object* to Jacques being a Jew? I don't understand.'

'But . . . you aren't *sure*, you said? It was never actually discussed?'

The intensity of her pleading stare shocked him. 'No. He never mentioned it to me. And it's quite likely that I could be wrong. But, Lily: I still don't see why it would make a difference to you one way or the other. You never cared before about other people's religions.' His eyes narrowed: 'Unless, of course, your husband's well-known ideas have finally gotten to you.'

She heard the unmistakable bitterness in his tone of voice, and sat back, as if slapped. She could sense tears forming, and starting to push behind her eye sockets. 'Dammit, Mark,' she cried, 'it isn't that at all! After all these years – after the time we spent together, when you said you loved me – you should know, better than anyone, that I'm not anti *anything!* It's just ... just ... that you don't *understand!*'

The tears had finally spilled out, and suddenly she stood up, almost knocking over her cup of coffee. Mark half rose, but she had already left, her footsteps quick, almost panicky, as she made her way to the corner of the street. His lips parted with bewilderment, he sat down again, his own breath raspy.

It was only five minutes later that he realized she'd left her package on the seat. Strangely troubled, he picked up the wrapped box, and fingered the ribbon. Maybe this was an omen.

'There's a Monsieur MacDonald in the study, waiting to see Madame la Princesse,' Arkhippe said to her.

'But – I don't really want to see him.' She felt a surge of nervousness, almost anger. 'Why did he come?'

'He says he'll wait, but he must see madame.'

'Thank you, Arkhippe.'

She stood uncertainly, wondering. She really wished he'd stayed out of her life. She'd been so glad to see him – until he'd mentioned that about Jacques. No, she wasn't going to think about it. It wasn't fair – the whole thing wasn't fair. Claire should have told her about it before, not let her hear it from someone else.

She walked, unsteadily, into the study. Mark stood up when he saw her, and she saw the package. She felt a wave of relief. 'Oh,' she said, 'thank you. I'd forgotten it, hadn't I?'

'Yes. I'm sorry to intrude on you. But – '

To prevent him from mentioning yesterday, she began a breathless monologue. 'Just a nightshirt for Kyra, and a sailor outfit for Nicky. You don't know my children – they're so cute. I'll have to ask Zelle to bring them in – '

'Lily,' he interrupted. 'I couldn't sleep last night. I didn't understand. What's wrong? I came to tell you that if you need someone to talk to . . . I'm here. I don't want you to feel alone, Lily. Please forgive me for coming here – but I simply had to. As your friend, who cares.'

She was weeping, her hands laced before her face. He put an arm around her. 'Lily – you must tell me what's troubling you. Maybe I can help.'

She lifted her face from her hands, and looked at him. Maybe he was right. She'd always felt that she could trust him. Long ago, she'd voiced all her intimate thoughts to him, all her hopes and insecurities, and he'd repaid her with his steadfast kindness and understanding. Pushing aside some of the awkwardness of their meeting the previous day, she concentrated instead on her tremendous need for honesty, for coming clean with someone. She needed to unburden herself, to let everything spill out – and providence, it seemed, had just happened to throw Mark back into her life. What better confidant than he?

'Look,' she said. 'It's a very private thing. I don't want *anybody* to know about it. You must swear to me.'

'I'll swear anything you like. Of course.'

'My mother's . . . Jewish. It's something she had to hide, when Papa was alive. And now – she knows she has to continue hiding it.'

'Why?'

She passed a hand over her wet face. 'Because. Claude, Misha. They'd reject her. And – Misha would reject me, too. And . . . our children.'

Mark was standing next to her, shaking his head in complete disbelief. 'It's incredible. Even in the South – in the United States – no one is that anti-Semitic. I think you and Claire are exaggerating.'

'I hardly think so. Just these past elections, the Jeunesses Patriotes were beating up members of the Socialist and Communist parties.'

'That's a different story.'

She asked, tentatively: 'Do you think so?'

'Sure. Look, Europe's in a state of flux. The economy's improved since Poincaré came back, in '26. The French aren't so afraid of Germany anymore. It looks as though, finally, war reparations will be paid. But there's a lot of fear of the Russians.'

'But in *L'Action Française*, Maurras is perpetually haranguing his readers against the Communists *and* the Jews.'

He raised his brows. 'You read this garbage?'

'No,' she admitted. 'But Misha does. I've glanced at some of the articles.'

'Well,' he said soothingly, 'Maurras is an old fool whose time is past. But perhaps the French are making a mistake, with the Russians. I don't like the fact that in Germany this man Hitler is growing in strength. *There's* a man who's bad for the Jews. The Russians haven't been asked to join the League of Nations. And now Germany's refusing to recognize the Czech and Polish borders. Perhaps more efforts should be made to put away fear of the Reds, to build a wall against the Huns.'

'But – Briand won the Nobel peace prize. Nobody wants another war – do they?'

Mark sighed. 'I guess not. However – French people aren't an anti-Semitic bunch, like the czarist Russians. I really don't believe the rioting in the streets has had anything much to do with anti-Jewish feeling, so much as anticommunism. You and Claire shouldn't worry.'

She said, with so much feeling that he was caught aback: 'But don't you understand? Misha and Ivan Vassilievitch *are* czarist Russians! You must promise me, Mark, never to let anyone know what I've told you. It's just – I had to tell someone.'

'And I'm glad I just happened to be the one. You mustn't be afraid, Lily.'

He came near her, and put his arm around her shoulder. She leaned against him, feeling exhausted. It was this way that Misha first came upon them when he returned home from work. Surprised, he stopped in the shadow of the open door. The scene, somehow, was so intimate. He stared, angry at his own inertia, and waited, anxiousness pressing against his heart. He'd never expected this – Mark MacDonald! All these years.

'You don't think so?' she whispered.

'No. But sooner or later, you'll have to break the news to Misha.'

She jerked her head up, her face white and taut, and cried: 'No! You know I can't.'

'But it's the only way.'

'He'll never know,' she said fervently. 'He'd never be able to forgive me this. You don't know my husband – but I do.'

'I can't believe he wouldn't understand.'

She pushed Mark away, and stated: 'But he wouldn't. It's just going to have to be my secret. And now, yours.'

'If this is what you want.'

Slowly, Lily put her fingers on Mark's face, and forced him to look at her. She said: 'Mark. For the sake of my children. And . . . of the child that hasn't been born yet. Think a little, Mark. I wouldn't ever want my children to be rejected.'

At that moment, Misha, against his better judgment, entered the room. He stood, very white, like a magnificent intruder on a very private scene. Lily's hands fell from Mark's face, and she began to tremble. Misha said, matter-of-factly: 'Hello, MacDonald. Care for a drink?'

'It's all right, your Excellency,' Mark replied, extending his hand. 'I just dropped in on Lily . . . to see how she was. I have to leave now.'

'Won't you stay for dinner? I'm sure Lily would be delighted.'

'No, thank you. I really must be going.'

The two men shook hands. Lily stared at them, frozen, her heart thumping. How long had Misha been listening?

And he was so pale, so quiet. She'd never seen him like this. When Mark left the room, she realized that she was filled with terror. She stood like a statue, unmoving, no words coming to her. Finally, Misha asked: 'Why was he here, Lily?'

'To drop off a package.'

'What package? A present, maybe?'

She shook her head, bewildered. 'No. Just some things I'd bought for the children.'

'And tell me, however did Mark MacDonald happen to have these items in his possession?'

'I – I had coffee with him, yesterday. And – I forgot the package on the chair of the café.'

'You had coffee with Mark, yesterday? Why didn't you tell me?'

His green eyes were like cold marbles, without feeling. Her mouth fell open. 'I – '

He came up to her then, and stood very close, towering over her. In a still, hard voice, he asked: 'And for how many weeks, months, years, have you been meeting Mr MacDonald?'

Then he *hadn't* heard. He'd only *seen* them, together. A flood of relief washed over her. She put her hand on Misha's shoulder, laughed hesitantly. 'I've never met him. I hadn't seen or heard from him since before we were married. But yesterday, in the street, we ran into each other. And so we stopped for a quick coffee, and I forgot the package.'

With a vehemence that she didn't expect, he pushed her savagely away from him. She fell back, caught herself on the back of a chair, stared at him with disbelief and naked fear. 'Misha – '

He grasped her arm, twisted it until she writhed in pain, then let it fall. 'You goddamned liar,' he said in a dead voice. 'Get out of my sight!'

Terrified, she ran from the room, blinded by her tears.

She hadn't moved since the terrible confrontation in the study. She sat on her bed, silent tears falling and falling over her cheeks, her body shaking. What had gone so wrong? He'd called her a liar. Then, he really believed she'd been ... with Mark. It didn't make any sense. He should have known she'd never be unfaithful. He knew *her*.

Misha had always been so gentle, so protective. Yet hours ago he'd been brutal and ugly. He'd been unfair. Lily wanted to run away from the house, to go to the safety of the Ritz, where Claire would be having a quiet dinner with Jacques –

But she couldn't leave the house, because her children were there, asleep.

The doorknob moved, silently, and she sat, mesmerized, staring at it. The door opened. Misha, his eyes bloodshot, entered the room. Instinctively, she recoiled on the bed.

'It's all right,' he said, in an unusual, singsong voice, blurred a little by alcohol. And he sat down beside her. 'I'm sorry I was rough with you, Lily.'

She said, blushing: 'But I told you the truth. Mark only came here to return a package. Our story ended years ago – and you know I was never really in love with him. He was always ... just a dear friend.'

'Relationships change. He's a clean-cut, attractive young man. Why shouldn't you have liked him?'

She stammered: 'But – I told you! I never liked him – as a man.'

'Then why did you ever become engaged?'

She turned away. 'Because Claude told me that *you* were already married.'

'And ... this time?'

'But, Misha, there is no "this time". I hadn't seen him in four years! *You must believe me!*'

Now his features set in the same ugly expression that

had so frightened her in the study. His green eyes seemed unfocused, his complexion too ruddy. Cords stood out on his neck. He seemed a man unhinged, and the nameless panic of the hunted animal seized Lily, paralysing her on the bed.

Leaning forward, his voice rose a pitch, and he cried out: 'But I *don't* believe you! I *heard* you! You're going to have *his baby*, Liliane. You slept with another man, and now you're carrying his child, wanting to pass it off as one of mine. Oh, God, God – why did you have to turn into a slut, like all the others? Why *you*, the only woman I ever loved?'

Her mouth fell open. In her shock, and disbelief at what she had just heard, she found no words to answer him. And then, to her mounting horror and amazement, she saw him sag against one of the posters of the bed, and, leaning his forehead against his arm, begin to sob.

Trembling uncontrollably, Lily stared at him, incapable of reacting. This had to be a nightmare. Things like this didn't happen. She recalled, in vivid images, some of her father's rages. They had been rainstorms compared to this tempest, which had ravaged her simple life and ripped it to pieces. Misha stood and sobbed, great racking sobs that sounded as savage as his accusing words, each a small sword thrust at their marriage. But she couldn't, wouldn't go to him. There were some things even she couldn't see forgiving, couldn't see explaining. How he could have *thought*, for a split second, that she could have betrayed her vows, betrayed not only him but herself, and then tried to pass off another man's baby as her husband's – this was beyond forgiveness! She, who had always refused to hear echoes of gossip about other women in his life, who had loved him more than mother, son, daughter, and God!

'Yes,' she said, her voice harsh and angry: 'I'm going to have another child. But not in this house. I'm going to take Nick and Kyra to my mother's, tomorrow!'

Slowly, his large, leonine head raised itself from his arm. There were ugly seams in his cheeks, and a dull flatness to his eyes. Remnants of tears clung absurdly to the pinpricks of his beard. She met his stare with one of her own, defiant now.

'You aren't going anywhere with Nick and Kyra,' he simply declared, no emotion at all in his voice.

'I'll go where I want to with my children. I'm their mother!'

'You're their *unfit* mother. And I think you'll see it my way, Lily: whatever you've done, you still love them both enough to wish to spare them an ugly scandal. I'll demolish you, and ruin Mark MacDonald – and you know I can, and will. *If* you try to leave this house with my son and daughter.'

She sat on the bed, shaking her head like a puppet: No, no! But no words came out, no cry, not even tears. She simply couldn't stop the shaking of her head like a mad puppet on a wild, uncontrolled string.

'And one more thing,' he said to her, swaying a little as he drew himself up to his full height. His pupils had shrunk to the tiniest of points in his irises. 'You'll go with me to a woman tomorrow, to have this pregnancy taken care of. I want to live in a clean house, do you hear me?'

All at once she found her voice, in a great, resounding shout: '*No!*'

He sighed, and pressed weary fingers to the bridge of his nose. 'You'll just have to balance this against the children,' he told her. 'Just as we both will have to live with this marriage. For the sake of Nick, and Kyrotchka.'

He turned the doorknob, and was outside before she could jump off the bed and do something, anything, to stop the nightmare. And so she stood, shivering, in the tasteful bedroom hung with raw silk, that denied, in its quiet decorum, that anything uncivilized had ever threatened the denizens of this household.

* * *

Misha paced the floor, fully dressed, his face flushed with perspiration. On the mantelpiece, the delicate Louis XVI ormolu clock, adorned with carved cupids, sat pitilessly ticking off the minutes of his life, irretrievable minutes that he felt dropping away inside his very body. He pulled at his stiff collar, drew it off, and tossed it down on the bed.

Never before had he been forced to examine his life with such unforgiving scrutiny. Misha found that tears, unexpected and unwelcome, were swelling his eyes. He'd felt secure with Lily, knowing that with the infinity of her love, she would always shield him, make him the centre of her existence without, like Vava, giving him cause to worry that she would leave him when the passions of her tempestuous libido would sway her to a new and more exciting partner. This was why, when he'd come upon her holding Mark's face, when he'd seen her eyes, so wide and filled with unabashed supplication, he'd felt doubly betrayed. She'd betrayed him once, as his wife; and twice, as the human being in this world he'd come closest to giving the key to his heart's emotions.

But I didn't hear everything, he thought. And afterwards, she'd seemed so sincere, so like the Lily he had always known. But all women, when it came to their self-preservation, were born dissemblers. Lily wasn't stupid. She would have known just how to sound convincing . . . just how to bring him back to her.

How could he know if Lily had lied?

He remembered what she'd said, about Mark MacDonald. That she'd agreed to marry him, four years ago, because he, Misha, had disappointed her expectations. That's what it had amounted to, anyway. His kind, sweet Lily had actually admitted that she'd consciously *used* a man, another human being. She'd come to a man she hadn't loved, Mark MacDonald, to soothe her own broken heart, to heal her own wounds. This didn't say much for Lily, then.

Or maybe this had also been a lie. He tried to recall the first time he'd taken her, in the prairie near the little chapel, in the Loire valley. She'd behaved exactly like a virgin. But, of course, these last four years he hadn't been with any virgins, and it was possible she'd fooled him. Maybe she'd loved MacDonald, and left him for reasons of her own. Maybe she'd listened to her father and brother, and decided that she'd have a better life as Princess Brasilova than as Mrs Mark MacDonald. *Still loving Mark.*

And if she'd *loved* the American novelist, that love might well have carried through into the years of her marriage to him, Misha. He sat down, uttering a sound of anguish as he envisaged them together, meeting time after time in small cafés . . . like yesterday. She must have been terribly agitated to forget her parcel, he thought.

Anger, outrage, and self-pity constricted his throat, and he could feel the blood vessels stretching. Of course she'd been beside herself. *She'd had to tell Mark about the baby!* And he had come today. Why? To clear things up? '. . . you'll have to break the news to Misha.'

I could still be wrong, he told himself. Maybe this is all circumstantial evidence stacked against her. But he'd seen her face. He'd seen how she had looked at Mark MacDonald: her whole life in her eyes, pleading. For what? Misha hunched over the bed, his hands falling limply between his legs. He thought: I am a pathetic animal, whimpering pitifully in the night.

All right, then. He had, after all, no real, tangible proof. She wanted this child. But the question would always remain: whose child was it? And so he had to ensure that the question would never come up again, that the memory of this traumatic night never be brought out again.

In his lifetime, many women he'd known had had abortions, carrying his children. He hadn't felt the least shame for this, as he hadn't loved them, and had promised them nothing. With Lily, it wasn't the same. He loved her; she was his wife. And *maybe* she was also innocent.

An abortion would profoundly scar her, he realized. She was such a devout Catholic. But what other solution *was* there, after all? He refused to bring up another man's son or daughter as his own, granting him or her the same privileges as Kyra and Nick. It was unthinkable.

Maybe I could forget, he thought. Maybe I could force my mind to reject what I hear tonight, and what I saw. And then this child could be born like the others, and it would be *ours*, like the others.

A memory was nagging at him. He remembered now. He'd had a good friend, Grisha Orlov, in Moscow. A law student a few years older than himself. Grisha had been married to a beautiful woman called Katya. Misha had known them both well, and felt welcome in their home. He remembered how deeply they had loved each other.

And then, one day, the delicate fabric of harmony had come undone. Grisha had received a letter. Anonymous, the way they always were. It said: 'Your wife doesn't love you.' Just those words. And after that, everything between Grisha and Katya had fallen apart.

She'd denied the implication, laughed it off and then become hysterical in her outrage that he might have believed it. She'd been pregnant. Misha had advised his friend to believe his wife, rather than the nonsense of an anonymous letter. Katya was beautiful: any jealous man might have written this, out of wishful thinking. And Grisha had agreed.

When the child was born, Katya had believed that finally her husband had forgotten about that abominable, faceless letter, and she'd tried to plunge ahead as a wife and mother. The child had been a splendid little girl, and Grisha had seemed proud to be her father. Until the day that he had sliced her head off, and then hanged himself from the beamed ceiling of his bedroom. Katya had lost her mind, and been institutionalized, and Misha had lost touch with her completely.

No, he thought: where doubt exists, it can never be forgotten. The child had to go – for everyone's sake, even its own. Better to end its life now, before it was begun, than the way Katya's daughter had ended hers, her head severed from her body at the age of two.

He would have to ask his God to forgive him for this. But there was no other alternative. Just as, he knew, his marriage to Lily would never be the same. He didn't trust her anymore, and would always remember how she had touched Mark MacDonald's face. Like a woman in love, carrying that man's baby.

God had paid him back in spades for his fun with Varvara, and with Rirette, and with the others who had never mattered. He'd *loved* Lily, in spite of them. And she'd turned out to have held the cards to destroy him in the most vulnerable part of his being.

Lily sat in bed, the sheet cool and crisp around her breasts, feeling nothing, her eyes wide open. Dawn was rising in its rose-petal colours, washing into her room through the half-parted curtains. Absently, she pressed the fingers of one hand over her smooth, flat belly. She couldn't feel the child, and nobody could see it. And tomorrow – today! – it would be gone.

It would never see its own apricot dawn, nor feel cool sheets against its tender skin. It would never be mourned, except by her. For only she, Mark, and Misha knew that it had even been conceived. Others would simply continue to see her stomach, hard and flat, and assume . . . assume . . .

Tears welled up, which she brushed off with the silk sleeve of her nightgown. She began a formless prayer, like a moan issuing from visceral parts of her. 'Dear God, you must understand, you must forgive me! I *can't* give up my

213

children, the children whom I have already brought to life!' A terrible fear clutched at her, numbing her insides. Misha could be a person's worst enemy when he was crossed. He could be as ruthless as she had seen him being kind, to her, to his children. And she knew, beyond the shadow of a doubt, that if she didn't sacrifice this baby, he would ruin everyone's life: Kyra's, Nick's, Mark's, not to speak of hers, and, incidentally, her mother's. He would destroy them all, and in so doing, destroy himself – all because of his doubt as to the paternity of this child.

A tremendous hardness set upon her, and anger so deep that she could feel no bottom to it. Very well. She'd have the abortion. She'd become an accomplice in this mortal sin, punishable by eternal Hell according to the teachings of her catechism. But he'd have to pay, too. She would live with him henceforth in name only – for the sake of Nick and Kyra, that was all.

And in this instant of decision, Lily Brasilova realized that she was capable of hate.

Book II
The Thirties

Chapter Ten

Lily couldn't sleep. She put down *Night Flight*, by Antoine de Saint-Exupéry – a book that moved her, with superb passages. This night of 2 May 1932, she had stayed up with Misha to hear the results of the Chamber elections. They'd stayed by the radio in the study, and Misha had called the servants to come and listen too. Together they had heard the returns: out of 615 deputies, 387 had been elected, and the rest had to be settled through a second-ballot vote. And it looked as though the Chamber was once again tilting to the Left.

She listened to the silence in the house. She'd spent the afternoon playing the piano with the children, and listening to their lessons. Two autumns ago, Misha hadn't objected to putting Nicky in the Lycée Janson, a first-rate institution. But this was Kyra's first year at the Lycée des Jeunes Filles nearby. He hadn't wanted to allow her – a girl – to attend a public school; but Lily had quietly insisted that what Kyra most needed was to be with other children. She needed to learn to share, to yield – and to listen to an authority that wasn't, in the final analysis, answerable to Mama and Papa. After seven months, Lily wondered how it was all going to turn out. Kyra was still as difficult, as capricious, and as headstrong as ever.

Nicky was an extraordinary child. He was an excellent student. His marks were the highest in the form, and he had even begun to learn Russian from his father and grandfather. He was well liked, always a diplomat, always kind and considerate. If there was a boy left out by the other pupils, Nicky would make it a point to befriend him:

and because they respected Nicky, the others would soon make overtures to include the outsider. Sudarskaya found him dexterous at the piano. He was a favourite with the servants, for he never forgot to be polite. And with his parents, he was loving and obedient.

Kyra, however, had been a problem since infancy, when she had steadfastly refused to eat and to sleep. She was a spectacularly beautiful child, with her green eyes and jet-black hair – and she was aware of her impact on people when they first saw her. Misha had never spoiled Nicky; but with Kyra, he couldn't resist. She would climb on his lap and cajole him, like a little woman – and he usually acquiesced to what she wanted, even against Lily's wishes. 'You're turning her into a little princess before she can know what it means,' she had told her husband.

'That's all right; she *is* one, isn't she?' Misha had retorted with a certain cold asperity that had taken Lily by surprise.

She'd felt . . . left out. Misha and Kyra were setting up camp together, in a land that they had barricaded against her. And after that, whenever she'd related Kyra's misdemeanours to Misha, Lily had expected to be supported only on the surface. Behind her back, he would rescind the punishments that she and Zelle had set – and make retribution for her punishment by slipping her spending money or sweets.

So many things had happened that year, to mark off a period of her life – of their life. They'd spent the Russian New Year's Eve dancing at the Grand Cercle Moscovite, where, once again, she'd felt a foreigner. They'd gone to the cinema to see *Marius*. They'd gone to the Salle Gaveau to hear the Ravel festival. Nights of richness of all sorts, to remember forever. And, binding them all together, a restlessness, an empty, floating feeling, as if she'd been disconnected from the whole world, and most particularly from her intimate family. A feeling that had taken several years to build up, but that, now that both children were at school and she had extra time to analyse it, had crystallised over the past few months.

Sometimes, like now, she perceived her whole body trembling, inside and out. She could feel the quaking, and her heart beating more rapidly. She remembered that this sensation had first come upon her four years before – after the abortion. She'd thought she'd done such a fine job of putting out the fire of her revolt, of accepting that she had to make this sacrifice to preserve her marriage. She'd tried not to think at all about it. And every time that the tears would mount, that she would touch her stomach or remember planning for this new child, she'd forced herself to do something else – not to analyse the pain, not to indulge it.

He'd treated her with the cool detachment of a haughty, slightly disdainful stranger, and she'd wanted to scream out her anger and her pain, to excoriate him. Instead, she'd held her tongue. He'd gone about his business, cold, absent – and she'd started to tremble, almost all the time. She'd become involved in five charitable organizations – not to think about herself, about them.

One day, Claire had said to her: 'Mark was here last night, and asked how you were feeling. For some reason, he seemed to think you were *expecting*.'

She'd smiled. 'Oh? Maybe, the day I ran into him near the Galeries, I looked a bit bloated. But men are funny, aren't they? They believe a woman should be "heavy with child" at least every two years!'

But her heart had knocked within her, frighteningly.

She hadn't seen him since that afternoon – and she hadn't spoken to her mother about any of it. Claire had gone to the South of France and quietly married Jacques Walter. They lived together in his suite at the Ritz, went to the theatre, travelled to the waters during the summer. Lily had scrutinized Jacques, at the beginning; he was such a kind, Old World gentleman, no different from any other refined, well-to-do retired businessman. She felt close to him – and glad for Claire. But, at the same time, he was part of the reason Misha had forced her to have the abortion, and she could never forgive him – nor her mother. If she hadn't been discussing Claire and Jacques with Mark, that day in '28 . . . She had paid for everything, from Claire's lies to her present marriage. Misha had never spoken one word to her about the abortion, nor about Mark; but she felt that this was his silent recognition that they'd struck a bargain: his pretence that nothing was changed, against her having the child taken care of. She'd been Job, proving her devotion beyond the point of human expectation – or perhaps Patient Griselda, loving in spite of perfidious treachery.

That first week, as soon as she'd been well, she'd gone to church. She'd kneeled on her side of the confessional, and murmured: 'Father, I have come here to obtain absolution. I have just committed a terrible crime.'

'How long has it been since your last confession?'

'Ten days.'

'Tell me how you have sinned, my child.'

The tears welling up, beginning to stream through the fingers she held as a shield before her eyes, she'd whispered: 'I . . . allowed my baby to be taken from me.'

'How did you do that?'

'I . . .' Overcome by anguish and shame, she'd tried to get the words out, knowing that God would not turn His back on her, and that, at last, she would find peace. 'Father, I let my husband take me to a woman – '

'You are married, then, my child?'

'Yes, Father. I let the woman . . . take the child.'

Confusion behind the grillwork. 'But – how?'

'With a knife, Father. She took the child from inside me.'

She hadn't expected the total silence, nor, when it broke,

the cold wrath in the priest's words. 'You have committed a mortal sin for which there is no absolution.'

'But Father – our Saviour, Jesus Christ, forgave all the sinners.'

'The Catholic Church excommunicates those who have sinned as you have.'

'But *I was not responsible!*'

'God granted man free choice, that he might know right from wrong. I cannot give you absolution for what you have done.'

She'd stumbled out of the confessional, blinded by tears, choked by sobs. Now, four years later, she recalled it all so vividly. Her last time in church. After that, she'd stayed away, the words *excommunicated* and *mortal sin* reverberating hollowly in her consciousness.

She'd tried to kneel and pray, time and again, but the words hadn't come, had stayed in her throat, stifling her. She'd felt cold, alone. God had rejected her. It was something she never, in her life, could have imagined possible. Her kind, loving God, the Father, had shut her out. Her Church had excommunicated her, banished her forever.

Tonight, she refused to think about it again, slamming the book down on the bedside table – trembling again. She thought, wildly, that if she could just have spoken to Wolf, he might have explained to her what had happened inside her, to make her feel this way. When God had shut her out – when the Church had refused her – she'd grown cold inside.

She turned out the light, lay in bed, listening to night sounds outside. Cars, on the street. People *feeling*, loving, hurting. And she? Tears pushed against the back of her eyes, and she swallowed them down, the way she always did.

Something had stopped inside her heart; a clock had stopped ticking. She lay on the smooth sheets like a starving person, dying from lack of food. Only she was well fed, in all aspects but one. Her soul was being starved. God had withheld absolution and turned her out into the street – like the worst of Dante's sinners, consigned to the Ninth Circle of Hell.

How was it possible, then, that life was continuing all around her, that people were living and dying, that they laughed with all their heart, that they could weep?

'Something is wrong here,' Misha declared. He passed a sheaf of papers to his father, and scratched his chin. 'I have a sick feeling in my stomach.'

'But these estimates ring fair,' Prince Ivan countered.

'I have to go to the Aisne Department and see for myself. Verlon says the materials are defective.'

'How is this possible?'

Misha filled his lungs with air, then let it out. His green eyes fastened on his father. 'When we first examined the plans and layouts for the new sugar refinery, I consulted the rules register, and found out that we would have to go to Germany again to get building materials. This seemed simple enough. I spoke to Claude, and he made the trip. When he returned with the estimates, he told me that he had found a new supplier – a small firm called Rabinovitch and Son. German Jews. He showed me the prices they wanted for bricks, for the ironwork frame, the wood, and the window-panes – and they concorded with those of first-quality materials. And now – our manager, Verlon, has cabled me that the materials that have arrived appear less than adequate.'

Prince Ivan fingered his Vandyke beard, and sat down opposite his son, who remained standing, a brooding giant behind his desk. 'Have you spoken to Claude?' he asked.

Misha shook his head. 'I wanted to speak with you first.'

'How did Claude find these people?'

'He has connections. I've never interfered with his area

of expertise – after all, you and I aren't contractors. But Rabinovitch was paid *before* delivery.'

'How did you permit this?'

'It was in the contract. Claude explained to me that they're a very small firm, and need to have their expenses fully covered. He said the old man was afraid of Hitler – that he might take power away from Hindenburg, and squeeze the Jews out.'

'But Hindenburg's just proved his strength last month: he won with nineteen million votes, and Hitler had only thirteen.'

'I don't really care about the German problem,' Misha cut in impatiently. 'But I have to verify what exactly's taken place in the Aisne. And I'm going to take Claude with me. We're dependent on quick construction of the refinery, or we won't be ready on time for the plantation – and then we'll lose all our revenues from the harvest.'

'And it seems to me that we're already late. There's no way to recuperate this time. How much do we stand to lose if we don't have a harvest?'

Misha said, his face dead white: 'Millions of francs.' He sat down at the desk and ran his fingers abstractedly through his hair. Then he picked up the telephone, and dialled a number.

'Lily?' he said. 'Pack a bag for me, please. I have to leave tonight for one of our building sites.'

Henri Verlon, the future manager of the refinery in progress, was close to sixty, tall, slender, distinguished – a fine man, Misha and Prince Ivan had always thought. This was to be his last post before retirement. Prince Ivan had set aside for him the manager's house, surrounded by a small garden, which came free of rent; and he had promised him a monthly pension for the remainder of his life, so that he might retire in peace after a few years. He had declared himself extremely grateful; he loved the country; he would cultivate his garden and live out his last years in security.

But now he hardly looked distinguished and at peace. His grey hair looked dishevelled, and his tie was loose below his Adam's apple. The terrain around the hastily put together office structure was loaded with bricks, metal frames, and glass. He waved at the tall heaps of materials, shaking his head; his blue eyes were rimmed with red. 'It's all below par,' he murmured. 'Every last brick.'

Misha stared across the yards of construction in progress, to the vast fields that seemed to stretch to the horizon – green, the grass blowing in the light breeze, and totally uncultivated. He could feel the blood stretching his arteries, and the perspiration pouring from his armpits. His stomach felt queasy. He turned to Claude, and asked: 'Is Verlon correct, in your opinion?'

His brother-in-law was standing beside him, almost rigid in his pearl grey suit and neat, shining spats. An incongruously urban figure among country dust and rubble. He nodded. 'I can't understand it,' he stated. 'What I saw in Germany – what Rabinovitch sold me on the books – wasn't this at all.'

'Then you'll simply have to return to Germany, and confront the Rabinovitches, father and son. I'll send one of the firm's lawyers with you. I don't see how we'll make the harvest on time – and I want to sue the bastards for compensation.'

Claude uttered a short, mirthless bark of laughter. 'Like the reparations France is still waiting for? You'll see, it won't work. The Germans have become very smart – especially the Jews. They're fighting for survival.'

Misha's eyes narrowed, and he said, quietly: 'Brasilov Enterprises is fighting for survival, too. We're hanging on by a shoestring; each operation is dependent on the successful completion of the one before it. If one fails, all the operations will come crashing down over our heads, like a house of dominoes.'

'That's ridiculous,' Claude answered. 'We're the most successful firm in town.'

Henry Verlon stood staring at the two of them, and the breeze lifted a few strands of his grey hair, like the comb of a madman. In the growing dusk, he looked like a very old man.

Lily hesitated in front of the closed panel of oak, behind which she could hear somebody existing, working, getting up and walking in the room. She'd left the children at home after school, and had come here by bus, feeling like a guilty child doing something behind her parents' back. But the need that impelled her was so strong, that she felt drawn as by a magnet to the office beyond the door.

She raised her gloved hand, knocked – her heart beating very fast. A man's voice said: 'Come in. Who is it?' Lily turned the knob and found herself face to face with Grand Rabbi Julien Weill, spectacles on his nose, writing on long sheets of paper at his desk. She felt herself blush. 'Rabbi – '

'Liliane Brasilova – Claire's daughter,' he said, in his measured, educated voice. 'Please – sit down.'

She sat. The small hat with its discreet feather felt tight over her pinned-up hair, and her shoes felt small. She was aware of her own awkwardness, of her height, of the way her hands were folded over her bag, as if clutching it for support. He smiled at her. He looked tired, drained. 'We were reintroduced at Diane de Rothschild's wedding, last Wednesday. Although I'd have remembered you from Marisa's wedding, seven years ago. You're a striking young woman. How old are you now, may I ask?'

From anyone else, this would have seemed the epitome of rudeness. But she felt that he was reacting sympathetically, wanting to know his old friend's child. 'I'm twenty-seven,' she answered.

'Claire and I have been friends for thirty-five years. She's a good woman: and an unusually strong one. She reminds me of those women in the Old Testament – Ruth, Esther – who were the mainstays of their families. I suppose you know that we go back a long way – or you wouldn't be here, would you?'

She smiled. She remembered looking at him curiously, at the Rothschild wedding. Hanging onto Misha's arm, but scouring the rooms for signs of Rabbi Weill. Odd how she'd been saving him for a last hope – as a last resort. Somehow she'd felt that he alone might understand – that he alone wouldn't judge her. He hadn't judged the mother – he wouldn't judge the daughter.

Diane de Rothschild came from one of the most important families in Paris. Her father, Robert, knew Misha; they had had some connections through the Bank of France. Unlike Marisa's wedding, this event had been a business necessity to attend, to see and be seen by *le tout-Paris*. Her mother had come, with Jacques, and Lily had tried to spend as little time with them as possible, sensing the danger of being in the same room with people who were sure to know that Jacques – Jacob, as Claire called him when Misha and Claude weren't there – was Jewish.

Diane had married Anatole Muhlstein, the gifts had been displayed on five enormous counters, the jewels in a glass-panelled showcase: a diamond pendant, a crescent of rubies, a pearl necklace, a river of diamonds and a necklace of three emeralds. Lily had examined the gems as if she'd been in a museum, and remembered when she'd asked Misha if they were rich enough 'never to feel anything'. She understood now the difference between the inexhaustible fortune of the Rothschilds, and the small, new French wealth of her husband and father-in-law.

It was then that she'd made up her mind to come and see Rabbi Weill – as she knew that her mother had, some thirty-three years ago, when she'd found out she was pregnant. Now she said, softly: 'I came here because of my trouble. I hope that you can hear me out. I know my mother's story – she told me everything, several years ago – before she married Jacques Walter. I know how much you helped her.'

'It was difficult to be of real help,' he said.

'When my mother told me, I was angry. I felt that she'd kept the truth from me, and betrayed my love. And also – I was angry because I was married to a man who . . . well . . . isn't particularly fond of the Jews. I was afraid he'd find out.'

'And would that be so terrible, Liliane?'

She leaned forward, her dark eyes wide with passion – fear? anger? he wasn't quite sure – and said: 'He's a terrible man! Rabbi Weill . . . you probably think I'm overdramatizing. But, oh, God – four years ago, he did something dreadful, for which I've never been able to forgive him! I was pregnant, and hadn't told him yet. A friend of mine, a man, was visiting me, and . . . well, the conversation between us was actually quite innocent, we were discussing my mother and Jacques . . . but Misha overheard some words that made him believe that this man and I had been having an affair. And so he took me to a woman . . . an *abortionist* . . . to force me to end my pregnancy. He was sure that I'd betrayed him and that my friend was really the father.'

Rabbi Weill removed his spectacles, and carefully wiped the lenses with his handkerchief. Then he looked at her. 'And? What did you do?'

She didn't look away, but whispered, with an emotion that seemed to reverberate through the room, like a sound: 'I went ahead with it.' And she sat back, waiting.

He slipped the glasses back over his ears and nose, and folded his hands together over the blotter on his desk. Still the dark eyes were on him, measuring him, testing the ground. He said: 'How did you feel, Liliane?'

'How do you suppose I felt, Rabbi? I had committed what, in my religion, was a cardinal sin. I'd done something which I condemned with all my heart – against which I rebelled with all my soul. Yet I'd let him do it, because – because I was afraid I'd lose my other children.'

'You're not saying that you did it because you loved him.'

She said, hotly: '*Loved* him? Rabbi Weill – at that moment I hated Mikhail Brasilov. I wanted *him* dead – not the baby.'

Again the eyes were glued to him. He smiled a little. 'You are expecting me to be shocked. I'm not. Life – and the actions of human beings – no longer shock me, my dear. Your husband behaved the way children do when they are at their most cruel – and yet, I suppose he did it as a soul in pain. Afterwards – what happened?'

He examined the upturned face, its skin white with tension, tension lines also around her lips and eyes. 'Afterwards, I felt as though I'd lost my life. I was a devout Catholic until that moment – but the priest refused me absolution. I have no church anymore. My husband killed the child inside me, and took away my salvation. Now I just live out the days. And he? He's continued as if nothing had ever happened. We've never discussed any part of it.'

Rabbi Weill cleared his throat. 'Well,' he stated. 'That's quite a story. You're Claire's daughter, all right. But if you have come here, it's for a reason. Tell me, Liliane, why you have confided in *me*, a relative stranger.'

She said, her voice shaking a little: 'I told you, I am no longer a Catholic. Not because I renounced my faith, but because my church no longer wanted *me*. But you see, Rabbi – I need faith. I need a religion. And I could never return to Catholicism. I came to confess, with my heart full; and the priest condemned me, without trying to hear my side of the story – without even asking if there was one.

I am so alone, without spiritual guidance; I can't survive like this, in this dry desert, with no God to pray to.'

'And so you thought that you would find out about your mother's religion.'

She nodded. 'Mama is so full of love for the Jewish faith. Yet, I know almost nothing about it. After she told me her story, I began to feel a connection with other Jews – but in my heart, in my worship, I remained a Catholic. Now, because of what happened, I want to know more about this religion. My grandparents were Jews – all my mother's family. I remember my grandpa: he was one of the kindest, gentlest men I ever met. Like an older, much older version of Wolf Steiner.'

'Don't make a grave mistake, Liliane. Judaism is a creed – a way of worship. It doesn't make people good, or bad. That's up to them.'

'The confessor told me the same thing. That God gave us free choice. But why is it that *you*'ve listened to me – that *you* haven't thrown me out? You're a better man, Rabbi. Maybe the Jewish religion allows people to be more human . . . less perfect.'

'I would say that this depends on the particular rabbi whom you are addressing. I've known intransigent rabbis who go entirely by the book – like some of the Catholic fathers. I've always believed that you have to see the wonder in every human being – in every one of God's creatures. I'm far from perfect, and I can't expect anybody else to be, either. But I love my God, and I love my religion. If you want, Liliane, you can come here every Thursday afternoon, and I shall try to teach you something about Judaism. Then, when you know enough, you'll be free to choose for yourself.'

His face was now lined with a beautiful, open smile. 'The Jews are not evangelists,' he said. 'We are even against the conversion of those of other faiths. We simply try to hang on to our own.'

'But in a sense, I *am* one of those,' she murmured.

He nodded, slowly. 'I suppose you are. In the Jewish religion, it's the mother's faith that counts. Claire was Jewish – and so you are, too – and your children. Even if they don't know it.'

She stood up, went across the room to shake his hand. He pressed hers between both of his. 'Don't be afraid,' he said softly.

'But Rabbi – you mustn't tell anyone.'

He patted her gloved hand. 'I know. After a while, when you know something about us, you may feel that you no longer wish to live in hiding. For Claire, this was the hardest thing in the world, and now, with Jacob, she feels a sense of release that's made her younger and much happier.'

In the street, a wind had started, lifting Lily's veil above her head. She looked around her, as if to check for familiar presences in the shadows. Nobody stopped her. She walked to the bus stop, suddenly free, suddenly happy. Somehow, she knew she had made a step in the right direction. Whichever way it turned out for her, this was the first time in four years she'd had the courage to speak, to unburden herself.

She let herself into the house, checking the time to make sure Misha hadn't yet come home. And then she remembered: he was in the Aisne, because of some problem. She was alone with her children, with the servants. Taking off her suit in her boudoir, she thought about the Lindbergh child, gone about nine weeks, and tried to imagine the anguish of his parents. If anybody ever tried to kidnap Kyra, or her beloved Nicky – she couldn't pursue the thought. But she realized that, in spite of everything, those two live children still bound her to Misha – that neither one of them would ever be willing to relinquish them.

For the first time in months – in years – her body wasn't quietly trembling, and her heart was beating normally. It

230

all had to do with Misha, then – with her feelings. She'd opened the door to Rabbi Weill, and told him about the anger and the hatred. She thought: I hate my husband. For four years, I've been living with a man I hate.

She slipped into a gown of soft satin, the edges trimmed with Brussels lace. She thought then of her grandfather, of the Rumanian grandmother she'd never known. All the women in our family have led tragic lives, she thought with consternation. One can't escape one's destiny. And she wondered about Kyra's future. Kyra, whom she'd always considered more Misha's child than hers. But she'd been wrong. This line of women was going to be carried on by Kyra, not by Nick. It would be she who, one day, would bring a new child into the tradition brought over to Western Europe by the young Rumanian girl who had married her grandfather.

She picked up the silver frame on the dressing-table and stared with strange detachment at the photograph of Prince Mikhail Ivanovitch Brasilov. Those arrogant eyes that thought they had all the answers – that cleft chin, which she'd thought vulnerable, but which, really, was just another point of vanity to him. She said, aloud, without passion: 'I hate you. But I'm not going to leave you. Because my children need me – and they need my mother, and Jacques. We don't think we're perfect, like the Brasilovs. But we know how to love, and how to express our love. I'll stay with you because I have to, because I don't know what else to do. But from now on, I'll never forget that you are the stranger – the outsider Wolf and my mother told me about. And I'll never let you touch my heart again, or betray my soul.'

Misha returned the night of the day that President Paul Doumer was murdered. In late afternoon, Lily opened the door to Sudarskaya, whose face was alive with an incredible excitement, and as the round little music teacher took off her jacket, she exclaimed: 'They've shot the President!'

Arkhippe, who had taken her coat, moved closer, disbelief on his features. 'It can't be true,' Lily said.

'But I swear it *is!* In the bus they said it was a Russian. They've lynched him.'

Nicky was running out into the hall, his hair still wet from his bath, his sister on his tail in her bathrobe. 'Mama! What happened?'

'You children stay quiet, and Arkhippe will go to the corner stand and bring us back a newspaper. Now, Raïssa Markovna is here to give you your piano lessons.'

Lily clasped the little woman's arm, and pressed it. Nicky had already turned around, in the direction of the living room, but Kyra, her eyes wide, had stayed at her side. Lily whispered: 'Raïssa Markovna, for God's sake, pull yourself together.'

But she realized that she, too, was shaking. Moments later, Arkhippe came back, holding a newspaper out to her: 'Madame Sudarskaya was right, Madame la Princesse. It was at the veterans' book sale. There were three, or four, or maybe five shots.'

'Is he dead?' she asked, feeling her voice quivering.

'Not yet, madame.'

Kyra pressed close to her. 'Mama, what happens when a President of the Republic dies?'

'The Chamber has to elect a new one. But we have to pray that President Doumer survives, darling.'

'Was he a good man?'

She looked up briefly to see Sudarskaya and her son, both seated on the piano bench, staring at her, their hands inert. Feeling ridiculous, she answered: 'I really don't know. I didn't know much about him. I'm sure he was a kind man, who loved his family. He was only our President for a year – and I don't always understand much about

232

politics. He was a man of the Right – like your Papa. He didn't deserve to be hurt.'

'I want Papa to come home,' Kyra said, beginning to cry.

Lily put an arm around her daughter, and sighed. 'Raïssa Markovna, it's useless to try to work today. Children – go to Zelle. You'll have your supper, and then you can come out to be with us a while. Raïssa Markovna – you'll stay and eat with me?'

There was a scramble as Nicky descended from the bench, and Sudarskaya waddled over, her cheeks red. The little boy took his sister's hand, started to pull her towards the hallway, but she resisted. 'I don't want to go to Zelle. I want to stay right here with Mama.'

Lily pressed a handkerchief over her eyes, and went to sit down in the study. The little group followed her. She didn't resist. The children sat beside her, huddling close to the warmth of her body. Sudarskaya said, in her wailing tone: 'What's the world coming to? Now the French will hate the Russians even more than before. We need them to protect us from the German menace. And what will this do to the Jews?'

Lily asked: 'What do you mean?'

'I'm speaking about that man Hitler, in Germany. He gained two million votes in the last election.'

'But he still lost to Hindenburg.'

'Fine difference,' Sudarskaya scoffed. 'A war criminal and a Nazi.'

'But the German chancellor just dissolved Hitler's private armies.'

'That was a risky thing to do. At the temple, they were speaking about Hitler, and about what he stands for – this super-race idea.'

'And you understood it?' Lily questioned gently.

The little music teacher shook her head. 'No. But I was afraid. There's no place anywhere for the Jews. That's one thing I do understand, Lily. In Russia, we were restricted to the Pale of Settlement, and we weren't granted citizenship. In Germany, there's an Austrian man who wants to get us out. And here – every day, there's a new article coming out with talk that links us with the Communists. We can't win for losing.'

'What's a Jew?' Kyra asked.

'A poor lost soul whom nobody wants,' Sudarskaya replied ironically. 'And you're lucky, my little girl, that your parents are Christian. That way, you'll never be hurt.'

'It sounds unfair,' Nicky said. 'At the lycée, there's a Jewish boy called Maurice. He's nice. We play together sometimes.'

'That's 'cause you *always* choose to go with kids nobody likes,' Kyra taunted him.

'But it's not true. Everybody likes Maurice.'

'And everybody likes my friend Marisa, and her husband. Raïssa Markovna was just teasing you right now. The Jews, Kyra, were some of the first people to believe in God. They wrote the Old Testament. Jesus Christ was a Jew.'

'And God knows, nobody liked *him*,' Sudarskaya cut in.

Lily said, to change the subject: 'My brother's in Germany right now. Misha sent him there for some business reason. Somehow, with those National Socialists, I'd prefer to have him home.'

'See? You don't like the Nazis any more than I do,' Sudarskaya declared. 'But you have no reason to be afraid. Your brother's not a Jew.'

Lily closed her eyes for a moment, and a mental image of Claude pressed across the inside of her eyelids. Claude, with his matt skin, and his dark eyes, and his aquiline nose. She thought, remembering Julien Weill's nose, and Wolf Steiner's father's skin colour: Claude is a Jew – one hundred per cent a Jew. And she wondered then if this

234

showed on his face, too. If so, had anyone else noticed it? And if they had . . . there was Nicky's face, too, so much like hers, so much like Claire's. Dark, Jewish faces, all of them.

'The whole world's a mess,' Sudarskaya sighed. 'If I could choose to be somewhere, I don't know where that would be.'

Hours later, with the children in bed, Lily and Sudarskaya stayed together in the study, listening to the radio. And when Misha came home, surprising them, Lily rushed to him without thinking, letting his arms go around her to protect her. He greeted Sudarskaya with unexpected warmth. 'I'm glad Lily wasn't alone,' he told her. 'Thank you for staying.'

After François had driven Sudarskaya home, Lily asked him about his trip, and for the first time noticed how exhausted he looked, how peaked and drained. He took her hand, stroked it absently. 'Things are very bad,' he murmured. 'Everywhere around me, the economy is collapsing. All the good that Poincaré accomplished seems to have been washed away. We're entering the slump that America and Great Britain felt before us.'

'And Brasilov Enterprises?'

He looked away. 'Somehow,' he said, 'we'll have to pull through. We've done it before, Lily. One missed harvest can't mean the end of the world.'

She sat watching him. Part of her wanted to be sympathetic, but she could feel a glass panel between herself and him, between what she vaguely felt she should do – open her arms to him, offer him comfort – and what, in effect, she felt capable of doing: absolutely nothing. She watched him suffer, and a sudden, vengeful flare came into her heart: suffer, Misha Brasilov, for your unimportant little Enterprises! What was this suffering worth, compared to her own sense of loss? He was speaking to her about a business, and she had lost a child, a living, human child!

And yet, when the flare died down, she did feel compelled to hold out her hand, in a halfhearted gesture of compassion. 'It's late,' she said. 'We should both go to sleep.'

The next day, Saturday 7 May, they learned that Paul Doumer had died at two forty in the morning, and that the man who had shot him was a Russian called Gorguloff. The authorities were certain that he was carrying false papers. He claimed to be from the Kuban River area, and had been a doctor in Prague, where he had been considered unbalanced. In France, he had been denied a residence permit, and had been living in Monaco since the previous autumn. Few people knew him, and his reputation was bad.

On 9 May Lily organized the children's piano practice, and went out in a glacial windstorm at three thirty, to see the President's body exposed in a coffin at the Élysée Palace. The crowd was thick, beginning at the Faubourg Saint-Honoré, extending along Rue de l'Élysée to the Avenue Gabriel Rue Boissy-d'Anglas. She left the car, and tried to forge her way through, but backs and hats blocked the view. And so she turned back, and had François drive her to the offices of Brasilov Enterprises. Misha was out, but her father-in-law, looking very gaunt, slipped on his overcoat and took her for tea at the Thé de la Madeleine. They tried to speak of the children, of women's fashions, of Claire and Jacques. But after half an hour, they both fell silent, looking at their hands.

On Tuesday 10 May, the Chamber at Versailles elected Albert Lebrun the new President of the Republic, and Lily met Misha for a quick dinner at the Restaurant Mozart. His face was drawn, and she could see he'd hardly slept. They held hands over the tablecloth, and he said: 'Hundreds of thousands of francs, Lily. The bastards have made off with hundreds of thousands of Brasilov francs. Not to speak of the harvest that will never be, and the millions lost there.'

'Who made off with this money, Misha?' She'd never heard him speak like this before, with such total discouragement. And it was the first time, too, that he had allowed himself to discuss his business with her.

'The Rabinovitches of Munich. Claude went to get the money back – they'd sold us first-quality materials, for the building of our refinery in the Aisne, and the things that arrived were all defective. But of course they'd left town, without a trace.'

She took this all in, feeling totally numb, and suddenly afraid. Hundreds of thousands of francs . . . millions. Sums that boggled the mind. Lost. 'You can't do anything?' she asked.

He stared at her, his eyes bloodshot, and made a fist that he banged upon the table. 'Goddamned kikes,' he whispered. 'They deserve everything that's in store for them!'

She blinked, growing cold. In a small voice, she asked: 'What's in store for them?'

But he had closed his eyes, and was pressing his fingers to his temples in a desperate gesture that moved her deep inside. He was a man, he was her husband, whom she'd married in love. She'd thought, many times, about how to manage without him – about how to leave him and take the children with her, escaping from the hypocrisy of their life together. But that night, at the Restaurant Mozart, she could only think of how lucky she was not to be Madame Paul Doumer, whose husband lay in a coffin. She whispered, urgently: 'It's going to be all right. We'll survive, somehow. Don't worry so much.'

And when he raised his eyes to her face, she forced herself to smile.

Chapter Eleven

Claude's apartment in the Avenue Kléber was spartanly furnished, to contrast with his father's lavishness in the Villa Persane. He had purchased the furniture at the Samaritaine, at a bargain; and the only point of fantasy were three prints of Henriette posing in Poiret gowns. The drapery was dark, the furniture of dark polished woods. Now he sat in the study with the papers in front of him, fingering the stem of his brandy glass.

It wasn't possible. All along, he hadn't wanted to believe Marguery. It was strange, but the little ferret-like man in his black suits had always represented, for Claude, a necessary evil. He was a small weasel whom Claude heartily disliked; but on the other hand, he was the best investigator in Paris. He brought bad news, but he was always right. And for that reason alone, it was difficult to like him.

Claude swallowed some brandy. He recalled vividly, with a painful, embarrassing sense of shame, the time, four years ago, when Marguery had finally brought him the dossier on Jacques Walter of Basel. It hadn't been easy, for the Swiss were a discreet, often secretive people, especially protective of their own. But Marguery had bribed and finagled his way to the necessary information.

Claude, overcome with dismay and a deep horror, had told Henriette about it over drinks at her flat. 'My mother's marrying a wealthy old Jew from Basel, and there's nothing I can do to stop her. Can you imagine? A *Jew!*'

Henriette had straddled him and fluffed his hair, like an

urchin. 'Come on . . . That's not so bad. What's wrong with the Jews, anyway? I like everybody.'

He'd become rigid and pushed her away. 'Don't be a smartass.'

She'd stepped down, and stood facing him, hands on her hips. 'No goddamned little prick is going to tell *me* what's wrong with me.' And then, narrowing her amber eyes, she'd tossed out: 'Why do you hate them, anyway? They haven't done anything to hurt you!'

He'd felt his cheeks turn crimson, and had faced her, his nostrils dilated. 'I hate them, that's all. They're . . . different. No country's ever liked them, and that's why they've always had to live on the outskirts. They chant their weird prayers like fanatics, with those funny caps on their heads, and their backs bent – it's disgusting!'

She'd started to laugh. 'Robert de Rothschild smells bad?'

Claude had stood up, shaking. 'Maybe not to you. But there's something unclean about all of them – the rich ones included. They rose from the gutters: all of them. They have the souls of slaves, because that's what they came from: slaves!'

Then she'd seen that he was really agitated, that the news about Walter had really shaken him, and she'd abandoned her angry pose and come to him, conciliatory. She'd been good to him. He'd felt relieved that he had spoken – and she'd respected his secret and never brought it up again. He'd trusted her. But, once again, Marguery had done his job well.

He scrutinized the papers, the photographs. Henriette – *his* woman, his only woman – with Misha. Walking in a small side street. Entering her apartment. Meeting elsewhere, in a Russian cabaret. For how long had it been going on this time? And what was he to do about it now?

He stood up, pulled on his jacket, went to the front closet and took out his overcoat. He must talk to her.

It was raining outside. The Renault wended its way to Clichy, then up the steep, curving streets of Montmartre. He parked the car.

He knocked on her door, hearing the gramophone blaring – a Negro jazz blues, heartrending in its melancholy. She opened, in her slip, her breasts naked underneath the filmy fabric. She stepped back, surprised. 'I didn't know that you were coming.'

'May I come in? Or are you expecting someone?'

She inclined her head, and he passed through. The apartment smelled of cloying incense, and a blue haze permeated the room. She was looking somewhat dishevelled and a little haggard. A half-empty plate lay on the dining room table, and an empty glass. He sat down on the comfortable sofa. 'I had to see you,' he said.

'That's nice.'

'I had to ask you just one question. *Why* Misha Brasilov? Why?'

She stepped back, her lips parting. He nodded, coldly. 'I know. You'd better tell me.'

'And what business is it of yours? I'm not your wife.'

Again, her familiar bad-girl stance, arrogant and aggressive. To cover up her own defencelessness. He felt a pang of pity, brushed it away. 'But you're my girl. Aren't you?'

She cocked her head, examined him. '*Am* I?'

'I thought you were. We had something very nice, Henriette. Didn't we? Don't we?'

She made a face. 'Look, Claude. Look at me. I'm no kid. I'm thirty-eight. That's almost middle-aged. In a few years Monsieur Poiret will kick me out, without thinking back, and that will be the end of that. Have you ever thought about that?'

He breathed in quickly. 'What is it you're trying to say?'

'That I've spent my life going from man to man, from cabaret to cabaret – and for what purpose? I don't have anything to show for it. Not like your sister, that *grande*

240

dame. She has two children! And money. Me? I have this small rundown flat, and a few nice dresses.'

'You want to get married?' he asked.

'You want to marry me? Claude, you're thirty-two! It doesn't make sense! Why?'

'Why not? If you want a child so much. I'd no idea.'

'You'd no idea of anything. I didn't want to marry you. You're a nice guy. But too French, too middle-class – too much like my father, in Meaux. You're a good guy to spend time with, to feel good with.'

'And isn't that enough between a man and a woman? You think my sister has more, with Misha Brasilov? He cheats on her, he keeps her his prisoner, he imposes his will in every matter: you think that's a dream life?'

She had very dilated pupils, and her face was pale. He glanced at the dining room table and saw the small pipe, looked again through the blue haze, and realized she'd been smoking. With him she never brought out the opium, knowing it would shock him and push him away. He felt small sensations of shock, right now. She was really very different. Maybe she was right – they didn't belong together. He'd always known it, deep inside. That was why he'd never proposed.

'Claude, I think Misha's a man in a million! He's a bastard. He lies and he cheats and he's a monster. But there's something about him – I can't explain. And anyway – it's too late. I'm pregnant.'

She was staring at him, almost taunting him. He felt the shock spreading, held on to the arm of the sofa. 'How do you know it's Misha's?' he whispered.

'Because I planned it. Otherwise, you'd better believe I'd have had this fixed. It wouldn't have been my first time.'

'You want to be pregnant by a man who's married?'

She sighed. 'I've waited for a long time, Claude. I don't intend to spend the rest of my life always looking back.'

'But he'd never divorce Lily!'

'Don't be so sure. Maybe it's Lily who will divorce *him!*'

Claude stood up, unable to answer. For a moment, he hesitated, struggling within himself. Then, abruptly, he picked up his coat, her eyes glued to him as he left the apartment.

Maybe she'd made a horrible mistake, but one had to gamble. Henriette shrugged, and went to curl up on the sofa. Outside, the raindrops continued to fall on the pavement, and she listened to their soothing rhythm.

On Tuesday 17 May, Lily rose early to have breakfast with the children and hear Nicky's lessons before he went off to school. While she was dressing, Madeleine knocked on her door and told her that a gentleman was here to see her. She quickly finished her toilette and went to receive him in the drawing room. He was young, well dressed, educated. He said to her, after he had introduced himself and she'd invited him to sit down: 'I've come about the Rolls-Royce, Madame la Princesse.'

She shook her head, smiling. 'I'm afraid I don't understand.'

He looked somewhat embarrassed, and stroked his trim beard. 'About . . . the keys. I've come to pick up the keys and take possession of the car.'

She felt a wave of blood rising to her face. 'Monsieur Brunville, why would you want the keys to my car? Is something wrong?'

He tried to smile, bit his lip thoughtfully, then plunged in. 'I'm sorry, madame. I had supposed your husband would have told you – Prince Brasilov sold me the car, three days ago. The paperwork was finished yesterday. Would you like to see it?'

A pulse was beating in her throat. Her voice trembling only slightly, she forced herself to look at this man and smile. 'You'll have to excuse me, monsieur,' she said. 'But

242

I know very little about business. These papers might mean nothing to me. I'd prefer to wait until my husband comes home for lunch. I'm sure he'll clear up this situation. Perhaps you could return . . . this evening?'

'Of course, madame. I'd be glad to.'

Stunned, she watched him leave. She couldn't believe what had just passed between them, and a premonitory chill passed through her, frightening her.

Later, around one o'clock, she heard Misha returning from the office. She waited for him in the bedroom, but he didn't come there. She found him in the study, nervously pacing, and when she closed the door, she finally faced him, forcing him to look at her directly.

'Brunville came here this morning?' he asked.

'Yes. And of course I wasn't expecting him. You *sold* my car?'

'I'm sorry, Lily – truly sorry.'

'It doesn't matter about the car,' she said. 'What matters is why you couldn't tell me, before.'

He wet his upper lip, compressed both lips together, stared at his finely manicured fingernails. 'Lily – the business isn't going well. I had no choice but to sell the Rolls. And . . . we're going to have to let the maïds go, and keep only Arkhippe, Madeleine, and Annette. There's no real need for François anymore. I'll tell him that of course he'll continue to live here, and that we'll help him to find work. And . . . we'll have to let Zelle go. The children are both in school now, and you, or Madeleine, can bring them to school and pick them up.'

She whispered: 'I don't mind. I can manage very well on a far more modest scale. But – if things aren't going well – you should have told me.'

'I'm sorry. Papa and I are on the lookout for new business ventures. It's this damned sugar harvest we missed . . . and all the money we lost in building materials. Now I've started to do some consulting work, putting firms together for deals, and advising bankrupt firms how to get back on their feet. The commissions on those will be large, and will help Brasilov Enterprises. I don't want you to worry.'

When he returned to the office, she went to her wardrobe and examined the rods laden with shimmering gowns, the shoe bags with dozens of brand-new shoes, some not even worn. She'd lived like a queen, without asking how, without asking if she deserved it – if it was right. She was twenty-seven, married eight years – and yet he'd treated her like a child, pretending everything was perfect in the magic kingdom, when in reality the magic potion that had kept the kingdom going had stopped working. Whose fault was it, then? Hers, for being spoiled? Or his, for making it seem as if by being spoiled, she was fulfilling his dream as well as her own?

She thought of separating the children from Zelle, who had become part of the family – and felt an ache inside. And François. He'd been her mainstay for so many years. All the day trips they'd taken together. How she'd loved her car . . .

It wasn't going to be easy, but she hadn't expected luxury, ever, even from her father. She'd been happier in Bougival than in that mausoleum in Boulogne. It was going to be much, much harder on Misha. He'd come to think that his world was lined with silver and gold, and paved with precious stones – that this was his destiny. Yet he'd made it work, when he'd come to Paris as a refugee. He, and Ivan Vassilievitch – the maker of empires, the founder of dynasties. For if Misha was the perfect administrator, it was the old man who possessed the genius of making businesses spring from ideas, and industries from businesses.

Lily shut the door of her wardrobe, and went out to tell Zelle that she would have to start looking for another job –

that she would have to leave the children she had come to love as if they'd been her own.

One morning, after the children had left for school, she sat at the piano, studying a piece by Stravinsky.

Arkhippe appeared. 'There is a lady to see Madame la Princesse.'

Lily asked, her hands poised over the keys: 'Someone I know?'

Arkhippe shook his head. Their eyes met, perplexed. These days, everything was moving so fast – and so many changes had occurred. Lily stood up, wondering if this was another messenger of bad news.

Arkhippe returned with someone whom Lily recognized at once. It was the slim, athletic model from Poiret's. She was dressed in a thin sheath of raw silk, and wore beads knotted below her breastbone. Her makeup was pronounced, and stark: crimson lips, kohl-rimmed eyes, cheekbones outlined with red blush over white powder. Lily felt a wave of revulsion. There was something so cold and shocking about this person – she couldn't really explain it. She looked to Lily a little like a circus performer: someone always on the edge of reality, teasing life by provoking fear, and shock. Lily smiled, and said: 'Please sit down, mademoiselle. As I haven't been to the Maison Poiret for quite some time ... perhaps you'll explain to me the purpose of your visit.'

The woman didn't smile. Her eyes were beautiful, and haunting: a strange amber colour, and long, like Chinese eyes. 'We've never actually met, Princess,' she said, opening her small beaded bag and extracting a gold cigarette case. She took out a long, thin cigarette, and lit it with an elegant gold lighter. Her strange eyes were on Lily, not letting her go, and their pull was oddly magnetic. 'My name is Henriette Rivière. I live in the Rue Lepic, in Montmartre. My apartment is very modest, because Poiret isn't known for being overly generous with his salaries . . . and because my lover is equally, shall we say, tight with his funds.'

Lily blinked, holding in her shock. Nobody she knew spoke in such raw terms. She was at a loss for words, and so she cleared her throat, just to cover the silence.

'I see that my blatancy has upset you,' the woman commented. 'But facts are facts, so why hide them behind euphemisms? For ten or eleven years, I have had a lover, who, depending on the other circumstances in his life – his work, his family – has seen me at least once or twice a week, and has given me an allowance and paid my rent.'

Lily's irritation mounted. She stood up. 'Mademoiselle,' she declared coldly, 'if you've come here to expose the particulars of your private life, I'm not the slightest bit interested. I do not and never have discussed what anybody does within the privacy of his home, and I don't really *care* who pays your rent. I don't even know you! I shall have to ask you to leave.'

'You aren't curious as to why I came?' Henriette Rivière sat nonchalantly smoking her cigarette, evidently quite at home.

Thoroughly annoyed, Lily declared: 'Frankly, I'd rather not know. It doesn't concern me, after all.'

'Oh?' Henriette arched her thin, pencilled brows. 'But my dear Princess: it *does* concern you . . . rather intimately, I'm afraid.'

Lily stared at her, profoundly unnerved. Carefully, she clenched and unclenched her fists at the sides of her legs. Then she sat down again, knowing, all along, that it would have been better to keep to her decision and throw out this person. 'How is it my business?' she asked.

The other blew out a cloud of blue smoke. 'Prince Mikhail, your husband, has been paying my rent for over ten years. I would think this might interest you – a lot.'

Lily felt a shot of adrenalin pump through her body. She

opened her mouth, could not speak. Henriette Rivière looked her squarely in the eye. 'Princess Brasilova, you have a splendid reputation. Your children bask in this reputation. How would they feel if everyone were told about your mother and stepfather?'

Lily shook her head. 'My mother? I don't understand.'

'You're a devout Catholic, madame. But Monsieur Walter is a Jew. How would the Prince, whose views are well known, react if suddenly all Paris heard that his mother-in-law was married to a Jew?'

Lily felt the wind being knocked out of her, and her heart missed a beat. Still, she said, her voice shaking: 'The barons de Gunzburg, de Rothschild, are Jews.'

'Maybe so. But they don't frequent the same circles as Prince Mikhail. What do you suppose Charles Maurras or Pierre Taittinger would say? He's supported the one's newspaper and the other's Jeunesses Patriotes for quite some time now.'

'Mademoiselle,' Lily said, making a superhuman effort to keep her voice still and strong: 'What do you want?'

The other smiled. 'I'm thirty-eight, Princess. And I've been waiting a long, long time. I'm expecting your husband's baby – and I intend to keep it.'

The room had begun to spin, tilting to one side. Lily clasped the arms of her *bergère* with all her strength, to fight off the nausea. Henriette Rivière's voice continued, piercing Lily's malaise. 'You wouldn't want your children to be destitute,' she was saying. 'Prince Brasilov's business depends on a few clients who are staunch French royalists – the kind who are making an exception even dealing with him, because he isn't a national. They aren't merely giving funds to *L'Action Française* and Taittinger's groups: they are solid mainstays of all pseudo-Fascist organizations to keep France clear of any "tainted blood". Mikhail Brasilov needs these clients – especially since it looks as though the slump has hit his company. You might not care about his future, or the future of Brasilov Enterprises: but I would think you'd care about your children, madame.'

I don't believe it, Lily thought. Many women like me, with important husbands, have been approached by cheap blackmailers. I'm sure Misha doesn't even *know* her! God only knows who is the father of her child – if there is even a pregnancy. She can't touch my home.

Gripping the arms of her chair, Lily demanded: 'But what exactly do you *want* from me? Even if what you say is true – you would then *know* my husband. He'd never marry you, even if I stepped out of the picture! Your child would continue to stay without a father.'

Henriette stubbed out her cigarette neatly and harshly. 'Look,' she said, her voice clipped and hard. 'I'm far too streetwise to expect *marriage* from this situation. But I want this baby. And whatever it takes, I'm going to make sure he has a name. I could do it nicely, without a fuss: just a quiet little talk between me and Misha. My discretion in return for his recognizing my child. *You'd* have your reputation, your children, and, I'm sure, a healthy pension; I'd have a child who was a Brasilov. And Misha would have a minimum of problems, considering how messy things could be if you don't give me what I need.'

Chilled, Lily asked: 'And what is that?'

'I have to have some money. I'll soon be losing my figure, and in my line of business, that's my livelihood. That's where *you* come in, Princess. You'll help me, I'm certain, because you wouldn't want a scandal anymore than Misha. But I wouldn't want to ask *him* for that. He might react in some unpredictable fashion, and then *all* our lives, all our reputations, would go down the drain. That's why I thought it infinitely more *civilized* for you and I to deal with this small aspect of the affair.'

Horrified, Lily held onto the arms of her chair to keep the room from spinning chaotically around her. She forced herself to concentrate on the red line of Henriette's lips. At length, the storm inside her body began to subside, and she found that she could breathe again without that wild sensation of shipwreck racking at her insides. 'No,' she stated. 'You're not going to tell my husband *anything*. I'll do what I can to get rid of you, but beyond this you're not going to touch us! And if you go against my wishes, and expose your dirty secret, I'll see to it, mademoiselle, that no *couturier* in this city ever hires your services again. Threats can work both ways.'

Henriette smiled, but not with her odd, amber eyes. 'My child has really put the fear of God into you,' she remarked. 'What is it about this small Brasilov that makes you so insecure?'

'Your child,' Lily said, 'is not and never will be a Brasilov. Whatever Misha has done to dishonour his name, is nothing to the disgrace that would come to it if my children were to be kin to yours. We have nothing in common, mademoiselle, and you had better understand this *now*.' Trembling, her fingers rose to her throat, and touched a heavy strand of pearls and emeralds. They moved to the clasp, and unfastened it. In one swift, almost violent movement, she thrust them at Henriette, and said: 'I . . . don't have access to cash. But these are worth a small fortune. They were a present from my father-in-law, and were purchased at Van Cleef and Arpels a few years ago.' She pulled a ruby ring off. 'Take this, too! But now leave me alone, and don't ever come back!'

Smiling, Henriette Rivière pocketed the jewels, and stood up. 'This is very little for the maintenance of a prince,' she murmured. 'We'll see how far it takes us, shan't we, Princess?'

Abruptly, she was gone. Lily felt the room closing in on her, and a sick, dizzying nausea pumped through her body, drenching her with acrid perspiration. She really didn't know where to turn.

During the hours that followed, time stopped for Lily.

She thought frantically about confronting Misha, about going to her mother and stepfather. If the Rivière woman's story was true, then it would be impossible to continue to live with Misha. She wondered about the eight years of their marriage. If, during all that time, he had been keeping this person in Montmartre, then their family life, their lovemaking, their entire relationship, had been a lie. To have lived over twenty years with a mother who had lied about the most fundamental part of herself, and after that, to find out one's whole marriage had been nothing but a sham, was overwhelming, mind-boggling. She could now forgive Claire. But what of Misha?

Marisa tried to warn me, she reminded herself, unrelenting. She tried to tell me he was seeing his ex-wife – when I was pregnant with Nicolas. And I refused to think about it. It wasn't that I refused to *believe* it: I hid my head in the sand and simply *refused to think!* I never asked him where he was, why he was sometimes late, why he didn't always keep appointments with me – why there were so many business conferences at night. I didn't see! But now that I've been forced to look at it, I do see. In colour. He was with this woman. And what about Varvara-Jeanne? Had he been with her too all these years?

'Mama, I got a nineteen out of twenty in my geography test!' Nicky was exclaiming. She jerked herself up, blinking at her son. Of course. It was Saturday, and school only went for half a day.

'Where's Kyra?' she asked. She wondered how her face looked, and if the children would detect that something was wrong.

'Madeleine took her to the kitchen for some bread and butter.'

In spite of her pain, Lily smiled. 'Well,' she remarked. 'That was good news about your test. But you always do well.'

'I'm just like Papa,' Nicky said, jumping off her. 'He

250

reads something once, and knows it. But if he wants to remember it, he'll read it two or three times.'

'That's fine,' she said, feeling her heart beginning to beat erratically. *I'm just like Papa.* Damn him – *damn* Misha!

'What's wrong, Mama?' Nicky was asking.

'Nothing, sweetheart. I was just thinking that it would be nice to take a trip: you, Kyra, and me. Would you like that, Nick?'

Nicolas looked up at her, perplexed. 'And Papa?'

She smiled, her hand on the crown of his head. 'No. Papa has to work.'

He asked: 'For the summer holidays?'

'Yes,' she answered. 'For the summer. Now go to the kitchen and ask Annette to make me a cup of tea.'

When Misha came home from work, he found his wife sitting in semi-darkness in the living room. He bent down to kiss her. Her skin felt cold – but moist, as if she'd perspired and the sweat had dried on her. 'Where are the children?' he asked.

'Madeleine took them by bus to see Mother. They'll stay for the night.'

He stepped back. 'Oh? Why?'

'I thought it would be good for them,' she answered.

He heard the dullness in her voice, and touched her forehead with the back of his hand. She wasn't running a fever. He sat down, and turned on a light. She was sitting slumped over, her hair somewhat dishevelled. 'Is something the matter?' he asked.

Suddenly she sat up, and he saw how brightly her eyes were shining. 'Everything's the matter,' she answered in a low voice that shook as if from fever. 'You've been lying to me for years, cheating all the years of our marriage. I've heard – about an affair you've been having since before our wedding. And it's not the first time I've heard rumours of your other women.'

Shocked, he could only stare at her, the blood slowly draining from his features. Finally, he said: 'But rumours, Lily . . . At some point, every marriage is bothered by its share of rumours.'

'Only this time, I know it was the truth. Don't tell me *how* I know. I just do. Just as, deep in your heart, you always knew that nothing whatsoever could have passed between me and Mark MacDonald, because I would have been incapable of betrayal.'

He stood completely still, his face deeply troubled. He'd never heard her quite so positive, so adamant. He was going to lose her. The episode with Mark still seared him, yet he now realized that his attachment to his wife ran deeper than any of his doubts. And now this. Just as he'd been sensing a kind of rapprochement in their relations, which had grown tense and cold after the abortion.

This time, there'd be nothing to fight back with, nothing to keep her and his children to him. She was right: too many rumours ran around Paris concerning him and his mistresses. Only . . . what was it she had heard? About Varvara?

'I'm going to leave you,' she was saying, quietly. 'If there's anything I can't stand, it's lies. And our whole marriage has been one big lie. I prefer to live alone, with Nick and Kyra, and to give piano lessons to support myself. I'm going to Vienna, Misha, to stay with Wolf and Marisa. And I don't know if, or when, I'll be back.'

All at once, he reached for her. The face that looked into hers was ravaged, the eyes full of tears. 'I *beg* you, Lily,' he whispered, 'not to go. I need you here. You, and the children. I – I can't survive without you! All around me, my world's falling apart. I can't go through this alone – don't leave me!'

'But I can't trust you. You never took our marriage seriously. You never respected me enough to honour your vows. I'm old-fashioned, but this matters to me.'

'Then I can change for you!' His desperation contracted his features into an expression of supplication that she suddenly could no longer stand to look at. She stood up, turning her back on him, and heard him cry: 'Forgive me, Lily! For everything I've done! I'm not the strong man you've taken me for. I'm just ... a man, who's found it difficult to resist temptation ... all sorts of temptations.'

'I'm afraid that's your problem,' she replied, very quietly. 'But mine is the pain I feel, and the humiliation. There's been too much already that I've been forced to live with – and you know what I'm talking about. It was *our* child, Misha, and you know it! But all the while that you were threatening me, that you were accusing me of having been with Mark, *you* were the one breaking your pledge, not I!'

She turned, her beautiful face set and calm, but underneath, nerves twitched and stomach churned. She felt as if the fibres of her life had finally come undone, and yet a strength, the presence of which she had not been aware of until this moment, was growing like a new skin.

'I never gave you reason to doubt me,' she said. 'And I never betrayed you. I thought you were the moon and the stars; I would have done anything for you. You know I did what no woman should ever have to do. Because of you I lost my God, and my sense of self. But at least I still have my dignity.'

All their years together, she hadn't been enough: stupid Lily, obedient Lily, patient Lily. He'd betrayed her for a common woman, hardly better than a call girl. Yes, thought Lily: my mistake was that I wasn't ever wilful enough, never assertive enough. Maybe even, she thought, feeling the poignant pain, not woman enough in the raw, sexual, come-hither fashion of this Rivière girl.

'I'll write to my mother from Austria,' she told him. 'And of course I won't tell her the reason for the breakup of our marriage. You're the children's father, and I don't want anything bad to be connected with you.'

'Then, if you feel this way, you still love me enough to put away the past.'

She smiled at him. It was the saddest smile he'd ever read on a person's face. And then she walked away, her shoulders shaking with silent sobs.

Chapter Twelve

In Vienna, life was far more civilized, Lily thought. She sat in her apartment in the large, romantic old mansion at number 2, Schwindgasse, sewing a button on one of Kyra's dresses. How smoothly life had flowed, since her arrival, haggard and distraught, with seven suitcases and two small children, almost a year before. She felt as though the Steiners, senior and junior, had taken over her entire life, shifting her burdens to their more capable shoulders and making sure that she and the children would have nothing left to worry about.

She hadn't wanted to explain anything, even to Marisa. The pain had been almost unbearable. The parting – Nick sobbing, Kyra's strange, silent tears, Misha turning away, his chin trembling – had been like a physical wrenching. She'd kept it all in during the train voyage. But in Vienna, once the children were asleep and she sat ensconced in an overstuffed velvet armchair, facing Wolf and Marisa, the tears had come. Marisa had quietly left, so that Wolf could be alone with Lily, holding her and listening. She wasn't sure if she'd made any sense; but the next day, the healing process had already begun, and a week later, Frau Steiner – Mina, Wolf's mother – had proudly shown her the beautiful little apartment upstairs from Marisa's, and told her it was hers for as long as she wanted it.

Lily had moved in, and Marisa had sent her a maid. Wolf and Marisa had a small daughter now, Nanni, an adorable two-year-old when the Brasilovs had arrived the year before; she had become the delight of Nick and Kyra. It was Nanni, more than anything else, who had helped them to get over the separation from their father. Misha had tried to force Lily to stay until the end of the school year; but she'd known that if she stayed in the same house, pretending for the children's sake that nothing was changed, she would become crazy. She'd left within the week, without even calling Claire and Jacques – unable to face their questions and their concern.

It was a pleasant life. She'd written to Claire that the marriage had ended, that she would stay in Vienna until she felt better. But it was now ten months, and she wasn't ready to return to Paris. Marisa was her best friend, and here, in the spacious old house with its sculpted balconies and trimmed garden, everybody lived together, the apartments separate for privacy but visits taking place with the informality of family. Nick and Kyra were always somewhere with Nanni, often at the home of the elder Steiners, who were, Lily thought, the warmest, gentlest people she had ever met. They had accepted her with her children without a single question. The gratitude she felt was immeasurable.

Old Herr Steiner had warned her against sending the children to school. Instead, he invited a gifted young man he knew to come to the house to tutor Nick and Kyra. In just a few months, they had both learned German. Lily's days were occupied with walks in the Prater, with matinée concerts with Marisa and Mina, and with trips to the local library to familiarize herself with German literature. She'd studied the language for a few years with the sisters, but now learned it with a diligence that won her the praise of Marisa's father-in-law. She had begun to read some Goethe, the dictionary by her side.

She'd wanted to find students, to help pay for the maintenance of her apartment and maid, and to take care of the tutor, young Herr Krapalik. But Wolf led her to understand that both he and his father would be insulted. She was their guest. She was much more: she was a part of their family. Overwhelmed, she wept. But she wrote to her mother, asking her to find out if there was a way to unlock some of the money from her dowry. Misha was sending her funds for the children: she had sent him back the first two cheques for herself, and he had understood, and not continued to include them in the mailings.

Jacques Walter answered her that Brasilov Enterprises was going through a difficult period, and that Misha had been forced to liquidate the apartment in the Rue Molitor, and to let the servants go. He wrote that her dowry was somehow tied into Brasilov Enterprises, and that, because of this, he and her mother preferred to take care of her themselves. After that, every month, he sent her a thousand francs. He was a fine man, and never asked why she had left her husband so suddenly. He and Claire wrote regularly, light, pleasant letters about their activities, the people they saw, the small trips they took. They were delicate enough never to mention Misha after that first reply from Jacques concerning her dowry.

With the money from her parents, and the cheques from her husband, she was able to start paying the tutor herself, as well as the maid. But when the Steiner servants went out to market, they made it a habit to buy for all the inhabitants of 2, Schwindgasse. She and the children lived in gracious luxury, all their needs met. It was almost as if she'd gone to sleep, and awakened in a world of good fairies who, by magic, had removed all the stress and heartache and replaced them with quiet, gentle kindness.

Still, it wasn't the same. Marisa's life was different from her own, because Marisa was happily married. In the late afternoon, she always rushed off to get dressed for Wolf, reappearing fresh and inviting. When he came home, Lily would feel a pinch in her heart: the two would hug each other, Wolf lifting his wife into a pirouette of joy, as if he'd been gone a month and not just a day. His office lay on the other side of the enormous house, but Marisa had always respected the mental barrier that separated her husband's workplace from the rest of the apartments. Wolf received his patients through an entrance on the side of the house, and had a nurse and secretary whose rooms were on the top floor of the building. But these women were seldom seen and never heard. When Wolf came home, he wanted to breathe freely, to let the troubled souls whom he was helping slide off his own, healthy one, for the evening. Then, in the morning, he would feel renewed by Marisa's love, and re-energized by Nanni's adoration and baby prattlings. Lily couldn't help but feel that she was an intruder in what otherwise constituted an intimate family setting; and sometimes, when she went to bed alone, in her own apartment, she yearned for a similar existence, with a man's loving caress and strong shoulder to lean on.

Lily hadn't wanted to tell Marisa too much. Her friend had always been outspoken, critical of any injustice. Especially, Marisa was loyal; if anybody hurt someone close to her, she responded with virulence against the one responsible. Lily was a little afraid that if she knew the truth, Marisa would never stop haranguing her about Misha's perfidy and unforgivable sins. Lily knew that this was one subject she couldn't bear to discuss. Yet she felt a need to speak about her pain. One day, she'd made an appointment with Wolf under an assumed name; and when she'd been the one to be ushered into the suite, Wolf had been surprised, but had immediately understood. She'd lain down on the couch and closed her eyes, and related everything that had happened over the last few years: what Claire had unveiled; the abortion; and finally, the degrading shame of learning that she had not been enough woman for her husband, and that another woman was carrying his child.

Wolf hadn't condemned Misha. He'd laced his fingers together and said: 'It wasn't that you were lacking, Lily; it was he who lacked confidence. Men who feel the constant

258

need to pursue other women, even when they are very happy with their wives, are insecure and want reaffirmation. This fits in with Misha's anti-Semitism. People who focus their animosities on a group outside their own lives, are simply afraid to face their own inadequacies. If a businessman can blame the slump on the Jews, it's because this way, he won't have to examine his own mistakes in helping to bring about economic disaster.'

She opened her eyes and asked, in a very small voice: 'But I was right to leave, wasn't I?'

Wolf had smiled. 'You were right to obey the signals of your own conscience. You were true to your values.'

'But . . . is that *good?*'

'Lily,' he had declared, 'in life there is no good and no evil. There is weak and strong, fair and unfair. We are each of us a finely tuned instrument whose sounds cannot be measured in general terms. You are not the soft young girl I met years ago. There's a resiliency in you that shows how healthy you are, in spite of all the injustice to which you've been subjected. You're going to be all right, sweetheart. But it's not going to be easy.'

She'd felt the tears running on to her cheeks, and had whispered: 'In a strange way, I miss him. At least I miss the life we had.'

'You miss what you thought you had. You miss what you perceive Marisa and I to have. Let's be frank, Lily: you miss a man's arms around you, and you have an unfulfilled physical need.'

'But he's the only man I've ever loved.'

'Maybe that's why, when your needs cry out, you tag them with his name. You have to realize that divorce isn't the black spot it used to be, nowadays. There are other, better-adjusted men who could make you happier – but for this, you have to accept your own actions, and not condemn yourself for leaving Misha.'

It was then that Lily had gone to a lawyer, in Vienna, to

instigate divorce proceedings. She'd felt it would be better to finish with this part as quickly as possible; that any lingering would simply cause the pain to remain that much more poignant.

The Steiners, after her visit to Wolf's office, began to make it a point to include her and the children in their Friday-night ritual. The first time, Wolf simply sent their maid to her apartment, to invite her to join them for the Sabbath meal. She'd understood. He wanted to continue what Rabbi Weill had begun. And so, her heart filled with gratitude, she went. Kyra had asked about the beautiful candles, and Nick had wanted to know about the language of the prayers. Wolf had said: 'Do you want to learn it? It's called Hebrew, and it has a special alphabet.'

'When I grow up, I want to speak twenty languages. I already know three: French, Russian, and German. Will you teach me Hebrew, Uncle Wolf?'

To Lily's amazement, the psychiatrist had reached over to caress Nick's cheek, and, in the softest voice, had answered that it would be his pleasure. And now, on Tuesdays and Thursdays, when Wolf finished his work, he always stopped off for two hours at Lily's apartment, where he would closet himself with the boy and teach him about this old biblical language, which rang with the wisdom and pain of thousands of years, and of a noble people who had wandered through the earth in search of a home.

In November, Lily had received a letter from Claire. Her mother was writing to announce Claude's marriage. Lily was flabbergasted. She was sitting in Marisa's parlour when Kyra had walked in with the mail. 'My brother's got married,' she said.

'To whom?'

'I don't know! Let me read the rest of the letter.' She sat forward and proceeded aloud:

> You will be as surprised as we were by the news.
> I had always hoped for a steady young woman, someone

with softness and charm, to bring out the tenderness that I feel exists in Claude's heart, though he seldom brings it out. This girl isn't a 'girl', actually; she's a mature woman, a number of years older than Claude; and she's streetwise. I'm not sure yet if I like her, for we were confronted with a fait accompli: they had just returned from getting married in the country, just like that!

I won't tell you that she's a lady, but I will say that she's sophisticated. A bit hard, but then, I imagine life hasn't been very good to her until this point. She isn't pretty, but she is most fashionable. In fact, she's had a job in fashion for over ten years. She's worked . . .

Lily had turned an awful shade of ghastly white, and the letter had shaken in her fingers. Marisa, openmouthed, had seized the vellum paper and taken up where Lily had left off:

She's worked for the Maison Poiret, as a model. We'll send you photographs when they come, and you'll be able to see for yourself what she looks like: rather exotic, I believe. Claude seems to adore her, and after all, that's the only thing that matters, isn't it?

Her name's Henriette, and there's another piece of news you will deduce from the photograph. The new Madame Bruisson is well on the way to having a baby! Life has a number of surprises in store for all of us. I'd never thought Claude could ever have fallen in love as hard as he seems to. She isn't my dream for a daughter-in-law, especially given the differences in background between them – and her age. But if Claude has chosen her, I shall welcome her with a full heart, and expect that you will also.

Marisa sat staring at Lily. 'Come on,' she said. 'An elopement is an elopement, what hey? Old Claude's done it after all – who'd have expected it? But it's no reason to look as if you'd seen a ghost!'

Lily had jumped up and run from the room, leaving a bewildered Marisa still holding Claire's letter. Later, when

Wolf had come home, she'd told him what had happened, and shown it to him. He hadn't hesitated for a moment. 'I'll be right back,' he'd murmured. 'I have to go and find Lily.'

He'd found her in her room, immobile, staring at the wall. When she saw who it was, she'd started to speak. 'She's passing Misha's child off as my brother's,' she'd said, her voice dull and thick.

Wolf sat down on her bed, and took her hand. 'Misha never wanted to marry this woman,' he remarked. 'Probably, when she came to him after you'd left, he sent her packing. I suppose your brother fell in love with her and was willing to accept the child as his own.'

Lily said, tears streaming down her face: 'History has a strange way of repeating itself. Now this horrible person is going to be in my family forever, and her child will always remind me of . . . of everything . . . Why? *Why* does it have to be this way, Wolf?'

He'd put an arm around her, and held her. '*You* don't have to live with her, Lily. You and your brother have always led separate lives. Maybe you should tell Claire the truth – and Marisa.'

She'd shaken free, and said: 'No. There's been enough mess, enough dirt as it is. Let Claude believe what he wants to believe. It isn't the first time a woman's lied to him.'

'At some point, you have to make a complete peace with your mother.'

'I thought I had.'

They stayed silent after that, listening to strains of Kyra's playing, on the baby grand piano in the sitting room. Then he'd said to her: 'At least there seems to be some good news these last few days. In Germany, all is going quietly and smoothly, after the scare of Chancellor von Papen's resignation. It looks as though Hindenburg's seeing Hitler, but people are inclined to believe there's little chance that he'll give him the cabinet to compose.'

'And . . . what do *you* think?'

'Hitler may not be the warmonger everybody expected. But I, for one, feel somewhat relieved. If all stays quiet in Germany, then nothing will be changed for the rest of us. We'll just continue our lives and make fun of his toothbrush moustache, and he'll become a parlour joke.'

Lily had smiled at him. He was so kind to her and the children; she thought of him as a benevolent brother, much closer to her than Claude had ever been. But she somehow couldn't relate to the problems in Germany – not on this day that she had learned the disastrous news about Henriette Rivière. She'd felt a little guilty, watching Wolf light a cigar and make himself comfortable in the parlour, afterwards. She'd needed him, and he'd given her the support that she'd been craving; but now, what she wanted was peace, not a political discussion.

And so, kissing him on the cheek, she'd closed the conversation, saying to him: 'Marisa said she received a letter from Léon Blum, and that he thought after the recent elections that Hitler is now excluded from all hope of power. So I suppose you must be right, and we can all relax again.'

Wolf had stayed for a few more minutes, talking of 'Uncle Léon', and of his prediction. The French, he said, were more removed than the Austrians from the German question. And they'd finally signed the nonaggression pact with Russia. They were the strongest country in Europe: their line of defensive forts, designed by André Maginot, and the kind treatment that Briand had shown towards Germany, seemed to protect them from fearing the monster with the toothbrush moustache. Wolf finished his cigar, and stood up, sighing. 'So if Uncle Léon has made this bold statement, it looks as if we shall remain a safe nation.'

She'd asked: 'You mean, the Austrians?'

263

And he had regarded her pointedly, and shaken his head. 'No,' he'd responded. 'I meant the Jews.'

The New Year had come. And then, to Wolf's profound surprise, Adolf Hitler had become Chancellor of Germany on the thirtieth of January. This was how 1933 had started off. In February, the household had been upset, reading in the news about a terrible snowstorm in England, which had buried alive some motorcyclists, while eighty children in a bus had completely disappeared. Mr Disengoff, the mayor of Tel Aviv, had come for a short visit, and Lily and the children had been included when the Steiners had fêted the dignitary by going to hear Artur Rubinstein playing Vivaldi. Then, on Tuesday, 28 February, while Lily, Mina and Marisa had been making masks for the three children to wear for the feast of Purim, Herr Steiner had walked in on them and announced that the Communists had set fire to the Reichstag in Berlin, and that one hundred and thirty of them had been arrested and a plot uncovered. At dinnertime, Wolf had argued with his father that no one knew for sure the Communists were responsible, and that, if a plot existed, he was inclined to suspect Hitler of inventing an excuse to blame his opposition and jail the members.

On the first of March, Claire cabled that a son had been born to Claude and Henriette, and that he would be baptized Alain Paul Bruisson. Lily sat alone in her room, holding the telegram – thinking of the child she'd wanted for her father, Misha's last child, which had been taken before its birth. She cried, moaning aloud and hugging her sides. Now Misha *had* a third child, and it wasn't hers; and it had been given her father's name, but she had not been the one to do it for him. Life was so cruel, so mocking! All her dreams, all her plans – all her *life!* – had come to nothing, while the woman who had shattered all was lying comfortably in her bed, holding the child she, Lily, would have given everything to hold. And the supreme irony was that Lily's mother, and Lily's stepfather, were probably at her side, making cooing noises to a baby that wasn't their grandchild, but which had been granted the right to live, and to live within Lily's own family – when it, and its mother, were the ones responsible for her pain and her children's.

On 7 March, one year to the day after Aristide Briand's death, Marisa and Lily had sat listening to the disturbing news of the suspension of the Austrian parliament; Dolfuss had just assumed semi-dictatorial powers, and all, it seemed, as part of the general wave of Nazi feeling in Germany. Then, on 10 March, they'd read about the possibility of a war in Poland, over the Free City of Danzig, which Hitler wanted. And Herr Steiner had said to the two young Frenchwomen: 'If there's a war, France will have to march.'

Mina Steiner had asked, in a hushed voice: 'Then, Isaac, shall we have to leave Vienna?'

There had ensued a horrible pause in which Marisa, Lily, and Wolf's mother had scrutinized the faces of the two men sitting in utmost seriousness on either side of the *Mehlspeise* pudding. Then Wolf had said: 'Don't you think we're all overdramatizing a bit? Danzig is very far away.'

And the women had sighed with relief, and Nicky had eaten two helpings of the thick rice pudding, and Kyra had consumed five apple fritters with jam.

The next day, they heard of a devastating earthquake in Hollywood, California. 'Where they make moving pictures?' Kyra had demanded.

'In all of Los Angeles, darling,' Wolf had answered.

'Did many people die?' Nick had asked.

'There were twenty-three tremors, and yes, many people were killed. The city suffered much destruction.'

'Uncle Wolf,' Kyra had piped up, 'does that mean there

won't be movies anymore? We won't get to see Spinelly and Noël-Noël?'

'But those are French actors,' Mina Steiner had replied indulgently.

And now, in the middle of the month, the world in revolt seemed to have calmed down. Yesterday, for Purim, the children had dressed up, and Kyra, in her long brown dress with ribbons of rope in her hair, had disappeared for three hours, returning with a button missing and a dirty face, and had stuck a match in the lock of the front door, which had become jammed. She'd cried angrily, when Lily had spanked her: 'But it's stupid to wear the same costume for eight days! I'm not even Jewish!'

Lily had stepped back, staring at the vivacious green eyes: Misha's arrogant eyes, and his cleft chin. She could hear again, like an echo, her answer to her rebellious daughter: 'In a sense we are all Jews, Kyra. Don't forget that Jesus Christ was a Jew, and that he was proud of it.'

'But if there's a war, I heard the man say on the radio that it was the fault of the dirty Jews!'

Lily, holding now the brown dress, recalled vividly her sense of shock and fear. She'd looked carefully at her child, and seen a small spoiled Russian princess. She'd reached over and touched Kyra, but the child had resisted. 'That man you heard must have forgotten that if he is a Christian, he has to be a Jew. The Jews began all Western religions, my darling.'

Now Lily set the dress aside and closed her eyes, suddenly weary. Everything had calmed down – even Kyra. But everywhere, in every country, people whispered about the possibility of war, and munitions were being transported. She wondered if she should take her children back to France, to remove them a step farther from Hitler. But then she decided that this was stupid. With acknowledged cowardice, she thought: Nobody knows we're Jews, anyway. Only Wolf, and he would never tell.

And immediately, she was ashamed, thinking of her best friends, of this family that had become her own, that had saved her from disaster. She thought: I'm glad that there is Jewish blood in our veins – we're in fine company.

Misha sat in the ante-room of the Baron Philippe de Chaynisart's offices on the ground floor of the Hotel Rovaro, 44 Rue Brunel. Around him glistened Lalique sculptures on low tables of glass and wood, splendid in the starkness of their simplicity. He glanced at his watch, perspiration beading his hairline. It was already two twenty; when he had been running Brasilov Enterprises from the Rue de Berri, he'd never kept anyone waiting: neither employee nor prospective client, neither the attaché of a minister nor a simple petitioner come to ask for a reprieve in paying a debt. But de Chaynisart had kept him waiting since a quarter to two.

He looked down at his suit. It had held up well, but in another two or three months it would need refurbishing. He couldn't see himself going to London to be fitted at Savile Row; the expense would not be justified. But the shoes, of Italian leather, had done better. He remembered how he'd gone through shoes all his life, every six months. He'd had to learn how to preserve his clothes. It had been only one of the things he'd had to learn, over the past year.

Had it been a year since Lily and the children had left? He laid his face in his hands, feeling a new wave of despair. Why was it that everything he touched seemed to spoil and rot? Lily. He'd been so happy with her, and she'd tried so hard, being exactly what he'd needed and desired. Why then hadn't he had the strength to stay faithful? He'd vowed to do this for her, when he'd proposed. But somehow, his resolve had wavered.

And then there was Claude. After the birth of the child, Misha had felt Claude becoming a shade more arrogant, and, at the same time, more distant, if that were possible.

The words between them now dropped like icicles from their lips, Claude's hatred barely veiled, and insolent in the fact that he no longer deemed it necessary to camouflage his feelings. They'd named the child Alain, as French a name as possible. He wondered if Rirette had told her husband of their former connection – and if Claude held this against him for Lily's sake, or for Rirette's. But perhaps she'd held her tongue, and Claude knew nothing of this. She'd been yet another of his own mistakes, he thought wryly.

Now that Brasilov Enterprises was floundering, Misha thought he sometimes detected a certain smugness in his brother-in-law. And yet, the Bruisson assets had been absorbed into Brasilov. If the latter failed, then Claude would find himself penniless too. He and his bride had moved into his apartment on the Avenue Kléber, and he'd heard that Rirette, after the baby's birth, had been going the rounds of antique shops. It seemed highly unreasonable; but then, Claude had probably saved while Misha had been entertaining lavishly. Misha couldn't help but wonder, too, at Claude's unexpected choice for a wife. Of all people . . . Rirette, who'd been *his* mistress. It made Misha uncomfortable. Too many questions posed themselves.

He'd left his father at the office, now just a small suite on the second floor of the Rue de Berri building, to deal as best he could with a series of creditors. Prince Ivan's reputation for cool judgment was exactly what was needed today. The sugar refinery in the Aisne would have to be liquidated; already, he'd put his lawyers to formulate a certificate of bankruptcy; Verlon would get to keep his little house, but the main buildings would be dismantled, and the land sold. Money was owed because the Brasilovs had been expecting a normal harvest, and had paid for materials with promises of funds that would come from the profits.

Of course, this was what had stopped the wheel from turning. Misha had always put money from one affiliate into another, borrowing from Peter to pay Paul; but before, his expectations had always been met, because they were reasonable. It hadn't been reasonable to foresee that the German materials would prove to be a swindle; and so, always one to take a calculated risk, he hadn't been prepared. His other affiliates hadn't been expecting a failure of such proportions in the Aisne deal. Prince Ivan had grown thinner, like a small reed, and his hair was almost completely white, and sparse; this downfall had been such a blow to him that it had felled him far more than the advent of Bolshevism to his motherland, and the consequent exodus.

Misha tried to think of what his life had become. He'd always been attracted to the glitter and the luxury of the *beau monde*. Now he had to live like a Puritan. He felt such hatred towards those who had brought about this state of affairs: those Jewish bastards in Germany, the Rabino-vitches; and whoever had spoken to Lily. They'd ruined his life.

Varvara, caustic, had shaken her head and said: 'Oh, no. You ruined it, my boy.' But he'd almost hit her then. Hit her in his helplessness – the way he'd wanted to hit Lily when he'd thought that she'd had an affair with Mark MacDonald.

He thought, overcome with anguish, that he might have been wrong; Lily would never have slept with another man. And the idea that he might have caused his own baby to be aborted tormented him. Sadly, he acknowledged that he had been the first chink in the armour of their marriage.

A balding young man came out of the inner offices, and said to him: 'If monsieur will follow me ... Monsieur le Baron will see you now.'

It was two thirty. Misha tugged on the edge of his lapels,

269

and was ushered into a clear, bright office decorated with brass and Cordoba leather. Philippe de Chaynisart was short, stocky, with bright blue eyes like a baby's. He was fiftyish, but with such cherubic men age was always hard to tell. Misha knew that there was no gossip surrounding the old, distinguished name; if anything the brothers de Chaynisart lived too much in retreat, minding their own business and the management of their old, old money.

'Sit down, sit down,' de Chaynisart said, gesticulating towards a comfortable leather armchair.

Misha complied, crossing his legs. 'I was most intrigued by your letter,' he stated.

'Well. It's become rather a mess. This hotel, I mean. My brother Charles and I sank a lot of money into it; as you shall see, it's the latest modern touch, and it's in the perfect location. But somehow . . . we aren't making the profit we'd expected.'

'This is interesting, my dear Baron. But why have you come to *me?* I am not a hotelier.'

De Chaynisart smiled. As he did so, he stuck a small white cigarette between his teeth, and motioned to light it with a solid silver lighter on his desk. The smile, therefore, had a certain subtlety that didn't escape Misha. 'True: you are not specifically a hotelier. But I've heard and read about you. Your business acumen has stretched over such multiple ventures that nothing, really, is beyond the scope of your possibilities.' De Chaynisart paused, puffed a moment on his cigarette, then laid it carefully on an ashtray of clear, cut crystal. 'And there's another thing. All Paris has heard of your, shall we say, stroke of bad luck. Pierre Taittinger was telling me about it a few months ago. You know Pierre quite well, don't you? A splendid fellow who knows the world goes around on action, not just pretty words. Your bad luck has touched the hearts of some of the hardest men in this fair city. We all know how you were swindled.'

270

Misha sat very still, making sure that his face did not betray him. He felt shocks of surprise. Raising one eyebrow, he inclined his head with a sardonic half smile. 'I hadn't realized that my misfortune was common knowledge.'

'Of course it is. As is my own – and my brother's. We're making a failure with this hotel. It was built in '27, and should have drawn all the rich young American expatriates who have come flocking to our shores. Perhaps you, better than we, will be able to determine why. I would like to hire you, Brasilov. If any man can, you can turn this enterprise into a profit for us.'

'And may I ask what's in it for me?'

De Chaynisart chuckled. 'I was attracted to your work when I learned of the success you'd had bringing together Michelin and Citroën. You're a good middleman. Now, if you can pull us out of the red, I shall pay you a fine commission – the same way the auto men did. Shall we say . . . fifty thousand francs?'

Misha smiled. 'That depends. If my work will take six months, that sum would suit me beautifully. But if I'm forced to stay over a year . . . that could be small payment for a lot of trouble, during which time I should not have been free to pursue other, more lucrative endeavours.'

'Very fair. Shall we agree on fifty thousand for up to one year, and, if the job lasts longer, the terms could be renegotiated?'

He was holding out his small white, porky hand, with its perfectly trimmed fingernails. Misha hesitated for three seconds; then he shook the hand in his own strong one. 'Agreed,' he declared.

The horse-chestnut trees were in full bloom outside Lily's window. She sat in the parlour, reading *The Crowned Fool*. Marisa had thrust it at her the week before, exclaiming that it was the most fascinating book she'd read in years.

Lily thought that the author, Cabanès, had told an interesting story from a historical viewpoint; but there were too many sexual details. She'd much preferred *A Sister's Story*, by Madame Augustus Craven, née de la Ferronays: fragments of diaries and letters reconstituting the life of an entire family from 1830 to 1848. How lucky were those who had the gift of words and plot!

For a moment she was wistful, and set the book down. The front door opened, and Marisa peeked in. 'Am I committing *lèse-majesté*?'

'I was reading,' Lily said, smiling.

Marisa, who still looked like a twelve-year-old elf, dressed in outrageously stylish wisps of nothing and high heels, came to perch on the edge of her armchair. 'You don't like it?' she asked, picking up the book.

'The sex part . . . bothers me.'

Marisa made a face. 'For God's sake, Lily! You always make me think of poor Héloïse in her abbey, waiting forever for Abélard. I don't want that for you, you know. Wolf would say it isn't healthy, but I'll just say it's a damn shame.'

'What are you talking about, Mari?'

'About sex, of course. A woman like you should have a lover. A marvellous, exciting, romantic lover. To sweep you off your feet.'

Lily burst out laughing. 'But it just isn't like me,' she said.

Marisa set the book down, and picked up Lily's hand resting on the other chair arm. The diamond and emeralds of her ring gave off blinding sparks. 'Isn't it time you had these reset?' she asked.

'Why should I, Mari? They were with me for nine years – Maybe I deserve to keep something from that time.'

'You have the children.'

Marisa jumped off, and went to the window. Looking out, she said: 'Guess who's in town? Mark MacDonald.

272

He's coming to dinner tonight. Mama and Papa Steiner haven't met him yet.'

Lily folded her hands together, and breathed in. 'Mark. Why is he here?'

Marisa turned, and shrugged: 'You can ask him yourself, this evening. But I suppose I don't believe his explanation. He said he came to visit Salzburg, which he didn't know – and decided to come over to pay us a call. What *I* personally think is that he came to see *you*.'

Lily chewed on her lower lip. Marisa declared: 'In any case, I don't want you to find some excuse not to eat at Mama's. She'll be expecting you at eight o'clock, as usual.' She started to walk away, wheeled about, and said: 'Wear something soft. I don't like the way you look in matronly things.'

She exited, closing the door delicately behind her. Lily sat thinking. Mark. What, exactly, had she ever felt for him? She'd been flattered; she'd liked him. She'd felt good around him. But in some way, she supposed, she also held him partly responsible for her abortion. Why had she followed her home?

But the question really was: why had she never contacted him again, to let him know what had ensued between her and Misha, following his visit? She'd been afraid that if she had, the door would have been opened to a tremendous explosion, which would have caused exactly the kind of scandal that Misha had threatened. And Mark would have been privy to her shame, and her children's. And so she'd buried Mark's visit with her engagement to him, keeping it sealed in the coffin of the past. She'd been sure she'd never see him again – that their paths would never cross, now that Marisa, the link between them, had settled in Vienna.

In a crystal bowl, cut gardenias sat on the small table by the window. Lily bent down and inhaled the sweetness of their centres. It promised to be such a good spring. She went into her room and lay down for a nap. But she

273

couldn't sleep. The trees made strange shadows over the bedspread, teasing her with their velvet softness. After a while she went into her closet and pulled out a simple vaporous dress of apricot chiffon. She thought: It's absurd. But it's true, I'm dressing for Mark. I haven't dressed for a man in a year; and he's my friend. It felt good, thinking about it. There was nothing ugly in this simple recognition.

The children didn't know him. She made sure that Hanneliese dressed them simply but carefully, and then, holding each one by the hand, she went out to the stairway and down to Mina and Isaac Steiner's high-ceilinged, large apartment. 'Mama, you look so pretty,' Nicky said. 'Like a movie star.'

When she walked in, everyone was already having cocktails. She felt a moment of acute embarrassment. Isaac Steiner was regarding her with lifted brows, and she could read, in Wolf's eyes, the same appreciation. 'Our little princess is here,' Isaac remarked. 'With our Dauphin and small Infanta.'

Mark stood up. 'Hello, Lily. It's nice to see you.'

She pushed Nicolas and Kyra in front of her, and said: 'You've never met my children. This is Nick and Kyra – Mr MacDonald.'

In a pleasant, easygoing fashion, he greeted them and had them sit beside him on the sofa. Lily felt the moment pass, and moved towards Isaac to accept a glass of sherry. It was almost as if no stranger were among them; but she felt him behind her, even as she chatted with Wolf and his father, and she could hear him entertaining her children.

During the dinner, Wolf told funny Viennese stories and Mark answered with Parisian anecdotes. They spoke of the Radical cabinet of Edouard Daladier, and of Schiaparelli's mounting offensive against the Maison Chanel. Carefully, the men avoided the topic of Hitler; and the women, in their relief, laughed openly, Lily too. Yes, he was her good friend, and she'd missed him; for who, in her life, had really been her friends? Just the Steiners, and Mark. And she'd lost Mark because of her marriage, understanding that Misha would never have tolerated him around her.

When the servants came to serve coffee in the study, three-year-old Nanni came running in, in her nightgown and slippers. Kyra picked her up, and somehow it was Mark who was granted the privilege of bringing her back to her governess. 'But I'll get lost in this vast house,' he said. 'Can't somebody show me the way?'

Nanni bit her lip. 'Auntie Lily can. She smells the nicest.' In the general laughter that ensued, Lily felt her cheeks warm and red, and her heart in her throat. Wolf said: 'Go on, then, the three of you. The rest of us want to proceed with our coffee.'

The small girl scampered ahead, and Lily found herself on the stairway beside Mark. They were silent. Outside Marisa's apartment, the Fräulein was waiting. Lily deposited Nanni in her arms, and kissed her. 'Good night, darling. See you tomorrow.'

'And will I see the nice man tomorrow?'

'The nice man promises to be here,' Mark replied.

'Well, then, thank you, Princess, and Herr MacDonald.' The Fräulein, Nanni in hand, closed the door. Mark found himself finally face-to-face with Lily. She could feel him looking at her; she knew, without any outward sign, that he, like Wolf and his father, appreciated the way she was dressed. She hadn't felt a man's eyes on her for so many months! And who better than a trusted old friend?

'I'd like to see the garden by starlight,' he said to her, taking her arm. 'Do you suppose we could just slip out and take a walk?'

She nodded. She wasn't afraid, being alone with him. As they made their way to the back door of the house, Lily remembered what Claire had told her: that friendship was the most important part of marriage. Somehow, she'd missed that with Misha. They'd been lovers – they'd been parents. But never really friends.

'You have a funny look on your face,' he said as they strolled along the gravelled pathway to a small gazebo. The Steiners kept their garden well lit, but the stars were like a shimmering mantle of diamonds protecting them. Sculpted Muses and Graces stood along the path, dripping sprinkles of clear water into granite bowls shaped like giant, scalloped shells. They reached the gazebo and sat down in wicker chairs.

'I was feeling pain,' she answered, averting her eyes. 'It comes on me, now and then. Memories, like an old lady.'

'It's been hard for you, hasn't it?'

She raised her eyes. 'It still is.'

'You know, he's had to give up the third floor and half the second, at the Rue de Berri. He's been in one hell of a mess.'

'Please,' she whispered, 'don't speak about him. It's over. The sooner the divorce comes through, the sooner I can begin to put my life in order.'

Mark lifted her fingers off the armrest, and played with them. She felt the warmth of his thumb and forefinger over her joints and knuckles. A friend, caring. 'It seems to me that it's already in order,' he commented.

'Not really. I can't stay forever dependent on Wolf and Mari, and Wolf's parents. This life – it's been like a healing rest. But soon I'm going to have to think about making a living. They've taken care of me and my children long enough.'

'You're not afraid?'

She smiled, sadly. 'Of course I am. But what else can I do?'

His face, so serious, was where it belonged, among the Grecian statues: his small, sculpted nose, his curls, his clear hazel eyes. It was a nice face, and he'd aged somewhat, dry lines showing around his eyes. After all, it was normal: he was thirty-three. 'And you?' she asked. 'No Hollywood film deals?'

'I'm not through with Paris yet. It's the most fascinating place to be. I've written a third book, and Scribner's has it. Let's hope I don't have to make too many editorial changes.'

She laughed. And then, hearing her own laughter, she suddenly stopped. She looked at him. Slowly, he placed his hands on the sides of her face, and brought his own face closer. She knew, of course, that he was going to kiss her; she knew, and didn't pull back. It felt right, somehow, that he should kiss her, and so, when it happened, she closed her eyes and felt the kiss, his lips upon her own, with quiet satisfaction. Something hard was melting inside her heart.

Then she felt him draw back, and realized that she was weeping, that the tears had fallen on his hands. 'What's the matter?' he asked quietly.

She stood up, shaking her head. 'I don't know. It's just that . . .'

He stood up too. He'd never been much taller than she, and she liked the fact that they could look directly at each other, equals. '*Is* it over?' he asked.

She let her shoulders rise and drop. 'You don't know,' she said, 'what happened between us. But yes, it's over. Because I want it to be. And maybe because he didn't need me as much as I'd thought, and didn't love me as much as I'd hoped. I don't think about it anymore all the time, the way I used to. Wolf helped me overcome that: the need to rake the wound.'

'And the man himself? Do you still think of him?'

Lily thrust her fingers through her hair. 'Sometimes.'

He put an arm around her shoulders, held her against him. 'Come,' he said softly. 'Nick and Kyra will be wondering what Nanni and I did to their mother.'

* * *

277

At breakfast, Prince Ivan wasn't hungry. It was drizzling outside. Since he had vacated his own apartment on the Rue Molitor and moved into his father's (now the street had been renamed the Avenue Paul Doumer), Misha had let the servants go, and now there was only the daily maid, Suzanne, to serve, cook, and clean. The old man looked around at the naked walls, marked by clear spots where all the paintings had hung. They had all been auctioned off. Soon it would be time to move to a smaller apartment in a less elegant neighbourhood. He had never had to experience anything like that in all seventy years of his life. Even after the exodus, it had been different. He'd known exactly what to do, and he'd had the sugar beets to work with. Now, what did they have? One failure after another: the domino effect, started by the Aisne débâcle.

He wondered briefly what his wife, Maria, would have thought, and was glad that he'd been able to spare her this defeat. Prince Ivan didn't like to go out anymore. He was afraid of reading pity in someone's eyes, or perhaps disdain. He was baffled by what had occurred. Somewhere at the back of his mind, an uneasy sense of distrust had built up.

Misha walked into the dining room, and sat down. Suzanne came in, her slippered feet flapping on the hardwood floor. 'M'sieur want some coffee?'

Misha reared his head and gave her a cold, piercing look. 'Suzanne,' he said. 'In this house you wear your uniform, and decent shoes.'

'*Oui, m'sieur.*' Prince Ivan could tell that she would open the back door later that day, and, her hands on her haunches, would recount, with derision, her employer's comment. Nobody was more cruel than servants, when ill fortune came.

'Aren't we supposed to receive the Michelin-Citroën commission soon?' Prince Ivan inquired.

Misha put down the newspaper, and said: 'I called yesterday. They were arguing over the percentage again.'

'But I thought it was all in writing. A legal contract.'

Misha picked up his cup, and saw the film of yesterday's coffee on the rim. He pushed it away. 'It was a strange contract, Papa. You see – I was to receive a certain sum of money contingent upon a particular agreement. As it was, the two parties did agree; but their merger was effectuated on somewhat different lines from what I had suggested; and so now they're saying that they'll pay me a finder's fee, but not the agreed-upon commission.'

Prince Ivan narrowed his eyes, and the fingers around the china cup began to shake. 'They really know when a person's desperate.'

'But with the Rovaro, we'll make ends meet. The de Chaynisart brothers are serious people who don't fool around with their money. And the hotel is sound. We should be able to make the restaurant work, too.'

Prince Ivan sighed. 'I don't know what you need me for,' he murmured. 'I sit in that small office day in and day out, and I'm accomplishing nothing.'

Misha sat back, thoughtful. All his life, Prince Ivan's small, wiry frame had seemed to him the most imposing figure in the world; and his perceptive, sharp mind, the most intelligent. In a word, his father had signified power. The sort of power that turned a small man into a giant, and allowed an older man to stay young forever. Now there was a hunch to the small shoulders that suddenly seemed frail; and a querulous tone to the resonant voice that said to him: This is an old man. Misha was filled with intense compassion and, immediately after, with deep, abysmal shame. He'd let his father down. In one short year, he'd let down everybody.

It was so easy to feel self-pity. The world had maligned him. When he'd come into success, he'd given work to many of his old friends from Moscow and Kiev, so many of whom had landed, like the Brasilovs and sixty thousand other White Russians, in Paris. The duck-liver factory had been given to manage to Banov, a destitute middle-aged count; the Metallurgy Works had been assigned to Lipavsky, a billiard player like himself and a companion from the old days. Banov had retired, and was living well with his new French wife. When life was good, everybody jumped on the bandwagon; and when it was bad, the rats jumped first off the sinking ship.

'Papa,' Misha said. 'Why don't you start coming with me to the hotel? Philippe de Chaynisart has set up an office for me. You can help me try to make a profit for them. And I could use your help, to tell you the truth.'

'Soon it will be June. Tourists will begin to come.'

There was a silence. Misha said: 'The Jews from Germany are flooding into the city.'

Prince Ivan blew his nose, and covered the moment. Every time there was a mention of the Jews of Germany, Misha's mind went to the Steiners of Austria. And of course to Lily. Now his father asked, in a soft voice: 'If they decide it's getting too close for comfort, *she'll* have to come home.'

Misha stood up abruptly, and reached into the inside of his jacket. He extracted some folded papers, threw them on the table. 'You think so?' he said sarcastically. 'I don't think she'll ever "come home". She's young, and she's a remarkable beauty. Do you suppose I believed for one minute that she went to Vienna to be with *Marisa?*'

Prince Ivan blinked, taken aback. 'Why else? Her heart was broken, and she had to find comfort somewhere.'

Misha made a grimace of disdain, and his face took on an ugly countenance. 'All women are the same,' he declared. 'She's signed all the papers, for the divorce. Nobody's pride is so intransigent.'

'What do you mean?' Prince Ivan demanded.

'That she's no different from all the rest! She didn't leave because of principles. She left because there was somebody else: another man.'

Horrified, Prince Ivan sat shaking his head from side to side, breathing in and out vociferously. At last he said: 'You're wrong. For once in your life, don't try to pin the blame on someone else! Lily is not responsible in any way, and you know it!'

Misha seized the papers on the table, and, with a savage noise in his throat, tore them into halves and then quarters, and threw the remains on the parquet floor. He cried: 'So now even my father's turned against me!'

Suzanne, her mouth open, a dishrag in her hand, watched goggle-eyed as the tall man thrust open the front door, then banged it behind himself. A small Delft figurine teetered on its wooden stand, and came clattering down, splitting in two. She crossed herself, and looked at Prince Ivan.

'I guess m'sieur's gone alone to the office?' she asked.

Prince Ivan smiled, folding his napkin. 'It's all right, Suzanne,' he stated: 'A little bit of rain never hurt a man my age. I think I'll take the bus: the exercise will do me good, and I like the leisure of the ride past the Palais de Chaillot.'

But when she had turned her back, shuffling into the kitchen, he pressed his hands over his heart.

Chapter Thirteen

After the first night, Lily thought with relief that Mark had only kissed her to be kind, and that he, realizing she was not ready, had put the whole episode behind them both, forging ahead with a friendship they both wanted.

It promised to be a month of peace and pleasure. The late May weather was warm and scented with the blossoms of many varieties of flowers. Kyra and Nick went with Marisa and Nanni and the Fräulein to the old castle in Tobitschau, and young Herr Krapalik followed, so no one would lag behind in his lessons. But Lily stayed behind, with Wolf and his parents. Mark MacDonald went to Tobitschau for two days and returned, declaring that he'd missed the symphony and hadn't come to Vienna to shut himself away in the country, however beautiful it was. And then Lily wondered again about him.

Lily's already abundant mass of dark, lustrous hair had grown to the middle of her back. She liked to walk in the Prater with her hair free, floating about her shoulders. Somehow, with the children gone and Marisa out of earshot, she felt singularly free, too. Isaac and Mina went to their weekend house in Baden, to take the waters, and Wolf took advantage of everyone's absence to begin research for a monograph. The first few days, Mark spent most of his days sight-seeing. And so no one intruded on Lily.

All her life, she'd lived surrounded by people, ruled by other people's needs. Her father's, the nuns', later Misha's, and, finally, the children's. She wondered guiltily if she had a right to be happy. After all, the divorce was well on its way, and she was looking ahead to a most uncertain future; Kyra, in particular, would cause her many problems; and she was a woman alone in what was still a man's world.

Yet she was content. She awakened with joy, her heart soaring with the birds. She walked everywhere, begging the driver to wait for her at the edge of the roads or streets. She stopped in the coffeehouses and ate ravenously, and, more and more, she saw single gentlemen turning to look at her, and sometimes tipping their hats in her direction. She laughed. Maybe this wasn't being very bold, by the standards of 1933; but for her, it seemed that way.

Her life was free, open, for the first time. Every time she thought of Misha, she remembered the constraints; how he'd never really understood her, never really listened – never really cared. He'd thought about his own problems and had seen the world from his own limited viewpoint. A man of black and white, whereas the real world was different shades of grey.

Maybe she'd changed; hadn't Marisa always accused *her* of acting on absolutes? And hadn't Wolf practically said the same thing when he'd tried to explain to her Claire's motivations, and the need for her to accept another human being's limitations? She'd learned that nothing was 'right' or 'wrong', but simply right for some and wrong for others.

She'd finally forgiven herself for her part in the abortion, understanding that when it had occurred, her need for the marriage had superseded her desire to have the child.

Mark said to her: 'I was thinking of taking a drive to the forest, tomorrow. Wolf's friend Hans von Bertelmann has an estate a few hours from here, and he's given Wolf the key while he's away in Switzerland.'

Lily had met Count von Bertelmann on several occasions. He was a member of the oldest Austrian aristocracy: an elegant man, a gentleman. She was not surprised that he would so generously have left his manor open to

283

his friends. And so she smiled, thinking of his kindness, of his good taste. And she felt curious to see his property.

When she had first arrived in Vienna, she'd been aware that the tall, fair-haired man who had been Wolf's university friend had looked at her as a woman. She'd felt his keen blue eyes resting on her, gently but with steadfast pressure. But she hadn't felt like a woman then, and had treated him as no more than a pleasant acquaintance. She'd appreciated the way he'd taken her lead, and acted the perfect Platonic companion on the next occasions when they had seen each other. 'I'm glad you've had a chance to meet Hans,' she said to Mark.

'He's one in a million.'

And when Mark suggested, casually, that she come along for the day, she paused only a moment before nodding her agreement. Wolf sat smiling to himself: Lily had definitely made moves to heal her scars.

The next morning, Mark was standing outside her door, waiting. Wolf's car was outside, its top down. She slipped her goggles on and wound a scarf around her hat, to shield her hair from the dust. Silently, he helped her inside, then took the wheel. She realized that they had never, even in the old days, taken a drive together.

On the way, Mark spoke about his new book, and about some of the ideas he had, and she listened, grateful for the impersonal quality of his subject. She had always been an avid reader. She told him about some of the books Wolf had lent her: *Show Boat*, by Edna Ferber, whose style hadn't always appealed to her; and André Maurois *Byron*, which had. He praised her judgment. Then they didn't speak. He drove on the open road, dust rising in motes, which bothered her more than him. For he sat humming the Brandenburg Concertos in the sun.

The old manor looked poetic, its balconies a bit rundown, its gables washed an opaque hue. The servants had prepared a splendid luncheon, and Lily, laughing at her own hunger, ate until the last bite. Mark teased her. 'One would think you were . . . in that condition.'

She turned red, lowered her eyes. 'I'll never have another child,' she murmured.

They stood up together, and began to walk on a winding path that went into the woods. Soon the sun was partly hidden through the twisting branches of saplings and young trees, and fell through to the ground in dotted patterns. Mark said: 'I've missed you, Lily.'

Something knotted her throat. He continued, his voice filled with tenderness: 'You left a terrible void in my life. There's no one else I've ever wanted to marry.'

His hand was on her elbow. She half turned, looking at him. His face was grave, and showed the passage of the years. He was no longer so . . . 'cherubic'. His regular features were somehow sharper, and there was less of the angel's softness in the line of his chin, not definite and masculine. All these small, half-related thoughts passed through her mind like quick, abrupt wildfire, as she took in the *proximity* of him – the sudden sensuality of him.

Dozens of strange men had smiled at her on the street, and she'd felt an odd stirring. Now Mark was standing so close that she could literally breathe him, and he was touching her.

In the narrow path, he bent over, and touched her lips with the soft fullness of his own. She could feel her heart hammering. She'd never responded like this in Paris. Why now? Why Mark?

And then, just as she felt his mouth on hers, the fear came. She drew away, her eyes wide with panic. It was ridiculous, there was no earthly reason to feel this nameless sense of fear – but yet it had risen like a wild thing between them. 'What's wrong?' he asked, blinking his surprise.

'I don't know. I didn't . . . expect – '

'You didn't expect to like it,' he finished for her. Thrusting his fingers through his tousled hair, she saw him struggle to regain his self-control. The flush on his face showed he'd been excited, and it frightened her.

'Look,' he said, his voice somewhat ragged, not looking at her. 'I know nothing about why you're divorcing Brasilov. And I don't care. While your marriage was going on, I lived my life. I stayed away, didn't I? But now there's no reason to shut off our feelings, is there, Lily? I love you; I want you. So . . . it's up to you.'

Part of her willed for him to try again, to take her in his arms; but something was still paralysing her. She didn't want to decide now. This had come too suddenly. She hadn't had time to think it through . . . the new feelings, the old. And her fear of being betrayed, still an open wound from her years with Misha, made her feel distrustful and wary.

His fingers rose to touch her cheek, and she shook her head. With a small cry, she moved away from him, running back along the path towards the house. He inhaled, let out the air, clamped his teeth together. 'Damn it,' he muttered, turning to follow her. But he didn't run. Instead he took his time, and when he emerged into the garden, found her seated in the car, goggles on and scarf tied. He opened his own door and stepped in without a word, his jaw set.

Misha glanced into the suite, making sure that all the light fixtures were working, and then made a note that truly, the Hotel Rovaro was in top condition. The accommodations were ultramodern. Rooms, suites, studios, gleamed with new paint, and the bathroom plumbing was adequate and hygienic. The curtains were of soft cottons and linens, and the light fixtures were tastefully set up, and handy to use. Every room had a pleasant view, and well-chosen reproductions on the walls.

He turned the key in the lock to close up the suite. It was strange, this feeling of power over the comings and goings of a hotel. Hotels were like small, self-sufficient islands, where hundreds of servants busied themselves daily, and where patrons ate, made love, and planned their next successes and their next betrayals. Hotels had always lured him, with their promise of anonymity. When he'd gone to the billiard halls in Moscow, he'd been searching for just that kind of anonymity: to stop being, for the moment, Prince Mikhail Ivanovitch Brasilov.

He stopped in the hallway, thinking, with sudden hunger, that it had been a long, long time since he'd been with a woman. Now, as the head of the Hotel Rovaro, he would have ample opportunity to take off a few hours to lie with someone for a brief pause in the inexorable machinery that was time, and his own life. But would that really be a pause? Time knew when people tried to cheat, and mocked them for their trouble. He realized that sweat was pouring profusely from his forehead, and he thought: I *have* no life. No love, no joy, no child, no mistress.

He went slowly down the stairs, and stopped at the restaurant. There were about twenty people seated at small tables with flower centrepieces. Around them, the waiters and wine stewards were dashing about with expertise and enthusiasm. He turned away, trying not to think of how many other tables had been empty. Of the three hundred rooms, only fifty were occupied at present.

If only he hadn't insulted his father! He opened the door to his office, next to Philippe de Chaynisart's. He sat down behind the desk and glanced at the pad of paper in front of him, filled with facts and figures.

At the Rovaro the bill at Les Halles for fresh food products ran to four thousand francs a day. The average take from the restaurant was two thousand gross. He twirled the pen in his fingers and chewed on the end. He thought: First of all, there are twenty-two employees that we don't need: maids, scullery people, telephone operators. Then, the menu à la carte was superfluous: the regular menu was ample enough. The daily expenses should run to no more than eighteen hundred, for Les Halles, the domestics, the housekeeping matrons, the cooks, the dishwashers, the wine cellar attendants, and the wine cellar. And the restaurant should be grossing ten thousand a day.

How to accomplish this? In the United States, there was a growing industry called advertising. This hotel was a product, like a soap or a chocolate cream. He'd known many men and women of great wealth, and somehow there had to be a way to let them know that the hotel existed.

I'll have to ask Papa to help me with this, he thought, happy suddenly at the idea of his father's face when he would realize how much his expertise was still needed. And for the first time that day, he felt the knot below his heart being released.

Hanneliese was asleep in the servants' quarters. The small apartment on the third floor was blessedly empty. Lily couldn't sleep. Restlessly, she pulled open all the windows, and went to sit in the living room in the dark. The view was of the large boulevard lined with trees in bloom, occasionally illuminated by an eerie streetlamp. Cars drove by, their chrome suddenly splashed by the yellow glow of the tall, sculpted lamps. She thought dreamily of the time when one drove in a horse-drawn coupé or victoria, and the only sound of travel was the clip-clop of hooves on the cobblestones. She wished she had been born twenty years before, when the world had been a quieter, more civilized place, and where men were gentlemen who knew the subtle art of courtship.

Directly below her, she could hear strains of chamber music. Wolf was playing the cello, and his friends from the Philharmonic were visiting. She'd made it her custom to play the piano with them; but when she wasn't present, a gaunt man from the Philharmonic came to play the viola, and a middle-aged woman, always clothed in dark velvet, came with the bass; from the beginning, a small, rotund man called Felix Klein had brought his Stradivarius, and now Lily could hear the perfect notes rising. These were professionals – even Wolf, who had taken lessons from Piatigorsky some years back. She listened, bewitched, imagining a large ballroom with high ceilings and delicate mouldings and fretwork, and a beautiful floor of polished oak – and lovely women in décolletages dancing on tiptoes in the expert arms of their escorts.

Slowly, she moved into her bedroom. It overlooked the garden, and so she leaned against the windowsill and gazed out. The manicured lawns pleased her, with their carved nymphs dripping water like the incessant tears of gods watching the erring humans. Somebody was there, walking, gravel crunching slightly beneath his feet. She knew, right away, that it had to be Mark; Wolf was downstairs, playing; and there was no one else in the house besides the servants. She watched him. He was walking in his shirt sleeves, his head bent, absorbed in thought. Lily, in her nightgown, leaned on the windowsill with her elbows. It was like watching a moving picture: the man, solitary, reflecting on his life, and maybe planning a chapter of his book. She wondered if Balzac had ever been watched this way, without his knowledge. It was strangely exciting.

Mark turned at the gazebo, and she saw his face in the light. It was a beautiful face, the face of an angel. She'd never actually given his looks that much attention. She'd always accepted him as a total being: Mark, kind, reliable, intelligent, gentle. Perhaps he'd been right when he'd been angry with her, for simply assuming that he could not be jarred, could not bleed inside, like other people. *I never really considered him at all!* she realized with sudden shame. He'd been right to be angry. She watched Mark carefully now, with different eyes. What had his life become? Was there a woman now, in Paris, whom he loved?

Surely, surely, someone with such sensitive eyes, with such beautiful hands, would make a woman want him. Not all would be as foolish as she. She could feel her heart beating. She tried to picture him with a woman: half clothed, his shirt haphazard on the bed, and his muscled torso gleaming with a thin film of perspiration. His hands on the girl's shoulders. Bending down to kiss her, tilting back her throat. Lily realized with sudden shock which way her thoughts were taking her, and stood up, her cheeks hot with embarrassment. But her hand remained on the moulding of the window, and her eyes were magnetized by the man walking alone, below her window, unaware of the emotions he was causing above him.

The curtain, moved by the breeze of the open window, began to flap. Lily secured it in its sash. She felt weak, her pulses beating, and her movements were jerky like a hesitant young colt's. Her elbow bumped against a bureau, and a small photograph of Kyra in a silver frame slid off its support and fell to the floor. The noise it made seemed disproportionate to the size of the object, and she felt the jolt inside, frightened. But, of course, when there was total silence, any small bump would be heard as a tearing crash. She bent down to pick up the frame, straightened up – and realized that, from the garden, Mark had also been alerted by the noise, and was now looking inside her room: staring straight at her in her filmy nightgown. For at least thirty seconds, their eyes remained locked, each surprised by the intrusion of the other into what had been, for either one, a private moment.

Prince Ivan sat in the office in his frock coat of crimson velvet, trying not to look at the papers in front of him. Two years ago, he'd been sitting in an office large as a ballroom, with paintings by Degas and Dufy on the walls. He glanced at his ruby cuff links and remembered when he'd been married, in Moscow, and had been invited to speak at a conference in London. Maria, bless her heart, had personally packed his suitcase. It had always been that way between them. She'd taken care of him with imperious protectiveness, in the area of food and clothing; and he'd protected her from the ills of life, as husbands owed it to their wives to do.

He'd gone with Misha, a very young man. They took a suite with adjoining rooms at Claridge's. Of course, they had brought tuxedos and frilled shirts with them for the evening events. The first night, he'd begun to dress, when, suddenly, his heart had missed a beat: where were his pearl shirt buttons? Maria had packed the cuff links, the collar button, the silk *pochette*, even the white scarf. But not the two small pearl buttons that were used to close a stuffed shirt.

He knocked on his son's door, and said to him: 'Misha: how many pairs of shirt buttons did you bring with you?'

The young man, puzzled, had shrugged: 'Just one. We're here for two days.'

'Your mother forgot to pack mine. I suppose you'll have to go down alone. I can't close my shirt.'

Misha had thought for a moment, then rung the bellboy. 'Could you go, as fast as possible, to buy my father two buttons for a stuffed shirt?'

'But sir,' the bellboy had protested, 'it's seven o'clock, and all the stores are closed.'

'Well, then, we'll give you a fine tip if you can go from door to door, and ask if perhaps another guest might have brought two pairs of shirt buttons and could lend one to my father.'

It had been a good idea. After fifteen minutes, the bellboy had reappeared, triumphant. 'Sir, I have here two buttons. But no one had a pair, so I had to borrow a single pearl from one gentleman, and a second from another.'

Prince Ivan recalled how joyful he had felt, until the boy had opened up his hand. On his palm lay, indeed, two pearls: but one was grey and the other white. 'I can't wear them,' he had groaned.

'But yes, you can,' Misha had contradicted. 'At the table, no one will notice; and in the reception hall, we shall be standing, and no one will see that the buttons are different. You'd better hurry up and finish dressing, Papa, because we're late.'

Prince Ivan hadn't felt reassured; but he'd travelled so far, that to stay in his room would have seemed preposterous. He returned to his room to put the finishing touches to his toilette. Then he had left with Misha.

Downstairs, waiting to be let into the banquet hall, groups of men gathered together in the reception hall. Prince Ivan had been approached by a British dignitary whom he knew. As they spoke, Prince Ivan had noticed that the other man's eyes were drawn, irresistibly, to his shirtfront. Instead of losing countenance, a brilliant idea had entered his head. 'I see you're looking at my buttons,' he declared. 'In Moscow, this is the latest fashion. We've started to wear unmatched buttons with our dress shirts. But the fashion is so new, I see it hasn't yet reached London.'

'What an original idea,' the Englishman said. 'It does give you quite an elegance ... Look here,' he'd cried, stopping a passing friend. 'This is the new Russian fashion, to wear shirt buttons of different shades. Isn't it nice?'

'Very,' the other asserted. 'One grey, one white. Looks most distinguished. The man who launched this had a great idea. Tomorrow, I'll purchase a grey pearl to put with my white.'

A fourth gentleman had come up to them, intrigued. 'I beg your pardon, but I overheard your conversation. May I see?'

Prince Ivan, and Misha too, had enjoyed themselves thoroughly. When it had been time to give his speech, the former hadn't felt the least bit embarrassed. And, to make matters more amusing, when he was invited to the British Consulate in Moscow for a formal dinner some three months later, he'd seen a remarkable sight: three of the guests, fresh from London, were wearing different shades of pearl buttons on their shirts. Princess Maria's forgetfulness had started a trend. But she'd felt guilty, and, to make up for having caused her husband a problem, had ordered a special pair of ruby and gold cuff links for him from the jeweller Fabergé.

Now that she was gone, Prince Ivan often wore them, never without being reminded of how he had begun an international fashion trend. He picked up a paper, dropped it listlessly again. Why bother to read what was obviously just another list of expenditures that went over budget, or an itemized bill that would require a dexterous juggling act to hold off the creditor? Lately, he'd caught himself thinking, more and more, about the past, especially about his wife. He was growing old; no, he'd grown old. His mind no longer was as sharp as it had been even a few years ago, and his morale was down, down, so that it wasn't possible for him to discuss facts and figures with Misha the way they'd always done, since he had taken the boy in as a partner.

There was a discreet knock on the door, and he answered, his voice poised and dignified. 'Come in.'

Rochefort stuck his head in, always conscious of protocol. 'There seems to be a problem out here, Monsieur le Prince,' he said hesitantly.

'Oh?' Prince Ivan wondered if another creditor had come for his due. He rose, on faltering legs. Lately, his knees seemed weaker, less stable. He went to the door and the secretary held it open deferentially. From the inside of his office, he could see two female clerks hovering near the staircase, and a man about ten years his junior, with a haggard expression and eyes that protruded oddly from his long, well-shaped head. The man looked ill, and agitated. 'It's Verlon,' Rochefort whispered. 'The ex-manager of the

Aisne refinery. He said he was looking for Prince Mikhail, but . . . something's wrong.'

Prince Ivan took a few steps into the hall, and smiled. With kindness, he motioned for the tall man to come up, and held out his hand. 'How do you do, Monsieur Verlon,' he murmured. 'I'm Ivan Vassilievitch Brasilov. How can I help you?'

Henri Verlon walked up, his stride jerky and abrupt, and Rochefort hovered near the Prince, a frown on his face. 'He wouldn't tell me why he's here,' he whispered to his employer.

'It's all right,' Prince Ivan said. 'Come in, monsieur. You've just come from your house in the Aisne, I presume, and you must be tired.'

Verlon, without a word, entered the office. Prince Ivan went to his desk, prepared to sit down. Rochefort had not left the room, but was standing awkwardly by the door. And suddenly, without warning, the tall, gaunt man moved his right hand into the inside pocket of his coat, and came out with a gleaming metal revolver. Prince Ivan's eyes widened with shock; his face turned white, and he clutched the edge of his desk. 'Monsieur,' he cried. 'Put that thing away – '

Rochefort jumped forward, but too late. Verlon, without warning, aimed at Prince Ivan and emptied the barrel of his gun into the small man's stomach. Prince Ivan collapsed in a pool of blood, his hands over the wounds, his mouth absurdly open. Rochefort fell on Verlon's back, but the other, though older, shook him off. At last he spoke.

'Don't come any closer!' he shouted, and whipped out a second gun as fast as he'd withdrawn the first. Rochefort began to run out. The two young girls had gathered on the threshold, and were screaming. Rochefort fell against them, slipped, and landed on the floor.

Then Henri Verlon turned to face him, pointed the revolver at his own temple, and fired.

* * *

When Lily received the telegram from her mother, she was struck with shock. It seemed so unbelievable . . . dear Ivan Vassilievitch, whom she'd always loved, hanging between life and death in the hospital. Henri Verlon? Misha had spoken quite highly of him. What, then, had really happened?

She envisaged Misha now, watching his father dying, as, seven years before, she'd watched her own. But Misha had always adored his father. Prince Ivan had been his best friend, his partner, his confidant. Where was the justice in life? She forced herself to actually see Misha's features: the pain, held back but poignant – the sense of despair. She got up from her table and went to the large closet in the hallway, and pulled out a suitcase. All her nerves were set on edge, and a tremendous restlessness had taken her over. It wasn't a time for thinking. You had to do what you had to do – that was all there was to it.

For Misha, the days were continuing in defiance of the fact that the world had stopped moving, that every human process – feeling, acting, thinking – had ceased. By the time he arrived at the Hôpital Beaujon, his father had been transported to the emergency ward, and he was only able to glimpse him from a half-open door. He rushed out to telephone the physicians he knew: Lebovici, Fildermann, and Simkov. When they arrived, he didn't even see them. They were immediately whisked away into the operating room.

He waited outside, on a hard bench, gnawing on his cuticles. After one and a half hours, Dr Basset, the chief of surgery, came out to tell him that his father had endured the operation quite well. They had put the patient under chloroform, and found eight intestinal wounds, three of them serious. One had to wait three or four days to be able to make a prognostication.

At eleven in the evening, exhausted and drenched with perspiration, Misha went home.

The next day the ground was frozen, and patterns of November frost had left designs on the windscreen of Misha's car. He had always meant to exchange the De Dion-Bouton for a more modern car, but instead, a few years back, he'd merely had the engine replaced. As he drove to the hospital, his eyes hurting from a sleepless night, he wondered how much he might be able to obtain for a car that was ten years old. It was better to think about the car than about his father; Misha couldn't bear to imagine his pain – or, worse, what might happen in the days to come. One had to drum up something – *anything* – to fill the cavities of one's mind: anything *not* to think, not to live in the absurd, cruel, senseless present.

Faces out of nowhere ballooned out at him, disconnected from reality: Rochefort; Claire and Jacques Walter; old friends from Russia who still loved Prince Ivan. If it was any consolation, his father had bound the people in his life to him, by his wisdom and kindness. But, oddly enough, it didn't matter. Nothing at all mattered, it seemed.

He went into the post-operative room, which was large and white, and filled with iron beds where patients of all ages lay, some moaning, others so silent that they presaged death. At the back of the room, two beds lay hidden, each behind a screen. Misha was directed to one of them, and drew back the screen. His father's eyes were open, and when he took the limp hand on the coverlet, he saw that the eyes had recognized him. He sat holding his father's hand until the nurse gently removed it, so that she might check the patient's temperature. It wasn't good: 38.8 Celsius, with a pulse of one hundred and twenty beats. She gave him water and told Misha that his tongue was dry.

A new doctor was on call, Marshak, and he told Misha that he was sorry, but that from now on, the patient would only be able to receive visitors between one and two in the afternoon. Also, one could go to the head nurse, and be taken to a door with two glass panes through which the patients could be observed.

Misha walked out like an automaton. Claire was standing alone, holding a cup of dark tea. She laid a gloved hand on his arm. 'Come,' she said. 'Drink this. You must! For *him*.'

He turned his green eyes to her, and she saw the circles around them, the intensity of his look. 'Do you know who lies on the other side of Papa?' he demanded. 'Verlon! They've put the assassin next to him!'

Claire didn't reply. She simply held the cup up to his lips.

After a while Claire seemed to have vanished, and he smelled an incongruously familiar perfume. He felt a hand on his shoulder. Almost angry at the intrusion, at the necessity of acknowledging yet another well-meaning friend, he turned to look up. Varvara, wrapped in grey astrakhan, with a fur bonnet on her red hair, was simply standing there. He breathed out with relief, and bowed his head. She sat down beside him, took his hand and played with it, soft caresses on his palm.

'It's in all the papers,' she said softly.

He didn't answer. Then she said: 'It's getting late. There's a café across the street, where we could get a bite to eat. Then you can return to see him through the glass panel.'

It would be his first meal in two days. Wearily, like a child being led by a wiser adult, he followed Varvara down the stairs and into the street. He could see some of the people he knew at the café, and felt, for a horrid moment, like running away in order not to face them. But Varvara's fingers were closed tightly over his elbow. She marched him through the tables, answering with a distant smile the worried questions that many pairs of eyes were addressing

297

to her. Then she sat down with Misha and ordered hot soup, and coffee.

'Speak to me,' he suddenly said, taking her hand and squeezing it in both of his. 'Say something about – anything! The theatre.'

'There's nothing to say about the theatre. I'm an old hand at it now. Watch me: I'll be like Sarah Bernhardt, or Réjane. I'll grow old with my admirers. Although there's nothing sadder than an old beauty queen.'

Then Varvara sighed, and patted Misha's hand. 'Oh, dear God,' she whispered. 'We all need a cause, don't we? With you, it's fighting the Communists; with me? I suppose it's staving off poverty and obscurity. It's not that I love the theatre: it's just that without it, who would I be? And there's a need to be somebody, isn't there?'

'I don't know anymore,' he replied, meeting her blue eyes with a strangely naked look.

They ate their soup, drank their coffee, and then she led him back up to the ward, where he peered at his father through a glass partition. This was all the life he could feel now: to touch the glass with his forehead and chin, and to observe a semiconscious figure lying immobile behind a screen, which, for the purpose of his eyes, had been partially turned aside. He felt Varvara's lips on the skin of his cheek, and then she was gone, only the warm scent of her perfume remaining. Varvara, Varvara. A woman like a river, ever changing yet forever constant.

He was conscious with a jolt that she was forty-seven, and that she had succeeded in warding off the cruelty of time. His father had had no such pretensions: he'd only wished to live, to eat, to speak, to read in the quiet of his study. And to hold in his lap his grandchildren, his tie to the future and to his past, another link to his beloved wife, dead in another land.

Misha thought, with so much pain that he had to turn away from the attendant: Where are these children now?

And will I ever see them again? He'd lost, now, everything: his country, his mother, his wife, his children, his position and fortune ... and, he felt with a peculiar intuitive certainty, his beloved father.

The next day the streets were covered with sheets of impenetrable ice. He realized, with shock, that he had let the days go by without keeping track of them, and that it was already Saturday 2 December. He was greeted in the hospital corridor by the head nurse, who told him that the night had been a difficult one, and that the patient was worse: his stomach was swollen like a hard balloon. Dr Marshak came at eleven, and looked pessimistic. Claire came, and sat with him outside the ward, then took him to the café across the street, where they shared a sandwich. Dr Simkov came to them there, with a slightly more optimistic prognostication. Claire returned inside with Misha and took up vigil with him until Dr Marshak returned at six thirty. The patient had a temperature of 38.8 Celsius, and his pulse beat one hundred and sixty times per minute. His stomach was still swollen.

Misha hadn't been allowed inside at all that day. In the evening the nurses purged his stomach, and the temperature went down to 38.2, with the pulse at one hundred and thirty. They told Misha that his father's tongue looked better than it had all day. He looked in through the glass panel, but nothing seemed changed.

At ten thirty, Dr Marshak told him that Henri Verlon had died, and that it seemed as if the story had come out, through some of his daughter's testimony as well as that of a gunsmith in the Aisne Department. The day before the fatal incident, Verlon had talked happily of his little house, and of how pleased he had been with the arrangements. Then, the next day, he'd gone out and bought two guns. He'd come to Paris looking for Prince Mikhail, and, according to Rochefort, had appeared definitely deranged. And for no apparent reason, he'd shot Prince Ivan, whom he had never seen in his life, and then himself. The only conclusion that could be inferred was that he had become temporarily insane, and had lost all contact with reality.

But Henri Verlon's daughter had another idea. She knew that when the refinery project had been let go, her father had lost all hope of ever getting out from the problems of making ends meet. He'd examined his life, and realized that his one hope had lain in making a great deal of money with the Brasilovs, as manager of the refinery. Instead of a small house in the country, he might have had a lifetime of cruises left for his old age. So that, having brooded for months upon the breakdown of his hopes, he had lost his mind in a paroxysm of frustration, and decided to shoot Prince Mikhail, whom he considered to be responsible. And when the younger man had been absent from his office, he had shot the father.

Misha nodded, but Marshak's words told him absolutely nothing. He didn't care. It really didn't make any difference who had tried to kill his father, or why. He was drained of all emotion, and put on his coat and walked out of the hospital.

Outside, he ran into Varvara and a young girl about eighteen years old, whom he didn't remember. Varvara said: 'Misha, this is Ida Chagall, the painter's daughter. I saw her at a benefit sale, and she particularly wanted to give you her sympathy.'

'Your father is a great man, Mikhail Ivanovitch,' the girl told him. He was staring at her blankly, not understanding. 'All the Russians in Paris admire him.'

Finally the words seemed to penetrate. He answered, softly, 'Thank you, Ida Markovna. But all the admiration in the world won't repair his intestine. Medicine hasn't found a way yet to mend such delicate organs. Today they refused to let me in to visit him.'

Ida Chagall turned her head aside, and Misha knew

300

that she had meant well. He said, curtly: 'I'm sorry, ladies, but I'm very tired. Good night.'

His footsteps crunched on the pavement, and he could almost feel Varvara's eyes boring holes into his back, trying to see inside his soul. She'd done the best she could; but still, she had her benefits to attend, her notoriety to uphold. Someone else's father was dying.

In the car, he thought: Even the Jews, then, admired Papa. And he felt strangely stirred, and touched.

In the morning the frost was less pronounced. Misha had gone to bed and been awakened by the telephone at midnight. Dr Marshak told him things looked worse. At 2.00 A.M. the telephone rang again, and again at four. Finally, at six, he washed and dressed and left the house. The night nurse and the head nurse both told him that the patient was extremely ill, and the screen had been put completely around the bed so that, when he tried to see his father, he saw only the wooden slats.

He tried to find Dr Basset, and when he did, was told that it might last till night-time. Misha went across the street to the café, and smoked half a packet of cigarettes. If this was the end, why then, good God, did it have to drag out this way?

At one, he was let into the ward, and led to the bed. Prince Ivan looked changed. His eyes were hollow, and his cheeks were like pale parchment dotted with unkempt points of grey where his beard had grown. What a proud man he'd always been! He would have felt ashamed to see his own appearance, now, on the edge of death. Misha held his hand, and thought that the lips began to move. He bent down, tried to hear the words, but no sound emerged. At two o'clock he was still sitting in the same position, holding his father's hand, trying to read his lips, and the nurse had to lift him half up before he realized that it was time to go.

He went into the hallway, and leaned wearily against

the wall. It was always draughty there, and he could feel himself trembling with a sort of fever. He half opened his eyes. Coming towards him, at the far end of the hall, was a woman in a dark coat, walking quickly. He watched her grow larger and larger, made out the long, well-shaped legs and the dark head of hair. And then his body was seized in a sort of paroxysm, and the dam ruptured. He felt the start of his own tears at the same moment that he felt her arms go about him.

At 4:00 P.M., when Dr Basset found him to tell him that this was the end, he found them sitting together, wordlessly, holding hands. They went in together, and sat on either side of Prince Ivan as he breathed his last agonizing moments. Then she bent down to close his eyes, and brushed his forehead with her lips. 'Goodnight, Papa,' she whispered, and the room was still.

Outside the grey of early morning greeted them, aureoled with pink. They walked aimlessly, holding each other tight, mute against the sharp sounds of the waking birds. Finally they sat down on a bench, and she held his head against the warmth of her neck. He was afraid to ask her if she planned to go away, now that it was over. And she didn't want to say, because her own grief had been so small compared to his. The enormity of life and death swayed over them both.

She held him until they entered the car, and when he inserted his key into the lock of the apartment, he went quickly into one of the bathrooms so as not to be in her way. But when he emerged, afraid, she wasn't in the living room. He called out her name, 'Lily!' and went, hesitantly, to his bedroom. She was already in bed, her dark hair loose about her shoulders.

And so he undressed, aware of the ticking sounds of time passing, and went to her. Under the cold sheets, he could feel the heat of her body near him. He was afraid to touch her, but the pain of death had been too strong, too

302

wrenching, and so he moved towards her, conscious that, in the same moment, she had moved towards him.

They welcomed the strength and power of their bodies merging, warding away the terror of death and reaffirming their own pulsing life, and as he fell asleep he remembered that he still hadn't asked her what her plans were. But her head lay in the crook of his neck, and her hair caressed his chest with the softness of pussywillows, and so he let his mind drift off in peace, for the first time in many months.

God had taken someone dear from him, but had given him back a treasure he had thought lost forever.

Chapter Fourteen

It was better for everybody to start a fresh life, and when Philippe de Chaynisart proposed to Misha that he move his family into a small suite at the Hotel Rovaro, this seemed to solve many problems at once. It would have been impossible to remain at the Avenue Paul-Doumer apartment, and to live surrounded by the mementos of Prince Ivan, knowing that he would never be with them again. Misha wasn't the kind of man to hang on to mementos: he preferred to turn the page, and thereby to accept his father's death. It seemed far better to let all his private memories live on in his spirit – and to keep only those few things that had a particular sentimental value to him. He kept the ruby cuff links, and a few other items. The rest was put up for public auction.

And, of course, the best part about the hotel was that there was no rent to pay. There were drawbacks, however. The suite was very small. In the bedroom was the big bed, and a small cot for Nick. Kyra slept on the divan in the living room. Misha marvelled within himself at the easy adaptability of his wife. She appeared not to miss the large apartment and the many servants. And because of her attitude, the children didn't question the arrangement, either.

Kyra and Nick had immediately gone exploring, discovering the kitchens and the multitude of servants always full of stories. They'd sat down Maurice, the old bellboy, and made him tell them all his anecdotes about the people who had lived at the hotel. There was the Pink Lady, dressed in shocking pink with boa feathers, who'd run out of her suite in the middle of the night, in a pink nightgown, screaming 'Fire! Fire!' only to have the Baron Charles discover that the 'flames' she'd seen had been her husband's red bathrobe left hanging in the bathroom, aureoled by a yellow lightbulb he'd forgotten to turn off. And the American heiress who'd asked Maurice why she couldn't seem to find the man she'd fallen in love with: they'd met on a ship, his name was André, and she'd walked up and down 'Main Street' looking for him. The children loved these tales of human foibles, and the old man in his red uniform with the elegant gold braiding on the shoulders and cuffs.

Lily usually took the children by bus to their lycées, at eight in the morning, and then walked home. At eleven she would walk again to pick them up for lunch, strolling back so that they would get their exercise. They lunched at the hotel, and often Misha joined them. Lunch was from twelve thirty to one o'clock. There were days when the rotund Philippe de Chaynisart stopped at their table to drink a cup of coffee. Lily liked him; he was not, she thought, as affable and congenial as he wanted others to believe he was. One had to stay on one's toes, but this was not a problem for the Brasilovs. He'd taken Misha under his wing, and had approved all the changes the latter had been making.

Lily had gone through her old belongings, and put everything up for auction with Prince Ivan's things. It hadn't been easy; but there was no choice anymore, and the suite was small. Claire had taken the Pleyel piano. Misha borrowed one of the small upright pianos from one of the lounges, where it was never used, and had it brought up to the living room. And so, twice a week, Raïssa Markovna Sudarskaya would come to give the two children their lessons.

Life was cramped, and there were almost no luxuries left. Sometimes, Lily thought back on the life she had left behind in Vienna. The Steiners had wrapped themselves around her like a warm matrix, yet she had been, for the first time in her life, on her own. She felt a twinge of regret, for those moments alone, for those moments with them . . . for the fact that there, she hadn't been somebody's wife, but just herself, Lily. Yet it felt good to be 'home', to sleep every night with Misha, to forget the hurts and the anguish that had separated them. She needed to be here, not just for herself and him as a couple, but to give the children a stability that they'd missed. They were completed by their father: without him, and his strong love, they'd been just a little disconnected, in spite of all the love that had come from other corners.

And Mark? Lily didn't have much free time for reflection, except when she was walking back and forth to the lycées. But then, watching the frostbitten trees, she would sometimes think back on that lovely spring, on the moments she had been with him, simply talking, or silent with memories. But Mark, like her own self-sufficiency, was part of the past – a stolen moment of friendship, of awakened hope, of . . . ? She couldn't tag a name to the sentiment.

The morning of 6 February 1934 began with a sharp, grey wind. After she had taken the children to school, Lily went to the Stock bookstore. When she came home, Claire telephoned and asked her to join them for dinner at the Hotel Crillon. A veterans' parade had been planned for the evening, but rumour had it that this would be the excuse to launch a massive riot to oust Premier Edouard Daladier and the other lame politicians whom the French Right was blaming for the Stavisky scandals. 'I don't know if I should leave the Rovaro,' Lily said hesitantly.

'Aunt Marthe is here, darling. You can't *not* come. She's very old now and only comes to Paris once or twice a year. Last year, and the year before, you were in Vienna.'

Aunt Marthe Bertholet was Paul's father's sister, and was at least seventy-three. She had married a man who had become an electrician, in Nantes, near the Loire. He had worked hard, and developed an invention dealing with storage batteries. Eventually he had patented this and opened a large factory, becoming quite wealthy. Then he had died, leaving his widow a considerable fortune. When one travelled through the fields of France, posters still greeted one's eye, saying BERTHOLET BATTERIES, at least as many as those that advertised the newspaper *Le Matin* and that other staple of the French marketplace, Amer Picon.

She was tall, thick, with the neck of a bull, a head that was round like a marble, with half-closed eyes and a potato nose that emerged from fat cheeks, and her mouth was crooked. For some reason, she had always believed that she was an irresistible beauty. Her husband, Uncle Alfred, had died twenty years before, and she had often wondered, out loud, why no rich and fascinating young man had presented himself in the interim. Lily found Aunt Marthe the most disagreeable woman she knew; but, once a year, she came to Paris and insisted on seeing her 'beloved family'. If she could avoid it, Lily skipped this rendezvous, and very rarely took the children. But Claire, out of a sense of duty because the old woman was alone in the world, always made it a point to meet with her and act as her companion during her week's visit. She always stayed at the Hotel Crillon, at the Place de la Concorde, midway between the Champs-Élysées and the Ile de la Cité across the Seine River. It was a stately mansion built in the late eighteenth century by the architect Gabriel, and Aunt Marthe felt that it was the only hotel in Paris good enough for her patronage. 'A *lady* can entertain so well there,' she would announce for all to hear, in her nasal voice.

Lily now said: 'But if there's going to be a demonstration, I won't bring the children. I'll just drop them off at Rovaro after school, and come to the Crillon by métro.'

'That's just as well. Tell Misha that he's welcome, of course, but I know he doesn't enjoy meeting Aunt Marthe.

You can spend the night with us: the Ritz is within walking distance, and if there's a riot, it would be good to have you near us.'

Lily passed her tongue over her dry lips, and asked: 'Claude isn't coming?'

This had always been the delicate point between them, now that Lily had returned to Paris. Lily, for a motive unknown to her mother, had made it very clear that she would never, under any circumstances, socialize with her brother's wife. When Claire, bewildered, had pressed the point, Lily had said to her, quietly but with intense emotion: 'It's a subject best not delved into. I'm happy Claude seems content with his marriage, and I wish the three of them well. But Henriette and I had words long ago, and I will never again be in the same room with her.'

Reluctantly, Claire accepted the situation.

In the afternoon, after the children had come home, Lily took her bath and put lotion on her hands. She trimmed her cuticles and polished her nails. Under no circumstance did she want her mother and Jacques – and above all, Aunt Marthe – to guess how strained the Brasilov finances really were. She pinned up her hair in a pomadour, and selected a simple bias-cut dress of dark blue velvet, with shoulder pads. Then she pinned a cameo at her throat and put a blue felt halo hat at the back of her head, to frame her face. 'Where are you going?' Kyra demanded.

'To have dinner with Aunt Marthe, at the Crillon.'

'Papa said there will be a riot,' Nicky said.

'Don't worry. I'll stay close to Grandpa Jacques. And you two will take your baths and eat your dinner with Papa, downstairs.'

On the ground floor, she went to find her husband in his office. He was standing in front of his desk, deep in conversation with the Baron Charles de Chaynisart. Philippe's brother was a few years older, a few pounds slimmer, and had a sharper set to his features. But the baby blue eyes were the same. 'Well, Princess,' he declared. 'You are without doubt the most elegant woman in Paris.'

Lily couldn't help feeling that the smooth compliment had been intended as an ironic slight. She didn't know why, but she was uncomfortable, and blushed. 'Thank you, Baron,' she answered. And then: 'I'll be going now, Misha.'

'I'd rather you skipped that,' her husband said, his voice tight. 'I don't want you out tonight.'

'But I promised. And I'll be with Jacques, and Mother.'

Charles de Chaynisart's lips curved into a sliver of a smile, and he said to Misha: 'My dear man, women today are so . . . independent. They aren't at all like our mothers and grandmothers. They fly over oceans and vote the Radicals into the Chamber, and know all about Monsieur Stavisky's dark past. Let her be! Do not clip her wings, they are too pretty to watch.'

'I'm sorry, but Lily is my wife. I can't allow her to go out into what is certain to be one of the most dangerous mob riots of our precarious times.'

'Well, then, I have an idea. Why don't you let me escort your fair lady to her destination? I was planning to leave shortly, anyway. There's a card game tonight, and I must go home to freshen up beforehand. My chauffeur can deposit the Princess on our way.'

Lily shook her head, confused and embarrassed. 'No, no. I can go alone, by métro – '

'Nonsense. I wouldn't hear of it.' Charles de Chaynisart grabbed his fitted overcoat from the back of an armchair, and put his hand on Lily's elbow. She turned, looking at Misha, and saw him nod imperceptibly. But there was a strange, closed look about his face that troubled her.

Charles de Chaynisart's car was a magnificent imported silver and blue Duesenberg Model J, spanking new. Lily stepped inside, all at once conscious of the shabbiness of her three-year-old suede shoes, and of the small bag that matched them. She could recall, eons ago in another life, sitting at a fashion show at the Maison Chanel, circling the numbers of the many gowns, dresses, and suits she was selecting. An unseen woman a few rows back had whispered audibly to her companion: 'Look! There's the Princess Brasilova. Isn't she a beauty? And so rich she could buy every outfit in this collection!' She thought, wryly, that perhaps God punished those who accepted their wealth without giving a thought to the millions of poor who didn't have enough to make ends meet in their daily lives.

The trim chauffeur started up the motor, and Charles, impeccable in his grey overcoat and grey homburg, was bending slightly in her direction. 'Frankly, madame, I won't be a bit sorry if there *is* an outburst tonight. Our country is going to the wolves – and to *Gospodin* Stalin. I say, let's get them all out: Daladier, Chautemps, and Blum, of course. He's the worst of the lot!'

'But you can't put the first two in the same category as Blum. They're Radicals, middle-of-the-roaders. He's a much more definite individual, less likely to compromise.'

'That's what makes him even more dangerous than the others. If that government should ever go socialist, I'll move to Italy. I rather like that little dandy over there – Mussolini. At least he knows how to be a man! He knows the meaning of strength.'

Lily couldn't help herself, and asked: 'And Hitler, Baron? Do you like him, too?'

He threw back his head and emitted a gurgle of leonine laughter. 'Adorable! I must say, you are adorable . . . Herr Hitler? He's an efficacious man, a leader. I wish we had someone like that in France. He knows how to get things done. Having admitted this, I do have to add that he strikes me as a touch too humourless. Life without humour can fade into dullness very quickly – don't you agree?'

'It depends in which sense you mean it. If the humour doesn't hurt others, and if it's gentle, it can be the most

310

healing agent in life. But there is also cruel, abusive humour. The kind that wounds so deeply, that sometimes the butt of the joke never fully recovers.'

They were slowing down near the Café Marignan, on the Champs-Élysées. It was five thirty, and the demonstration was not expected for another hour and a half. But already the pavements were congested, and the streets guarded by a battery of uniformed policemen. Lily shuddered, and was sorry she hadn't stayed with Misha at the hotel. This would be worse than she had imagined.

Charles de Chaynisart picked up her gloved hand in one of his own, and turned it over. She felt a moment of electric shock, and wanted to remove it at once; but the pressure of his fingers was so slight, that she chided herself for reacting like a prude. He was the kind of man who toyed with any object that came into his line of vision. She'd seen him pick up pencils, feel their tips with momentary curiosity, then set them down, only to seize a paperweight next to them and idly fondle its smoothness. There had obviously not been any thought on his part when he had turned her hand over so cavalierly, as if it had been a card left behind on somebody's sofa.

The noise around them was thick, and he asked: 'You aren't afraid?'

She smiled, perfunctorily. 'A little, yes.'

He regarded her levelly with his baby blue eyes, in which, she felt with a sudden shiver, there wasn't the slightest trace of babyish naïveté. 'Not me,' he said, in a still, slightly bemused voice. 'Nothing frightens me. That makes me a mite peculiar, don't you think? My brother, for example, is frightened by mice, and by women who scream, and by wars. But I seem to have been born without the ability to fear. I'm not sure if this is a quality, or a detriment. What is your opinion?'

She felt somewhat confused, and shook her head. 'I don't know.'

311

'That makes two of us, then.'

They were quiet, looking around them as the chauffeur wended his way through the crowd. Charles de Chaynisart bent again towards her, and she could smell the slight odour of vinegar on his breath. She sat perfectly still, waiting, knowing that something she didn't want to happen was about to occur, yet not knowing what this would consist of. He murmured: 'I'm glad we had this unexpected opportunity to make friends. I'd never been alone with you, madame. I've been enjoying your company.'

She answered, almost stammering: 'Thank you for bringing me. I would have had a lot of trouble manoeuvring alone, on foot.'

'A splendid woman of your type should never have to manoeuvre alone, anywhere. You deserve a palace, and three footmen, like a fairy princess, and not the wife of a fallen, decaying prince who doesn't carry the price of a taxi fare in his worn-out pocket.'

She couldn't believe she had heard him correctly. The harsh, crude words rang through her skull, stunning her. He smiled. 'You're a desirable woman,' he said in a soft, low voice – a mellifluous voice. 'I've observed you many times, from afar. You wear your poverty with dignity and pride, the same way that before, you wore your wealth. But everyone in town knows about your husband. It's a shame, really, that he allowed you to come home and be dragged down with him.'

The shouts and disorder outside were like pellets of sound falling all over her head and ears. There was a ringing noise drilling through her brain. Not knowing whether it came from the people massed on the streets, or from the cacophony within herself, she cried out: 'Monsieur de Chaynisart, I don't know what "everyone in town" has to say about Misha. He is an honourable man, and if his luck has turned, it's not through any fault of his, but due to the bad faith of others. He works, holding his head up,

312

although now I wish that he were working somewhere else – anywhere, but not for you! And if you can't feel respect for him, then at least you should be gallant enough not to speak badly of him to me, of all people!'

'My dear Princess, I did not think to offend you. Please forgive me if I stepped out of line. But Mikhail Brasilov has a very bad reputation, and it hurts me to see you slandered along with him. It is a shame his father was killed, by that madman. For Prince Ivan was a strength, a power among men, and his son doesn't match him.'

'My husband doesn't have a bad reputation,' Lily said, near tears. 'He's simply going through a difficult time. And if he did suffer from the dirt that others might have tossed on him, he suffered inside, like a gentleman. Why, monsieur, did you hire my husband, if you felt that he was a bad man?'

Charles raised his brows. 'I never said that he was *evil*, madame. "A bad man . . ." That's too strong a term. But I shall be blunt. My brother hired him, not I. Philippe thought that Prince Mikhail had an excellent head for running businesses. And since I prefer to train my horses and to attend to my card games, I allowed Philippe to hire whom he pleased. But what I know is that Prince Mikhail borrowed a lot of money, when he first arrived here. He set up quite a train of life, and let things slip by him. Then, when the Aisne refinery disaster occurred, a number of influential people lost many hundreds of thousands of francs, along with him and his father.'

'It can't be true,' Lily countered. 'He built his firm around the first sugar beets he brought with him from Russia.'

'That's a fact. But people had to invest in his idea. And because – to be quite crude – he spent a great deal of money on the women of this fair city, the businesses began to suffer from attrition. Some say, dear Princess, that his divorce from Jeanne Dalbret isn't even legal, and that she stayed his mistress long after his bigamous marriage to you.'

Lily felt a tremendous urge to vomit, and swallowed several times. Her whole body was shaking. The chauffeur was just coming to the Place de la Concorde, and with a sudden, jerky motion, she opened her door, letting a wave of cold air into the car. Charles de Chaynisart's fingers closed about her elbow, restraining her, and he whispered, urgently: 'Don't get out, Liliane, because you are angry with me. But you're hardly a child now, are you? Don't forget that I am your friend. I want to stay your friend. I couldn't care less about Brasilov, but about you, I could care a great deal. And, Liliane, if you allowed me to *really* care for you . . . there would be no limit to what I could and would do, to make your life a little more like the life of the fairy princess we were speaking about before.'

With all the strength that she could work up, Lily wrenched herself free of his hand, and jumped out of the car, which had stopped momentarily. She began to run, her heel catching on a rut of the pavement, and she fell, ripping her silk stocking at the knee. She realized, with a moment of shock, that she had forgotten her small bag inside de Chaynisart's Duesenberg. But it felt so good to be out of there, breathing clean air, that she refused to think about this now.

A policeman had grabbed her arm, and was pushing her back, among the crowd of onlookers that had gathered at the Concorde. She could see the majestic Crillon, where her parents and old aunt were waiting, undoubtedly worried about her. But there was no way to cross the square. Machine guns were stationed in the middle, near the tall, spindly granite obelisk. A man near her said: 'It's starting: look! The veterans are coming!'

It was six forty-five. She could see the time on someone's watch, his arm raised in salute to the veterans. They were marching from this very Concorde, with grand old men

314

who had served in 1871, in neat rows, coordinated and in charge. 'Where are they going?' Lily asked the man with the watch.

'To the Palais-Bourbon, to get the idiots out of the Chamber.'

She was quiet, overwhelmed. A woman behind her cried: 'Down with Stavisky! Down with the Jewish Masonic Mafia! Down with Léon Blum and the barbaric Soviets! Down with the government!'

'What do they want?' Lily asked, perspiration wetting her forehead.

'They want an end to this hocus parliamentary government, that does nothing but take bribes,' the man with the watch said. His eyes were strangely vacant, the pupils tiny dots. She could see a vein throbbing on his right temple.

The marchers kept coming, like well-ordered battalions that didn't stop. The daylight was giving way to night, and soon Lily could see the veterans outlined by the yellow glow of a multitude of streetlamps. She realized that thousands of men had passed through, and that it was probably eight o'clock. She hadn't eaten since noon, and now her stomach grumbled. She thought with mixed apprehension of Aunt Marthe's certain outrage, and of the moment they were all living through.

From the Concorde, she could see the Rond-Point des Champs-Élysées on one side, ending the great avenue, and, on the other, the Concorde Bridge that led right to the Chamber of Deputies. The man with the watch, now a warm blur at her side, was saying: 'It was terrible over there, but they deserved it. They beat up Herriot, the President of the Chamber, and they say Daladier escaped through the back, on foot. They burst in, shouting cries of "Murderers!" and "Thieves!"'

But the well-kept order of the veterans was starting to break up in all directions. Mounted police with cocked hats and feathers were rushing up to bar the entrance to the bridge, and to the Faubourg Saint-Honoré. The veterans were assaulting the police with the same kind of brutality she would have expected from anarchists. 'Who is leading these people?' she asked in a hushed voice.

'There are many right-wing groups, lady. The Colonel de la Rocque with his Cross of Fire; the Jeunesses Patriotes; the assault section of the secretive Hood. And the King's Servitors, an old Royalist organization.'

She shivered, thinking of the day the Communists of Berlin had attacked the Reichstag, and its bloody aftermath. The mounted cavalry, feathers flying in the air, was rushing at a group of men in uniform, swords brandished and swishing. 'Those are the King's Servitors,' the man told her. He seemed to have appointed himself her interpreter of current events.

'Look!' someone to the left of them cried. 'On the terrace of the Tuileries Gardens!'

Old men in military uniforms were up there, throwing bricks at the cavalry, which, in turn, was assaulting young men in boots and berets. Lily could feel the tension all around her, and the tremendous sense of exhilaration. It was a kind of demented joy that something, at last, was being done out in the open, airing out all anger within the hearts and minds of the Parisians.

A chant had risen, to the right of her, way in the distance. She could hardly distinguish the men who were coming down the Avenue des Champs-Élysées, but they seemed to be singing the *Marseillaise*. After what seemed an eternity, she made out stronger sounds of breaking glass and clicking boots. There were men in all the trees, helping the veterans fight the police, who had finally opened fire. Lily realized that she had seized the sleeve of the man with the watch, and that she was hanging on to it for dear life. Her hat had fallen off and was hanging down her back.

She thought, suddenly, that she heard a muffled voice, among the thousands raised close to her, calling out hoarsely, 'Lily! Lily!' She turned, and a man's elbow came crashing down on her head, sending the hat catapulting among the caterpillar legs of the crowd. She raised herself on tiptoes, trying to make out who might be calling her – if, indeed, someone had said her name, and if he had been looking for her and not another person by the same name. She saw, fighting his way through to her, a tall, thin man with dishevelled white hair, and, with an outpouring of relief, screamed out: 'Jacques! Here, near the front!'

The men marching down the Champs-Élysées had reached the Rond-Point, and now she could see that their chests were studded with metallic spikes, and that the canes they were using to walk with had knives on their ends. They were coming closer and closer, singing the national anthem at the top of their lungs. She didn't care who they were: the fact was that she was truly terrified, as she had never been in her twenty-eight years of existence. 'Yes,' the man next to her murmured, as if he were drugged, 'that's exactly what France needs. Law and order.'

She stared at him, bewildered. But he continued: 'Ah, Hitler could hurt us. But you've got to take your hat off to the fellow. He knows how to *control*.'

Hadn't she heard nearly the same words, just recently? Then it came to her: Charles de Chaynisart. She began to tremble again, recalling what he'd said, about Misha, about her – and how she'd been forced to jump from the moving car into this great, greasy, animal crowd. A hand grabbed her, and her heart flew into her throat, her legs turning to puddles of warm gelatin, but, just in time, she felt herself being steadied and held up, and a man's strong arms about her. 'It's all right, darling,' Jacques Walter said. 'It's all right. I'm here, and we're going to get you out into a safe room with warm food and a glass of brandy.',

* * *

'There were at least forty, maybe up to one hundred thousand people at the Concorde,' Claire was saying.

Lily was lying on a velvet divan in a large, elegant suite at the Hotel Crillon. She couldn't really remember how she had got there. She did recall being in Jacques' arms, feeling bounced around, and then, a deep, deep sleep. 'You lost consciousness, poor little lamb,' Aunt Marthe explained, bending her head towards her.

'What time is it now?' Lily asked.

'Three in the morning. An officer of the *gendarmerie*, a Colonel Simon, finally managed to break up the riots. There was shooting in the Faubourg, and the men with metallic breast plates stormed the Palace of the Élysée to eject President Lebrun, but his guards held up. There were seventeen people killed, and many dead policemen.'

'I should have stayed in Nantes,' Aunt Marthe wailed. 'This is preposterous. I knew the Communists had to be at the bottom of this. They took the métro to the Étoile, and then walked down the avenue breaking windows and looting. They made a real mess at the Claridge, where Stavisky had lived – but that's more understandable. Damned Reds!'

'You sound like the people who planned this,' Lily remarked. 'It wasn't the Communists. It was the Fascist groups. I suppose the others were just retaliating.'

'I don't know and I don't care. The Reds are always wrong, that's what *I* say. The Reds, the politicians, and the Jews.'

Claire said, quietly: 'Aunt Marthe, that sort of thinking brought Hitler to Germany. You know that, first of all, those groups are hardly interconnected. You've probably read some of the propaganda papers, which don't explain things well.'

'I have no need for any propaganda, my child. I know what I know. The Reds were fighting at the Madeleine, and on the Boulevard Sébastopol, and they say in some parts, they're still at it. I used up three sachets of smelling salts tonight, didn't I, Claire?'

'There were six burned buses, and they set fire to some private cars that were nearby, by lighting some spilled petrol. They brought in several wounded people. One of the chambermaids here was killed. The Café Wéber was turned into some kind of casualty centre for the wounded.' Jacques poured himself a glass of Hennessy cognac, and asked, suddenly: 'Do you know a Baron Charles de Chaynisart? Isn't that the fellow who owns the Rovaro?'

Lily sat up, her pulse beating in her throat. 'Yes. One of the brothers. Why?'

'His was one of the cars that was set on fire. Near here somewhere. He and his driver were pulled out, and they lit up his gas tank. He came into the lobby here looking like a madman. We spoke for a few minutes.'

She couldn't resist. All at once the laughter came pouring out of her in hysterical gulps, and she continued laughing while her mother, concerned, tried to contain her. Then she asked: 'You mean, the beautiful Duesenberg is no more?'

'He had a *Duesenberg?*' Aunt Marthe cried out. 'The abominable devils! Such wonderful cars ... like shining jewels ...' Her half-closed eyes reflected a sudden hungry envy.

Ever so slightly, Jacques Walter turned away from her, and took a sip of cognac. 'From what he told me, the beautiful Duesenberg is now a pile of charred metal. He said he'd had it specially shipped from the United States. He was almost crying – and here you are, laughing. Probably we would all feel better with a good laugh though, wouldn't we?' And he smiled at Lily and handed her his half-empty glass.

With the back of her hand, his stepdaughter wiped the tears that had been streaming down her face, and then she took the glass in her long, slender fingers. For a moment their eyes met in unspoken complicity, and then she raised the glass to him and said, softly: 'To the few strong men who still exist in the Republic.'

'Well, they certainly saved the day,' Aunt Marthe exclaimed. 'Those King's Servitors and that simply marvellous Colonel de la Rocque! How they helped our good Parisian *gendarmes* to keep up law and order against Maurice Thorez and that damned Blum!'

Lily saw Claire's shoulders rise and then drop in exasperation. Jacques Walter was looking at his wife with a fond, understanding smile. Lily cleared her throat. 'I didn't mean them, Aunt Marthe,' she explained. 'I was speaking of the few men who can still think for themselves, and who can preserve the rights of man against a sudden flood of mob hysterics.'

'Oh, the French are basically a good, sensible people, like the Swiss,' Jacques remarked. 'Here, a Hitler and a Mussolini could never reach a position of power. I still believe in the French, in spite of tonight, in spite of the last two months. These riots were like the revolt of every adolescent democracy. Because, really, Western democracy is still very young, and therefore isn't yet understood by all.'

'I think we should all try to sleep now,' Claire said to her husband. 'If you think it's all right, darling, then the three of us will leave you, Aunt Marthe, and walk on back to the Ritz.'

The old woman turned a querulous face to her. 'You'll be here tomorrow? For breakfast at seven?'

Claire nodded, wearily, and put on her coat.

Chapter Fifteen

The year 1935 began strangely, like an electric current giving off some small, startling sparks along the way, signalling defective wiring yet not actually causing fear of imminent short circuit. Lily, in the sober objectivity of hindsight, would recall every one of these small explosions, and wonder why she, along with the others, hadn't understood all these telltale warnings and stood far back, to protect themselves.

On 13 January, the rich coal-mining region of the Saar basin, hitherto an independent province administered by France, voted by an overwhelming majority of 477,109 to 46,513 to be returned to Germany. This was hailed across the Rhine by an explosion of martial exhilaration. Flowers were hurled upon the Brown Shirts as they marched. Pierre Laval, the unprepossessing foreign minister from Auvergne, had begun his career as a shrewd lawyer whose cases were most often settled out of court. He had entered the political arena as a Socialist deputy, had long since moved from Left to Right, and, along with Premier Pierre-Etienne Flandin, still thought that Germany was less dangerous than a rapprochement with Communist Russia. Nevertheless, in March, conscription was increased to eighteen months for those entering the army that year, and to two years for the recruits that would enter over the following four. Immediately, cries went up from the Left that this step would provoke the Germans. Daladier and Blum were among the most vociferous.

Lily remembered how, in Vienna, the Steiners had pretended not to be afraid of Hitler. There was something so savage, so unconditional, surrounding this small man and his followers, that when she thought about them, she recoiled and immediately filled her mind with something else. At the end of 1934, he had incorporated the air force into the Wehrmacht, showing Europe that he was blatantly remilitarizing in violation of the Treaty of Versailles. But the days when this treaty had been regarded seriously were so far behind that no one – not the French, not the British – could react with the proper outrage and counter-reaction.

A French colonel named Charles de Gaulle spoke out about the need for an army composed of small units ready to act and move very quickly, but he was ignored. The tacticians were smugly relying on the defensive line of forts set up by André Maginot, which extended into Belgium along the German frontier.

The German retaliation against France's extension of its military service was to completely renege on the Versailles agreements to keep its army to one hundred thousand. Hitler reintroduced conscription, and not long afterward, Belgium declared its often-practised neutrality. The Maginot Line was brought up short at the Belgian border. The Russian newspaper *Pravda* announced that France was no longer able actively to contain the German hordes.

Finally, in early May, Pierre Laval signed a mutual-assistance pact with Joseph Stalin. From Russia, approval came for the extension of military service. Simultaneously, the extreme Left changed its tone, and Misha, pushing an arrangement of straw potatoes around on his plate, said to his wife: 'Now doom has really set in.'

'The French can't survive without a strong ally like the Soviet Union,' Lily countered gently.

'France is caught between Scylla and Charybdis,' he said, sullenly throwing down his napkin and standing up. 'I'm going downstairs, to see what's going on.'

She nodded, and removed the plates, arranging them on a dinner tray and putting it outside her door for removal.

The children were spending a night with Claire, and so she followed Misha to the top of the stairs, feeling an inexplicable pang of anxiety.

'What do you have to do tonight?' she asked.

'The restaurant made twelve thousand francs today – fifteen hundred at the *thé dansant*. We laid two hundred place settings for lunch and dinner. Not bad for a Monday.'

'Then what's the problem?'

He regarded her circumspectly, and she tried to read the sea-green eyes with their tiny, pinpoint pupils. And she felt herself grow uneasy. Putting a hand on his arm, she retained him and said: 'Tell me, Misha. It's better to know the truth.'

He shrugged, impatiently. 'It's nothing. Just that the de Chaynisarts have been stalling over a new contract. They claim the hotel didn't develop as fully as they'd hoped, and that I disappointed their expectations.'

She cried, outraged: 'But that's not true! The general economy is bad – not just the hotel business. And you've done wonders for the Rovaro!'

He sighed. 'But not enough wonders. They refused to pay me when Papa died the full amount we'd agreed upon – they kept putting it off, and saying there was a cash-flow problem. Last year they gave me twenty-five thousand francs, without writing up a new contract. And this year, just seven thousand to date. We can't survive this way, Lily . . .'

She blinked. 'But – from the first and second payments . . . we should have savings to live on. We've done nothing costly, for eighteen months. The rent is free and food is inexpensive.'

The green in his eyes appeared to freeze over. He loosened her grasp, stood up straight. 'Brasilov Enterprises is no more, Lily. What was left were the debts. I had to pay off all the creditors.'

'But . . . . Claude? He still has his office, and his clients.'

'He formed a new company, in his own name. And brought in some of our old clients, who trusted him, a Frenchman, and not me – a suspect foreigner.'

She stepped back, stunned. So the Brasilov dynasty had really collapsed, and her own brother, Claude, had made off with the spoils. Overwhelmed, she ran back towards their suite. Misha was a desperate man, and for the first time she was really afraid, of the future, of destiny. She thought of what he'd said about the de Chaynisarts, and wondered, briefly, whether Charles had done something to influence his brother, in revenge for her rude rejection of his proposition. No – it seemed too much, even for him. And he hadn't come around for such a long time.

It had to be bad luck, and nothing else.

For the summer, Claire and Jacques Walter rented a beautiful villa on the Riviera, in the city of Cannes. Misha seemed almost relieved to send his wife and children there with them. The villa had an enormous garden, which the children used for intense, imaginative games played in teams, recruiting neighbouring children to form a large, joyful group. Lily read, took walks along the Croisette by the sea, and spent time with her mother and stepfather. In the evenings they dined on the terrace, under the stars, or drove to Nice or Monte Carlo. Lily almost forgot the heavy problems of the city. It was Kyra who said it: 'With Grandma and Grandpa Jacques, it's as if we were rich again.'

Only the clothes were different, Lily thought, walking one August day on the famous Croisette and watching the elegant women, pencil thin, as was the fashion, with their clown's hats by Schiaparelli, and their men's tailored summer trousers, by Chanel. She was wearing a loose-draped dress of soft green linen, left over from Vienna, and had tied her straw hat down with a silk scarf, to protect her from the sand and too much sun. She was, she decided, definitely out of the picture; her figure was wrong, her clothes not quite chic enough – and she worried that a touch of tan would turn her sultry skin unbecomingly dark. The Jewish strain, from Eastern Europe, she thought.

A gentleman she hadn't noticed tipped his hat to her. She met his eye on a level, for they were almost the same height. She stopped in her tracks, suddenly cold on this hot day, her skin rising in delicate goose bumps. '*Chère Princesse*,' Charles de Chaynisart said, with that slightly ironic tone, and his somewhat twisted smile. 'So you too are vacationing at this charming resort? I didn't know. Did you take a villa?'

She could feel the ice in the sharp blue of his eyes, although he was as polite as ever. 'No,' she demurred. 'My children and I are staying with my parents.'

'How very agreeable. Monsieur and Madame Walter, am I not correct? Tell me,' he added, bending forward just a little to look directly into her face: '*Walter*. What kind of name *is* that, my dear Princess? We were wondering the other day, my friends and I, over a game of poker. I voted for Alsatian. Was I right?'

Lily's stomach contracted, and she noticed, rather than felt, her knees begin to shake. To steady herself and work away from this most profound dismay, she pretended to adjust the scarf around her hat, thereby shielding her dead-white face from Charles de Chaynisart. Then she looked at him, and smiled. 'I'm afraid you were wrong. My stepfather is a Swiss-German.'

She could hear her own heartbeat in the moment that followed. De Chaynisart, up-to-the-minute elegant in his white duck suit, inclined his head in mock sadness. 'Oh, dear, dear. Well, you win some, you lose some. I shall simply have to tell my friends that the most lovely woman in Paris has declared me lacking.'

She wondered then who these 'friends' might be, and felt the purest fear of her life. 'Swiss-German.' That had sounded good enough, she wagered. Now she knew that she had to acknowledge the compliment. How she hated this man! But she replied easily enough. 'Hardly "lacking", monsieur. For indeed, the Swiss names often have the same Germanic resonance as those from Alsace. And I'm afraid you're laughing at me. I'm in no way the loveliest woman in Paris.' She motioned with her chin to the sandy beach below, where long-limbed beauties were reclining in the sun. 'To others belongs that title.'

His eyes narrowed for a split second, and then he was once more the debonair man of the world that he had always affected to be. 'Do you believe that Mussolini will take his troops on that "African adventure" he promised them?' he asked casually.

Lily let her shoulders rise and fall, and held out her hands palms up. 'I don't know. I've never been very clever at politics. But . . .' She hesitated, remembering with acid clarity that he had spoken of the Italian dictator with a certain unabashed admiration that day of the February riots. 'I heard that today, Léon Blum spoke out quite strongly against Italian aggression in Abyssinia. He said that no one would be able to limit its damage.'

The Baron's eyebrows shot up, and he chuckled. 'My, my. And do you remember, dear Princess Brasilova, what Maurras wrote back in April, concerning Monsieur Blum? That he should be shot in the back, to get rid of him.'

Lily said nothing. The words seemed caught in her throat. And so he shrugged lightly, and remarked softly: '*La France aux Français*. France belongs to its own, don't you think? Have you heard this slogan? It was coined by François Coty, I believe – the owner of *Le Figaro*, a fine newspaper if ever we had one. It has such a nice clear resonance, don't you agree? *La France aux Français* . . .'

'And Monsieur Blum isn't French?' she couldn't help interjecting, feeling a sudden anger filling her.

'Who knows, *chère madame*. You and I, we are pure

French, that is for sure. But some of the others? One never knows, does one now?'

The blue eyes reflected the sun, the beach with its gaily coloured umbrellas, and the dancing waves: symbols of a peaceful summer that nobody wanted to ruin on account of the broken Treaty of Versailles. Lily held on to her hat as a gust of wind rose unexpectedly, and declared: 'I must be getting home now, if you'll excuse me.'

'Why, certainly, beautiful Princess Brasilova.'

As she walked away with hurried footsteps, she knocked his words about in her head. *France belongs to its own. Beautiful Princess Brasilova.* He had rolled his *r*'s with a humorous hint of drama, but now she remembered this with awe. When he had spoken of foreigners . . . whom had he meant? Jacques Walter, about whose name bets had been placed? Or her husband, Prince Mikhail, whose contract still had not been written? *La France aux Français.* And in January, forty-eight hundred foreign residents of Paris had been suddenly expelled without trial, without explanation.

Lily ran towards the first taxi that she saw, and gave the name of her villa, lying back against the cushions with relief.

Misha sat in his office, his eyes bloodshot, the pulse in his throat hurting with its intensity. In front of him lay sheafs of invoices, which he now pushed aside with an almost listless gesture of hopelessness. This morning, while he'd been having breakfast in the dining room, with Philippe de Chaynisart, a strange, yet now familiar figure had approached their table, unceremoniously. Strange, because he'd never laid eyes on this particular messenger of fate, and familiar, because he'd come to recognize the telltale signs of their ominous presence every time one of them had come up to him: the ubiquitous bill collectors sent to confront him and humiliate him like scum at their feet.

327

He'd seen this one before Philippe, and had straightened up, his face a mask of imperious hauteur, hiding the fear that gripped his stomach.

'Mikhail Brasilov?' the small, rotund man had demanded.

'Yes, it is I.'

'I have an order to repossess your furniture for nonpayment of debts.'

'Nonpayment to whom?'

'To the Bouleaud Funeral Services.'

Misha had registered this with a small inward shock. So they were planning to collect on his father's coffin and embalmment. But this was natural: funerals, after all, were part of business. He had sighed once, shortly, and then said: 'But I have no furniture.'

'Then, unless you possess other valuables, I shall be obliged to put a lien on your earnings, to attach a part of your salary until the debt is cleared.'

Philippe de Chaynisart's bright blue eyes had rapidly gone from the *huissier* to Misha, then back to the *huissier* in embarrassment. His baby face had turned a shade of pink. Clearly, he'd been in sympathy . . . or *had* he? It was always more difficult to read Philippe than the cunning snake who was his brother.

Misha had rapidly considered the alternatives. If they attached his salary, Lily and the children would suffer every day. On the other hand . . . Lily still owned a few pieces of jewellery. She'd kept the tear-shaped diamond flanked by two emeralds, the Cartier ring he had given her for their engagement. To give away this piece, which wasn't his to give, while she was in Cannes, had seemed abhorrent to him. Yet less abhorrent than to force his family to live on half nothing for the next half year. And so he'd gone upstairs and relinquished the ring.

He was now sitting in the comfortable Louis XIV *bergère*, thinking. The situation had gone from bad to worse. And still, no contract. He wondered about this, again. Philippe had always appeared on his side. Yet men like him were first and foremost businessmen ... like the *huissier*. They might like you, they might spend time with you, but when business was bad, they forgot about you so rapidly that you wondered what chair had been seized from under you when you landed with a thump on your rear end.

He'd spent every spare penny fortifying the Jeunesses Patriotes, whose ranks had swelled to almost one hundred thousand members. But to what avail? France now needed Russia, for the French stood, on weak, scared legs in the shadow of Great Britain, which made all joint decisions. The decisions of cowards, always afraid to speak out against the affronts of Hitler and Mussolini. And in the meantime, Léon Blum sounded off about a forty-hour workweek and collective contracts. Misha had spent his money ... his family's money ... to fight against a Blum takeover, and now he felt pangs of dismay and shame. He'd never told Lily he'd done this, because she'd needed the cash. He'd thought he'd been doing something altruistic, sacrificing the comfort of his family ... for nothing. To reach this point.

There was a knock on the door, and almost immediately it swung open. Philippe was standing in the doorway, his shoulders inside his immaculate jacket of beige raw silk looking oddly hunched, his face drawn – a tired cherub with bloodless lips. 'Is something wrong?' Misha asked, rising. 'You look ill.'

Philippe stilled him with a wave of his hand. 'No, no. Just a bit of the heat, probably. But I'm going home to rest. I've been thinking ... about this morning.'

He edged into the room, and passed a monogrammed linen handkerchief over his brow. 'Misha, your problems have touched me. Of course, you must understand why Charles and I didn't feel it was right to renew your original contract. The restaurant hasn't done as well as you'd led us to expect. But we have every hope that come September, you will work wonders for us. Really – our confidence is still high; I want you to know that.'

Misha said, his voice hard and low: 'But you still owe me money from the first year.'

Philippe sighed. 'Yes. And that's why I decided to stop in this afternoon. Charles and I just made an enormous profit on a property we sold in Auvergne. It's time you collected the money we owe you. And while the cash flow is good, I'd like you to take an extra ten thousand francs, as an advance and a show of confidence on our part.'

Misha said, without smiling: 'Thank you, Philippe.'

His hand on the doorknob, the Baron added: 'From the hotel safe, of course, Misha. Use your keys, as always, and leave an invoice on my desk.'

When he had left, Misha organized the papers in his office, locked the door behind him, and went to the small alcove in the basement where the hotel safe reposed behind two heavy steel panels. Only three people possessed keys to unlock it: the two de Chaynisart brothers, and he himself. Now he looked carefully behind him, saw that no one was there, and unlocked the first panel. He then inserted a second, serrated key into the lock of the second panel. The safe stood open before him, revealing sheafs of paper money neatly arranged in numbered piles.

Misha counted out the eighteen thousand francs that was owed to him, and the additional ten thousand that Philippe had told him to take. He was trembling inside, with a cold, dark anger. Philippe had let him give Lily's ring to the *huissier*, without lifting a finger. Only afterwards had he felt a twinge of personal guilt. Damn it, Misha thought, I should have insisted on back pay when the man appeared before us. It was my right, as much as it was that funeral parlour's, to collect on what was owed to me. But he hadn't done this. He had remained, as always, the prince, the gentleman, just as Philippe had expected him to. Another might have turned the tables and humiliated de Chaynisart – but not he.

Philippe, under this guise of kindness and comprehension, had merely paid him hush money not to make a scandal. But also, Misha realized, he'd always known that the Brasilovs were now totally destitute, and therefore totally dependent on Misha's position as manager of the Hotel Rovaro. Misha, who had always worked for the pleasure of making money, now worked because he had a family to feed. For even if the de Chaynisarts were lax in their payments, they did provide the Brasilovs with free accommodation. And in the eyes of Paris society, Prince Mikhail was a hotel manager, which, whatever way one looked at it, was still an honourable profession.

They'll bleed me to death because they know I can't cry out, he thought angrily, putting the bills in his pocket and locking the safe doors.

In the morning, as he was shaving, there was an urgent knocking at the door, and when he went to open it, his face full of lather, he saw Merpert, Philippe's balding young office clerk, his eyes nearly popping out of their sockets. 'Your Excellency,' Merpert said, his teeth beginning to chatter. 'Monsieur Philippe is dead.'

Misha stepped back, unbelieving. 'Dead? But – how?'

'He died of a massive heart attack in the middle of the night. His *maître d'hôtel* had to call Monsieur Charles, at the Hotel Majestic in Cannes . . .'

'Charles is in Cannes?' Misha said. It seemed to him an unhappy coincidence. With this new development, he'd have to call Lily and the children back too. He needed their warm presence around him. With Charles, the going wouldn't be easy. He said to the young clerk: 'Go downstairs, Merpert, and act like a man. This is the first order of business. It's your job, yours and mine, to keep the hotel going smoothly. The guests are not to be alarmed, do you hear?'

But as he watched the retreating form of Merpert's back, he wondered why, suddenly, he felt so uneasy. Philippe hadn't exactly been a friend, but he'd been among the more trustworthy business relations he had had to deal with over the past years. Not a bad man, fundamentally. He felt sad. He'd never really come to know the man, to see him in his intimate surroundings – but he had to admit that he'd liked him. They'd liked each other. Without Philippe, what would happen to the Rovaro? Charles wouldn't want to keep it, Misha supposed, finishing his shaving and smoothing talcum powder over his jaw and chin. Or would he?

And once again, the sensation of discomfort returned, like a dark cloud.

'I'm so sorry for Philippe,' Lily said, picking up her cup of tea. 'He was young, like my father. But, Misha – I don't really want to stay here if there's just Charles. I don't like him.'

Misha smiled, wryly. 'Neither do I. I wonder if anyone does, actually. But look here: I've had an offer to renovate the Hotel Carlton, on the Champs-Élysées. They especially need to do something about the café. Do you remember which hotel it is?'

She nodded. 'On the Champs-Élysées, near the Étoile. On the shady side of the avenue. Are you sure they really want you, Misha?'

He stared at her, confounded. But she hadn't meant to belittle him with her remark. She'd merely wished to be reassured that he was speaking about a concrete offer, and not just a dim possibility. He glanced at the fingers of her right hand, singularly naked and tanned from the Cannes sun, and felt a moment of terrible shame that he had given her ring to the *huissier*. But she'd stilled his remorse when he had admitted this, upon her return. 'The wedding ring is all I need,' she'd said quietly, and where another woman might have said the words to make a good impression, he knew she'd been sincere.

'When will you tell Charles that we're going?' she asked softly, her dark, liquid eyes on his face.

'As soon as I can. He's been going over all the invoices, all the books.'

Lily sighed with relief. In all probability, life would begin to take a brighter colour once they made the move. She wondered again what kind of man Charles really was, remembering the time she'd jumped from his car, and that other time, so recently, when she'd encountered him on the Croisette at Cannes.

And then, with true horror, she asked herself whether he might know, through some fluke of fate, that she was half-Jewish. Things were so good now between her and Misha. And then, just as she was musing about the closeness between them since Prince Ivan's death, she sat up with sudden horror. 'Misha,' she whispered. 'Mama told me, a few weeks ago, that Claude and Rirette had sold their apartment, and had decided to live in a hotel. Mama said they had chosen the Carlton. And you know how badly we all get along . . .'

He shifted his eyes from her face to the tea tray at her side, then back again to her direct, brown eyes, filled with mute appeal. Very gently, he said: 'Lily, a job's a job. We have no other choice now, do we?'

'No other choice at all, in all of Paris?'

He said, harshly: 'I told you: no choice at all. So I will have to become manager of the Carlton. But I'll find you and the children some other place to live. Though on the tiny salary they're offering, I wonder how the hell I'll be able to afford it!'

* * *

333

The children loved the Hotel Carlton. It stood in perpetual shade at 119–121 Avenue des Champs-Élysées, tall, stately, and, like a decayed aristocrat who has seen better times, somewhat gone to seed. The Persian carpets in the lounge needed to be cleaned and renovated. The walls needed new paint. And, as Misha had said, the outdoor café needed the most work of all. And so the first thing that he did was to order tables, chairs, and a series of gaily coloured parasols to shade the already shady tables. His hope was that during the hot season, passersby would stop in to hide from the sun on the opposite side of the street.

Kyra revelled in the marble columns of the reception hall, and in the fretwork around the moulded ceilings of all the downstairs rooms. Often, on Thursday afternoons when all French children were off from school, her father brought her over from the *pension* a few blocks away on the Rue Lord-Byron, where he had set Lily and his children up in a small room with three beds. Nicolas didn't always come. This autumn of 1935, he was almost eleven, and in the sixth form, which was the first serious class, when one had to choose between a classical or a modern course of study. He had chosen classical, because, as he'd announced to his parents, anyone could master science, but not everyone could read Greek and Latin. And so, many a Thursday, he stayed at home with Lily to polish up his homework.

But Lily knew that there was another reason why he didn't like to go to the Carlton without her. He'd run into his Aunt Henriette one day in the lobby, and had come away with an odd sensation of repulsion. She'd fondled him, and tousled his hair, and sent her small son, Alain, to play with him; yet he'd felt her strange, amber eyes like a lizard's stare, and had told his mother he didn't like his aunt. And so, while the old hotel held as much charm for him as it did for his sister, it also made him a little apprehensive about meeting this lady whom he hadn't

334

liked. When his mother and aunt passed each other, they merely nodded and moved on.

Kyra, on the other hand, was different. There was a side to her nature that sought the forbidden, that liked to toy with danger and high adventure. She'd always sat on the very edge of her seat at the circus, when the lion and tiger trainers performed, almost hoping that something unexpected would occur, to test the bravery of man against beast. She didn't care a hoot about adult problems. If Papa and Uncle Claude had disagreed, this had nothing to do with her. On the contrary, it suddenly made her somewhat insipid uncle more interesting to her. And she guessed, with her child's intuition, that the mysterious lady he had married lay at the root of the question. So, when she went to have lunch with her father at the Carlton, she kept her eyes open for Henriette.

She'd seen them once, all three of them. Uncle Claude, dark and handsome in his perfectly tailored brown pin-striped suit; the small boy, dark like his father, but with curiously moss-green eyes, not unlike her own, Kyra had thought: decked out like Little Lord Fauntleroy in a cute sailor suit and patent leather shoes. But the lady had been extraordinary. She had an oval face, very delicate, and slanted eyes of a queer amber colour, like light topazes. Her hair, styled in a pageboy bob of the latest fashion, had been topped by a marvellous heart-shaped dark green hat, to match her velvet suit with its padded shoulders and fitted skirt that came to just below the knee. What slender, elegant legs had emerged from that tight skirt, and so daintily shod in patent leather green shoes that went just perfectly with her patent leather bag! Kyra had been amazed by the colour of her hair: a burnished burgundy that contrasted dramatically with the pallor of her somewhat sunken cheeks. 'She looks like an actress,' Kyra had breathed.

And then Christmas came, eclipsing all else behind it,

and they went to Grandma's at the Ritz, and opened presents at midnight. Kyra received a brand-new silk nightgown, and a silver-backed toothbrush and comb from Grandma and Grandpa Jacques. Aunt Marthe had sent five books by the Comtesse de Ségur. Mama had made her a blue velvet dress, with an embroidered, hand-crocheted collar. Papa gave her his own Bible, its leather cover embossed with gold print. And then there was the mystery present, which had come to the Ritz addressed to 'Princess Kyra Brasilova, in care of Madame Jacques Walter'. It had said 'Fragile: To Be Opened at Once', and so Grandma hadn't waited, and removed the wrapping.

Grandma and Grandpa had found themselves staring at a small gilded cage, in which sat two lovebirds, terrified and soundless. By the time Kyra arrived, they'd started to sing, and she fed them from the two boxes of special seeds that had been included in the package. Everyone had wondered who had sent this most wonderful of gifts, but Kyra, in her heart of hearts, had known.

She had no doubt that the beautiful woman in the green velvet suit, her Aunt Henriette, had sent her the lovebirds. But she was afraid to tell anybody, even Nicky, about her secret knowledge.

Chapter Sixteen

On 13 February 1936, Misha walked both his children to their lycées, and went bright and early to the Hotel Carlton. The *maître d'hôtel*, Carvalho, greeted him with a sombre expression. 'Your Excellency, business was bad yesterday. The café only made eleven thousand francs. And now Marcel, the chef, is ill. Jean-Paul, the assistant chef, has never yet been on his own, and he's got the worst case of stage fright you could imagine.'

Misha sighed. 'Well, then, I shall have to reanimate him. Where is he?'

'In the pantry, sir.'

Misha smiled, and walked resolutely past Carvalho. The Portuguese was a fine *maître d'hôtel*, but he didn't know how to handle his subordinates. Misha strode into the pantry, and past some sinks to the row of closed doors that stored bins of dry goods. 'Jean-Paul,' he called gently. 'I won't allow you to let us down. But more than this: I won't allow you to let *yourself* down. Every assistant chef waits like a nervous frog for the moment when his superior will fall sick. Because that's when his own worth will emerge. Many reputations have been built during a chef's sick leave. Do you intend to remain an assistant for the rest of your days?'

A man, inside one of the closets, coughed. 'But your Excellency, if I fail . . .'

Misha let the thought hang in midair. 'How do you think I ever got started in this dratted country?' he retorted. 'It took a lot of guts and a strong stomach. I was scared, just like you. At least you're a born Frenchman, Jean-Paul.

337

You know the tastes here. Come on, man. There's a small crowd waiting for breakfast, and we can't keep feeding them yesterday's leftover croissants. They desire small miracles, which only you can accomplish.'

Jean-Paul's voice said, faltering: '"Small miracles"? But what could these people possibly want, at eight thirty in the morning? The bread is ready. With coddled eggs, or soufflés, or at most sugared crêpes, they ought to call themselves lucky! Why, your Excellency, we were up till four, baking brioches and croissants and small chocolate breads. Tell me what other miracles they might have in mind?'

Misha stifled a laugh. 'Oh, wait and see, *mon cher*. But to start with, I'd say you had the kitchen well in hand. The only item missing from the menu is the brilliant man to put these foods together. You wouldn't want us to rely on Aristide now, would you?'

He heard the door being savagely pushed out, and watched as Jean-Paul, outraged, stepped forward. '*Aristide?!* Your Excellency wishes the Carlton guests to die of food poisoning at eight thirty in the morning? If you please, let me through to wash my hands. Just to *think* of that little lame-brain touching my pots and ladles! I don't want to get an attack of the runs!'

Misha patted him twice on the shoulder, and made his exit. He walked through the lobby, exchanging greetings with the desk clerk, and went into the main lounge. He wanted to examine the new panelling that had been put in, and the new frames he had ordered for the paintings of President Lebrun and Raymond Poincaré, dead two years now, whom the owner of the Carlton still felt to have been France's greatest statesman. Misha peered now into the plain, somewhat dour face, and thought: How far astray has your great nation swerved, Raymond . . . how divided it lies. There was no longer a Bloc National, with its solid centrist majority. The conservatives had turned fiercely to the extreme Right, and the Left . . . well, one hardly needed to document *its* ideals. The Popular Front, composed of Radicals, Socialists, and Communists, had swelled to such a point that in the April elections, it was likely to win a majority against the National Front.

Misha suppressed a rising disgust, and turned to scrutinize the fine oak woodwork. He was glad of his selection. The panelling had the look of age, including the right patina. But it was new, and therefore a lot less costly. A team of young carpenters he had known had given him, in fact, a fine rebate.

'I beg your pardon, your Excellency – but this man is insisting on speaking with you . . .' Émile, the desk clerk, elderly, myopic, and full of decorum, was trying, by the look on his face, to convey to Misha his deep apologies. At his side stood a bailiff in uniform, erect and inscrutable as befitted his profession.

Misha started, then recovered his composure. What other money did he owe that he had now forgotten about, and that had now come to haunt him at his new job? He felt a moment of complete anguish, but said: 'Thank you, Émile. I can handle this matter, I'm sure.' But in reality, he wasn't so sure. He felt years older than his forty-five calendar years: older, more tired, and less in control.

When the old man had departed, Misha extended his hand for the papers that the process server was holding out to him. 'You must sign here,' the man said, pulling out a ledger from a thin briefcase. Misha complied, grimly. France, bureaucratic and punctilious, appeared to be embodied in the person of this ramrod-straight public official. One couldn't hate him: he was merely doing his job. But when he had turned his back to leave, a terrible nervousness took possession of Misha. He wanted to be alone to see what this was about, and when, finally, he saw the bailiff disappear into the front lobby, he tore open the envelope with fingers that shook.

Misha read the form once, twice, then leaned against the oak panelling and read it through again. He couldn't believe this. His stomach was tight as a knot, and he could feel his scalp tingling, as if a million tiny needles, touched with fire, had been dancing over the thin skin under his hair. Very quickly, he tried to think over his last few months at the Hotel Rovaro. For it looked as if Charles de Chaynisart had instigated legal action against him, for theft. *Theft.* Misha knew that in forty-five years, he had never committed a single instance of theft. Only the lowest of the low committed theft. Like the Rabinovitches. Men reared in the slums, devoid of any basic values. He felt outraged, revolted – and horribly ashamed, that any man would dare to call him a thief.

He thought for a moment of going home, to that miserable room that was the only home he had at this point, and of telling Lily what had happened. Then he rejected this idea. She'd suffered enough. It had never been his style to tell his wife of his business problems, if it could be avoided. It was up to him to protect her – not to burden her.

In this instant, he missed his father with an acuteness that pierced through him with its poignancy, and he had to steady himself against the wall. Who, then? Because he knew he had to talk this through, to try to comprehend. There was only one person, of course. And so he put his coat on and told Émile not to worry, he had a pressing engagement outside but would return before lunch.

Outside, Misha felt the nipping cold and pulled the collar of his overcoat up to protect his neck. He began to walk, briskly, in giant strides, down the Champs-Élysées. It wasn't that he was trying to economize on bus fare; but the exercise helped to clear his mind. Before he knew it, he had reached the Place de la Concorde and was making his way east along the Quai du Louvre. Colourful little stalls

340

displaying old books and watercolours met his eye, distracted him for the breath of a second, and then he sank his gaze into the murky, grey-green Seine, drowning his sense of helpless despair in its age-old waters, as the disconsolate had been doing for time eternal. Soon he had reached the Pont Louis-Philippe. He checked his watch: he had been on foot one and a half hours. He crossed the bridge, and soon had reached his destination, the elegant stone mansion on the Quai de Bourbon built by Le Vau in the seventeenth century, which had come to be known as the 'Maison Dalbret' in the Paris vernacular.

Dragi, the Negro butler, gave him a wide, bright smile as he let him in. Misha felt his heart lift a twinge, in this incredible palace that seemed, like the Taj Mahal, to belong to a different world from that which had brought him down. But it amazed him, too, to consider Varvara. She was fifty now, and yet she still held Parisians enthralled, on the edge of their seats as they watched her perform, whether an outrageous comedy by Georges Feydeau, or as Medea, in the grand tragedy by Corneille. She'd done it all alone. Probably, if he'd treated her as a real wife, she wouldn't have had the need to become an actress. So he had, by his own neglect and injustice, done her an enormous favour. He smiled, wryly, wondering if Lily, left to her own devices, would have risen to the occasion, like Vava, and become one of France's most renowned pianists.

He was led once again to the red silk bedroom, where he found her in front of her dressing-table, an intricate piece of Chinese lacquered wood, surmounted by a huge mirror with a spotlight. Behind her, an effeminate young man sat trimming red curls, and he stepped back, his face appalled by the sudden intrusion. 'It's all right, my pet,' Varvara said to the coiffeur. 'Dragi will take you to the kitchen, where I'm sure the cook will find something wonderful to feed you. You can come back in an hour.'

With the door shut upon the backs of Dragi and the

hairdresser, Varvara stood up, and shook óff the hairs that had fallen all over her shoulders and neck. She smiled, and said: '*Il faut souffrir pour être belle* – right, Misha? But for God's sake: what's wrong?'

He sat down on one of the Chinese chairs, and replied, steepling his fingers: 'I'm not exactly sure. Charles de Chaynisart has accused me of grand theft, and is bringing me to trial. But I don't understand where he could have got his ammunition. He claims I stole ten thousand francs. I don't even recall taking such an amount from the hotel safe. It was always in smaller or larger doses, but uneven ones, as befitted the occasion.'

'And you received no explanation of the notice?'

'Of course not. By Napoleonic law, anyway, a man is guilty until proven innocent – an odd process, to be sure.'

'I know him a little – your Baron Charles. He's a strange, perverted man. Likes to hire whores to enact little scenarios for him: you know the type. But always impeccable to the outside world. But *think*, Misha. What did you ever do without his knowledge, that he could now legally hold against you?'

Misha said, 'But I always dealt with Philippe – almost never with Charles. As a matter of fact, the last thing that Philippe ever told me was to pay myself. I took eighteen thousand francs from the safe, and left him a memorandum on his desk, as was our custom.'

'And you made a note of this in a ledger?'

'Naturally.'

'Tell me,' she said, 'these memoranda – they were specific, detailed? The last one, for example. What did it say?'

He shrugged, irritated. 'Vava, Philippe and I had no reason to distrust each other. I can't recall the exact wording. But it went something like this: "As per your instructions of today, I removed eighteen thousand francs, to reimburse myself."'

'No greater *detail*, Misha? To reimburse yourself for what? For when?'

'For the money he owed me by our original contract, plus a sum of ten thousand he should have paid me after that, along the way, for services rendered. He hadn't paid me for months, and actually owed me far more than this.'

'But not by any signed agreement.'

'No. He'd kept stalling. I think his brother was to blame for that.'

Varvara sighed. She stood, unpretentious, in a white terry-cloth robe that enveloped her totally, hiding the feline curves of her body. But her unpainted eyes, clear blue and wide, were arresting in their beauty, so that no one noticed the small creases at their edges. Her neck was perfectly smooth, her skin translucent. There were some lines on her forehead, but these were in no way unpleasant tributes to the passage of time. She announced: 'Misha, that's the crux of the problem. You aren't going to have an easy time proving you were entitled to this money. And don't forget: we shall always be foreigners, my love. The French are chauvinists. To them, you and I are "exotic", when they want to use us; but when we're the ones in need, we're pure and simple outsiders. A court of law will give de Chaynisart the benefit of the doubt, not you – no matter how plausible your story sounds. The de Chaynisart name is old, and full of nobility.'

Misha stood up, trembling, and cried: 'Then what you're advising me to do, between the lines, is to *leave France*, because I won't get a fair trial here?'

She thrust her fingers through her hair, then stretched. 'I'm not giving you *any* advice. I'm not a lawyer, Misha. You need a good lawyer.'

'I *am* a lawyer.'

'*Were*, my pet. You're not a member of the French bar. Get yourself someone good. Someone who'll settle out of court, preferably.'

He said, outraged: 'But I can't afford a good lawyer! And I can't afford to settle out of court!'

She raised her thin, arched brows. 'Look, Misha. Find yourself a lawyer. There are always ... friends ... who will help you to pay him – or her. You've helped enough people in your day for them to want to help you now. And you've had your share of crocodiles nipping at your shirttails.'

He took this in, and fell silent, acutely embarrassed. She was offering to come to his rescue ... like Jacques Walter, earlier. He'd never been in a position to accept anybody's charity. Suddenly, he asked her about something that had been on his mind for a while: 'Why is it that Claude is doing so well? Brasilov Enterprises completely collapsed. I smell a rat.'

Slowly, Varvara inhaled, then exhaled, turning around on tiptoe. She turned back to Misha, her face oddly set, composed. 'How many years did it take you to realize this, darling?' she demanded. 'The facts stared you right in the eye. Who was it that made the initial connection between you and the Rabinovitches? Claude. Who was it who went back, trying to find them, and reported that they'd vanished into thin air? Claude. Who was it who lived like a successful businessman when you were falling to ruin? Whose wife wears all the new Schiaparelli outfits, and vacations in the palace hotels? I'm asking *you*.'

Misha's lips parted, in an ashen face. 'You think *Claude* actually stole from me? That he was partner in crime with the Rabinovitches?'

Varvara yawned, and covered her mouth with the back of her hand, sensually. 'I'm just an actress. I can only suppose, like any half-wit, from the facts that you presented to me, years ago.'

'Then, if Claude did this, he, along with these Jews, wrecked the Aisne project and catapulted us into ruin. He ruined his own sister. I can't believe it.'

She said, hardly: 'Believe it. He was envious of you, and envious of Lily. As long as you were necessary to his own success, he played your game. It's what I told you: when you ceased to be essential, he saw you as an outsider, and threw you out. He used Lily, too, to hook you with. But now he couldn't care less about her, because she's just the wife of a poor man. Go home, Misha. And tomorrow, find yourself a good solicitor to handle your affairs. Don't spare expense. There are those who will help.'

When he departed from the Dalbret house, he was conscious of a pang of hunger, and looked at the sky. It was already late afternoon. Exhausted, baffled, at his wits' end, Misha hailed a bus and got into it. But he didn't know what he would tell Lily when he got home. For what was worse? That Charles was suing him, and had labelled him a common thief, or that her only brother had helped destroy her husband.

When he walked into the room at the boarding-house, Lily came towards him, her hair dishevelled, and tears running from her eyes. His first thought, as he closed his arms around her, pressing her close, was that somehow she already knew. But then, realizing this impossibility, he stepped back, his eyes questioning.

'Léon Blum is in hospital,' she said. 'Some King's Servitors and people from the Action Française forced him from his car, beat him up, and left him for dead. Some workmen found him and took him to a clinic – but he's very bad.'

'You're weeping for Léon *Blum?*' he asked, disbelieving.

She shrugged, her face contracting. 'I'm crying because I'm afraid, because people have lost their heads, because Eliane and David Robinson have packed their bags to move to the United States with their son, to join David's sister. They're *afraid* to stay here. Last year, Jacques said that he still had faith in the French – that they would never go completely mad, like the Germans and the Italians. But now, when a man can't feel safe to proclaim his ideas, when some impassioned savages can break into his car and nearly kill him – I think Jacques was wrong. And these were *your* people, Misha. People *you* paid for, to fight against normal, decent men like Blum, who wouldn't hurt a fly.'

Completely taken aback, he stammered: 'I never paid anyone to hurt another human being. You know this as well as I do, Lily. You're being unfair.'

'*I'm* being unfair? *You* paid them, Misha! Enough money for us to have lived quite well on for two or three years. I heard you, on the telephone, years and years ago – giving away money to this Fascistic organization, to this man Taittinger. And now look what's happening to France!'

He shook his head, speechless. He couldn't remember ever having seen her so distraught. His cool, composed Lily, falling apart over a man like Blum – a Socialist, who could bring France to its knees.

'You hate him because he's a Jew,' she was saying, accusingly.

'I don't really *hate* him. I never wished personal harm on him. And I'd dislike him just as much if he were a Christian.'

'That isn't true. You hate all Jews.'

He cried out then, after the day he'd had, with all his rancour and desperation: 'It was the Jews who did me in, Lily! The Rabinovitches! They started the whole ball rolling, and now we're here. Don't ask me to be a Jew-lover: I can't be, that's all.'

And then he left the room, slamming the door behind him, not trusting himself to keep silent about Claude's part in their downfall, and about the lawsuit. He could hear her crying in the room, but he didn't go back in. No, he hadn't wanted to hurt anyone – not even a political menace like Blum. He'd thought Taittinger would keep France from going the way of Moscow, that was all. And now, on top of

Charles, on top of Claude, there was his wife, who held him responsible for all the ills that had befallen France. Where, then, might he turn? And where was the justice he'd always believed in?

On 26 April, in the pouring rain, the French voted the Popular Front into office. The elections had underscored the polarity now existing in French politics. The Popular Front was elected by over 5.5 million votes, while the right-wing National Front received 4.5 million. Although the French Communist party, which had doubled its membership to 1.5 million members, refused to participate in the new government, Léon Blum decided to accept the post of premier, even without the majority he had always felt he would need if he were to head a cabinet. The threat of Fascism had made him drop his earlier reservations.

Yet France still closed its eyes in the matter of Hitler. Jean Dobler, the French consul in Cologne, repeatedly sent dispatches about the rearming of Germany, and the way its airfields were increasing. The Quai d'Orsay ignored his alarm. On 7 March, Hitler's Reichswehr had penetrated into the Rhineland, which had been declared a demilitarized zone after Poincaré's troops had left in 1923. But the French, cowering behind their Maginot Line, refused to strike back at this obvious offensive. And now, with the first Socialist premier voted into office, France let loose its energies only in the matter of internal affairs.

Misha didn't comment about the election of Léon Blum. He was too preoccupied with his personal problems to be able to think about the world's. When Lily told him that Wolf and Marisa were having problems convincing his parents to leave Austria with them, he merely shrugged. He didn't care about the Steiners. Because, in the middle of April, the owner of the Hotel Carlton had told him that he would have to relinquish his post as manager. People had begun to hear about Baron Charles's allegations, and these were hurting business at the hotel, where a manager accused of theft was a black mark held against it.

Misha was out of a job. He went to all his old clients, trying to drum up business as a mediator between companies, and as a finder for new business. But on the whole, Parisians shunned him. He'd lost his wealth, and now he'd also lost his reputation. The afternoon when Kyra ran home from school, in tears, crying that a friend had called her father a 'dirty thief', stayed in his mind like an imprint of his shame. He felt responsible. And yet, of course, he had done nothing wrong. In fact, he had worked for many months at the Rovaro without any pay, and only free board.

He'd put off finding a lawyer, despite Varvara's pleas, because, in his mind, he couldn't really believe that this matter would ever come to trial. It was so incredible – so preposterous. He'd built his reputation on his integrity. He had been forced, however, to tell Lily the truth. And she had listened, her face set, her eyes hard, unmoved by any real surprise. At thirty-one, she was already well acquainted with the perfidy of men.

But on the whole, the children were still happy. On Sundays, Lily packed a picnic basket, and the four of them boarded the bus with their games, a ball, and some books to go to the Bois de Boulogne. Near a shady bush they spread a blanket, sat or lay on it and remained there from noon to dusk, just like poor people. For the Brasilovs were poor now. But for the first time in their lives, the children had their Papa home every night, early, and he played with them. Lily tried to laugh and joke with her family, for brooding didn't help. And so, when they were all together, she tried to close the drawers of trouble in her brain, and to open those that were full of joy.

They owed money to the boarding-house. Lily begged the owner to allow them not to take their meals there, which was a custom in all French boarding-houses. Kindly, the rotund little bourgeoise acquiesced. And so their debts became smaller. Whenever Misha was paid one hundred francs, Lily paid half to the landlady, and kept fifty for their food. She had made an arrangement with the Restaurant Moscou, where Misha and his cronies had been habitual patrons during the days of wine and roses. They'd eaten oysters, pheasant, and drunk champagne, and left the restaurant huge sums of money. Now she asked the owners if, in memory of those splendid times, they could help him out a little. And so, at noon, she went there with a closed pot and was given a large portion of good food for the children. In the evening they ate a light meal, but at noon, Misha and Lily frequently went without food in order to give to Kyra and Nicolas whatever was left over. Lily and Misha never discussed it. But sometimes, when it was lunchtime and there wasn't anything to eat, one would look at the other and shrug, saying: 'I don't think I'm hungry today. We'll have an early dinner.' And the other would nod, and agree.

Between September and Christmas, an eruption of right-wing reprisals occurred in Paris. The Secret Committees for Revolutionary Action, more commonly known as the Hood, undertook the murder of an Italian anti-Fascist newspaperman and his brother, and blew up the head-quarters of the Employers' Association. And just before the holidays, Italy and Germany left the League of Nations. Lily wrote to Marisa: 'Things have become so ugly, I wonder now if you wouldn't be better off following your parents to America. At least there, one's civil liberties are respected, and there's no threat of war.' But Wolf replied that if his own mother and father still refused to heed the signs of danger, he would be forced to get out of Austria without them, bringing Marisa and Nanni to the South of France. For, he told Lily, many of his Jewish patients were now leaving in droves, and many had ended up on the

French Riviera. A semblance of gracious living still seemed to be maintained there.

'You must understand how we feel, Lily,' he wrote. 'For the Jews of Europe, it is most important to stay together at this time of fear and horror. We feel threatened in our very existence by Hitler. In Nice, we shall at least have the illusion of being in a safe enclave among our own kind.'

She'd felt a shock, reading his lines. She wondered if Claire and Jacques felt this way, too. After the summer, they had remained in Cannes, in their rented villa. She thought: Then there can be no more escape. And thought again: I am Jewish, too. For how long will Paris remain safe for me, and for my children? And in this moment, she *felt* her Jewishness. It was in her bones, in her flesh, making her identify with the thousands who, like the Steiners, were fleeing from lives of comfort and grace, in Germany and Austria, in order to keep one step ahead of the small, puffy-faced man with his toothbrush moustache.

Lily had strengthened her friendship with Rabbi Weill. Because she was no longer free to come and go as she pleased, having no one to supervise her children if she was out, her visits to the temple in the Rue de la Victoire had had to be spaced out to fit an erratic schedule. But the Grand Rabbi of Paris had taught her a great deal. Lily yearned to share her new religion with her son, who was turning thirteen – but, of course, it was impossible. And there were still many times when the tug of her old religion continued to pull her in the opposite direction: at Christmas, at Easter. She was familiar with the most minute details of Catholicism, and only with the rudiments of Judaism. Sometimes she prayed to God, the God of all religions, to give her guidance, to tell her who and what she was. But no direction came. And so she felt like a curious hybrid, a nomad in a confusing no-man's-land. She was a Jew, and yet not completely; she was still a Catholic, though without right to take the sacraments.

With the end of the year, of course, there were her children's birthdays. Claire and Jacques came home, and reintegrated their suite at the Ritz. With them in the city, Lily felt oddly relieved. She helped her mother plan a birthday dinner for Kyra, whose birthday came first; and then one for Nick. And, as they set the table and wrapped packages, the two women's eyes met, knowing without having to say the words that this boy would not have the bar mitzvah of his ancestors. He didn't even know he was a Jew.

Kyra's day had come and gone in a pretence of joy, characterized by the girl herself, full of exuberance and fire as she had tried on her grandmother's coral necklace, and had pinned her hair up like a young lady to view herself in the mirror. The faces around the table had been wreathed in smiles, but the smiles had been like painted curves on the faces of wooden dolls. Nobody spoke of Misha's problems; but he hadn't worked in months, hadn't been paid in almost as long. Elegant and stately, strands of white mixed with the shining black of his hair, he had sat between both his children, ever the proud father. But then, when Kyra had fallen asleep on her grandmother's bed, and Lily and Claire had covered her with a mohair blanket, he'd slipped out of the suite, to walk in the cool night air, snow falling about his shoulders, neck, and hair. He'd found it suddenly hard to breathe, surrounded by all these people who meant well, who loved him – and whom he had cruelly disappointed. He wondered what might have occurred if his father had not been killed, four years before. Lily and the children might have stayed in Austria, and who knows? she might even have married another man, and now been living in a vast, comfortable house, as she so richly deserved. He wished then that he had had the courage to kill himself, or at least to exit from the lives of his loved ones. By staying, he had hurt them ten times more deeply.

On the day of Nick's thirteenth birthday, he left the

house with the last hundred francs he had saved. Months ago, he'd felt forced to pawn his father's ruby cuff links, but now he hoped to redeem them. Maybe, if he left the pawnbroker the hundred-franc note, the man might make an exception and let Misha take them back. He knew that the rubies alone were worth five thousand francs. But the man had given him a mere four hundred for them, which Lily had accepted with a beggar's relish at the time. He'd offer him one hundred up front, and the rest payable within the year. For surely, in the space of twelve months, a job would crop up. And if it didn't, he'd forget his pride and go to work in the kitchen of a restaurant, or as a bellboy. Anything, so that Lily wouldn't speak again about going out into the streets of Paris, like that poor, obsequious, forever famished Sudarskaya, looking for piano students.

He didn't tell Lily where he was going, but told her, instead, that he would join her at the Ritz. And so, when he appeared there in the evening, freshly shaved and dressed for his son's birthday, she wasn't surprised. He went out frequently to look for clients, to try to drum up business; she had ceased to question him about it, in order not to depress him when the answer was inevitably negative. They all had dinner in the suite, and Jacques had ordered Mumm Cordon Rouge champagne, to toast the young man. The entire evening had been rich in warmth, more subdued than Kyra's night, but at the same time, more real. Lily felt, as she looked around the table at her mother, now fifty-seven, and at the white-haired man who had come to be more of a father to her than Paul had ever been, that her heart was full of gratitude that they had never let her down, that during all her misfortunes, they had stood solidly behind her, giving her two beautiful children a sense of permanence and strength.

When it was time to open the presents, Nick felt his father's eyes upon him, and, with his innate sense of intuition, he set aside the small wrapped box that Misha had brought with him. It was only after he had disposed of his other gifts that he slowly, carefully, removed the coloured paper from his father's. A velvet box appeared, and Kyra cried: 'Open it! It's a piece of jewellery!' as excited as if it had been for herself. Misha's heart contracted; how rarely, now, did his children have the opportunity to see anything of value.

Nick worked the catch, and the box opened. His grandfather's ruby cuff links, set in Florentine gold, gazed up at him from their velvet bed. He picked them up, a slow smile forming on his smooth boy's face. And when he unhooked his simple metal studs to slip the new ones through the buttonholes of his white cambric shirt, Misha noticed that his wide brown eyes, duplicates of Lily's, were liquid with unsuppressed tears.

He'd always had a slight penchant towards his daughter; but on this December night of 1937, Mikhail Brasilov saw, across the table from him, the young man who would redeem his honour, and make good again the ancient, proud name of Brasilov.

Claire prevailed on them to leave the children with her, and so Misha and Lily went home alone, walking in the moonlight, his arm tight around her in the cold. And when she went to sleep, her head safe in the crook of his arm, she had no way of knowing that on this very night of their son's thirteenth birthday, Misha had given up the last tenuous hope to which he had been clinging. In the morning, when she rose, he had already left the room, and so she went downstairs alone to share a cup of coffee with Madame Antiquet, the landlady.

They sat together in the small, cheerful kitchen of the *pension*, watching the snowflakes dancing down on the streets of Paris. When Léone, the young maid, ushered in a uniformed bailiff, Madame Antiquet frowned, puzzled and not a little irritated at this unpleasant appearance. But

Lily saw him with a sinking of the heart, knowing that he had come to cause her husband yet another problem. So she rose, a little unsteadily, and said: 'I'm Princess Brasilova. Are you looking for me?'

The bailiff bowed slightly, and replied, with some embarrassment, 'I beg your pardon, madame, but it was your husband I was searching for. Do you know where I could find him, or when he is due home?'

Madame Antiquet, plumping out her pigeon breast, said sharply: 'When are you people going to leave the Brasilovs alone? It's Christmastime. Why do you want the Prince, anyway?'

The bailiff looked down at the polished linoleum of the neat little bourgeois kitchen. Then he raised his eyes to Lily's, and, ignoring the landlady, declared: 'I have come to arrest him, madame. As of nine o'clock this morning, he became a fugitive from justice.'

'What on earth are you talking about?' Lily cried. Suddenly her forehead was moist, and a pulse was rapidly beating in her throat. A dreadful anxiety enveloped her senses, and she felt dizzy.

'I'm really terribly sorry. But the Prince was supposed to appear before a court of law, regarding the de Chaynisart affair, first thing this morning. He was sent a summons some weeks ago.' In a softer tone, the bailiff asked: 'You didn't know?'

Lily shook her head, mutely. Next to her, Madame Antiquet was holding her arm – holding her up, she realized with shock. Because she couldn't feel her toes, and then, her knees.

'Get out,' the landlady said. The bailiff raised his brows, stunned, but then, understanding, he began to beat a hasty retreat to the front door. When they were finally alone, Madame Antiquet forced Lily to sit down. 'You mean, you really didn't know?' she inquired.

'No. And I have no idea where Misha's gone. I don't

know where to go, to warn him not to come back – to find a hideaway, somewhere else – ' Her voice broke off, and she began to sob, her head at last bending into her hands, her fingers forming a woven screen across her eyes.

Hours later, after Léone had escorted her back upstairs to her own room, Lily lay down on the bed, trying to sort things out. She was certain that no summons had been sent to the *pension*. Madame Antiquet would have known about it, and told her, even if Misha had been trying to hide the truth from her. Why, he hadn't even gone to speak to a lawyer . . . ! She felt her eyes fill up anew, and buried her face in the pillows, letting her grief pour out naturally, silently.

After a while, she became aware that a steady knocking was coming from the door. Afraid of more bad news, and another bailiff, she pushed the hair from her forehead and went to open it. On the threshold stood a superb woman with red hair, wearing a black sable coat and a matching toque. Lily's surprise made her step back inside the room, momentarily caught completely off guard. She'd recognized her at once.

'Please,' Varvara said, coming in and closing the door herself. 'Don't be angry that I've come. I had a number of things to tell you, and I felt that if we talked, you might perhaps better understand.'

Bewildered, her heart hammering inside her chest, Lily nodded, bereft of words. Varvara untied the belt of her coat, and let it drop from her shoulders. She sat down on a narrow wooden chair with a straight back, and said, softly: 'Madame – we don't really know each other, but we are not enemies. In fact, through Misha's descriptions, through so many of the touching things he's told me about you over the years, I feel that I've come to know you.'

The tears threatened to spill once more, and so Lily swallowed hard to keep a composed face. 'Madame,' she said. 'I don't quite know what to reply. I . . . hadn't realized that you . . . and Misha . . .'

'. . . stayed very good friends. You see, Lily . . . if I may call you that . . . I always loved Misha. But he married me largely out of loneliness, because I was a familiar object in a foreign world, when he ended up in France. It was never a real marriage, as I'm sure you know.'

Again, Lily nodded, still at a loss for words. And so Varvara continued. 'You mustn't be upset that we stayed friends, and that he never told you. I'm sure he felt that you might have judged our friendship to be . . . something else. Be that as it may, when he was hit by the de Chaynisart lawsuit, he came to me, and told me about it. And so, just a few days ago, I concluded arrangements for *Maître* Maurice Garçon to represent him in this matter.'

Lily's lips parted. Maurice Garçon was one of France's foremost trial lawyers. But the surge of hope that had lifted her heart was immediately replaced by a new feeling of despair. 'Under normal circumstances, madame,' she stammered, 'I would be dancing with joy at your generous kindness. But – a few hours ago, a bailiff came to find Misha, because he failed to appear in court. The start of the trial, it seems, was *today* – and we never received a summons.'

Varvara was playing with the clasp of a large gold bracelet on her right wrist. She said, in such a soft voice that it was hard to hear her: 'He's left, Lily.' The words hung in the room like a diaphanous cloud, breaking up and reforming, then, like a thunderstorm, hitting Lily about the shoulders with the power of their significance. And all the while, Varvara's blue eyes stayed glued to her face: her serious eyes, full of the wisdom of the ages.

'What do you mean?' Lily finally cried.

'What I've just said. Misha left the country this morning. He knew nothing about the summons, you can be sure. He left because his heart had broken – because he didn't have any courage left, and he didn't want you to continue to carry the burden of his presence in your life.'

'No!' Lily screamed. She stood up, her whole body trembling, the tears spurting out so that she could no longer see Varvara. 'No! He would never leave us! We were together, last night, in this room – '

'I told him the same thing, Lily. I advised him to stay with you, to come to you for the strength to face the problems in his life. But he was always too proud to bring you down to his level. He didn't want you to suffer any more, on account of him. He wants you to get a divorce,' she added, folding her arms around the other, taller woman, and starting to caress Lily's hair, loose on her back. 'He wishes for you and the children to forget him.'

Slowly, with infinite gentleness, she manoeuvred Lily to the bed and forced her to lie down. 'He didn't care about Maurice Garçon, at this stage of the game,' Varvara explained, holding Lily's hand. 'He felt that he would lose, no matter who represented him.'

Lily struggled to sit up, and asked: 'Where has he gone?'

'To Belgium, to begin with. But he wants very much to sail to the United States.'

'He has no money. I have seventy francs, for our food, and that's all.'

'He has some money,' Varvara declared, looking away from Lily at the doll on Kyra's bed. 'Enough for his trip, and to get himself started.'

'But if you love him – why did you let him go?' Lily cried.

Then Varvara stood up, and smoothed down her skirt. Looking down at Lily, she sighed, and murmured: 'Because, when a woman loves Misha Brasilov, she has to learn that he will always do what he feels is best. I tried to keep him once, and I learned this lesson long ago. I was young then, though that's a few years older than you are now. But maybe you can find it in your heart to understand

357

his pain, and also to forgive him. He didn't leave you because he didn't love you enough; he left you, on the contrary, because he felt that he loved you too much.'

Unclasping her alligator bag, Varvara withdrew an envelope. 'He left you this letter,' she said gently, laying it on the bed near Lily. 'Perhaps his words will mean more to you than anything *I* can tell you, from the outside.'

At the door, struggling into her fur coat, Varvara added: 'I can be a good friend to you, Lily. Don't judge the world too harshly. It takes more years than those you've lived to digest the infinity of someone's pain, when, like Misha's, it comes clothed in an excess of pride.'

She opened the door, crossed the threshold, and closed it carefully behind her. Lily was left alone, her nerves on fire, all of her being in revolt. It couldn't be true, that he had left her, just like that. It couldn't be true.

She ran to the window, and saw the trim figure of Varvara Trubetskaya being helped into a taxi by the driver. Then the taxi pulled away, and Lily stood staring into an empty street on which the snow, oblivious to her suffering, continued to fall like a cascade of magic crystals. It was the heart of the Christmas season – almost fourteen years since she had met her husband, at the Comtesse de Béhague's lavish reception in January of 1924. In the neighbourhood, a church bell began to peal.

She sat down on her bed, and picked up the envelope. Her fingers tore it open, pulling out a single sheet of creamy vellum. Tears blurred her sight as she began to read, and she had to blink them down her cheeks in order to make out what Misha had written.

My beloved wife

I can no longer continue to disgrace you and our children. I know that once I'm gone, Jacques and Claire will take better care of you than I have, for the past few years. I shan't ask you to wait for me; that wouldn't be fair. I've brought you nothing but heartache. But I do want to let you know that I'm going to make something of my life, in my new country. And only when I shall have restored my honour, will I return or send for you.

Until then, I won't write to you. I don't wish to make you remember a man who was a failure. But you and the children will be in my thoughts, each and every day. I couldn't have faced saying goodbye to you all. I knew that if I did, I'd lose the courage to part from you. So please, take care. And if you ever need anything, Varvara will take care of you. She's good, and dependable . . . which is more than I can say for myself.

I'll always love you. And I mean for us all to be together, in the future.

Misha

And then she felt, inside her body, that Misha had truly left her. In spite of his final words, she was sure that she and her children would never see him again.

Chapter Seventeen

The average Frenchman had not been much surprised when Camille Chautemps, on 10 March 1938, had walked out of the Chamber of Deputies, and resigned as premier. Tired and even bored with the constant pendular swings between the Right and Left, this French Everyman had been more preoccupied with the advent of spring, signalled by the sudden blooms of anemones in the Bois de Boulogne.

It was a national habit to listen to the news broadcasts on the radio. And so, when Everyman turned on his radio on 12 March he was shocked to learn that Adolf Hitler had marched into Austria, to claim it as part of the German Reich. Chancellor Kurt von Schuschnigg had resigned, as Hitler had demanded in return for maintaining the peace. But still, the German troops stationed at the border had come through, proclaiming the beginning of the *Anschluss*, or reintegration of Austria into what Hitler called 'the Fatherland'.

Lily, huddled with her children near their small wireless set at the Pension Lord-Byron, heard the news with a dreadful sense of doom. She saw the same expression forming on Nick's face as he asked, voicing aloud her fears: 'And the Steiners? What's going to happen to them now that the Nazis have taken over Austria?'

'Why didn't they leave before?' Kyra demanded.

'It isn't easy to persuade old people to leave their homeland,' Lily answered softly. 'Mina and Isaac didn't want to start anew, in a place they didn't know. And, of course, whatever Wolf had written us, you know that he and Marisa would never have left without their parents.'

360

Nevertheless, a month later, Marisa and Nanni arrived, alone. The Brasilovs hurried to the Ritz, to meet their friends in Jacques and Claire's suite. For now, with Marisa's parents in America, the Walters were the closest to family for her. While Nick and Kyra dragged Nanni into the bedroom, their eyes popping out with amazement that the three-year-old toddler whom they had so loved had turned, miraculously, into this blooming girl of eight, with her father's brown hair and her mother's beautiful blue eyes, the Walters and Lily surrounded Marisa to hear what was really happening in Austria.

'It's incredible,' Marisa said, her voice low but vibrant with anger. 'Chamberlain and the French don't give a damn about the Jews. They just didn't want to intervene to help Austria stay independent: and now it's too late. The plebiscite showed more than ninety-nine per cent in favour of the *Anschluss*. And all the anti-Semites have come out of the woodwork. They're only too happy to apply the laws of the Reich to their own Jews.'

'We hadn't heard it was that bad,' Jacques countered mildly.

'It's worse. Wolf and Papa had been active in the Social Democrat party, and now we're terribly afraid of reprisals. On April first, nine days before the plebiscite, the Nazis sent the first trainload of political prisoners to Dachau.'

'What's in Dachau?' Claire asked.

'They call it a "concentration camp". We're really not sure what it is. Probably a kind of prison. And anyway, there are already thousands of Jews waiting to hear about their fates in the jails of the Gestapo. They're forcing some to emigrate, selling their businesses at a huge deficit. Wolf was able to sell some of our family holdings a while back, and when things got bad, he decided that I must leave, since I'm a French citizen and Nanni is my child. I've brought with me a sum totalling thousands of schillings, Jacques – you must please help me to put it away for us.

Because though it's only a fraction of what we own, it was all I could possibly smuggle out.'

'But Wolf will be here soon, dear,' Claire said softly.

Marisa's blue eyes stayed on Claire's, with a steadfast, ardent quality to them that finally unnerved the older woman. Claire looked down then, and nervously began to twist the cord of her silk belt. An odd, pregnant silence filled the room like a wet mist that chilled the bones. And then the children came in, singing an old Viennese nursery rhyme that they had all sung five years before, at the Schwindgasse house.

'Do you know what the German Storm Troopers sing when they're marching?' Marisa asked, her voice kept down. '"When Jewish blood comes spurting from the knife, then things go twice as well!"'

It was a strange summer for everyone. Once more, Claire took her villa in Cannes, and this time everyone followed her: Lily and her two children, Marisa and Nanni. And although Nick, Kyra, and the small Austrian girl filled the house with noise and games, the adults didn't have their hearts in the vacation.

Since Misha had left, Lily had not heard from him. Once or twice Varvara Trubetskaya had come to see her. She'd told Lily that Misha had arrived in New York, and had found some work. But she didn't elaborate on what kind of work, and Lily didn't ask. It was still too raw and too sudden for her. She felt bewildered, out of kilter, as if she'd been hit by a blunt object while calmly walking down a peaceful street. She was overwhelmed with sadness, imagining Misha alone, struggling with his guilt. He'd made a decision, thinking to shield her and the children from additional pain and shame; but, she felt, he'd made the wrong decision. For, when she'd returned to him after Prince Ivan's death, she'd made the commitment to stand by him no matter what. He simply hadn't thought her strong enough for this.

The beginning had been a nightmare. When she'd left him because of Rirette, she'd felt outraged and betrayed. Now, however, she felt worse. She felt totally, completely alone. Immediately, Jacques had begun to pay her a stipend of a thousand francs per month, as before, in Austria. Varvara, too, had offered to help her out, but Lily had thanked her and explained that this was in no way necessary. Jacques had thought of buying a house, finally, so that they might all live together. But Lily had turned this down, too. She knew that though they both loved the children, communal living would be a difficult adjustment for Claire and her stepfather. She preferred to continue at the boarding-house, and to venture out a few hours a day to give piano lessons to supplement her income.

She'd felt the most wrenching heartache of her life. She *needed* to teach these pupils, because only when strangers were around her was she forced not to dwell on her own misery. Nick's bitter eyes, the hurt and understanding shining out, silently, haunted her wherever she went. No matter how often she had tried to make him see why Misha had decided to leave, Nick's interpretation came out the same: his father had abandoned them out of cowardice and fear of facing the consequences of his trial. He never wished to set eyes on Misha again.

With Kyra, it was a different manifestation, but one equally difficult to deal with. She *hadn't* understood – at all. She'd tried to pin the blame on everything and everyone else, to make her father seem the victim. And then, every night, when she said her prayers, came the inevitable plea: 'Please, God, make my Papa come home. Make us a family again.'

Nick had said: 'Mama, I'm the man of the family now, and I'll protect you and Kyra. Don't be afraid.' But *he'd* been afraid, uncertain what to do, uncertain how to help.

Whenever Kyra awakened, screaming, having dreamed of Misha, it was Nick, rather than Lily, who rushed to hold and reassure her. In those moments, Kyra needed to feel that there was still a man who cared, and she clung to her brother with a strange, pitiful desperation. No, she hadn't understood. And she, like Nick, like Lily herself, lay outside the boundaries of help. No one could make it easier for any of them.

Just one time, Nicolas had declared, bitterly: 'Well, if he doesn't write to us, then he truly does want us to forget him. And if that's what he wants . . . then I, for one, shall do my best to put him outside my heart.'

'How could you be so disloyal?' Kyra had cried.

'Disloyal? He was disloyal,' Nick had replied, and gone to sit quietly at the large desk. He'd opened a book and started to read, but Lily had noticed the tears on the edge of his curling black lashes. And she'd felt a sword running through her stomach, taking all her own courage away.

Now, in Cannes, they listened to Daladier, premier since 10 April, and to news of the visit of the British king and queen, sealing the already strong bond between the two countries. It seemed, Jacques commented, that France, and particularly the timid Radicals, didn't know how to take a breath without the British showing them how to do it. Strange, distant rumours reached them about the Germans' fortification of their Siegfried Line, along the Rhine, to match the Maginot. And Wolf wrote, explaining his notion that aeroplanes and tanks were being built at increasing speed, in increasing quantities. But around Cannes, the vacationers didn't appear to care. They went to the casino and gambled gaily, and the ladies paraded down the Croisette, the handsome promenade by the beach, in loose caftans of gypsy design.

In the spring, Adolf Hitler had begun to make noises concerning the Sudetenland, a region in the northern part of Czechoslovakia whose three and a quarter million inhabitants spoke German. He had spoken of injustices and prejudice levelled at these 'Germans', and, during the royal visit to France, Lord Runciman had been delegated to Prague from Britain to mediate between the Czechs and Hitler. A plebiscite had been suggested, to decide the fate of the Sudeteners. In mid-September, the French radio spoke of fortifications in Paris against enemy aircraft. And then, Hitler declared that he refused the idea of the plebiscite, and that the Czechs must give him the Sudetenland. This news threw all the French into profound shock, and after that, fear. 'If the Czechs refuse,' Jacques said, 'there will be war.' For Czechoslovakia had signed a firm alliance with France.

Hurriedly, Claire and her entourage of friends and family packed their bags to move back into the capital. All at once, the pretence of being on holiday had dissipated. It was important to return home, and to stay close to the wireless for news.

Marisa had taken a smaller suite at the Ritz, near the Walters. She'd confided in Claire that she didn't want to move to the Riviera, when Wolf came to join her with his parents. Eliane had written to her repeatedly, begging her to come at once to the United States, where there was no anti-Semitism and psychiatrists were always welcome. But Marisa didn't want to leave Paris. She'd been reared there, and Nanni felt at home with Kyra and Nick – and besides, the United States seemed so remote that it was difficult to imagine what life would be like there for people as fundamentally European as she and Wolf and the two old people.

As tensions mounted, it was Marisa who became the focal point of the group. Although Lily had lost her husband, the two women's situations were palpably different. Misha had left of his own free will, and was absolutely safe in the United States. Lily might mourn her marriage, but with or without Hitler's intervention, Misha's plans to go would have been the same. Marisa, on the other hand, had a husband who loved her, from whom she was estranged only by circumstance. War had already struck her and her family. And so, as afraid as the others might be, they realized that she, and she alone, had experienced this war; and she alone knew exactly who Hitler was and what he could do. The situation was much worse than anyone in France could possibly have conceived.

Wolf had written to her in Ma , explaining that Mina had caught pneumonia and that, because of this, they would not be able to join her as soon as they had planned. He begged her not to worry. But the tone of his letters betrayed the anguish he was living with, and so she'd begged him to tell her the truth. He'd sent her by the next mail a long missive that she had to share with Lily and her parents. It was too dreadful to bear alone.

> For years the Austrians have been suppressing the hatred they have felt for the Jews, and now they have unlocked the door and let it out, in full force. Hitler's laws are being applied, without mercy for the old and the very young. We must display a yellow star of David on our clothing; we are severely rationed, and our children can no longer attend public schools. Our radios have been confiscated, and we have a curfew. We are not even allowed to go to the theatre anymore.

As an afterthought, he had added: 'We in the big cities have not yet been physically assaulted, and of course, as long as there is Jewish money, it will be possible to help along our situation. Our plight is therefore less pitiful than that of our poorer co-religionists.'

Marisa had cried: 'And for how long will this Jewish money last, before they take him away like all those others?'

Horrified, Claire, Jacques, and Lily had stared at her, their lips parted. Nobody dared to ask where 'all those others' had been taken, but they remembered what Marisa had told them about Dachau.

On 24 September, under a sky of molten pewter, Daladier and President Lebrun ordered the immediate mobilization of the reserves, without relying on individual notification. Hitler responded by giving the Czech leader, Eduard Beneş, until 1 October to comply with his demands. It was the eve of Rosh Hashanah. France lay quiet, its ministers called to London. 'Aren't we going to the synagogue, Mama?' Nanni asked.

'I don't know if I can summon up the right prayer,' Marisa sighed. 'Where is the God of Israel, who must protect His people?'

Jacques looked down at the carpet, and Claire watched him, from lowered lids. She knew that at this moment he was struggling with an enormous weight that she, above all, had placed on his shoulders when they had first met, ten years before. His religion had been kept a guarded secret, with only a few men knowing about it from the temple on the Rue de la Victoire. Eliane and David had known – but not Marisa. And Jacques, who had always been a devout Jew, had never again broached the subject of disclosure to his wife.

Together, they had lit the candles on the Sabbath; and, when possible, they had slipped out, Claire heavily veiled, to a smaller, less conspicuous synagogue than that in the Rue de la Victoire. She felt a weighty guilt about all this, and now, with Misha gone from all their lives, and the imminent threat of Hitler, she longed to let the secret out. Placing her hand on her husband's, she murmured: 'Tell her that she is not alone – that we are all with her.'

Lily felt her body tense, and looked at Marisa. The young woman was leaning slightly forward, a puzzled expression on her face. Then Lily examined the children. Nanni, leaning against her mother, seemed a bit restless, and bored. But Nick's eyes were sharp, glued to his stepgrandfather. Kyra had moved instinctively to his side, alert and perhaps suspicious.

367

Jacques released a long, low sigh. 'My darling Marisa,' he declared softly. 'At a time like this, all the Jews of Europe need to draw together. We are Jewish, my dear: Claire, and I. Lily has known for quite some time, but it was impossible to announce it to the world. Misha, and the people he worked for, were stringently anti-Semitic. And of course, you can remember what some of the papers said just a few years ago? "Better Hitler than Blum." Don't forget, that's what Claude believed – and still does.'

It was her children that Lily was watching, not her friend. Nick's face appeared suddenly suffused with a joy, like the day breaking. But Kyra held back, stiff and haughty, her green eyes filled with reproach and fear. Marisa was saying, 'But . . . for so many years . . . I'd thought that Lily was a stringent Catholic. I wish I'd known.'

'Wolf knew,' Lily said softly. 'I had to confide in some-one, and so I told him, in Vienna.'

'Then that was why he decided to teach me Hebrew!' Nick exclaimed. 'I'd assumed it was because I was so curious, and loved languages. Mama – I'd no idea.' Then he added, shyly: 'But . . . I'm glad. All those evenings when we sat at Aunt Mina's Sabbath table . . . they meant so much to me. From somewhere deep inside. I like the Jewish religion. Frankly, now that I'm not afraid to admit it, Catholicism always made me feel cold. I mean . . . it's so *forbidding*. Confession and the priests and all the stark whiteness of everything – d'you know what I mean? It's like being in a hospital. You think you're never going to get out.'

Lily smiled. She could see Marisa grinning too, and Claire's eyes, so gentle upon her grandson. Then Kyra said, her voice very cold: 'But I don't want to be a Jew.'

The silence prolonged itself, and the shock on the four adult faces. Nanni asked: 'Why not, Kyra? I'm Jewish. There's nothing wrong with being Jewish.'

Nick turned to her, his face at once curious and protective. He touched her on the neck, a strangely adult gesture, and said: 'I think we should be proud that we're partly Jewish. It's Grandma's part, and that's the best we've got inside us. Don't you see?'

Unexpectedly, Kyra buried her face into her brother's chest, and started to sob. Nick murmured to Nanni, whose great blue eyes stood wide open with shock, 'Kyrotchka didn't mean to hurt your feelings. Or anybody's. It's just that it's . . . hard without our father.'

'With Hitler around the corner, it's all at once become most important to know what to do about it,' Jacques broke in. 'Right now is hardly the moment to tell our acquaintances about this. There's been a curious reversal in political attitudes these last few months. The Right, which was always fiercely antagonistic to any foreign attempt to tread on France's toes, has been oddly placatory of Hitler; and the Left, always the peace-loving element of society, has stopped wanting to yield all in order to avoid war. Because the Left has been from time immemorial the opponent of Fascism, Nazism, and the like. We can't tell which side will win, but if it's the Right, France, too, will grow unkind to its Jews.'

Claire added: 'It's better to keep very quiet, my children. At the moment, I don't want Claude to know anything about this. He . . . well, he goes around with some people I definitely feel afraid of. Arch-reactionaries. And besides, it would be difficult to . . . explain it to him.'

Lily nodded, remembering Rirette's threats six years before. But Jacques was saying: 'Let us at least say a prayer for our people. It's the start of a new year, and maybe, after all, things will smooth out. Tell me, Nicky – do you remember enough Hebrew to say the words aloud with me?'

And in the hush that followed, the thirteen-year-old boy rose and took his place by his step-grandfather. They began to intone the magic words by which millions of Jews, for thousands of years, had been committing their fates into the hands of their God. Claire's voice joined in, and then Marisa's, and finally Lily's. Instinctively, Marisa held her hand out to her friend, and clasped Lily's strongly in hers. They prayed with tears in their eyes, and when they stopped, they saw, in the corner, Nanni and Kyra standing together, the older girl's two arms brought down over the little one's shoulders.

'Happy New Year,' Marisa said.

On Wednesday 28 September, Madame Antiquet received an official visitor from the Foundation of Auxiliary Shelters. He had come to examine the building, to see whether it might qualify as a possible bomb shelter. Lily accompanied them to the attic, with which he was pleased, because its floor was made of concrete. 'You're going to have to remove all the papers and bolts of material,' he announced. 'But you can keep the trunks.' In the basement, he told them that more space needed to be cleared out, to be able to fit more people in.

In the afternoon, the handyman came with three others to bring down the excess furniture from the attic. 'If there's a bombing, nothing loose can be left up there,' Madame Antiquet said to Lily. 'It could clatter around like an old man's loose teeth.' Then, with a resigned shrug, she added: 'But the house is an old Parisian house, with concrete everywhere. You'd think *that* would make a difference if a bomb should hit it square in the face. But watch: it won't matter a pin. It'll just topple down like a house of cards, and we'll be crushed alive, concrete or no concrete.'

'But presumably, we'll already have run into the basement,' Lily countered.

'People have died in basements, too,' the plump landlady grumbled. 'Of suffocation, like helpless swine.'

Lily didn't sleep all night, wondering which God to pray

370

to, the Jehovah of the Jews, or the Father of the Holy Trinity.

On the twenty-ninth, the Brasilovs went to the Ritz, to listen on Jacques's radio to the results of the Munich Conference. The French, the British, and the Italian heads of state were meeting with Hitler in an effort to avoid a major European catastrophe. The Soviets, conspicuously left out, had not even rearmed. But in Paris, Maurice Thorez and his Communist Party had staged a noisy campaign against Nazism and Germany. Through the early evening, the TSF put off its report, announcing that the powers were still in conference. Finally, at 10:00 P.M., the broadcaster came through, jubilantly declaring that an agreement had been reached. Lily sighed, packed up her tired children, and went to bed, where she slept, though fitfully, dreaming of Wolf and his parents, and of her own children. In the early morning, she awakened as if hit by a bolt of lightning. Kyra and Nick were asleep, each dark head on its own pillow. And Lily crossed herself, as always when a danger had been narrowly avoided.

The next morning, the weather was so clear and the sky so blue, that her heart soared when she pulled the curtains aside. But the morning newspapers were still not carrying the full story.

In the afternoon, Madame Antiquet came to pull her away from some handiwork, and together they rushed out to the Champs-Élysées, to watch the procession of cars to the Élysée Palace: Daladier returning triumphant, on his way to receive his laurels from President Lebrun. The crowds were thick, and it was difficult to see. Women were throwing flowers that splintered off into a rainbow of petals as they hit the black cars; men chanted the *Marseillaise* in voices half drunk with the sheer exhilaration of relief. Finally, long after the passage of the procession, Lily and her landlady turned away and walked the short distance home.

Kyra and Nick were waiting for her, their young faces bright with excitement. Their friends from school, Jacqueline and Pierre Rublon, had invited them to watch from the balcony of their father's firm, which stood on the great tree-lined avenue. 'It was better than Bastille Day!' Kyra cried.

But still, Lily had not read the confirmation of this day's events, and last night's signed agreement in Munich. She longed for the details in an afternoon daily. Kyra went to the nearby stand and bought a batch of different ones, and came bounding in, like a light-hearted young doe, brandishing them. 'Look, Mama!' she exclaimed. 'The headlines are all the same: "*Peace!*"'

Lily took the first one from her daughter, and skimmed the front page rapidly. 'The agreement was signed at one thirty-five A.M.,' she said. 'And look: here are the pictures of the returning "heroes". Mussolini, Chamberlain, and Daladier. They were *all* received with ovations.'

'So there won't be war,' Nick remarked, peering over her shoulder.

In the evening they listened to a broadcast of the return of the three chiefs of state. But the Poles were disturbed, and the Hungarians and Soviets were complaining. 'Everywhere else, however, a veritable delirium of joy is raining down,' the newscaster said, his voice concluding on a definite lilt.

'Those other countries are so far away, they hardly seem to make a difference, do they?' Kyra commented brightly.

'Czechoslovakia was their neighbour,' her brother reminded her. 'And the Soviet Union is a monster. Remember what our father used to say? "Russia is like the Hydra: cut off its head, and it will grow two back again."'

'I thought you put Papa's ideas alongside those of madmen and children,' Kyra said ironically.

'Maybe I've learned to sort through them for their reality,' the young boy said. Although his voice was devoid of the pomposity of youth, it vibrated with a new self-confidence. Lily gazed at him, reminding herself that he was not yet fourteen, and was surprised, as always, by his strange maturity.

'May Kyra and I go outside to ride our bicycles?' he asked, his eyes suddenly bright and hopeful. Claire had given both children shining new cycles for the resumption of school, so that they might ride together to the lycée and not hinder their mother's piano-teaching schedule.

'Don't go far,' Lily answered, but they had already raced out of the door. She moved to the small window, and peered out. Nicolas and Kyra, hand in hand, were carrying two bicycles from the house to the pavement, setting them down, and eagerly mounting. Kyra's long hair, loose on her back, gleamed in the glow of the setting sun. They were still children, she thought, with a pinching of the heart: children, in need of her protection, whose father had abandoned them as orphans. And she was swept by bitterness, wondering if, in that other country so far away, he had even considered what this September had done to them all.

On Monday 7 November, a young German Jew, Herschel Grynszpan, whose parents had been living in Hanover for forty years, shot the first secretary at the German Embassy, Ernst von Rath. Two days later, on Wednesday 9 November, von Rath was dead.

The Grynszpans were tailors, who had lived well. But since the advent of Hitler, they had been obliged to close down their shop, and were buying secondhand clothes that they repaired at night, in order to resell them in the morning. Two of Herschel's brothers had died, one in front of his eyes, mowed down by a car. Another brother, a mechanic, and his sister, a typist, had lost their jobs the previous year. He, just seventeen, had been advised to spend a year with an uncle in Paris, but he had been unable to find work there. When at last he had received his notification of expulsion, he had lost his head and gone to the embassy. All doors had been left open, as if the Germans had been awaiting just this kind of incident. He had not been stopped on his way to von Rath, and when he had shot him, nothing could have forewarned him that by his incensed action, he would be giving the Reich its first martyr.

And so, because a traumatized young Jewish boy had fought back against the very thought of being forced to return to a Nazi hellhole, a flood of rage was set loose in all the cities of the German Reich. Since the shooting, Wolf and his father had transported their beds to his office at the back of the house, and sat huddled near the wireless set that they kept hidden in the basement. As Jews, they were more afraid now than ever since the *Anschluss*. But they thought that if anything were to happen, they would be safer in the office than in the spacious apartment giving right onto the thoroughfare of the Schwindgasse.

Wolf hadn't spelled out to Marisa how he had bribed every official in Vienna to retain his house, and how, in spite of the millions of schillings he had distributed, the Nazis had reduced their living quarters to the office, and half the former apartment where his parents had lived. Upstairs, where he and Marisa had resided, and where Lily and her children had spent a year, Austrian Aryans had moved in. Daily, Mina wrung her hands at the thought of the fine things she had been forced to leave behind; strangers were drinking from her Steuben crystal, and eating from her Meissen porcelain. Strangers were sleeping in her Louis XIV four-poster, and bathing in her marble bathtubs. And each day, when she peered out into her precious garden, she would see the children of others trampling her flowerbeds.

Isaac, resigned, seldom complained. Always conscious of his wife's well-being, he wanted only to spare her as much pain as possible. Her recovery from pneumonia had been slow; she'd been fearful of opening the windows, afraid that passersby would take this opportunity to taunt her or even to step through and pilfer from the apartment. Next door, where the living room had been, a family of peasants had taken over the premises, and kept her up half the night chanting martial tunes. And, of course, fresh produce was no longer available on the Jewish ration cards. Sometimes, Wolf managed to bribe one of the other tenants into bringing back an extra apple or cherry. For a single cherry had become the *ne plus ultra* of luxuries.

The night of 9 November, Isaac didn't want to go to sleep, as his son had suggested. Since the seventh, they'd been expecting the worst, and stayed up all night. They tucked Mina into her bed, and closed all the blinds in the house. At this moment, Wolf felt a sharp stab of guilt. Why hadn't he thought to move his parents right out of the house, where it was known that the richest Jews in Vienna had been residing for centuries? His shirt lay against his skin like a wet cloth, and he realized that perspiration had formed on every part of his body. Some inner premonition told him that tonight would be the night of the Reich's vengeance. Across from him, his mother lay, her eyes closed; and on the other side, sitting hunched over on the analysis couch, his father, suddenly a very old man, held the radio in hands that trembled. 'They're going to want our blood for this Rath's life,' Isaac intoned, but his voice held no strength, and was quivering.

'Our bags are packed,' Wolf reminded him. 'If there's the slightest sound of a mob, we'll wake Mama up and run from the side door.'

'Where they'll be waiting for us,' his father cut in.

Irritated, Wolf shrugged slightly. It was nearing midnight. He felt tired, exhausted, in fact; but tension kept him up, like the old man. They sat looking at each other, silent, pretending to listen to the radio. But in their bones, they felt the dread of which they were afraid to speak.

Wolf had almost decided to go to sleep for an hour's quick nap, when, near two in the morning, he heard a noise. It was the sound of glass shattering, and of men's voices raised. Electrified, he sat bolt upright, and ran to shake his mother awake. She was breathing heavily, with difficulty, and so, as he shook her shoulders, he felt enormous compassion. 'We have to go now, Mama,' he said urgently.

Slowly, as if in a dream, Isaac rose too, and together they helped Mina to her feet. She cowered against her son. 'Where are they coming from?' she asked.

'Everywhere. We'd better run now, through this door – '

Now the screaming had risen to a wild, swimming roar, and Wolf could feel the floor beneath his feet starting to shake. The noise of breaking glass seemed to be coming from this very house, although he knew that this could not actually be so. But he surmised that thousands of crazed men were coming through the Schwindgasse, thousands of men whose blood-lust for the Jews had taken possession of their very humanity. It was going to be worse than he had even anticipated.

To his horror, Mina had started to weep, refusing to move. Wolf opened the door, pushed out the suitcases, and went back to his parents. 'We could hide in the garden, between the bushes,' he murmured. 'They won't think to find us there. But we don't have a second to lose.'

Mutely, Isaac's face stared up at him. On the intelligent bearded face, a stunned expression was painted. Wolf recognized the signs of shock, and took over. Firmly, he seized his mother and father by the arms they were holding linked together, and pushed them out onto the small side street. Around them the din had become deafening, and he knew that every Jewish house along the way had been brutally destroyed. But it didn't matter, compared to the preciousness of their three lives. He propelled his parents to the small gate of the garden, and pushed them through. Then, directed by starlight and memory, he guided them to the far back, where some tall, manicured bushes loomed large and sheltering. He pushed his mother and father down into a crouching position, between two large shrubs, and squeezed behind them.

The hordes of frenzied Nazis were singing the Troopers' marching song, and bits and pieces of others. Now, for sure, Wolf knew that they had reached his house. He whispered, 'Maybe they won't be so rough, because Aryans have been living here too.' But he realized that he was just trying to reassure himself that this was a nightmare that would pass, and to bring some paltry comfort to his weeping, frightened parents.

And then they saw them. Or, more precisely, they saw blazing torches, and barely human forms discernible in their lights. Mina opened her mouth, and immediately Wolf clamped his hand down over it. The cry was muffled. Their bodies frozen in horror, they listened as windows were broken, as furniture was hurled out of the windows, as priceless objets d'art were crunched beneath the feet of the looters. Aghast, they saw, from the light of the torches, a medieval tapestry being ripped apart. 'Let Judah die!' the shouting came, ferocious, like the roaring of a hundred mountain lions let loose inside a fragile, age-old cathedral.

Mina Steiner, crouching like a fugitive, watched as savages she'd never met literally lifted the beams off the ceiling of the house she had come to as a bride. And Isaac, in a hushed whisper, said, stupefied, 'For centuries, Steiners have been born here, and Steiners have died here. I wanted you to have a son, Wolfgang, so that he, like I, and like yourself, might one day bring his bride to live in this house . . . *my* house.' There were tears streaming down the seams of his proud old face, and he held his wife's hand tenderly in his own, understanding that her thoughts, as always, had been synchronized to his.

Wolf, viewing the destruction of his birthplace, found himself unable to speak. He thought of Marisa, her beautiful eyes so filled with love, anxiety drawn into her small features, as he had last seen her at the train station. His own bride, for whom, during the past thirteen years, he had thanked God each bright morning of his life. He wondered then, for the first time, if he would *live* to hold her again in his arms, and if he would be granted the privilege of watching his Nanni grow into the full bloom of womanhood. With the terror of death, a great calm was taking over his senses. If he was to die, then so be it. He was strong enough to face the end. But for his parents, he whispered a prayer. God, he knew, would shield them.

Then he remained glued to the ground, his hands poised over the heads of his mother and father. The first band of looters was coming through the side gate, into the garden. He hadn't expected this. He'd been so sure that they would be in a hurry to continue down the Schwindgasse on their trail of destruction, that he'd taken it for granted that here the Steiners would be safe from harm. Mina's mouth was still open, but no sound emerged. He saw that she had wet the earth with her fear, the fear of an animal at bay, knowing it would not escape the bloodhounds on its trail.

'Look!' one man cried, pointing to the gazebo. 'Israel and Sarah had their little nesting place, too! Let's see what we can do to all of this!' And then a group of them ran forward, torches first. When the blaze began, they danced up and down, hurling broken pieces of the stone statues into the fire, crazed laughter emanating from mouths that seemed demented, out of proportion, like demons' lips.

The fire crunched on, and the looters remained one step ahead of it, taunting it to swallow up the entire garden. Wolf knew that if they stayed where they were, they would be burned alive, along with the bushes. He cursed himself, and with the desperation of self-preservation, whispered to his father: 'We'll have to run for the street, and hope that if we keep to the shadows, they won't see us. Because they're not expecting to find us here.'

But his father wasn't moving. Wolf, horrified, saw again the signs of deep shock, and knew that he would not be able to reason with Isaac. Pulling his mother up, he held her hand firmly, and said in the lowest of voices: 'You heard me, Mama. You'll have to try to make it alone. I'll have to carry Papa – he's not responding . . . Now, when I tell you: *run!*'

From the corner of his eye, he saw his mother scramble forward, hugging the darkness of the hedge. He lifted his father into his arms, and followed, quickly. But his mother's foot had caught on something, and in her terror, she let out the smallest of cries as she fell forward on the ground. Suddenly there was an enormous shout, and Wolf knew that they had been found out, that the end had come. He bent down then, and, with the utmost gentleness, pulled his mother up and towards him with one arm, cradling his father to his breast with all the strength left in his other arm. The crazed men were now surrounding them completely, yelling obscenities, and he guessed that this would be the last moment of his freedom. He felt the strange, repulsive hands pull Mina away, and wrench the limp body of Isaac from his arms. And then he was pushed down, headfirst, onto the gravel.

For a single moment, Wolf imagined that they would leave the Steiners to perish in the fire. But no, they were now shoving them out into the street. He felt blows around his head and ears, and all over his body. 'God, give me strength,' he begged. Ahead of him, they were throwing stones at his father, who was barely crawling on his knees. Wolf's eyes filled with tears. He couldn't cry out, for he knew that this would only incense them more. But he continued to pray for his father and mother.

Then he heard the voice. 'Keep the young one for later,' it said, in the accents of authority. 'And the old bitch. She isn't going to last the night, the way she looks. But the old geezer will have to go. He's done enough to fight our presence in Vienna.'

Only at this moment did Wolf use his voice. It was early dawn, and he could see that the street was littered with millions of shards of broken glass, like shining crystals in the roseate light. Wolf asked, 'Where are you going to send my father? He's never hurt anyone in his life.'

'He helped pollute the earth with his vile Jewish body,' another man replied. 'He'll be going with the rest of the political prisoners to Dachau. We know all about you Steiners. You went against the Reich, and paid money to keep us from power.'

'Why can't you send *me*, instead of him?'

'Because,' the authoritative voice came back, sardonically, 'you'll lead us to the rest of the money. He's too old and decrepit to have known where you put it.'

Somewhere near him, he heard his mother cry out as Isaac was pushed into a crowd of malevolent faces and hands. Only once did the old man turn; and then, Wolf saw that the shock had passed, and that he was in complete control of his senses. His magnificent brown eyes bore into him, filled with their love and unconditional understanding. And then, his father disappeared between two large, fierce men.

He couldn't see his mother, but Wolf knew that from this moment on, they would have to think only about the two of them. Isaac Steiner had passed into another existence, from which they, helpless victims also, would not be able to extricate him.

When the political prisoners, many of them still in their nightshirts, were pushed outside the sealed train, they saw before them barbed wire, and a hedge of uniformed bodies.

380

As they lifted their eyes to those bodies, they discerned long, corded whips in every hand. On either side of the barricade, a double row of men armed with whips was guarding the entrance to the camp outside the city of Dachau.

Isaac Steiner was among the first to be sent out into the live hedge. On his back was only a thin cambric shirt; on his lower part, the remains of serge trousers. He felt the immense fist going into the small of his back, hurling him face forward into the raised whips. The sky was suffused with a dusky sundown, and the strips of leather, curled into the clouds, made a funny swirling pattern against this dusk. Isaac had no time to think before he felt the slashes, burning into his already pummelled body like live flames, cutting into his skin to the muscle, through the veins and right down to the bone. He was sixty-eight, and had never, even as a child, experienced any physical punishment.

Other men were coming behind him, pushing him ever forward, bent in half and only semiconscious, into the live hedge. The ground was spattered with blood – *his* blood, he knew, but still he felt himself being propelled farther. Was there to be no end to this pain, so excruciating that now he could no longer see the ground before him? 'Jehovah, sweet Lord of my people, save me,' he whispered, or thought that he was whispering as he fell, and the wind was knocked out of him. And then, the pain miraculously ebbed away. Isaac's face, in the rictus of death, could not erase his own responsive smile.

God had saved him from the gates of Dachau.

The next day, Wolf and Mina were released from the SS prison where they had been taken, and they were told that Wolf's old friend, Hans von Bertelmann, had paid fifty thousand schillings for each of them. With hundreds of other Jews, dressed as they had been taken, Wolf and his mother were forced into the streets and made to clean up the remains of the damage. Shards of glass pierced their hands, and boots kicked their legs as they were bending down to do their slaves' work. On the streets, remnants of their normal lives stared at them, ripped apart to the point of disfigurement. They had been born children of God; and now they had lost their humanity.

Wolf and his mother had no house of their own in which to take refuge. And so, when darkness came, they directed their footsteps, cautiously, to the main thoroughfare of the Ringstrasse, where their friend Count von Bertelmann resided. The row of trees, bare-limbed and white with snowy crystals, seemed a painful, almost ironic reminder of the previous night. But here, for the most part, the damage had been minimal; not many Jews lived in these tall stone mansions full of Old World style and character.

Hans von Bertelmann was a stately middle-aged man who had been Wolf's friend from time immemorial. They had met at university, and had continued a close friendship thereafter. Von Bertelmann was a poet; he had been born to sufficient riches to indulge his pleasures, and so he wrote odes and ballads that he published himself, and distributed to his acquaintances. He was an elegant, fair man, who had never been married; and, with Wolf, he had fought to uphold the Social Democrats against the rising power of the Nazis. He'd believed in saving his country from Hitler. And so now, afraid of reprisals, although there wasn't a drop of Jewish blood in him, he lived discreetly, out of the public eye, in his ancestral home.

Wolf, not wishing to incriminate his friend further, knocked quietly at his back door. Within seconds, it seemed, it opened. A young maid let them in, and in the hallway Hans himself met them, hands outstretched. 'I alerted Helga to your coming,' he stated.

Wolf, pressing the strong, good hands, could only murmur, 'It was dangerous, Hans. Terribly dangerous to go out on a limb for some Jews. By the way – how did you know where we were being held?'

'I knew you had to be *some*where. To determine exactly where only required a certain persistency and diligence. No genius, I'm afraid.' Dropping his tone, he added: 'The girl's okay. But you'll have to live in the wine cellar for a few days until I can make arrangements to get you out. Every day, it seems, I get some unexpected visitors . . . checking to see if I'm up to something they could pounce on to deport me. My name is too old, too well-known for them to send me away for something other than high treason – and so they're hoping to indict me for *that*, if they can catch me.'

'Why don't you leave the country?' Wolf asked. 'Your parents aren't alive . . . you have no ties.' His own eyes welled up with tears, remembering Isaac.

Hans touched his shoulder, sympathetically. 'We'll do all we can to find him,' he assured them. 'But I *do* have ties. To my country. I'm not going to allow Hitler to destroy Austria. I have to stay – if for no other reason than to help the Jewish underground.'

He led the way to a small, recessed staircase, and Wolf held his mother up so that she could go down. After her bout of pneumonia, the events of the past forty-eight hours had reduced her to a weak, wobbly state, and her cheeks were slack, her eyes glazed, her chin trembling. Downstairs were three enormous cellars, very cold and damp, and entirely lined with bottles of exquisite vintage wines. Mina started to weep, against her son's shoulder.

Against one of the walls of the last cellar, two beds had been placed. A small oak table stood between them, laden with fruits forbidden to the Jews. 'I'll raise the temperature of the whole house,' Hans told them. 'That should help. And I'll come down whenever possible.'

'No one will look for us here?' Mina asked, her voice hollow with fear.

'Not at this point. None of my visitors has come this far. The house is very quiet, and I appear to lead a most uneventful existence. And of course, this is the first time I shall be hiding anyone.' He added, grimly: 'But I'm sure not the last.'

Mina touched his sleeve, imploringly. 'Please, Hans. I can't leave ... without Isaac. And if ... the worst has happened, then I don't want to continue living. We've been together all our adult lives. I can't survive without him.'

In the cavernous cellar, her voice rang out, echoing her heart. Hans only said: 'My dear Mina, I'll do what I can. You know I will. But you must do something for *me*, too. You must listen to me, and when I have completed the preparations for your departure, you must go. Isaac will follow you. I'll make myself responsible to you on this matter.'

'Do you suppose we'll be able to get out legally?' Wolf asked.

'I don't think so. Since Hitler's seizure of Austria, the friendly countries have been deluged with Jewish refugees. Australia and the United States are refusing to accept more than five thousand. Brazil, just a few thousand. Britain and France will only take children. And the Reich is allowing each Jew to take with him ten deutschmarks; that's two hundred French francs.'

'Marisa's waiting for us in Paris,' Wolf murmured softly. His chest felt tight with a strange lump that wouldn't dissolve. Mina had sunk down on one of the beds, and lay weeping silently, her body curved like that of a small child.

Seeming to read his mind, Count Hans von Bertelmann looked into Wolf's eyes, and said: 'You're going to see them again, my friend. Marisa, and your small Nanni. Thank God that they are safe.

'I'm not quite sure how we'll get you out, nor to which country you will have to be sent. But get you out we shall.

And you'll be safe, like Marisa and Nanni, and able to join up with them somewhere.'

Long after he had departed, Wolf kept hearing Hans's word, *somewhere*. It rang cold and indefinite, chilling him infinitely more than the temperature of the cellar. But for the moment, he and his mother were safe. That was all that counted.

For Wolfgang Steiner realized that if the Reich were to flourish, it could do so only over the slaughtered corpses of the Jewish people. They had escaped, this time, because the Nazis had gone easy on them, releasing them for a fortune. He was certain, then, that such had not been his father's good fortune. Isaac had been one of the first casualties of the Nazi ordeal. Just as the night of 9 November, named *Kristallnacht* in memory of all the broken glass shattered in the cities of the Reich, symbolized only the beginning.

But he would have to keep these thoughts to himself, if he expected his mother not to fall apart.

Chapter Eighteen

Throughout November and December, Marisa Steiner waited for her husband. A flow of legal and illegal Jewish refugees was pouring into Paris. Raïssa Sudarskaya burst in on Claire, to beg for clothes for an old lady who had arrived with only her nightgown on her back. The refugees, who had been professionals of standing in Germany and Austria, were arriving in droves, two hundred francs in their pockets, or none at all if they had been smuggled out. The *Kristallnacht* had left no hope of justice under Hitler, and so the Jews who came, as beggars, were glad just to have escaped intact. Many had left members of their families in concentration camps. This term had come to signal terror in every German-speaking Jew.

They came, telling tales of such ghastly horror that those who listened felt their tears brimming over, and hackles rising on their skin. Only Marisa's face stayed carved in perfect, clear lines of immutable hardness. She listened, but she did not weep. She had pushed out the immediacy of her pain and thought only of Wolf's agony, and that of his parents. For him, she had to stay whole; and for him, she had to contain her own anguish. She simply waited for him. He'd promised to come to her, and she knew he would. But in the meantime, she didn't sleep, and hardly tasted the food that Claire insisted she order. Every minute of every day, she sat, taut and expectant, waiting for word of Wolf. She didn't even know where he might be, at this point. But she prayed for his safety, for the preservation of his life. This was the only meaning to her own existence: to know he had survived.

And so the new year came, wrapped in a cloud of unknowing. Lily wondered how Marisa could stand it. They never spoke out loud about their fears and hopes. But every time word came about a man who might have been Wolf, or of two older people who might have been Mina and Isaac, Marisa's eyes would light up with intensity, and she would lean forward, hoping. Only to have her hopes dashed down by the discovery that it hadn't been her husband or his parents, but somebody else's husband, somebody else's parents.

Holding Nanni in her arms one evening, Kyra said, a strange, faraway intonation in her young voice: 'I know how hard it is to be without your Papa. But at least, when you go to sleep, you know that wherever he is, he loves you. My father's gone, just like yours, and we don't know where he is. But he left because he didn't love us enough – because we weren't that important to him.'

She was thirteen, already five feet three inches tall, with hard young breasts that pushed through her school uniform, and the long legs of a ballerina. Many times, strangers had thought she was sixteen. But the look of pure hurt on her triangular face was the look of a wounded child. She had crossed a threshold, from adoring daughter to rejected child, from still hoping to resigned. Nick heard and saw her, and the look he gave her was one of sheer empathy. Now she could understand where he had been for the last year, and stop condemning him for not keeping the fires burning.

They played with the Rublon children, Pierre and Jacqueline. They took Nanni for walks, and exclaimed over birthday presents. They were still children, but Lily often wondered for how long. Nick, in particular, had skipped that wonderful, carefree part of childhood that she'd wanted for him; at fourteen, he was the best student in his ninth form. He was taller than his mother, topping her at five feet eleven inches; he shaved, although not every day.

And his voice had deepened, acquiring a resonance that made her think, at the oddest moments, of Misha. This boy, who had never resembled his father at all, now had his rich, Russian voice, with its enchanting, melodic, powerful timbre. She could close her eyes and hear her son, and think again of the days when Misha had courted her, reliving those halcyon days with poignant clarity, much better forgotten. For it was infinitely easier not to see one's own unhappiness when one didn't compare it to a better life.

At the end of January 1939, Barcelona fell to General Francisco Franco's Fascist troops. Daladier halfheartedly permitted about half a million Spanish refugees to flood into France. By the end of February, those who had sought refuge in the city of Perpignan had behaved in such a despicable fashion that the cost of damage to the host city had risen to two million francs. Wood placed at their disposal for the construction of barracks had been set afire, and the pumps that had been set up were now plugged up and impossible to use. But it looked as if the war was winding down to a close, and many of the renegades were returning home. How different from the German and Austrian Jews, who would never see their homeland again!

On 2 March, Cardinal Eugenio Pacelli, who had been Pope Pius XI's secretary of state, was elected in a single day to become the new Pope Pius XII. Lily felt an old stirring of excitement. The Catholic Church, with its myriad traditions that dated back far beyond the Middle Ages, could still grip her soul. On the tenth, she listened to a broadcast of his five-hour consecration; forty thousand of the faithful had crowded into the cathedral to watch, and he came out for the coronation, that the many more who were gathered outside might witness this holiest of moments. She leaned against the little radio, captivated, and remembered that when she'd been sixteen, she had thought, with some seriousness, of entering a convent. Now she was thirty-three, at the midpoint of her life, and hadn't been to church in eleven years.

It was actually strange, but she felt more and more Jewish, hearing the stories of those who had escaped death at the hands of the Nazis; and less and less a Catholic, even in those moments when, alone, she lay in bed and thought about God.

On 15 March, Hitler's army moved into Prague, and the invasion of Czechoslovakia was on. On the eighteenth, the Führer confiscated all the Jewish money in the banks of Prague. That same day, a Viennese couple came to the Ritz, to see Marisa. Their name was Schwarz, and they had been no more than vague acquaintances. They came with some small paintings that, obviously, could have been worth no more than a hundred francs each. Marisa gave them money for their hotel, and waited, her lips parted, for them to tell her something ... anything at all concerning Wolf.

But Herr Schwarz merely shook his head, and bit his lower lip. 'We hear so little,' he told her, his voice low and trembling. 'Sometimes, a titbit. A man told me that your husband was alive, that he and his mother had been hidden somewhere by a Viennese *goy* – an aristocrat.'

'Hans? Count von Bertelmann? Was it him?'

Embarrassed at the fire of hope, so naked and glowing, in Marisa's eyes, Schwarz raised his hands palms up, helplessly. 'I can't say. But the old lady – *if* it's your mother-in-law – isn't well, and isn't fit to travel. Yet the longer they stay ...' His sentence hung in mid-air, ominously sinking in. Marisa nodded, her face numb, her heart knocking wildly inside her.

'And the old man? Herr Isaac Steiner? You didn't speak of him.'

'There was no old man, from the small snatch of news that reached my ears. And of course, I can't be certain of the accuracy of what I've told you.'

389

Marisa reached into her small alligator bag, and withdrew a cheque-book. Silently, she wrote out a cheque, handed it to Schwarz. If what he'd said was true, then it was likely that Hans von Bertelmann had saved Wolf and Mina. But what of Papa? she thought, the tears coming at last in a rebellious spurt. Where could he be now?

'There are still good gentiles in the Reich,' she said, thinking of the tall, fair poet who had shared his university days with her husband.

After that, she began to live somewhat more easily, believing that Wolf lived, breathed, existed somewhere: it didn't matter where. When news came that two hundred and fifty Czech officers had committed suicide, and that twelve thousand Jews of Prague had been sent to concentration camps, she almost didn't pay attention. But she wept at the fate of the children who would be reared as slaves to the great German Reich.

The night of 29 March, Edouard Daladier spoke to the French people. He announced that he would not give a single acre of French land, nor one right over it, to the Italians, and he commended the Moslems of Tunisia for upholding their religion and their civilization. He said that France was strong, and united, that she would do all for peace, but that if the need came, she would rise in one movement to defend her rights and her freedom.

On the night of 2 April, the sound of a bugle, and a broadcast on the radio brought the news, at eleven fifteen, that the Spanish war had ended. And on 5 April, in Versailles, Parliament re-elected Albert Lebrun President of the French Republic. But on Good Friday, Mussolini invaded Albania. That month, Franklin D. Roosevelt, President of the United States, sent a message to Hitler and Mussolini, demanding that they cease their invasion of independent peoples, and begging them to promise not to touch thirty-one independent nations, and to begin at once to speak of disarmament and the resumption of international trade. Hitler reacted with anger, and Italy was silent. But the British started a register of volunteers twenty and twenty-one years of age, which yielded three hundred and ten thousand soldiers-to-be; and, in Château-Thierry, in France, a general mobilization occurred.

Finally, after thirteen days of tension, Hitler answered Roosevelt. He had announced that only on the twenty-eighth would he make his reply. The world stood on tenterhooks, but for some reason, not the French. In fact, when Lily and Nick tried to hear the speech on the radio, they discovered it had not even been broadcast. But in the evening, the newspapers were full of his good intentions. He said he wanted peace, the liberty of states, and that he wished to open talks with Great Britain. General amazement met his words. Maybe, then, there wouldn't have to be a war. And Lily was thankful, thinking with sudden anguish of her almost fifteen-year-old son: in three years, he would be called up to defend his country. It was better that this country should not have to be defended, like that of the Steiners.

Relaxation was short lived. On 22 May, the Axis pact was formally consolidated. The French newspapers spoke of 'Italy's subordination to Germany'. Nick took his mother's hand, his dark eyes troubled. And then he said in a strangely adult voice: 'This time there is no going back. Eventually, he'll have to be stopped. And it's better that it happen soon. This war, Mama, isn't going to be "civilized", like the last one when you were a girl.'

It's you who should be in America, my strong, brave young son, she thought. It's you, my Nicky, who needs to be protected, in a country that will not go to war again to save her European allies. And she wondered once more, as she had so many times, why her husband had left her, why life had turned against him – and why he'd never said goodbye.

* * *

'Why *Cuba?*' Mina Steiner implored, her brown eyes filled with fear. 'It's so far away, and we know no one there – and Isaac, when he gets out, won't know where to find us!'

Wolf was very tired. Since the *Kristallnacht*, he had lost twenty pounds. His mother, however, had completely wasted away. All his life, he'd watched her, plump, rosy, bursting with liveliness, full of opinions and of joie de vivre. Her round face ringed with auburn curls had soothed away, by its mere presence, hundreds of youthful hurts. Now she weighed one hundred pounds, and her cheekbones jutted out below huge, bloodshot eyes that were afraid, all the time afraid.

And for good reason, Wolf thought. He stood on the lower deck of the medium-sized German ship *Saint Louis*, watching the infinity of ocean spread before him, and he blessed the memory of his friend Hans. Slowly, Wolf closed his eyes, allowing himself to remember the days spent like rats in that damp cellar, and his mother's recurring illness. Hans had somehow managed to sneak a doctor – a real doctor, with medicines – down to visit her. At length she'd started to improve, but every day, every hour, it seemed, she'd wailed for Isaac, branding that cherished name into his brain like molten iron. Because he'd known, after a few months, that it was useless to hope. Either his father had already died at Dachau, or he would soon do so. Isaac was frail, a gentle man; and Wolf knew the Nazis well enough to understand that they would have no mercy.

But he couldn't voice his opinion to his mother. He had to keep her alive until they were reunited with Marisa and Nanni. After that, his little daughter would give her a reason for living. Wolf wondered now, with an acute anguish, when he would see his loved ones again. There was no way of communicating with them. Hans had tried, through the underground, to send news, but he hadn't been at all confident that it would reach Marisa in Paris.

Finally, then, Mina had felt well enough to travel. But

the only hope of immediate refuge that Hans had been able to arrange for them had been on this old ship, bound for Cuba. Nine hundred and eighteen Jews were aboard, because the Cuban authorities had granted them permission to land. Their visas were legal; Wolf remembered with horror how they had been forced to cross into Germany, to board this ship in Hamburg. Most of the other emigrants were German Jews. But Hans had planned well, and the trip from Vienna had gone smoothly enough. And now, they were on their way to freedom.

'To me, Cuba sounds like the Garden of Eden,' he said, smiling, putting an arm around his mother.

They'd been sailing for weeks, it seemed. Wolf tried to count the number of days, spent crowded in the hold, or sometimes, for rare moments like these, pushing against the railing on the deck, smelling the sea. Three weeks. It had to be three weeks now. He hadn't had a bath in at least that long, and his beard was straggly, unkempt. But this morning, he'd heard the rumour that they were going to land, and so he'd brought his mother out, to watch. 'Some say Cuba is a beautiful island,' he said. 'And the Jews there are rich, and respected.'

They remained there, leaving only to retrieve some food. It was incredible to think that they would really be landing . . . without fear of the Nazis. In the afternoon, the vague outline of the island had appeared, and the hundreds of immigrants, many of whom had sold their last possession to be able to make this trip to freedom, crowded each other to catch a glimpse of their future refuge. Towards dusk they had finally entered the port, and dropped anchor. The captain had gone on land to prepare for the unloading of his passengers.

'It's very strange,' a small, bald man next to him murmured to Wolf. 'Usually the disembarkation is very speedy. But our captain seems to have been gone for hours.'

393

'This is a different world,' Wolf smiled back. 'Everything is *mañana*.'

But he couldn't help feeling a pinprick of apprehension. Holding his mother close to him, he prayed to God for a safe landing, and gave himself up to destiny.

When at last the captain returned, his face, as he turned to his passengers, was dark, troubled. 'There's been a coup d'état,' he announced in German. His voice rang clear through, although a mumbling noise had risen up from the hold. 'And so we've got unexpected problems. The consuls who signed your visas are no longer consuls. And so the governor of the island has refused to take you.'

Wolf shut his ears against the cries, and held his mother close to him. Was this possible? A panic was pushing through the ranks around him, and he could literally smell the fear on the breaths of those who were screaming it out. After some hours, the captain went ashore, and the old Jewish men began to pray aloud, in unison. Wolf joined in, his voice tied in a knot.

That night, it was almost impossible to sleep. Wolf could hear murmurs all around him, voicing speculation back and forth in the large hold. The next day, the captain went back for another discussion with the authorities. Rumours went around that the Jews of Cuba, as well as prominent Americans such as Mrs Gould and her New York Co-ordination Committee, and even President Roosevelt, had sent ardent pleas to the governor of Cuba on behalf of the emigrants. But the governor sent the captain back with another staunch refusal.

Slowly, shock passed into horror as the captain narrated the situation. Wolf was aware of a sudden hush, and of all the minds that thought in unison: we are alone. He recalled that when he'd gone to temple as a child, he'd sometimes felt, in his own veins, the empathetic presence of others, all thinking alike, all holding hands with their minds. It had given him goose bumps to sense such a strong human bond. He'd supposed, later, that Catholics who came to the Vatican to listen to the Pope probably felt the same, joint awe. So it wasn't just being a Jew. But now, at forty-six, a practising, licensed psychiatrist, he had to recognize that fear, more than awe, could bind people to one another. The nine hundred and eighteen refugees all felt the same fear, and it had reduced them to animals, smelling death. Even his mother had the appearance of a wild animal at bay, her nostrils slightly quivering, her eyes vacant, her body hunched together in instinctive self-protection.

Suddenly there was a terrible cry, and he saw a woman gesticulating. There was a commotion at the back, and, like all the others, Wolf strove to press forward, to catch what was happening. 'It's Chaim!' the woman was screaming, tearing at her hair, pointing to the huge double doors on the other side of the hold. 'Didn't anybody see him? He's slashed his wrists! He's out on deck!'

Wolf reacted within seconds. 'Let me through!' he cried, loudly, pushing through the crowded room. 'I'm a doctor! For God's sake! Aren't there any other doctors in here? A man's tried to kill himself!' Around him, he could barely make out the hushed faces, the stunned eyes, and one man said: 'So what? We're all going to die.' But they did try to make room for him, and when he reached the double doors, he felt a man tugging at his sleeve, trying to catch up with him.

'I'm a doctor, too,' he said. 'Where is this Chaim?'

Dishevelled and perspiring, Wolf and the other ran on deck, their hearts palpitating. And then, against the railing, they saw him. To Wolf's amazement, it was the small bald man who had stood beside him the day before, waiting for the return of the captain. Wolf held up a hand, cried: 'Wait! Chaim! What's the good of all this? You can't admit defeat, like a coward. We're coming to treat your cuts.'

But the small man was shaking his head, in a rhythmic, hysterical fashion. His eyes were streaming tears. Blood was dripping onto his trousers from his wrists. And all at once, he bolted around, and with what was left of his strength, hoisted himself over the railing, and with a great yell, threw himself overboard. 'My God,' Wolf said. 'He's gone mad.'

'He just doesn't want to live. Maybe we're the ones that are mad.'

In unison, Wolf and his companion had begun to discard their shoes and their excess clothing. By now, the deck was full, the captain holding the screaming woman, people peering into the water where Chaim had landed, like a popped balloon. Wolf and the other doctor jumped over the railing, and threw themselves after him, one landing on each side. Within minutes they were holding him up, trying to stop the wounds with their shirttails, while the captain was lowering a lifeboat into the water.

And then it was over. Chaim was being taken ashore, on a stretcher, bandages over his wrists, and the captain was attempting to explain to the frantic woman that later, perhaps, she and her children might be allowed to visit him in the hospital. But this privilege was never granted. The port authorities, aggravated at the notion that one man had succeeded, in spite of their edict, in gaining access to Cuban soil, sent back the message that no one else, not even the grieving family of the wounded man, would be accepted ashore. The faces of the nine hundred and seventeen remaining Jews on board registered the news with a strange, silent resignation. They'd stopped expecting to be treated with compassion by those who were on the outside. They were no more to Cuban eyes than a shipload of caged animals, whom nobody wanted to take care of.

'All my life I thought God loved me,' Mina whispered, awed. 'But perhaps now I believe He hates us all.'

'It isn't God who hates us, Mama. It's men. Human beings.' He felt a deep chill after his earlier exploits, and a slight fever. Never had the future appeared so uncertain.

How right he'd been, to have sent Marisa and Nanni to France when he had done so! He would never have forgiven himself if they'd been with him, sharing this terrifying uncertainty.

At length the ship lifted anchor. Men and women wept openly. The captain had at least been able to obtain from the Cubans a replenishment of food and water. 'We're going to the United States,' somebody said. There seemed to be a new surge of hope, and he allowed himself to go with it, thinking of Eliane and David, his parents-in-law. They'd been the smartest of all, leaving Europe entirely behind them.

By now their ship, the *Saint Louis*, was famous. When it crossed to the United States, and set anchor, the captain wasn't allowed off the ship without official escorts. Hopes ran high once more. The Americans, always so fair, would surely be able to admit so few of them, under a thousand. President Roosevelt would never turn them away. The Jews were being closely watched, so that no one would get the idea of jumping off to gain illegal access to the country. But surely, Mrs Gould and her group would force her cohorts to open their doors, and their hearts, to these unfortunates fleeing from the Nazis.

After a while, the captain came back to the *Saint Louis* with bad news. Roosevelt had declared that their near-thousand exceeded the quota for German immigrants. Exhausted, at his wits' end, the captain announced that since no place wanted them, he had no choice but to turn around and return to Hamburg.

Then the tall man came to Wolf, and held out his pen. 'There are over a hundred of us who have already signed,' he said, his cultured voice smooth and low. 'If we are to be thrown back to the Nazis, we shall commit suicide upon arrival. But we refuse to be sent back to Hell. Better death, than Dachau.'

Wolf waited half one minute, scrutinizing the writing on

the paper. Certainly, they were right. And yet . . . Marisa. If he agreed to end his life, he would be agreeing never to see his wife and daughter again. While he was thinking, he saw his mother's delicate hand jut out, take the pen from the tall man's fingers, and begin to write. 'Mama, no,' he cried, wrenching it from her hand.

'Your mother's right: what choice have we?' the man murmured. But Wolf turned away, his eyes suddenly filling up with tears.

The captain, before setting off, went back on land, and made a public declaration of his intentions, and of the suicide pact that had been signed, finally, by two hundred of his passengers. He made a valiant plea, heard over the broadcasts of many nations. And on the twelfth of June, France announced its permission to land the ship in Cherbourg. The Netherlands would accept two hundred Jews, Belgium one hundred and fifty, and France and Great Britain the rest.

The Joint Distribution Committee had given fourteen million francs, or five hundred pounds sterling per head, to help the various governments to make room for the nine hundred and seventeen. But Wolf didn't forget that his mother had signed the suicide pact, her fingers firm and unwavering.

'God sent trials and misfortunes to Job, His disciple. But in the end He showed him that He hadn't deserted him. We have to have faith, Mama,' he said, his voice tight.

The old woman was silent, but he knew she didn't believe him. The past few months had been too trying for her, and she was on the verge of forgetting her God. Wolf said, urgently: 'Mama. For Papa's sake, you must have hope! Every day, you must force your heart to feel the hope, even if it's so tenuous you can hardly sense it inside you.'

'For Papa's sake?' she repeated, meeting his eyes for the first time. And he had to step back, her eyes were so cold.

398

'Papa's dead, Wolfgang. This is what I felt in my heart, instead of your hope. He's dead, and we can't even sit shiva for him.'

And she turned away from him, her shoulders contracting in spasms of silent sobs.

In the night-time, he held her, his compassion so great that his insides felt twisted. For as much as he'd adored his father, Isaac had been Mina's life. He understood then why she had signed the pact. He still had Marisa, and Nanni; but for her, the core of her being was gone.

While the fate of the Jews on the *Saint Louis* had been widely discussed, and the entire world had listened to the progress of their story, Marisa still had no idea that her husband and mother-in-law were among them. That summer, Claire had decided not to go to the Riviera. Instead, for a bracing change of climate, she chose the small Normandy community of Saint-Aubin-sur-Mer, in the Department of Calvados. She and Lily selected a spacious villa with many bedrooms, anticipating that friends from Paris would want to come for weekends. Nick had already invited Pierre Rublon, and Sudarskaya had expressed the wistful desire to come for a part of the summer. Her little marble eyes had shone so brightly that no one had had the heart to refuse her.

One afternoon, Lily and Kyra went to the Ritz to have tea with Claire and Marisa, and when they arrived, they found the young woman in the midst of her packing, open cartons strewn all over the sitting room of her suite unheeded, while she sat, hands folded in her lap, tears streaking her cheeks. Next to her, dapper and smart, stood, of all people, Mark MacDonald. I should have known I'd most likely run into him here, one day, Lily thought at once, conscious of his presence like a small dart into her chest. Her discomfort was such that at first, her friend's distraught attitude didn't even register. Claire was standing behind Marisa, her hands on the young woman's shoulders, and it was she who said: 'Mark received word that Wolf and Frau Steiner are going to land at Cherbourg. They've been . . . on that ship that returned from Cuba.'

Marisa lifted her eyes to Lily, and held her hands out to her friend. Lily ran to her, and they embraced. 'He's safe,' Marisa whispered, tears falling on Lily's hair. 'Thank God, thank God.'

Lily fought the growing lump in her own throat, and, disengaging herself from Marisa, looked at Mark. He met her gaze with his perceptive hazel eyes, direct and probing. He reads into me, she thought, disturbed again as she always was when encountering him for the first time after many years. Her own dark eyes expressed nothing but gratitude, and she asked, softly: 'How did you find them, Mark?'

'Through the AP wire service,' he replied. 'I still have many connections. A reporter friend called me, and said he remembered that I had had Jewish friends in Austria. He suggested that I come down to the offices of the *Figaro* to look through the passenger list they had received . . . to check if any of the names were familiar. I found them, almost immediately, and came here at once.'

Claire cleared her throat, said, 'I've ordered the tea,' took Kyra by the hand, and disappeared into another room. Marisa rose, hurriedly. 'It's such a mess in here,' she breathed. 'But I – I've got to meet the train, tomorrow. He's coming home . . . tomorrow.' She turned her head aside, wiped her nose, and followed Claire.

'It's miraculous news for her,' Lily remarked, finding herself alone with Mark. She glanced down at her feet, fidgeted with her ring, her wedding ring, she realized with a start. She was still wearing it, although *he'd* been gone a year and a half. Raising her eyes, she found him looking at her again, and coloured. 'Where have you been?' she asked then. 'Marisa's been in Paris for fourteen months. Yet I have never seen you here, until today.'

'I didn't think you'd want to see me,' he answered, always direct. 'So when I wanted to see Mari, or even your mother, I made it a point to invite them out. I have a nice apartment now, much nicer than the old one, on the Avenue Montaigne, near the Rond-Point des Champs-Élysées. So I'm not far away, and there are many good restaurants to choose from in the area.'

Lily was profoundly shaken. That someone would go to such extremes, only to respect her feelings, suddenly embarrassed her. She said, 'But why, Mark? There were no problems between you and me. It would have been . . . nice . . . to see you once in a while. To be friends with you.' God knows, she thought, how much I needed friends.

He shrugged. 'Well. Let's let that one lie, shall we? Kyra's certainly a beautiful, grown-up girl. A far cry from the gangly kid I met in Vienna, six years ago. Could it have been that long, Lily?'

'I don't think she remembers you. Besides, she was in Tobitschau for part of your visit, with Marisa and Nanni.'

'She *was*, at that, wasn't she?'

They stood silently appraising one another, each one vividly recalling the night when he had caught her looking at him, in the garden. Lily felt herself turn red, down to the roots of her hair. Stupidly, she stammered: 'We were still young then, weren't we? And there was no war. And the Jews . . .' Her sentence was left off, and she made a face, tears starting to well up. 'Damn it!' she murmured. 'It was another life, and Wolf was home, and we were happy.'

He had come close, was touching her on the arm, was drawing her close. Unexpectedly, she buried her face in the lapels of his jacket, and wept, unashamed. 'Yes,' he whispered, smelling the soft fragrance of her hair. 'We were, in a certain sense, happy. At any rate, Mari was.

401

You were betwixt and between, and I . . . who knows *where* I was? On my third book. Thank God for them: the books, I mean. I've learned to count the years by the number of my novels.'

'Has your life been that empty?' she asked, raising her face to him, appalled.

Embarrassed, he began to laugh, self-deprecatingly. 'Well, nothing as dramatic as you might think. I was no hermit on my mountaintop. But you know, loneliness can exist even in a room full of sympathetic people.'

'I should know,' she agreed.

'And it grew worse, after Vienna. Because when we were together at the Steiners', I felt that something new had developed between us. Something that we'd never had, when we were engaged.'

She was chewing on her lower lip, reflecting. 'But, Mark . . . after that, Misha's father died, and I came back to him. Anything else had to stop.'

'I understood.'

'And now? Can you understand that the last thing on my mind is a new involvement? My dear, dear Mark: I need you as a friend, as a *confidant*. It wouldn't be fair for me to tie up your feelings at this point. Because you see, *I* can't feel anything. I'm still reacting to having been abandoned.'

Tears clouded her vision, and she brushed them off with tired fingers. 'Sometimes, I actually find myself *hating* Misha. And yet, I understand how he might have felt so disgraced, that no other door seemed open to him. But it was *wrong* – his leaving without us. Marriage is supposed to be for better or for worse . . . I'm sorry,' she added, smiling lamely. 'These are *my* problems, and I shouldn't be burdening you with them.'

'It's never a burden to listen to you. But I'm a man, too. And even now, when you're speaking about him with bitterness and anger, I can't help feeling jealous. He took you away from me when we were engaged. And then, when you and I might have had another chance . . .'

'Then, it was *my* decision to return to him. You *can't* feel jealous, Mark. And please, don't let's talk about this anymore. The point is that you shouldn't love me, Mark. My life's in disarray, and it would be the wrong time to try to make something work between us.'

Gently, he caressed the line of her cheekbone. 'If that's the way you want it,' he whispered. 'But I guess I've been like those fools I've always despised: in spite of the years, in spite of your husband . . . even in spite of you yourself, I've never stopped caring. I've met my share of interesting women, and I've lived a normal life. But there's been no one, Lily, to replace you. That tug at my heart: I've felt it for you, through the years, whenever we've been thrown together. It has to mean something, doesn't it?'

She looked down, feeling the silence of the room around them.

'And you?' he asked. 'Haven't you ever wondered why we've been able to pick up, time after time, exactly where we'd left off the last time we'd seen each other?'

'We could be "soul mates",' she said, smiling suddenly to lighten his mood, and to dispel her own sense of discomfort and uncertainty.

'Soul mates make the best lovers,' he countered seriously. 'I wish you'd think about it, Lily. You and Brasilov never understood each other. And perhaps what you'd like to think was a great love affair, was really only a moment of passion. Don't be so quick to reject the idea of *us*. It *could* work. You might even be happy!'

He'd wanted to smile, but couldn't. Near him, he could feel her drawing away, pulling back inside herself. 'Look,' he said. 'Maybe you're right. Maybe it *is* the wrong time. And maybe I should stop trying to make it right between us. I've handled enough rejection for an afternoon, haven't I?'

In the total silence, she could feel her heart beat. Abruptly she turned away, walked briskly to the other room, opened the door. 'Marisa, Mama,' she called. 'Hasn't the tea tray come yet?'

But when she came back to the sofa, holding Kyra, his eyes were still on her, burning brightly. And she felt what they were spelling out to her: You can't escape now, Lily. You can't hold on any longer to what's not there for you. To what perhaps was *never* there. And her heart pounded in a maddening roar, like waves crashing on a craggy shore.

Saint-Aubin-sur-Mer lay on the coast of Normandy, and its houses looked onto a narrow seawall where no cars could pass. One could cross directly from the villa to the beach. The village was still rather primitive, and was pervaded by a scent of the sea, and of seaweeds. The beach was composed of the finest sand, and shells of all types and shapes, with fine designs and inlays of mother-of-pearl, were spread across its banks.

The old gabled house that Claire had rented was filled with small, oddly shaped rooms, and was almost like a boarding-house. And perhaps this was indeed the best way for Wolf and Mina Steiner to readjust to normal civilization, after the horrors that they had experienced in Vienna and on the ship. Mina had become a quiet, introspective woman, with a haunted expression in her brown eyes. But the presence of Sudarskaya, tactless and ebullient, helped to draw her a little outside herself. And for Wolf, the sun, the sea breeze, and the relative privacy of the beach provided a warm atmosphere in which, little by little, he learned to relax.

Nanni's joy at being reunited with her father helped him. For the first few days after his arrival from Cherbourg, where Marisa had gone to meet them, he was strangely silent, even hostile. Marisa went in tears to Lily, saying

404

that he had closed himself off, that he was no longer the kind, gentle Wolf whom she had loved and married. At night, he stayed on his own side of the bed, immobile and isolated, and when she snuggled up to him, she could feel him stiffen. But on the fourth day he drew her softly to him, and, caressing her mass of golden curls, murmured: 'You must give me time, Mari. You can't understand the hell we lived through. I never thought . . . never imagined, even after the intensive classes I took in human behaviour and psychosis, that man could behave thus against man, crushing out the soul.' And then he'd wept, and she'd rocked him in her arms, understanding at last, and weeping for him and with him at the indignity he had witnessed.

There was a casino in one of the hotels, and sometimes, at the weekend, Jacques would invite his guests to go there for supper, and he would order Dom Pérignon champagne and oysters on the half shell, and treat the ladies to some gambling at the baccarat and roulette tables. For Sudarskaya, this brush with the world of distinction and luxury was almost too much, and she would glance swiftly across the table, then quickly rifle through the hors d'oeuvres tray and gobble up mounds of fresh Beluga caviar on small toast points. Everyone pretended not to notice, and Mina, who had hobnobbed only with the cream of Viennese society, smiled indulgently, accepting the small piano teacher with an openness she would never have been capable of displaying on her own turf. But times had changed, and it was best not to think of old Vienna. If she did, sometimes, then it reminded her of the house on the Schwindgasse, and the *Kristallnacht*.

But everybody felt the ghost of Isaac Steiner like a cloud hanging over them, not allowing them to forget. Even the children felt his absence almost like a silent *presence* in the room with them. 'My Grandpa's going to appear one day, out of nowhere,' Nanni had said, expressing what everyone else felt, and what they all hoped. Yet Wolf had told his wife that he was certain that his father had died.

The older children played tennis and ping-pong. Pierre Rublon, Nick's friend from school, was a medium-sized young boy of sixteen, with well-developed muscles and a pleasant, tanned face sprinkled with freckles. His blond hair and shining blue eyes made him look like a child of the sea, sun-washed and salt-streaked. Lily liked him, because he was always carefree. He drew Nick out, and was good for him. And Kyra, shy around her brother's friends, seemed less put off by him, and went along, playing with them. Lily watched her, hanging on the outskirts of the group of young boys that Nick and Pierre had gathered from neighbouring villas. She felt sudden pleasure and embarrassment when her brother asked her to join them.

One afternoon, when Nick had accompanied his mother and grandmother into town for groceries, Pierre found Kyra alone on the beach, kicking the soft, round pebbles with the stub of her naked toe. 'Bored?' he asked, edging towards her, and picking up a shell.

'Sort of. Everybody's gone.'

She didn't dare to look at him, and was oddly conscious of a flush going through her body. Keeping her eyes resolutely averted from him, she said: 'Don't you find us a strange group? I mean, Uncle Wolf and Aunt Mina, with the queer looks they sometimes exchange when they think no one else is looking. And Raïssa Markovna, who eats like a starved piglet. And then, my mother. She always looks so sad, and you know the story, about my father's leaving.'

He shrugged, grinning. 'I like it here. I used to get bored a lot, with my sister, doing nothing on the beach. But now it's fun with you and Nick here.'

She laughed, and for the first time, dared to look at him. Her brilliant green eyes seemed to touch him deep inside. His smile faded, and he stood watching her, his own eyes strangely expressive in the golden afternoon sunlight. Then

Kyra abruptly turned away and sprinted back towards the house, leaving him, baffled, staring after her.

It was the start of the month of July, and in the evening, the men hovered near the radio. The question of rights to the Free City of Danzig was starting to come up more and more frequently, and Great Britain was starting to growl back at the encroaching fingers of the Reich. Kyra stood behind her brother, and listened to the tense words of the broadcaster without really hearing them. She was glancing down at the back of Pierre Rublon's head, remembering their brief moment together, alone, on the beach. And she hoped that war wouldn't come, so that they might all stay here, in Saint-Aubin, until the end of September.

On 4 July, the voice of the broadcaster was lifted in hope. Germany, he reported, was being quiet, reacting to Britain's anger. And so the small group began to relax. Wolf's face remained the only dark, tense one. 'One can never underestimate Hitler,' he said, and then Kyra was afraid. She walked alone on the edge of the water, wondering what a war could be about, and remembering all that she had heard from Wolf and his mother, and even Marisa.

When Nick and Pierre came to join her, it was already dusk, and the sky over the seawall was a soft coral hue lined with threads of orange gold. She knew that the adults hadn't meant to be overheard, but now she said to her brother: 'They send the Jews away to horrible places. And – we're – ' The sentence died in her throat, as she remembered that Pierre was there, and that her grandparents hadn't wanted anyone to know that they were part Jewish.

'It's all right,' Pierre said gently. 'Nick already told me. You're Jews.'

'On my mother's side. We're only one-quarter Jewish, really,' she added defensively.

'Don't worry about it, Kyra. I don't care about what you are – or Nicky. I like you both. You're my friends.'

'But if your parents knew, they wouldn't let you stay with us,' she accused him.

He regarded her blankly. 'My parents aren't like that,' he said, a twinge of hurt creeping into his voice.

'Oh.' She fumbled with the sash of her sun dress. Suddenly she cried: 'My father hates the Jews! Maybe that's why he went away! Because *we're* Jews, too!'

For a moment the two young boys stood staring at her, and then Nick turned away, striding off towards the house. 'You've made him angry,' Pierre chided her. 'He doesn't like to speak endlessly about your father, and why he might or might not have left. How can you know, Kyra? People act strangely sometimes, and we don't know why.'

Her young face crumpled, and she said: 'But I can't help it! There are moments when I hate the memory of Papa. But other times . . . I wish he'd send for me, so I could be with him again. You don't know! You don't know how he loved me! He didn't love Nicky in the same way, and so it's easier for him to hate him. But nobody's ever going to love me the way my father did.'

The wind was blowing around her face, and soft wisps of hair rose and fell about her neck and cheeks. In the setting sun, her dark green eyes were so ineffably sad that he was certain they were the saddest eyes he'd ever seen. Without knowing why he did it, he let his hand go to her face, his fingers touching her cheek.

Like a frightened cat, she drew back, and the green eyes blazed her shock at his touch. He shook his head, puzzled by his own behaviour, and abruptly asked: 'How old are you now, Kyra?'

'Fourteen.'

He breathed in and out, and turned aside. He could feel her near him, like a shadow.

Smiling, he looked at her then, and shook his head. 'I don't know.' He sighed, and continued: 'But I'm scared, Kyra. I don't want there to be a war. Because if there is . . .

408

Nick and I will be called up within two or three years. And I don't want to die, like the million and a half that died in the last war.' When he finished speaking, he wasn't smiling anymore, and his tanned, healthy young face seemed contemplative and almost brooding.

Impulsively, Kyra moved closer to him, and began to play the piano on his arm, lightly. 'Don't think about it,' she said quickly. 'That's what being grown up is all about. Sadness, and death. Think about the sand, and the sea. If Nick's still angry with me, will you go swimming with me tomorrow?'

He moved with sudden sureness, and caught her deft fingers in his own hand. Slowly he pulled her close to him, and peered into her eyes, his own breath held. Then he bent down, and touched her lips with his own. When he released her, she was still staring at him, and she said: 'Don't leave us, Pierre. Always be our friend.'

'How could I leave,' he replied, 'when you're the most beautiful part of my summer?'

But neither of them knew that by the end of August, their summer would be over. It wasn't till the first of September that it hit them all, adults and young alike. At 1:00 P.M., a general mobilization was announced in reply to the German invasion of Poland. Posters were pasted on the walls of all public buildings in the village, requisitioning all horses and all vehicles. And on Sunday the third, though the picturesque streets of Saint-Aubin remained calm and normal, war was officially declared by the French government, and news came that there was heavy fighting in Poland already.

Pierre's father came, to take his son back to Paris, and stayed two days. There was fighting on the Siegfried Line. Warsaw was being heavily bombed. Jacques, Monsieur Rublon, and Wolf stayed by the radio, anxiety painted on their faces. And then Lily announced that her stepfather, Sudarskaya, and the Steiners would have to go to the city hall to be officially fingerprinted, with the other foreigners of Saint-Aubin. And everybody laughed, sudden mirth erupting among them, as Nanni said: 'Is it like playing Thief? Do they really think we're *thieves?*'

And then Monsieur Rublon and Pierre, surrounded by luggage, were standing in front of their car, and everyone was crowding around them. Nick stood close to his sister, and she thought, I'll never be alone with him again. It's over, everything is *over*. The car door was opening, Monsieur Rublon was stepping inside, and then she saw Pierre's eyes, on her, on her only. For no more than three seconds, he looked at her, and she stared back intently. And briefly, he smiled, and nodded, imperceptibly. Then he opened his own door, and sat down, and closed the door, and the car revved its motor and took off in lifting specks of dust and sand.

Later, in the house, she took the dishes in and soaked them under the hot water, letting the heat scald her soft hands, as if in punishment. She felt her mother near her, but kept her face averted, to the sink. Lily's hand touched the back of her neck, and she murmured, 'Time will pass quickly, my darling. You'll see him again – soon.'

Kyra turned, and Lily saw the fresh tears on her cheeks. 'But with the war . . . Are we going to go back to Paris? And maybe he'll forget me. I'm just his friend's little sister.'

Lily sighed. 'I really don't know what we're going to do, Kyra. Grandma and Grandpa, and the Steiners, want to go home. But I'm afraid. I feel we'd be safer here, away from everything . . . far away from any possible fighting. There's talk around the beaches about setting up five lycées in the reception rooms of the large hotels on the coastal area near Caen. Many vacationers, like us, were caught by the war, and are electing to remain here. And some teachers on holiday don't want to go back to the capital, so there wouldn't be a staffing problem for you young people.'

Kyra bit her lip, and shook her hands free of the soapsuds. 'But . . . if we stay here . . . then Pierre – ' Her voice suddenly broke, and she cried, 'He really will forget me! And maybe we won't ever see each other again!'

Intensely moved, Lily wrapped her arms around her young daughter, and held her silently. The strength of Kyra's despair made her feel how far away she'd come from her own youth, from her own first love. But had there ever been a puppy love, like Kyra's now? Or had she lived so far removed from the mainstream of society that the first time her heart had felt the rapture and the fears of romantic involvement, had been when she'd met Misha Brasilov? She tried to cast her mind back to her years in the convent school, to the time when she'd been, like Kyra, close to fifteen. She decided that both her children, because of the instability of life around them, had grown up much faster than she had. Their childhood was gone, and suddenly, she regretted it.

Lily knew that Kyra was expecting her to say something, and so, tangling her fingers in the girl's long hair, she finally whispered: 'I wish I could tell you when you'll see him again. War changes all sorts of plans and habits, turns people's lives upside down sometimes. But there *is* one thing I *can* promise you: he will always remember, Kyra.'

Then she closed her eyes against her own overwhelming sadness, a nameless sorrow.

Claire said to Lily: 'But you'll be so alone here, just with Sudarskaya. I don't feel it's right, your staying behind.'

'I can't explain it, Mama, but I just don't want to return to Paris. And I wish you and Jacques, and Wolf, wouldn't insist on going back. The butcher said it was a madhouse there, with fighting in the streets and the constant clamour of gunfire. People are going crazy over there! But here . . . we can hardly feel the difference. We can't *feel* the war.'

'At least, in Paris, we'll feel connected. We'll know

411

exactly what's going on. And Wolf says he has some patients there, emigrants like himself. It's important for him not to lose contact with his profession.'

'I remember the last war. Papa kept me in Brittany, and there, with the nuns, I felt protected. I don't want Kyra and Nicky to have their lives completely disrupted by riots, and by food shortages, and other ways Paris will be affected. We'll stay here, at least for a few months. And because it will be the off-season, the villa will cost us very little.'

Claire shrugged, clamping down on her irritation. 'Sometimes,' she remarked tersely, 'you're a very stubborn woman, Lily.'

Lily smiled. 'It's an inherited trait.' She walked out to the living room, where everyone else stood around piled-up boxes and stacked-up luggage. She felt strangely relieved that she had made her decision. But she was sad that everyone was leaving, except for the small Russian piano teacher.

'Well,' Jacques declared. 'The car's ready, and I suppose there isn't any reason to dawdle. The roads are clogged up enough as it is, and we'll be on the road for days.' Taking two suitcases in his hands, he began to walk out to the large Rolls-Royce that stood waiting. Behind it was Wolf's smaller Peugeot.

'I'll miss you, Aunt Lily,' Nanni cried, throwing her arms around her neck. 'But you'll write, won't you?'

'Of course, darling. And we're not at the other end of the world, you know.' Gently, she helped the little girl climb inside the Peugeot. The small, plump hand stayed entwined with hers, and Lily felt a tremendous pang of sadness. Still, she'd made up her mind.

Hours later, when the children had helped her tidy up the house, she felt the silence of the empty rooms. Sudarskaya, sidling in beside her, said: 'It won't be the same without them. Such a jolly time, all of us together. I was thinking,

412

when the war ends, you and I could start running a *pension* together. The children would love it, and it's a good business.'

'And when will the war end, Raïssa Markovna?' Lily smiled at her, suddenly grateful for her company.

'It will end when the powers that be take a good look around them, and decide that enough young men have died. Like the last time.'

But last time, the war lasted four years, Lily thought, a dreadful anxiety twisting her heart. And in four years Nicky will be nearly twenty. They'll take him in *two years!*

'Are you all right, Lily?' Sudarskaya was asking. 'Is anything wrong?'

'I'm glad you're here,' Lily said, and squeezed her arm. 'We'll keep each other company.'

Sudarskaya sighed. 'I have no one else,' she simply stated. 'That's why I stayed.'

After a few days, Lily discovered that they hadn't brought enough heavy clothing, and she decided, come what may, to take the train back to Paris and pack up some things. Besides, she had to make storage arrangements with Madame Antiquet. Reaching the capital after a trip of starts and stops, in a train filled with people who were returning to Paris after an initial hesitation, she discovered that, although the city was certainly in turmoil, the butcher had greatly exaggerated his description of the situation. Most of the stores had reopened, and transportation could be obtained. But, on the train, they'd passed another train full of soldiers, and had seen more soldiers with horses at the station in Cagny. She'd even seen what appeared to be aeroplanes in camouflage after the city of Evreux. There could be no mistake: France was at war.

After a short visit to her mother, Lily went to the boarding-house. Madame Antiquet helped her to look through her things, and they put together warm clothing, topcoats, and some books. The *pension* looked like a blind replica of itself, with bands of paper covering all the windows, and sacks blocking all the air vents. The two women ate cabbage and rice, and then Lily went upstairs to sleep.

At one thirty, she was awakened by sounds of aircraft, but when she went to the window, she saw nothing. At four twenty, an air-raid siren began to shrill, and she quickly dressed in the dark and joined Madame Antiquet and the young maid in the cellar. They sat in total obscurity and talked, their words reassuring against their fear, and at five twenty the siren signalled the end of the raid. Quickly the young maid heated a pot of coffee, and they had breakfast. Then the two women helped Lily with her baggage, and she took the métro to the Gare Saint-Lazare, from which she intended to take the six twenty-five train. This would take her to the city of Caen, from which she would have to board a smaller train to Saint-Aubin. The trip was supposed to take less than six hours, but with the crowds and the air raids in Paris, it was difficult to tell when she would finally arrive.

After purchasing her ticket, Lily made a passage for herself and her luggage, and settled down on the platform among thousands of wives whose husbands had already been called to arms. She sat down on a battered leather suitcase, exhausted. All at once she saw a man pushing through the crowd, head forward, and she realized with a start that it was Mark MacDonald. She stood up, called out to him, raising her arm above the heads of the people. She saw him stop, lift his head, catch a glimpse of her . . . and then proceed at a faster pace. She felt a tremendous joy when he reached her side, a great relief that in this sea of strange faces, she'd found a friend.

'You came here just to find me?' she asked him, incredulous. 'But you might have missed me entirely, if I'd been glancing the other way and hadn't spotted you first. It's ghastly here.'

'But I had to try. I never did say goodbye to you, Lily, when you left for the summer. And I wanted to see you.' He added, in a less personal tone of voice, 'Who knows, anyway, when you will be back? Maybe you're right to keep the children out of Paris.'

'I experienced my first air-raid warning last night,' she said. 'Have there been many?'

'Several times a day.'

'And . . . you aren't going to try to return to the States?'

'Not for the moment. I'd never be able to arrange it, anyway. I guess I'll just stay put where I am. I might resume my writing for the *Clarion*, now that war's on. The folks back home will be crazy for news of wartime Paris. There's nothing like a safe, faraway disaster to make some people salivate.' He gave her a lopsided, ironic half smile.

Impulsively, she said, looking into his eyes: 'And if you feel like it, do come and see us. We have a huge house, and we'd love it if you came. If you want a semblance of peace, that is. Or a place to write your novel.'

He smiled. 'It's a charming invitation in the midst of all this pandemonium. I'll keep it mind, fair lady. But I don't imagine either one of us will be travelling around much over the next few months.' He added, his hazel eyes serious and earnest in the grey dawn: 'That's really why I wanted to say goodbye to you now. You'll be okay there, won't you?'

She nodded, trying for lightness. 'Thank you for caring, Mark. Keep up with my parents, will you please? It would relieve my mind to know that should they need something, you'd be nearby.'

'Of course.'

For a moment they were awkwardly silent, pressed together by the hordes of waiting passengers. She could feel his thigh against hers, his hand poised on her arm, his

415

breath warm against the cold air. Oh, God, she suddenly wondered, and when will I see him again? When will I see my parents, Marisa and Wolf – all the people I'm leaving behind? And, with an absurd juxtaposition of memory, she saw him turn again in the black of night, illumined by the garden lights of the house on the Schwindgasse – turn and look up into her bedroom, discovering her watching him, in her nightgown. The remembrance suddenly shamed her, and she turned her face so that he wouldn't see the mounting colour in her cheeks.

The shrill of a train whistle startled them both, and, very quickly, almost without looking at her, he kissed her on the neck. 'Take care,' he murmured, and then, as she bent down to pick up her packages, they were separated by a fat young woman and two children, moving forward. She tried to hold her ground, to turn back to catch a glimpse of him. But in the sea of faces that pressed in on her, she realized she'd lost him.

Afterwards, in the corridor of the train, sitting on her suitcase, she thought of what she'd said to Kyra in the kitchen in Saint-Aubin. War did turn people's lives upside down. What would happen to Mark MacDonald, who had loved her as a young girl, and who had, in a tenuous fashion, remained connected to her life for nearly sixteen years?

And she was conscious that she hadn't thought at all about Misha, not for the last part of the summer. Dear Mark, she thought, with a stirring of her heart. Throughout the years, how carelessly I often forgot you. But you never once forgot me, did you?

Life was inexplicable. One man had given her two children, lived with her for more than ten years, and left her without even saying goodbye. And another, who had never been her husband, nor even an intimate part of her life, had come through a war-clogged city at six in the morning, *just* to say goodbye. How, then, was she supposed to explain this life, with all its unexpected twists and turns, to the two adolescents who looked to her for answers?

I have no answers, Lily thought. And she felt a terrible aloneness descend upon her, and she was afraid.

Book III
The Forties

Chapter Nineteen

Some Paris institutions, afraid, had transferred their personnel and offices to the southwest. Some had come as far as Bordeaux; others had stopped on the way to set down temporary roots. Still others, uncertain as to the future, had remained in Paris.

Saint-Aubin and its neighbouring beach resorts, Langrune and Luc-sur-Mer, had, during the summer of 1939, seen many vacationing employees who, that September, hadn't known what to do. The mail was still working, in spite of common sense, which would have predicted a total stop in postal communications. But for most of these people, a trip to Paris just to check out the situation had seemed too expensive. If their office stayed open, they would be expected back; on the other hand if it was moving, they would have no way of learning where to – and would therefore be better off staying put and renewing the lease on their summer rooms. The atmosphere was pervaded with anguish and anxiety.

Lily had not had to worry. Jacques had sent her a sum of money to last her a few months, in case the mail was suddenly stopped and she was left stranded without funds. But another problem faced her. Nicolas was due to enter the tenth form, Kyra the ninth. Other parents wondered if the lycées of Paris would continue to function, in the dire eventuality that the capital was invaded. And if they *didn't*: wouldn't it be better to stay in Saint-Aubin? Many people shared Lily's concern for her children's education. Those resolving to stay were afraid that their young people would lose a whole school year.

And suddenly, word came that a referendum would be held to determine how many children would thus be left over at the end of summer. If a school was opened on the coast, would the parents be willing to send their children there, however makeshift this operation turned out to be? The results were striking: all the families that had resolved to stay put, answered in the affirmative. All along the littoral, which stretched from Villabella to Arromanches, the total of young people in need of schools numbered over two thousand.

It was decided that five lycées would be formed. They would draw their teachers from all the ones who had not reintegrated their own communities, but who had, like the vacationing parents, stayed behind in fear of the Germans. In the Brasilovs' area, the large hotel in Langrune, now closed for the off-season, donated its dining room and restaurant. There wouldn't be any heating; but then, no one was expecting miracles in a summer resort during a wartime winter.

It took time to set up desks and chairs and to send for books and notebooks, and there wasn't sufficient space to hold all the students at the same time; and so the boys were thrown in with the girls, in the American fashion; and the older students worked from nine to noon, the younger ones from two to five. And to replace a certain lack of hours, classes were also held on Thursday, which, until then, had always been France's free day for students.

All the young people of Saint-Aubin would gather together at the tail end of the village, and walked as a group the two kilometres to the hotel in neighbouring Langrune. Lily, watching them sometimes, was reminded of a marching regiment, and her skin would rise up in gooseflesh.

One didn't really feel the war. But friendships that otherwise might not have flourished among the restrained, reserved French, developed over the fences of the summer cottages. Normandy, that autumn, was grey, smelling of salt that clung to the skin. Lily and Sudarskaya gave some piano lessons, and stayed for warm mugs of coffee and radio bulletins in their students' homes. And while Poland was being savagely defeated, the women knitted to ward off the bitter chill – and people laughed, to hear the echo of their own voices raised in joy: to ward off worry and fear.

Almost from the beginning, Nick and Kyra brought their friends home to study with them. Lily, who had so seldom been permitted, as a child, to bring anybody home, never pointed out that food was expensive, and that, at noon, there were often extra places to set. Raïssa Sudarskaya loved young people. She played the piano for them and told them outrageous stories of her youth in Russia, thrusting out her pigeon breast and proudly recounting tales of former glory. They laughed, but with, not at her. She was the village eccentric, and it took several months before some conservative parents stopped thinking of her as a flaming Red. Lily had made a point to let it be known that they were French – all of them; but still, people referred to them as 'the Russians', because of the sonority of their names, and were at first diffident about befriending them. Like Misha, Sudarskaya had never changed her citizenship; but Lily felt it would do no good to let people know this. Nick spoke perfect German, and had been promoted to a higher level in this course. His teacher was a middle-aged man called Gauthier Voizon, whom Lily had only perceived from afar. In the group of students that walked to and from school together, there was a young girl a little older than Nicolas, who sometimes stopped in for a bite, or to study with him. Her name was, absurdly, Trotti. Nick had explained to his mother that she was the daughter of his German teacher, and that her real name was Raymonde. As a toddler, she'd trotted everywhere: hence the odd nickname. She was tall, somewhat large of frame, and her nose was just a little too long, her mouth a little too generous, for her to have been pretty. But she possessed a cascading mane of luxuriant black hair, beautiful dark eyes, straight white teeth, and a clear, healthy complexion. 'She's very smart,' Nick told Lily. 'She's first in the eleventh form, and we're tied for first place in German. Her dad's especially tough on her – so I think that in Paris, she would have beaten me outright.' But he said it with a rather happy smile.

Trotti's manners were nothing if not excellent. At the beginning she was hardly a regular visitor, and Lily paid little attention to her. And then, slowly but surely, she began to make her presence felt. She would sit at the large kitchen table and help Kyra with her algebra. Or she and Nick would take their German books into the living room, and work together by the small oil lamp. Sudarskaya said one day: 'I made rice pudding today, and Trotti didn't come for a snack. What happened?' And it was then that Lily came to with a jolt: Trotti Voizon had, imperceptibly, fitted herself into all their lives. She wondered if this was for the good, or a questionable situation.

She had never met Trotti's mother, but had seen her several mornings at the market. She'd recognized her by the little dog with long yellow hair that Nick had described. Trotti was an only child. Sometime in November, Madame Voizon smiled at her and tilted her head: undoubtedly, Trotti had described *her* too. But the families' socializing stopped at that. Afterwards Lily and Trotti's mother always exchanged smiles – but nothing further.

Nick and Trotti were together for a large portion of every day, and for almost every evening. More often than not, he would go to her house after supper, some books under his arm. 'Do you think he loves her?' Kyra asked, her green eyes suddenly intense. '*She* loves *him* – you can tell immediately!'

Lily blinked. Was it then so obvious that even a little sister could perceive it? But, strangely enough, Kyra was way ahead of her brother in the matter of the opposite sex. Lily thought, with poignancy, of the letters Pierre Rublon had carefully sent to them *all*: letters that inquired about his best friend, Nick, about his best friend's mother, even about Sudarskaya. Then, somewhere in the middle, a specific question directed at Kyra.

Nick would read the letters aloud, then leave them on the table, casually. And Kyra, clearing up the dishes, would remove the onionskin papers with quick, deft fingers, then disappear for forty-five minutes in the bathroom. Sometimes she emerged with red-rimmed eyes; but she never spoke about it. She had her father's secretiveness, and also, Lily suspected, his wounding vulnerability.

Nick, turning fifteen, looked older, but was still an innocent. Like Lily, he was of a much more trusting nature. Shortly before the winter vacation, he seemed troubled. When they were alone at the kitchen table, he glanced down at his hands, cleared his throat, and asked: 'Mama . . . do you think I can kiss Trotti? Or would she be angry?'

The open naïveté of the question took her breath away. She felt certain that Pierre had already kissed her daughter, and that *she* hadn't thought to confer with her mother about it. But she answered, in an even voice: 'Darling, you must know this better than I. I'm not sure where you two are in your relationship at this moment. Maybe she's expecting a kiss – or perhaps it *would* affront her. It's up to you to figure this out, and to feel if the right moment has come.'

The next day, he came into the house, his face alight with pleasure. 'Mama!' he cried, somewhat breathlessly. 'I kissed her!' Shyly, he turned slightly aside and added: 'And she was happy.'

The winter of 1939–40 proved uneventful on the western front. The war still appeared to be acted out in the dim

425

distance. It was difficult to summon excitement over the fate of the distant Finns, invaded by the Soviet Union. Sudarskaya, still a Russian citizen in spite of Lily's assurances to the contrary, had had to be fingerprinted at the police station. Edouard Daladier was forced to resign in favour of the economist Paul Reynaud, over his failure to send help to Helsinki. But still, he remained in the Cabinet as defence minister. Old Marshal Henri Pétain was given the post of vice-premier.

In April, the improvised force sent by the French and British to help the Norwegians defend themselves against Hitler, was roundly defeated. Chamberlain was unseated, but Reynaud remained. Nick said to his mother: 'The French don't care. All this is still too far away.'

From the start of the school year, Nicolas had amazed all his teachers with the agility of his mind, his gift for languages, and his astounding memory. Then, towards Christmas, he spoke to Lily. 'With the war on, I want to make sure I get as far as I can with my studies,' he explained. 'Who knows how long I'll have the luxury of being a student?'

'*Don't*, Nick.'

'But we have to face reality. Mama, I already had a discussion with our principal. He's going to let me accelerate, so I can take my first *baccalauréat* exam this June, instead of next.'

For the students, the *bacs* were trial by fire. They lived in dread of them all through their high school years, and many brilliant students failed them unexpectedly. Lily considered Nick's age: at fifteen, he wanted to forge ahead, taking on a monstrous load. But he was right. She didn't want to think that he might eventually be drafted. She preferred to imagine that they might have to flee from Saint-Aubin in the middle of an important semester. Had it been Kyra, she would have vetoed the acceleration. But she knew that Nick could handle this strain, and even thrive under it. And besides . . . now he would be thrown in with Trotti Voizon all the time.

'If this is what you feel you can do, it's all right with me,' she told him, smiling.

Marisa had written that in Paris it was becoming more and more difficult to admit to being a Jew. Left and right, their Jewish friends were running away, to the United States and to Britain. Yet the quotas were so tight that many of them were being turned away. Wolf didn't want to move. 'It's as if his experience in Vienna has emptied him out,' she wrote to Lily, honestly adding: 'He's changed so much that half the time, I don't recognize my husband, always so vibrantly alive, in this still, frozen shell of a man . . . suddenly so old.'

It was then that Lily's mind captured the thought, holding it like a palpable object, that she hadn't been with a man in over two years. And the image that came to her was, strange as it may seem, a remembrance of Mark walking through the garden of the Schwindgasse, one hot night in Vienna. How long ago had this moment been? *Six years ago.* She'd been lonely then, too, without the warmth of a man's body in the night, without the thrill of a man's fingers running trails over the languorous softness of her skin. All at once, thinking about this aroused her. Filled with an unaccustomed bitterness, she sat down, momentarily defeated. Years ago . . . sixteen, to be exact . . . she'd unburdened herself at confession of her physical desire for a man. Now, she thought, she'd hardly know what to say anymore to a Catholic priest. She'd let her old religion fall like a relic by the wayside . . . like a broken object for which she had no further use. She could recite all the Jewish prayers, like delectable incantations. But she couldn't put feeling into the Pater Noster nor the Ave Maria. And she didn't feel guilty now about wanting to be touched, wanting to be loved, wanting to love a man with all her body and soul.

Later in the spring, Nick and Trotti had their first serious disagreement. Some of their friends had planned a bicycling outing to the city of Caen. 'We'll go, too, with picnic lunches,' the young girl said.

'I can't. I have to prepare for the physics exam.'

'But we'll study together, on Saturday! *Everyone's* going to go . . . and it's time we spent a day together, without our parents around.'

Her black eyes, insistent, bored into him. She placed a hand on his arm. 'Come on, Nick.'

He was aware that her insistence was over more than just a trip to the big city. He could feel her strength, her *femaleness*, so close to him, and it caused strange stirrings inside him. Part of him was suddenly, mystically excited; but the other part, the mental one, seemed to fight back. Trotti wanted to do things her own way. She was older. And he didn't intend to let himself be manipulated. Suddenly, the fact that her breasts were only inches away from his elbow, was a reason to withdraw, instead of responding. 'Look,' he told her, his voice tight, 'I've got two years to do in one. It won't be enough for me to study on Saturday. I skipped a grade so I could pass my *bac*, and to me, that's the most important thing in the world.'

She folded her arms over her chest, and said, sarcastically: 'How pretentious, Nick! And . . . how unromantic. I thought you'd be sweet enough to spare my feelings, and at least *pretend* that *I'm* the most important thing in your life!'

Turning red, he replied: 'You're not a "thing", anyway, Trotti. You're a person, and you know I like you. But I'm not going to let you bully me into an outing when I know I'd be risking a poor grade in physics. It's my worst subject.'

'We never do *anything*,' she shot back at him. 'All the others go places and have fun, and we just study. Don't you know that they make fun of us at school?'

His brown eyes met hers, calm and steady. He was not about to show her how her stinging words had hurt him. Instead, he sighed. 'Look, Trotti. I know you're disappointed. I'll try to make it up to you sometime when I'm not swamped with work. But – ' Suddenly, his control broke. '*You can't understand!* I *have* to pass my *bac*, I have to start my life, because I'm the only one who can do anything for my family! You've *got* a father. Mine abandoned us! That's the reason I wanted to rush through my studies ... so I can start earning some money for Mother and Kyra.'

But Trotti merely shrugged, still sullen. And then, seeing that his concerns, his *life*, seemed less important to her than an afternoon with her friends, he turned his back on her and strode into his house, feeling an ache so deep that for a moment, tears burned on the edges of his lashes.

In the weeks that ensued, Nick's habitual evenings at the Voizons' were not resumed. Madame Voizon, for the first time, stepped out of the line for fresh bread, and walked up to Lily and Sudarskaya, who were waiting for a pound of dry beans. 'I'm not sure what's happened,' she said, and Lily noted how cultured her voice was, and how soft-spoken. Trotti's was harsher, somehow: she didn't possess her mother's refinement. 'We miss Nick. My mother had taken to him, and used to play a game of dominoes with him every night. And then ... he was so considerate. To save us all from the humid nocturnal air, he made it his job to walk the dog before going home.'

Lily was surprised. If Trotti had inserted herself into the Brasilov household, how much more, it seemed, had Nick into the Voizons'! Trotti was sixteen, Nick a year younger. She wondered then how hard her son must be taking the separation. Her heart contracted for him.

That noon, when he returned home from school, his face was pale, drawn, with unnatural circles beneath his eyes. She waited for him to confide in her; when he didn't, she remained tactfully silent. For the next few days, she watched him circumspectly. He was eating very little, and appearing distracted and, she thought, distressed. Was it all over this headstrong young girl? Lily asked herself.

That evening, she took her daughter aside, and asked: 'Do you have any idea what's been upsetting your brother? Was it something at school?'

Kyra shook her head. 'He had an argument with Trotti. Now she won't even speak to him. But he hasn't told me why.'

'Then, do me a favour,' Lily said, on an impulse. 'Ask her to come by the house tomorrow afternoon. I'll send Nick on an errand, and she and I will talk.'

Lily wondered if she was doing the right thing. Nick was fifteen, and might resent her unbidden interference. Yet she also knew that her son's unhappiness could only be resolved by an adult's getting to the heart of the matter. She wasn't sure Trotti would come, and she wasn't even sure she liked the girl. But she knew that adolescent pain could sometimes run deeper than the situation warranted.

The next afternoon, she sent Sudarskaya out with both her children, in the hope that Trotti would come. And she did, promptly and politely. Lily took her jacket and drew her into the kitchen, where she'd put out teacups and a brewing pot. 'Kyra said it was important, madame,' she said, a bit awkwardly. It was the first time that the two of them were alone, speaking one-to-one.

'You and Nick have quarrelled,' Lily stated. 'And now he's broken-hearted. I just wondered, Trotti, if there was any way I could help.'

The girl appeared surprised. 'Help? But how? Nick just doesn't want to do *anything* fun. I like him, really I do – but I'd also like to go out sometimes, with our friends. He's so . . . intent . . . so *obsessive*, about his studies.'

'Perhaps the fault is mine. Nick's taken on more than his share of responsibilities. But he's *always* been ambitious, Trotti. He's so conscientious. He knows that the only sort of man who can succeed in a career is the one who'll work diligently to achieve it.'

'He says it's because he has no father.'

Lily was shocked. Trotti's face had set into lines that were almost ugly. It was, Lily realized, as if she'd just accused *her* of putting too much on Nick's shoulders. And maybe she was right. 'It's been difficult for all of us,' she answered, her voice trembling. 'But hardest of all, I suspect, on Nick. He's such a fine young man, Trotti! He wants to take care of us ... even of the old piano teacher, Raïssa Markovna. You have to admire him for this, not criticize him. He doesn't give up where most adults would have, months ago. And this business of two grades in one has been a big burden.'

'Then ... why d'you let him go ahead with it?'

'Because,' Lily replied quietly, 'he's old enough to make some important decisions on his own.'

She poured them each a fresh cup of tea, then eyed the girl levelly. 'You and Nick had such a nice, open friendship. I suggest that you make up your disagreement, instead of letting it ruin the rest of the year for both of you. And, Trotti – don't make him the focal point of your free time. Enjoy yourself. You have other friends. If Nick has studying to do, there's no reason you shouldn't be out with Diane Boucher, or Charles, or Émile. You're a nice group that's always doing things together.'

'But excursions aren't the same when he's not with us.'

'Each of us has to do what's right for himself. Don't ruin a perfectly good relationship over such a small matter. You're older than he is, Trotti: it's up to you to be the wise one.'

Lily smiled then, and Trotti, shrugging, had to smile back.

In the days that followed, slowly but surely Trotti and Nick began to put back the jigsaw pieces of their friendship.

And, two weeks later, what his mother had hoped for took place: once more, after dinner, Nick went to play dominoes with the old grandmother, and Trotti stopped by to borrow his German grammar book because she'd left hers at school.

The friendship had resumed, although of course not with its initial trusting freshness. On 10 May 1940, Hitler made a clean sweep through the Netherlands and Belgium, and on through the Maginot Line. It seemed inevitable now, given the paucity of resistance the Germans had encountered, that they would eventually penetrate to Paris. Now the war was felt, and everybody quaked. But Nick and Trotti were busy preparing for their *baccalauréat* examinations, and almost as busy with each other. Lily saw their heads touching, their hands linked together. It might no longer have been the intense emotional communion they had shared in the beginning: but now the two young people appeared to have gained a new physical awareness of each other. A new phase of the relationship had opened up.

One night, Lily felt compelled to have a talk with her son. 'I'm worried,' she said, wetting her upper lip and feeling for the right words. 'You and Trotti have become . . . so *attached*. And there's a war on. Who knows where you'll end up – and where she will. Before you choose a bride, there will be many other Trottis, Nicky. Don't fall too hard: cushion yourself by withdrawing now, just a little. She's a compelling girl – a very strong, wilful girl, who can turn a boy's head and make him forget his common sense, his hopes for the future.'

Brown eyes encountered their match, silent and expressive. 'You don't like her,' he remarked finally.

'I have no reason not to like her. She comes from a good family, with good values. It's you I'm worried about. You're younger than she is. If you let yourself become carried away . . .'

'You don't have to be worried, Mama,' he countered

gently. 'It's not that way between me and Trotti.' Seeing her relax, he looked thoughtful, then said, 'And . . . there's something else. Ever since I found out about Grandma, I've felt . . . differently about religion. I've been reading about the Jewish faith . . . and I like it. It makes sense to me. I think, Mama, that when the war ends, I'll try to learn more about it. Catholicism was always too . . . well, mystical for me. Judaism's more down-to-earth.'

Lily nodded, speechless. 'Trotti's a devout Catholic. I don't think I could be happy with a wife who put such faith into being granted absolution by a priest. She and I have discussed it, many times. To me, priests are just men, and I think that whole ritual is a bit ridiculous. One day, I'll meet someone who's going to share more than just a snack by the oceanfront. It isn't just the bit with the priest . . . it's all that it tells me about Trotti. She needs someone who'll understand her ways, and I need . . .'

Laughing, he shook his head in self-mockery. 'I need to finish my homework.'

That night, Lily lay in bed thinking of her children. How different they were! Nick had a deep understanding of human nature, but, like all young people, he tended to go to extremes. He soared in his beliefs, in his altruism . . . even in his newly formed religious convictions. She, at eighteen, as sure as she'd felt about her unshakable faith, hadn't thought to exclude either Mark or Misha as a possible husband, though one had been Protestant and the other, Russian Orthodox. But in Catholicism, as long as one promised to rear the children in the faith, it wasn't so important that one marry within it. Among Jews, there tended to be more of a community feeling . . . Wolf had called it the sense of 'the unbroken chain'. And her son had become imbued with this feeling. In spite of his conditioning, in spite of her own efforts to the contrary – in spite, even, of his father's ardent anti-Semitism – the essential spirit in his family's ancestral archetypes had pierced triumphantly through aversion, deception, and even religious education. He had *known* who and what he was.

Kyra was a different matter. She would love according to her flights of fancy, and according to the call of the flesh. She would never, like Nick, be able to 'cushion her fall'. Even now, at fourteen and a half, she still clung, fiercely, to the memory of Pierre Rublon – and Lily knew that unless Pierre deceived her, broke her illusions, or otherwise forgot her, she would pledge her heart and soul to him. Unless, of course, somebody else came out of the blue yonder to completely captivate her, cancelling out each and every previous emotion. Kyra was like Misha: vulnerable through the tender parts of her being, parts that so few people even knew existed, seeing only the hard carapace that covered them.

At least, Lily thought, beginning to drift off to sleep, she wouldn't have to worry about Nick and Trotti – or not as much as she'd been doing.

'Mama,' Nicolas announced. 'The time has come to leave. We don't have a moment to lose. You and Kyra and Raïssa Markovna will leave at six A.M. tomorrow, and I shall make the trip by bicycle. This will mean one less person on the trains, which are packed like sardine tins.'

It was 11 June 1940. Just last night, they'd heard, in horrified silence, that Italy had declared war on the French and British. For some time now, the Germans had been advancing into France. Some Belgians, and some inhabitants of the Department of the North, had passed through Saint-Aubin in motorcars jammed with people and baggage, with several mattresses heaped one on top of the other, tied with rope to the tops of their cars. Some had found lodgings there and stayed.

But now they were leaving again. And the citizens

434

of Saint-Aubin, both permanent and seasonal, were also speaking of leaving town, and were preparing their luggage. Even Lily's landlady had moved to the home of some relatives in Brittany.

The advance of the German troops had been stopped at the River Seine, where the French were furiously fighting. For several days, the Brasilovs had been hearing bombings over Le Havre. And two days before, from 11:00 A.M. to 5:00 P.M., total obscurity had fallen over the town, so that lamps had had to be turned on. Lily and Kyra had gone to the seawall to watch the ship lights and the lighthouse beams, in the middle of the day, as if it had been in the dead of night. They'd thought it had been the battle of Dunkirk that had reached them, invading the entire skyline. But the next morning, they'd learned that the darkness had been caused by the bridges and kerosene vats that the French had set on fire in the city of Rouen, and which had been burning. It was rumoured that the flaming oil spreading all over the Seine had made the immense river look as if it had been made of pure fire.

On the morning of the eleventh, Nick had gone to school as usual, but having heard that it was imperative to leave now, he'd scooped his sister from her class and run home to warn his mother to pack their bags. He'd waited until the last possible moment – hoping against hope that the Germans would be stopped. His plans for taking the *bac* later that month had had to be shelved: survival alone mattered.

The night before, just in case, Lily and Sudarskaya had packed the things they knew they wouldn't be needing: household pots and kitchen utensils, linens and towels. They'd stuck these crates in the attic, to be left there. For on the ninth, they'd received word from Claire that she had found a small house to rent in Arès, near Bordeaux, on the bay of Arcachon. In spite of the crowds pressing to

435

buy tickets at the Gare d'Austerlitz in Paris, Jacques had found them room on a sleeper.

Lily had decided that they would go to Arès, and had already sought an exit permit from the city hall, which had to be sent to be registered at the township of La Délivrande, several miles from Saint-Aubin and of which the latter was an administrative dependant. Nick had gone to La Délivrande in the morning, but had returned empty-handed. So, at noon, Lily went to the city hall, and learned with dismay that as yet, no one had even bothered to send her permit to La Délivrande. And now time was of the essence. In the chaos of wartime travel, one felt a great deal less helpless with an official document on one's person.

After a quick lunch, Nick went to Caen to buy himself a new bicycle saddle and to see how the trains looked and what people were up to. He took the permit with him, hoping to get it registered there. But the mayor of Saint-Aubin hadn't signed it, and Lily barely had time to reach the city hall before it closed at five.

She had packed all day, with the help of Kyra and Sudarskaya. From the city hall, they made the rounds of the few friends who were left, and said their goodbyes. At the Voizons' house, Madame begged Lily to take her and Trotti and the grandmother with them, as her husband had gone on ahead to Royan, and since they were both going to the same area, she preferred to share the travel with some friends. Lily accepted; she was hardly thrilled at the prospect of travelling with an elderly person, who might complain; but she felt that she had no choice.

Nick's account of what he had seen had been quick and to the point. 'The main thing is going to be to leave the Caen train station. It's like hell down there. Hundreds of families have settled there, waiting for their turn. Most have folding seats, hot plates, and pillows. Some have been stationed there for three days already! Because all the people from the beaches, stretching from Deauville to

Courseulles, have gathered at Caen. So you must inch your way to the platform, and under no circumstance stay in place – or you'll be staying forever! You'll get on the first train that comes, whatever its destination. It doesn't matter where you'll end up: the important thing is to leave Caen. And of course, no trains are going east.'

Watching her son, Lily's heart grew heavy. Fifteen, and with full responsibility for his family. As always when her thoughts took her in this direction, she became filled with rancour, remembering that Misha had left without even a word of farewell – or of explanation: leaving his former wife to explain it to Lily. Poor Nick was so exhausted from his day's pilgrimage that she sent him, along with his sister, early to bed.

She and the little Russian piano teacher packed Nick's rucksack, the large suitcase that they would bring with them, and many bags. In the suitcase they put clothes and shoes; in a large plaid blanket, two smaller rugs and a change of personal linen for all three women; in one sack, food to eat on the way, in a second one, dry goods, and in a third, cans and biscuit tins, as well as cutlery for everyone. In a small bag they put pharmaceutical products, in a paper sack some knitting wool, and finally, in Lily's enormous bag, legal documents, stationery, and some sewing things. The two women washed the dishes and cleaned up the pantry, but gave up on sweeping the floors. Too bad: the landlady would have to do it when she came home, and God only knew how many months ahead that would be! They finally tumbled into bed, falling into a dreamless sleep as thick as fog.

At 4:00 A.M. Lily arose, washed and dressed herself, and went downstairs to prepare Nick's breakfast. She woke him fifteen minutes later, and when he had finished eating, he took his leave of his mother. Holding her to him, he steadied her with his young, virile strength. She started to ask: 'When shall we see each other again, and shall we all be safe and sound?' but he placed his index finger over her dry lips, and shook his head. 'When Kyrotchka and Raïssa Markovna awake, kiss them for me,' he said. 'And, Mama: *bon voyage* to you, too.' He closed up his rucksack, jumped on the saddle of his bicycle, turned to Lily and waved. He had begun his long journey, all alone.

At five, she awakened Sudarskaya and Kyra, fed them, and made the beds. Then they took as much luggage as possible to the railway station. The Voizon women were already there, the old lady more poised and cheerful than her daughter and granddaughter. 'You stay here with the ladies,' Lily said to Sudarskaya. 'Kyra and I have one trip left to fetch the last of our baggage.'

When they returned, the small local train in the city of Caen was already whistling its imminent departure. Kyra and Lily jumped aboard, and found the Voizons and Sudarskaya sitting on their suitcases in the long corridor. But Lily knew that after they reached Caen, real troubles would begin. Nick had forewarned them.

But she had not pictured the enormity of the situation. Caen station was swarming with a crowd of people that took up every square inch of space. Remembering Nick's advice, Lily took the lead, pushing herself through the pressed bodies towards the platform. There, a blessed quiet reigned. Few had possessed the audacity to burst forth without waiting for their turn. They found room on a bench, and sat down. 'Kyra and Trotti can go inside to buy our tickets,' Lily said, handing some notes to her daughter.

'You're quite bold, Madame Brasilova,' Madame Voizon remarked, with a smile. 'I wouldn't have dared to come this far, if you hadn't been with us.'

Twenty minutes later, Kyra and Trotti returned, empty-handed and dishevelled. Their cheeks glowed with perspiration. 'The hall was full of people. We barely pushed our way to a ticket counter, only to find it closed. The ones next to it were, too. To return here, we both had to shove our elbows into the crowd, not caring whom we hit.'

Lily shrugged. Turning to Trotti's mother, she said, sighing: 'It doesn't matter, then. We'll just have to travel without tickets.'

'We heard somebody say that a train was half expected, on its way to Laval,' Kyra ventured.

Lily thought about her permit. 'Well,' she said, 'if we lose this train, we'll wait for the next one. Maybe if I go to the police station here, I could change our permit for a safe-conduct.'

But at the police station, a harried employee took a single look at the permit, and exploded. 'What the hell do you think *I* can do to help you? This bloody paper's not even been signed by the police station of La Délivrande! There isn't a thing I can do!'

She returned to the train station, where she was greeted with the news that there would be no train that day. 'I'm going to go back to Saint-Aubin,' she announced wearily. 'The local train leaves at eleven, and it's almost that now. There, if I can find a car, I'll hire it to take me to Lison; on the way, I'll stop at La Délivrande and get my permit signed. In Caen, I'll try to get it exchanged for a safe-conduct, and then I'll stop here to pick you all up, and we'll go to Lison in the car. Of course, there are so few cars left that it's likely I won't find one; if so, I'll walk to La Délivrande and take the four P.M. little train back to Caen.'

She went then to the small train that was waiting, almost empty, to return to Saint-Aubin. She felt feverish, but it wasn't the moment to admit illness. At least she was sitting down. Suddenly Kyra appeared in the doorway. 'Come quick, Mama!' she cried. 'The train to Lison has just arrived, unexpectedly!'

A train? So much, then, for the safe-conduct. In the chaos that reigned, perhaps there wouldn't be such great need for it. Lily gathered up her belongings and followed her daughter out of the small train.

From the platform, they could observe the train. It consisted of a locomotive and two railway cars crammed full of people, and not even a matchstick could have been squeezed in there. A railcar, however, was coming to the back, and it was being hooked on to the second car. Immediately, hundreds of people pushed forward. 'There's Trotti, getting on now,' Kyra said. And she edged onward, straining, holding on tightly to her mother's hand as Lily followed through the crowd.

They were being propelled with the others towards the train. Just in time, they climbed onto the stepladder, and heard Trotti cry: 'Look! Over there!'

And they saw, on the platform, Sudarskaya immobile by the luggage. 'She'll never be able to get on,' Lily said, her voice suddenly faltering. 'And absolutely no one will hand us our bags.'

'Besides, there's no room for so many parcels,' Kyra added.

Across many heads, Lily spoke to Florence Voizon. 'You all stay; but we have to get off, because we can't leave her, and these bags are our only possessions.'

And seizing Kyra's hand, she painfully stepped down from the stepladder. She could hear the echo of Florence Voizon's voice, but not what she was saying. And she was sorry to have lost her company.

On the platform, they found the small piano teacher, and went to sit on their bench. They unwrapped some bread and fruit, and started to eat. 'If there's been one train, another may come, too,' Lily remarked, trying to infuse hope into their hearts. But she felt discouraged, and tired.

But all at once, forty-five minutes later, a train did pull in. It was a freight train; but there were two empty compartments, their large doors open. This time, all three

440

women grabbed as many packages as they could, and threw them ahead into the train. Then they hoisted themselves inside. The step in a freight train is placed very high, and so it was difficult to reach it. But a gentleman helped, holding out his hand, and soon they were all three safely inside the car.

Slowly, with much huffing and puffing, the train started to move. Lily could see the faces around her lose their tight, worried looks. Everyone was happy to have at last left Caen. Then Kyra said: 'Mama, we're eighty-eight in here. I've just counted.' And they had grabbed the best places, by the door but not directly in front of it. They had enough air, and were quite comfortably seated on their packages. But if someone pushed them, they would not run the risk of falling out. Feeling privileged, they exchanged small smiles.

After two hours, the train pulled into Lison, and it was learned that a train for the city of Nantes would be leaving at seven the next morning. Lily found out that there were two cafés that had rooms to let, but when she went there, of course all the rooms had already been rented out. And so all three women settled down in the waiting room of the train station, on a bench. Kyra went to a grocery store and purchased some fresh food, and then they unwrapped their plaid blanket, took out the rugs, and stretched out, preparing to sleep.

At eight in the evening, a railcar left for Féligny. Then a train bound for Dol was announced for 9:00 P.M. Several people scrambled to their feet, and they heard hurried footsteps on the platform: many people were hastening to catch this train. Lily stopped a man and asked: 'Why is this particular train, bound for a city that's so close by, suddenly so popular? The one in the morning is going all the way to the west of Brittany!'

'No, you've been misinformed on both counts,' the man replied. 'The line which has just formed *is* for the train due to leave at seven A.M. And it's only going as far as Dol. If you don't take it, God knows when another will come.'

They stood up, quickly folding their blankets together. 'Oh, well,' Lily said. 'Dol is still one step farther in the right direction.'

The three women had already lost ten precious minutes. The train was full, but people let them in, and in the corridor, they found two unoccupied flap-seats. Sudarskaya took one, and Lily the other, but she pulled Kyra onto her lap. They positioned their feet over some of the bags. People kept climbing in, more and more desperate, until finally the entire corridor was filled.

But, instead of departing at seven the next morning, they left at eight thirty. When they reached Dol, it was announced that the train would continue, and that there was no need to get off and wait again. But still more people, smelling of sweat and grime, climbed aboard. Many were turned away.

A group of young soldiers, pleasant and joyful, who had fought in Belgium and at Dunkirk, slipped in through the open window of the corridor, and found space standing up, squeezing close together. Then, somebody passed a one-month-old baby through the same window. But its mother had to go through the door. Everybody tried to help, but goodwill was not enough. Finally she was inside, and the baby was handed to her over Lily's head. She couldn't tell how they settled down, but the mother had possessed, as her only luggage, a small bag. How would she change her baby on the way?

All through the night at Lison, and at each stop during the day, those who could get out did so, to refill water bottles at the fountain. Others handed them theirs through opened windows. The stops lasted a long time, and in the train the air was stale, and it was so hot that drizzles of soot and perspiration ran down everyone's face. When people had appeased their thirst, they would dab a few drops of water on a linen cloth, and press it over their tired faces. The cloth turned instantly black, but it was the only way to obtain some relief. The presence of so many humans pressed together was suffocating.

Going to the lavatory was quite a different odyssey. One had to reach the end of the corridor, stepping over all sorts of packages, side-stepping people's legs and even people's bodies. Once there, one had to dislodge the three men who had taken possession of the small room, one sitting on the toilet seat and the two others standing, leaning on the walls. They were more than willing to move: the problem was to find space for them outside.

In Avranches, many people left, and Sudarskaya slid into a compartment where one real seat had been vacated. After a while, a man signalled to Lily to come to the same compartment. 'Here,' he said gently. 'Sit down in my place for an hour.' And so, at last, she was able to sit high enough so that her legs could rest. For, on the low flap-seat, all the weight of her body had shifted to her feet, which were now swollen and aching.

At three thirty, the train stopped in the middle of a field. The station of Rennes lay in the distance, and after an hour and a half, they started to inch forward at a snail's pace, in fits and starts. It wasn't until five thirty in the evening that they pulled into the station.

Lily, Sudarskaya, and Kyra moved all their baggage out, and walked to the other side of the platform where, quite far down, stood the train bound for Nantes. 'Maybe we should stop there, in Nantes, and stay with Aunt Marthe,' Kyra suggested.

Lily shook her head. 'Absolutely not! She's a hateful old woman, and I want to stay with my mother.'

Kyra stared at her, dumbfounded. She'd rarely heard her mother speak against anyone, or be excited. Lily was always cool, poised, in control. Absurdly, Kyra burst out laughing.

443

They found some room in a compartment. Some well-thinking official had removed the partition between two compartments, and a greater flow of air circulated inside. They sat down on the floor between the torn-down partition and the corridor. Sudarskaya leaned her head forward, closed her eyes, and started to snore lightly.

Shortly after that, some ladies from the welcoming centre managed to enter the cars and hand every passenger some bread and chicken broth.

At around seven, the train departed, and arrived much later at Nantes station. Lily and Kyra went outside for some coffee, dragging all their bags outside and half dragging the sleepy little piano teacher with them. They sat on their packages, leaning against the wall.

There wasn't any thought of falling asleep. From time to time they would doze off, feeling thankful that, for once, they weren't being pressed on all sides by human flesh. At four in the morning, the stationmaster announced that a train would be leaving for Bordeaux in one or two hours. He wasn't in charge anymore, but was simply relaying the orders of the military authorities.

All of a sudden, rumours spread that yesterday's train from Rennes was ready to leave. Everybody rushed back inside. It hadn't been worth it to leave it and spend the night outside – but last night already seemed part of the past. Kyra found a third-class compartment that was still half empty, and next door, they heard their agreeable companions, the soldiers from Dunkirk. The train pulled out at five thirty, and each turn of the wheels was bringing them a step closer to Bordeaux.

The day of Friday 14 June passed quickly. They stopped several times, for a long time, and once two young soldiers popped their heads in to ask if Lily and Kyra wanted to share some dried fruit with them. Lily knew that her daughter was still burning with resentment, and she also realized, with an odd jolt, that to these young men of eighteen, she, at thirty-five, seemed an old woman. She looked at her daughter, noting her small waist, her round, plump breasts, and her lovely legs. It seemed a shame to waste this period of her life, when she should have been enjoying her first flirtation, and learning to dance and to be courted. 'You go, darling,' she said softly. 'I'm not hungry.'

Afterwards Kyra came back, her cheeks shining with pleasure. 'There wasn't any dried fruit,' she explained, her resentment miraculously evaporated. 'We just ate the bread and coffee that the welcome-centre ladies handed out. But it was fun. They've seen *so much!*'

Lily had always thought that bread and water was considered harsh punishment because it deprived the offender of good food. Now, after hours with nothing else to eat but dry bread and horrid *ersatz* coffee, she realized that the bread was sticking to her throat, and she pictured the pleasure it would be to eat a bowl of macaroni. Bread alone could fill a person, but never satisfy him.

La Rochelle passed, then Jonzac, where they stopped for an hour and refilled their water bottles. One old woman was left at the fountain when the train departed, and the alarm was pulled. The passengers were shaken by a case of crazy, liberating laughter, watching her running to catch up with the train.

At Saintes, at 1:00 P.M., everyone was forced off the train. Horrified, Lily heard that all trains for Bordeaux had been forbidden. They could sleep in Saintes – but what then? Their money, too, was running out, and they had no more food left. But somewhat later, they learned that in the morning there had been an accident, and that they were clearing the rails – and that eventually a train would arrive, and not, as had been supposed, that the military authorities had cancelled all further travel.

Then a train appeared. They rushed towards the first open car, along with two ladies holding a huge cage containing nine finches. Some soldiers from the territory of the Landes sat with them, talking their own dialect. Their chatter, mixed with the chirping of the finches, brought a sense of joy into the atmosphere. The train set off from Saintes at three o'clock, and stopped, like its predecessors, many times for long halts. At 2:00 A.M. it pulled into Bordeaux station.

Arès was now only thirty miles away. Lily, Kyra, and Sudarskaya went to the welcome centre, and drank some coffee. 'This is our last punishment meal,' Kyra whispered conspiratorially. 'The next time we eat, we shall be sitting at Grandma's table!'

Suddenly, Lily said: 'My God! We registered our large suitcase in Lison ... but we've changed trains so many times, no one will know where to send it on! It's lost!'

'Pierre's letters were in it – all of them.' Kyra's face, ashwhite, stared back at her, horrified.

Lily felt a dead weight landing in the pit of her stomach. 'All our clothes ... all our shoes ... *everything!*'

Unexpectedly, Sudarskaya snorted, shrugging. 'Shoes! We'll never be able to fit into any of our old shoes, my girls. Look how swollen our feet are! And as for Pierre ... young men never lose their hand at writing. Just think: maybe next time, little one, he'll address himself to you alone – instead of writing to your brother, like a goose.'

Five hours later, weary and nerve-racked, Lily was halfdozing on the *quai* when Kyra drew her out of her fog. 'The train is forming, Mama,' Kyra said. It was seven in the morning, and she saw that several old third class wagons had been pulled together. Hoisting themselves on, they walked directly into the same compartment as their cheerful soldiers from the Landes. And again, as with the boys from Dunkirk, Lily was conscious of their eyes upon her daughter.

At the town of Facture, the Brasilovs and Sudarskaya got off the train, waving goodbye to the pleasant soldiers.

They were going on to Arcachon. One of them winked at Kyra, who blushed and smiled. Lily's heart contracted: she wondered how many of these young men would die at the front before the war was ended.

The railcar only left at nine o'clock. It ran its course through a densely wooded region, stopping several times. Then, all at once, they saw the sign: *Arès!* They had arrived at their destination!

Leaving almost all their baggage in the cloakroom, they took with them only their dry goods, which might please Claire and Jacques, and the plaid cover. They wondered if their other belongings would be waiting for them, or if they would be stolen. But at this point, they hardly cared. They looked at Claire's directions, and set out on foot. They were walking with slow, small steps, their poor feet hurting from days of swelling and disuse. And the villa was far.

'What do you think Mama will say when she sees us, dirty, dishevelled, our clothes and shoes caked with dust? We look like vagabonds,' Lily said.

'Well, we've been on the road forever, haven't we? We left on Wednesday, at six A.M., and now it's already Saturday noon. Three and a half days without washing or brushing our hair – in trains where we've perspired in the soot, along with thousands of other . . . vagabonds.' Kyra laughed, but her voice shook with exhaustion.

And here, at long last, was the villa. It stood behind a small garden, riotous with flowers. Lily pushed the gate open, and, in front of the door, rang the doorbell. She could hear somebody pulling back the bolt, swinging open the door – and Claire's face, her white hair neatly piled on top of her head, her brown eyes round in her head, widened in astonishment, stood staring at them. 'Oh, my God,' she whispered, taking Kyra in her arms and holding her tightly against her.

When they were all seated in the small mahogany *salon*, drinking hot milk and relishing a thick purée of white butterbeans, Claire leaned forward in the green velvet wing chair, and asked: '*Where's Nick?*'

Lily blinked. Pushing back a greasy strand of her dirty hair, she thought: of course; she doesn't know! 'He's coming, by bicycle. He should be here in two or three days.' And she, in turn, asked: 'How long have *you* been here?'

'We arrived five days ago. We've been waiting for you ever since. Paris is occupied.'

'I beg your pardon?'

'The Germans have invaded Paris. And Mussolini's declared war on us, too.'

But this she'd known; Il Duce's belligerence had been the last piece of news she'd listened to on the radio.

'There's going to be an armistice,' Jacques spoke up grimly. 'The French have lost the war.'

Lily sat speechless. In a stunned, exhausted silence, she listened as her parents told her what had happened during her voyage. People had come from all parts to Arès, and rooms were hard to get. They'd hired a girl from the town to help them cook and clean, but she went home at night. Mark had gone to the market to bring back some fresh vegetables and fruits.

'Mark?' Lily echoed.

'He came with us, because he didn't want us travelling alone. I only wish Marisa, Wolf, and Nanni had come too.'

'They're still in Paris?'

'Wolf's had a setback: he's worse than last summer, an emotional piece of ice – nothing seems to move him.'

'With the Germans . . . the Nazis . . . in Paris?'

'What can I tell you? He's changed, Lily, since the *Saint Louis*. But surely, before Mark comes back and we settle you down, you'll be wanting to use the bathroom. You too, Raïssa Markovna – and Kyrotchka.'

A bathroom. It seemed too good to be true. With great difficulty, the three women tried to remove their shoes.

Their ankles were as large as their calves. Lily stretched out in the tub, soaping herself with languorous relish. But when she stood up and looked down, she was horrified. The entire surface of the bathwater was black and oily.

They unwrapped the plaid blanket, and removed their changes of underwear. Claire brought out several pairs of house slippers, because they all needed softness around their tender feet. Then they stretched out on the small but cosy beds in the guest room, and fell asleep.

Hours later, when she awakened, Lily padded downstairs to find her mother. Her clean hair floated down her back, and she could smell her own warm, soapy smell. Claire was standing in the small kitchen, explaining something to a young girl in a simple uniform. 'Mark went to the cloakroom and brought back your bags,' she said. 'Nothing was stolen, after all. And I've got a nice lunch prepared – a kind of English high tea, really, because of the hour. I'll bring it in a few minutes to the *salon*.' They stood smiling at each other, happy to be together.

Lily was aware that she'd been standing there, not moving, for several minutes. Ask, then, she thought. Ask about Mark, who came all the way from Paris to save your parents from trouble. Ask about Mark . . . because you've thought about him a lot lately. You've thought about him *all the time*. But her throat felt strangled, and her feet couldn't move.

'Hello, Lily,' he then said, framing the doorway, and when she turned to face him, her face colouring, she noted at once that he had changed. He'd aged. He was as old as the century: forty years old. And his curled, sandy hair had turned salt and pepper above his ears. He was more attractive than he'd been as a perfectly chiselled young man of twenty-four, when they'd first met in the living room of the Robinson family home.

'Hello, Mark,' she answered, holding out her hands and walking gingerly towards him. She felt the tears burning the rims of her eyes, all the tears of exhaustion and frustration that she'd kept inside all through this dreadful week of tribulation.

When she felt him seize her hands and draw her to him, Lily saw the room begin to tilt to one side, and when he caught her going down, it had become a revolving arena of red and golden stars afire in her head. But it would be all right ... all right ... because she could feel his hands under her arms, his virile strength holding her.

Chapter Twenty

'But you're not a Frenchman,' Lily said to Mark.

They were standing together in the grocery store, listening to the radio. It was Monday 17 June. That morning, Nick had finally arrived on his bicycle, and they had left him at home with his sister and grandparents.

The news, blared over the store, had brought all the shoppers to a halt. 'That's Marshal Pétain's voice, unmistakably,' someone had whispered. And then they'd heard him say that France could no longer continue to fight, and demanded peace.

Mark had moved closer to Lily, encircling her shoulders with one arm. She'd burst into tears. And then, tremulously, the owner of the grocery store had started to intone the *Marseillaise*. And all the assembled patrons, one by one, had joined in – Lily's voice, tremulous but clear, for three rounds of the same patriotic hymn. His own cheeks had been wet, his own throat knotted, his own voice merging with all of theirs.

'I'm a human being, and a free man,' he now answered softly. 'And I've been living on French soil for seventeen years.'

She felt herself melting with affection for him. 'Look,' he told her. 'Maybe it's just a German station. It could be a false bulletin.'

She shook her head, despondent. They paid for their groceries and left. Outside, it was drizzling in a suffocating heat. The seashore loomed green-grey, and turbulent. They walked home in silence, weighed down by the news and by the weather.

Over the next few days, news bulletins followed one another, bringing confusing and contradictory news. Jacques stationed himself in the small *salon*, near their wireless. It was cramped in the little villa. The three women slept in the guest room, Mark and Nicolas in sleeping bags in the *salon*. There was never any place for a moment of privacy. And yet, the feeling of being all together, as a family, was overwhelmingly appreciated. How strange, Lily thought, Sudarskaya's become a fixture among us. And Mark . . . Mark was like a big brother for Nick, a companion, old enough to be his father but never making this age gap felt. And the Walters treated him with such casual familiarity, as if his presence was a natural fact of their own lives, that everyone else simply had to follow suit.

Yes, she admitted: in Austria, we were awkward around each other. I was in a transitional stage of life, and neither one of us knew what I wanted. I *had* to try again with Misha. If his father hadn't been killed, something else would surely have come up to give our marriage another chance. But now . . . he'll never come back, and if he did . . . I wouldn't be the same woman, the same wife. I probably would not be prepared to accept him.

And yet there *was* an awkwardness. As long as there were other people around, Mark and Lily could extend their fondness for the group in a more or less natural fashion to each other. But when they were alone, electric sparks were in the air, which were hard to ignore. Yet they did try to ignore them. If their fingers touched by mistake, they tried to avoid each other's eyes. It was the eye contact that was the most deadly. She made an effort to look at his nose, at his hairline . . . at anything but the hazel eyes that revealed her own self, as he saw her. My God, she thought, deeply perturbed: he still cares.

It didn't make any sense for him to care. She'd never been in love with him, as a young girl. She'd loved him, yes, but as a dear, close friend . . . a relative, almost. But

452

now . . . since Vienna, actually . . . she saw him differently. She noticed his compact, trim body, his proportioned arms and legs, his muscled torso. She learned how he blinked his eyes, how he smiled with a certain amused irony. And at night, she tossed restlessly in her narrow bed, seeing him in her mind's eye.

Nick learned that Trotti and her family were in nearby Toussat, and he started to make daily trips there on his bicycle. Both had missed taking their *baccalauréat* examination in June, and, having compressed two years into one just for this, Nick, especially, wanted to take the re-sit that was being offered in Caen in July. Normally, there was always a re-sit in September for those who had failed their orals in June. But, because so many people's lives had been upset by the sudden disaster of Dunkirk, and by the German invasion, a special test was being set up for those who had studied in the region of Caen. Nick and Trotti had heard about this from a friend who had remained in Saint-Aubin.

Nick therefore decided that come what may, he would find his way back there to take the exam, and to bring back the boxes that Lily and Sudarskaya had left in the attic of their house. Lily's first reaction was one of pure horror. All the Normandy coast had been set off limits by the Germans, who were re-arming for their attack on Britain. A person could not penetrate this region without special papers issued only by the Germans to those who possessed a connection with them.

'How on earth do you intend to get through?' she'd asked.

'I don't know. I'll have to invent something at the station in Nantes. But don't worry, Mama. It's not dangerous — just problematic. Who knows how long we'll stay in Arès? I don't want to fall behind. And besides . . . we need the things you left at the house.'

She'd had no choice but to shrug in defeat. Mark told

her, afterwards: 'He'll never get past the line of demarcation. So don't worry. He'll be sent home, but at least he'll have done his utmost to accomplish what he wants. This is so important to him!'

Trotti at first seemed excited, wanting to go with him. But as time passed, she became afraid, probably discouraged by her parents. 'I'm sure we'll go back to Paris soon,' she said to Nick. 'And I'll just take the *bac* in the autumn.'

'But we don't know what Paris is like. At least, in Normandy, we *know* what to expect.' He swallowed his disappointment, then smiled crookedly: 'Hey,' he told her. 'It's okay this way. I'll be a *bachelier* and you'll still be a green schoolgirl!'

And so the month was progressing.

But with Nick so often at Trotti's, the little house appeared that much more spacious. Lily and Mark ran into each other in corridors and the kitchen, or going in and out of the house, and without Nick near Mark, acting as a buffer, their eyes met, more and more frequently. Like electric sparks – quick, magnetic, fiery – then gone.

On 20 June, Hitler and Mussolini met in Munich to discuss terms for the peace, and Bordeaux was bombed, killing nearly fifty people. The Germans were in Rennes, Niort, going towards Vichy. On Saturday the twenty-second, they had reached Clermont-Ferrand, and because of the frantic movement of the troops, all passenger trains were requisitioned. Germany let it be known that it would ask for the total neutralizing of the French armed forces, so that it might hurl itself at Great Britain without fear of French intervention. 'Why doesn't he ask for the colonies?' Jacques demanded, suspiciously. And that day, France signed the dreaded, shameful Armistice, and in the Walter household there was unrestrained weeping.

On 23 June the rumour spread that the Germans wanted eighty billion francs, and all the colonies. The British were furious at the French for capitulating, and in Arès, the

English tourists had all packed up and left the territory. The next day, news came that the Germans planned to enter Arès at eleven. But they didn't come.

Kyra had settled on the living room sofa, her knees tucked under her, and was reading a novel. Outside, a light rain was falling, and Nick was staying in Toussat, where he'd bicycled over to have lunch with Trotti's family. The young girl could hear her mother and Mark moving in the kitchen: talking, and perhaps preparing food. She set her book down and leaned back, suddenly alert.

Mark. What was he doing here anyway, with her family? She could feel a wave of resentment building inside her, just thinking about it. Years ago, she'd liked him. He'd come to see the Steiners in Vienna, the year that they'd been separated from her father. Kyra still didn't understand about that year: why Lily had left Misha. So much had happened that no one had ever thought to explain to her.

But now she was less confused. She *knew*, just *knew*, that if Mark continued to stay, her parents would never be able to put their life back together again. She had dreams of going to America, to her father – of all of them being together again. But Mark! He'd ruin everything.

Lily came out of the kitchen, wiping her hands on a clean washcloth. She looked tired, but there was an unusual glow on her face that irritated Kyra. Her mother was middle-aged, much too old for flirtation. And obviously, Mark had been flirting with her. Kyra could feel the anger welling up, the tension.

'What's the matter, darling?' her mother was asking. 'You look upset.'

'It's nothing.' And then, all at once, all of it tumbled out of her. 'That's a lie. I just don't like it when you're with Mark. I don't like *him!* Mama, he acts as though he's a part of this family – and he *isn't!* I wish . . . I wish you'd just tell him to go away.'

Lily stood dumbfounded in front of her daughter. 'But Kyra, that's so unfair! Mark's been more attentive to Grandma and Grandpa than Uncle Claude ever was. We've all come to depend on him . . . to need him.'

'*I* don't,' the young girl said almost viciously. She could feel tears coming, and her heart ached again for her father, for their special times together. 'I don't think any of us needs Mark MacDonald! You just think you do, because he's always following you around like a puppy dog. But Papa's going to send for us, I know he will, and *he'll* take care of us – not some *stranger!*'

To Lily's horror, she saw that Mark had come into the room, and was standing quietly next to her. 'You apologize, young lady,' she addressed Kyra, her voice tight with anger. 'You apologize at once to Mark! You had no right to speak this way!'

Mark laid a hand over her forearm. 'It's okay, Lily. She voiced her feelings, that's all. No harm done.'

'She voices her feelings whenever she pleases, regardless of whom she hurts! That's been Kyra, all her life. And I won't have her insulting you.'

Kyra stood up, her chin jutting out defiantly. 'I'm *not* sorry. Mark's a stranger. I didn't say anything that wasn't true!' And she ran from the room, slamming the front door behind her. They saw her running out into the street, under the rain, her long hair streaming dramatically behind her.

Mark took Lily to the sofa, holding her to him, and then said: 'She's right, you know. She's seen what you and I have tried not to see. That we want to be together. And she still sees you as a married woman . . . married to her father.'

Lily raised her eyes to his, and answered: 'But I *am* married. Whether or not we may want to be together . . . I'm still married to Misha.'

He stood up, his face tightening. 'And what do you intend to do about this . . . Princess Brasilova?'

She took a deep breath, trying to deflect his irony and the pain in his voice. 'I don't know.'

'But you don't love him, and you don't want him back.'

'We're in the middle of a war, Mark. It's not exactly the right time to decide whether or not to get a divorce. Soon the Germans will be swarming all over, and we'll be scrounging for food. I'm not in the proper frame of mind to decide my future. A divorce is something over which one should deliberate with peace of mind.'

'But we can't give you that. So you have to decide what you're going to do about your present – our present. You're thirty-five. Stop trying to be perfectly fair to him, and start thinking a little of yourself . . . of your youth, of your beauty, of your *present*. It seems to me you haven't had any fun in many, many years. I'd love to promise you the world, Lily, but I can't. As you yourself said . . . it's not the right moment.'

'What, then?'

Her brown eyes had never seemed so nakedly appealing. She was dressed simply, in a beige cotton dress, and she had swept her hair up, more carelessly than usually, so that now, strands of the strong, vibrant tendrils were curling around her oval face. She rarely wore makeup. Now, in that clear, honest face, the only thing that he could read was her naked plea to decide for them both . . . to spare her any future guilt over her own choice.

'I want for us to be together,' he said, fervently, taking her hands in his and kissing her fingertips.

He could see her face accepting this, like a new gospel. She was still so childlike, so innocent! The young girl who had run to the confessional, in need of reassurance, still sat before him, so little changed that something powerful stirred inside him. 'God,' he said. 'How I love you!'

That evening, Kyra avoided her mother. Both were ill at

ease, and guarded. Jacques turned the radio on. It was Tuesday, the twenty-fifth. At 9:00 P.M., Marshal Henri-Philippe Pétain spoke. The conditions of the armistice were: the country would be occupied from above Lyons, through Bourges, to the Spanish frontier; the three armies would be demobilized. Everyone was supposed to go home, and the French government would remain independent.

'It's a day of national mourning,' Claire said softly. Her face was wet with tears. In the small room, nobody spoke. Jacques moved to turn off the TSF programme, his face long and lugubrious.

Then Kyra said: 'Mama and I are the only genuine French here. Raïssa Markovna is Russian; Grandma was born Belgian; Grandpa's Swiss, and Mark's American.'

'But this is more our country than any other,' Sudarskaya replied. 'We can weep for it, too.'

'Let's go to bed, Kyra,' Lily said, holding out her hand as a peace offering to her daughter. Grudgingly, the girl took it. But her eyes flashed one second at Mark, and he could read in the bright green irises her triumph over him. She had scored a point because of her uncanny understanding of her mother's vulnerability. And he, like the once proud French nation, had no choice but to capitulate.

But I'm not going to, he thought angrily. Not this time.

Nightmare days had begun. The next day, there were no news bulletins; all had been cancelled, the station seized by the Germans. A few days later, a decree came that, in the near future, all pastry shops and sweet-shops would be closed down. Bread would have to be made from five grains, including split pea and dried bean. It would be sold stale, and new food cards would specify how much a person, or a family, could buy.

In the meantime, the Soviet Union made an ultimatum to Rumania, demanding Bessarabia and Bukovina, all its oil, and control of the mouth of the Danube River. 'There's going to be trouble all over the world,' Jacques remarked.

But the newspaper *Paris-Soir* ran four pages on how well the Germans were behaving in Paris. Bakers would have the right to work on Saturdays and Sundays, and the radio would be French, after all.

Lily and Kyra saw one German soldier on a motorcycle, and a German officer in a kind of carriage with a swastika painted on its side. They were arriving in trucks to look for lodgings, evacuating from their homes some of the people that the Walters and Brasilovs had met in Arès.

The German time was one hour ahead, and the French had to set their clocks in accordance with it.

Great Britain gave an ultimatum to the French fleet in Oran, to go over to them; and when it refused, the British opened fire. Diplomatic relations with England were severed.

Already, during the tenure of Paul Reynaud, British Prime Minister Winston Churchill had asked that the fleet of their weakened French ally go to the security of some British ports. He'd feared that the Germans would conquer all of France, and demand its fleet as well – a fleet that the British might put to good use. Reynaud had refused. Churchill had repeated this request, via the proper diplomatic channels, to Marshal Pétain; but the latter had failed to be informed of this; and was therefore unaware that an answer was required. The British, of course, were insulted.

Then, probably motivated by a certain degree of shame, the French had not immediately informed their British ally of the terms of the armistice. Already on guard, and put out, Churchill assumed that the French had therefore made an arrangement with Germany involving their fleet. And these were the reasons that the disaster of the port of Mers-el-Kébir, near Oran, took place on the third of July. The fleet was sunk, more than a thousand French sailors were killed or reported missing, and hundreds were wounded. A

459

wave of shock swept over France at what was deemed a British betrayal.

Already, anti-British feelings in France had been almost as strong as the anti-Jewish sentiments that had slowly but surely spread over the last years before the Occupation. With the severing of relations between Great Britain and France, those like Vice-Premier Pierre Laval could set to work to actively undermine their former ally from across the Channel. For men like Laval, it seemed far safer for France to come to an agreement with Germany, than to do so with a nation that had traditionally been France's fiercest enemy throughout the ages.

And then, on the fourth of July, the Germans mysteriously disappeared. Rumours ran rife, that the Americans had threatened them with war; that they had passed over the Spanish frontier to fight the British; that they had left Bordeaux with Orléans as their next destination.

On Wednesday 10 July a unanimous vote was taken to revise the Constitution of 1875. And on Thursday, the Senate and the Chamber of Deputies convened in Vichy, where the French government had transferred its seat, now that Paris was occupied. On the eleventh, Marshal Pétain, who was eighty-four, was named chief of state, encompassing the duties of both the Premier and the President of the Republic. His powers stretched over a vast territory, like those of a monarch. His Cabinet was to be composed of twelve ministers, with Pierre Laval as his vice-premier. The Senate and the Chamber adjourned, and said their good-byes to Albert Lebrun.

'Listen to this: one of Pétain's new laws bars anyone who doesn't have a French father from taking any administrative post.' Nick seemed disgusted, and tossed the tabloid he'd been reading aside. 'Now I wonder if there's any use in pursuing a future in this country!'

Kyra took in her breath, appalled. 'What do you mean?'

'I mean, that on Monday I have to retrace my steps,

and start my journey back to Caen, to pass the exams on Thursday. And for what? Our father is Russian. It doesn't matter that he abandoned us like stray dogs. He'll still hold us back, in our careers. It's only the beginning! Pétain may remove all other privileges from us, in time!'

Kyra fought back tears of fear and horror. Nick, the calmest of human beings, her security blanket, her love, her protector, was losing his hold on reality. Or was he? What if he was right? He was standing now, thoroughly agitated, his shirt soaked with undue perspiration. 'Maybe Papa was right!' he cried out finally. 'Maybe in the United States, there's justice, and freedom. Those goddamned swastikas make my blood run cold. *We're Jewish*, Kyrotchka. And a demon, a madman from Austria, whose own grandfather was probably a Jew, is going to try to annex this country, where you and I were born – the same way he did Austria, and Poland. We have to fight him, Kyra! We *have* to.'

'But . . . how, Nicky?'

'General de Gaulle, in England, has started a movement of the Free French.'

She was silent. Then, softly, she laid her hand on his arm. 'Don't talk like this,' she begged him. 'You've got to be careful. I want you to succeed in your exams. And then, Nicky, we'll need you with us. Mama and I – you know we can't manage alone. Grandpa's too old to help.'

'There's always Mark.'

She turned her head aside. '*Don't*. Mark isn't a member of our family. I wish you, and everybody else, wouldn't treat him as such.'

Surprised, Nick examined his sister circumspectly. 'Why don't you like him?' he asked.

'Because.' She bit down on her lower lip, then wheeled about, her prominent cheekbones bright red. 'He's in love with Mama.'

For the first time, Nicolas smiled. 'And? Doesn't she

deserve to be loved by a peaceful, kind, considerate man? Stop being so possessive of our mother, Kyrotchka. She's a woman first; and our mother second. And she's had a dog's life.'

Kyra said nothing. 'But I won't go to England,' he continued gently. 'At least, not now that the French and the British are no longer on speaking terms, and now that the Germans are preparing their big offensive. I love my country, and I believe in de Gaulle. But I also want to save my skin, and I'm not prepared to lose it crossing the English Channel at this moment. You don't have to worry.'

'But I feel you . . . restless.'

'Maybe so. I'm afraid, Kyra. Really afraid. These new laws, I told you, are only the beginning.'

'And nobody knows we're Jewish,' she said hesitantly.

His brown eyes narrowed. 'It was wrong, what Grandma and Mama did. It was Papa's fault. I wish they'd told us from the start, so we could have been what we are, proudly, openly. But now, perhaps this deception will save us. I worry much more about the Steiners, and Sudarskaya.'

They stared at each other, both of them unsmiling. Then he shrugged, and smiled. 'Hey,' he told her. 'And what if I fail my *bac?* Will you still love me?'

She wound her arms around his neck and laughed. 'I'll always love you.'

By the twenty-third of July, all but twenty customs officials of the Germans stationed in Arès had departed.

Lord Halifax and Churchill had harsh words for both the Germans and their former French allies.

Later in the week, it was announced that several important Frenchmen had, in absentia, been deprived of their citizenship, for having left their country between 30 May and 30 June. These included Edouard Daladier, Yvon Delbos, the directors of the Institute of Art and of the National Library. General de Gaulle was condemned to death; but, if anything, his insurgent movement in London only continued to flourish – as if the general were laughing at the Vichy leaders. Meanwhile, the French fleet was being reorganized.

Kyra received a postcard from her brother, from Saint-Aubin. He had reached La Rochelle on Monday night, Nantes on Tuesday, Caen on Wednesday . . . and had now returned to 'their' small town with the other *baccalauréat* candidates. He planned to bring home the boxes Lily had left behind in their Saint-Aubin house.

That day, it was declared that no more correspondence would be permitted between the Free and Occupied Zones.

On the second of August, Lily received a letter from her son that perhaps, on the fifteenth of that month, the entire coastline would be opened up. He suggested that he attempt to return to Paris alone, and that the small group in Arès pack up and try to do the same from their end.

'But Paris is chaos,' Claire countered. 'There are no cars, not even bicycles . . . people are stranded in their homes.'

'The métro is working,' Lily reassured her. 'Slowly . . . but surely.'

In Bordeaux, the bridge had been so full of troops going northward, that no civilian had been able to pass through. Then, on Sunday the fourth, a great movement of soldiers passed through Arès. People said that the Germans had tried, the previous week, to launch a tremendous offensive against Britain, but that the English had thrown tar into the sea, burning the rubber ship covers, and repelling the magnetic mines. Fifty thousand Germans had perished.

Claire and Jacques found a neighbour, Madame Catti, who was planning to drive home to Paris at the end of the month. She had room to take three other people, but no more. So Mark decided that Sudarskaya and the Walters should travel with her, and that he, Lily, and Kyra would leave in the middle of the month, by other means of transportation. Nick had written that he would leave Normandy between the fifteenth and the twentieth.

Madame Catti summed up their feelings accurately. 'If we're going to have to live under Nazi rule, we may as well be doing it at home,' she commented. Nick had added in his note that Trotti's family was also planning to return to their apartment on the Ile de la Cité, so that Trotti might attend the Sorbonne if she had passed her *baccalauréat*.

In those lingering last days, under the beating August sun, Lily felt that a period in her life was coming to a close. Her year in Normandy had helped her come to terms with the past. Always before, when she'd met Mark, Misha had clouded the issue in her mind. Now, she knew that he no longer did – that she had closed the chapter on their marriage. But the romance that had been flourishing between her and Mark, thwarted by her own fears and her daughter's hostility, was coming to an end. Soon, they would all be once more in the capital. Would there be time to see him? Wouldn't other problems take priority? For here, in Arès, they lived in the same house. In Paris, where transportation was so erratic, they wouldn't be so close anymore.

Almost as if he'd read her mind, Mark suggested that they take a walk through the nearby forest of Andernos. There, in the thick woods, she remembered their walk in Austria, through the shrubbery annexed to Hans von Bertelmann's *Schloss*. She'd run away from him then, to escape from her own guilt in having hurt him as a young girl. And now she felt guilty, too. She'd put him off. Although, even if she hadn't . . . where would they have gone? The house was too small for them to have arranged to be there alone at any time.

The limbs on the tall trees of the forest bent towards each other to form a trellised pattern of strangely shaped leaves, throwing the moss-scaped ground into Chinese relief. Mark and Lily walked slowly, hand in hand, their heads bent down. 'It's so beautiful here,' she said softly. 'Almost as if there were no war around us.'

He made no reply. Instead, he stayed her arm with his hand, and turned her towards him. Once again, he was breathless before her pure beauty, her face with its extraordinary, wise eyes. He brought his arms around her, and simply held her to him.

It was she who lifted her chin, whose parted lips encountered his like the silky wings of a butterfly brushing against his skin. Filled with the urge to possess all of her, he turned the tentative exploring of her lips into a hungry plunge, his hands moving simultaneously to unhook the back of her dress.

She uttered one small, throaty cry of surprise, then gave herself up to the moment. They could hear children laughing, calling out to one another, in the far distance. But around them, only birds and squirrels chirped and fluttered, their sounds the emissaries of a benevolent god who wished them well.

With fingers that only hesitated for a moment, he pulled the dress off her shoulders, letting it slip to the damp ground. She stepped out of it, and out of her sandals.

She wanted to be with him, but she was afraid. A dreadful nervousness had taken hold of her. She felt his hands on her hips, and turned again to him. He was standing nude, waiting for her to take off the rest of her clothes. And he was looking at her, a serious expression in his eyes.

'What if somebody catches us?' she whispered, clinging to him.

'Do you suppose they'd put us in jail?' He said it with gentle mockery. But she shook her head, seriously.

'Mark,' she reminded him. 'I'm a married woman. This isn't at all easy for me.'

She could feel the strength of his erection, pushing against her stomach. And suddenly she pulled off her brassière, rolled down her silk panties. She was recalling with a memory that seared her flesh how it had felt to be with a man, to merge and move together. Yes, years ago Wolf had been right: what she'd thought had been her need for Misha had, in reality, been her need to be possessed by a loving man. And Mark, in every way, was certainly loving.

He pressed her then against a tree, to feel every part of her soft, long-limbed beauty. And he guided her hands over his muscled chest, over the small nipples, over his firm stomach. By then she wanted to feel all of him, and so they slid together to their carpet of emerald moss, and made full and complete love, until both were drenched with perspiration and their bodies trembled with release and exhaustion.

Afterwards they sat together, covering each other with odd bits of clothing, her dress, his shirt, and they laughed, with that new intimacy of couples who have first possessed each other. He brushed strands of her hair over his neck, and said: 'I don't ever want to leave you, Lily.'

'Nor I you. How I *wish* – '

He placed his index finger over her lips, and shook his head. 'You can wish the present, or the future. But never the past, my love. We each did what we had to do.'

'But you? Why didn't you ever marry anyone, Mark?'

He let one shoulder rise and fall. 'I couldn't tell you. I loved writing. I didn't particularly care about a family, so unless I found the magic girl, I didn't see the point in forcing the issue of marriage. Don't forget: I'd found her, once. But it was wrong then, for both of us. Because I understand now: you didn't love me.'

She nodded, sadly. 'It's true. I really was in love with my husband. But . . . it's over now. I'm glad it happened. I have my children, and I learned to defend myself, to survive.'

466

'I promised you never to clip your wings. Don't you remember that, sweetness?'

She smiled at him. But the years had slipped between them, eclipsing the shimmering beauty of today. And now they were both a little depressed, a little afraid for the future. She felt old. Then she thought about her two children, who had grown up well. She'd loved them like two strong seedlings taking root and blooming.

After that marvellous experience, they walked home quietly through the woods. Jacques greeted them on the steps of the house, his face grave in the early evening. 'Rumania's a real part of the Axis powers,' he said to them. 'And they've expelled all Jewish students from the student unions, and sent a large number of Jews to Bessarabia and Dobruja. They've divided their Jewish population into those whose families have been established there since 1800, since before 1914, and all the others.'

Lily and Mark gazed at him, awestruck. 'Like Austria, like Poland,' she finally murmured.

'And here, another mockery of justice is about to take place. The Vichy government's rounded up some of the ministers of the Third Republic who it feels were responsible for starting the war. Blum, Renaud, Daladier, and many others have been interned in Riom to await special trials for their "war crimes".'

'But . . . it's insanity!' Lily cried. 'Pétain's turned justice into a sick joke!'

Jacques sighed, and held the front door open for them. Lily passed through, then Mark. They found themselves face-to-face with Claire, Sudarskaya, and Kyra, all seated on the couch, their hands in their laps. Lily felt her daughter's eyes burning holes into her, accusingly.

'When are we going to leave?' the young girl finally asked, her small face white and taut. 'There were Germans at the Hôtel des Voyageurs, laughing it up over some beer steins. They're on the roads . . . everywhere!'

'I'm afraid you'll find them just as much "around" in Paris,' Mark replied gently. 'But we can leave for Bordeaux on the sixteenth, and from there, the next day. It's hard to tell how long we'll take to get back.'

'I want to go to my old school,' Kyra said, nervously biting a nail. 'I'm sick of being rootless – like a sack of wheat nobody wants!'

Had it just been an hour ago that she and Mark had lain entwined together, their eyes full of hope and love? Lily wondered. In the small room, an undercurrent of impatience, discouragement and irritation crackled, like a powder keg about to explode. For a mere second, she thought that all these people – her parents, her daughter, her old friend – knew, beyond a doubt, that she and Mark had made love together. They'd read it in their faces, in their shining eyes. And now, they were trying to ruin the magic, to break open the crystal ball in which she and Mark had taken refuge.

But no. Of course it wasn't so. There was just no time, that was all. No time left for lovers to love, for emotions to flourish and for bodies to stretch, twining and merging together. The war was all around, and she and Mark were needed by the older generation, which felt at loose ends, and by the restless young, unchannelled and afraid to meet their future.

She was tired of having to act brave for everybody else. But now there was Mark. He'd entered her life, and she wasn't about to let him go. With him she didn't ever have to act. She could simply be herself, and know that he would never be disappointed.

Lily's eyes sought out the man who had, after seventeen years, become her lover. And quickly, just by looking at him, she told him that she loved him.

Thursday, Assumption Day, the feast of the Virgin Mary, was usually a big holiday in France. Now, however, some of the offices were still functioning in Arès. It was the last day when the French people would be allowed to use their cars in the city, except, of course, for doctors, priests, and some commercial cars that would be permitted.

Lily, Kyra, and Mark took care of tying up all their loose ends. They packed their books, and mailed them to their Paris address from the post office. But the city hall was closed. In the evening, Kyra went to the house of the adjunct to the mayor, and had him stamp their departure papers. All was now set for them to leave the next day.

Their goodbyes to the family were quick, because at seven, the bus for Bordeaux was departing promptly on schedule. Mark took a seat across the aisle from Lily and Kyra, and they didn't speak, watching the progression of small towns of the Guyenne passing by the side of the road: Andernos, Blagon, Saint-Jean d'Illac. They arrived in Bordeaux in midmorning, left their bags in a store across the way, and proceeded at once to the train station.

Since the new regime had set up stricter rules, one no longer could simply get on the train of one's choice, no matter how crowded it appeared to be. One had to go to the counter and buy a numbered ticket. The number helped the clerk to determine if the train of one's preference was already full; if it was, then he could schedule the passenger on a later train. Lily and Kyra stayed back, in the midst of other waiting people surrounded by baggage. And when Mark returned, it was with the news that they would not be able to get onto the Paris train until Sunday morning.

Mark found them two rooms at the Hôtel du Petit Poucet. In the lift, posters outlined where to go in case of an air raid warning.

When they'd travelled with Sudarskaya from Saint-Aubin to Arès, Lily had been forced to assume all the expenses, and to shoulder all the burdens. Now it was Mark who, with complete naturalness, was taking care of everything. Lily had a fleeting memory of the days when she'd known nothing of what was spent, only of what was bought. The days when she'd changed clothes three times a day, not out of vanity, but because her social schedule, set by her husband's desires, had required her to. She didn't, in fact, regret those days. She'd been a child then, playing the role of spoiled young princess. Now all she had left was the title. With it, or without it, the price of a train ticket stayed the same.

She was exhausted, and excused herself to take a nap. Kyra made as if to follow her, but Mark stopped her with a hand on her shoulder. 'Let's you and I have a snack at the Restaurant de la Terrasse,' he suggested. 'I'm starved, and it would be more fun to go together.'

They stood alone in the hallway, in front of Lily's door. Kyra's green eyes gleamed impertinently at him. 'What *you'd* consider fun would be to go with Mother,' she retorted acerbicly.

He smiled, fielding the barb. 'Well? Shall we go?'

Kyra shrugged, and followed him.

At the café, they ordered cake and hot chocolate. Kyra pointedly avoided meeting his eyes, but she licked her fingers lustily, picking up the crumbs from her plate. 'I'm sure in Paris you can't find this kind of food anymore,' he remarked.

'And in America?'

He was jolted, wondering if she was trying to send him home, or finding an excuse to stir her father into the conversation. Whichever it was, however, was immaterial: he knew which way her mind was working.

'Kyra,' he said, gently. 'I don't want my presence to cause problems for you. I'm not trying to come between you and your mother. But you've got to be fair, too. I've known Lily half my life, even before you were born. I've always loved her. And while she was married, I never interfered in any way.'

470

'Then why are you interfering now?'

'Because,' he answered patiently, 'now it's no longer an interference. Your parents have separated, Kyra.'

'It's not the first time it happened. And they mended things then.'

He wasn't sure how far he might push it . . . how much she was ready for. 'Kyra,' he said, 'I'll do whatever your mother wants me to do. But it *is* her choice. Your mother is a decent, honest person. She'd never do anything dishonourable, or wrong, or unfair, if she could help it. She wanted your father to stay. But if circumstances forced him to have other ideas, it doesn't mean that she can't be allowed any new happiness. She's your mother, Kyra: but she's still young. And what I'd like to offer her is my affection, and my care. And to you, too, and to your brother.'

He sighed, looking deeply into her eyes, which were now silently fastened on his face. 'I'm not trying to take Misha's place. Not in her life, and not in yours. But I'd like to be your friend. Your trusted friend. And maybe,' he added, with a smile, 'I need your friendship, too.'

Kyra's face tightened into a vulnerable mask of fear and pain. 'It's so easy for you to come up with all the right formulas,' she finally said. 'But it's . . . it's . . .' Abruptly, she turned aside so that he wouldn't catch her weeping.

She felt his fingers pressing softly into the crook of her neck. 'Just give things a chance, darling,' he murmured. 'Your mother. Me. And yourself. We all want the same thing, Kyra: to find a place where we can fit, where we can feel loved, fulfilled, wanted. Try to relax a little, will you?'

She surprised him by suddenly laughing, although the sound was a little like a nervous sob.

It was at least a beginning.

Their train left Bordeaux on Sunday morning at eleven sixteen. Because of the numbered tickets, they were able to find a compartment with three seats together. They ate in the dining car when they approached Angoulême, and found the *café au lait* expensive. Their fellow passengers engaged in a heated debate over the Germans and the Vichy government, and about de Gaulle and what he was doing in London. Kyra joined in, vibrating emotion. 'My brother says de Gaulle is the only real patriot left,' she said. 'That Pétain sold us down the drain, and Laval gave back the payment.'

Lily gazed at her, a strange thrill seizing her. 'Nick said that?'

'Yes! And he's right! If it hadn't been for Vichy, there would never have had to be a Mers-el-Kébir!'

She'd gone too far, and Mark had to rescue her. Personally, Lily applauded her, and knew that Mark did, too. But she allowed him to appease their fellow passengers, afraid of unpleasant consequences. These were not days when the young, or the old, were free to speak their minds.

At eight forty-five, the train pulled into the Gare d'Austerlitz in Paris. They had some problems with the luggage, because the baggage room was refusing to take any bags. But at length, after many trips, they collected all that was theirs on the pavement outside. But the métro stopped functioning at ten fifteen, and it was now ten thirty. A man offered to help them carry everything to the small hotel across the street.

In the morning, Lily and Kyra left Mark with the baggage, and took the métro to the Pension Lord-Byron. Léone, the young maid, flung open the door, her face all welcoming smiles. And Madame Antiquet threw her arms around them, saying, conspiratorially: 'I have a surprise for you two!'

In the dining room, Nick was sitting at the table, stirring a cup of *café au lait*. Before he knew it, his sister had toppled him off his chair, and was hugging him so tightly that they both fell to the floor, laughing. Lily felt a moment

472

of weakness, the room blurring before her eyes. He was safe. God – whichever one, the Catholic or the Jewish one – had let him come home safe.

'What happened over there? Did you run into any problems? When did you arrive?' she asked him, words tumbling out haphazardly in her excitement.

'Yesterday morning. I had no trouble getting out, and the exam was tough, but all right. I gave them both addresses, here and in Arès, just in case – so they can let me know if I passed. My problem was getting there: in Nantes I reached the ticket counter at the station, and the woman refused to send me through without a German permit. So, with great emotion, I took my identity card and shoved it the window. I'd judiciously spat on it a few times, smudging the writing, to look like tears. I told her that my brother was dying in Caen, and had requested one last visit from me. There were tears in my eyes and my voice was shaking. And, guess what?' He grinned at them, his large brown eyes shining with pride: '*She let me through without a permit!*'

Lily was holding herself in, trying not to let her emotions gush out. She felt on the ragged edge, not knowing whether to laugh or cry. 'You alone, Nick, would have made your way into a forbidden zone in order to take an *exam* . . . and you alone would have invented a story like that one! I'm not sure whether you deserve a standing ovation, or a thorough whipping.'

'Paris is certainly a shambles, though,' he commented. 'I've tried to help Madame Antiquet a little. Five German officers have requisitioned rooms here. She's had to move us into her own apartment, for the moment, to make extra space.' And then he asked: 'Where's Mark?'

'He's in a small hotel by the Gare d'Austerlitz, with our baggage. There was too much for us to carry by hand.'

'Then I'll get Gustave, the handyman, and we'll go over there to help him. Madame Antiquet – perhaps you'd let us use your two carts? The three of us should have no trouble going through the métro with the bags in those carts.'

'I'll go with you,' Kyra offered.

When they had departed, their young energies radiating joy through the boardinghouse, Madame Antiquet turned to Lily, and, her hands on her hips, asked: 'Who's "Mark"?'

'A family friend who came with us on the train.'

The plump woman made a face, shrugged, and made a gesture of 'I give up.' 'I'd hoped for something more, Lily,' she said. 'War or no war, it's good to have you back – with a bloom in your cheeks.'

Following her into the kitchen, Lily felt her heart constrict. The long trip was over, and Mark would be returning to his own apartment. She was on the verge of confiding in Madame Antiquet, and then held back. She'd always hated women who gossiped, spilling their guts out. All her life, she'd been forced to keep other people's secrets: her mother's, Misha's, Claude's. And now she had a secret of her own. She owed it as much discretion as the others.

God had a way of deciding the fate of everyone. Lily would have to let Mark go, like the kind friend he was supposed to be. For, in occupied Paris, survival had to take first priority.

Chapter Twenty-one

The children were back at the lycée, Nick in his final year and Kyra in the tenth form. But for everyone else, life in Paris had turned into a kind of nightmare. The Germans paraded around town, obstreperous and arrogant, as if they'd always owned the graceful boulevards and picturesque avenues – their martial boots clicking, their harsh, clipped accents jarring the quiet beauty of the old city. The French found themselves quivering, shrinking against the façades of buildings to make way for the strutting conquerors – as if they were a lower echelon of person in the face of the Nazi occupiers.

Everywhere, there was evidence of Teutonic supremacy. The city walls were plastered with posters of cabaret acts with flashy, seminude attractions, their captions in German. Varvara Trubetskaya's heart-shaped face, its saucer eyes of forget-me-not blue winking provocatively as her red curls bounced, smiled invitingly at German lieutenants young enough to be her sons. It was rumoured that she'd gone to a clinic in Switzerland to get her face lifted, though most women weren't sure what that meant, and some said it was Sweden, not Switzerland. She looked twenty years younger than her fifty-five, though she graciously admitted ten. But the Germans loved her; she spoke their language fluently, and crooned to them from the stages of the Olympia, the Gaîté-Lyrique, and even the Opéra Comique theatres.

Lily was too busy surviving to dwell for long on her husband's first wife. Yet she was becoming frightened by the Jewish question. Street names that were Jewish had

475

been changed. The signposts around the city were no longer in French. By October, even the Vichy regime had expelled the French Jews who had held public employ, and was preparing to try, in a special court, those ministers of the Third Republic whom it had interned in Riom. Pétain wanted to placate the Germans, and to let France fit into Hitler's European plan, which visualized Germany as its centre of industry, and all the other countries providing it with their raw materials. The old marshal had surrounded himself with Maurras's *Action Française* clique, and preached a simplification of life to his 'subjects', a return to old values and strict moral codes. French life had become, in effect, a thinly cloaked version of what existed in the Reich.

Already, the Reich rule that had forced all Jews to register at their city halls had come into practice. The Steiners and Sudarskaya, known to be Jewish by all their acquaintances, had been obliged to comply; the Walters had not, hoping to avoid detection ... glad at last that Claire had never been open about their religion. Yet Lily saw the large red *J* on her friends' identification cards, and her stomach twisted with worry. How much longer, then, she asked herself with sudden terror, before the French Jews, like those of Germany, Austria, and Poland, were plucked from their homes to be sent without warning to places with strange names.

Jacques Walter, for one, agreed with her. He told Claire that he would do his best to straighten out the red tape that would allow her to travel back to Switzerland with him, as soon as possible. The small neutral country was filled to the brim with Jewish refugees, and Claire wasn't Swiss, but a naturalized French citizen. 'We don't have to go,' she reassured him. 'All my married life with Paul, I was known to be a good Catholic.'

'Your maiden name was Leven. It's on all your papers. And "Walter" rings Jewish.'

'Most people think you're a Swiss-German.'

476

'But a Nazi would know better.'

And so, with as little fuss as possible, they left their elegant suite at the Ritz for a less conspicuous apartment in the suburb of Auteuil, not far from where Claire had lived with Paul at the Villa Persane. They selected a large apartment on Boulevard Exelmans, which the previous tenants, who had left in a hurry for Spain, had furnished with taste in Louis XIV and Louis XVI, delicate *bergères* and inlaid consoles, with velvet upholstery in chartreuse, mustard, and coral hues. Jacques had obtained all this at a bargain. They were not far from the Bois de Boulogne, but not at the centre of Paris. And when they took their lease, they signed it 'Monsieur and Madame Walton.' 'It's totally un-Jewish, and sounds Anglo-Saxon,' he explained to Lily. 'Right now, having British connections isn't exactly the best thing, but we didn't want to go too far off. We can plead an English ancestor, and leave it at that.'

She understood. Claire didn't want to think about leaving her beloved Paris, and she, Lily, had nowhere else to go, so the question of emigration didn't even occur. Sudarskaya, a foreigner and a Jew, had had a large red *J* plastered to the front of her identification card, and felt afraid to walk the streets in daylight. The Steiners, on the other hand, had not left the Ritz. Marisa had wrung her hands and pleaded, but Wolf hadn't responded. He'd changed almost beyond recognition from the firm, compassionate friend she'd turned to in every personal emergency. He'd become quiet, withdrawn, spending his days poring over old books, shutting himself away from his wife and daughter. The momentary resurgence of life that they'd all noticed in Saint-Aubin, when they'd thought he was healing, had dwindled down and died. Marisa wept, furiously and piteously, seeking Lily out with nervous frenzy. 'I can't go on,' she said. 'It's as if I'm all alone, only much worse. He's here . . . yet he's not here at all. Sometimes, Lily – oh, God! I'm so ashamed! – sometimes I find myself

477

wishing for the days when I'd spend all my time wanting to be with him again ... the days when he and Mama were still in Vienna. Because then, I could live on my memories, whereas now ... I have only the fearsome present.'

But for the moment, the Steiners were still safe. Mina had done her best to adjust, but her life was behind her, in another land, with a man she'd stopped hoping to see again. She functioned, but that was all. With their Austrian papers, all slashed with the big red *J*, they continued to be seen around the city, as if Paris had not been full of those same Nazis who had broken into their home on the Schwindgasse, and sent Isaac Steiner to his death. 'You've got to make Eliane and David send you an affidavit from America,' Lily pleaded with her friend. 'But for that, you'd have to find a way to the Free Zone, to communicate with them.'

Marisa's small hands fluttered in the air. 'I've tried to convince Wolf. But he says he won't go, that the Americans turned him away once, and he won't risk going on a ship another time, and perhaps being sent back to Austria.'

It had become impossible to communicate from the Occupied Zone to most foreign countries. If one was in touch with a special courier, or with a consul, clandestine messages could be delivered. But for a Jew without proper contacts, relatives outside the Reich might as well have been dead. And even between the two zones in France itself, communication was heavily censored. One was only permitted to send special cards with preprinted questions, which one then had the right to fill in as briefly as possible. This constituted the only system of mail now available, though the Free Zone had no problems communicating abroad.

The Germans had taken over French industry and its treasury, and were buying foodstuffs with French money, so that there was now a serious food shortage all over

478

France, but especially in the capital. For those who could work with the black market, some luxuries were still available. But the others had to survive on ration cards, and queue up at dawn to obtain whatever products had been left over from the Germans.

There were different types of ration cards. The bread cards were divided into tiny squares bearing the thirty or thirty-one dates of the month. When a person bought some bread, the cashier of the bakery cut out one small square, and at the end of the day, had to line up all the small squares she had cut out, and paste them on special sheets of paper which she had to bring to the city hall.

There were food ration cards divided into the same little squares, but these were numbered consecutively and went to forty. With these cards, which were also dispensed each month, one could obtain meat (48 grams of boneless, or 62 grams with bone per week); dry foodstuffs, wine (one bottle per month), paraffin (1 litre per month), coal (145 kilos per month), shoe coupons (one pair per year), tea (almost 14 grams per month), and eggs (one or two a month). If one saved four coupons of a certain type, one could purchase a dish; with all the coupons marked for textiles, accumulated over five or six cards, a dress or a coat; with a single textile coupon, one handkerchief.

There were six card-categories: *E (Enfants)* for babies up to three years of age who received milk, flour, and rice, but no wine or meat; *J (Jeunes) 1*, for older children from three to seven; *J2*, from seven to twelve. *J3*, from twelve to twenty, was the most interesting one, for it was between these ages that human beings developed, needing good nutrition. The *J3s* possessed some advantages: they could receive one cup of milk a day, and two eggs a month.

At the rate of one egg per Frenchman a month, the Food Ministry distributed forty million eggs, which were most difficult to obtain; for the Germans, figuring that a hen laid once every other day, purchased ahead of time all the eggs that would be laid per week, leaving nothing for the farmers to consume, or to send to town.

Then came the *A* cards for adults, from twenty to sixty, and finally the *Vs (Vieux)*, the senior citizens from whom certain products were subtracted and others added, such as a larger quantity of sugar, jam, and so forth.

At the markets, vegetables were sold without cards, but the vendors rationed their customers themselves in order to be able to serve more of them. And they knew tricks. Leeks were weighed wet and with mud still clinging to them, which meant that when one returned home, and washed them, one was left with half the weight for which one had paid. Carrots were weighed with their tops, and then the greengrocer would slice them off to feed to rabbits. Most often, these too would be sold embedded in clumps of moist earth. The cupidity of the vendors respected few boundaries.

The Germans forbade anyone from being on the street before five in the morning. Anyone not in Nazi military garb found outside before this, was instantly arrested. The stores opened at nine, but they possessed only a limited amount of merchandise. One had to be among the first sixty in the queue to be sure of obtaining something. The queues began early, in the midst of the blackout. Each was afraid that others would come ahead of him or her.

Lily didn't dare go out before five, but two minutes before, she was downstairs near the entrance to the *pension*, the bolt drawn back and ready to go, the young chambermaid Léone at her side. At the first sound of five on a nearby church bell, they would bound out into the cold and the pitch-darkness. They had their shopping bags, their wallets, and the ration cards of everybody for whom they were buying. Mark had found Lily a pair of wooden clogs, for the cold ground froze the soles of her feet, and this way they were more insulated.

In the dark, they couldn't walk fast. They had to feel for

the kerbstones, and hope that the moon's rays would help them along the way. Positioned so centrally, the markets were far. They would reach the bakery queue, join it, and instantly others would follow. Each minute was precious. Five extra people ahead of one could mean no food. Frozen, these people waited silently for the daylight to come. By seven the sky would be clear and half the waiting would be over.

Being out in the daylight, one could see ahead and behind. If they were forty-eighth or -ninth, it was very good; but if sixty-ninth or even seventy-second, they could hardly risk leaving. There might have been a portion left that they would miss if they deserted the queue. But, once in the open light, people began to speak, recognizing friends and neighbours. Léone, who had worked for Madame Antiquet since she'd been sixteen, often saw maids from other hotels whom she knew, and would say to Lily: 'Hold my place, please, Madame la Princesse. I want to go and talk to Estelle.' And she would dart away for five minutes, returning bright and rosy-cheeked.

Sometimes those who had gone to chat with their friends would try to cheat, returning a few places ahead of where they belonged. And then there was always a lot of shouting. Lily enjoyed these small scandals; to her, they provided a diversion that helped to while the time away.

People were allowed to replace tired members of their families, and sometimes Madame Antiquet came at seven to relieve Lily or Léone. Other stores too opened at nine, but some, like the dairy where one could obtain 14 grams of butter and cheese per person, were not open every day; and the fish market delivered without taking coupons, but only according to the number of cards, for fish, too, was rationed.

Only in front of the bakery did the queue begin at five. The other stores formed queues around seven. But if one waited to buy one's bread before queuing up for milk, one could be certain of reaching the dairy too late, after two hundred other people, and of finding nothing left. Lily and Léone discovered an unwritten law of the jungle that allowed them to stay awhile in one line and then queue in another, asking the person in front to save their places for them before returning to the first queue after a quarter of an hour or so. If they started to queue up for milk before eight, and then had to get back into the bread queue, by the time they had been given bread, their turn would have come and gone at the dairy. The trick, therefore, was to know just when to start the second queue.

Finally, three or four minutes before nine o'clock, a salesboy would go out from the back door of the bakery, open the iron curtain that closed the front entrance and the other that shut out the display window, and, stationing himself by the front door, would let in ten people whom he carefully counted, closing the door behind them and remaining on guard.

But the main line did not diminish by ten; while it continued to spread out to the left of the pavement, another queue was forming, with just fifteen to twenty people. These were the 'priority cases'. Pregnant women, and those with small babies whom no one else could watch, were able to obtain official certificates. In the beginning, they had to be served before anyone from the main line; but after a few months, this created such an uproar that a compromise was thought up: for every priority case, two people from the main line were let in. And so, in five or six admissions of ten, no one was left from the priority queue. Somehow, this way was considered fair for everybody, and became a practice at all the stores.

After a few weeks of frantic scrambling for places, Lily suggested to Léone that they stand in line for each other, alternating days at the bread queue. With blessed relief, Lily would allow herself to sleep till six on the mornings when Léone stood at the bakery. Léone bought for Madame

482

Antiquet, the handyman, Gustave, and two or three elderly boarders; Lily bought for herself and her two children.

Queuing for food took up her entire morning, and after that, she gave a few piano lessons around town to augment her income. Then, around four each afternoon, she looked by the apartment Boulevard Exelmans to check up on her parents. The young maid who worked for them bought them their rations, but Lily liked to assure herself personally that all was properly taken care of for Claire and Jacques. More and more, she felt anxious about their thin disguise as Monsieur and Madame Jacques Walton, reminding herself of how secure the Steiners had felt in Vienna until the very moment of the *Anschluss*.

The Steiners gave her more concern than anyone. She met Marisa frequently in town, and, braving her own dark, secret fear, tried to go to the Ritz once a week to visit Wolf. Yet, try as she might, every time she went, her heart would hammer inside her chest, and her tongue would go curiously dry. It was as though Wolf, who was more a brother to her than Claude had ever been, was attempting to bait the Nazis with his presence in Paris's most luxurious hotel. She found excuses to postpone her visits, for, every time a German officer's admiring glance casually fell on her tall figure in the street, she wondered if he was reading 'Jewess' into her almond-shaped brown eyes and her light copper complexion.

During these strange days of the Nazi occupation, Lily had come to feel self-conscious about her appearance. She walked with her head hung forward, averting her eyes from those around her. Jews were like skunks to the average pro-Vichy Frenchman: they emitted their own disgusting odour. She was terrified of being found out, while, at the same time, her innate sense of honour made her ashamed of her continued efforts at dissimulation.

All around her, everything was changed. Even the young people existed on tenterhooks, their nerves rubbed raw.

Nick had renewed his friendship with Pierre Rublon, who, before, had been in the class ahead of his and now was in the same one. The Rublons lived in an enclave of protected vine-covered houses behind a wrought-iron gate that faced onto small, neat Rue de la Pompe. Pierre's sister Jacqueline was in Kyra's class at the Lycée des Jeunes Filles, and so it had seemed perfectly normal for the four young people to be thrown together frequently. But now, in the autumn, Pierre became less reserved and began to walk Kyra home from school, and to appear at the Pension Lord-Byron when he knew that Nick would be absent.

Because of the rationing of food, he never stayed to dinner. But frequently, when Lily returned from Boulevard Exelmans, she would find a note from her daughter that she and Pierre had gone out for a walk. She knew, then, not to expect her home till dark. Kyra had never been a willing student, and now she was neglecting her books to spend time with Pierre. Yet Lily hesitated to reproach her. Her heart pinched at the image of the two young people, ambling through the streets of Paris with nowhere to go, their hearts and minds on fire, with each other and with the events around them.

Pierre spoke to Kyra at length about de Gaulle, just as Nick had in Arès. They would sit, hand in hand, on the parapet that lined the Seine, and watch it idle by them in lazy splendour. Her green eyes burned into his pleasant, freckled face, and she would breathe his words into her soul, accepting them for being heroic and grand. 'If there hadn't been a war,' she asked him one day, 'would you still have wanted to be with me?'

He reached for her cleft chin, and ran his fingers over her cheeks. 'You're the only girl I've ever loved,' he answered simply.

And then the intensity grew too strong, and they both had to look away, afraid of each other and of themselves.

'What will your father say when you go to London?' she asked, abruptly changing the subject.

'He's never encouraged me to go, but he'll be glad. In his heart, he's all for what de Gaulle is doing.'

'But he hasn't the courage to face his own feelings.'

They sat staring at each other, understanding all. 'He's like my grandmother,' she remarked softly. 'All her life, she was afraid to admit she was a Jew. And now . . . it's too late.'

'Thank God she never did,' he said with uncommon bitterness. And then they rose, as in common accord, and laced their arms around each other. She wondered how much longer he would be here to spend time with, yet in the same moment, understood that he had to do what his conscience dictated.

She felt strangely adult, loving a man. Because in her mind, the muscular, blond Pierre, now seventeen, was without doubt a man. He was going to find a way to England, to join the Free French movement. None of her friends at school could boast of such a love. She wanted it to last and last between them . . . but also, willed him to leave quickly, that he might come back a hero all the sooner.

She rarely expressed her feelings to her family. They *knew*. Nobody pried, and Lily was unusually understanding about Kyra's lack of discipline in her school work. She was so different from Nick, who, even now, spent all his evenings poring over textbooks in readiness to pass his final *bac* at the end of the school year. Pierre was, like her, a casual student. He thought only of de Gaulle and of freeing his country.

'Will you tell them when you leave?' she asked him one evening.

'My parents? I'll tell them when everything's set, just before I go. But I'll tell *you* in plenty of time.'

'And . . . before you go . . .' The words hovered in the

cool breeze between them. He found her so beautiful, so exquisitely, extraordinarily beautiful, that it did not matter that she wasn't yet fifteen, two months younger than his sister. He laced his fingers through hers, playing with them. 'Don't you *want* to, Pierre?'

He smiled, gently. 'I do and I don't. I love you, Kyra. I don't want to do something that might not be right.'

'What do you want to do about us?' she persisted.

'I want to go to England, and help win France back for the French. And when I come back, I want to marry you.'

It was the first time she had heard him mouth the words. She took them into her body like an electric shock that startled and quickened her. Then she threw her arms around his neck, burying her face against his neck. 'Oh, Pierre, Pierre!'

His hand caressing the silken strands of her hair soothed her, calmed her. 'We're both a little crazy,' he said softly.

'But I'll wait for you. And . . . I want . . .'

He drew away, regarding her seriously. 'I don't want to hurt you,' he told her. 'And if we make love, it will hurt us both so much more when we're apart.'

'And Trotti and Nick? I wonder if they kiss each other,' Kyra asked.

'Nick's discreet, and so am I. We've never discussed it. But I'm sure his plans don't include her.'

'Why not?'

'Because Nick's a serious fellow. He's got his own plans brewing, which have nothing whatsoever to do with any girl.' Suddenly he turned away, hiding his shame. Without meaning to, prodded on by this quixotic, thrilling girl, he'd spilled his best friend's confidences, revealing a whole Pandora's box of problems he'd had no right to disclose.

She was staring at him, her wide eyes full of questioning, fearful light. 'What plans, Pierre?'

'Oh, his studies and all. You know . . . "man talk".' He

486

smiled self-deprecatingly, shrugging lightly. He felt deeply sorry for what he had said.

'You're lying. Pierre: Nicky's going with you, isn't he? To London?'

Now he was able to answer truthfully. 'No. Don't forget, Kyra. One Jewish grandparent is enough to get a person labelled a Jew. Who knows who might give him away? It wouldn't do for him to try to get across the Channel. If caught, he'd probably be tortured. And he's a year younger than I am. The Free French wouldn't accept him.'

She felt oddly reassured. It was one thing for Pierre to go – Pierre who was well connected and strong, whom she would one day marry, who would always be there to protect her – and quite another for her brother to go. It might be romantic to have a lover in the resistance movement, but a brother was something different. A brother couldn't always stand alone. Her thoughts were confused, and she felt a point of acute misery.

'Come on,' he whispered, 'your mother will be getting worried. It's time to go home.'

The boy stood, irresolute, looking beyond the arched passage into the well-groomed victory garden where once, trim rose bushes had drooped themselves around slender poles. The white granite mansion loomed enormous to him, like the palace it had been built to be. Yet he had come on a mission, and he had to plunge forward.

He crossed to the immense black door, and rang the bell. His heart fluttered inside him. He wondered briefly about the victory garden. Everybody *knew* that she was a *collabo*, a detested German collaborator. He could feel revulsion passing through him, and also naked fear. The *collabos* turned in more Jews than the Gestapo these days. Since it had become patently obvious that the Germans had failed in their attempt to break the British through their repeated bombings, the occupiers had seemed infinitely less placid. Vicious stories were propagated about new atrocities each day, and it was well known that some of the best German agents were Russian citizens working for the Soviet Consulate.

The door swung silently open, and the young man found himself nose to nose with a slender black man whose head had been tightly wrapped in a turban of cloth of gold. 'Yes?' he asked, in an unctuous, whispering tone.

'I'd like to see Madame Dalbret. My name is Nicolas Brasilov.'

The dark man raised one thin, arched brow, and smiled. 'Prince Mikhail's . . . son?'

Nick felt himself colour. 'Yes. Madame Dalbret has never met me, but it's important that I talk with her. I won't take up much of her time.'

'Do come in.' Nick stepped into the oddest decor he had ever encountered, or dreamed of encountering, in France. A cloying scent of incense pervaded the air, and he was stopped by a life-size Buddha exhaling water into a scalloped shell filled with goldfish. He was elaborately ushered into a Chinese living room three steps below the entrance hall, and as he raised his head, a dazzling composition of tiny fitted mirrors blinded him. The entire ceiling, dome-shaped like a church cupola, was encrusted with these mirrors where he saw himself, lean and long and conservative in his brown suit, reflected behind the black manservant.

'Madame will be with you in a moment,' he was told, and then he was alone in the strange room, on a low settee adorned with at least twelve small velvet cushions, each of a different bright colour. Coromandel screens faced him, and paintings on shimmering silks in lacquered frames. He wondered if he'd made a big mistake, coming here, and puzzled once again over his father's past. He couldn't for the life of him picture his mother in a house like this.

So engrossed was he in his own thoughts that he failed

to hear the tiny footsteps on the thick, plush Persian carpet. But the rich, throaty voice roused him blushing to his feet. 'Hello there,' she said. 'Welcome to my humble home. And tell me if you like the effect. Grotesque, isn't it?'

He'd seen her on stage several times, but had never realized how small she was. Her face was like Kyra's, heart-shaped, and round blue eyes like aquamarines dominated it. Her mouth was sensual and bright red, matching a cap of curls that surrounded that elfin face, rendering it unexpectedly vulnerable. She was wearing an Indian sari of turquoise woven with silver, and a huge silver and turquoise pendant drooped into her cleavage. The hand she extended was tiny and delicate, its Chinese-red nails perfectly tended into squared-off ovals.

Intensely embarrassed, he took the hand and brought it to his lips. He'd already forgotten his fears and his disgust at her reputation as a *collabo*. He was finding himself in the same position as all the men who had ever met Varvara Trubetskaya. Young, middle-aged, or old, they had inevitably felt the adrenalin begin to pump furiously through their systems.

She was a living legend, besides being the most incredible woman Nick had ever seen. 'Well?' she pressed, smiling. 'Admit it, Nicolas. It's grotesque. But I like it.'

And suddenly he could visualize his father here, too. There'd been in Misha Brasilov an untamed quality that he had seldom brought home, but that, in the right sort of atmosphere, might have flourished wildly.

Without waiting for his answer, she had curled into a lacquered armchair and draped her arm over its edge. 'Yes,' she said, solemnly. 'You're what I expected. Not at all like Misha, and exactly like your mother. You're a Frenchman.'

'These days, madame, I'm not certain whether that's an advantage or not. Our poor country. . .'

She cut him off peremptorily. 'Look, Nicolas, please

understand me. It does no good to speak around the subject, over and over. Old Marshal Pétain's half lost his marbles, and Laval has persuaded half of France that the Nazis are less to be feared than the sons of *perfide Albion*. I became a naturalized citizen ten years ago, but you may have heard that all the naturalizations that were performed after '27 are now being looked into. I have no wish to offend the ruling Boche. My idea is to smile broadly at them, in the hope that they . . . and the Vichy government . . . will continue to allow me to live as I please.'

'In other words,' he shot back, anger suffusing his cheeks with crimson, 'honour is of no matter to you — just expediency!'

She simply raised her brows. '*Honestly*, Nicolas. I was looking forward to this little meeting, but now . . . you disappoint me.' She held one nail up to the light, and peered at it. 'A Brasilov shouldn't mouth clichés. Especially without knowing all the facts.' Suddenly she regarded him with a look that pierced right through him, and he saw a blue vein throb in her neck. 'I lived through one revolution. I lost everything I had! And I had little then, compared to now. I was a wealthy Muscovite matron, but not a personality. Here, I don't have to depend on any man to keep me. I'm *Jeanne Dalbret!*' Her nostrils quivered slightly, and she took a deep gulp of air. 'But even Jeanne Dalbret, without an audience, is *nothing*. And I can't survive being just another nothing.'

'My mother has a great talent, though no one knows about it and she's poor as a churchmouse. But she survives on her sense of loyalty and decency.'

'And who are you to tell me I've no decency?' She stood up now, powerful in her fury. He remembered why he'd come, and rose too. Conversations with Pierre, with Mark, who could no longer send his stories in because the Germans had censored all newspapers, reverberated through his head. He answered, evenly, keeping his own anger well controlled, the way his mother did: 'Madame, I'm sorry I intruded. I meant no offence. I came because I had a personal problem, and thought you might be the single person in Paris to be able to help me.'

She held her hands up to the sides of her face, ran her fingers through her red curls, her face all at once lined and haggard. He saw despair in those small, sharp features, and stood stock still with surprise. He'd thought her the epitome of poise and savoir-faire, the kind of woman who would always be in control, never dominated by people or events. Now he saw a distraught woman of fifty-five who looked damned good for her age, but not the glamour queen he had encountered moments ago. He found himself liking her, and not yet understanding why.

'*How* do you suppose I could help you?' she asked, a sarcastic bite to her voice. 'Do you have dreams of becoming a *jeune premier?*'

His brown eyes, almond-shaped like Lily's, rested on her with an intense, unabashed honesty. He wasn't going to play games with her. 'Madame,' he said. 'You are the only one who knows where to contact my father, in New York.'

It was her turn to blink back her amazement. 'You want to find Misha? *Now?* Why, for God's sake? He's been gone three years!'

'Believe me, it's not because I miss him.' Now the brown eyes were unreadable, guarded. He's been badly wounded, she thought, and the scars are still hurting. 'It's for a purely practical reason. The Nazis are beginning to take young men of seventeen into Germany, forcing them into labour camps to manufacture arms for the Reich. To put it bluntly, *I'd rather die.* I can't, like you, envisage a peaceful coexistence. And so, since my seventeenth birthday is next year . . . I've decided that the only way out is to go to the Free Zone, and from there, to the United States. I need my father to send an affidavit for my visa to the American Consulate in Nice.'

She breathed in and out, and wet her lips. 'That's quite a plan. But tell me, my patriotic young Galahad: I thought most of your contemporaries were thinking of joining the Resistance, or de Gaulle directly – not of running as fast as their legs could carry them into another land.'

The blow was full force but he withstood it. Again she noted, and was impressed by, the composure of his oval face. 'If I could do so without implicating my family, I'd have left already,' he replied. 'But ... I'm Jewish. My father doesn't know this to this day. Most people don't know, and our family didn't register at the city hall. I don't want to run any risks that would later alert the Germans to my mother and sister. If I can leave, quietly, for Nice, and from there for the United States, the Boche won't even know I'm gone. In the Resistance, I'd be found out, sooner or later, and reprisals might occur.'

Very softly, she murmured: 'I'd heard about it, Nicolas. There are some who like to speculate on the racial origins of illustrious people. Your mother, my dear, as poor as she may be, was in her youth a luminary, and much talked about. She's still the Princess Brasilova. And many envied her, and still do.'

'Envy my mother? She gives piano lessons to subsist, and leads a life a dog would spit on! Why would anyone envy her?'

'Because she was once a fairy princess, with seven servants and wardrobes full of elegant clothes. And because she still is one of the most radiant beauties of Paris.'

'Mama's beautiful, but who's there to notice? Her dresses are old, and she's too thin, and all her rich friends have forgotten her.'

'Still, Nick. And some say that she's Jewish. I personally never cared to pry into the religion of others. Jews, Moslems, Catholics – who gives a damn? Yet today, Nick, a lot of people do. They'll brand others "Jews" just to make sure nobody will brand *them* as "Jews". People want to save their own skins. And me too.'

'But . . . who could have told you this?' he demanded, perplexed and horrified. 'I thought *nobody* knew!'

'Nobody "knows", exactly. But some suppose. Your step-grandfather is one, that's for certain. People have looked into that. And so questions are being asked about your grandmother.'

He decided not to press the issue, but his earlier resolve seemed shattered. Varvara Trubetskaya touched his hand in a sudden gesture of deep compassion. 'It's all right,' she said. 'I told you: your mother's the Princess Brasilova. She's still married to one of the world's most vituperative anti-Semites. Misha's hatred is her strongest shield, odd as this may seem. And you can't blame your father. He came from an anti-Semitic father, and an anti-Semitic country. He only reflected the culture he was born into.'

'So we may as well forgive the Nazis, too. They also are mere reflections of Hitler's dictates and standards.'

She smiled at his mordant tone. 'I'll write to Misha,' she declared. 'I'm friends with enough influential people that the letter will be sure to leave posthaste, by diplomatic pouch to Vichy, and then by air to New York. And I'll do better yet. I'll provide you with an *Ausweis*, to allow you to move from the Occupied to the Free Zone. I have a friend at the *Kommandantur*.'

His lips parted, but she cut him off before he had a chance to answer her. 'You may have to wait as long as a year in Nice, or Marseilles, wherever you decide to go. Visas take time, you know.' She started to continue, then stopped, and abruptly decided to plunge in again. 'You see,' she murmured, 'how useful it can be not to offend the Germans?'

And then, with a graceful movement of her tousled head, she gestured that the interview had come to an end. 'I hope,' she said, 'that you'll try to work things out with Misha. He needs you, you know.'

In early December 1940, Nick left Paris with two suitcases and a small bag, and the all-important *Ausweis* from Varvara, which was needed to cross the border from Occupied to Free France. He carried in his wallet five thousand francs from Jacques, which were supposed to last him the year they surmised it would take to obtain his visa of entry into the United States. His train journey was uneventful, and he arrived in Nice well rested and only a little saddened by his separation from his family. The way he looked at it, as soon as he was established in New York, he would send for all of them.

The winter on the Riviera was mild, and he felt curiously free and adult, on his own in a strange city. He knew exactly what had to be done. First, he rented a small room in a boarding-house, and then registered himself at the lycée. In the summer, he would be passing his final *baccalauréat*, and he felt that with this achievement to his name, life would be infinitely easier in the United States. The *bac* was well respected all over the world.

Yet, as the December days wore on, a gloom set upon him. It hit him all at once that he was cut off from the whole world. Even the mockery of correspondence that was permitted between the two zones took ten days, and an ache formed in his chest for his mother and sister, whose cards he anxiously awaited. He knew absolutely no one in Nice, and even at the lycée, his companions had already formed and established friendships. They looked at him with a curiosity mingled with sympathy, and once in a while someone would invite him to lunch on a Thursday, and he would be forced to undergo yet another polite but unrelenting interrogation concerning his family: Who were they? What did they do? Why was he alone? He longed then to escape once more to his small room, where at least he could dwell in peace without facing his fears.

Because, of course, he *was* afraid. He wondered whether his father, that strange enigma of a man, would send him the affidavit.

Did Nick *want* to see his father again? Sometimes, closing his schoolbooks, he would withdraw the ruby and gold cuff links from their box, and caress them tenderly. Yes, Misha had loved him; yet that hadn't prevented him from deserting all of them. Nick would feel the anger burn anew, his heart pressing upward and out with the swelling of bitter resentment. I hate the man, he'd think, shaken by the power of his own emotions. But he had no other choice. Sooner or later, the Gestapo would come after him to send him to Germany, and it made more sense to swallow his pride and go to Misha.

Anyway, he'd think, covering his slender young body with the harsh, bleached sheet from the boarding-house: I won't have to stay with him. I'll find a job, and take care of myself, and send for Kyra, Mama, and my grandparents.

How easy everything seemed, if he could only get to New York! The worst thing was the clawing loneliness. But at the end of December, the affidavit arrived, eclipsing the news of the moment in the highest circles of Vichy politics. Marshal Pétain, whose collaboration with the Germans had been one of resignation, had found himself once too often gainsaying Pierre Laval's enthusiastic embrace of their Nazi victors, and had, on 13 December, dismissed his vice-premier, whom he had never liked, going so far as to place him under house arrest in his property of Châteldon. But Hitler's Ambassador Abetz had demanded Laval's release, and had refused to acknowledge the new foreign minister, Pierre-Étienne Flandin . . . pointedly ignoring his presence in the Cabinet. For two weeks now, newspapers had revealed more than the customary censorship had allowed, and France was speculating about Germany's increased intervention in Vichy politics. But Nick,

495

normally the first to rush to the radio or to devour a tabloid, had still not digested this series of events. For him, an immense relief had lifted the tension with which he had been living: his father had not rejected him, and this was tantamount to having a foot on the gangplank to a vessel that would bear him safe and sound to a continent where he could stop being afraid.

All that he needed was to go to the American Consulate in Nice, show his affidavit and his new passport, and sign the necessary papers to apply for a visa. Then he would have to wait. And so, one December morning, he took himself there instead of to school, and asked what he had to do. The consul was the son of Sholem Asch, the Polish-American writer who wrote in Yiddish. Nick was surprised to see him in person, checking up on his employees. Here was a known Jew, just paces from the Nazis, operating as if he were merely going through the customary steps of his everyday work. Nick was duly awed.

A young woman with a bun pressed to the back of her skull said to him: 'We'll need your birth certificate, monsieur . . . Prince Brasilov. And then we can proceed, and forward these papers to the embassy in Vichy. Usually, for a French citizen, a visa takes three months, but the way things are right now . . .'

Nick nodded, still trying to follow the consul's movements in a small room to the right of where he himself was standing. He felt himself colour; it had been so long since anyone had called him 'Prince' that the title felt uncomfortable on his shoulders. Then the sense of what she was telling him penetrated. His *birth certificate?*

Nick tried to itemize, in his head, all the things he had brought with him to Nice. Mechanically, he laid out his identification card, his French passport, and some extra photographs on the counter, but his heart was pounding erratically. 'I don't think my mother gave it to me,' he said. 'In fact . . . the only time I've ever needed it was to obtain this passport. We thought it would be sufficient.'

The young woman's mouth became a thin line. 'We can't proceed without the birth certificate,' she said brusquely. 'Anyone can forge another person's identification card, and even his passport. We need the authorization of both the French and the German governments in order to issue someone a visa.'

All at once, as the bottom seemed to be falling out of the floor where he was standing, Nick had a dizzying sensation of why Consul Asch was able to walk around fearlessly. The Americans were protected by an inviolable wall that separated them from the rest of the world. He understood then how it was that Wolf Steiner's ship of immigrants had been casually turned away. Perhaps they, too, had left their birth certificates behind. A quick anger sweeping through him, he left the building, his feet making quick, clattering sounds on the outer steps.

What to do? Because of the censored nature of communication between the two zones, he would not be able to ask his mother to send the document. Time was of the essence if he wanted to file his papers rapidly. He'd simply have to tempt fate and return to Paris – without the benefit of an *Ausweis*. He'd come all this way for nothing!

There was no other choice. Quickly, without warning anyone at the *pension*, he packed a few things into a small bag, and went to the train station. He was able to purchase a ticket for Châteauroux, near the border to the Occupied Zone, and took his seat in a stuffy third-class compartment. Across from him, a rotund, middle-aged man sat picking his teeth. 'Morning,' he told Nick cheerfully. 'My name's Bagnard – Jean-Marie to the ladies.'

Politely, Nick nodded. They were the only ones in the compartment, and he felt vaguely ill at ease under the scrutiny of this coarse man, whom under normal circumstances he might never have encountered. Bagnard persisted. 'What're you doing here, all alone? Where're you going?'

Briefly, Nick looked up. 'To Châteauroux,' he replied.

'Me, I'm on my way to Paris. I've been gone long enough.'

Nick realized that he was being trapped into conversation. The man continued, winking: 'I've been gone from my business too long. Boches or no Boches, a working man has his job to do and his pay to collect.'

Inwardly sighing, Nick closed his book and laid it on his lap. 'You're not interested,' Bagnard inquired, 'to find out what kind of work I'm in? But then, you're such a refined sort, you might just thumb your nose at me.'

'I hope I'll never do that to any man,' Nick countered, blushing.

The man relaxed, lit a cigarette, and, sitting back on the hard wooden seat, shifted his weight and declared: 'Well, then, that's a good sign! I take care of girls.'

Nick blinked. 'I'm sorry. I didn't catch that.'

'Perhaps you're too young and too clean to understand me. I work a stable of girls in Clichy. Or at least, I used to. Got caught by the war in my mother's house, on the coast. Only now, I'm getting hungry for the old life, for the hard sound of the coins against my hip pocket.'

Nick felt at a loss for words. Not unkindly, Bagnard asked: 'Ever done it with a girl? Listen, if you're in the mood, I'll give you a card. And if ever you're in Paris, come to see me. I'll let you have a turn on the house.'

All at once, Nick burst into laughter. The tension that had been crippling his stomach since his visit to the United States Consulate gave way, and he found himself helplessly gasping for air. He'd left Paris with hardly a farewell to Trotti, the girl he'd cared for the most in his life, because too many essentials of survival had crowded his brain; he hadn't allowed himself to think of her too much in the three weeks since he'd arrived in Nice, in order not to be distracted from his course of action by heart-tugging reminders of their romance. And now, in the midst of a clandestine journey home, he was being offered a prostitute by a fellow traveller to whom he'd lied about his destination. The irony of his last month was hitting him fully.

'Hey!' Bagnard was protesting. 'My girls ain't nothing to make jokes about!'

For a reason he would never comprehend, Nick turned to the small man and said, very gently: 'I'm not laughing at you, Monsieur Bagnard. I'm laughing because I'm afraid, and can't hold it in any longer.'

The pimp stubbed his cigarette out and stared at the young man, a long and hard stare that took in his fine features, his dark eyes, his excellent posture. 'Yes,' he murmured. 'Of course you'd be scared. You're going to Paris, too, aren't you?'

Nick nodded. 'I don't have an *Ausweis*.'

'I'm not going to ask you why you're going. But me too – I don't have one, either. So I'll tell you what: just before Châteauroux, when the train slows down, we're going to jump out and find our own way across the border. Then we'll just take the first train out of the station. The hitch will be to get around the frontier guards.'

Somehow, it seemed less formidable a plan because there were two of them now, and because the middle-aged pimp was familiar with the ways of the underworld. Nick was glad that he hadn't shown his dismay, and that he'd blurted out his frightened confession. Bagnard was getting out a pack of cards, and saying: 'Know how to play poker? It helps to pass the time away.'

As the train wound slowly northward, the third-class compartment began to fill, and Bagnard and Nick, concentrating on endless poker games, tried to keep themselves apart from the noise and conversations that sprouted up around them. Nick found that his companion possessed a smart street sense that he himself, from lack of experience, had never developed; and, though his profession was still a mind-stopper to the sixteen-year-old boy, Nick had to admit that he liked Bagnard. The older man, without an excess of verbiage, had somehow conveyed his own self-confidence to Nick.

The train took three days before reaching the Department of Indre, of which the capital was Châteauroux, set inside a vast, well-tended forest. During stops for sandwiches and coffee, at various stations along the way, all of which looked the same to the young man, Bagnard extracted his family background from him. Nick, reticent at first, had wanted to change the subject. But the little pimp had pressed. 'Brasilov? *Brasilov?* That name's familiar. It sure doesn't sound French, though!'

Nick had been forced to tell him it was a Russian name, and then the surmises had started all over again. White Russian, or Red? Nick had plunged in, explaining that he was going to New York to join his father, but that his mother and sister were in Paris. He felt a huge wave of relief when the stationmaster had announced the need to climb back on board. 'You sure don't like to talk about your people,' Bagnard had grumbled. 'And mighty fine people they seem, from the little you've told me.'

Then, steepling his long, slender fingers, Nick had replied: 'You're a nice man, Jean-Marie. I don't know what your girls think of you, but I like you. So you see, clichés can be wrong. If not all men of your profession are thieves and abusers, then maybe you can understand that having a title of nobility doesn't always make a man noble.'

'You're speaking of your father?'

All at once deeply ashamed to have betrayed his parent, Nick shrugged impatiently. 'Let's just not discuss our family,' he told the other.

After that, they played silently, and over their *ersatz* coffee, spoke of Pétain, Laval, and the sights and sounds

500

of Paris. Bagnard adored Jeanne Dalbret, and his eyes protruded when Nick mentioned knowing her. To make up for his earlier aloofness, the young man meticulously described her house, its decoration, and the sinuous, exotic Dragi. He did not tell Bagnard of his family's connection to the *comédienne*.

In the afternoon of the third day, the train passed into a thick, emerald-green forest, and Bagnard, drawing out his packet of Gauloises, held a cigarette out to his companion. 'Well, Nicky boy,' he said, with his street-wise bravado: 'Let's take a breather in the corridor for a few smokes.'

Too late, Nicolas realized that it was time to jump, and that his small bag was still on the ledge above his seat in the compartment. Bagnard was still offering him a cigarette. 'One last drag?'

'I don't smoke, thanks.'

Bagnard shrugged. Nick felt incredibly young, naïve, and unworldly, but he had never learned to dissimulate in order to give himself a veneer of sophistication.

'Now,' Bagnard was saying, tersely. 'We're getting ready to pull into Châteauroux, and the train's going to slow down.'

Without a word, Nick followed him. Bagnard opened the door connecting two cars, and they stood in the whipping wind, watching the wheels below them turning with deafening noise. It seemed to Nick as if the train was slowing down, but imperceptibly, so that he thought he was imagining it. But the small pimp looked at him, nodded, and suddenly hurled himself, curling into a small ball, to the side of the embankment. Nick stood staring down at the turning wheels, paralysed.

Then, out of the nightmare, he heard the laughing voice of a woman. People were approaching in the corridor, perhaps seeking the dining car, and the imminence of their coming upon him now finally galvanized him into action. Drenched with perspiration, he jumped. remembering in

501

the last instant to curl up like Bagnard so that he would hit the ground with his side. But the blow of the ground hitting up at him was blinding, and as he felt himself rolling down the small hill, his right shoulder and hip shot bolts of sheer agony through every layer of muscle and nerve.

At long last he stopped rolling, and sat up, dazed. Gingerly, he touched his right side, wincing. He was at the foot of some shrubbery, in what appeared to be the forest of Châteauroux. He was, mercifully, still alive. But where was Bagnard?

Nick rose, unsteadily. He could walk, so nothing was broken. Or was it? Perhaps his damned shoulder. Rubbing its tenderness, he began to retrace his steps to where it seemed logical that the small pimp had jumped. But there was no sign of him. Discouraged, Nick entered the forest, thinking to find a way to the border by himself . . . *some* way.

Half an hour later, he had to admit that he was hopelessly lost. Exhausted, he sat down on the cold, winter ground. Above him, white branches laden with snow moved in the wind, dispersing some of the white powder on his head. Suddenly, he heard a voice.

'You all right?' a stranger was asking.

Nick looked up, and saw a tramp. He blinked, amazed. But truly, the variety of man staring back at him could best have been found lying on a bench along the banks of the Seine, or on the cobbled pavement under its ancient bridges, an empty bottle of wine dangling from his hand. He could hardly have ventured to guess at the tramp's age. Dressed like a scarecrow in dark pants and a tattered dark overcoat, his unshaven face and brilliant dark eyes reminded Nick of a dishevelled, modern-day Christ. 'My God,' he said softly. 'Where am I? And – who are you?'

'Arnaud. Arnaud de la Tour du Bellay. But that's a

little beside the point, isn't it now? Etiquette is for better days. You're the pimp's friend?'

Still in shock, his shoulder hurting badly, Nick nodded, scrambling to his feet. 'I didn't think I'd ever find him again,' he said. 'I jumped too late.'

'Well, we're going to cross together: you, me, the pimp, and Richard. Richard's an escaped soldier from the Vichy army. And Bagnard says you want to get to the other side as badly as we do.'

'How did you find him?' Nick asked.

The tramp shrugged. 'It was easy. We saw him trying to get across the border, over there, a quarter of a mile west of here, and we went to warn him about the soldier stationed under the tall birch tree. We've been waiting for the changing of the guard to slip ourselves between the wiring. We'll have a better chance at night.'

And so it was that when night fell, Nicolas Brasilov crossed the border between the Free and the Occupied Zones with a pimp, a tramp from the Paris sewers, and a defecting soldier from the Vichy army. It turned out that Arnaud and Richard had been turned away by a border guard somewhere else in the area, and had decided that this particular stretch of land was the least well guarded, particularly during the change of shifts among the guards.

The next morning, the four boarded a train to Paris, and played four-handed poker for the rest of the journey. By night-time, they'd reached the Gare de Lyons, and Nick parted from his newfound friends with genuine warmth. Bagnard pressed a card on him, reminding him that if he wanted, there'd always be a girl on the house for him.

He took the métro, grateful for its logical, familiar route, letting his head rest on the back of his seat. His mother thought that he was safe in Nice, and would not be expecting him, particularly in this shape, his shoulder swollen and his hip bruised. A slight rustling noise near him roused him, and, before he could properly react, he saw, as the train eased to a stop, a thin man in a nondescript raincoat hurrying through the car and then out the door and onto the platform. The man was holding a worn black wallet. Then a surge of people boarding eclipsed him from Nick's sight, and the next moment, the train began to move again.

His heart thundering, Nick felt for the bulge in his trouser pocket, and realized that his fears were well founded. The thin man had, effortlessly, lifted his wallet while he'd been dozing. Nick sat down again. After all that had happened, he almost didn't care anymore. New York loomed like a mirage in the far distance, unattainable and dim. Now all he wanted was to lie down in a real bed, and to eat something warm and thick.

When he rapped on the door of the Pension Lord-Byron, he'd even forgotten about the food and bed. The cold, icy streets had frozen the soles of his feet, and his ungloved fingers were red and blistered. He couldn't tell which female voice greeted him, nor whose arms supported him into the hallway and onto a bed, or a couch. Fingers pressed at his shoulder, massaged his face. With blessed relief, he sank into unconsciousness, letting slip the single thing he'd kept with him from his travel: Bagnard's card, printed in garish red, with his own scrawled, uneducated writing: *The plumpest, the juiciest, the most depraved – you want it, I've got it for you, old buddy.*

Lily never asked about the card, and Nick's vivid account of his travels edited the part about Bagnard's profession. But he found himself telling a respectful audience composed of his mother, his sister, and Trotti Voizon about the tramp, the escaped soldier, the barbed-wire border, and his own mad jump, over and over until he had tired of repeating himself to answer their multiple questions.

Then Lily and Kyra left him alone with Trotti, and she sat close to him, holding his hand. Her lovely dark eyes shone with her affection, and he felt himself being drawn into them, with the concurrent surge of excitement that pumped through his body whenever she was near him. He was sixteen, she a year older. And so she said, her voice plaintive and eloquent: 'I'd hoped you'd come back. But it isn't for long, is it?'

The excitement bubbled and broke, like champagne bubbles reaching the edge of a glass. He could feel it seeping away, minute by minute. Her eyes were so beautiful, like his mother's, and her heavy breasts lay pressed against his arm, and he could smell her own clean yet special scent, like wild lemons on the tree. Yet the wild, animal passion had dwindled of its own, and as he looked at her, he felt sorrow – for her, for him, for both of them.

'No,' he answered gently. 'I'm going back as soon as I get my new *Ausweis*. I have to get the paperwork started for my visa, in Nice.'

'Madame Dalbret?' she asked, her voice husky.

Turning slightly from those probing eyes, he replied, somewhat crisply: 'Mama went to her. I almost wish she hadn't. I . . . I don't want us to owe her for another favour.'

'Oh, Nicky,' she cried. 'You always take everything so seriously! People *can* help each other, can't they, without having to draw up lists? Madame Dalbret was simply being nice. Can't you just accept this, and let it be?'

He smiled, ruefully. 'I suppose you're right. But then, I've always had a hard time taking things lightly . . . all sorts of things.'

'Don't I know it.'

Their eyes met. 'I wish you'd ask me to wait for you,' she said impulsively.

He sighed. 'Oh, Trotti. I don't know what to say. But . . . it wouldn't be fair. We're both much too young to know what we want . . . or who we'll turn into. You might

505

decide that Nick at twenty-two is not at all the Nick you'd envisaged. It wouldn't make sense to tie you down.'

'You're saying that because of the religion.'

'No. I'm saying that because I just don't know anything at all about the future.'

'But Pierre and Kyra – they made a commitment. And she's much younger than I am.'

He looked at her. She looked back, intensely. 'Trotti, I want us to remember how beautiful it was, and that we loved each other. Please understand . . .'

'. . . that I'm really "not the one?"'

'I wouldn't want to change you. We are who we are. If I wanted you different, I'd have loved someone else – not asked you to change.'

She stared at him, uncomprehending. 'So . . . you're telling me you love me, but it can't work?'

Unexpectedly, he hugged her close to him, letting her thick hair form a soft curtain over the back of his head. And he thought: Let me always remember this, let me always cherish what there was. When he pulled away, he saw that tears had gathered on the edge of her lashes, and he could feel his own, way back, behind his eyeballs.

'Damn it,' he said. 'I wish we didn't have to say goodbye.'

Chapter Twenty-two

In the spring of 1941, Marisa Steiner sat her husband down in their opulent suite at the Ritz and, wringing her delicate, small-boned hands, pleaded with him to leave the country. She was thirty-six, he twelve years her senior; and Mina Steiner was seventy-five, a shadow of her former ebullient self.

'You haven't worked since you arrived here,' Marisa reproved him. 'And Mama wrote that in New York, there are many psychiatrists ... many Jewish refugees, who've set up good practices. We could try to emigrate, like Nick, from Nice or Marseilles.'

Marisa had last heard from her parents days before the French armistice, when all transatlantic mail had effectively been blocked. David and Eliane Robinson had informed their daughter of their move to cosmopolitan New York, where, it appeared, a market for fine French biscuits was thriving. They'd renewed their acquaintanceship with many old friends, such as the Baronesses Lucy and Yvonne de Gunzburg, living in grand style at the Carlyle. The Robinsons had purchased a penthouse on Central Park West, in the best part of Manhattan.

This news, however, was stale by now after eighteen months.

'If you want to go there, through the Free Zone, you can try,' Wolf told her, his patient voice edging slightly. 'But you'll find it a problem to leave Paris, first of all. And then — '

'You know I won't leave you!' Perspiration sprang out

507

under her arms and over her brow, beading out over her upper lip.

'It's not so simple,' he said. 'Look at the problems Nick is having. And he's not known to be a Jew. The Germans will probably give the American Consulate permission for his visa. But what about us? Who would give *us* an *Ausweis*? And with a large, red *J* on our Austrian passports, would they allow us even so far as Nice?'

His logic stilled her, with its irrefutable base of truth. Effectively, they were trapped in Occupied France. A wave of hopelessness enveloped her, and she started to cry. Small sobs wracked her shoulders and she slumped, a diminutive figure of defeat.

In former times, Wolf would have bridged the gap between them in half a second, to hold and comfort her and breathe quiet confidence into her. In Vienna, he'd protected her, his immense strength like a rampart against any outside evil. Yet here she wept, alone, while he gazed at her, immobile. Since his presence on the ship that had floated, unwanted by any free land, almost two years before – since his witnessing of the man Chaim's jump overboard into Cuba's hostile waters – he'd lost the ability to react. Part of him seemed paralysed into inaction.

In front of him lay an old Torah, and a red pencil. He was quietly reading, as was his wont now, oblivious to the presence of his wife and even of his child when she was home, as he underscored passages that appealed to him. He had completely abstracted himself from reality in the here and now of Paris, 1941.

Mina appeared, her back stooped. 'Where is Nanni?' she asked.

Without shame, Marisa raised her tear-filled eyes to her mother-in-law. 'She went to visit Lily and Kyra. I don't want her around, Mama. We don't have a family life anymore, and she can't bear to see Wolf like this!'

Mina smiled. 'Perhaps Isaac will have a talk with him,

dear,' she answered softly. 'Wolf always listens to his father.'

Marisa's lips parted, her face paled. In complete desperation, she turned her back and went into her bedroom, and lay down fully clothed on the bed. There were no tears left to spill.

When the rap on the door came, the Steiners were having breakfast. Even at the Ritz, rations were in effect, and food was scant and unappetizing. Marisa went to open her pink satin robe flowing around her like a regal train, its delicate lace trim emphasizing her tiny elegance. She stepped back, shock piercing to the marrow of her bones, deadening even her fear. In front of her stood two Gestapo officers, their hair closely cropped under their neat caps, their backs ramrod straight.

'Madame Steiner?'

Marisa nodded, speechless.

'We've come for your husband,' one of them said. She wasn't sure which one, because her vision had blurred and they appeared like mirror images of each other.

Wolf was standing up, pushing back his chair, a questioning look on his sad, intelligent face. 'Yes?' he asked softly.

'You are Wolfgang Steiner?'

'I am Dr Steiner, yes. What do you want?'

'We have been ordered to take you. You are an Austrian citizen?'

Nanni, who was eleven, jumped up, spilling some precious milk over the lace tablecloth. She was ready for school, in her trim uniform, her hair neatly plaited. At eleven, she was two inches shorter than her mother, but she gave an impression of sturdiness that was more Steiner than Robinson. Clutching her mother's robe, she pressed against her. 'Why do you want my Papa?'

'It's not your business, little girl.'

509

'I won't go if you don't tell us why,' Wolf said mildly.

'You have no choice. We've been ordered to round up all foreign Jewish lawyers.'

'But my husband isn't a lawyer, he's a psychiatrist,' Marisa explained, relief flooding her. 'Surely you've made a mistake!'

'The Gestapo never makes *mistakes*,' one of the officers countered, sarcasm cutting the air. They had been speaking German, and now the other added: 'In 1930, was your husband not awarded an honorary law degree from the University of Heidelberg?' A thin smile creased his face, but his eyes were cold.

Marisa started to say something, outrage and terror blocking each other in her mind and body. She was trembling like a leaf. 'You can't take my Papa!' Nanni was crying. Marisa tried to restrain her, tightening her fingers around the little girl's arm, but Nanni refused to stay put, and jumped forward, thrusting herself between Wolf and the officers. 'You can't! He hasn't *done* anything!'

'He is a Jew,' the first declared, with a smug satisfaction that stopped even Nanni.

And then, Wolf stepped forward, calmly, his overcoat over his arm. 'I'm ready,' he stated. There was a quiet dignity about him that made Marisa remember her husband in Vienna, when their love had been complete and their understanding total. She was frozen in place, overwhelmed by the unexpected sequence of events, yet also moved to the core of her being by the simplicity of his manhood, which, even faced by the Gestapo, remained undaunted. Why, *why* hadn't he reacted when she'd told him to flee? They could have been in Nice, in Spain . . . anywhere but here on this cold spring morning of 1941.

He bent down to touch her forehead with his warm lips, and she threw her arms around his neck, hysteria pulsing through her veins until she screamed his name, blinded by tears, and felt the Gestapo officers pulling them brutally

510

apart. She was conscious of Nanni darting out from her side, following the small group, hurling herself down the staircase of the Ritz, her voice a shriek that curdled the blood. Mina was dragging Marisa away from the door, to the window, and she saw her husband being thrown into a car, just as the little girl arrived on the pavement, arms outstretched towards the departing vehicle bearing her father. 'Papa! Papa!' she was yelling, and Mina whispered to Marisa: 'We have to bring her upstairs, dear. There's a crowd out there, watching. And I can't find Isaac.'

The stillness of the room surrounded them, shrouding them. Marisa's hysteria had died down completely, and she could feel a dreadful calm imposing itself on her. To act. She had to *act*. Thinking could come later.

'Mama,' she ordered, 'you go downstairs to pick up Nanni. And then we're getting out of here, as fast as we can!'

In the minutes that followed, Marisa threw open two large suitcases, and opened all the closets and cabinets. Then, pell-mell, she tossed, unfolded, all the clothes that would fit in. She pulled jewellery boxes out of drawers, emptied their contents haphazardly into the open luggage, and when there was no space left, she zipped the two valises up and dragged them to the threshold of the suite.

Nanni and Mina, hand in hand, their faces set with the pall of loss, were coming up the stairs, staring at her. 'Come on!' Marisa cried, her arms and legs taut and twitching with nervous energy. 'Help me with these bags!'

Without a word, Mina and Nanni took the second suitcase between them, following her to the lift. The beribboned operator stared at them, his moustache wobbling over parted lips. They hurried past amazed hotel guests into the street, and Marisa jumped forward, sidestepping the horrified doorman, into the first taxi that presented itself. 'Where are we going, Mama?' Nanni ventured to ask, in a hushed voice.

The driver was waiting, and she gave them the Walters' address in the Boulevard Exelmans. 'We're going to Aunt Claire's?' Nanni asked. 'Why?'

'Because,' her mother replied fiercely, 'from now on we're not safe! They've taken Wolf, and the next time, they'll come for all of us!'

It was only then that she realized that she was still dressed in her satin bathrobe, and that she understood why all these strangers, unaware of her plight, had been staring at her uncomprehendingly.

Marisa Steiner began to shiver, while silent tears glistened in her blue eyes.

'Princess Brasilova.'

Lily, crossing the street towards the boarding-house, stopped, the chill of recognition going like lead into the pit of her stomach. She was coming home after a long day, teaching the piano in different parts of the city, an ache of exhaustion pervading her limbs. Already the sky over the Champs-Élysées had darkened, and when she looked in the direction of the voice, the man's aquiline features had taken on the sinister shadows of evening. Baron Charles de Chaynisart, inclining his head, stood smiling at her, his bowler lifted in a gesture of courtliness.

'Monsieur de Chaynisart.'

She could feel his blue eyes piercing through the worn suit she was wearing, which had seen smarter days. 'Lovely spring weather, don't you think?' he remarked, immediately taking her elbow and guiding her safely to the opposite side of the wide, tree-lined avenue.

'Very pleasant, yes,' she murmured. What did he want? She felt an acute embarrassment, thinking of herself running from his car after the improper proposal he had made to her in 1934. She'd seen him just once after that, on the Croisette in Cannes. He'd implied such dreadful things about Jacques, that just thinking of it made her suddenly afraid. 'My daughter is waiting for me,' she murmured, smiling apologetically. 'I'm afraid I don't have time to stay.'

'Herbert von Karajan will be conducting the Berlin Opera in *Tristan et Ysolde* at our Opéra, on the twenty-second. I should like you to be my guest at the performance. To hear Wagner's music of love and sacrifice being interpreted through the baton of a genius like von Karajan, could only be topped by sitting near the most beautiful woman in Paris, enjoying the experience together.'

Lily's lips parted, and she was speechless. For months now, she'd been scraping by, refusing to accept Jacques's offer to help her buy food on the black market. Out of principle, she wanted nothing more than she was allowed, nothing more than the other hungry of Paris. Marisa, whose family had moved in with the Walters, had fewer scruples. She wanted Nanni to eat an occasional strawberry, and her mother-in-law to get her fill of protein. Yet even the Steiners bought such luxuries reluctantly; there was the shame, of course, but also the fear of being noticed in these times when anonymity, for every Jew, was often worth a life.

Now this man, whom she'd always found repulsive, was offering her an evening of German music. She'd heard, from Mark, that the Berlin Opera had been bombed by the British, and that its members had come to give a series of performances in Paris. She knew that many of her former associates, socialites she had known during the early part of her marriage, had made accommodations for the fact that high-placed German officials now took part in all the artistic and social events of *le tout-Paris*. She'd viewed this with a total revulsion. These were the people who, in spite of restrictions, still heated their mansions; the ones who still frequented Maxim's and La Tour d'Argent, whose clothes were still make of silk, while she, like most French women, wore rayon stockings and old clothes.

Evidently, Baron Charles was one of those; she could feel her gorge rising, and breathed quickly to calm herself. With her anger, fear lay mixed. This was the man who'd prosecuted Misha, unjustly; and who, in only a half-veiled fashion, had threatened her family. How much did he really know?

'I'm still a married woman,' she told him, her eyes level with his.

Still smiling, he nodded his agreement. 'Indeed. I know this. But a married woman who spends agreeable hours at the Avenue Montaigne, in the company of a charming American. Since Lend Lease went into effect two months ago, our government, and our friendly occupants, no longer consider the Americans personae gratae.'

She found herself gasping for breath, her windpipe constricted. 'Mr MacDonald has been a friend of my family for almost twenty years,' she whispered.

'Quite so. I just felt it wise to . . . warn you, shall we say, because, after all, *we're* friends too, aren't we? Or if we aren't yet, I should like to remedy this sad lack. Monsieur MacDonald's remaining in Paris is a silly romantic gesture, at this point in the war, when you and I both know the Germans will win. But it's a shame that your other friend, Frau Steiner of Vienna, wasn't smart enough to emigrate when it was still possible.'

He *knows*, Lily thought, appalled and terrified. He knows *all about me* . . . about all of us!

'The twenty-second of May is just two days away,' he said, his blue eyes narrowing, icy wedges of light in the indigo dusk. 'You must give me your answer *now*.'

Wolf, she thought, panicking. Wolf, held in the detention camp at Compiègne. She had to make sure he stayed alive . . . as long as possible. How much longer would they keep him there? Marisa had heard nothing further . . . just that the foreign Jewish lawyers were being interned in Compiègne.

It looked as if Baron Charles de Chaynisart was close to the Germans. He must be doing business with them, she calculated. Her eyes sought his, and she nodded, her fingers tight over her small bag. 'Yes,' she said, but the sound came out strangled, guttural. She couldn't add the normal niceties – that would have been too much. Oh, Mark, she thought, her heart stirring with pain: if only you could help me out of this one!

He was lifting her work-roughened hand to his lips. 'I have to go,' she said, and without a farewell, began to run towards Rue Lord-Byron.

Lily's body was held so tensely that the ligaments in her long, graceful neck stood out. This Opéra, where she had sat through countless performances at Misha's side, now seemed a like a foreign battlefield, the red velvet of its loggias and curtains a clear contrast to the *feldgrau* uniforms of the German officers. Next to her, his hand carelessly draped over the back of her chair, sat the Baron Charles de Chaynisart, in a tuxedo and frilled shirt.

Amid the sea of green-grey uniforms, familiar faces of the Parisian aristocracy beamed back at her: various Princes de Polignac, a Murat, the philosopher Henry de Montherlant. She could see other famous faces from the arts: Marie Laurencin, the painter, in a sweeping gown of pink and blue gauze; Serge Lifar, the *danseur*; and Varvara Trubetskaya, rubies at her ears, in something with feathers and paillettes, on the arm of a stately German. 'That's General Hanesse of the Luftwaffe,' de Chaynisart whispered to her, handing her his opera glasses.

How had he known? Even the direction of her gaze was not a mystery to him. Inwardly, she was quaking with a mixture of fear and horror at even being in such company. But outwardly, she displayed only a polite coolness, hoping that this subtle wall would be enough to protect her. For she felt naked and vulnerable, though to which particular danger she was still unsure. The Germans around her, laughing as they exited to the foyer to drink champagne at the interval, seemed harmless enough. Yet . . . she was an impostor, a Jew parading as a gentile in a world where Jews were no longer considered human beings, so that their rights were being stripped from them as if they'd been animals. She'd heard rumours.

Horribly ashamed, she'd nevertheless forced herself to tell Kyra about the invitation. And then they'd looked through her wardrobe, and realized, with yet more dismay, that she owned nothing suitable for such a soirée. But yesterday, when she'd returned from her mother's, Madame Antiquet had shown her the big box that had arrived that morning. In it had lain a gown of the softest emerald silk, trimmed with seed pearls; a pair of exquisite silk pumps, to match, and a small silver bag. And so, feeling like a condemned prisoner mounting the scaffold, Lily had clothed herself as he . . . this diabolical man she detested . . . had willed for her to appear at his side, for all Paris to witness.

'You look superb,' he'd said, picking her up in a royal blue six-cylinder Mercedes-Benz, as sumptuous as a limousine.

'Thank you . . . for your generosity.'

'I simply wanted you to know how I think of you. You are a *queen*, my dear Princess . . . and I should like to treat you so.'

Now she peered through the mother-of-pearl glasses, suddenly immersed in a child's game of searching for famous faces. Faces from her past, faces that should not have been here, faces that, creased in obsequious smiles, had lost every trace of their former dignity. Did I live in such a world, among such venal people? she asked herself, shocked.

'Let's take a walk into the foyer,' de Chaynisart was whispering to her, bending very close. She wanted to shrivel against her seat, but merely nodded, and rose. The perfect gown fell in graceful folds to the floor, and she had no choice but to lay her gloved hand on his proffered arm.

The foyer, brightly lit from its crystal chandeliers, was alive with elegant people. Charles de Chaynisart ordered champagne, and began to stroll among groups of people. He was playing at nonchalance . . . wanting to be seen with her, she knew. Desperately, she kept her eyes averted from anyone who seemed familiar, until, finally, a woman rushed up and embraced her. 'Lily! Good God, you'd dropped out of existence!' It was Marie-Laure de Noailles, one of the upper crust with whom Misha had once been on friendly terms. A hostess whose father was a Jew, but who now was an accommodating collaborationist.

Others were pressing by. 'It's the loveliest woman in Paris,' a man declared. She recognized Léon Daudet, a right-wing intellectual. He'd echoed de Chaynisart, but in her youth *le tout-Paris* had called her this. Mechanically, she smiled, like a puppet. And de Chaynisart beamed, possessively.

And then it was the turn of a youngish man in a trim tuxedo, whose face Lily was certain she'd seen before. De Chaynisart was thrusting his hand out, colour jumping to his cheekbones. 'My dear Otto,' he was declaring. 'The spectacle is wonderful . . . von Karajan is the best!'

Lily, in spite of herself, watched, fascinated. She knew now who this was, even before the Baron formally introduced them. 'Herr Otto Abetz, the ambassador from the Reich . . . Madame la Princesse Liliane Brasilova.'

Abetz was, she thought, no older than Mark, or her brother. He was bringing her hand to his lips, and she did not feel afraid, as she did with de Chaynisart himself. Abetz looked distinctive, subtle, intellectual . . . not at all like the German soldiers who were strutting about everywhere. Had he not been connected with the Führer, he might have been a likeable man, a gentleman. 'Your reputation precedes you,' he was saying to her, his smile sincere. 'It's true, what Daudet said: you are the loveliest woman here. I'd heard of you – who hasn't? – but had never had the pleasure of seeing, firsthand, one of the wonders of the world.'

'A wonder that belongs to *me*,' the Baron specified.

Lily felt the shivers going up and down her spine, and she turned to the two men and smiled. 'I beg your pardon,' she said, 'but today, no woman belongs to a man. She belongs to herself. The most loving gift a man can bring her is to recognize this freedom, and hope that she will come to him of her own free choice.'

She hadn't intended to deliver a speech, especially in front of the German ambassador. But the evening, and all the months since France had been conquered, had been pressing her further and further to the wall, until now, suffocating from many indignities, she hadn't checked herself. But when she'd finished, she felt the blood racing to her face, and flooding it. De Chaynisart looked grey, the colour of papyrus, and his nostrils were twitching. She felt an odd exhilaration, having, for a brief instant, humiliated him.

Otto Abetz started to laugh. 'Bravo, Princess! I quite agree. Which is one of the reasons I married a French-woman. You know your own worth. I admire that.' Turning to the Baron, he added: 'And I assume that you and the Princess will be coming later to our small gathering at the embassy? For a light supper, my dear Charles.'

Afterwards, while de Chaynisart strutted back with her to their box, he remarked, with obvious pride: 'You charmed him. Very good *indeed*. When you were married to Mikhail Brasilov, you had quite another reputation: you were meek, cowed, and mild. I believe his departure freed the best part of you . . . dearest Lily.'

What have I *done*? she thought, appalled. I've invited myself to the hornet's nest . . .

* * *

518

The reception halls of the German Embassy were of a luxury that insulted her. Only this morning, she'd queued for four hours and returned home with a loaf of bread that was ninety-eight per cent inedible, composed of pea-meal and various bean flours. The French . . . the honest people, who didn't prostitute themselves to the conqueror, were starving. Marisa had paid fifteen francs on the black market for an extra egg for Nanni. And here, on sideboards that stretched for metres and metres, on lace, hand-embroidered lengths of cloth, silver and crystal trays displayed caviar, smoked salmon, roast venison, and domed platters exhibited pheasant surrounded by tiny artichokes. On yet another table, pushed against a far wall, stood mounds of tiny, glazed petit fours, and three charlotte russes topped with whipped cream in stiff, white peaks. A bartender was taking orders, and Charles de Chaynisart requested two *coupes* of Dom Pérignon 1916.

He seemed to know everybody. He bowed to Alice Epting, wife of the director of the German Institute, and to various uniformed Nazis ramrod straight in their *feldgraus*. Lily remained by the door to the library, hoping not to be noticed.

From where she stood, the front entrance was clearly in her line of vision. A butler was letting in the late-comers. Who, she wondered, had opted not to come crawling, as sycophants, to the Reich's envoy? With cool disgust, she now watched, fascinated by a sight that no longer surprised, simply confirmed her sadness for the fall of the French. Even Jean Cocteau, the writer, was here.

For a moment, Charles's form eclipsed the sight of those entering. 'I've brought you a little of everything,' he was murmuring, holding out a dish of the finest Limoges china, filled to the brim with delicacies. 'The venison isn't quite up to par. But I have a castle in the Loire. If you like, we'll go there, and hunt together. You must look ravishing as Diana.'

'I've always hated the sight of blood,' she replied. 'I've never hunted in my life.'

'Then I shall have to initiate you. It's hypocritical, my dear Lily, to turn from the slaughter of animals, when we are all carnivores. *Somebody*, you realize, has to bring down the deer, or shoot the partridge.'

He was blocking the view, and so she did not see the front door opening once more, and a couple being helped out of their elegant outdoor clothing. The woman was bone-thin, with magnificent legs encased in perfect silk stockings. She was wearing a cocktail-length dress of burgundy taffeta, cut low, trimly hugging her sides, with a shimmer of ruffles on the hips. Around her neck was a choker of gleaming pearls and garnets. Her oval face was hard, its cheekbones pronounced, her eyes almost oriental slits of a strange, amber hue. Her hair was jet black, pushed into a knot of stiff curls that emerged below a burgundy turban.

Near her, a tall, handsome, dark man in his early middle age fussed with his gloves. His hair was neatly pomaded, and his long, slightly aquiline nose gave his great, dark eyes a certain sinister detachment. He looked like a Roman diplomat. But Lily hadn't noticed him, concentrating instead on the ruffle of Charles's stiff shirt. Trying to tune out the insidiousness of his tone, while forcing her eyes to steady her through the tiny focal point of an innocuous shirt ruffle: he can't hurt me. We're at a party. No one can hurt me here . . . not tonight.

'Goodness,' Charles was saying. 'Familiar faces, my dear.'

She looked over, surprised. A complete stillness settled over her. Across the room, the tall dark man in his tuxedo, his arm protecting the shoulders of the thin woman in the turban, had frozen too, his eyes on Lily. For barely three seconds, he hesitated. And then, patting his companion quickly on the hand, he strode over.

'Lily,' he said, in front of her now.

'Hello, Claude.'

'Baron . . . how do you do?'

De Chaynisart acknowledged Lily's brother with a tilt of his head.

'Nice to see you again,' Charles said, his ironic smile like a moon crescent on his smooth face. 'Henriette looks so attractive with her new, dark hair. Almost . . . Asiatic.'

Claude was laughing. 'She'll appreciate your remark. The last thing my wife wants to be is a typical French bourgeoise.'

There lingered a moment of awkwardness. De Chaynisart brought his immaculate fingers to Lily's long, swan's neck, and caressed the inviting crook of her shoulder. 'Enjoy yourselves, children,' he said amiably. 'I haven't spent a quiet moment with Madame Bruisson since . . . when was that, Claude? Oh, yes – General Hanesse's last banquet . . . three weeks ago.'

Lily watched him glide over to Rirette, and lead her into one of the reception rooms. Claude's face seemed marbled, chilled, suddenly withdrawn. 'I never thought I'd find *you* here,' she said at last, her vibrant tone catching in her throat.

'Nor I you. I had no idea . . . Baron Charles de Chaynisart . . .'

'The man who set my husband up. Did you know this, Claude?'

'Lily,' he broke in, 'we haven't seen each other for several years. Misha's gone now – all the better for you, I always thought. Why can't we, for once, try to keep things pleasant between us? Let's not talk of the past.'

Colour jumped to her cheeks. 'Tell me, then!' she cried. 'You seem to know this man very well! And all the German high society! How, Claude? What have you been doing, for them to include you in every dinner, in every party? And

521

you look good. Not like a hungry Frenchman suffering from restrictions.'

Claude's nostrils distended. 'Lily, you were always naïve. Germany is going to win this war, and the new Europe will be, as Laval predicted, with the Reich at its centre, controlling all, and the other countries feeding it its raw materials. If the French play the game well, then we shall have a more prominent place in this reworked society.'

'And you . . . believe in this?'

He shrugged, and let his shoulders rise and fall. 'I believe in not getting left out. And, to tell you the truth, after the disasters of the Third Republic, and particularly of Blum's year, the Nazi ideal suits me fine. France *needs* Fascism, Lily. The Fascists . . . the Nazis . . . believe in ironclad discipline, and in a strict oligarchy. I've lost my faith in democracy. The Communists have proved to me that in any democracy, they will take over. And I much prefer Hitler to Stalin.'

'They're exactly the same.'

'No, they aren't. Hitler sees to it that the smart man profits. A man can get somewhere in Nazism . . . not in Communism.'

'And Dachau? You approve of that, too?'

His upper lip rose in a sneer of derision. 'The Jews have controlled the world long enough,' he declared. 'Now it's time the real élite took over. Yes, Lily: I believe in purifying the world. The Jews are selfish, ugly people who have conspired with Communism through the century. I'd like them all gone, absolutely! No more golden ghettos, no more Rothschilds, no more kike regime behind the Bank of France. The Jews are upstarts, and intruders in our country. They had no right to immigrate and take over our banks, our industry. They had no right to marry their sons to our clean, French daughters.'

Her temples beating, Lily stood immobile, entranced by her brother's words. His face was a strange red hue brought on by the exhilaration of his own words, of his own powerful emotion of hatred. Good God, she thought: all his life, this has been the only feeling that has moved him. He hated me, and had to get the best of me; he hated Misha, and had to eliminate him. He married a woman who could strengthen his hatred, his jealousy, his anger. But most of all, he hates himself, and doesn't even know it.

He hates the Jews, without realizing that he is *one hundred per cent a Jew.*

'I'm pleased to see you here,' he was telling her, a touch of warmth coming to his voice. 'The Baron is a powerful man, and very rich and influential. This is exactly the sort of man you need, Lily. As beautiful as you are, it should be easy to win him, if you haven't already done so.'

'I'm not remotely interested in Charles de Chaynisart,' she said, in a low whisper, her eyes filling with tears. 'And the only reason I'm here is that I was afraid of him . . . for . . . Marisa . . .'

'. . . and Jacques, our Jew stepfather.'

'I'll *never* tell Mama I saw you here! She'd be so ashamed, knowing you came of your own free will, and not like me, out of terror. I want to spare our mother that . . . and to spare her your philosophy! What have you come to, Claude?'

'I've come,' he said, 'to my senses. And I do wish you'd come to yours. At thirty-six, you're hardly a girl anymore. If you're going to strike a bargain with a powerful man, you'll have to do it soon. You have no choice. The Germans are *here to stay*, little sister, and if we don't play the game their way, we'll end up like all those poor slobs who queue for hours for a slice of nauseating bean bread.'

'I'm one of those,' she said quietly. 'At least I sleep at night.'

'And so do I. In a bed with satin sheets and down pillows, courtesy of our occupiers. They're not half bad, those Germans – not half!'

Afterwards, inside the royal blue Mercedes, she couldn't resist questioning Charles de Chaynisart. 'You know my brother well?'

'Passably. He's made quite a killing from the Occupation. He was one of the first to buy from the deserting Jews who were fleeing our country, one step ahead of Hitler's armies. Buildings, at first, and then businesses. And naturally, the kikes were selling at ten per cent of what these enterprises were worth!' He laughed, a brief, mirthless chuckle. 'And now he's set all this at the disposal of the Reich. His factories help to grind out war *matériel*, his fields help to yield crops to feed the Germans. And his buildings house official Nazi headquarters, and the mistresses of Nazi generals. I'd say he's made cool millions, Liliane. A young man to admire, for his quick thinking.'

Like a jackal, feeding off the carcasses of dead animals, she thought, wanting to cry with shame. And when he stopped in front of her boarding-house, she did burst into sudden, involuntary tears, and ran quickly past him and into the building.

Madame Antiquet, her night bonnet astride silver curls, was waiting for her. 'A man's here to see you,' she announced, her mouth set in the cold, disapproving line it had when unexpected happenings came to disturb her. 'I've never seen him before. A *black* man.'

The tears still streaking her cheeks, Lily followed her worriedly into the parlour. And, indeed, a wiry black man, his salt-and-pepper hair closely cropped around his small head, jumped to attention. In that instant, she recognized him, though his attire was completely different from what she had seen him in previously. In a simple suit and tie, he looked absurdly normal . . . like the American jazz player he had once been. 'Dragi,' she said, blinking with bewilderment. 'What are *you* doing here, at this hour?'

'Madame sent me,' he replied, smiling with embarrassment.

'Madame Dalbret? I saw her tonight. We spoke, briefly. Is anything wrong?'

Dragi looked around him, as if to make certain that Madame Antiquet had not lingered outside the door. 'Madame feels that it isn't safe for you and your daughter to remain in Paris. She thinks the only way out for you is to quietly ... disappear. That way, the Baron will not know where you are, and won't be able ... to hurt you.'

One hand holding her throat, she sat down, weak-kneed. '*Hurt* me? How?'

'She said: "The Princess has no option left, if she stays. By displaying her so obviously to all of Paris tonight, he's made it clear that she's his mistress." And, your Excellency – if I may add my opinion to that of my fair lady ... if one thwarts a man like the Baron de Chaynisart, he has a whole German Embassy to avenge his wounded pride.'

'But ...' Lily began. 'I ... have nowhere else to go! Does she suppose I can move in with my mother? The apartment's too full as it is!'

The small butler extracted a slip of paper from his waistcoat pocket. 'Madame has written here an address, in Chaumontel, near the forest of Chantilly. It's a small village, not far from Paris. She knows a Madame Portier, who owns a small house with some rooms to let. She'll contact this person, and you are to leave tomorrow morning, with Miss Kyra.'

It sounded like a bad scenario from a horror film, and Lily, on the verge of tears, started to laugh. Her body bent in two, she laughed silently until her face was moist from the release. Her shoulders were shaking. Then she felt the warm, comforting hand of the black butler, lightly touching her arm. 'It's not so bad,' he said to her. 'Chaumontel is a very pleasant place, and this is no town for a woman like you, now.'

'What do you mean ... "like *me*"?'

He shook his head, trying to decide whether it was safe

525

to proceed. 'Your son,' he finally said, 'told madame . . . about your religion. She'll protect your secret, but if you become conspicuous, and if the German Embassy becomes curious . . . you understand that they'd have ways of finding out, too.'

Later, in the bedroom she shared with Kyra, they packed their suitcases, silently. Lily was thinking that the following morning, before leaving, she'd stop off at Mark's to alert him to her change of address. And he'd communicate it to her family at the Boulevard Exelmans.

Dear Mark, how long before you, too, will have to leave? she asked him in her mind.

And thought of her son, who had returned to Nice, and who was waiting, alone, for his American visa. Her loved ones were dispersing themselves, like scattering seeds in the winds of a storm. Kyra touched her hand, and said, softly: 'Let's go to sleep, Mama. I'm very tired.'

Pierre Rublon consulted his directions, and decided that Montsoult was the right station for getting off the train to Chantilly. As if to confirm this, he spotted the local train to Luzarches sitting on the opposite track. The young man, now almost six feet tall, had the massive shoulders of an athlete, but his clear blue eyes brought an unexpected, candid softness to his serious face. Stepping into an empty compartment, he sat down by the window and absently fingered the signet ring on his left ring finger. Almost immediately, the little train started up, and the entrancing forest landscape hypnotized him into tranquillity.

At three months short of his eighteenth birthday, Pierre's future loomed ahead of him, grim and full of risks. His blond hair fell over his forehead, and impatiently he brushed it aside with his hand. His freckles, so engaging two years ago in the sun and salt of Saint-Aubin, had paled in the Paris air. He knew that he was by no means handsome, and, as always, pondered his good luck to have won himself a splendid girl like Kyra. But he had seldom suffered from insecurity; he'd grown up in a home where intelligence and honesty had always been prized. He'd realized, from the beginning, that his friend Nick too came from this sort of family. Kyra's values had been fashioned in the same mould.

If she promised not to forget him, then she would keep her word. Yet, for the first time, his youthful fears came to the surface, and he was swept with a shameful relief that this passionate, exultant, moody girl was hidden away in a small village like Chaumontel, away from the sophisticated world of her Paris peers.

If the recent German attack on its former ally, the Soviet Union, was any indication of the future, Pierre had to feel a resurgence of confidence in a Nazi defeat. You've made Napoleon's mistake, *mein Führer*, he thought. And then, if all went well, the war would last only a few years more. He'd return man enough to marry his girl.

The train pulled into the station of Luzarches, the last stop on its short route, and Pierre was one of the first to jump off. A rural road led towards the village of Chaumontel, and Pierre, walking rapidly, noticed that the only people to cross his path were hardened French peasants – no German soldiers. He thought, with another surge of relief, that the Brasilovs were well hidden there, for the road was a mere thread through vast, cultivated fields where labourers ploughed and tended the crops.

The hamlet was composed of small houses tiled with red roofs, webbing out from the main road. Pierre had never come here, but he had been in countless other French villages like it. Every house had its back yard with long, unmowed grass, and its wooden outhouse. He stopped at the tobacco shop and asked for Madame Portier's house. The old man behind the counter smiled a wide, toothless grin, and remarked: 'You've come for the pretty young lady, haven't you?'

527

Pierre blushed. 'Yes.'

'They're nice people. Here in Chaumontel, nobody asks any questions. They're not registered, and so aren't entitled to food cards, but the butcher, the baker, the dairyman don't care, and the police and the priest pass over their existence. We know they're fugitives, and probably Jews – but we'll never give them away. It's our village pride that we protect our own – and these ladies have become ours, too.'

Pierre smiled his gratitude, and proceeded to the side street to which the old tobacconist had sent him. The Portier house was unprepossessing, to say the least – and for a moment, he almost recoiled. It stood, low, grey, and squat, dark curtains rimming its small windows. But he pressed the doorbell, and waited, his heart pounding.

The door swung open, and he saw Kyra's mother, a kerchief around her dark hair, her face clear and inviting as he remembered it. It wasn't so difficult to imagine her as the fabled princess his parents had told him about: rich, elegant, worldly. She still carried herself, even in this old brown skirt and blouse, like a proud Athena. My girl is a *princess*, he thought; in many ways, she is above me, even though my family is old French money, and dates back to the Huguenots. Lily was holding her hands out to him, drawing him in. 'Pierre! We weren't expecting you!'

He had to walk down a step into the corridor, which was dank and gloomy. But Lily's animated voice cheered up the almost sordid surroundings. She led the way into a room that was at once kitchen and parlour. In the centre stood a large wooden table, and welded to the back wall was an enormous cement sink for washing clothes. Next to it, an old iron stove jutted out. The only other furnishings were four battered chairs and an oak cupboard filled with kitchen utensils. Lily was sitting down, and he did the same, opposite her.

'It's quite nice here,' she said. 'We don't have to queue

up for food, and there are fresh vegetables, eggs, and milk, which were so scarce in Paris. Four hours to bring home one hundred grams of tomatoes! Here, because we didn't dare register, they give us what's available, and when the constable from Luzarches comes once a week to verify the ration tickets at the bakery, he overlooks our purchases. Once we passed him on the street, and he just tipped his hat and went on his way.'

How old was the Princess Brasilova? Pierre wondered. He'd always known her this way, serene and engaging, but almost destitute. There were no creases around her eyes, which were mesmerizing pools of darkness, warm chocolate brown. 'But you didn't come all the way out here just to listen to me prattle on and on,' she declared. 'Kyra's in the small wood, gathering up some dry twigs for the fire. You wouldn't believe this: but here, in late June, the nights are still chilly, and the walls ooze moisture.'

He realized that he was standing, horribly embarrassed, his eagerness to find Kyra painted in bold red all over his face. She took his arm and walked with him through the damp corridor to the back door. 'It's not far,' she was saying. 'Over there, to the right.'

His heart hammering, he strode towards the small thicket. A light rain had begun to drizzle, but he ignored it. He passed through some brushwood into thick foliage, then found himself lost under a dome of green leaves where the top branches of stately old trees had met and tangled. Not more than twenty steps away, she was bending down to pick up dead wood, her dark, brilliant hair falling over her shoulders and arms. He called out: 'Kyra! Over here!'

She flung down her basket, and her young, pliant body sprang forward, eager and lithe like a sprinting panther's. In a minute she was in his arms, flinging kisses all over his face, her hands messing up his hair, her tears on his cheeks. 'Hey,' he said gently, '*hey* . . . I've missed you.'

Her hand in his, she brushed off a tree stump and pulled

529

him down beside her. 'I wondered when you'd come,' she told him. 'And then, I thought you'd forgotten. Your life's so complicated, so full of plans – and I'm out here, living like a peasant. I go to the school in Luzarches, and there are only twelve girls in my class ... all daughters of labourers.'

'At least you're safe. Things are becoming very scary for the Jews, in Paris. The Germans have begun to round them up, during the night, going by the addresses they gave when they registered. It's as if they signed their own death warrants, without knowing it.'

'You know,' she said, 'I used to feel angry that my grandma was Jewish. It was always different with Nick. Maybe because he and Papa never got along so well, and Nick was rebelling, he became quite religious at the end. But not me. I wasn't reared in the religion, and I don't feel the need for it. God's in my heart ... in the forest here, with us, wherever there is life. But the Germans have made me change. I love my grandparents, and Aunt Marisa. I respect their old traditions. And so now, I understand my mother's feelings. There's a subtle bond that ties us all together, we, the hunted, the persecuted ... the Jews.'

'But it's not just the Jews ... it's also the others, like me, who can't accept France's abnegation. It's *we* against *them* – the Boches, the Vichy cowards, and all the other *collabos* who have teamed up with Abetz out of cupidity or hatred. You have to hate your fellow man to become a Nazi, Kyra.'

'My uncle Claude's a *collabo*,' she said.

'Every family seems to have one. But I'm convinced the British, with the help of the Americans and their Lend Lease policy, will prove victorious. And General de Gaulle's troops are swelling now.' He stared for a moment at his hands, then looked frankly at her. 'Kyra – I came to say goodbye.'

Tears hovered on the edges of her long, curled lashes.

She'd known, the moment she'd seen him here, why he had made the trip. 'When?' she asked. 'How?'

'I'm going to make my way to Spain, across the Pyrenees. The Basque underground is quite organized. Every night, six or seven guides take fugitives across the mountains. It would be impossible to find one's way without them. They know every inch of the thirteen thousand feet of sharp peaks that must be crossed, and often, there's a thick fog that blocks all the reference points, but which doesn't seem to bother *them*. Then, from neutral Spain, I'm to take a small, clandestine boat to London, with a handful of other Free French volunteers. It's all been arranged, down to the last detail.'

She sat, silent, reflecting. 'And then? Are you going to fight in North Africa?'

He shrugged. 'I don't know. They'll tell me when I get to headquarters, in London. They might also assign me to Intelligence, and keep me there.'

The two young people sat, hunched by the enormity of his immediate plans, sad and speechless. Kyra could feel her heart aching inside her. Her nerves were alive. Tears welled up in her eyes. In that moment, she experienced the same desolation she had felt, almost four years ago, when the first man she had ever passionately loved – her father – had abruptly ripped himself from her existence.

But now it was different: she understood what Pierre was doing, why he was leaving. But it didn't lessen the wrenching pain. He was suddenly kneeling in front of her, his large, strong hands on both her shoulders, and she had the absurd desire to pull herself away and hurl herself far into the thicket, to be alone with her desolation. But he wasn't about to let her escape.

The only sound around them was the rain, which was so light that they had hardly felt it, protected as they were by the limbs and leaves of the trees above. 'Don't,' he was pleading. 'Don't cry so, Kyra! It makes me feel I've made the wrong decision, that I'm a coward, leaving you. . . .'

'All the men I've loved have left me: my father, my brother, now you! How d'you *expect* me to feel, Pierre?'

His voice, so tender and low, assaulted her with its own, respondent hurt: 'But I'm not abandoning you. For that matter, neither did Nick. You have to get over your father. It's not fair to Nick, it's not fair to me, and, most important, it's not fair to yourself.'

She shook her head, her hair tumbling about her face. 'I'm sorry,' she said contritely. 'All my life, my family's told me I was selfish. I didn't mean that. Forgive me.'

His hands had tightened over her shoulders, and he had drawn himself up to her level. Impulsively, she slid off the stump and into his arms, her lips seeking his, her weight pushing him down onto the summer earth. She felt his hands fumbling on her breasts, and responded with a sweep of passion, her own fingers parting the soft cambric of his shirt, nestling over the circles of his nipples. With the rain beating time to her own rush of excitement, she unfastened her cotton skirt, unbuttoned her blouse, and waited for him to lie naked beside her. And she watched him struggling with clasps and zippers, her green eyes like two blazing emeralds, holding him so that he could do nothing else but respond to this girl of fifteen whom he had loved for two years with unswerving devotion.

His body was tight, muscled, and compact, as she'd expected. Blond, blond, the soft, curling hairs on his chest and around his unmasked erection. She held out her arms, and he nestled there, his head between her full breasts. He will remember, she thought, fervently. I won't let him forget this day! And so when finally he pushed himself onto his elbows, above her, she lay ready, her eyes wide open, unafraid. She'd been afraid of being left, not of being filled, by this young man, and so she received him with only a silent biting of her lower lip as his manhood entered her for the first time.

When he had exerted himself and finally collapsed, his perspiring face lying between her neck and shoulder, the quiet told her that the rain had stopped, and that, indeed, this moment would remain indelible in his mind. And she felt, for the first time that afternoon, for the first time in many months, a serene security within herself. He was asking her, suddenly ashamed: 'You're not sorry? I hadn't planned this . . . Are you sure it's all right?'

She nodded, unblinking. 'Now I can let you go,' she murmured, and her voice was almost detached, far away, as if, for her, the magic moments had already been locked up in their treasure box. For she and Pierre had passed a threshold, and now she wouldn't be alone anymore. She wouldn't have to be afraid. He'd have to come back – God owed this to her now.

Chapter Twenty-three

Claude stood, tall and straight in his dark grey suit, his face almost scornful in its removed, withdrawn expression. Claire, on the small sofa, smoothed out a pleat in her skirt, and reflected, as she had so many times in the past, that, had he allowed emotion to penetrate his features, he would have been, like Lily, a most handsome individual. But there was a woodenness about him. Even she, whose love for him had flowed in spite of his flaws, felt an edge of apprehension, watching him.

'I wanted you to know at once,' he stated. 'But I also felt certain you wouldn't approve. So I waited, until it could wait no longer. I'll be leaving on the fourth of September for a German training camp in Poland, with the first contingent of the Legion of French Volunteers to fight the Red army in Russia.'

Claire shook her head. 'You can't be serious. Claude – it isn't true!'

'I've admired the Germans for many years, Mother. And I approve of the way Hitler wants to run Europe. Father always said that the worst plague of all was the Red plague from the Soviet Union. If there's something I can finally do to help, then I must sacrifice my comfort, and enlist. I've already enlisted, in fact. And received my commission as lieutenant.'

Claire's face was so pale that one could see a vein beating at her temple. 'But the Legion will be fighting on the side of the Reich – the Reich that ploughed into our country and demolished it, and has now subjugated it into an affiliate state. *You* . . . my *son!* want to fight with *them*,

534

with the Nazis – it's more than I can bear, Claude! You've disappointed me before . . . but never have you ripped the heart from me, until now.'

Claude's eyes were the only proof of life in that icy face, and now they shone with an odd, disquieting light, like twin embers. He clenched and unclenched his fists. 'I came for you to send me away as mothers always do, with a show of maternal affection! But I suppose I was wrong! I should have known you'd be against me – as you always were. All my life, you preferred Lily. All my life, I had to feel like an unwanted member of the family. Even after I married Henrietta, you put Lily and her children first, before us and our child! But what could I have expected, from a woman who'd marry a *Jew*?'

Claire stood up, upending a small tray of odds and ends that had been lying in front of her on the long coffee table. 'What do you know about the Jews?' she whispered, her heart beating twice as fast. 'You, a traitor to your country, a collaborationist? You thought perhaps I didn't know. But I had to learn of it, sooner or later. Jacques found out! Yet still, I loved you enough to try to pretend that this was just a phase you were passing through! I've never been so deeply ashamed as I am today.'

His cheekbones gleamed red and shiny. '*Jacques! A kike!* It's I who am ashamed, Mother, that you'd lower yourself to marry a Jew. How could you have done that?'

Her eyes on his, she said, her voice trembling with rage: 'How? I married a Jew, Claude, because I *am* one. And because I'm proud to be a member of an old and venerable tribe that has remained, through the ages, pure and honourable. Jesus was a Jew, a fact that Hitler has chosen to forget! But *I* never have forgotten. I am a Jew, and *you* are a Jew. It's time you knew this and digested it, and came to your senses.'

Claude stood stock still, incredulity painted on his face. 'No,' he said.

'Yes. You've joined up with a reactionary group that wants to kill us all, to wipe us from the face of this earth. But you can't hate the Jews without hating yourself. You're as Jewish as Jacques.'

'But Father was a Christian,' Claude finally countered, his chin jutting out in defiance. He could feel his legs going weak at the knees. His mother . . . his own *mother* . . . Jewish. It was beyond his imagination.

Claire, sixty-one years old, her white hair swept into a fine French knot, her composed, cameo face set in an unaccustomed hardness, declared: 'That's not exactly true. *Lily's* father was a Christian. You accused me of always having loved her best. But you were wrong! I always loved you more, Claude, because you, not she, were conceived in love.' Unrelenting, she pursued, her eyes holding his: 'You are not Paul Bruisson's child. Your father was a Jewish man, whom I knew before I ever met Paul. So you see, you are one hundred per cent Jewish. There's no escape, Claude. You're going to have to live with it, and come to your own terms.'

He was backing away, shaking his head, grasping the door handle with a blind man's desperation. 'No! You're just telling me lies, to prevent me from going to Russia!'

'I'm telling you the truth. My greatest mistake was not to have told it to you before. Then, I might have stopped you from committing the gravest error of your life.'

'I'll never believe it!' he cried. 'But nothing will hold me back from the Legion, not even your disgusting lies! You are no longer my mother! I abhor you, and wish you were dead! But you'll be sorry, when I come back a hero and you'll be left out, like a dog!'

When he had left, and she was alone in the apartment, Claire sat, shaking. Why had she told him the truth, just like that, out of anger? Had it really been necessary? Tears welled up in her eyes, and she let them fall, a terrible agony. She'd lost her son.

But then, she'd never really had him. Their relationship had been based on that first, inexcusable lie, and if today he had become a man whose values were a twisted web of anger and hatred, then she could only blame herself.

Yes, she'd given in to the right impulse, telling him. It had been not only necessary, but, at this late date, even unavoidable.

Maybe he'll reconsider, she thought, a surge of hope cresting. But she knew, as surely as she breathed, that the truth had come too late for Claude ... too late, perhaps, for all of them.

At forty-one, he was one of the oldest Legionnaires, and, at Camp Deba in Poland, he'd felt his age and his lack of physical preparation. He hadn't known what to expect, but had looked forward to the rigours of training in order to forget himself, his aching mind and heart. When Henriette had seen him off, he hadn't been able to look at her. *I am a Jew, I am a Jew*: these words had kept reverberating in his head, and a dull fever had throbbed through his body.

On the way to Poland, he'd listened to his companions exalting their mission, and trying to get over their own disappointment at the lack of support the Legion was receiving in France. He'd listened, but as if a veil had parted him from them. His intense shame had kept him quiet, even more so than was usual for him. But then, crossing the cleanliness of Germany, his spirits had momentarily been revived. *She'd lied*; it was as simple as that; and his duty was to return a hero of the French people, to show her that there was no way he, Claude Bruisson, could have had Jewish blood coursing through the vessels of his fine, Aryan body. She'd lied, to show him the full extent of her rejection of him. What better way to have humiliated him, than to have insulted his very birth, labelling him *one hundred per cent a Jew?*

She wasn't Jewish, of this he was certain, as well. She'd been a Belgian Catholic, lapsed but still believing. And, of course, he wasn't a bastard, but the son of stolid, conservative, unimaginative Paul Bruisson.

At Deba, the Germans had put them through muscle-wrenching exercises, but he'd welcomed the pain, hoping it would obliterate the searing memory of what his mother had told him – the horrid lie. It had been strange: all the French had expected the Germans to be grateful for their help, but instead, had found them barely tolerant of their brothers-at-arms. A multitude of uniforms had paraded together, each the emblem of a partisan group from another nation; but only the French had been forced into the *feldgrau* of the Reich itself. Some of Claude's fellow Legionnaires had balked at this, and later, at the oath that they'd had to swear to the Führer. But he hadn't balked. To him, his willingness to be clothed as a Nazi, and to swear allegiance to the Nazi ruler, had seemed only another, ultimate proof that he could not possibly have been a Jew.

Later, they'd been put on yet another train, to Smolensk. The cold was so great that now, crouching behind machine guns in the bleak afternoon, Claude thought that never had he felt such burning pain as that which was paralysing his fingers and joints. They were on the road from Golo-kovo, and Moscow, their destination, seemed continents away: though, in fact, it was less than fifty miles from where they were advancing, inch by inch, through snow so deep that his feet had stopped hurting, stopped reacting to the frostbite, and he could not feel his extremities at all.

How long had this absurd march been going on? And which day was it now? The day before, they'd taken a small village, killing three Russians. But five of the Legionnaires had died of cold. This morning, when he'd tried to relieve himself, and had removed a glove, his fingers had almost turned to ice, and a companion had had

538

to rub them immediately to revive them. How had the Russians learned to endure such a glacial climate?

At night, they huddled inside peasant huts owned by partisans, everyone around the stove at the centre of the miserable single room. But tonight he had guard duty, by the machine guns. He and the young sergeant who could have been his son ate their bowls of soup and left the warmth of the small dwelling, their breath curdling in front of them, their noses immediately sending shoots of pain through their nervous systems. 'Which day are we?' Claude asked.

'It's the night of December the first,' the young man told him.

Behind the machine gun, Claude prayed: I've never been a believer, but, dear Lord, if you exist, remove me from this cold. The sergeant, whose name was Marcel Lepuis, was crying softly into his gloved hands. 'I'm going to die,' he moaned. 'I'm from Provence, where the heather blooms and the tomatoes grow large, and where the sun flirts with you like a pretty girl, way into the winter season. But I'll never see the sun again . . .'

'Shut up,' Claude said roughly. He didn't want to think of his family: of his wife, whom he'd always loved, of the child, Alain, now eight years old, to whom he'd given his name – even of his sister, who'd always been a victim, because of the stupidity of her convictions. He didn't want to think of his mother, the beautiful, the betrayer. Above all, he didn't want to think of her.

'I can't *see!*' Lepuis was screaming, and Claude, immersed in his own physical anguish, had to move to take a look at him. Horrified, he saw that the sergeant's tears had frozen over his eyes.

'You idiot,' he spat out, but nevertheless a surge of compassion filled him. He took the young man's face in his own gloved hands, and gently massaged his cheekbones, until the movement seemed to thaw the shards of ice. 'This isn't the moment to indulge in any excess of emotion,' Claude admonished him. 'We have to keep our circulation going, or we'll die.' His own voice sounded ominous in the dark gloom, and he asked himself why he had left the comfort of his plush apartment at the Carlton to risk his life at the ends of the earth ... battling the cold, rather than the Bolsheviks.

After a while, enveloped by silence, Claude felt himself drift off into a torpor. He blessed the fact that neither his feet nor his hands had any feeling anymore: the excruciating pain appeared to have numbed them. Perhaps they'll have to amputate a limb, he thought, but even this eventuality failed to rouse him. He simply prayed for the day to dawn and this tormenting vigil to come to an end.

I should shift positions, he warned himself. *Keep the circulation going.* But his legs refused to budge beneath his weight. *I can't move!* Marcel Lepuis was making no sound, not even the slightest whisper of a breath, and Claude called out: 'Hey! Sergeant! Answer me!' But only the steady, wheezing wind replied, with its inhuman lack of pity.

My God, he's dead! like the five bastards from the night before. Claude had a visual image of the hut, with his companions huddled around the stove. How cold was it now? Probably at least minus ten degrees Fahrenheit. In Paris, a person shivered when the temperature fell below sixty, and when it descended to fifty, piled thermal blankets one on top of the other to block out the chill.

But this, here, was no chill: it was deadly cold, and Claude knew beyond the shadow of a doubt that his young companion had frozen to death at his side.

Claude felt no pain inside his heart, for really, this lad had been nothing to him. *And if I went, would anyone miss me?* Only his thoughts now stood between him and the black abyss of nothingness ... his thoughts, and his hatred. Misha Brasilov, the bête noire of his existence, whose child he, Claude Bruisson, had reared as his own son, had been born in this enormous land, where night lasted four hours and bleak daylight, twenty. Already the white light of dawn had risen, outlining miles and miles of white, unchanging landscape, and the bowed figure of Marcel Lepuis near Claude. Like Lot's wife, turned overnight into a pillar of salt . . . only, Lepuis was ice.

For a moment, he thought again of his family.

They'd all used him, and then thrown him away.

Even his mother.

Now the wind no longer whistled, and Claude's mind was alive with a giant buzzing, as if a thousand bees had set up housekeeping in his head. He could feel nothing, no part of his body, and he thought: Thank you, God. No feet, no hands, no legs, no arms, no ears, no nose.

He thought he'd fallen asleep, and that an angel, with blond hair and a straight nose, had come to take him away to the Aryan heaven. He tried to part his lips, willing himself to speak. But there was no need for words: the angel understood. The angel knew that Claude Bruisson, one hundred per cent Aryan, one hundred per cent pure, honest, and true, deserved, at last, to be loved unconditionally. No more picking up other people's broken toys; no more sister, no more mother, no more wife in love with an enemy brother-in-law who, for no reason, had wanted him, Claude, out of the way.

The angel was reaching a long, elegant hand towards him, to pull him up. Claude's heart felt as if it had burst, as if all inside him had combusted; and it felt good, like a release, like the ultimate orgasm shuddering through his body. And he said to the angel: *Don't leave without me*.

When his companions came to relieve them, they found both Sergeant Marcel Lepuis and Lieutenant Claude Bruisson dead, like frozen statues, behind the machine gun they had been guarding. But the Nazi colonel who commanded them had no time for an Aryan burial. He kicked them twice with his boot to unjam the wheels under the machine gun, and left them to be buried by God under fresh piles of newborn snow.

Nicolas leaned over the railing, hailing in the New Year with a silent toast, his eyes lifted to the star-sprinkled winter night. The tiny *Gonçalo Velho*, a bare fifteen hundred tons, was carrying him and twelve other passengers to the New World . . . to a new life. His heart felt heavy, and for a moment, fear strangled him. Perhaps he should have gone along with Pierre, to London, instead of embarking on this strange expedition. Pierre, he'd heard in Madrid, had reached his destination. And would be doing something to help his country.

He, Nick, had received his visa just in time, before his seventeenth birthday. For the line of demarcation between the two zones had become officially closed to all men over that age. He'd taken a train to Madrid, a transit visa for Spain and Portugal safely tucked in his wallet, along with his exit visa from the Vichy government. He'd left Nice, and his studies, with hardly a regret. The *baccalauréat*, which had seemed so important to him a year ago, now mattered very little. He'd had to interrupt his last year of high school, without passing the second *bac* – but now, it looked as if, for a Jewish boy, only survival mattered, which, in France, was a risky business.

His train to Spain had been the last before Pearl Harbor. The sudden entry of the United States into the war had blocked all travel out of France, for no one knew how long. So on the one hand the late December date of his birthday, and on the other, the Japanese attack, had wedged his trip into the only possible period when he could still have departed, legally.

Nick had paid forty pounds sterling to reach Lisbon from Spain, and then, the outrageous price of four hundred additional pounds to embark on the small Portuguese ship, the *Gonçalo Velho*. Now, leaning to smell the sharp salt of the sea, he thought how unpredictable life could be. When he'd returned from Paris to Nice, he'd found that the landlady had given his room away at the boarding-house. In a panic, he'd wandered through the streets until he'd seen a sign in the window of a slim, badly lit building: ROOM TO LET. He'd walked in, and asked, and been given a key. It hadn't been until three weeks later that he'd become aware that the small hotel, where pretty, made-up girls waved him their friendly greetings every day on the worn-down staircase, had been, in fact, a brothel, and the pleasant girls, prostitutes. But then, none of *them* had supposed that they'd had a real prince in their bawdy house . . .

Nick smiled, remembering Myriam, the thirty-year-old blonde who'd made it her business, after six months, to see to it that he became initiated into the rites of manhood. He'd only once thought of Trotti, during their encounter in the whore's narrow room. Now he wondered about his sister; war turned some timid virgins into passionate mistresses, and Kyra had never been timid. But things had been more serious between her and Pierre, and Trotti had told him of a commitment between his sister and his best friend. And if he could trust anyone not to harm Kyra, it had to be Pierre: kind, truthful Pierre.

Not the man Papa would want for her, he thought, suddenly bitter. But Kyra's life is in her own hands now. Misha, by leaving the country, had allowed his daughter to blossom into the giving, valorous girl he, Nick, had always known she could become. With their father around . . . who knows? Kyra might have remained the selfish, spoiled little Russian princess, her Papa's toy child.

Yesterday, they'd had a scare on board ship: they'd been stopped by a United States destroyer. But when the Americans had verified the cargo: thirteen passengers and a hold full of cork, they'd allowed the *Gonçalo Velho* to continue its journey. And so now, New York was only a few days away; they'd already been sailing for over two weeks.

The only problem was the salt cod. For the first days, the food had been delicious, but now, reality had set in. For breakfast, lunch and dinner, the passengers and crew knew what to expect: salt cod and potatoes, with only water to wash them down.

The God of the Jews knows how to save His people, Nick thought, gratefully. If his visa had come just two days later, he would still, now, be stuck in France, held back by Pearl Harbor and his seventeen years. And if, somehow, through the help of Jeanne Dalbret, he hadn't received that extra few hundred pounds ... he'd never have had the money for this voyage.

The Vichy man who had brought him the funds had also left him an uncensored letter. Claude had shocked the family, and joined the Legion. And old Aunt Mina, her mind already three-quarters warped, had gently passed away one Sunday morning. Nick still felt a deep sadness whenever he thought of her; for old Papa and Mama Steiner had brightened his youth, and given him and Kyra the best year of their childhood.

'Hey, young man, happy New Year!' the captain called out, his form appearing next to him, outlined by the moon. 'What's that you're holding in your hand? A button?'

'My cuff link. It fell off at dinner.' And gently, Nick caressed the sharp planes of the ruby, recalling another holiday season, four years ago, when a man had paid his last sou to redeem this family heirloom. For him, Nick: Prince Nicolas Brasilov. He'd never live that legend, as his father had, and even his mother, and his sister. The fabled title meant nothing to him, a modern young man concerned more with his future than his ancestral escutcheon.

And yet ... could one ever escape the pull of one's blood, whether worthy or venal? Nick only understood that

544

within his thin form, two mighty heritages, as opposite as night and day, had found a common vessel into which to pour the elixir of life.

'Happy New Year, Captain,' he said softly, pocketing the gold and ruby piece, and breathing in the clear, new air in front of him.

Because of the lack of petrol, the trains and métros were few and far between, and only a fraction of the peacetime taxis were running. Twice a week, on Mondays and Thursdays, Lily came to Paris, visited her parents, and purchased some of the dry goods, dairy products, and meat to which her ration cards from the Rue Lord-Byron still entitled her. But mostly, she made the trip to spend an afternoon with Mark. Usually, they were able to stay together only for an hour, for Lily wanted to be on her way home by six, in order to run no risk of being caught after the curfew of 8:00 P.M., after which identity cards were checked, and only proven gentiles were released in peace.

Rommel was suffering setbacks in North Africa, and Marshal Pétain had regained some support among his people by refusing any further military aid to the Reich. In Paris, the Germans were no longer behaving like civilized overlords. One heard of terrible reprisals, and the French underground, the Resistance, was manifesting itself more and more often, blowing up trains to slow down communications among the Germans. It was said that these underground groups were being directed by de Gaulle's Free French headquarters, in London.

But April, in the capital, had come with the full rush of early spring, the horse chestnut trees in bloom, the skies intermittently azure blue, or torn with storms, the Seine swollen and ripe beneath a sun that was moody, uncertain whether to dim or to brighten the ancient city. It seemed poignantly ironic that the weather was ignoring the war and the occupation.

On a certain Thursday afternoon, Lily knocked on Mark's door, and was let in by her lover himself, in his shirt sleeves. He made it a habit to let his maid off on Mondays and Thursdays, when he knew that Lily tried to come. In spite of the fact that their lovemaking had become a constant, passionate part of their lives, they both still maintained the delicacy of discretion. She did, for her daughter's sake; and he, to make her comings and goings less noticeable to an outside world that had grown increasingly more hostile. Who knew which spies de Chaynisart employed, to tail her or to watch this house? For his link to the Gestapo and the German Embassy was a well-known fact.

Mark's apartment, on the second floor of a spacious old building, was decorated unpretentiously, for comfort. Lily thought that it was the exact opposite of what Misha had wanted for Rue Molitor. The furniture was modern, its tones warm and autumnal, and the paintings Mark had chosen for his walls were two original Chagalls and a Picasso nude, from the master's Blue Period. Lily felt her spirits rise, an enormous warmth filling her, as soon as she stepped inside this apartment, which, to her, had been more of a 'home' than either the Villa Persane or the immaculate, too perfect Rue Molitor.

Avenue Montaigne was where she was accepted and loved, however she was dressed, and in whatever mood she arrived.

Now he drew her inside, and hungrily covered her throat and lips with a small flutter of kisses. The afternoon sun filtered through the mustard-coloured raw silk curtains, falling with mellow generosity over the polished parquet floor. She thought, her heart reaching out through tender fingers in the tight curls of his hair, that, in spite of the war, in spite of the daily fear she experienced concerning de Chaynisart and the Gestapo, she had never felt so full, so happy, as now, in her thirty-eighth year, with this man who acted as if their lives were bound forever, as naturally as grapes to the vine.

He took her by the hand to his low, curved Art Nouveau sofa, and, gratefully, she pushed her shoes off and curled up, taking the pins out of her hair and lying back in his arms. 'Lily,' he said, his voice strangely awkward. 'I don't know how to tell you this, darling . . . but . . .'

Shaking her hair loose, her muscles suddenly alive, and the warm inner glow receding, giving way to a gnawing apprehension, she asked: 'You're leaving?'

De Chaynisart had said it all: Lend Lease had made Americans unpopular even before Pearl Harbor. Now, to the Germans, they were the enemy. No American was going to stay in France if he could help it. Mark's hand stayed on her shoulder, and he said, his hazel eyes intently on her: 'Darling, the situation is worsening here in Paris, especially for you and Kyra. If I'm out of the country, it will be easier, through my connections, to get both of you out also.'

She watched, through a film of tears, the anxious expression on his face. He cared. He really *cared*: he wanted her with him. But she felt a tremendous sense of bereavement, listening to him. 'Lily,' he repeated, stroking the softness of her hair: 'I want us to be together, when all this is over. I want us to live together, to be married. But right now, I can't take you with me, because we're *not* legally married. You've got to trust me to do it from Spain. Things aren't safe here . . . especially for Jews. But from Paris, there's almost nothing I can do for you, or for Kyra.'

She found it impossible to reply. Not looking at her, in order to avoid facing their heartbreak, he added, in a low voice: 'And besides . . . it's a little shameful not to be making any contribution to my country, now that it, too, is at war.'

She nodded, a coldness descending like ice water from her head to the pit of her stomach. She thought, though she didn't mention it, that Mark and Claude would have been the same age, too old, really, for warfare, at forty-two. But her brother had burned a searing scar into their mother's heart, so that, when news had come of his death on the Russian front, Claire's face had remained stone cold. She'd banished him from her heart when he had left with the Legion.

And now Mark was speaking of leaving, of wanting to serve his country. She spoke hesitantly: 'What are your plans?'

'Nothing too dangerous. I'm going to Spain, Lily, with the Associated Press, as war correspondent in a neutral territory. There's still a lot to be written about the Spanish; Franco's neutrality is heavily tilted towards the Axis powers, and the folks back home want to read all about it. There are spy rings in the Pyrenees, and inside the country itself. How long they'll keep me there, I don't know; they might want to send me to North Africa, after a while. And I'll go wherever they feel I'm needed.'

She didn't know what to say. Her throat hurt from trying not to let out her anguish in a great, relieving cry, and the back of her eyeballs stung from contained tears. His fingers played with hers, but she could tell how uncomfortable he was, how pained, how suddenly unsure and confused. And so, to ease it for him, she said, quietly: 'It's true; you should go.'

All at once, the comfortable room began to close in, and the Picasso nude to leer at her, pressing her back against the silk nub of the sofa cushions. Her chest felt tight and hard.

Only then did she burst into sobs, a dam rupturing inside her. Mark was holding her head, playing with the soft strands of her long hair, and she could feel the warmth from his fingers, the warmth of his presence. 'You still have me,' he stated. 'You'll always have me, Lily, for as long as you want me in your life.'

'I'll never *stop* wanting you,' she whispered, letting her tears fall on his chest. 'You're my heart, Mark . . . my life.'

'And I'll get you and Kyra out, just as soon as I can. We'll be a family.'

For a long time, they remained entwined on the sofa, until it was time for her to leave. They'd felt too empty, their emotions on the ragged edge, for lovemaking, content just to let the dying sun caress their limbs as they'd held each other. And when he held the front door open to let her out, she simply kissed him once, fully on the mouth, and then walked down the stairs without turning back.

But when he pulled back the curtains to see her crossing the street, her shoulders were hunched and she was holding a handkerchief to shield her face. His own grief a strangling knot, Mark MacDonald shut his eyes and pounded a fist into the palm of his other hand.

They hadn't said goodbye, on purpose.

Raïssa Markovna Sudarskaya lived in a mansard room under the eaves, on the Rue des Sablons near the suburb of Neuilly. The entire floor of her apartment house, once an enormous attic, had been divided into twenty-two tiny rooms now occupied by maids and students. In a corner stood her Bunsen burner, and an old sink, its enamel badly chipped and its iron pipe a glaring ugliness that could not be hidden.

She led a quiet, undisturbed existence, living on her earnings as a piano teacher. By ten o'clock she was always asleep, especially now, when Jews were not allowed outside after eight o'clock. Her single luxury was the beautiful ebony piano that occupied half her room. Now that Claire lived in the Boulevard Exelmans, she sometimes visited her there, and, once in a while, Lily stopped off to see her. Otherwise, her social life was a blank. She was even afraid to go to the temple in the Rue de la Victoire, because of the Germans who were surely keeping it under surveillance.

She was old, almost seventy. Her brilliant life as a student at the Moscow Conservatory seemed like a hazy dream to her now, and she, the talented student, a fairytale princess as unlike herself as the crone is unlike the virgin. But still, her life continued.

It was May 1942. Raïssa Markovna had washed her small plate and braided her sparse, yellow-white hair, and gone to bed. Outside, a downpour of rain clattered against her window and the pavement, lulling her to sleep. The alarm was set for seven thirty, for that gave her just enough time to prepare herself for her first lesson at nine o'clock, in Saint-Cloud.

Sudarskaya was a light sleeper. During the Bolshevik Revolution, she'd learned to awaken at the smallest sound, in case the Bolsheviks arrived and an immediate escape was necessary. So, when she heard the raised voices at her door, in what seemed to be the middle of the night, she sat up at once, her heart flying into her throat. The alarm clock read five in the morning.

The concierge, whom she had known for over twenty years, was saying, loudly: 'I repeat, she isn't here!' Sudarskaya pulled the sheet and blanket over her head, her breath suddenly short.

A metallic male voice answered: 'Turn the knob.' Sudarskaya had never felt such terror in all her life; if the Bolsheviks had brought fear to all White Russians, the Nazis were worse. For the Reds could have done no worse than to kill her, while the Nazis were known to send you to places like Auschwitz and Bergen-Belsen, names that were starting to mean a fate *worse* than death: slow torture, or . . . She couldn't think, wouldn't think, as she felt the doorknob being moved.

But of course it didn't give. She'd turned the key herself, before going to bed. But the German voice persisted: 'Surely there's a passkey, or a master. Go and get it. The corporal will accompany you, and I shall wait here.'

Raïssa Markovna lay, petrified, under the covers. For one flash of a moment, she considered tiptoeing to put the key back into the lock, and thus block the mechanism on the other side. But this would have alerted the officer on guard to her definite presence in the room. Then, they'd have kicked the door in.

A Jewish man she knew from synagogue had been taken to Drancy, the collecting camp from which sealed trains departed every few days, for parts unknown, except for their dreaded names: Bergen-Belsen, Treblinka, Auschwitz, Dachau. What did those names mean? And was it true that lampshades were being fashioned out of the skins of dead Jews there? This nice Jewish man had been seized from his house, in the early dawn . . . just like this, a few days ago.

The little piano teacher was well over the 'legal' age of fifteen to fifty-five, for deporting Jews in France. But then again, the Nazis were well known for their disregard of all but their lust to kill Jews. Now heavy steps were resounding down the corridor, and she heard the concierge say, feebly: 'I found the passkey.'

She thought that for sure, her final hour had come. There could be no escape. She heard the metal key being inserted into her lock, and shut her eyes tightly. But the door did not give way.

'See for yourself, officer,' the concierge said. 'This is supposed to open any door on this floor. But it's not working. And, I told you, Madame Sudarskaya left a few days ago.'

'Well, if we can't open, then we may as well be on our way,' the German voice remarked. 'It hardly seems worthwhile to expend energy on someone who's skipped town. But we'll return tomorrow, to make sure you haven't lied to protect this old Jewess.'

When the steps had stopped reverberating in the hall-way, and she was sure that they had gone, Sudarskaya bounded out of bed, grabbed the same dress she had laid out the night before, and, without bothering to find her shoes or to comb her hair, dashed out like a possessed spirit towards the service staircase.

On the third-floor landing, she found herself face-to-face with the concierge, a little old man from Brittany. 'Madame Sudarskaya, you'd better leave at once,' he told her. 'It was just your luck that we fumigated your floor last week. The chemical must have rusted the lock. Your small key could turn because its contours exactly fit those of the lock – but the larger passkey was stopped. Your life was saved by the cockroaches, so to speak.'

She stared at him, gaping. 'And . . . they're *gone*?'

With a resigned shrug, the old man made an evasive sign. 'But find somewhere else to sleep from now on. Somewhere where they won't be able to trace you. Go to a friend's house . . . anywhere. But not near Neuilly, if I were you.'

Sudarskaya nodded, mutely, and ran down the rest of the staircase. She wondered if the Jews had a special prayer for roaches, and didn't begin to relax until she was sitting comfortably in a taxi, on its way to Boulevard Exelmans.

'But there's no extra room to let,' Madame Portier said, sighing. 'And Madame Dalbret told me you had no money to pay another person's rent. As it is, madame, you and your daughter have raised few questions among the peaceful inhabitants of our small village. But another refugee, old and foreign, surely would.'

'What other choice do we have?' Lily asked. She clasped and unclasped her long, slender fingers. 'Our friend has no one else in the world. We can't turn her away.'

'If it makes any difference,' Kyra interrupted, 'then we'll tell her she's not to leave the house. Like this, no one will even know she's here. She can sleep in the bed with Mama, and I'll take the lounge chair for myself.'

Madame Portier clicked her false teeth. 'Well ... I wouldn't want anyone to think I was a *collabo*. I guess she can come. But you'll have to speak yourselves to the priest, the baker, and the butcher. It'll be up to *them*.'

On the threshold, she turned around, her small eyes like piercing rivets. 'You're all Jews, aren't you?' she murmured, her face unreadable.

Lily and Kyra stared at her, and for a moment, a taut silence almost crackled like an electric field. Then Kyra stepped forward, her chin raised defiantly. 'What's wrong with *that*?' she demanded.

Madame Portier scratched a large mole. 'I didn't say there was anything wrong,' she replied, and moved towards the door. 'Just make sure there's no spilled garbage, and that this old lady doesn't start a fire in the kitchen, as some old folks do, burning their cereal.' And she closed the door.

Marisa Steiner had gone each Wednesday to Compiègne, by train, bringing fruit and vegetables that she'd purchased on the black market, for Wolf. But the German guards refused to let her see the prisoner. There was a strict rule by which no one was permitted an interview with the inmates, and in spite of her charming smiles, and of the crisp bills that she unfailingly slipped to the security SS officer, she was repeatedly turned away.

Yet, undaunted, she would repeat her trip, leaving love letters from herself and Nanni for her husband. Once, in the autumn of 1941, she had been allowed to glimpse Wolf from a distance, across glass panelling and barbed wire. She'd told the guard that her husband's mother had passed away, and that she wished to relay this news to him personally. For five hundred francs, a note had been taken to Wolf, and he was brought one hundred yards away.

She'd seen him, but wondered if he had seen her. He'd been between two guards, his shoulders hunched, his hair considerably thinned out, his face strangely jaundiced and bony. Always, Wolf had been slightly plump, with the face of a good child; and to see him now, looking far more than his forty-nine years, and weighing forty pounds less than when the Gestapo had taken him away, had shocked Marisa so profoundly that she'd fallen back on her wooden chair, unable to force a smile to her lips.

His mother had died, and the guards had not allowed him to ask about her, nor to seek comfort for the first time in six months simply by being able to hold his wife's hands in his own. And so Marisa had gone home, and hadn't seen him since. Now it was already August, and more than fifteen months had passed since his incarceration at the detention camp.

When Marisa arrived that Wednesday, with her basket of goods, the SS officer informed her that Dr Steiner would be leaving, along with all the other foreign attorneys, for a camp in Poland. 'Resettlement,' he called it; she knew it to be *deportation*. She felt glued to the ground, unable to move. 'They'll be leaving the fifteenth of this month, at seven in the morning,' he told her. 'If you wish to see him, come with the other wives to the Compiègne station.'

'Will they let us talk to our husbands?'

'I doubt it. But at least you'll see him.'

Marisa fumbled in her purse, her fingers icy as she slipped the twenty-franc note into the officer's uniform pocket. 'I just wish to know one thing,' she pleaded, her voice vibrant with despair. 'Is my husband well?'

The German touched his moustache, rubbed his chin. 'Your husband is the psychiatrist, isn't he? From Vienna?'

'That's right.' She supposed that among the hundreds of prisoners, few were doctors as well as lawyers.

'He's been ill. He's had an ulcer, and some form of colitis. But be there on the fifteenth, if you want to see for yourself.'

Marisa returned in tears, unable to function. Claire put her to bed and pressed cold, wet facecloths to her forehead, holding her like a daughter. Marisa had never been alone. All her childhood, her parents had surrounded her with warmth, love, and support. Then it had been Wolf's turn. And these past fifteen months, waiting for him to finally be released, had eroded her core of resistance, which had never been strong, like Lily's or Claire's. And now she'd learned that she'd been living for a dream that was the opposite of reality: Wolf, instead of coming home, whole and complete, was about to be deported, his digestive system already destroyed.

On the night of the fourteenth, Lily came to Paris and spent the night in Claire's guest room, in Marisa's bed, hugging her as the tears emptied silently out of her friend. And Lily thought with gratitude that Mark had left France safe and sound, and that Misha was in New York, with their son. She was alone with Kyra, but none of the men she had loved was in the hands of the Nazis. She hugged Marisa, feeling a twin fear for the man she had depended on and loved, and whom she now felt helpless to rescue.

At five the next morning, they arose, dressed, and fed a quick breakfast to Nanni. At twelve years of age, she had become a handsome girl with a quick mind and a comforting, steady presence for her mother. She was old enough, Lily had felt – making all the decisions for a distraught Marisa – to see her father off, for God only knew how long.

At the train station in Compiègne, at six thirty, several hundred women and children were parked behind a grill-work from which the platform of the special German train could be observed. Lily, taller than most, determinedly edged her way through the crowd, to find them a place towards the front, from which the diminutive Marisa would be visible. She pushed her friend in front of her, holding on to Nanni's hand as she forged them a path.

At the grillwork, she turned to Marisa. 'No tears,' she declared. 'He has to *see* that you're strong, for him. You

555

must stand on your tiptoes, and smile, and wave. It's the only farewell he's going to get.'

Marisa nodded, almost catatonic. Lily pressed against the fence, straining to see. But it was not until a quarter to seven that noises were heard, and that SS officers marshalled forward these lawyers who had been imprisoned fifteen months. Most of them were thin, pale, and tripped as they were pushed onto the platform by their guards. 'My God,' Marisa whispered.

The other women were calling out names, and husbands were turning to catch a final glimpse of a beloved face. The sudden note of hope on these resigned features sent a thrill of compassion through Lily. These men, herded like sheep, deprived of their humanity, would remember a smile and a shouted farewell all during their voyage.

'Aunt Lily,' Nanni said quietly. A skeleton of a man, his head completely bald, was being shoved forward by a bayonet, held in the arms of a rigid SS lieutenant. Lily's instinctive intake of breath was filled with horror, and she had a moment of difficulty before being able to grasp Marisa's shoulders. 'Now, Mari,' she whispered.

Tears, though forbidden, were streaming from Marisa's eyes. Lily pushed her against the grillwork, and yelled out: 'Wolf! *Wolf! Look* at us, for God's sake!'

Nanni, sobbing, was screaming too: 'Papa! Papa!'

For a moment, it seemed as though the human skeleton, who looked a hundred years old, was searching through the crowd. But the eyes were vacant, glazed. And then he fell. Many others had tripped, but this man, Wolfgang Steiner, merely keeled over like a door falling off its hinges. Marisa screamed. But the man on the platform remained down, and it was only after all the others, every last one, had been shepherded inside the ominous, dark railway cars that two SS officers returned to the fallen human vestige, and seized him under the arms and at the ankles. He was the last to be thrown aboard. Then the Germans descended, and the engine sounded, and the cars departed, like consecutive hearses.

'I couldn't help it, I couldn't *help* myself.' Marisa was sobbing, holding on to Lily with the tenacity of a drowning woman to her saviour.

'It's all right,' her friend replied, her voice low and strangely devoid of tonality. 'He wouldn't have seen you, just as he didn't hear Nanni and me.'

With a sudden hope painted on her small face, Marisa asked: 'Do you think he'll die on the way . . . today?'

Nanni cried out: '*Mama!* How can you *say* this?'

'Because,' Marisa replied, all at once calm and forceful, 'if he dies, and I pray he does, then he won't have to suffer through the rest!' She turned to Lily, and asked, her voice hard but steady: Will you sit shiva with us? It's only supposed to be the family, but you were so close to him! And will Jacques say the kaddish for him?'

'Papa's still alive,' Nanni countered, outraged.

Lily put an arm around both their shoulders, and stated: 'We'll pick up Jacques, and Mama, and go to the synagogue today . . . spies or no spies. And Rabbi Weill will lead the prayers.'

New York, this autumn of 1942, was a strangely populated metropolis, for all the young men had gone to war, and the immigrants thronged the streets and the coffee shops. Nick looked one last time at his reflection in the mirror, and scrutinized the shadow of the beard he had just finished shaving around his jawline and chin, and the trim brown moustache, which he'd let grow to give himself more countenance, at seventeen. He felt pleased with the poise of his face . . . just the right poise for an encounter with his father.

Nick pulled on the lapels of his square-shouldered blazer, and checked to see if his round-toed shoes were well polished, and his trousers pressed on the bias. Then he glanced around the small apartment that he shared with Charley Blum, a young Belgian Jew whom he had met shortly after his arrival, nine months ago. Charley was handsome, secure, and a ladies' man, which meant that the dapper apartment in the Oliver Cromwell Building, between Central Park West and Columbus Avenue, was often Nick's alone. Charley was older and more sophisticated, and, had he been less honest and less of a 'good guy', Nick would have compared him to a younger version of his father. But he liked his roommate too much to hazard this comparison.

The beds were made, the dishes stacked in the strainer on the small kitchen counter. Nick closed the front door and locked it, went down the lift, and walked out into a hazy sunshine.

He liked this teeming monster of a city, so different from his native Paris that at first he had felt sure that he would hate it here. Paris was cultivated, elegant, and old; New York was unchecked, young, and bursting with energy. Nick had been surprised at how fast he had grown to enjoy it, to find its challenge exactly what he needed.

And he also didn't miss his schooling. As soon as he'd arrived, Misha had declared that he would enrol him in a top Ivy League men's college in the autumn, giving him a semester at the French Lycée to pass his *bac*. Nick had felt a quick anger rising. He hadn't wanted Misha's help, hadn't wanted the advantages that his father could easily have offered him. For Prince Mikhail Brasilov, now a United States citizen, had passed the New York bar examination and now practised law in a small but elegant office on Wall Street. The profession he had prepared for but never exercised, in his early youth, had, ironically, opened up for him in this new country. And, slowly but surely, the glamour of his name as well as his quick, adaptable mind, had generated a small but steady clientele.

Nick stepped onto a bus, and let the scenes change as

the driver took them from 72nd Street to 56th. There, he stepped down, and took the crosstown bus a short way to Fifth Avenue. Even with wartime shortages, this most elegant part of New York still reeked of an unheard-of luxury, comparable, Nick thought, only to the Faubourg Saint-Honoré or the Rue Royale, in Paris. One day, he thought, Kyra and my mother will come, and I shall put them up at the Plaza, or the St Regis.

It was at the St Regis Hotel, on Fifth Avenue, that he was due to meet his father. Any coffee shop or Horn of Hardart self-service cafeteria would have been fine, Nick thought – but Misha was still trying to impress his son with his success, and woo him back with offers of the same, if the young man re-entered the fold. But Nick would never do that. He would make his own success, and he felt certain that he would do so.

His first disappointment had been with the Free French army, which had rejected him because of the discovery of a heart murmur. Later, the United States Army Recruiting Office had sent him away with a 4-F classification, for the same reason. He knew that his father had been relieved; but he had wished to fight, and had felt humiliated at this double rejection. He hadn't come to New York to be a coward.

He and Charley had talked, when they'd first met, at a party. With both Belgium and the Netherlands out of commission, a great need now existed in New York for diamond cutters. They had decided to become partners, twenty-year-old Blum and seventeen-year-old Nick, and they had each paid three hundred dollars to an old-timer on 42nd Street, to teach them the business. Nick had been forced to accept at least this much financial aid from his father. They had gone to work in a large gem-cutting workshop for three months, then had felt confident to open their own tiny shop – again, with a minimum of financial help from Mikhail Brasilov.

But now, earning the incredible amount of two hundred to two hundred and twenty-five dollars a week, Nick had a cheque in his pocket to reimburse part of this debt. He had called Misha to arrange the encounter, and Misha had told him to meet him for breakfast at the main dining room of the stately old hotel.

Nick had mixed emotions about this meeting. It would be the first time he and his father would actually share a meal together since his arrival in the United States. Until now, the young man had refused to have the slightest social contact with Misha. They'd met in his father's office, because Nick hadn't wanted any intimacy to permeate their relationship. He'd pushed Misha out of his thoughts, not wanting to feel anything but the old anger, the old hatred that had replaced the love and trust he had felt as a boy for this magnetic, controversial man who was his parent. But now, too, there was the grim satisfaction of one-upmanship: he'd be meeting Misha to pay his debt, and to show him, once and for all, how unimportant he had become in his grown son's existence. It was a victory of sorts, and one that the young man was not above savouring, like an old battle scar to prove that the old soldier had fought in, and survived, the war.

His father, a snap-brim felt hat on his grey head, walked in two minutes after Nick, and waved, his leonine face suddenly creased in smiles. Nick stood up, formally, and let the older man embrace him. He could sense a slight, though numb, pain, feeling the strong arms, and the scent of his father's cologne. 'You look good, Nicolas,' Misha said.

The waiter came to bring menus. Nick waited, then answered: 'Thank you, Father.'

Misha's suit of Saxony tweed was cut perfectly over a Brooks Brothers shirt, and a silk tie adorned its front. For some reason, this latest business fashion looked remarkably good on the tall, broad Russian, and Nick felt a familiar, gnawing resentment. His father's success irked him, angered him, thinking of Lily and Kyra standing in queues at five each morning, in Paris.

They ordered, and made polite conversation until their steaming scrambled eggs and sausage were delivered with a flourish, with freshly pressed orange juice and aromatic coffee. Nick was ashamed, eating this way during a war. But he was also very hungry. Neither he nor Charley was a good cook, and the places where they went for dinner were usually inexpensive and served *ersatz*, tasteless meals. This was an unaccustomed treat.

It was only over his second coffee that Nick withdrew his wallet, and laid the thousand-dollar cheque in front of his father. 'I told you I'd have it before the New Year,' he said proudly.

'And I told you, Nicky, that it wasn't necessary ever to repay me.'

An awkwardness permeated the air between them. 'I'm not a charity case,' the young man said tightly, only too well aware that he was mouthing the worst of clichés.

'I'm your father.' Misha's face, his still gleaming green eyes expressive and magnetic, appeared to wince, and, leaning forward, he said, gently: 'I know why you hate me. But adults learn to forgive their parents, Nicky. If you want to be a man, then you must forgive like one, too.'

'Like Jesus Christ?' Nick snapped, sarcastically. How he detested himself for falling into the trap, and becoming mean and churlish, like a peevish boy! But where Misha was concerned, a raw nerve always lay at the edge of his skin, ready to be touched off.

'Why not? Have you anything against Him, son?'

Nick breathed in, and touched his moustache. 'I'm not a Christian, Father, and you know it,' he said at length.

If Misha felt the blow, his face did not reveal it. 'So you've been telling me over and over again, these past nine months,' he replied. 'But you *know* I didn't know Lily was half Jewish. I had to learn it from you, when you came here.' Then, regarding his son, he forced himself to add: 'At your age, I had chosen my way. I wouldn't try to influence you.'

'You wouldn't succeed! I might only have toyed with Judaism, had it not been for this war! But the Occupation forced me to define my choice. I wouldn't be surprised if Kyra, too, didn't adopt our grandmother's religion.'

He had planned to shock his father with his last words. And this time, Misha did draw back, his face a silent wound. 'You left us,' Nick murmured, his voice insistent and low, like a gentle yet pressing hum. 'And when you left us, the three of us had to grow up . . . my mother, too. We each made our own way.'

Misha closed his eyes and bowed his head. Then, looking once more at his son, he said, fervently: 'I've told you how my letters were returned, how I tried to find out where you had moved to. More than anything, I hoped to get you all out here, away from the carnage. I *wanted* us to be together again.'

'Madame Dalbret always knew where we were.'

'But *my letters were returned!* You know how Vichy has seen fit to interfere with all mail. You're not being fair, Nick. What else could I have done? Besides,' he added, 'Varvara had her own skin to save. I couldn't have asked her for more than what she did.'

Nick's anger surfaced again. 'She helped plenty. But if you'd *never left in the first place* . . . we'd have stayed a family, and my mother and sister would be safe and protected! You thought only of your own wounded pride, and left Mother the bad debts and hardly any means of support.'

'Don't you suppose I had the money to send her? But I couldn't locate you! And you know yourself that we can't send money to Occupied France!'

Nick read the desperation on his father's face. Suddenly,

he felt very young and helpless. 'Look,' he declared, 'leave Mother and Kyra to me from now on. Kyra's in love with Pierre Rublon, my best friend . . . and if he survives this war, I'm sure they'll get married. But you may as well forget about Mama. She's your wife in name only. Your claims to her ended the day you walked out, without so much as a farewell. I want Mama to come, too: but to be with me . . . and with the others here, who love her.'

'The Robinsons . . .'

'Mark MacDonald. He's good, and he's kind, and he made Mama very happy, those last years. I only hope he had the sense to get out, after Pearl Harbor. If she and Kyra had to stay, at least *he* should have had a chance to escape.'

'It's perfectly legal for a United States citizen to leave any country he pleases.'

'As long as he isn't interned by a hostile power.'

Brown eyes met green, the brown ones hostile, the green luminous and filled with a naked pain that made Nick suddenly flinch, and look down at his hands.

He abruptly rose, his heart pounding frantically, and he declared quickly: 'I'm late. Charley's alone at the shop. See you, Father.'

As he walked rapidly across the room, he could feel the tears pushing at his eyes, and he bent his head low, in case they showed around the rims. He didn't want to see his father's face, that vulnerable ache, pre-eminent on his memory. It made him want to give in, to forgive, and to accept the hand being offered to him.

I'll change my name, he thought, in four years, when I become a citizen. I'll drop the ridiculous title, and take my mother's maiden name . . . or my grandmother's.

And in the vast, sumptuous dining room of the St Regis, Prince Mikhail Brasilov bowed his head and wept, unashamed.

Chapter Twenty-four

The young blond sergeant of the Free French army sat down at a small table in the dusty café, and removed his cap. In front of him, a typical Algiers afternoon was unfurling its endless resource of attractions, which were acted out with all the rehearsed choreography of a medieval passion play in front of his amused eye. A turbaned carpet seller had set up 'shop' in one corner of the street, and bejewelled, dark women with Moslem veils were stopping by, fingering the wool and exchanging quick, sometimes loud words. Street urchins darted between the carpet vendor and an old man offering up baskets of fresh fruits set on a tiny, overloaded stand, a monkey playing at his side. The young man ordered Turkish coffee and a strange, syrupy cake, and watched, fascinated.

'You're Pierre, aren't you?'

The question, spoken in the flawless French of those who had learned it as educated, meticulous adults, jarred him. Since he'd left Paris almost three years ago, he'd heard this tone and accent many times: in London, where he'd been stationed, working in Intelligence and coordinating the efforts of the Resistance underground in Occupied France, most of his British contacts had talked like this; and here, he'd run into many Americans and English, too, especially since the Allied victory in North Africa. But the familiarity of this voice penetrated through him like a hot liquid on an empty stomach, producing shock. He looked up, slowly, squinting. In front of him, standing, was a medium-size middle-aged civilian, his shirt sleeves rolled up, his handsome face tanned under a crop of white-grey curls.

'Mr . . . MacDonald?'

The older man smiled. 'May I join you?'

'Of course.' Pierre remembered this man more from Kyra's words than from his actual memory of him, for they had only met occasionally, and then for brief moments as one of them had come and the other gone from the *pension*. But Kyra had resented him, her dislike thinly veiled, while Nick, on the contrary, had been all 'for' him.

The journalist didn't seem at all surprised to see him here, and Pierre felt puzzled. He said, 'I'd never have expected to run into you. What's brought you to North Africa?'

Mark sighed. 'I'm a war correspondent for the Associated Press. Before that, I was investigating the spy rings in Spain and Portugal. But for six months, I've been in these parts, following the action. And a few days ago, I heard your name mentioned at an officers' meeting I attended. It seems you've made yourself noticed. Your reports have been appreciated by the brass.' He smiled. 'And so I've had you on my mind. The sergeant on duty at headquarters told me I might be able to find you here.'

Pierre leaned forward, nerves tingling like electric wires. 'Mr MacDonald,' he said, 'have you heard *anything* about . . . the situation in Paris?'

The journalist recognized the signs. He himself had gone through all this . . . was still, in fact, going through this. 'I wish to God I could give you news of them,' he replied. 'As far as I know, they're all right, in Chaumontel. I've gone the rounds, trying to find a way to get them both out . . . Lily and Kyra. I've spoken to consuls and ambassadors, and powerful businessmen and members of the Free French military. But there are two problems. The first is that someone *there* would have to smuggle them out – and I don't know who'd do this, with the Krauts swarming the city.'

'So you're telling me that there's nothing either of us can do?'

Mark didn't answer. But his face had set into hard, grim lines. 'I'm not going to give up trying,' he finally stated. Then, to change the painful subject, he asked: 'You fought here, in North Africa?'

'At first I spent time in London, and then, last year, they shipped me out to help beat back Rommel. But now that we've won, I'm at headquarters.'

The thin, amber-coloured waiter deposited a cup of the thick, aromatic Turkish coffee in front of Mark. 'With Italy's surrender, can the Reich last much longer?' he demanded. 'There's word from on high that there's to be a massive Allied landing in France, later this year.'

'I've heard rumours.'

'But of course, you won't tell a reporter.' Mark smiled, giving his face a sudden, boyish look that appealed to Pierre.

Then his face hardened again. 'Things are really getting bad, in France,' he said tightly. 'The general hunger can only be compared to the terror the French have to live through, under the rule of a regime that knows its days are numbered. Even poor old Pétain is being hustled from castle to castle, and his government has lost all pretence at ruling the country. The Germans, and the last of the collaborationists, have grown so vicious that they remind me of wounded lions and tigers, intent on lashing out all around them, to cause the most harm until the moment when, inevitably, they will be slain.'

Pierre Rublon didn't answer. His blunt, strong fingers were playing with his cap. So young, so beautiful, his girl. She had to be spared. He'd done all this for *her*, for *them*. 'You really love her, don't you?' the journalist was asking, his voice soft, yet incisive.

The young man looked into that tanned, weathered yet boyish face, and felt as if at last he had found a companion with whom to be open. He nodded. 'We made promises to each other. Maybe it was foolish – she wasn't yet sixteen – but we talked of marriage, of a future together.'

Mark MacDonald's eyes were distant, their pupils like pinpoints in the hazel irises. 'So did we,' he finally said, the words tight, hard, and infinitely pained.

Then the two men drank the sweet, dark coffee, bound by their shared hopes, fears, and daily remembrances.

As soon as the Germans, losing ground at Stalingrad in autumn 1942, and giving way to the Allies in North Africa, had invaded Vichy and taken the existing reins of control from the weakened old marshal, Aunt Marthe Bertholet packed her bags and moved to the capital. Nantes, she told Claire, was no longer bearable; she needed her family around her, and besides, she was eighty-three and suffered from four debilitating illnesses. She had her furniture sent from Nantes to a vast apartment Claire had found for her at 33 Rue de la Tour, in the same Passy area where Prince Ivan Brasilov had lived, years ago; and she hired a maid, Rosine.

All her life, Aunt Marthe had adored the accoutrements of the First Empire; her crates unwrapped the inlaid, overwrought consoles, cabinets, bed, and other furniture of the epoch, as well as paintings, chandeliers, knicknacks, and dishware of Napoleon's style. The house in the Rue de la Tour had a narrow façade, and only two rooms stood at the front; but the courtyard behind was large and airy, and the seven rooms that bordered it were agreeable. The kitchen lay at the tail end, near the service staircase; it had two windows, and at its centre, a table four yards long; an electric stove, an enormous sink, and an icebox seemed lost among all the cupboards, sideboards, armoires, and small pieces that lined the walls. One could have lived in this large room alone.

Aunt Marthe had furnished the room adjoining the kitchen for Rosine, and had converted all but the master bedroom into storage rooms where all her bric-a-brac lay piled together, from the much vaster space of the Nantes house. Boxes and trunks were heaped pell-mell on top of each other. The old woman was pleased not to have had to rent space from a professional storage company, and was content to live in her ornate bedroom, most often under piles of blankets in her gilt four-poster bed.

Now that Mark was gone, Lily tried to squeeze Aunt Marthe into her tight schedule whenever she came to Paris. She sometimes shopped for her too when she queued for her own allotment of sugar, salami and matches, for it seemed that Rosine was forever 'forgetting' important purchases. She now brought carrots, leeks, and onions for the old woman as well as for her parents and Marisa, from Chaumontel. Lily found her old relative egotistical and demanding, but forced herself to visit Aunt Marthe to save her mother from coming every day. And, every time she came, the sick woman pressed butter cookies and port wine on her, from a seemingly endless supply that she had brought from Nantes in tins and crates. The sweet wine would remain on Lily's stomach, nauseating her all the way home; but to refuse Aunt Marthe would have been futile; she was a domineering old woman whose chief pleasure consisted in imposing her will on the few people with whom she still had contact.

Early in May 1944, Lily decided not to go to Paris for the Thursday visit. She'd been suffering from influenza, and, though for the most part recovered, didn't wish to take chances with a two-hour train ride. The previous June, Kyra had passed her second *baccalauréat*, and in September, had started taking some courses at a child-care centre in Paris. She was going into town three times a week, to learn to become a nursery-school teacher. Like her mother, she was careful not to be on the street after eight o'clock, and carried an identification card that listed her religion as 'Eastern Orthodox Christian'. And so, when Lily couldn't leave Chaumontel on Thursday, Kyra decided that, when her classes were finished the next day, she would stop by Aunt Marthe's apartment with the fresh vegetables.

Kyra was eighteen. She'd grown to five feet seven inches, and had a full, supple figure. But otherwise, she still bore a striking resemblance to her father. Her green eyes, unmixed with any other hue, were like emerald flames, their shape exotic, tilted at the corners. She walked like Misha, too, in a bold stride, and usually disliked her itinerary when she left Chaumontel; for, on the slowed-down métro, and out on the open streets, her arresting figure often drew the admiring catcalls of men of all ages, and of German soldiers. When stopped by one of them, she would respond politely, but with the cold hauteur that had been character-istic of her father. So far, she had encountered no special trouble. Her identification card, though bearing her Rus-sian surname, also listed her as being a French national.

After school, she wrapped her books together in some twine, and took the métro to her old aunt's neighbourhood. She was dressed in the blue and white uniform of the child-care school, her hair braided around her head, and also carried a fishnet bag full of the fresh vegetables from her village. She too found Aunt Marthe a horrid old witch, but had had less contact with her through the ages than Lily. She was able to find the house with no trouble, and went up to the second storey.

Rosine opened the door. 'I'm Kyra Brasilova, Princess Liliane's daughter,' the young woman said.

'Come in, mademoiselle. Madame Bertholet is with Madame Bruisson, in the bedroom.'

Kyra felt her heart beat faster. Mixed feelings assailed

her. Madame Bruisson had to be Uncle Claude's wife, Henriette, whom she hadn't seen since that single encounter in the lobby of the Carlton, when her father had managed the old hotel. She'd been . . . how old? Ten? And the lady had smiled so beautifully, at *her*, alone. And what about the lovebirds? Yet a dark secret had kept Claude Bruisson's family segregated from the Brasilovs, and her uncle had been a *collabo*, and a member of the reactionary, anti-Semitic Legion of French Volunteers.

'Maybe I shouldn't disturb them,' she murmured. 'Perhaps you could just give Aunt Marthe these vegetables – '

'Who are you?'

Kyra found herself staring beyond the lobby, into the eyes of a ten- or eleven-year-old child, with her own black hair, triangular face, and piercing, almond-shaped eyes. She blinked, her mouth dry, her lips falling open. The sensation of staring in the mirror was so great that she laid a steadying hand on an inlaid sideboard.

'My name is Kyra Brasilova,' she said. 'And you?'

'Alain. Alain Paul Bruisson. I'm Aunt Marthe's great-nephew.'

Of course. The boy. She'd barely noticed him, that time eight or nine years ago when she'd seen Claude and Henriette with him, in the Carlton lobby. Kyra's throat hurt from a tremendous lump, and she could feel tears coming. 'I'm your cousin, then,' she said. 'My Mama and your Papa were sister and brother.'

'I come every Friday,' he declared. 'Come on. They've got cakes in the bedroom. It stinks in there, from *her*, the old horror – but the cakes are super!'

She found herself following, while Rosine took the string bag into the kitchen. He was striding through the corridor, his young body already tall and well defined, and she watched him, hypnotically. At the door, he pushed it open and, suddenly gallant, smiled, inclined his head, and made a mock courtly gesture to let her pass first. She would have laughed, had this joking flourish not hit her in the stomach with the poignancy of a remembered dream.

'Mama, Auntie!' he was calling out. 'Look who *I've* found! A *cousin!*'

The master bedroom was like a mausoleum. The immense four-poster dominated the scene, its brocade curtains matching the covers of the seats of the *bergères* and the ottoman. Tables perched everywhere: a large one, set with a heavy silver tea tray, and four or five scattered occasional stands, all inlaid with mother-of-pearl. From the bed, old Marthe Bertholet, propped against an impressive array of cushions, stared at her from her half-closed eyes, her potato nose twitching.

Her stomach queasy, Kyra tried to speak, overwhelmed by the room, the ugly old woman, and the boy. 'Hello, Kyra,' a resonant, attractive female voice intoned, and she turned. On the opposite side of the tea table sat Alain's mother, her slender face perfectly made up, the amber eyes still arresting beneath jet black hair pulled into a topknot that frizzed in permanently-waved curls onto her forehead. The woman was probably fifty, but, like all rich women, had known how to protect herself from the onset of age. She was elegant, unusual, and, Kyra found herself guessing, vibrating sensuality.

'Well, come in, don't stand there like an overgrown oaf,' Aunt Marthe called. 'Your mother didn't come yesterday?'

'Mama's been ill,' Kyra responded, deciding that she, too, hated the petulant old relative. But she forced herself to walk to the bed, and to kiss the withered cheek. It allowed her to compose herself for the other. When she made her way to the seated woman, she was smiling politely. 'Madame,' she said, extending her hand.

'I'm your Aunt Henriette. Don't you remember? We met when you were younger than Alain, at the Carlton. And I thought then that you were the most exquisite little girl I'd ever seen. You've turned into a stunning woman.'

Not knowing what to say, Kyra smiled again, her mouth twitching in a nervous spasm. Why was this woman being so pleasant? She'd always wondered about the feud, but now pushed the whole business resolutely away, with sudden frenzy. She wished that she might exit immediately, to avoid any further complications. Still, her heart thumped erratically, and she was grateful for the cup of steaming tea that Claude's widow was proffering to her.

Aunt Marthe then entered into a series of complaints, followed by ceaseless questioning. All the time that she was answering, Kyra felt Henriette's eyes upon her. Kyra wished that Nick were with her, for she knew that he, loyal to the bone, would have found a graceful exit line. At length, she noticed that the old woman's head had fallen forward, wobbling like a large marble on the end of a stick, and that snores were escaping her lips. 'Aunt Marthe has this habit of falling asleep in the middle of a sentence,' Henriette remarked sotto voce. 'Come. I'd like a chance to talk with you, Kyra. We'll go to the kitchen.'

There was no way to refuse, short of being rude. Alain darted ahead of them, calling Rosine, and disappeared into the young maid's room. 'Good,' Henriette stated. 'That way, we'll be alone. The kitchen's comfortable, like a parlour furnished by Frankenstein . . . but we can sit there, a bit.'

Kyra, feeling like a puppet without a will of its own, nodded. She wanted to escape, for myriad reasons . . . yet, now that she was trapped, her old curiosity about this woman flared up. Henriette took a seat by the large table, and she sat with her hands folded in front of her.

'So now you know,' Henriette began. The amber eyes stayed on Kyra's face, not letting go.

Kyra blushed. 'I – '

'I could see it painted on your beautiful, expressive, Russian face. You saw Alain. Another might have ignored the facts, but *you* couldn't. Because you saw your own face in his face: your own face, so exactly like *his* face . . . your father's face.'

Kyra's throat was parched, her temples beating. 'But – '

'I was his mistress for many years. He was my lifeblood. When he didn't want my child, or me, I married your uncle.'

Trembling, the young girl said: 'But – Papa was married to my mother then. Wasn't he?'

'I came before he even met your mother. And it wasn't fair. She left him, yet he refused to have anything to do with me. I wasn't young, Kyra: almost forty. I'd taken a great risk, to have his child. Because I loved him more than life itself, and because I thought that he loved me, too.'

Henriette's voice, low and calm, hit a nerve inside Kyra. She remembered so many things, haphazardly: herself, naked in the small wood, with Pierre, willing him to leave her pregnant; her mother, suffering in Vienna; her mother, suffering again, alone, in Paris. And her own anger, her stubborn refusal to accept Mark MacDonald. 'Your grandmother tells me that you, too, are in love, with a young man of twenty-one,' Henriette was saying. 'You aren't a child anymore. You *have to try to understand!*'

'Why?' Kyra whispered.

'Because Claude is *dead*, and Alain is your brother. And because you're both so much like Misha, that you have to be my friend, you have to help me!'

Kyra plunged her fingers through the pins to her scalp, scouring the soft skin as if to punish herself for being caught here, listening to this dreadful, painful story – painful for all. 'My grandmother: does she know?' she asked.

'Claire is a strange, reserved woman. But I'd say yes, she's guessed. Before, the resemblance was only on the surface. Alain was a small boy, plump and rosy. But now, he's begun to grow lean and tall, and to take on some of the mannerisms of Misha. Claire would have had to be blind not to notice. But she's never brought it up.'

'What is it you actually want of me?' Kyra demanded.

Henriette was staring at her, her long, narrow eyes gleaming with a strange, unremitting passion. 'Claude told me *everything*,' she murmured. 'Before he left for Russia. About how your grandmother . . . *that great lady* . . . gave birth to him illegitimately, just as I did to Alain. And about how she was a Jew, and Claude's natural father was one, too.'

Kyra didn't answer, but she could feel new waves of shock unfurling inside her. She repeated, her voice suddenly like her father's, haughty and cold: 'What's your point, Aunt Henriette?'

'I want you to promise to help me. The tide is turning, Kyra, and my side is losing. Surely your mother's told you about how Claude and I . . . collaborated with the Germans. There will be severe reprisals . . . and I could lose everything. Everything I ever worked for!'

Revulsion was twisting Kyra's stomach. 'If reprisals come, it's going to be important to have you on my side. I know all about the young officer you're in love with. He's a Rublon. His family's always been prominent. I want you to vouch for me, to deny to one and all that I ever collaborated.'

Now the anger exploded from within Kyra. 'Why should I protect you?' she cried. 'My whole family has stood in danger because of people like you and my uncle Claude! Why should I lie for you?'

Henriette's reply came, unexpectedly soft, belying the strange gleam in her eyes. 'Because,' she whispered, 'I've been lying for *you*. When this is all over, I thought we might be friends. It would be to all our advantage.'

Kyra's expression remained defiant.

Henriette breathed in slowly, straightening her shoulders. She was shorter than Kyra, but the latter was still seated, and so she looked down at her, deeply into her eyes. 'I see I placed my bet on the wrong horse,' she declared, and walked proudly out of the room.

Slowly, like a sleepwalker, Kyra stood up and went to the entrance hall to retrieve her books and her bag. Then, without going back into the house, she opened the front door and slipped out, shutting the large black panel quietly behind her. Outside, darkness had fallen, and she knew that it was past six o'clock, and that she'd get home late.

She'd invent a story to tell Lily: that Aunt Marthe had not let her go, and that, thirsty for companionship, she'd pried and prodded until she'd made Kyra miss her train.

The following Wednesday, Kyra took the train from Luzarches, on her way to school, as was her custom. She left Lily and Sudarskaya bringing water in from the fountain in the courtyard, while Madame Portier cleaned the kitchen.

At eleven that same morning, while Lily and the landlady were peeling potatoes and Sudarskaya quietly sewing in the bedroom, there was a persistent knocking at the front door. When Madame Portier opened, Lily behind her, drying her hands on her apron, they saw the two nice policemen from Luzarches, and, between them, a captain of the German Gestapo. Lily's fingers numbed over the clean cotton of the apron. The Germans never came to Chaumontel, a peasant village of no consequence to them. 'We're sorry to have to disturb you, madame,' one of the *gendarmes* told the landlady. 'But there was no avoiding it.'

His face seemed to be pleading forgiveness. Madame Portier, her chin defiantly jutting forward, swung the door more widely to let them through. Lily still stood, stunned, in the hallway.

'We've come to check your papers,' the captain of the Gestapo stated, his metallic eyes narrowed at her. 'We've heard you didn't register at Luzarches. You *are* Liliane Brasilova?'

575

Lily nodded, and went into the bedroom. As soon as she saw her, Sudarskaya realized that something was terribly wrong. Lily pressed her finger to her lips, and took her bag out of the closet. Then she left, closing the door behind herself. Sudarskaya, alarmed, cowered on the bed, listening for sounds.

Extracting her identification card from her wallet, Lily handed it to the captain. 'It's not in order,' he declared. 'You don't have a *J* stamped across it. And I see you're not displaying the yellow star on your clothing.'

'Madame Brasilova isn't Jewish,' Madame Portier countered.

'Then why didn't she register for food cards?'

'She just came here for a short vacation.'

'Our information is different. The Princess Liliane Brasilova is a Jew, and she came here to hide, with her daughter. Where is Princess Kyra?'

'She went into Paris.' Lily wondered who had given them away, and hoped that there would be a way to contact Kyra, to prevent her from returning home. There was obviously no escape. Even the nice policemen, their eyes betraying compassion, no longer could help her. 'I have a certificate of baptism,' Lily announced.

'It makes no difference. You are half a Jew. Your daughter is one-quarter Jewish. By law, you both should wear the Star of David. You have broken the law by not registering your religion. You are to come with us right away, Princess – as soon as I've searched the grounds for any further evidence of your daughter's whereabouts.'

Lily felt a tremendous calm spreading through her body, after the sudden burst of adrenalin. It was over. There was nothing left to do now, except hope to save Sudarskaya. She'd find some way of alerting Kyra – maybe through the nice policemen at the Luzarches station. But already the German officer was marching through the corridor, throwing doors open.

When she heard the strange, martial footsteps outside their room, Sudarskaya, like a terrified animal, leaped from the bed and over to behind the door. When the captain pushed it open, the tiny piano teacher pressed herself against the wall. 'There's nobody here,' she heard, and then she glimpsed, through the crack, the retreating form of the Gestapo man. He hadn't checked behind the door!

In the living room, one of the policemen was murmuring to Lily: 'We did all we could, madame. But we had no choice.'

Urgently, her voice a mere whisper, Lily said, her fingers pressing the sleeve of the young *gendarme*: 'My daughter will come home by the last train, to Luzarches. If you could meet her there, and send her back immediately . . .'

'Consider it done.'

The Gestapo captain was re-entering the room, his face impassive and hard, like a closed door. 'Very well,' he announced. 'I'll be back in the morning, for the young one. We are leaving now.'

Outside, between the captain and one of the *gendarmes*, Lily walked, her head bent, her legs moving mechanically over the dirt road that she had come to know by heart. It was over. *Over.* She shut her eyes against the memory of Wolf, bald and skeletal, falling on the platform at Compiègne. And she hoped that he had died on the way.

Sudarskaya had been saved, for the second time, by Providence. And she knew that the young *gendarme* would meet Kyra at the station, and warn her not to come home.

When the doorbell sounded, Jacques, in his shirt sleeves, went to open it. Four officers of the Gestapo stood on the threshold. 'Jacob Walter?' one of them demanded.

The seventy-four-year-old man's eyes widened. Slowly, it dawned on him that they knew all about him, and he nodded. When they came in, he went to sit down on the living room sofa, and watched as they took several plastic bags into the master bedroom. He understood what they had come to do, and waited for them, resting against the soft cushions. It was the maid's day off, and Marisa and Claire had gone together to pick Nanni up from school. He was absolutely alone in the apartment, but he was not afraid, simply expectant, feeling in his bones that his peaceful, dignified existence was about to be irrevocably violated.

He could hear them prying open the floorboards in his and Claire's room. Obviously, the maid had finally told on them. She was a young girl from Brittany, whose brothers had joined the Resistance, and he found it difficult to accept her betrayal. But no other explanation presented itself.

My God, he thought: I have to stop Claire and Marisa, somehow! On tiptoe, he walked from the living room onto the balcony, and stood leaning over the railing. And then he felt a hand clamping down on his shoulder, and a German voice saying: 'It's no good, Herr Walter. We have two men stationed downstairs, in front of the lift. They'll have taken them by now.'

'What are you going to do?' he asked, calmly.

'With you? There isn't much we *can* do, Herr Walter. You're Swiss. We'll just have to send you back home, on tomorrow's first train, with a minimal sum of money in your pocket. We've found your silver, and your wife's jewellery, and all the money and gems Frau Steiner hid around the house. But we can't touch you, because of Switzerland's neutrality.'

'And . . . my wife?'

'Your wife is French. She is a citizen of a country the Reich is occupying. That's a different story.'

They walked back into the living room, and Jacques sat down, his whole body trembling, tears gathering in his eyes.

Claire and Marisa were led into the Walters' apartment,

a Gestapo man on each side of them, while Nanni stood between her mother and Claire, her face ashen. 'Jacob!' Claire cried, when she saw her husband coming towards her, tears streaming down his face. Throwing off the officer's hand, she ran across the room and hurled herself into Jacques's arms, hugging him tightly.

Marisa, numb, simply stood limply while her daughter massaged her hand, an expression of defeat painted on her elfin face. At thirty-eight, Marisa now looked older. The skin had tightened over her small features, and her golden hair no longer shone with magic lustre. Wolf's departure from Compiègne had taken the last ounce of fighting spirit out of her, so that now that doom had come, she was simply yielding up to it, much in the same way that Wolf himself had given in after his experience on the *Saint Louis*.

But Claire had been a survivor since her early youth. Her arm still tight around her husband's waist, she asked, defiantly: 'Who turned us in?'

'It's not our business to inform the Jews.'

'But you *knew*. You came in here looking for our silver, and our jewellery. Only our family was aware of where they were – yet you knew exactly where to go!'

'It had to be Marie,' Jacques said, his voice hushed. 'Who else but our family – ?'

'No. Marie's brother was killed last week, in a partisan fight. She'd never collaborate.'

'You'll have to come with us now, Madame Walter. You're under arrest.'

Jacques's fingers twined in hers, Claire shook her head. 'I'm never going to leave my husband. Where he goes, I go.'

'It's not so simple. We have to send Herr Walter back to Switzerland. But you and the others will be deported to a family work camp. Resettlement,' he specified, the sharp, clear word electrifying Marisa with her memories.

Nanni uttered a piercing cry, and Claire moved between

her husband and her friends. 'You can't take this *child* away!' she exclaimed. 'She isn't of legal age, anyway. She's not fifteen yet!'

'It's for us to judge,' the first officer snapped.

'Aunt Claire, I am the only one here of legal age,' Marisa said at length, her voice toneless. 'You're too old, and Nanni's too young. Take *me*, officers. I don't care what happens to me now, in any case. Without Wolf, I – ' Her voice broke off, and she hunched over, hiding her face in both her hands.

'We don't intend to waste the whole day persuading you Jews to leave quietly. Madame Walter, either you come with us, without any further fuss, or I shall have to shoot you down.'

Jacques stepped back, his mouth falling open. The Gestapo officer, a captain, had placed his right hand on his holster, and was drawing a pistol out, threatening Claire. The old man cried, 'No!' and positioned himself directly in front of his wife. 'Darling,' he said, 'when I reach Basel, I'll take all the necessary steps to have you released. You *must* do as they tell you. You *know* that I'll get you out . . . there's no question – '

'But I don't care if he shoots me down. I'm not going to be separated from you, Jacob. I can't let them take Nanni, either. There are laws . . .'

Claire was sixty-four. Still full-figured and elegant, her white hair swept into a French knot at the back of her head, she continued to hold her husband's hand. She'd lived out her life, hurting and being hurt; she'd made her sacrifices, and endured her pain. Now, the gun aimed at her, she stood unafraid, her mind clear, her heart intact. 'You won't take me to a concentration camp,' she told the officer quietly. 'All my adult life, I had to hide being a Jew. And now I'm proud to tell you what I am. I am not a coward, and I'll stay with Jacob, because he's old and sick, and I'm his wife. And, as long as I live, I shall not let you take an innocent Jewish girl of fourteen, when the law reads, clearly, that you can only take those between the ages of fifteen and fifty-five.'

'Then, madame, you leave me no choice.'

In the minute that ensued, Claire's mind took in chaotic parts of a single scene, seeing Nanni running towards her, Marisa collapsing, and Jacques trying to jump in front of her. She saw the officer's finger on the trigger, watched his face as he pulled it. And then, the scene exploded into myriad red splashes, and she felt the jagged pain searing her insides, and felt her legs give beneath her. Conscious of a pungent odour, she knew, too, that she had voided her intestines, and as she fell, she saw Jacques bending towards her, this loving man; and she thought that she heard Lily's voice, and Claude's, and Paul's, all calling to her.

Jacques Walter, his face streaked with tears, the front of his shirt splattered with his wife's blood, was crying, from where he knelt over Claire's dead body: 'You didn't have to do that! She would have gone with you! She simply meant to say goodbye!'

'She was a pig Jewess, and tried to resist an officer of the Reich.'

'You don't understand,' Jacques whispered, his hand caressing Claire's white cheek. 'We'd never been separated. We were married sixteen years, and she's the only woman I ever loved.'

A nervous tick twisting his face, the Gestapo captain simply turned aside, and Jacques saw him clench and unclench his hands at his sides. 'Hurry up,' he called crisply to his underlings. 'Clean up this mess, and let's get out of here.'

On the other side of the room, Marisa and Nanni were holding each other. Jacques could smell the gunpowder in the air, and felt as if his lungs were about to burst. His worst punishment, he thought, was in not having been allowed to be the one to die.

A sergeant was pulling him to his feet, and yet another man was throwing a sheet over Claire's body. Jacques Walter's lips formed in the kaddish, and, silently, he mouthed the words of the Hebrew prayer for the dead.

When Kyra stepped off the train at the Luzarches station, the young *gendarme* moved out of the shadows into the lamplight, and she saw him approach her, surprise registering in her mind. 'You're Princess Kyra?' he asked, his voice low and pressing.

She nodded. 'What's going on?'

'The Gestapo came to our headquarters, this morning, and sent two of us out with a German captain, to arrest you and your mother. She told me to meet you here and to tell you not to come home, because they'll return tomorrow.'

For a moment, her legs weakened. 'Where's my mother?' she whispered.

'They've taken her to Paris. The captain didn't even let her pack. But apparently, he didn't know anything about the old lady – Madame Sudarskaya. She hid behind the door, and since he wasn't looking for her, he didn't pursue the search. It was you they were after.'

The young policeman, full of pity, put his arm around Kyra, and led her to a bench on the platform. She was weeping softly, her head bent forward. 'Do you have anywhere to go?' he insisted.

'My grandma's, in Paris. Unless . . .' Her eyes, huge and green, burned into his heart. 'And Raïssa Markovna – I can't leave her here. There's my great-aunt, who isn't Jewish, and who's old and sick. I suppose I could go there, for a few days.'

'Then I'll go and get Madame Sudarskaya, and bring her here. Don't move. I'll stay with you tonight, to make sure nothing happens to you. And in the morning, you'll both go to this aunt's on the dawn train.'

'Thank you,' she whispered, feeling as if the universe

had collapsed around her. She'd never been without her mother. Everyone had left her: Misha, Nick, Pierre. But Lily . . . She'd always taken it for granted that they'd be together; she'd taken her *mother* for granted, all her life. And now . . .

'But the war's almost over,' she said, new tears forming. 'Why did they have to do this *now?*'

'Because somebody told the Germans about you,' the *gendarme* explained. 'Somebody well placed, in Paris.'

Kyra nodded, at last understanding.

The concierge of the Boulevard Exelmans apartment stood with an arm around Marie, the little maid, who was sobbing. 'When I returned from my day off, they'd already come,' she gasped, fresh tears appearing on the edges of her lashes. 'It was horrible. Poor Madame Walton . . .'

Kyra's own eyes were dry, though red-rimmed. Next to her, Sudarskaya was wringing her hands, her face a mask of uncomprehending agony. She looked, Kyra thought, like one's stereotype of the suffering Jew, mobile features twisted with ancestral pain. The young girl's hand reached out to grasp the gnarled, nervous fingers, to calm her old friend down. 'I knew Claire before I ever met your Mama,' the old woman said. 'She was thirty-seven. She helped me to get my first students. She was my only friend.'

'I know, Raïssa Markovna.'

'Who could have alerted the Germans? Do *you* know?' The small piano teacher searched Marie's face, anxiously.

But it was Kyra who answered. 'It's all right, Marie. *I* know who it was.' But her grim expression revealed nothing to the three expectant faces watching her.

Rosine opened the door, and when she saw who it was, let out an audible sigh and stepped back to let the two women enter. 'I'm so glad it's you, Mademoiselle Kyra,' she cried. Her hat sat firmly planted on her head, as if she'd been caught on the verge of leaving. 'If you hadn't come, I don't know *what* I'd have done!'

Her face was flushed, and she seemed curiously breathless. Kyra said: 'This lady is my friend. What's happening here, Rosine?'

'It's Madame Bertholet. She thinks she can treat me like a slave, putting me to wait on her day and night, with no time off and only six hours to sleep. Well . . . I've decided to quit, *right now!* I'm going to go to my brother's house, in Vaucresson. I can't take another day of this!'

'It's all right,' Kyra told her. 'My aunt's known to be an impossible person. I'll see what I can do to find her a replacement. You can go, Rosine.' Turning to Sudarskaya, she said: 'Wait for me in the kitchen, please, Raïssa Markovna. I'll speak to Aunt Marthe.'

In the master bedroom, confusion reigned. The old woman sat propped against the usual array of pillows, and a tray rested on the slipcovers. 'Good morning, Auntie,' Kyra said. She tried not to breathe the stale air of the sickroom. With the tips of her lips, she brushed the old woman's cheek.

'There's not a damned thing good about it!' Marthe Bertholet muttered. 'That idiot girl says she wants to quit! Who'm I going to find in the middle of a war, will you tell me, to come and work here?'

'Perhaps I can look for someone,' Kyra replied.

'Everybody's abandoned me! I came here to be with my family, and I haven't set eyes on Claire since the day before yesterday. And your mother was supposed to come this morning – promised me to be here to check on the food! What have I done to deserve such a forgetful, selfish set of relations?'

Her voice calm but hard, Kyra said: 'My grandmother's dead, Aunt Marthe.'

Aunt Marthe blinked, horrified. 'Claire? *Dead?* What happened?'

Kyra twisted her hands together, and tears came. Above all, she didn't want to weep in front of this dreadful old woman. But swallowing didn't help. The tears fell. 'She died of a heart attack,' she said, quickly. And then: 'My mother hasn't been well, and won't be able to come to see you for a few months. But I'm here, and I can stay, if you need me.'

The round head tilted to the side, and the slitty eyes examined her circumspectly. Finally, Aunt Marthe replied. 'You're too young, and I don't know you well enough. But I suppose you'll have to do. I'm tired of paying wages to a stupid servant. It's time I had a relative to do my cooking and cleaning – not some illiterate stranger!'

Stilling a gasp, Kyra nodded. 'All right, then.'

'But no extended visits from anyone,' the old woman ordered, her voice edgy with petulance. 'You can have an occasional hour off, or a friend to sit with you. But for no longer than half an hour. I can't afford to feed anyone else – not even for a cup of tea. My resources are limited,' she whined, 'and anyway, I don't like strangers in my house. Rosine was enough to last me till my death. Do you understand?'

'I understand,' Kyra answered.

In the corridor, she stilled the anguish within her. Sudarskaya met her in the entrance hall. 'Well?' she murmured.

'I'm to be her next servant. And she wants no "extended visitors". Raïssa Markovna, you're just going to have to keep very quiet. We're the only ones left now, and it isn't right for us to separate.' Turning to the coat stand, she pulled down a small felt hat. 'I don't know whose this is, though I seem to remember Grandma having one of these. But from now on, during the day, you'll keep this on your head at all times. Like this, on the off chance that she'll get out of bed, we'll tell her that you're just a friend passing through.'

'But . . . where will I sleep?'

'With me, in Rosine's old room. It'll be more comfortable than in Chaumontel, and you'll be safe. But from now on, your name will be Madame Soudaire. "Sudarskaya" is Russian, and the old hen is as anticommunist as she's anti-Semitic. She can't tell the difference between a White and a Red Russian, and we can't run any new risks. I didn't tell her about Mama, and the details about Grandma. She's never to learn that we are Jews.'

Silenced by the enormity of Kyra's command, the small piano teacher simply inclined her head.

Anything was better than her mother's fate, Kyra thought, carrying the dirty tray to the kitchen sink. And she wondered how she'd deal with Henriette Bruisson, who came to visit every Friday. For she knew beyond a doubt that it was she who had set the Germans on her mother's tail, and who was responsible for her grandmother's death.

There had to be a way to stall her, to prevent her from coming here and learning that Kyra, a fugitive from the Nazis, was now living here, with an old Russian Jewess who had miraculously escaped deportation twice, and of whose existence Aunt Marthe was totally ignorant.

She'd simply have to confide in the concierge, who'd always been fond of her mother, and who had much experience in the clandestine. Lily had told her daughter that on the first floor, an escaped prisoner lived; on the third, a British family whose existence was not known, and who should long ago have left the country; and on the top floor, two men who had been sent to Germany for forced labour, and who had escaped.

Kyra fingered the small gold heart that she wore on a chain around her neck, and that her grandmother had given her on her last birthday. At its centre lay a tiny diamond. It was the only thing she possessed with which she might bribe the concierge. But she'd have to trust that it would be enough.

Chapter Twenty-five

One had to train oneself *not to think*. Lily's background as a
Roman Catholic, dwelling among the nuns whose lives had
been defined by abnegation and renunciation, by strict
obedience and poverty, had perhaps prepared her better
than some of her fellow deportees. She remembered staying
up endless nights in her narrow stone room at the convent,
reciting Hail Marys and rosaries, making lists of sins 'of
the mind' that prevented her from falling asleep; and with
the discipline of her adolescent days, she had tried to throw
her mind into another gear, so that she would cease to
exist on this plane, and her five senses cease to register
what was happening around her.

Otherwise, allowing herself to remember the near present, since the Gestapo captain had come to arrest her,
might have reduced her to craziness . . . like the old man
in the corner, whose trousers had dropped, and who had
repeatedly defecated over the shoes of the woman next to
him. Or she might have sunk into total despair.

A kaleidoscope of events crowded her brain. She'd spent
a night in a Paris police station, and been told that if she
wanted, she might alert Madame Portier to put together
fifty kilograms – one hundred and ten pounds – of clothing,
jewellery, books, furs, and foodstuffs, which would be
allotted to her for the journey. She'd felt in a constant state
of panic, dislocated from her family and in terror as to
where she would be taken next. Deportation. They killed
the Jews, though exactly how was still a mystery. And, she
now realized, she *was* a Jew: free choice in this matter had
long since ceased to exist.

She'd shaken her head. When Misha had left, Lily's last vestige of interest in material goods had left with him. She preferred to go alone, without any ties. And besides, she had no idea what had happened to Kyra and Sudarskaya. She'd wanted to leave the house in Chaumontel as swiftly as possible, to prevent the captain from deciding to recheck the rooms. Her heart squeezed into a tight knot, she worried about her daughter, and asked herself over and over whether the young *gendarme* had met her and warned her.

Kyra had never been alone.

After a few days, she'd been sent with other prisoners, old people in fur coats, their backs bent with fear, in a small van with grilled windows used to transport derelicts and disorderly whores after their arrests. They'd been taken to the enormous Vel' d'Hiv', the Vélodrome d'Hiver, a stadium that had been filled, not with eager spectators, but with frightened men, women, and children, who, like her, had wondered where they were being uprooted to.

Horribly alone, Lily had stood, without baggage, and for one terrible moment, had almost asked to send a message to Ambassador Abetz. Had she not been stupid to refuse Charles de Chaynisart? And then, strength returned. Not because Lily was so valiant, so upright and noble – but because, in the crowd, she'd thought she'd seen the bright, auburn curls of Nanni Steiner, her young figure proud and light, in a trim sealskin coat, heavy for the May weather. Lily's heart had turned over, and she'd pushed her way through the crowds, trying to guess where the person had stood that she'd assumed to be Nanni.

At long length, exhausted and perspiring, she'd elbowed herself into a dense group of wailing old people who didn't understand her need to get through. Maybe she'd imagined Nanni; she hoped so with all the might of her heart. For if Nanni was here, her parents might be, too, and Marisa.

But, if it *had* been Nanni . . . she had to admit a wish not to be alone at this desperate time.

They'd left on buses, and had arrived a few hours later at Drancy, a suburban town that, Lily knew, had been converted by the Germans into some kind of detention station for Jews, like that of Compiègne. 'A way station,' she'd been told. And it was there, finally, that she'd been reunited with Marisa and Nanni.

It was in the refectory that she'd seen them, and they her. The young girl had come running, throwing her arms around her. And later, Marisa, her face white and drawn, had burst into sobs and told her about her mother. Lily had sat like a stone, willing the pain to lift from her heart. She hadn't wept. She'd pushed this death far back, telling herself she'd deal with it later. Because Marisa needed her. She'd seen the barely masked hysteria in her friend's eyes, and rallied to bring forth some hope, as vain and as stupid as she knew her words to sound.

The next morning, the Germans had driven thirty-five hundred of them to a train station far removed from the beaten track, and she'd found herself being shoved to the back of a cattle car. She'd remembered Raïssa Markovna's joy, explaining to Kyra how her wish to travel on a freight train had finally been fulfilled. But this was no joke. Fifty, seventy, maybe one hundred people were being crowded into a boxcar built to accommodate eight cows or fifteen pigs. Lily had held tightly to Marisa's hand, and to Nanni's, feeling her back pushing against the wooden planks, and her neck onto an iron bar. And then the doors had been shut, bolted . . . and almost total blackness had come over the doomed passengers, relieved only by tiny windows, like slits, high above Lily's head.

How many days had they travelled? They'd been pressed tight, one against the other, in a fashion so monstrous that some had begun to scream, from lack of air. And then, they'd received only fourteen ounces of food for the first three days. After that, only an isolated piece of bread. Starving had been less painful, however, than thirst. Once a day, at some station where, amid big jolts, the boxcar had come to a stop, perhaps to be hooked up to a different convoy, or to move to a side rail, a water bottle had been flung through the slit windows, and had been seized by anxious hands. Often, the will to survive had obliterated all other human sentiments, and the contents of the bottle had been gulped before it was ever passed to the ones near the door.

And the only sanitation facility had been a covered bucket, soon uncovered, soon overflowing. The worst part was that few people could ever reach it. For many hours, the young, the valiant, had held out. And then, Nanni had said: 'I can't. I have to go, here.' And Lily had told her to go ahead. There'd been no point in helping her to squat, or to remove her panties. They hardly had the room to stand. And so Nanni had wet her pants, and after that, Lily and Marisa had done the same, like incontinent animals.

Amid the pungent odours of excreta, old men vomited, and a baby suffocated. In front of them, an old woman tried to collapse, but couldn't, her dying body maintained upright by other living bodies. We don't even have the room to *die*, Lily thought. And then she wondered how she had steeled herself . . . how young Nanni had known *how* to steel herself, to accept death, decay, and ignominy. Perhaps the losses Lily had sustained, and her last years of poverty, had helped her; but she marvelled at Nanni's inner strength, she who was still a child, and who had always known comfort.

It had turned cold, and, standing on tiptoe, Lily had seen a bleak landscape. And now they were clanging into a station, she could feel it, and her fingers tightened over Nanni's, and she said to Marisa: 'Fresh air. We'll have fresh air.'

590

Only Marisa didn't answer. She'd long ago ceased to speak, her head on Lily's shoulder, her blue eyes unseeing . . . dazed by hunger and shame, and abysmal fear.

All at once, the door to the outside was flung open, and the prisoners, momentarily blinded by the strong white light, stood shakily hooding their eyes. 'Out!' came the brisk order in German, and slowly, the fatigued people made their way to the platform. Lily, Marisa, and Nanni, at the back of the boxcar, were among the last to leave.

They were standing on a platform set against a grey background. Across some tracks, they could see barbed wire held up by myriad fence stanchions, and, beyond, an A-frame grey house with chimneys that belched smoke. But on the platform itself, SS guards, dressed in black uniforms, with silver pistols and batons, were busy marshalling the prisoners together. And then, men in blue-and-white striped jackets and trousers, with matching caps on their shaven heads, stood gathering together the luggage being heaved off the wagons.

The SS men were lining the deportees into rows of fives. Lily noticed that the women and children had already been divided from the men. She found herself pushed, between Nanni and Marisa, next to a young woman carrying a baby. In front of them, two older women, in elegant clothes, stood clutching each other's hands. One of them turned, and asked Lily: 'Why are we here? What are they going to do to us?'

'I have no idea,' Lily answered, smiling to give herself, as well as her interlocutress, courage.

'They're selecting us for work or the family camp,' the young woman next to Lily told her.

In the ensuing silence, Nanni stood fidgeting with the buttons of her coat. Lily faced Marisa, and began to fluff up her lifeless hair, to pinch her cheeks. 'Whatever this is, you'll need to look strong,' she told her, tersely. 'We all must, if we want to stay together.'

591

The line was moving forward rapidly, and now they could see a tall, handsome man in a form-fitting uniform waving each person to the left or right with a flick of his thumb. He reminded Lily of the dandies she had known in Paris – younger versions of Charles de Chaynisart, always a little nonchalant and careless in their exquisite, perfumed elegance. The contrast between this man, clearly not yet forty, and the bedraggled prisoners who were parading in front of him, their throats parched with thirst and their clothes soiled and smelly, shocked her to the core of her being.

What have we done to deserve this? she asked herself, a deep revolt forming. We've committed no crime, any of us! And yet we're being stripped of our dignity, brought here on cattle trains like soulless animals . . . just because we are Jewish.

A young boy, looking barely older than Nanni, was loading some luggage into a truck. He was bone-thin and dressed in the pathetic blue-and-white striped uniform, yet one could tell that his smooth, pleasant features, and his bright brown eyes, would, in a normal setting, have made him good-looking. Nanni put her hand out, and touched him. Instinctively, a fearful animal, he jumped back.

'I didn't mean to frighten you,' she said, her voice trembling slightly. 'But . . . what's going to happen to us?'

Glancing quickly around, he asked, in a low, hurried voice. 'How old are you?'

'Fourteen. And you?'

He shook his head, fear making him impatient. 'Just remember this: if the selector, Dr Mengele, asks you the same question, you will tell him you are eighteen. Then he will send you with the able-bodied women to be a slave labourer.'

'But . . . isn't he going to check the records?'

The boy laughed, but the sound was totally mirthless.

'He never does. The secret in this place is never to look weak, old, or sick . . . and not to be a child.'

'Why not?' Her grave blue eyes searched his face.

'I have to go,' he said, taking hold of a rucksack and throwing it into the truck.

'What's your name?' she asked, hesitantly.

'Mihai. Mihai Berkovits. You?'

'Anna Steiner, from Vienna. My family calls me "Nanni". And you, where are you from . . . Mihai?'

'From Hungary . . . Transylvania. But look – '

'Will we see each other again?'

'That's not likely. The men are kept separate from the women, and almost never come together. Try to get placed into this work detail. It's the best. We call it "Canada", because of all the loot we have to sort through.'

'But . . . aren't those *our* things?' she asked, with dismay.

'I could get one hundred and fifty strokes of the whip for even having spoken to you,' he mumbled. 'Just remember, Anna . . . you have to be *eighteen* . . . just like me.'

'You're eighteen?'

'If I weren't,' he told her, his dark eyes fastening on her, 'I certainly wouldn't be here, talking to you, and risking my life.'

Then he quickly moved away, an emaciated young boy among loads of heavy parcels. Nanni watched his receding back, and felt Lily's hand around her wrist. 'You've made a friend?'

'I'll probably never see him again,' the young girl said. 'But he gave me precious advice. I'm to be eighteen. Tell Mama.'

It was their turn. Lily held tightly to Marisa's arm, feeling her about to faint with fright. She herself could feel her knees weakening. The elegant man had taken a single look at the boy on their far right side, and had flicked him and the woman with the baby to the left, following the two older women from the line ahead. Now he was scrutinizing

593

Marisa. 'Tell me,' he asked, smiling. 'Are you strong? Perhaps you would prefer the family camp. You appear to be . . . well . . . delicate.'

'She's really very strong,' Lily spoke up, in her flawless German. 'Small bones run in the family. But she's never been sick in her life.'

He shrugged. 'Well, then, to the right. You, too,' he added, a trifle impatiently, flicking his thumb at Lily.

The two women hesitated, waiting for Nanni, but an SS lieutenant waved them on, brusquely. Behind them, as they walked away, they heard the selector ask: 'And how old are you?'

Her head proudly raised, Nanni replied, unflinching: 'Eighteen.'

He placed his fingers over her shoulders, felt the firm young muscles, and nodded. Not ungently, he turned her resolutely to the right. She started to run, to catch up with her mother and Lily, her face breaking into a smile. Reaching them, she announced: 'I made it!'

'And all the others?' Marisa asked. 'Where are *they* going?'

'It doesn't matter, does it? We're going to be together,' Lily replied. And, linking arms, they entered a long line of able-bodied women, moving slowly across the tracks.

Lily, who had never undressed in front of anyone, not even Misha and Mark, felt the mortification spread through her, ripping away the last threads of self-respect to which she had been clinging. Naked, she had been pushed into a room where SS men stood leering at the nude women parading before them. At a large wooden table, three girls, in coarse grey dresses, kerchiefs around their heads, sat holding scissors and razors. Their faces were hard, closed, rough.

'Next!' the SS captain called.

Marisa moved forward, trembling, her thin body caving

in already. The first girl seized her by the hair, and cut it off in a series of blunt snips, and then, with a razor, shaved the rest of it off. Lily stood staring, agape, at the friend she had known all her life, and whom she now could hardly recognize. But the second girl was busy shaving off Marisa's pubic hair, so harshly that at one time, Marisa cried out. The SS captain, slightly unsteady, laughed. 'Jewish whore,' he said in German.

The third woman was daubing Marisa's pubis, and her shaven head, with a pungent, acrid liquid. Lily stepped forward, chin firm. And then the captain said: 'This one. Save this one for us. I like the way she looks.' Lily could smell the odour of whisky on his breath.

'She's too old,' another countered. 'When we can have them young and pliant, why take this old broad? Let her go.'

Impatient at the wait, the first girl called to Lily with a strange accent ... perhaps Slovakian? The Czechs had been here longer than anyone but the Poles, Lily had guessed. She moved up, and the beautiful brown hair that she had never shorn in all her life, was snipped off as if it had been the mane of a horse. Lily shut her brain again, travelling back in space to that small, prim convent room, and began to whisper the words of the Ave Maria.

'What's she mumbling?' the Captain asked.

'It's a Hail Mary,' Lily replied, in her accentless German.

The man stepped up, swung back his arm, and slapped her suddenly across the face, bringing tears of surprise and pain to her eyes. 'That's one of ours, not one of yours, you Jewish sow,' he spat at her.

Behind her, Nanni was standing, almost in front of the hair cropper. Lily's pubis was being shaved, the girl's hand harsh and careless as she slashed the razor across the sensitive area. The captain was eyeing Nanni with interest. 'Blue eyes and dark hair, young, plump, and rosy,' he stated. 'Not so striking as the other, but with the right outfit, she could be a beauty. How old are you?' he demanded.

'Eighteen.'

'Virgin?'

Lily felt the shock passing through her, but Nanni's voice was perfectly calm and assured, as she replied. 'Yes.'

'Then get out of this line. Heinz, you take her with you. We've selected three from this batch, and that's enough.'

Nanni's arm was roughly gripped, and she was pulled out of the line. Behind her, Marisa, a hairless, nude animal, was asking, her voice congealed with fear: 'Where are they taking her?'

The Slovak girl who was daubing Lily's scalp answered, in bad German, her voice a hard whisper: 'To the whores' barracks. She's lucky . . . luckier than any of us. And she doesn't look like anything special, if you ask me!'

Their exchange had lasted a mere few seconds. With a hard push, a young SS officer forced the two new deportees to exit into another room, where they were subjected to scalding baths followed by brutally cold showers. Another set of grim-faced women watched over them, moving them in and out with the precision of drill sergeants. When they were dry, their skins burning from the hard chemicals, Marisa and Lily were issued the same kind of rough, grey, tattered rags that the Slovakian girls were wearing. Lily's was tight and short, showing vast expanses of her thighs, while Marisa's, on the other hand, floated around her, dropping to midway between her knees and her feet. They were handed wooden clogs, reminiscent of what Dutch children wore in holiday pictures. Then they followed a young woman out of the back door, along a path lined by low stone huts and a fence of wiring and stanchions.

'Lily, Lily,' Marisa cried. 'What are those men going to *do* to Nanni? They're going to rape her – '

'She's alive.' Lily surprised herself with the hard tone of her voice, cutting into her friend's words. 'They didn't make her cut her hair. That awful woman at the table told us she was one of the lucky ones. Just remember that, Mari. One of the lucky ones.'

After a walk of perhaps half a mile, they found themselves, in their absurd clothes, lining up again in rows of fives, to be counted. Behind them stood a long, low building with three chimneys, from which emanated odours of food. A well-fed, strong woman of about thirty, her red hair curling around her face, her body clothed in an attractive skirt and blouse, was saying to them, in a loud voice: 'My name is Malka Sandikova. I am a Slovak. I am your *Kapo* – your trustee. The Germans are going to count you. Every morning, and every evening, you will be counted. I have been here since '39, and you are all to be my responsibility. You are to do everything I tell you. If you disobey, I shall punish you. I report directly to the *Oberscharführerin*, Irma Griese, who is in charge of all of us . . . groups and groups of us; and if you do something she doesn't like, then I too shall have to pay. So you see, I want to make sure you do exactly what she wants . . . what they all want.'

And then, in the oncoming dusk, the three hundred women were counted like sheep, in front of the kitchens. It was only after that that they were finally taken to their hut. In front of the long, low stone building, Malka Sandikova looked quickly around, and then pointed to an area behind the women's heads. 'You're just fodder for the ovens,' she hissed at them, her face contorted into a grimace beyond humanity. 'Whenever you get the illusion you're still a person . . . check the smokestacks going day and night!'

Uncomprehending, Marisa stared at Lily. But Lily quickly shook her head, and reassured her with the light pressure of her fingers. 'The point is, Mari,' she whispered, 'never to disobey, and never to think. It's the way we're going to survive.'

'And Nanni?'

But someone was poking them in the back, and so they entered, leaving behind them any hope beyond that of simply pulling through.

Sudarskaya, Rosine's black and white uniform splitting around her fat hips, opened the front door, keeping the chain on. 'Yes?' she demanded, a deep frown forming between her brows. Atop her white-streaked red hair crested a small, starched white cap.

The thin, fashionable woman, her dark hair hidden beneath a velvet strip mounted by a froth of egret feathers, blinked, startled. 'Madame Bertholet is expecting me,' she stated. 'Who are *you?* Where is Rosine?'

Sudarskaya's chest expanded in a lugubrious, long sigh. 'I'm Rosine's cousin. Her mother's cousin, that is. Rosine had to go home, unexpectedly, to help out. And so I came. Madame Bertholet's quite ill, I'm afraid. The doctor's come and gone, and has requested that no visitors be admitted. She needs absolute rest.'

Nervous fingers massaging her throat, the other hesitated. 'But ... I'm her niece ... I always come, on Fridays.'

In her best imitation of a French peasant woman, the tiny Muscovite piano teacher shrugged, making a compassionate face. 'I beg madame to excuse me, then,' she declared. 'But ... orders are orders. Especially when they come from Madame Bertholet. When she heard the doctor ... madame should have been here! "Raymonde!" she cried. That's my name: Raymonde Soudaire, at madame's service. "Raymonde! I don't want to die! You are not to let a living soul in, under any circumstances." And madame knows Madame Bertholet: what she wants, she gets. So all that I can say is that if madame will leave her name and telephone number on this piece of paper, I shall be glad to call her every week to give her a precise health report on Madame Bertholet.'

Perplexed, the other nodded. 'But – perhaps I should speak to the doctor . . . directly.'

'Oh, no!' Sudarskaya cried, almost losing her cap in her excitement. 'Madame Bertholet would never forgive madame, and would fire me, for interfering in her life!' Again she added, conspiratorially: 'Madame *knows* my esteemed employer.'

'Madame', on the other side of the chained door, remained perplexed under this barrage of third-person explanations, still trying to figure out who had said what to whom. At long length she lifted a helpless hand. 'All right, then. Perhaps you're right, Raymonde, and my aunt would be angry. Here's my card. Call me every Friday morning, and if Aunt Marthe gets better, I'll come right over.'

'Madame's generosity will be most appreciated by Madame Bertholet.' And without waiting for a farewell, the small Russian closed the door firmly in Henriette Bruisson's face, and leaned against it, mopping her wet forehead.

Kyra was emerging from the kitchen, her face pale, her heart pounding. 'How did it go?' she whispered.

The old woman plumped out her pigeon breast, and smirked. 'I should have gone to Petersburg, Kyrotchka,' she stated. 'To the Imperial School of Dramatic Arts. I would have made a *grand* career, not like your Jeanne Dalbret, who has only her legs to boast of!'

Suddenly relaxing, Kyra steadied herself against an end table, and smiled. 'But I'm afraid you'd have made a lousy *coiffeuse*, Raïssa Markovna,' she added.

Tilting her round head to the side, Sudarskaya examined the young woman. Her lustrous black hair had been cut off at her chin, then bleached in cheap peroxide to a strange, reddish-blond hue; and then it had been subjected to a makeshift permanent wave, executed in Aunt Marthe's

599

bathroom. 'You do look different,' Sudarskaya remarked. 'And that's the whole point, isn't it, little one?'

'My own brother wouldn't recognize me,' Kyra said, and suddenly they were both still, thinking of all the ones they loved who were completely out of reach to them.

But the buzzer was screeching, and Kyra hurried off to Aunt Marthe's room, already out of breath.

The barrack looked like a stable for no more than fifty horses, the purpose for which it had originally been intended; but close to one thousand women slept in it. Entering, one passed the small room occupied by the *Blockälteste*, or senior block prisoner, and then proceeded into the long room illuminated only by a thin strip of clerestory windows. A single stove stood in the centre, and, proceeding outward, were never-ending three-tiered bunk beds, their wooden slats fitted unevenly, with only scant mattresses scattered around. The women slept five to a tier, in simple night-shirts, with only a single, thin cover, and, at night, were not allowed outside to the bathrooms, and had to use a covered pail. Even in the spring and summer, the floors and walls oozed with dank moisture. This was home for Marisa and Lily.

Several days after their arrival, they were taken to yet another grey house, where they stood in line in front of several young girls. When it was Lily's turn, the girl in front of her asked her for her left forearm, and, with a small needle, punctured a series of numbers onto her skin. Lily held her breath, the dreadful burning branding her, she realized, forever. But she made it a decision not to flinch, and not to cry out. These women who had come here years before had learned to protect themselves by dropping all human sensitivity; she would have to survive by never giving in to her moral or physical pain, keeping it all inside.

Outside, in the bleak, white sunlight, she examined her

fresh skin. In bold blue letters, she had been stamped *B-14448*. Gone was her identity except as that tattooed number. She was hairless, shapeless, and without name.

She waited for Marisa, and together they took their places in the usual lineup by rows of fives. Next to them stood a reed-thin girl from Budapest, who had introduced herself as Magda on the first day. She'd arrived only weeks before, as part of a tremendous deportation of Jews from her country. They'd spoken French together, and German, for it seemed that upper-class Hungarians were fluent in these languages. She was a quick, bright creature, in her early thirties, and had been assigned to the coveted 'Canada' brigade. She'd been a dancer in the ballet, and had struck up an immediate rapport especially with Lily. It was good to know where they were, what would be going on, and how they should behave, because it looked as if Magda, before them, had already gleaned a great deal of precious information.

'Canada' was not, as Lily had thought, a place where they sorted through incoming luggage to ensure delivery to its varied owners. Instead, the brigade of grey-dressed women and blue-and-white striped men sorted through all kinds of riches, and set them aside in different groupings to be mailed back to the Reich. Sometimes, one was able to find a special something that could be hidden under a skirt, if the watchful SS guards were just a trifle drunk.

Magda had explained to them that the tattooing occurred irregularly. Sometimes it happened on the first day; other times, as much as two months later. Now the three of them stood in line, and marched back to the barrack. Marisa had tears of shame in her eyes, but Magda's head was proudly lifted in an attitude of defiance. 'It's a badge of courage,' she said to them. 'They're daring us not to burn, or die of starvation.'

The starvation, Lily and Marisa already could attest to. In the morning, before the dreaded roll call, or *Zeile Appell*, when the entire camp of thirty thousand women was counted, they were handed a cup of black, thin *ersatz*, an imitation coffee to which no milk or sugar could be added. Sometimes, but not always, a piece of bread was added. 'Hannah in the kitchen *Kommando* told me that it's made with parsnips and sawdust,' Magda had informed them. And it was nearly inedible, tasting like blotting paper. At noon, on the job, they received their ration of soup ('made with grass, water, flour, and one potato for seventy gallons'), and sometimes bread with one and a half ounces of sugar beet jam. At night, after the far more lengthy, far more trying *Appell*, they would be given an occasional strip of sausage or a piece of cheese, and a cup of soup. Magda had already lost twenty pounds since her arrival.

One learned to feel the hunger pangs at each and every moment, and to still them by thinking of something else.

Now Marisa asked: 'Why does everyone always speak of burning? Malka tried to frighten us with that, and I thought she was crazy.'

Glancing around furtively, Magda leaned towards them and whispered: 'She's mean, but hardly crazy. Look, to the west end of camp, at the smokestacks. I learned, from my work companions, what goes on there. There are five ovens, in Auschwitz – four large, modern ones here in the new camp, and one less evolved in the old. Underground, below each oven, is a huge gas chamber. And every day, the SS gas six thousand Jews – the ones that got sent to the left at the first selection, and all the ones who get too weak to pass all the next ones. The ovens burn the bodies of all the Jews who were gassed . . . day and night.'

Marisa's lips had fallen open, and she said, awed: 'That man, at the ramp . . . He asked me if I felt strong, or if I wanted to be sent to the family camp. You mean that . . .?'

Lily, as usual, had a firm arm around her shoulders, steadying her. She spoke firmly, staunchly. 'What did you mean . . . "all the *next* ones"? You mean that there will be other selections?'

With a short laugh, the Hungarian dancer made a face. 'Auschwitz, and especially Birkenau, the new camp, is a death factory, Lily. They don't have to look for excuses to slaughter us. Josef Mengele, the man at the station, goes up and down the Lagerstrasse looking for blocks where weak people seem to predominate. And then, swiftly, he makes it a point to descend on that block with some kind of trumped-up inspection.'

A few minutes later, she broke the silence again, her chin aimed in the direction of a skeletal woman leaning against a cart, her dark eyes vacant, her face smeared with dust and dirt, her nails like claws. 'See that one?' she murmured. 'We call them "Musulmen". They're the ones who've stopped being human, who defecate in the middle of the barrack, or who haven't washed in months. The ones who've turned senile at twenty-five. The ones who weigh sixty pounds and are dying of typhus or of dysentery. And, sooner or later, we'll all end up that way. Our only hope is that before we reach that point, the Allies will come swooping down in their magnificent shiny aeroplanes, and save us. Because the Musulmen are prime targets for immediate gassing. The Germans want working slaves, not slobbering idiots.'

'Surely, surely my husband died on the transport,' Marisa said, her voice ragged. 'I don't know where they were taking him, but if they have ovens here, wouldn't they have them elsewhere, too?'

'Preferably outside the Reich. But many died in the boxcars, when we came from Hungary, and thus were spared, Mari.'

Bending her head, Marisa let the tears fall on Lily's hand, and, impulsively, the young dancer hugged her. 'But we're alive,' she said, vibrating courage. 'And *we'll* never see the inside of those gas chambers.'

* * *

The barrack looked nothing like the others. It had proper beds, curtains, heating, and even potted plants. A movable bar had been installed, set up with liquor bottles and fine crystal glasses.

And the girls. Girls, all of them, not women. Young, one lovelier than the next, ranging in years from late teens to early twenties. Nanni, who was the youngest, looked at her reflection in the gilded mirror, and was amazed. She'd never considered herself beautiful. Her mother, and her Aunt Lily, were beautiful women. She had just been a girl, with good skin, glossy brown hair, normal, symmetrical features, and intelligent blue eyes. Not bad, but certainly nothing to dream about.

Now she saw a small *woman*, the silk dress cinching her tiny waist and revealing the fine, muscled legs encased in kid boots. For, even in the summer, Auschwitz-Birkenau was damp and cold and grey, and its paths filled with ugly marshes through which one could catch cold.

Wanda, one of the Polish girls, had combed Nanni's long hair so that it fell in great, dark swoops around her shoulders. And the contrast between her hair and eye colours drew attention. Nanni realized, with shock and a certain youthful pride, that in her person had been captured the best elements of both Robinsons and Steiners.

'You're such a pretty girl,' Heinz Kleinert said, motioning for her to sit down next to him. 'When I saw the dress this morning, I had to bring it to you at once. Perhaps I'm falling in love with you.'

Nanni blushed. Suddenly, because of the young boy at the train ramp, she had been propelled into a world for which she felt totally unprepared. She found it both a horror and a strange, kaleidoscopic mirage . . . nothing at all like the boxcars, nor like what she'd seen happen to her mother and Lily. She tried not to think of them, because inevitably, the gnawing anxiety sprang up, and the pain of missing them.

She and her mother had never been separated, even for one night, until now. Poor Mama . . .! She'd aged so much, and all that fine, vibrant, naughty spirit had been washed out of her, leaving only an exhausted, frightened woman approaching middle age, whose tears flowed incessantly.

She went to sit on the bed, next to Heinz. Like this, in the late afternoon light, he seemed just like any young man she might have known in Vienna. He was even handsome. But when he started to push himself on her, when he forced that part of his body, so engorged and disgusting, purple and veined, into her most private enclave – she wanted to scream with anger and shame, and with the searing pain of her violation.

'Accept it gladly,' Wanda had advised her. She was a tall, voluptuous blonde, older than Nanni by eight years. 'Remember that when they tire of us, they'll make sure we never live to discuss what happened here.'

Perhaps her father would have preferred for her to die. As she let Heinz's hand travel from her shoulder to her breast, the profound shame overwhelmed her, and she froze. 'What's wrong?' he asked.

'Nothing. I was thinking of my father. I'm sure he's dead now.'

'I'm sorry.' Heinz Kleinert gently pushed her onto the satin coverlet, and started to massage the tips of her nipples. 'Your father was not a Jew. Of course not. What did he do? Did he plot against the Reich?'

Wanda had warned her never to say anything that might displease their SS lovers. And so, swallowing her anguish, she said, tears in her eyes: 'He worked with the Social Democrats against the *Anschluss*.' Which, of course, was the truth.

'And so they sent you here because of this?'

Tears swam up and engulfed her. He took this to mean an affirmation, and, in sympathy, buried his face between her breasts. She'd heard of some inmates who carried poison capsules on them, and wished, now, that all this might be over.

He had removed his pants, and now she saw, through the haze of her tears, that tremendous, obscene organ, throbbing with a life of its own. He was bringing it close to her, and she could smell the odour of his flesh, of that slight perspiration combined with sex and urine. 'Kiss me now,' he told her, his voice oddly thick, the way it was each time he mounted her. Only this time, he hadn't touched her once in her tender parts.

She started to sit up, but with a motion of his hand, he stayed her. 'No, Anna,' he said. 'Kiss me *there*. I want to feel your warm, sweet lips around *him*. *He* wants you just as much as I do.'

Her eyes widened with incredulity. Heinz had this horrid habit of personalizing his organ. Sometimes he called it 'Hermann.' And she was supposed to call it 'Hermann', and to caress it gently. But to *kiss* it?

Holding her breath, she planted one short, dry kiss on the tip of Heinz's penis. He began to laugh. 'Open your mouth,' he ordered, though the words still came in that polite, kind tone of voice he always used with her. She parted her lips. And then, with full force, he thrust his penis inside her mouth, to the far back of her throat, and she felt herself gag uncontrollably.

Nanni held her breath, counted to ten in German and in French, in order not to vomit. And then he spewed out his liquid, and her mouth was filled with warm, thick matter, and she wanted to spit it out but didn't know where. He had thrown himself exhausted on top of her, and now asked: 'Did you swallow me? Swallow me, Anna. I want you to have all of me, because I love you, I love your purity, and because I knew from the beginning that you couldn't possibly be a Jew.'

Nanni swallowed.

* * *

Slowly, Marisa and Lily learned most of what there was to know about the strange city where they were interned. It was fifty miles west of Cracow, occupying a city the Poles had called Oświęcem. The first concentration camp, Auschwitz I, contained the prisoners of war and other, mostly non-Jewish inmates. On Monowice stood the industrial plants. And Lily and Marisa, along with some two hundred thousand other men and women, the vast majority being deported Jews from various countries of Europe, lived in Birkenau, named after the alley of slim pines and birches through which the condemned had to pass on their way to the gas chambers.

Auschwitz occupied 1,150 acres, on which hundreds of barracks and blockhouses were strewn in complexes set apart from one another by electrified fences. Farther away, munitions factories had been set up, as well as farming fields and mining camps, all worked by squadrons, or *Kommandos*, of slave labourers. It was considered a privilege to be sent out of Birkenau to work in the synthetics plants, or in the factories. Because this way, one avoided the constant selections that took place 'on the home grounds'.

In retreat from all of this, the camp commandant, Rudolf Höss, and the SS officers under him, including the beautiful Irma Griese and the trim, dandified Dr Mengele, dwelled in smart houses set inside blooming gardens. There were about forty-five hundred SS guards for the hundreds of thousands of inmates, yet the latter knew better than to try to escape. The electrified fences, the Alsatian dogs, and the watchful eye of silver-pistoled guards prevented almost any successful escape. Those who tried were inevitably caught, tortured, and killed, in front of the whole camp.

There were no children around, and no old people. Their absence stayed conspicuously on everyone's mind. And, under Lily's eyes, women who had come with them from France turned from refined, respected ladies into animals slavering at the mouth. There were never enough plates for

607

the soup, and sometimes a single bowl had to be passed among several dozen women. Few were those who waited patiently for their turns.

It was almost impossible, at first, to go to sleep. The barrack was alive with cries of pain, as women, five abreast, tossed and turned upon each other. The sick groaned, and voided their intestines before reaching the pail. But after a few days, Lily's exhaustion was such that she fell asleep without feeling the hardness of the slats of wood.

At around five, whistles awakened them. The women had only half an hour in which to wash, clothe themselves in their single rag, and clean the barrack. The washroom was a hut in which a pipe with holes oozed drops of water, and the toilet, a slat of wood set on a trough, with holes drilled through the wood. Thirty seconds was the most time allowed per person, to visit these two huts. And so the most fastidious women dipped into the dew on the grass, or into the ubiquitous puddles, or soaked the hems of their dresses in the rain, in order to maintain cleanliness. One learned to brush one's teeth with a finger held under the dripping pipe.

After cleanup, breakfast came, and then, the morning roll call, held under yellow lights because the sun had not yet come up. Often, the camp band played delicate Bach variations, or joyful martial music, while the Jews were counted.

At the end of roll call, certain prisoner numbers would be called out, and one waited with held breath, hoping that one would be spared.

The weak hid their weakness, the sick their illness. And one tried to avoid using the bar of soap that had been issued on the first day. Because by now it was known that this soap had been made with the fat from Jewish bodies, right on the premises of Birkenau.

After roll call, the labour *Kommandos* were formed, and those headed for the munitions plants filed out singing loud songs under the direction and jeering of the SS. Marisa and Lily had been selected to help put together endless parts of rubber tubing.

They worked in long, silent rows, punished by lashes of the whip if they spoke to offer encouragement to each other. Marisa's fingers shook, and she often did not fulfil her quota of hose parts. But Lily, next to her, worked with dexterous hands, and finished off her friend's work so that no one noticed.

They drank their soup in the courtyard, and had half an hour. Then they returned to work until five.

Evening roll call took a long time, and by then, dusk had fallen and a cold wind had risen. The SS shouted, whipped, and threatened. Even those who had died of natural causes had to be dragged out into piles, and accounted for. Only when all the numbers tallied by the prisoner clerks had been verified, could the exhausted women return to their barracks, and eat their night's ration of undigestible food.

After dinner, a certain amount of free time was allotted, and the inmates could wander about on the Lagerstrasse, or retire early. Lily, from the start, had become a centre of attention. By her quiet, unwaveringly positive voice, she had made friends among the sad and sorry inmates of her barrack. She spoke to them about the need to hold onto their faith, and to pray to God to help them through each day.

'There is no God,' a middle-aged woman named Hannah countered. 'No God would allow the ovens.'

'God allowed Christ, the best of men, to die. We have to learn not to give in to death, without becoming like the Musulmen. We can only do so by believing.'

But she herself felt her faith wavering as the days continued, the starvation gnawing deep within her reserves of strength. Before her eyes, Marisa's face had hollowed out, her stomach had caved in. Lily refused to think about what she herself might look like. She kept up her gentle encouragement, but now she did it to keep from thinking, to keep her own thoughts away. She spoke the words without believing them.

The principal thing was to avoid being selected for the ovens, which belched red flames and sweet-smelling odours of burning meat into the dark night skies, and into the grey daytime heavens.

By July, Aunt Marthe had started to weaken. She suffered from four illnesses, and, once a week, Kyra, in the disguise provided by her new hairstyle, crossed town on the métro to obtain a certain precious medicine at the laboratory that manufactured it. She had to make her journey despite the many air raid warnings that were a daily occurrence in Paris; if outside, she had to dart into the first building she saw, and wait out the alert. And if on the métro, she would have to sit in total darkness while the minutes ticked by. Her trips to Ménilmontant took at least three hours.

One afternoon, when she came home at four, she was surprised not to find Sudarskaya waiting for her in their 'sitting room', the large kitchen. Alarmed, she went to check on her aunt. When she opened the door, a strange panorama unfolded before her. Aunt Marthe, propped up in bed, was drinking a cup of beef broth, the small piano teacher seated by her side.

'Oh, Kyrotchka!' Sudarskaya cried, preventing the young woman from speaking first. 'I did exactly as you instructed when you left me here for a few hours. Madame Bertholet rang her bell, and I came to see what I could do. She wanted a hot beverage.'

'Your friend is very pleasant,' Aunt Marthe declared. 'Of course, I disapprove of people coming here to visit you without my permission ... but we've had our broth together, and talked about the Communists. I didn't know you had any White Russian friends, who feel, just like me, that the world is actually protected from the Reds by that man Hitler.'

'Madame Soudaire is an old friend of Papa's,' Kyra ad-libbed. A tremendous amusement swept over her. 'You *know* how *he* used to feel! Why, I do believe that when they were both young, in Moscow, Papa and Raymonde had a small romance. But Raymonde has been a solid French citizen for as long as I can remember, voting for the Right.'

Sudarskaya, who had always lived in dread of Misha, allowed her lips to part. But Aunt Marthe merely raised her brows. Then Sudarskaya, her small hat firmly planted on her head, looking very much the visitor, rose, patting her skirt into place. 'It was a charming afternoon, even if you and I missed chatting together, Kyra,' she announced. 'And now I'll say my goodbyes.'

Outside, in the hallway, the two women breathed out their relief. The small visitor's hat had stood them in good stead; just as the fact that Sudarskaya's weekly reports, filled with gloom, had kept Henriette and Alain away from the apartment. Furthermore, Kyra was certain that no one from her old life, seeing her in the street, would have recognized her with her blond hair. And so they felt a measure of safety in their ingenuity.

The next few days were topsy-turvy. Aunt Marthe, barely conscious, rang for Kyra and demanded her favourite beef broth. For neither coffee, tea, nor milk was any longer available in the capital. When the young girl arrived with the steaming cup, the old woman burst out furiously: 'Why did you bring me this? I hate it! Take it back!' But before she could reach the doorstep, Aunt Marthe called out, querulously: 'Open the window! It's stuffy in here!'

Accordingly, Kyra complied without protest. She moved once more towards the door. 'Girl, close that damned window!' Aunt Marthe screeched. 'Do you intend to kill me with this draught?'

It was the beginning of three days of constant capriciousness, and of a steady decline. Kyra took up her vigil by her aunt's side, feeling that the end was approaching. On Tuesday 18 July she began to cough, and the next morning, started to vomit on an empty stomach. Kyra went to fetch the doctor, who applied suction cups to the old woman's back, and who sent her niece out to purchase cotton wool.

Several days passed, punctuated by the doctor's visits and by errands. On the morning of the twenty-second, Kyra was just leaving the apartment, when a troop of German Gestapo officers, the concierge in their midst, blocked her way on the staircase. The concierge smiled at her. 'Hello, Mademoiselle Brasseur,' he remarked gaily. And the leader of the Gestapo men raised his cap and inclined his head.

Kyra waited, a nameless terror in her chest. Perhaps ten minutes ensued. Then she saw them reappear, their upstairs neighbour manacled among them. 'Another Jew apprehended. Well, have a pleasant day, mademoiselle,' the Gestapo captain said.

She wondered how her small gold heart had swayed the heads of the pair of collaborationist concierges, and allowed herself to fall back against the door panel, sweat on her forehead.

That night, at eleven, Aunt Marthe's breathing began to sound like dried peas shaken in a bowl. Twenty minutes later, the dreadful rasping stopped. On unsteady feet, Kyra took a small hand-mirror and held it to Aunt Marthe's lips. No mist appeared. And so she went to her bedroom and roused Sudarskaya. 'Aunt Marthe is dead,' she announced, her voice oddly detached and cold.

They padded back to the master bedroom, and Sudarskaya instructed the girl on how to help move the dead body so that it could lie in a proper supine position. They pulled out Aunt Marthe's legs, crossed her arms over her chest, removed all but a single pillow, and closed the windows. And then they faced each other, horrified.

'If we announce the death, the authorities will come to seal off the apartment,' Kyra declared.

'Worse than that: this Henriette person will arrive, and we'll have to go into hiding God knows where.'

Close to tears, Kyra said: 'But we can't keep a dead body here! I'll just have to go to the concierge, and beg him to help us.'

'What have we to offer? He's the one who reported the upstairs neighbour.'

Kyra shook her head, overcome by the impossibility of the situation. 'I used to hate the old biddy,' she cried. 'But why did she have to die on us?'

And then, her face brightened. 'Raïssa Markovna,' she said. 'We have an apartment full of riches here. If they held their tongue because of a small gold pendant, think how they'd help us if we offered them a chance at Aunt Marthe's things!'

Two days later, in the middle of the night, the concierge and one of his friends removed the dead body, presumably to bury it. The next morning, the same man returned to disinfect the dead woman's room. And, in the afternoon, the concierge and his wife rifled through all the piles of Bertholet antiques, and departed with four sacks full of jewellery and objets d'art.

Kyra, continuing to buy food on Aunt Marthe's ration cards, felt the uneasiness of guilt gnawing at her. They had just performed an inhuman, dishonest act. But then the Germans, occupying France, had performed worse in the name of the Reich.

She felt she'd had no choice, if she and Sudarskaya wished to continue to hide out in peace, and to eat without fear of being seized by the Gestapo. For she was sure that the Germans were on the lookout for them in their old neighbourhoods, where they'd registered for ration cards.

And Sudarskaya continued, punctually every Friday morning, to telephone Henriette Bruisson to give her this week's bulletin on her aunt's state of health.

Chapter Twenty-six

By August, the marshes of the Auschwitz swamp had begun to fester with disease, and many of the women, stooping to lap up the fetid liquid to slake their thirst, caught dysentery. Lily, at ninety pounds, was still relatively healthy; but Marisa weighed a bare sixty-eight, and looked hardly better than a Musulman.

Occasionally, in the evening on the Lagerstrasse, they encountered Nanni. Yet they were not able to speak to her in private, as a young lieutenant of the SS was always with her, his arm possessively around her. She looked lustrous, healthy, and even beautiful in the finery with which she paraded down the main avenue of Birkenau. But her face was infinitely sad, and she tried to look at the ground whenever she was near them.

By 15 August, it seemed as if Marisa was very sick indeed. Her scalp was covered with eczema, and her hands had swollen, so that it was difficult to accomplish even half of her task at the factory. Lily was finding it impossible to make ends meet for two people. And so one afternoon, Lily begged Malka to arrange another work detail for her friend.

'You'll have to pay me,' the Slovakian announced, small eyes narrowed.

Lily felt new despair gnaw into her heart. She was sure that Marisa, if not helped, would soon wither away. She had no personal belongings to swap with the *Kapo* for an easier detail. And so she decided that only Nanni would be able to help.

Winding her way through the complexes of huts and

615

fences, Lily, understanding that she was risking twenty-five lashes for being in a forbidden area, kept her head bent. In front of the whores' barrack, a terrible sense of shame spread through her. These were young women, many of them, like Nanni, girls of good family; but she'd seen them on the street, their carriage proud as they kicked at the others who, like herself, were slave labourers. Lily felt ashamed because the Nazis had transformed these tender young women into hard, predatory animals, who boasted of their good fortune with all the delicacy of sadistic monsters. And yet this 'good fortune' had to be one of the most degrading forms of slavery. Nanni, barely fourteen, had been raped and used, and Lily could feel this degradation inside the pit of her own stomach.

Shyly, she knocked on the door. An SS officer, his shirt undone, swung it open, his face turning purple at the sight of her. But behind him, she saw Nanni. The young girl thrust herself between the man and Lily, and kneeled before him with the subservience of a practised geisha. 'Please,' she begged, her voice low and pleading. 'This woman is my aunt. I must speak with her.'

'One minute only,' the man snapped, drawing back.

Nanni stepped outside. She was wearing a silk dress and a long gold chain with a cluster of rubies hanging from it. 'Is it Mama?' she whispered.

Overwhelmed by pity, Lily drew the girl close to her, and held her. 'Your mother has dysentery. She can't work anymore, and Malka wants something to barter for a change of assignment.'

'I'll see what I can do,' Nanni said. Her face was darkened with anguish, as if she couldn't wait to be away from Lily, away from a confrontation with what she had been turned into.

Lily nodded. Impulsively, Nanni removed a small gold charm bracelet, and closed Lily's fingers over it. 'Heinz

616

gave this to me,' she whispered. 'But I don't want it. I don't want any of the gifts he gives me.'

Her hand over the cool gold links, Lily's mind suddenly turned over, and a swift anger filled her. 'They've given you gifts?' she echoed, pushing the astonished girl away from her with surprising vehemence. 'Anna Steiner, your mother is dying from lack of nutrition, and we are all working our hearts out, merely to escape being selected out! And you are *here*, sharing absolutely nothing! In your place, another would have smuggled anything she found, to help her sisters!'

Aghast, Nanni's eyes filled with tears. 'But . . . Heinz . . . I'm never alone,' she finally murmured, her face crumpling.

'I'd have gone to the washroom. I'd have thought of *something!* Where do you suppose your fine Heinz has purchased these gifts of his . . . these expensive, exquisite gifts?'

'I'm not sure.'

Lily stared at the girl, her own breath coming ragged with excitement. Nanni's face was masked with sorrow, the nameless sorrow of the ageless, of mourners. 'You know very well,' Lily stammered in a low, hard voice. 'They were unpacked by the "Canada" brigade, from suitcases of gassed women!'

Before Nanni could reply, Lily strode away, the gold bracelet safely tucked in a fold of a makeshift belt she had made from the hem of a smaller woman's ragged uniform.

All night long, Lily could not sleep. Her heart hammered inside her, and vivid images of Nanni in her whore's outfit kept passing through her mind. All pity had been snuffed out. Next to her, moaning in a trance, Marisa lay huddled like a trusting, ailing child, her body wracked by shivers. Already five times, Lily had had to help her void her intestines into the small food bowl they had found in one of the garbage pails, and which Lily had dumped into the communal night bucket, and wiped clean.

617

Left and right, women were dropping off like insects, brought down by the insanitary conditions, by the contagion, and by malnutrition. Lily did all she could to keep clean, for herself and Marisa. And it was becoming increasingly difficult, at night, with fifteen women tossing together on the thin wooden slats to get the proper rest to keep strong. There were repeated incidents of broken tiers collapsing, of inmates crashing on top of their companions on the bunk below. Now, to help Marisa with her diarrhoea, Lily had to carry her friend like a baby, climbing with utmost care over the sleeping bodies of the others, to do their business on the dank, wooden floor.

In the morning, Lily slipped the gold chain into a quarter of her slice of bread, and handed it to Malka. And in the evening, the Slovakian *Kapo* informed them that Marisa had been transferred to the kitchen detail. Then Lily went to Hannah, the girl she knew from this *Kommando*, and gave her the beautifully crafted charms. 'That's to make sure Marisa eats proper food, not this slop,' she whispered.

Hannah's eyes widened with disbelief, but she nodded, mutely. In Auschwitz-Birkenau, one had no personal use for beautiful gems; but one could trade them for food, or for special favours.

And at night, Lily reflected on how much they all had changed: she, Marisa, and Nanni. She was most surprised at herself. For now, she felt such a powerful hatred in her heart for all that threatened their survival, that she found it difficult to recognize the person she had been in Paris, when she had found excuses for all kinds of infamy, and forgiven with an open spirit.

'Why did you want to come here?' Heinz asked.

Nanni slowly let her shoulders rise and drop. 'I wanted to see this operation,' she answered sweetly. 'Are you angry?'

The young man shook his head, and sighed. 'Not angry. But I don't like it when you become curious . . . like all the others. They just want *things*. With you, it's different. I think you care about who I am.'

Nanni's large eyes, so like her mother's, rested on him in their calm, gentle fashion. In a sense, she had to like him. This was such an inhuman place, where every value had been sacrificed or distorted for reasons of cupidity, that a simple person like Heinz Kleinert, who only wished to stay near her, seemed like the least offensive participant in a world where cruelty was the norm, and torture the pleasure.

'I do care,' she told him softly. 'And I only came here because . . . I heard that all the presents that we receive come from *here*.'

'And what of it?' he retorted, suddenly Prussian and aloof, his eyes cold and defensive. 'Do we have any sort of garrison town in this camp, for us to purchase presents for our girls?'

Putting her hand on his arm, she said: 'Just let me look around, all right? I'm not going to get in anybody's way.'

Suspicious, Heinz nevertheless allowed her to step out into the busy workroom of 'Canada'. Emaciated inmates in stripes and rags, stood sorting through rucksacks and suitcases. Nanni spotted Mihai Berkovits at once, and, casually, stopping here and there to pick up a lady's slip or a furry wrap, wended her way to where the young boy sat working, alone, with a pile of men's shoes. She bent down, picked up a moccasin, examined the leather sole, and whispered, continuing her scrutiny: 'I threw a paper wrapped around a stone into the men's camp, two weeks ago. And when you didn't answer, I asked my mother's friend, Magda, to contact you. She worked on this detail, too.'

Mihai said nothing, but kept on working. 'Today I learned that Magda came down with typhoid fever, and was sent to the infirmary. So I suppose she never told you.

I need help,' Nanni said urgently, tossing the shoe aside and lifting another from the pile.

Mihai's brown eyes fell fully on her face, and she was touched by the intelligence in them, and the undisguised torment. 'Why should I help you?' he asked. 'You seem to have done plenty well enough alone.'

Stemming the tears before they could spill out, Nanni said: 'You saved my life. I wanted to see you, to speak with you, to walk a little beside you on the other side of the barbed fence ... but you never answered my messages. And now my mother is dying. She has dysentery. They put her on the kitchen detail, and she's being well fed. But the *Kapo's* an Austrian peasant, and she's decided to let my mother suffer for all the years when we were rich, on the Schwindgasse, and her family was poor. So she's made Mama carry the coffee and soup urns back and forth from the huts, with only one other woman to help her. The urns weigh more than she does, and my aunt Lily's afraid she'll collapse.'

'My father was gassed the first day,' Mihai declared. 'And my mother was sent to the soap factory, with my sister. We wash with the fat from their bodies.'

With the back of her hand, Nanni flicked off the moisture from her cheeks. She was angry with herself for giving in to tears. Her young voice suddenly hard, she said: 'I'll do anything you want, Mihai Berkovits. I'll meet you in the washroom and make love to you. I'll let you sell me to your friends. But you have to help me. You have to send me *something* I can give this *Kapo*, to prevent her from killing my mother. Magda can't help us now.'

The boy stopped making piles of shoes, and reached over her to pick up a child's slipper. Deliberately, his hand brushed against her leg, and she could feel the warmth. 'Anna,' he murmured. 'Of course I'll help. It won't be easy, but I'll help because we all need our mothers, and I've lost mine. You don't have to treat me like an SS pig,

620

and yourself like a whore. You're *not* a whore; they've just chosen you for that particular work detail.'

'I wish I could die,' she whispered, fervently.

Again his brown eyes fastened on her. 'No, you don't,' he said.

In the middle of the night, the lights were suddenly turned on, and the elegant form of *Oberscharführerin* Irma Griese, a vision of feminine loveliness with her thick, white-blond hair and her eyes of periwinkle blue, came striding in, her silver pistol aimed at the ceiling. 'She looks like an angel,' Magda had told Lily, repeating the camp cliché. 'But she's more cruel than Mengele.'

'Out of bed, you Jewish sows!' she called, her assistants swinging their clubs randomly through the tiered pallets. '*Selection!* Take off your nightshirts, raise your arms, and run one by one in front of me!'

Dazed, their hearts thumping, the thousand women trampled over each other in their effort to prove their strength. But Marisa had not moved from the bed. Lily jostled her, whispering urgently that they had to get down, that time was of the essence. 'I don't care,' Marisa whispered, her face so white that every small capillary seemed clearly delineated like a thick river on the map of a plain. 'Let them take me.'

Summoning every particle of strength within her, Lily pulled her friend towards her, and stepped off the bunk. She deposited Marisa on the floor, and held her up beneath her arms. 'Just for a few minutes,' she entreated. 'Do it for me, and for Nanni. Without you, and with Magda in the infirmary, I'd be too alone to continue.'

Marisa swayed on her feet, then appeared to regain a modicum of stamina. She's a Musulman already, Lily thought, terrified. How many times this week, Lily had washed her face for her, and helped to clean the urine from the sides of her legs. She could remember her young mother, explaining to her in her childhood that the body was the soul's mirror: that how we treated our bodies was a reflection of the way we saw ourselves as individuals. And Marisa was, bit by bit, forgetting who she was.

'I know you.' Irma Griese was standing in front of her, a charming smile on her perfectly chiselled features. 'What's your name?'

She reached out, and her fingers turned Lily's forearm over, to read her number. 'B-14448. And what *was* your name?'

'Liliane Brasilova.'

Still that exquisite face smiled, and the blue eyes sparkled. Then, all at once, Irma Griese punched Lily with her fist, right under her diaphragm. The breath knocked out of her, Lily was bent in half. 'That's for your activities in "Canada",' she said softly. 'We apprehended the other ... Magda? the Hungarian. Who were you selling those goodies to, B-14448?'

Marisa, her eyes enormous in her haggard face, tiptoed up, like a wraith. She fell to her knees, and seized the hem of the *Oberscharführerin*'s skirt, raising it abjectly to her parched lips. 'It was for me, *gnädige Frau*', she murmured. Her voice was a toneless and hollow tube, devoid of will or of strength. 'She did it to save my life.'

Irma Griese looked down at the human skeleton on the floor, and started to laugh, a low, merry chuckle. Immediately, Malka the *Kapo* began to laugh, and soon the entire barrack was resounding with the jarring, harsh laughter of animals turning on a weaker species. Then, with the tip of her dark, polished boot, she kicked out once. Marisa fell away, like a dead fly, and did not get up.

Irma Griese touched Lily's cheek with a well-manicured nail. 'Well, my lovely,' she declared softly. 'You shall have your wish. What a sad challenge to put to sleep one such as your friend. Musulmen finish themselves off, sooner or later, in any case. I shall not select her. But you, my dear, shall report to the gatehouse tomorrow, after *Zeile Appell*.'

Within minutes, the *Oberscharführerin* had selected twenty other names, and had turned her erect back and walked out. 'Back to bed!' Malka called out, and in the mad scrambling that ensued, Lily found herself jostled next to the Slovakian *Kapo*.

'Why did you do it?' she asked.

'Because you and Magda thought you were smarter than I. You only gave me what you wanted. But that hospital ward, where they put her, is worse than any other barrack. Mengele starts there when he makes his selections!'

Lily, like a stone, lay down on the hard wooden pallet, next to Marisa. She knew, beyond a doubt, that there was to be no exit from this situation. In the morning, she would be sent out to be gassed.

For the rest of the night, Lily lay awake, listening to the groans of her companions, and images of her parents, her children, Mark, Misha slid into her mind like turning pages of a family album. She was too terrified to weep, and her mind felt congealed. At length, towards dawn, she began to whisper the words of the *shma* just to keep from hearing her heart beat.

After the twentieth of August, everyone knew that the liberation of Paris was imminent. The French and the Allies had recaptured almost all of Normandy, although the fighting was still fierce there, and the Germans savage in the defence of this territory.

In Paris itself, the Germans were already packing up. Truckloads of soldiers rolled away as fast as they could, followed by tanks, all bound for the East or the western fronts. Towards the East, they were hoping to cross the border into their own country, and to the west they were headed for Brittany, where a heavy German contingent awaited them. The Parisians watched them with stupefaction, but didn't dare mock them aloud.

Rumour ran that Paris had been mined in several places, and that Abetz had been ordered to destroy the city when he left it. The Parisians were therefore living in fear of being blown up at any moment. But this rumour proved to have been false. (Either the ambassador had no time to fulfil his instructions, or, married as he was to a Frenchwoman, he allowed his scruples to overrule his devotion to the Reich.)

For several days now, the atmosphere had noticeably lightened, as a five-year hope seemed about to come true. All around, Parisians were making flags to hang outside when the time would come. Kyra found a small piece of blue cloth, then a torn red rag, and she sewed them together, adding parts of a white handkerchief to form the three stripes. But she was afraid to hang her flag outside, for fear that some of the Germans who had not yet departed might make a last-minute raid through Rue de la Tour, and shoot the ones who had adorned their balconies.

The next morning, on the twenty-fifth, Kyra was on her way to the laundress when a group of running people almost knocked her down. 'They're here!' she heard. 'They arrived this morning, and are going up the Avenue Mozart!'

A tremendous lump rose in Kyra's throat. Her first impulse was to follow these excited people; but she thought of Sudarskaya, waiting at home, and wanted her to witness this with her own eyes. To hell with the laundress, she thought, and ran back to the house, taking the stairs two at a time.

Inside the apartment, she seized Sudarskaya, and told her the news. Together they hung the small flag from their balcony, and then raced down the stairs outside. The entire street was adorned with red, white, and blue material, dancing in the wind.

Already, a grumbling noise could be heard growing in

intensity as it approached. Hand in hand, the young woman and the small Russian piano teacher made their way to the corner of Avenue Mozart. Bumper to bumper, enormous tanks were rolling up, in a slow, uninterrupted march. The crowd, pressed together, began to shout and clap, and Kyra and Sudarskaya joined in, as loudly as they could, tears flowing freely down their open faces.

The tanks were the colour of sand, and on their flanks were scrawled, in large black letters, their war names. Most were geographic appellations: Normandy, Poitou, Rheims, Loire; or of fighter animals: lion, panther, falcon; or, finally, the names of women: Pauline, Jeannette, Valérie, Suzanne. There were no more than four or five men in each tank: tired men, harassed men, tanned, dirty, and unshaven men, so exhausted that only their eyes seemed alive in their heads. But how intensely their eyes shone! The Parisians at the side of the street shouted tender, grateful epithets, and, since the procession was infinitely slow, with many stops and starts, young girls were climbing on the tanks and winding their arms around the heroes, and middle-aged matrons were applying resounding kisses on those unshaven cheeks.

They had been travelling since the previous morning. They had fought and crossed the cities and towns of Normandy, and, knowing that the Americans had stopped at the Porte Saint-Cloud and at the Porte d'Orléans in order to let the French be the first to enter their city, they had allowed themselves no rest.

After several hours, Kyra, feeling hungry, put her arm around Sudarskaya's shoulders and turned back towards home. 'You are stupid not to climb aboard, like the other girls,' Raïssa Markovna chided her. 'Just think . . . Pierre might be among them!'

But at that moment, a sudden rain of bullets crashed onto the pavement of the small street where they had been walking. Kyra and Sudarskaya flattened themselves against the façade of a granite building, terrified. An old man, huddled near them, said sotto voce: 'It's the collaborationist militia, trying to get its revenge. Look – on the roof!'

Kyra shaded her eyes, and peered upward at the house directly opposite them. Men were crouched behind machine guns, firing where they could, haphazardly. But after a few minutes she felt her courage return, and led the way, keeping close to the walls, to Avenue Paul-Doumer. There, the torrent of bullets seemed far too dense, and the two women waited for half an hour.

Confused, Kyra wondered what to do. And then Sudarskaya cried: 'Let God protect us!' and, grabbing Kyra's hand, ran as fast as she could across the dangerous street. They kept their heads bent, as if this would have helped had they been hit. But, standing on the opposite pavement, they realized that they were still intact.

'God has been protecting us for many months now, Raïssa Markovna,' Kyra murmured, a stream of perspiration matting her curious red-blond hair. 'I think it's time for us to do what's long overdue. On the Sabbath, we'll go to services at the temple on the Rue de la Victoire, and pay our homage to Rabbi Weill.'

Abstractedly, she gazed down at the back of her right hand. It was dripping blood, and the skin was gashed and pulpy. With the hem of her skirt, she dabbed at it. It hardly hurt. 'I guess I've been wounded, like a good soldier,' she said, and smiled, the corners of her mouth trembling only a little.

It had begun as a very strange proceeding. SS men and women had handed out postcards to the four hundred women assembled at the gatehouse, and someone had barked out the order to write down their full names and addresses on the back, in neat block letters. And so the women, who had come from all parts of Europe, had done as they were told, wondering what the cards would be used for.

And now Josef Mengele, an ironic smile giving his face the look of a bored, detached aristocrat deigning to supervise an inept staff, walked among the four hundred exhausted, skeletal women. Disseminated among the group were the black-clad, well-fed, muscular SS.

Raising his left hand, he made a signal with his thumb, pointing to the door.

At once, the SS moved to marshal the prisoners out. Five abreast as usual, these sad-looking Musulmen shuffled their feet into the rain, and sloshed through the mud to a building they had never seen before. An SS lieutenant held a wooden door open, and the others prodded the women through by jamming the barrels of their rifles into the small of their backs. As soon as all had come inside, the lieutenant locked the door with several bolts and a padlock, and, from the darkened interior, the women heard the SS departing, chatting and laughing easily together as they shared a casual joke.

The boots of the SS slipping on the mud, and receding into the distance, resounded like the last fragment of hope for these four hundred. They were sure they had been abandoned to die. They found themselves in a long but low enclosure, its wooden walls soggy with moisture, its roof leaking rain. There were no beds, only the hard floor, as wet as the street. Lily was too tall to stand up straight, and the situation reminded her of the boxcars, when one hundred had been crammed inside without food or air. She thought of Magda, in the makeshift infirmary; perhaps she was already on her way to the gas chamber. She felt waves of sadness for this new friend who had done all she could to help Marisa, and who was paying with her own life.

Yet Lily, of the four hundred jammed together in the dark barrack, was probably the only one who felt an enormous sense of reprieve. In the morning, following roll call, she'd been certain that a truck, disguised as a Red Cross ambulance, would drive up to take her and her companions to be gassed. Instead, they were here . . . still alive. A fervent hope crested in her chest. If she'd survived this far, she owed it to God to survive till the end.

But after several hours, the hope began to ebb away as thirst, and a beseeching hunger, crept through her body. Aware that she was among the healthier of the inmates, she made an effort to resist without succumbing to the moaning and groaning of her neighbours. Some were women she knew, from her barrack. She moved quietly to them, finding them in the light from the ripped ceiling, and from tiny clerestory apertures. And then, sitting near them, she tried to speak, to soothe, to calm. By busying herself with women who were really sick, some of whom she knew were dying, from their weakness, the drought, and the closed quarters without air, food, or water, Lily kept herself from going crazy, and proceeded in her idea that the secret of survival lay in doing, not thinking.

She stopped trying to figure out how many hours had passed when, next to her, a young Greek girl passed away. From the clerestory windows, no more light appeared. There were seldom any stars in the Auschwitz-Birkenau skies, so Lily could see nothing. A tremendous sense of futility fell upon her, and she lay on the ground, spreading the dead woman's ripped skirt as a blanket between herself and the muddy floor.

After the second day with no food and water, Lily fell into a kind of dreamless haze, and, like an animal, crawled among her companions, the living and the dead, to lick the moisture from the wooden walls.

And then, on the third day, the door was suddenly thrown open, and Mengele, a riding crop impatiently tapping his freshly pressed trousers, was outlined against the clear, even grey that blinded those who, still alive, could still distinguish forms in their line of vision. He wrinkled his nose. Lily sat up, her lips parted with thirst. It had been so long since she'd smelled the odours around her, that the view of human faeces spread around, and of decomposing, bloated bodies, maggots already feeding from them, failed to make an impression. But to Mengele, walking in from the outside, the odours and the sight must have been overpowering. '*Scheisse!*' he exclaimed, reeling slightly.

After that, chaos took over. Some of the slave labourers came in, dragging corpses out with strange, twisted hooks, which they'd passed through the heads of the dead. Lily recognized her own *Kapo* Malka Sandikova, and some of the others from neighbouring barracks. One of the *Kapos* was saying to Mengele: 'Some of these women are still good for work, *Herr Oberarzt*. We could use them.'

Carelessly, Mengele shrugged. 'Very well, then. Bring them for one final selection, in Facility Number Two.'

A tremor passed through Lily. She had accepted Magda's stories of the gas chambers and crematoria, though there were still some who believed that the red flames were bursting from a bakery, or a gigantic factory. The smell of burning flesh was perceptible every day, whether the wind had risen or not. Facility Number Two contained a gas chamber in its west wing, below the ground; and on the first floor, the bodies of the gassed were cremated, their ashes to be dispersed later as fertilizer for the fields. *One final selection.* Josef Mengele had made his ultimate joke, laughing at the Jewish *Kapo* and at what remained of the four hundred women interned for three days and nights without food, water, or sanitary facilities. They'd been left to rot, and the majority had done just that.

Only about one hundred women remained alive, and all in sorry condition. A young female SS, her strong hips swaying, escorted them into the birch grove, where tall, delicate, and poetic pines and birches rose to form a cluster evocative in its distilled sadness. Lily was walking next to a woman her own age, who, surprisingly, was clutching a Bible. Its leather binding was ripped, but its gold-leaved pages attested to its presence in a loving family over several generations. 'Which way do you think they will condemn us to death?' she asked Lily, her cultured voice hard and toneless, the way all women learned to speak after a few months.

Lily was afraid to answer. The woman, her bony face still luminous, said softly, 'My name is Edna Rosenthal, and I'm a Belgian. If I don't make it, and you do, will you tell my daughter? She's in Barrack Twenty-six.'

Lily smiled. In French, she murmured: 'Don't speak this way. You've somehow managed to hold on to your Bible; you'll hold on to your life.'

'They told me this is the way the people walk when they're sent to the left at the arriving ramp,' Edna said, her voice calm. 'But I don't think we'll live to talk about our own walk. They call it the grove of the condemned.' After a while, she spoke again. 'I saw one of the cards we filled out, in Dr Mengele's hand. And in his handwriting, had been scrawled: "Dead from scarlet fever". They made us sign our own death certificates.'

The straggly group of women had reached the entrance to Killing Facility Number Two, which, on the outside resembled the neat mansion of an English country squire. Its brick façade was disconcerting. But the flames belching from its chimney petrified the hundred. Almost in a trance, they walked inside.

They were told to go down some stairs. Now, Lily thought, no escape was possible anymore, for downstairs were the gas chambers, where the innocents who were taken directly there on arrival were told that they would shower. They stood in a room where signs explained that one had to remember where one left one's clothes, and that, upon returning from the showers, the diabetics would have to report their condition. But this was all right for the naïve first arrivals; for seasoned inmates of Auschwitz-Birkenau, like them, there was no need to disguise the truth. They knew where they stood.

'Take off your clothes,' the female SS ordered.

A young French girl had once hidden under a pile of clothes, and been saved by a member of the *Sonderkommando* who had come to collect the discarded outfits. But Lily was a tall woman, and besides, in a commotion involving three thousand, one person might do some quick thinking. Here, with only one hundred prisoners, ten SS stood on guard, and Dr Mengele sat at a table in the front of the room, his eyes alert and not at all bored now.

Lily stepped out of her prison-grey dress, and she saw Edna slip the Bible between the folds of hers. The doors to the gas chamber lay open, to the right. This meant that, under no condition, would anyone sent *right* be able to survive.

Mengele, this time, seemed more thorough than he had been at the station ramp. He made each of the prisoners walk up and down, then lie down on the floor. He felt their bodies for odd lumps or crevices. Lily felt the fear knot her stomach. Like most of the others, she had abruptly ceased menstruating less than a month after arrival, which, she thought, was lucky, since no underwear had been provided, and no extra materials to wipe the blood. She was sure malnutrition was the culprit, though some said their food was being drugged. But lately, she'd felt a tremendous pain in her left side, at her waist, and she'd been certain she had developed a hernia.

In Birkenau, one never brought up one's illnesses; one made every effort to pretend one was in tiptop condition. But with Mengele's prodding, she would never be able to hide the hernia.

The women were being waved to the right, or out a back door on the left. She noticed that there were two armed SS to push in the recalcitrant ones who refused to put themselves into the gas chamber . . . such a tiny group for such an enormous room, capable of holding three thousand.

Edna passed in front of her, and walked up and down. Mengele nodded. 'Now lie down.' After three days without food or drink, this forty-year-old woman wasn't doing badly. She lay down. With a resigned sigh, Mengele called her forward.

They had all been counting. Already, forty-eight women had been sent right. Lily guessed that Mengele, with his odd sense of proportion and symmetry, would require fifty. But most of those pronounced healthy seemed to have been much younger than she and Edna: eighteen-, nineteen-year-old girls, with better resistance.

Mengele palped the shrivelled raisins that had once been Edna's breasts. In his cultured, dandified voice, he tossed out: 'This one has a tumour. Right!'

Lily felt herself freeze with horror. Edna turned once, her beautiful green eyes eloquent with anguish, fear, and a bravery that Lily could not match. She made a gesture with her chin towards her dress, which still covered her Bible. Lily opened her mouth, but no sound came out. She watched, transfixed, as her Belgian companion, friend of an hour, proudly stepped into the gas chamber.

'Next,' Mengele said.

Lily stepped in front of him, began her walk, lay down, and stood up for him to probe. There was absolutely no exit. She wondered frantically about a confession, or about speaking to a rabbi . . . the old religious confusion returning. Next to Mengele, one of the Polish *Kapos* was saying: 'This one's healthy; I know her.'

'She has a nascent hernia.'

He'd said it. He'd pronounced her dead. But the female SS was saying: '*Herr Oberarzt*, I think we should close the doors. We don't want a commotion, and there's an old one in there . . .'

Josef Mengele looked up from his probe of Lily, and frowned. The Polish woman said, 'All the others are young, and relatively healthy. We need them for work details.'

He moved away, fingering his chin. Lily, nude, still stood right in front of him, her once beautiful body reduced to skin, bones, and the hernia.

'All right,' he stated. 'Shut the doors, Lieutenant. Tell the boys to get the cyanide capsules ready to drop through the ceiling.'

The Polish *Kapo* moved her head roughly to the piles of discarded prison garb, and called out: 'Get dressed, all you swine! You're late for work!'

It was only when she was outside, wedged in the middle of the row of five, that somebody spoke to Lily. 'I heard them say it's the first time anyone's walked away alive from the gas chambers.'

'There are fifty-one of us.'

A long column of seven hundred men was coming up the path from the birch grove, their heads bent and knowing. Mengele, whistling to himself, was sprinting jauntily away on the other side. And then Lily remembered that she had forgotten Edna's Bible among the clothes of those who had gone in to die, and at last, she wept.

Nanni kicked at one of the ubiquitous stones of the *Lager*, with the toe of a beautiful patent leather pump. Across the vast divider of the electrified barbed-wire fence, Mihai Berkovits was keeping pace with her, his eyes like shining olives in the white, sickly paste of his skin. She could feel her heart flying out of her, to this young boy she knew so little, whose hand she'd never held. In many ways, she felt that she was much older, though in fact they were both fourteen. But she felt like a divided being: half of her still almost a child, wanting to trust and hope; the other, a tough girl, who had learned how to protect herself from the SS.

'What did you do, in Transylvania?' she asked him.

He shrugged. 'My father owned a small business. We were eight children. Now we're just four, and both our parents have been gassed.'

She nodded. 'My father was a neuropsychiatrist, in Vienna. But in Paris, he couldn't practise. And then the Gestapo put him away, in a detention camp in Compiègne, for over a year. On the station, as he was being deported from there, he collapsed.'

'The best people die,' Mihai said with unexpected vehemence.

'And when you get out, what will you want to become?'

'I like cars. I'd like to have a car repair shop.' His eyes fastened on her, and he smiled. 'Hardly a boyfriend for you, Anna Steiner.'

'For a prostitute?' She stopped, picked up a small pebble, and tossed it neatly between the barbed wire. 'Mihai,' she said. 'I can't even look at my mother. I know she's staying alive out of love for me. Our families were old, respected names in Western Europe. Her family ranked among the first three Jewish families in Paris.' Each seemed to want to speak in a direct line about himself, finding in the other a listener without preconceptions and prejudice. Now the young boy said: 'I'm not a Hungarian. I'm actually a Rumanian, but our province was recaptured by Horthy's regime. The Hungarians have sent all their Jews away to Nazi concentration camps. The Rumanians protected us.'

'When you return, you'll see a better life, Mihai,' she reassured him, smiling tremulously. 'Wait: reach over, between these two wires, and take my hand.' Her cheeks red, she carefully inserted her small, plump hand through an aperture in the fence, daring the wires to touch her. He stood staring at the delicate, well-tended fingers, for a moment angry at their health and good care. Then, shrugging, he took her hand in his own bony one, feeling the warmth radiating out from her fingers to his. She was still

634

smiling, and he imagined her in her house in Vienna, maybe sitting by a blazing fireplace, roasting chestnuts, her hair plaited like a schoolgirl's.

Liking the image, he smiled back.

'What are you doing here, Anna?'

The German voice broke into their thoughts like shards of glass thrust through tender skin. She almost jumped, and remembered in time that the slightest wrong move would electrocute both her and the boy. Slowly, judiciously, their fingers came apart. She faced Heinz Kleinert, standing with his hands clenched into fists, pounding into the flesh of his thighs, as if to punish himself for loving her.

Mihai Berkovits waited, and with the back of one of her hands, she signalled that it would be best for all if he left the scene at once. 'I was just speaking to a companion,' she said, softly.

'You are just a whore. If there weren't a fence, you'd have been in bed with him! I was a fool to think you were different. You like all men . . . like a real *gutter* whore.'

Her blue eyes blazed with a quiet, inner fire. Perhaps because she was challenging danger, or perhaps because this contact with the young Rumanian had so profoundly touched her, awakening her spirit, she answered him. 'No, Heinz. I'm not, and have never been, a whore. You know I was a virgin, you know I was only with you. You know I never liked it, and was ashamed! But you forced me to be with you . . . and I had no choice!'

'You're telling me that you didn't want me?'

At this precise instant, he was not a twenty-three-year-old lieutenant in the SS, and she a fourteen-year-old slave prisoner. They were two young people, confronting each other. She was totally unafraid. 'It isn't that I didn't want *you*,' she explained. 'It's that I had no choice.'

'I would have married you,' he retorted, his eyelids narrowed over sharp, light-blue irises, lighter and colder than hers.

635

'But you were not the man I dreamed of, to spend the rest of my life with.'

'You wanted a Jew. Not me, but a Jew. A low-down, dirty Jew with a hooked nose. Right, Anna . . . *Hannah*?'

'Hannah happens to be my Hebrew name. And I am not ashamed of it.'

'But *I* am ashamed of *myself*,' he declared, 'that I ever allowed a Jewish whore to corrupt me, to make me betray every ideal I have fought for and respected. Goodbye, Anna Steiner. My love is now dead.'

With her strange maturity, she stared at him, smouldering. 'Thank you, Heinz Kleinert,' she murmured. 'For you have just set me free.'

Nanni stood naked in the smallish square room, looking with terror at the other women. There were only a hundred of them, and she had heard all the stories about the gas chambers, and the crematoria. Except in Auschwitz I, the death room accommodated three thousand. And these people here were all *different*. They were all plump, some of them actually tubs of lard. How was this possible?

In the *Lager*, nobody except the privileged, like herself, could eat proper meals. She'd been told about people suffering from glandular diseases, and supposed these poor, shaking women were fat because of this. And though she, at one hundred and five pounds, was not nearly fat, by Auschwitz-Birkenau standards she was well overweight.

She wanted to cry, but terror so paralysed her that her throat had become constricted. She wanted her mother. She wanted to be near Lily, near somebody who loved her and had known her all her life. Above all, she didn't want to die.

Above them were the same shower spigots that she had been warned about. Now she closed her eyes, wishing it to be over. The glass door was being shut, and she turned, in spite of herself, and saw the SS guards peering out at them, one hundred unfortunate Jewish women, condemned to death. It was going to happen. *Now.*

She could hear the soft hiss of the gas being released . . . cyanide capsules, she'd been told. And then she smelled the strange, odious smell, and waited for it to kill her. But it wasn't doing that. Instead, she felt oddly euphoric, and good. Suddenly life was pleasant again, and she felt like laughing aloud . . . and she actually laughed aloud, and heard respondent laughter. They'd all been *spared*, as if by a supreme joke, the SS had fooled them again, as they liked to do!

An outside door was opening, and she saw the bright summer light, welcoming her back to the realm of humanity. Heinz had relented, and would be waiting for her, with a nice gift from 'Canada'. He hadn't meant it, about his love being dead. In front of her, rows and rows of fat women were running towards the beckoning light, and, filled with excitement, she followed, a little dazed by the odd gas that she had just breathed. Everyone was laughing.

Anna Steiner skipped out into the late August sunlight, her small feet light as those of a doe in springtime. She skipped, and was surprised, because it seemed as if the ground had receded, and was not present to receive her. Her last moment of consciousness, before landing in the gigantic cauldron of boiling water, was that, somehow, Heinz had deceived her after all.

'I have some news about your daughter,' the tall, handsome young lieutenant of the SS said to Marisa.

The woman turned, and stared at him, disbelieving. She was nothing more than a skeleton, with white skin drawn tight over the bones, and a shaved skull. But the eyes were the same as Anna's and their huge, saucer-like proportions, with their periwinkle irises, hit him suddenly below the belt.

'You're Anna's mother, aren't you?' he demanded brutally. The Musulman nodded, speechless.

'This morning, your daughter was boiled alive, and fat from her body was melted into a bar of soap.'

The wraithlike creature shook her head. She was like a caricature of a death's-head. Heinz Kleinert hated her with all his might, this Jewish bitch who had poisoned his girl into turning from him, and from their love. Their pure, unique love that had flourished here, among the smokestacks and the gassings, among the Musulmen and the fat, nauseating *Kapos*.

He held out his hand, and the whitish-grey material, inscribed *R.I.F.*, gleamed in the sunlight. The woman again shook her head, and so, anguished beyond words, he threw the cake of human soap right into her face, hitting her brow and causing her to raise both hands to protect herself.

Retching, he turned away, striding off as quickly as his legs would carry him. His pistol jangled in its holster, and perspiration drenched his shirt. By the side of the barrack, he had to bend over to vomit.

The Musulman still stood shaking her head, and touching her forehead. And then, she tiptoed across the Lagerstrasse, and stood for a minute or two in front of the barbed-wire divider. He was mopping his mouth with a clean white handkerchief when he heard the bloodcurdling yell, and wheeled about immediately.

The sight was no different from that which he'd witnessed many times before. A woman, turned black by the electroshock, had killed herself by flinging her body, arms out, upon the wires.

At roll call on 18 January 1945, Camp Commander Höss suddenly bellowed everybody to attention. Those who could walk one hundred and forty miles should move to one side, those who believed they would not succeed, should move to the other. Magda, who had somehow survived her bout of typhoid fever, and who had not, after all, been selected for the gas chamber, whispered to Lily: 'The Russians are approaching so fast, I'm afraid that if we admit our weakness and stay here, we shall be shot or blown up with the whole camp, by the SS.' For it was now a well-known fact, propagated through the underground, that the Allies had all but won the war, and that the panicking Nazis were disbanding all the *Lagers* outside the Reich, and marching as many prisoners as they could back into Germany, one step ahead of the Russian army.

Lily weighed no more than sixty pounds. Her hair had stopped attempting to grow back, and her stomach had swollen from malnutrition. But still, every morning, she went to the washroom and waited while the drops of polluted water dripped out of the pipe, so that she might clean herself as best she could.

Her general exhaustion was such that she had not been able to see clearly for some time now. It had been all the more difficult to fight, when she'd returned from the gas chamber selection and been informed of the double deaths of Marisa and Nanni. Now her connection to the living was completely severed. She clung only to the hope that Nick was alive, in America; for of Kyra she knew absolutely nothing. Sometimes, when an Allied victory came to her ears (for there was at least one homemade radio in the *Lager* underground, from which news travelled by word of mouth), she wondered what might have happened to Mark. But her interest was only casual. She really had stopped caring. The normal feelings and opinions of a human being were now foreign to her world.

'I couldn't make it,' she whispered back.

'You *have* to,' Magda pressed.

Magda's fingers curved over Lily's arm, and they moved together to the side of the strong. A side composed of some sixty thousand men and women, eaten away by dirt, disease, and starvation. In the sub-zero chill of the Polish winter, they shivered in their scant clothing. Lily had acquired, through Magda's theft from the 'Canada' brigade, a short alpaca jacket. Magda herself hugged a woollen coat, three sizes too large, to her bones.

And so, linking arms, the two friends joined into a row of five other women, and the procession began. The SS escorted them, comfortably ensconced in horse-drawn carts. The men and women trudged through the deep snow in their wooden clogs, slipping on the icy roads, holding on to one another.

The nervousness of the SS was apparent. They reacted like predators who knew that, just around the corner, a hunter lay in wait to kill them. In the last throes of their power, they vented their helpless rage on the poor thousands marching like exhausted automatons over the frozen roads of Poland, westward, ever more westward towards the safety of the Fatherland.

Lily and Magda had forgotten which day it was, and why they were marching. They were given a bare five minutes every few hours to lie down, in the snow, to take the load off their feet. Lily thought that, perhaps, her days walking all over Paris had helped her to build up a resistance that some of her more spoiled companions had never experienced, but on which she still knew how to draw. The rows of fives were diminishing every hour. Whenever someone faltered, an SS guard would shoot him or her at once, leaving the body in the snow.

On the fourth day, when the reserves of sawdust bread and margarine had been consumed, Lily's strength gave out at last. Magda, in the 'Canada' brigade, had never been so physically taxed as she, in the factory. 'Just leave me here,' Lily murmured. 'I don't care. But I can't continue for another mile.'

She knew that they had crossed the border into Germany, for that morning, they had crossed a village and been given milk by some of the women, who had addressed them in the language of their captors. But Magda was adamant. 'We're going to carry you,' she asserted. 'But we're not leaving you here to die.'

The young Rumanian girl on Lily's other side took hold of Magda's hand, and together they lifted Lily's torso from under her arms. After that, she lost consciousness, and they dragged her body until, two days later, she awakened once more.

'We've arrived somewhere,' Magda said. 'It's some kind of camp, I think.'

Of the sixty thousand, perhaps fifteen thousand were still alive. Lily could hardly make out their surroundings, but she could see a courtyard and barracks. Another prison opening up its gates to the dregs of the world, the wandering Jews whom nobody would claim and who were hated and derided by all. Overwhelmed by bitterness, she followed the long line of exhausted women to their next home.

They worked underground, manufacturing bombs to be used against the British. Their heads shaved, in their tattered dresses, they stood side by side, their fingers putting the tiny pieces together like automatons. Lily's hands were swollen, and she knew that her sight was probably permanently impaired. She was forty years old, but felt sixty-five. Her skin was blotched with eczema, and a tick kept bringing down the right corner of her lip.

Magda, younger and healthier, in spite of her bout of typhoid fever was less adept with her fingers. By the end of the long day, when they returned above ground to the barracks, she was always in tears, certain that her mistakes would sooner or later catch up with her. One hundred and twenty thousand Jews were working as slave labourers in the factory of Ludwigschutz, and, although they had one free day per week, and there were no crematoria to haunt them, they worked in terror; for at lunchtime, those who had broken a piece of machinery were lined up by the Germans, and hanged in front of the whole group.

In the morning, they marched to work to the sound of the *Lager* orchestra. They felt as if their hearts had shrunk, as if all the hope that had animated them during those last few weeks at Auschwitz had been for naught. The Russians might have saved those who had remained in the death camp; but the Allies were not aware of the hundred and twenty thousand lost souls in Ludwigschutz.

Magda told Lily that, even if the Allies came to save them, she would have no home to which to return. 'You have your children,' she despaired. 'But my parents are dead, and there's no reason for me to return to Budapest. The ballet would never be able to use me.'

Lily could offer few words of comfort; Magda had spoken the truth. They would never, any one of the survivors, be able to resume a normal life.

And then, one morning at the beginning of April, Magda, her hands shaking uncontrollably, dropped a small hammer, and saw it land on an infinitesimal plastic wedge. Her eyes widened with horror, and she could not move to retrieve it. Lily, in the flash of a second, had dropped to her knees, her vision blurry as she tried to find the shattered piece of plastic. But immediately, an SS guard stepped between her and her quarry. The plump, sturdy SS sergeant, his eyes cold and bright amid creases of fat, had his hand on Magda's arm, and then was bludgeoning her about the shoulders and neck with his cudgel. She was taken away, screaming her pain and fright, and Lily remained frozen in position, blinking back her own tears.

With sympathy, her companions allowed her to stay in place, immobile, until the lunchtime break, each taking more than her share of work so that the SS would not notice her lack of productivity. The young Rumanian who had helped drag her through the snow, Cornelia Ionescu, put an arm about Lily's shoulder and walked outside into the courtyard with her. In the concrete square, gallows had been set up, as they were every day. Only this time, Magda was standing with the condemned.

Lily watched, through her dimmed eyes, as the SS put a noose around the neck of each of the victims. She remembered sitting in Claire's room, as a small girl, and being read to from *Les Misérables*. A crust of stolen bread, a piece of broken plastic. And then, an explosion occurred inside her own head, and dots of jagged red filled her line of vision. With a sudden scream, she darted forward, her hands outstretched to the brave, kind young ballerina she had grown to love in the Dantesque horrors of Birkenau.

She heard Cornelia screaming: 'Lily! Get back!' and then fell forward, her wooden clog catching on a bramble. She felt the ground rise up to meet her just as the SS bullet went through her shoulder. At the same instant that Magda Gaspar was choked to death by the hangman's noose, Lily Brasilova lost consciousness, her blood seeping like Indian ink into the eternal grey of the German *Lager* yard. She missed hearing the sudden, shrill sound of an air raid siren, and seeing the German guards scamper for cover.

When she opened her eyes, she had a sensation of infinite softness, of a cleanliness only dreams could be made of. She blinked, saw the unknown female face bending over her, and heard strange words in a strange voice. American English. It had been years since she had heard that kind of accent. The truth was that she spoke very little English, only enough to get along, but . . . an *American accent?*

'Hospital,' the unknown woman was saying, intonating for her. '*Hôpital?* You're French, aren't you?'

Lily nodded, and tried to move her right hand to touch her face. But a terrible pain went through her, and she realized that something was resisting her freedom of movement. The woman said, in hesitant French: 'You're in an

643

American hospital, in the American sector of Berlin. You were found among a handful of survivors, in the courtyard of a Nazi munitions factory. You were delirious, you had pneumonia, and your shoulder had been damaged by a bullet. But you were alive. The Red Cross brought you first to the Russian sector, and then, three weeks ago, they sent you here, thinking we might have more success finding out who you are.'

Lily shook her head, and started to form a scream. But the woman touched her face with gentle fingers, and said: 'I know. We saw the number tattooed on your forearm. They used fake Red Cross ambulances to take the condemned to the gas chambers. But this time, a real ambulance took you to a real hospital. We've been feeding you intravenously, and this is the first time you've regained consciousness. We knew only that you were French, because, in your delirium, you said a lot of things in your language.'

Lily could see the woman's face, better than she had seen her own hands during the last months in Auschwitz and Ludwigschutz. She opened her mouth, to ask. But . . . for *whom?* Marisa was dead, Nanni was dead, Magda was dead. Her mother was dead, and her husband had ceased to live for her many years before. This kind woman would know nothing of Kyra, or of Nicky.

She felt the tears come, oceans and oceans of tears, and the woman knelt before her and put two strong arms around her. 'It's all right,' she murmured, over and over again. 'You'll be all right. Try to tell us who you are. We'll do what we can for you, to help you to go home.'

The American journalist, his curly grey hair tousled and dishevelled, his shirt rumpled and stained with perspiration, let his raincoat drop on the counter, and leaned forward, eagerly. 'Tell me about her,' he demanded.

'She doesn't seem to want to tell us who she is. She's

been wounded in the shoulder. She was so emaciated, at first we couldn't tell how old she might have been, or even if she'd be likely to recover. Her eyesight is still blurred, but she seems able to focus. And she's been gaining weight. Before all this, she must have been a beautiful woman. She still has marvellous brown eyes.'

The journalist felt a moment of dizziness, and used the wall to steady himself. He was exhausted. From the time when he'd found Kyra, in Paris, and been told what had happened, he hadn't stopped long enough to rest properly. All their friends had tried to talk them both out of finding Lily; in all probability, she hadn't survived. But for Mark and Kyra, nothing had seemed impossible. And so she'd gone her way and he'd gone his, stopping at all the hospitals of Western Europe where they had heard that camp survivors had been sheltered.

In the process, he'd seen so many ravaged women, barely more than breathing skeletons, that he was almost afraid to think of the condition she'd be in if she *had* survived. But he had to continue, until all leads had been followed. And there had been so many moments of hope, so many times he'd *thought* it might be she, and instead, he'd been faced with a total stranger with eyes that had begged for him to claim her . . . not to abandon her. He owed it to all these women that nobody would claim, owed it to them too to pursue the trail to the woman who belonged to him.

'What makes you think she might be the Princess Brasilova?' he asked.

'Those names she kept repeating, in her delirium. The same as those you mentioned: Kyra, Nick, Marisa.' The middle-aged nurse chewed on her lower lip. 'And once, at the beginning, she called out "Mark!"'

He couldn't speak. And so she led the way, into the long hospital dormitory. Her crêpe-soled shoes made squeaky noises on the linoleum floor. She wove between beds until she was standing in front of a screen. 'She doesn't like anyone to see her,' she whispered. And she tapped. 'It's me, Nurse Angela. And I brought a friend.'

With expert fingers, the nurse moved the screen so that they might both pass through. She let Mark go first, and remained only for a minute behind him. Because when he saw the patient, and fell to his knees to clasp her to him, Nurse Angela Pryor knew that, at last, her 'dark lady' had been found.

Epilogue
The Fifties

The elegant middle-aged woman made a stunning impression on the head nurse in the maternity ward of the Beth Israel Hospital, in New York. She was tall and extremely slender – a touch too thin, actually. Her raw silk duster, its large collar turned back to reveal a pearl choker at her neck, was belted at the waist, and its sleeves were becomingly cuffed just above her elbow. The duster was of deep emerald green, and her small, veiled hat matched perfectly. The elbow-length kid gloves did not obstruct the length and grace of her tapered fingers, now closed over a large bouquet of springtime flowers.

The woman, whose face, beyond the delicate netting of her hat, was definitely exotic with its large, almond-shaped eyes the colour of rich coffee, hesitated in front of the glass windows of the nursery. The head nurse tiptoed over. 'Which one are you trying to find?' she asked, kindly.

The woman turned, and smiled. Before, her face had been touched with a strange, mysterious sort of sadness, like an unconscious grief in spite of her will. But now there was a glow to it. 'The Brasilov baby,' she said softly.

'That's him – over in the corner. He's kept us all quite busy, I can tell you. Jack, isn't it? Are you . . .?'

'His grandmother. Would you ask someone to hold him up? He doesn't seem to be asleep, and I've never been alone with him.'

The head nurse nodded, sympathetic. The elegant woman spoke with a French accent. The head nurse went inside, and after a moment, returned with a bundle in her arms. 'Here,' she said. 'I've done one better. You can hold him, Grandma.'

With infinite care, the two women exchanged flowers and baby. The French woman held the tiny infant, wrapped in his blanket, and cradled him with absolute awe and parted lips. 'He's beautiful, isn't he?' she said. 'He looks like my son.'

The head nurse laughed. 'He looks like *you*. I've seen your son, and he's just like you, too. He's such a pleasant, considerate young man ... so attentive to his wife, so loving to his baby. We chatted together, yesterday. His wife's parents were with her, and he didn't want to crowd her. He told me about his import-export business, and about how he met his wife at a party, two years ago. Is Jack your first grandchild, Mrs Brasilov?'

The woman smiled, looking up from the baby. 'It's "MacDonald": Lily MacDonald. Jack – Jacques – is my first grandson. But I have a two-year-old granddaughter, in Paris. My daughter's child. Her name is Marie-Claire ... Marie-Claire Rublon.'

The head nurse hesitated. Then, wetting her lips, she plunged in. 'I'm sorry if I'm nosy,' she declared. 'But ... I think I've seen your photograph, in the society section of the *Times*. Aren't you the novelist Mark MacDonald's wife?'

Her face bent close to the tiny face of her grandson, the woman asked, softly: 'Have you read his books?'

'All of them.'

The baby began to cry. Again, the two women exchanged charges, and, apologetically, the head nurse made her exit back into the nursery. The elegant woman resumed her walk towards her daughter-in-law's room, her face once again setting into its serene yet melancholy expression.

'Lily.'

She heard the voice, and turned, not really surprised. Misha Brasilov, as elegant as always in his dark blue spring suit, had aged since the last time she had seen him. His thick crest of hair was now completely white. But this was normal; after all, if, this May of 1952, she was forty-seven, he was a good sixty-one. He'd borne up well, she thought, and was surprised at how little bitterness she could summon up at this point in her life . . . in both their lives.

'I'm sorry. But I hadn't thought to find *you* here, alone.' A certain awkwardness had edged into his voice. 'I knew how you must feel; it's why I didn't attend Nick's wedding. I'm sure I'm the last person you wanted to see.'

'Adina's a dear, sweet girl,' Lily said after a brief pause.

'I'm fond of her too.'

'Even if she's one hundred per cent Jewish?'

Misha bit his lower lip, and glanced away. 'Lily,' he said. 'I never really understood, in those days. But you weren't fair, either: you never told me.'

'You'd never have accepted. But it was wrong of me to have lacked the courage to be open about it. In those days,' she added, 'I was a much weaker person.'

It was an awkward moment. Misha took her hand. 'I'm the one who made the mistakes,' he said softly.

She let him hold her hand, but her eyes were oddly veiled, and he knew that she was thinking of the baby that had never been born to them. 'Lily, Lily,' he said, his voice full of pain. 'I made every effort to find you and the children, during the war. Didn't Nick, or Varvara, ever tell you? But it was impossible at the time.'

She nodded. 'Nick told me.'

'I wanted you back! I didn't leave you because I'd stopped loving you. I left because I was ashamed of the mess I'd made in our life . . . in all our lives. And I didn't want you to keep paying for my troubles.'

Her brown eyes fastened on him, and she smiled . . . a smile that was bittersweet, and that pierced through his anguish. 'I know why you left. I wept for you and wanted

651

to die, but of course I didn't. I had Nick, and Kyra. But you were wrong, Misha, not to have given me a chance to come through for you. If you'd given me the opportunity to be a real wife, and not a porcelain doll, both our lives would have ended up differently.'

He dropped her hand, and turned aside. 'My life's been empty,' he declared 'I've never wanted to remarry. In my heart, you'll always be my wife.'

She could feel a burning sensation in her eyes. Quickly, to lighten the atmosphere, she said: 'Your life will never be empty. We have grandchildren, Misha. Jacques lives on in Nick's son, and both our mothers in Kyra's daughter. She called her "Marie-Claire", you know, after both of them. You'd be so proud of Kyra, if you saw her now! She makes Pierre a tender, loving wife.'

Misha fumbled with a button of his jacket, and cleared his throat. 'One thing that I have never quite understood is why she's taken your brother's son under her wing. She has enough responsibilities with her own family doesn't she?'

Lily's mouth hardened, but only for an instant, then relaxed again. 'She and Pierre felt sorry for the boy. Henriette, you know, endured a public shame. She was paraded around the city, and her head was shaved, like the other women who'd been collaborators. And Kyra, who has more heart than either you or I, felt that Alain needed to know that the rest of his family had not forgotten him.'

The air was thick with unspoken memories, and she was glad then that she'd never told him what had really happened between her and Rirette. Somehow, what had seemed cataclysmic then, now appeared almost unimportant. After the camps, she'd learned to put aside all her old ideas of right, wrong, good or bad. She would never be the same, nor would she ever feel the need to share, absolutely, in the life of another human being. Her experience in Auschwitz had set her apart, and no one, not even Mark, could now penetrate to the core of her being. She couldn't help this: she had changed.

'Do you think you'll ever really forgive me?' Misha was asking her. 'And what about our children?'

Lily MacDonald looked directly into his green eyes. 'We've all forgiven you,' she replied. 'Perhaps it's time you forgave yourself.'

And she held out her graceful, gloved hand to the man who had been her first love, nearly thirty years before, on another continent, in another life, before the veil of her innocence had been snatched from her.

She could forgive, because there was a God who had kept her alive, and who had given her two precious children and two grandchildren. And inwardly, she smiled at the ultimate irony of this family. For her first grandson, who would continue the line of Brasilov, was a living link in the unbroken chain of Judaism.

The keepers of the walls had wounded her, as they had all the Jews of Europe. But she had survived, in spite of them, to help bring forth a new generation.

Yet she would never stop mourning the ones who should have been alive to share in her triumph.